ZOMBIES

ZOMBIES

ENCOUNTERS WITH THE HUNGRY DEAD

Edited and with Commentary by

JOHN SKIPP

BLACK DOG
& LEVENTHAL
PUBLISHERS
NEW YORK

Copyright page continued on page 700

Library of Congress Cataloging-in-Publication Data available upon request.

Published by Black Dog & Leventhal Publishers, Inc.
151 West 19th Street, New York, NY 10011

Distributed by Workman Publishing Company
225 Varick Street, New York, NY 10014

Design by Red Herring Design

Printed in the United States

ISBN: 978-1-57912-828-9

h g f e d

PART TWO:

POST EMANCIPATION 247

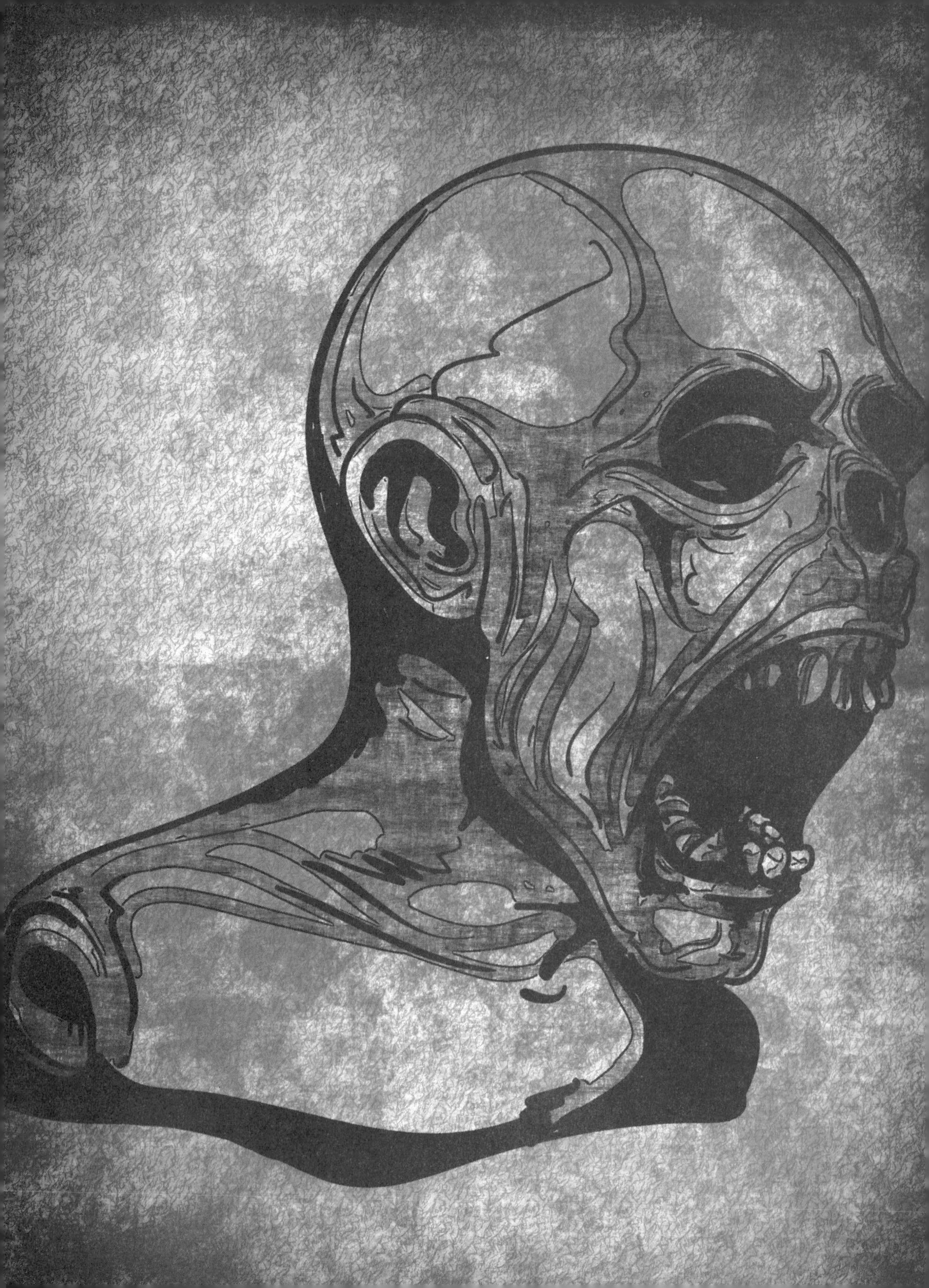

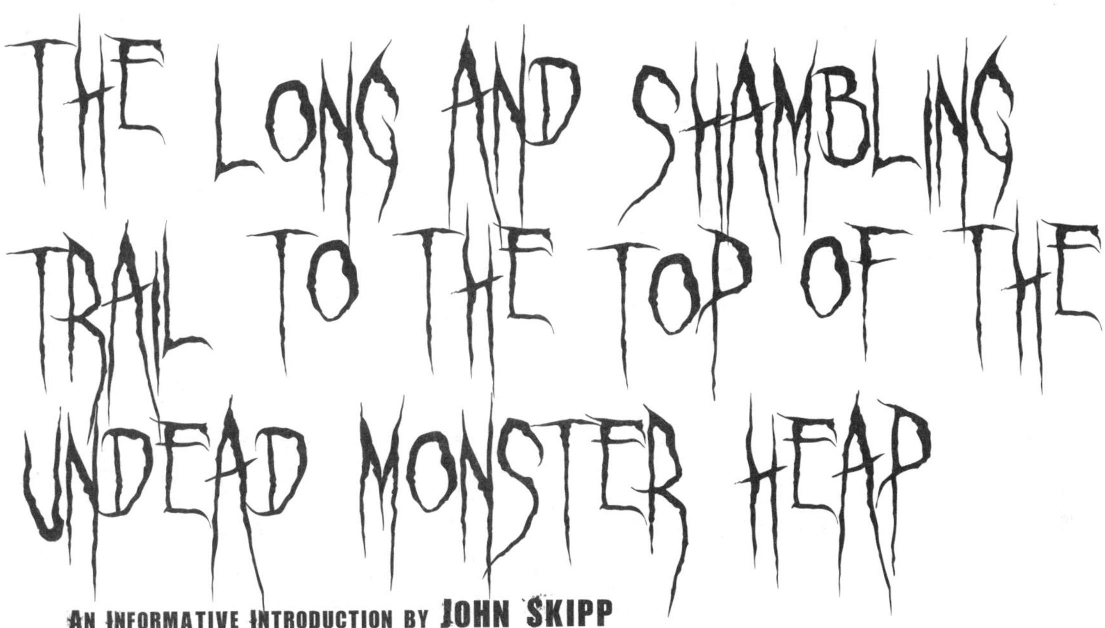

The Long and Shambling Trail to the Top of the Undead Monster Heap

An Informative Introduction by **John Skipp**

WELL, IT FINALLY HAPPENED. *GO, TEAM ZOMBIE!*

Never thought I'd see the day.

I don't know about you, but I'm one of those guys who always root for the underdog. Doesn't matter what manner of story it is; the specifics aren't really the point. I *just want 'em to win, that's all.* That's the cut of my DNA.

I like underdogs because they're scrappy, forever rising up against impossible odds. You knock 'em down, they get right back up. They're not big on taking no for an answer. Their tests and travails feel so much like my own—and like those of so many of us, struggling through these troubled times—that when one of them makes it, their triumph feels like *everybody's* triumph.

So I can't say that I'm not delighted for the zombies, now that they've taken over the earth or at least the popular consciousness. Lord knows they've worked hard for the distinction. It's been a long time coming.

And since suddenly the whole world wants to know who they are, where they come from, what they're like, and how to stop them, it's a great honor to bring you this book.

In it, you'll find the widest, wildest brain-popping cavalcade of multi-perspective zombie lore ever assembled—a soup-to-nuts of the shambling dead, from shadowy beginning to dear-God-please-be-merciful end—in a single volume so massive it can also be used for staving in heads (although I gotta tell ya that old standby, the tire iron, still gets my heartiest recommendation).

But before you hurtle into the meat of the matter, let's just take a minute, shall we? Grab a drink, a smoke, a snack, or at least a deep breath.

And let me get you up to speed on the living dead.

Ah, zombies. Those poor dumb reeking bastards. They've always been the low men on the evolutionary chart of monsterdom. One step above blobs and giant bugs, perhaps, by virtue of their former humanity; but put 'em in a lineup with vampires, werewolves, demons, ghosts, pod people, and plain old psychotic serial killers, and zombies are the skanky, vacant-eyed bottom feeders that nobody voluntarily asks to the dance. The ones you wouldn't even let wash your car.

Unless, of course, you were *making* them wash your car.

Because that's the tragic truth about zombies: They started out as slaves. Either raised from the dead to do some vile master's bidding, or somehow mesmerized into mindless subservience, zombies were the husked-out shells of humanity whose sole purpose was to do the degrading shit no willful soul would do.

In that sense, they were the *ultimate* slaves, in that they had no will of their own.

The first use of the z-word in English lit came from the poet Robert Southey, in a letter to the visionary Samuel Taylor Coleridge, way back in 1819. Fans of *Rime of the Ancient Mariner* and *Kubla Khan* will no doubt see why that's a cool backstage glimpse.

But it didn't enter the popular canon until another mystically inclined gent named W. B. Seabrook wrote a colorful account of his time in Haiti, *The Magic Island*, 110 years later.

One excerpt from this—". . . Dead Men Working in the Cane Fields" (included in this volume)—incited a slew of exotic zombie voodoo yarns, most of them staggeringly racist and not very insightfully written.

". . . Dead Men Working in the Cane Fields" also inspired the first "official" zombie film: 1932's *White Zombie*, starring Bela Legosi with a nod toward Faustin

E. Wirkus, the "White King of la Gonave." (Do yourself a favor and look that story up sometime. Who knew that *White Zombie* and *Apocalypse Now* had so much in common?)

Meanwhile, it could be argued that the poor mesmerized patsy in the 1920 classic *The Cabinet of Dr. Caligari* was the first great old-style zombie of film. But let's face it—some people just like to argue.

From there, zombies would pop up from time to time, mostly in pulps and B pictures and comic books. But they were never all that popular. They lacked the elegance and sex appeal of vampires, the peekaboo hijinks and classicism of ghosts, the unbridled id and robust physicality of werewolves and Mr. Hyde.

The perception was that zombies were definitely creepy, but mostly just kind of sad. They couldn't do squat until someone told them to. They were the brokenest of the broken: monsters with no self-esteem, their empty eyes haunted by the ghosts that had fled them, stripping all personality in a wispy vapor trail, leaving only the moldering skin and bones.

Poor zombies, I thought. I *hope you pull your shit together.* Cuz I *definitely sense potential here.*

Then came 1968 and the Great Zombie Emancipation.

It was a sneak attack, from the seemingly out-of-nowhere known as Pittsburgh, Pennsylvania. Spearheaded by a humble, brilliant, unsuspecting filmmaker by the name of George A. Romero. A director of commercials at the time—in fact, the inventor of the legendary "Tidy Bowl Man"—who got together with a bunch of his friends and, for less than one hundred grand, made a film that transformed both zombie self-image and the future of horror forever.

This was not Romero's intention. He just wanted to do something cool and creative, have fun with his crew, maybe make a couple bucks and a little name for himself. The fact that he cast a handsome black man as his lead wasn't even politically calculated: Duane Jones was simply the best actor he auditioned.

And it may be that his socio-commercial inadvertence—the simple desire to just *do something cool*—is no small part of the reason why his little black-and-white drive-in exploitation flick achieved such cultural transcendence. He was just surfing his unconscious, noting his influences, and riding the tide of the times. But he also thoroughly grasped the gestalt, and juicily pulled it all together in ways that none before him had ever come close to.

George has cited '50s-era EC Comics such as *Tales From the Crypt* as a seminal horror influence—with a nod to the look and feel of Herk Harvey's 1962 *Carnival of Souls*—but spotlights Richard Matheson's 1959 novel *I Am Legend* as the pivotal inspiration. And indeed, no analysis of the zombies we know and love today can proceed without name-checking Matheson's book.

Matheson was the first to postulate an undead pandemic, set in the modern America he knew. His monsters were cast as vampires, but stripped of aristocracy: no longer of the manor born, á la Bram Stoker's trend setting *Dracula*, but instead reenvisioned as clamoring hordes-next-door in a godless populist free-for-all.

Romero didn't do vampires. But he wasn't doing classic zombies, either. In fact, his original title was *Night of the Flesh-Eaters*, harkening more unto ghouls: the other underloved shamblers of yore.

Which opens up a whole 'nother bag of worms.

Because the fear of cannibalism—*of being eaten by your own kind*—is far older than voodoo, or magic of any stripe. Trust me. Long before we were sophisticated enough to pray, conjure, or even scrape two sticks together, we were eating each other. You can bet your ass on that.

As such, the human social contract has been a looooong time evolving. We've gradually set up basic rules along the way. *Thou shalt not lie. Thou shalt not steal. Thou shalt not rape. Thou shalt not kill.*

But once you get to *thou shalt not rip big squirting chunks out of each other with your goddam teeth*, you'd think you were stating the obvious. How much clearer could the social contract get?

Romero's zombies broke that contract. Moreover, they did it on *camera*: right in front of you, en masse, and with guileless purity. Which makes them part of a far older tradition.

Let's take, for example, this little four-thousand-year-old ditty from the epic *Gilgamesh*:

Ishtar spoke to her father, Anu, saying:
"Father, give me the Bull of Heaven,
so he can kill Gilgamesh in his dwelling.
If you do not give me the Bull of Heaven,
I will knock down the Gates of the Netherworld,
I will smash the door posts, and leave the doors flat down,
and will let the dead go up to eat the living!
And the dead will outnumber the living!"

Man, talk about foreshadowing!

The fact is that most of the world's religious and mythic traditions are crawling with representations of the hungry dead. (See Appendix A for further details.) They were all ghosts, ghouls, demons, or some other weirdo subspecies, either

a) cursed to roam the earth with their insatiable hunger, or;

b) needing live flesh to somehow *ground them* in this reality. Make them more physical. Retain a toehold in this world.

Then there were the grand Dionysian meatfests, wherein his loyal devotees would get so fucking hammered that orgies were no longer enough. Drink a gallon of wine, and the next thing you know, you're eating some poor pixilated chowderhead alive. *Woe unto Orpheus! Praise Dionysus!*

And let's not forget that Christ's whole sacrament came down to, "Take this and eat, for this is my body. Take this and drink, for this is my blood."

About which, for starters, I just gotta say it was a smart maneuver to make the body bread, and the blood wine, neatly shifting the focus to the symbolic.

But I also find myself wondering sometimes if he wasn't actually saying, "Please stop eating other people. *Eat me instead.*"

Which strikes me as a very Christian move.

All of this lays the foundation and such, but is largely tangential to the central fact underlying the Great Zombie Emancipation of '68.

And this is the kicker:

From that moment on, it suddenly became clear that *no one was running the show*. No spooky witch doctor. No creepy guy with a skinny little moustache and a Hypno-Wheel. No social contract. And seemingly, no God.

For the first time ever, the zombies were totally on their own. Self-determining at last.

Only their self was gone, too.

So what did they do? With nobody home, they became machines set on *chomp*: not regaining their souls, but simply reduced to broken meatbots, mindlessly consuming all they encountered.

Then the people they killed got up and killed.

Now *we* are the underdogs, hanging onto our humanity while, from every direction, we are being rent asunder.

It's frankly not the outcome I was hoping for; and in retrospect, I almost wish I hadn't rooted so hard for the zombies. It always sucks when your team turns out to be jerks.

But whaddaya gonna do?

Go, Team Zombie! I love you guys!

Now please stop eating us!

Finally, about this book . . .

What I've done is assembled thirty-odd pieces of my favorite zombie prose—some time-honored classics, some freshly cut gems—in an attempt to capture the full breadth and depth of the booming zombie phenomenon.

Movies are great. Games and comics are, too. But there's something about the written word that is uniquely suited to exploring these horrors: not just the surface, but the resonant depths. Elucidating profundities that might otherwise be missed.

Not to mention rocking the fucking house.

Trust me: there is world-class talent on tap here. You are in extremely good hands. Lovers of great writing will be amply rewarded. And zombie freaks? Prepare to have your world expanded.

Because the gamut is so vast—from the subtle and haunting to the truly, deeply, shockingly transgressive—the odds are extremely good that you'll love some and hate some. That's just the way it goes.

And that's the thing about zombies. *They are not pretty.* They unearth deep reservoirs of darkness within us, and the things they have to tell us are often raw and excruciating.

No matter how tough you think you are—what a first-class badass on *Left 4 Dead* or one of the other incredible zombie shoot-'em-up games currently selling a bajillion units worldwide—there will be points in this book where you're apt to go, "*Dude, that's just too much!*" As well you should.

It means you still have a heart.

And that, I think, is why zombies have become such an important metaphor for our time: effortlessly careening from comedy to tragedy to full-tilt atrocity, until even our global economy sports the z-word writ large.

Because they put our humanity into such stark relief.

They are *us*, stripped of everything that makes life worth living. Heart. Soul. Intelligence. Compassion. Joy. Laughs. Loyalty. Sense of purpose. All gone.

And they force us to live, if for no other reason than to differentiate ourselves from their dumb rotting asses.

But questions remain: Why are they so popular now? What has happened to them? And more important, *what has happened to us?*

This book closes with a second appendix that provides an in-depth analysis of the zombie in popular culture, revealing their myriad forms and the sheer measure of their impact. I think you'll find it enlightening indeed.

The end result of all this is my best attempt at one-stop shopping for all things zombie. A touchstone for inquiring minds. An anchor for the faithful. And a collection you'll treasure for years to come.

Thanks for lending your living minds to the undead nightmares parlayed herein. I hope you enjoy, and through the course of it arrive at your own best survival strategy.

Myself, I vote for empathy, every single time. Because if you lose that, you're just another one of them.

But keep a tire iron handy, just in case.

And know that I'm rootin' for you.

PART ONE:

ZOMBIES OF THE OLD SCHOOL

Lazarus

By Leonid Andreyev

Translated by Abraham Yarmolinsky

Where better to start than with the world's second-most-famous resurrected dead guy? And how better to start than with this 1906 stunner, which extends Christ's miracle past its initial delight into a woefully unfathomable darkness?

Leonid Andreyev was an artful, profound, subversive Expressionist pre-Soviet writer, dramatist, and photographer, who had an inarguable gift for persuasively bumming people out with the hard truths of life. When the Revolution came, it destroyed him completely, driving him to madness and a destitute death.

As such—in keeping with the grand Russian literary tradition of sunshiney highjinks and boisterous laughter—"Lazarus" is grim as grim can possibly get.

And yet—throughout this staggering work—he unstintingly takes note of the joys of living, if only to forensically dismantle them.

What stuns me most about this piece is its vastness of scope and economy of prose. It's one of those profoundly rare short stories that manages to simultaneously address the entirety of the human condition while always hewing close to the narrative bone. Which is to say that every strata of civilization introduced is yet a deeper plot point in the unfolding tale of poor Lazarus: his experience, his vision, and its impact on the world.

And yes, this is a zombie story.

WHEN LAZARUS ROSE FROM THE GRAVE, after three days and nights in the mysterious thralldom of death, and returned alive to his home, it was a long time before anyone noticed the evil peculiarities in him that were later to make his very name terrible. His friends and relatives were jubilant that he had come back to life. They surrounded him with tenderness, they were lavish of their eager attentions, spending the greatest care upon his food and drink and the new garments they made for him. They clad him gorgeously in the glowing colors of hope and laughter, and when, arrayed like a bridegroom, he sat at table with them again, ate again, and drank again, they wept fondly and summoned the neighbors to look upon the man miraculously raised from the dead.

The neighbors came and were moved with joy. Strangers arrived from distant cities and villages to worship the miracle. They burst into stormy exclamations, and buzzed around the house of Mary and Martha, like so many bees.

That which was new in Lazarus' face and gestures they explained naturally, as the traces of his severe illness and the shock he had passed through. It was evident that the disintegration of the body had been halted by a miraculous power, but that the restoration had not been complete; that death had left upon his face and body the effect of an artist's unfinished sketch seen through a thin glass. On his temples, under his eyes, and in the hollow of his cheek lay a thick, earthy blue. His fingers were blue, too, and under his nails, which had grown long in the grave, the blue had turned livid. Here and there on his lips and body, the skin, blistered in the grave, had burst open and left reddish glistening cracks, as if covered with a thin, glassy slime. And he had grown exceedingly stout. His body was horribly bloated and suggested the fetid, damp smell of putrefaction. But the cadaverous, heavy odor that clung to his burial garments and, as it seemed, to his very body, soon wore off, and after some time the blue of his hands and face softened, and the reddish cracks of his skin smoothed out, though they never disappeared completely. Such was the aspect of Lazarus in his second life. It looked natural only to those who had seen him buried.

Not merely Lazarus' face, but his very character, it seemed, had changed;

though it astonished no one and did not attract the attention it deserved. Before his death Lazarus had been cheerful and careless, a lover of laughter and harmless jest. It was because of his good humor, pleasant and equable, his freedom from meanness and gloom, that he had been so beloved by the Master. Now he was grave and silent; neither he himself jested nor did he laugh at the jests of others; and the words he spoke occasionally were simple, ordinary and necessary words—words as much devoid of sense and depth as are the sounds with which an animal expresses pain and pleasure, thirst and hunger. Such words a man may speak all his life and no one would ever know the sorrows and joys that dwelt within him.

Thus it was that Lazarus sat at the festive table among his friends and relatives—his face the face of a corpse over which, for three days, death had reigned in darkness, his garments gorgeous and festive, glittering with gold, bloody-red and purple; his mien heavy and silent. He was horribly changed and strange, but as yet undiscovered. In high waves, now mild, now stormy, the festivities went on around him. Warm glances of love caressed his face, still cold with the touch of the grave; and a friend's warm hand patted his bluish, heavy hand. And the music played joyous tunes mingled of the sounds of the tympanum, the pipe, the zither and the dulcimer. It was as if bees were humming, locusts buzzing and birds singing over the happy home of Mary and Martha.

II

Someone recklessly lifted the veil. By one breath of an uttered word he destroyed the serene charm, and uncovered the truth in its ugly nakedness. No thought was clearly defined in his mind, when his lips smilingly asked: "Why do you not tell us, Lazarus, what was There?" And all became silent, struck with the question. Only now it seemed to have occurred to them that for three days Lazarus had been dead; and they looked with curiosity, awaiting an answer. But Lazarus remained silent.

"You will not tell us?" wondered the inquirer. "Is it so terrible There?"

Again his thought lagged behind his words. Had it preceded them, he would not have asked the question, for, at the very moment he uttered it, his heart sank with a dread fear. All grew restless; they awaited the words of

Lazarus anxiously. But he was silent, cold and severe, and his eyes were cast down. And now, as if for the first time, they perceived the horrible bluishness of his face and the loathsome corpulence of his body. On the table, as if forgotten by Lazarus, lay his livid blue hand, and all eyes were riveted upon it, as though expecting the desired answer from that hand. The musicians still played; then silence fell upon them, too, and the gay sounds died down, as scattered coals are extinguished by water. The pipe became mute, and the ringing tympanum and the murmuring dulcimer; and as though a chord were broken, as though song itself were dying, the zither echoed a trembling broken sound. Then all was quiet.

"You will not?" repeated the inquirer, unable to restrain his babbling tongue. Silence reigned, and the livid blue hand lay motionless. It moved slightly, and the company sighed with relief and raised their eyes. Lazarus, risen from the dead, was looking straight at them, embracing all with one glance, heavy and terrible.

This was on the third day after Lazarus had arisen from the grave. Since then many had felt that his gaze was the gaze of destruction, but neither those who had been forever crushed by it, nor those who in the prime of life (mysterious even as death) had found the will to resist his glance, could ever explain the terror that lay immovable in the depths of his black pupils. He looked quiet and simple. One felt that he had no intention to hide anything, but also no intention to tell anything. His look was cold, as of one who is entirely indifferent to all that is alive. And many careless people who pressed around him, and did not notice him, later learned with wonder and fear the name of this stout, quiet man who brushed against them with his sumptuous, gaudy garments. The sun did not stop shining when he looked, neither did the fountain cease playing, and the Eastern sky remained cloudless and blue as always; but the man who fell under his inscrutable gaze could no longer feel the sun, nor hear the fountain, nor recognize his native sky. Sometimes he would cry bitterly, sometimes tear his hair in despair and madly call for help; but generally it happened that the men thus stricken by the gaze of Lazarus began to fade away listlessly and quietly and pass into a slow death lasting many long years. They died in the presence of everybody, colorless, haggard, and gloomy, like trees withering on rocky ground. Those who screamed in madness sometimes came back to life; but the others, never.

"So you will not tell us, Lazarus, what you saw There?" the inquirer repeated for the third time. But now his voice was dull, and a dead, gray weariness looked stupidly from out his eyes. The faces of all present were also covered by the same dead gray weariness like a mist. The guests stared at one another stupidly, not knowing why they had come together or why they sat around this rich table. They stopped talking, and vaguely felt it was time to leave; but they could not overcome the lassitude that spread through their muscles. So they continued to sit there, each one isolated, like little dim lights scattered in the darkness of night.

The musicians were paid to play, and they again took up the instruments, and again played gay or mournful airs. But it was music made to order, always the same tunes, and the guests listened wonderingly. Why was this music necessary, they thought, why was it necessary and what good did it do for people to pull at strings and blow their cheeks into thin pipes, and produce varied and strange-sounding noises?

"How badly they play!" said someone.

The musicians were insulted and left. Then the guests departed one by one, for it was nearing night. And when the quiet darkness enveloped them, and it became easier to breathe, the image of Lazarus suddenly arose before each one in stern splendor. There he stood, with the blue face of a corpse and the raiment of a bridegroom, sumptuous and resplendent, in his eyes that cold stare in the depths of which lurked *The Horrible!* They stood still as if turned into stone. The darkness surrounded them, and in the midst of this darkness flamed up the horrible apparition, the supernatural vision, of the one who for three days had lain under the measureless power of death. Three days he had been dead. Thrice had the sun risen and set—and he had lain dead. The children had played, the water had murmured as it streamed over the rocks, the hot dust had clouded the highway—and he had been dead. And now he was among men again—touched them—looked at them—*looked at them!* And through the black rings of his pupils, as through dark glasses, the unfathomable *There* gazed upon humanity.

III

No one took care of Lazarus, and no friends or kindred remained with him. Only the great desert, enfolding the Holy City, came close to the threshold of his abode. It entered his home, and lay down on his couch like a spouse, and put out all the fires. No one cared for Lazarus. One after the other went away, even his sisters, Mary and Martha. For a long while Martha did not want to leave him, for she knew not who would nurse him or take care of him; and she cried and prayed. But one night, when the wind was roaming about the desert, and the rustling cypress trees were bending over the roof, she dressed herself quietly, and quietly went away. Lazarus probably heard how the door was slammed—it had not shut properly and the wind kept knocking it continually against the post—but he did not rise, did not go out, did not try to find out the reason. And the whole night until the morning the cypress trees hissed over his head, and the door swung to and fro, allowing the cold, greedily prowling desert to enter his dwelling. Everybody shunned him as though he were a leper. They wanted to put a bell on his neck to avoid meeting him. But some one, turning pale, remarked it would be terrible if at night, under the windows. one should happen to hear Lazarus' bell, and all grew pale and assented.

Since he did nothing for himself, he would probably have starved had not his neighbors, in trepidation, saved some food for him. Children brought it to him. They did not fear him, neither did they laugh at him in the innocent cruelty in which children often laugh at unfortunates. They were indifferent to him, and Lazarus showed the same indifference to them. He showed no desire to thank them for their services; he did not try to pat the dark hands and look into the simple shining little eyes. Abandoned to the ravages of time and the desert, his house was falling to ruins, and his hungry, bleating goats had long been scattered among his neighbors. His wedding garments had grown old. He wore them without changing them, as he had donned them on that happy day when the musicians played. He did not see the difference between old and new, between torn and whole. The brilliant colors were burnt and faded; the vicious dogs of the city and the sharp thorns of the desert had rent the fine clothes to shreds.

During the day, when the sun beat down mercilessly upon all living things, and even the scorpions hid under the stones, convulsed with a mad desire to sting, he sat motionless in the burning rays, lifting high his blue face and shaggy wild beard.

While yet the people were unafraid to speak to him, some one had asked him: "Poor Lazarus! Do you find it pleasant to sit so, and look at the sun?" And he answered: "Yes, it is pleasant."

The thought suggested itself to people that the cold of the three days in the grave had been so intense, its darkness so deep, that there was not in all the earth enough heat or light to warm Lazarus and lighten the gloom of his eyes; and inquirers turned away with a sigh.

And when the setting sun, flat and purple-red, descended to earth, Lazarus went into the desert and walked straight toward it, as though intending to reach it. Always he walked directly toward the sun, and those who tried to follow him and find out what he did at night in the desert had indelibly imprinted upon their mind's vision the black silhouette of a tall, stout man against the red background of an immense disk. The horrors of the night drove them away, and so they never found out what Lazarus did in the desert; but the image of the black form against the red was burned forever into their brains. Like an animal with a cinder in its eye, which furiously rubs its muzzle against its paws, they foolishly rubbed their eyes; but the impression left by Lazarus was ineffaceable, forgotten only in death.

There were people living far away who never saw Lazarus and only heard of him. With an audacious curiosity, which is stronger than fear and feeds on fear, with a secret sneer in their hearts, some of them came to him one day as he basked in the sun, and entered into conversation with him. At that time his appearance had changed for the better and was not so frightful. At first the visitors snapped their fingers and thought disapprovingly of the foolish inhabitants of the Holy City. But when the short talk came to an end and they went home, their expression was such that the inhabitants of the Holy City at once knew their errand and said: "Here go some more madmen at whom Lazarus has looked." The speakers raised their hands in silent pity.

Other visitors came; among them brave warriors in clinking armor, who knew not fear, and happy youths who made merry with laughter and song. Busy merchants, jingling their coins, ran in for awhile, and proud attendants at the Temple placed their staffs at Lazarus' door. But no one returned the same as he came. A frightful shadow fell upon their souls, and gave a new appearance to the old familiar world.

Those who felt any desire to speak, after they had been stricken by the gaze of Lazarus, described the change that had come over them somewhat like this:

All objects seen by the eye and palpable to the hand became empty, light and transparent, as though they were light shadows in the darkness; and this darkness enveloped the whole universe. It was dispelled neither by the sun, nor by the moon, nor by the stars, but embraced the earth like a mother, and clothed it in a boundless black veil.

Into all bodies it penetrated, even into iron and stone; and the particles of the body lost their unity and became lonely. Even to the heart of the particles it penetrated, and the particles of the particles became lonely.

The vast emptiness which surrounds the universe, was not filled with things seen, with sun or moon or stars; it stretched boundless, penetrating everywhere, disuniting everything, body from body, particle from particle.

In emptiness the trees spread their roots, themselves empty; in emptiness rose phantom temples, palaces and houses—all empty; and in the emptiness moved restless Man, himself empty and light, like a shadow.

There was no more a sense of time; the beginning of all things and their end merged into one. In the very moment when a building was being erected and one could hear the builders striking with their hammers, one seemed already to see its ruins, and then emptiness where the ruins were.

A man was just born, and funeral candles were already lighted at his head, and then were extinguished; and soon there was emptiness where before had been the man and the candles.

And surrounded by Darkness and Empty Waste, Man trembled hopelessly before the dread of the Infinite.

So spoke those who had a desire to speak. But much more could probably have been told by those who did not want to talk, and who died in silence.

III.

At that time there lived in Rome a celebrated sculptor by the name of Aurelius. Out of clay, marble, and bronze he created forms of gods and men of such beauty that this beauty was proclaimed immortal. But he himself was not satisfied, and said there was a supreme beauty that he had never succeeded in expressing in marble or bronze. "I have not yet gathered the radiance of the moon," he said; "I have not yet caught glare of the sun. There is no soul in my marble, there is no life in my beautiful bronze." And when by moonlight he would slowly wander along the roads, crossing the black shadows of the cypress-trees, his white tunic flashing in the moonlight, those he met used to laugh good-naturedly and say: "Is it moonlight that you are gathering, Aurelius? Why did you not bring some baskets along?"

And he, too, would laugh and point to his eyes and say: "Here are the baskets in which I gather the light of the moon and the radiance of the sun."

And that was the truth. In his eyes shone moon and sun. But he could not transmit the radiance to marble. Therein lay the greatest tragedy of his life. He was a descendant of an ancient race of patricians, had a good wife and children, and except in this one respect, lacked nothing.

When the dark rumor about Lazarus reached him, he consulted his wife and friends and decided to make the long voyage to Judea, in order that he might look upon the man miraculously raised from the dead. He felt lonely in those days and hoped on the way to renew his jaded energies. What they told him about Lazarus did not frighten him. He had meditated much upon death. He did not like it, nor did he like those who tried to harmonies it with life. On this side, beautiful life; on the other, mysterious death, he reasoned, and no better lot could befall a man than to live—to enjoy life and the beauty of living. And he already had conceived a desire to convince Lazarus of the truth of this view and to return his soul to life even as his body had been returned. This task did not appear impossible, for the reports about Lazarus, fearsome and strange as they were, did not tell the whole truth about him, but only carried a vague warning against something awful.

Lazarus was getting up from a stone to follow in the path of the setting sun, on the evening when the rich Roman, accompanied by an armed slave, approached him, and in a ringing voice called to him: "Lazarus!"

Lazarus saw a proud and beautiful face, made radiant by fame, and white garments and precious jewels shining in the sunlight. The ruddy rays of the sun lent to the head and face a likeness to dimly shining bronze—that was what Lazarus saw. He sank back to his seat obediently, and wearily lowered his eyes.

"It is true you are not beautiful, my poor Lazarus," said the Roman quietly, playing with his gold chain. "You are even frightful, my poor friend; and death was not lazy the day when you so carelessly fell into its arms. But you are as fat as a barrel, and 'Fat people are not bad,' as the great Caesar said. I do not understand why people are so afraid of you. You will permit me to stay with you over night? It is already late, and I have no abode."

Nobody had ever asked Lazarus to be allowed to pass the night with him.

"I have no bed," said he.

"I am somewhat of a warrior and can sleep sitting," replied the Roman. "We shall make a light."

"I have no light."

"Then we will converse in the darkness like two friends. I suppose you have some wine?"

"I have no wine."

The Roman laughed.

"Now I understand why you are so gloomy and why you do not like your second life. No wine? Well, we shall do without. You know there are words that go to one's head even as Falernian wine."

With a motion of his head he dismissed the slave, and they were alone. And again the sculptor spoke, but it seemed as though the sinking sun had penetrated into his words. They faded, pale and empty, as if trembling on weak feet, as if slipping and falling, drunk with the wine of anguish and despair. And black chasms appeared between the two men—like remote hints of vast emptiness and vast darkness.

"Now I am your guest and you will not ill-treat me, Lazarus!" said the Roman. "Hospitality is binding even upon those who have been three days dead. Three days, I am told, you were in the grave. It must have been cold there . . . and it is from there that you have brought this bad habit of doing without light and wine. I like a light. It gets dark so quickly here. Your eyebrows and forehead have an interesting line: even as the ruins of castles covered with the ashes of an earthquake. But why in such strange, ugly clothes? I have seen the bridegrooms of your country, they wear clothes like that—such ridiculous clothes—such awful garments . . . Are you a bridegroom?"

Already the sun had disappeared. A gigantic black shadow was approaching fast from the west, as if prodigious bare feet were rustling over the sand. And the chill breezes stole up behind.

"In the darkness you seem even bigger, Lazarus, as though you had grown stouter in these few minutes. Do you feed on darkness, perchance? . . . And I would like a light . . . just a small light . . . just a small light. And I am cold. The nights here are so barbarously cold . . . If it were not so dark, I should say you were looking at me, Lazarus. Yes, it seems, you are looking. You are looking. *You are looking at me!* . . . I feel it—now you are smiling."

The night had come, and a heavy blackness filled the air.

"How good it will be when the sun rises again to-morrow . . . You know I am a great sculptor . . . so my friends call me. I create, yes, they say I create, but for that daylight is necessary. I give life to cold marble. I melt the ringing bronze in the fire, in a bright, hot fire. Why did you touch me with your hand?"

"Come," said Lazarus, "you are my guest." And they went into the house. And the shadows of the long evening fell on the earth . . .

The slave at last grew tired waiting for his master, and when the sun stood high he came to the house. And he saw, directly under its burning rays, Lazarus and his master sitting close together. They looked straight up and were silent.

The slave wept and cried aloud: "Master, what ails you, Master!"

The same day Aurelius left for Rome. The whole way he was thoughtful and silent, attentively examining everything, the people, the ship, and the sea, as though endeavoring to recall something. On the sea a great storm overtook them, and all the while Aurelius remained on deck and gazed eagerly at the approaching and falling waves. When he reached home his family were shocked at the terrible change in his demeanor, but he calmed them with the words: "I have found it!"

In the dusty clothes, which he had worn during the entire journey and had not changed, he began his work, and the marble ringingly responded to the resounding blows of the hammer. Long and eagerly he worked, admitting no one. At last, one morning, he announced that the work was ready, and gave instructions that all his friends, and the severe critics and judges of art, be called together. Then he donned gorgeous garments, shining with gold, glowing with the purple of the byssin.

"Here is what I have created," he said thoughtfully.

His friends looked, and immediately the shadow of deep sorrow covered their faces. It was a thing monstrous, possessing none of the forms familiar to the eye, yet not devoid of a hint of some new unknown form. On a thin tortuous little branch, or rather an ugly likeness of one, lay crooked, strange, unsightly, shapeless heaps of something turned outside in, or something turned inside out—wild fragments, which seemed to be feebly trying to get away from themselves. And, accidentally, under one of the wild projections, they noticed a wonderfully sculptured butterfly, with transparent wings, trembling as though with a weak longing to fly.

"Why that wonderful butterfly, Aurelius?" timidly asked some one.

"I do not know," answered the sculptor.

The truth had to be told, and one of his friends, the one who loved Aurelius best, said: "This is ugly, my poor friend. It must be destroyed. Give me the hammer." And with two blows he destroyed the monstrous mass, leaving only the wonderfully sculptured butterfly.

After that Aurelius created nothing. He looked with absolute indifference at marble and at bronze and at his own divine creations, in which dwelt immortal beauty. In the hope of breathing into him once again the old flame of inspiration, with the idea of awakening his dead soul, his friends led him to see the beautiful creations of others, but he remained indifferent and no smile warmed his closed lips. And only after they spoke to him much and long of beauty, he would reply wearily:

"But all this is—a lie."

And in the daytime, when the sun was shining, he would go into his rich and beautifully laid-out garden, and finding a place where there was no shadow, would expose his bare head and his dull eyes to the glitter and burning heat of the sun. Red and white butterflies fluttered around; down into the marble cistern ran splashing water from the crooked mouth of a blissfully drunken Satyr; but he sat motionless, like a pale shadow of that other one who, in a far land, at the very gates of the stony desert, also sat motionless under the fiery sun.

V

And it came about finally that Lazarus was summoned to Rome by the great Augustus.

They dressed him in gorgeous garments, as though it had been ordained that he was to remain a bridegroom to an unknown bride until the very day of his death. It was as if an old coffin, rotten and falling apart, were regilded over and over, and gay tassels were hung on it. And solemnly they conducted him in gala attire, as though in truth it were a bridal procession, the runners loudly sounding the trumpet that the way be made for the ambassadors of the Emperor. But the roads along which he passed were deserted. His entire native land cursed the execrable name of Lazarus, the man miraculously brought to life, and the people scattered at the mere report of his horrible approach. The trumpeters blew lonely blasts, and only the desert answered with a dying echo.

Then they carried him across the sea on the saddest and most gorgeous ship that was ever mirrored in the azure waves of the Mediterranean. There were many people aboard, but the ship was silent and still as a coffin, and the water seemed to moan as it parted before the short curved prow. Lazarus sat lonely, baring his head to the sun, and listening in silence to the splashing of the waters. Further away the seamen and the ambassadors gathered like a crowd of distressed shadows. If a thunderstorm had happened to burst upon them at that time or the wind had overwhelmed the red sails, the ship would probably have perished, for none of those who were on her had strength or desire enough to fight for life. With supreme effort some went to the side of the ship and eagerly gazed at the blue, transparent abyss. Perhaps they imagined they saw a naiad flashing a pink shoulder through the waves, or an insanely joyous and drunken centaur galloping by, splashing up the water with his hoofs. But the sea was deserted and mute, and so was the watery abyss.

Listlessly Lazarus set foot on the streets of the Eternal City, as though all its riches, all the majesty of its gigantic edifices, all the luster and beauty and music of refined life, were simply the echo of the wind in the desert, or the misty images of hot running sand. Chariots whirled by; the crowd of strong, beautiful, haughty men passed on, builders of the Eternal City and proud partakers of its life; songs rang out; fountains laughed; pearly laughter of women filled the air, while the drunkard philosophized and the sober ones smilingly listened; horseshoes rattled on the pavement. And surrounded on all sides by glad sounds, a fat, heavy man moved through the centre of the city like a cold spot of silence, sowing in his path grief, anger and vague, carking distress. Who dared to be sad in Rome? Indignantly demanded frowning citizens; and in two days the swift-tongued Rome knew of Lazarus, the man miraculously raised from the grave, and timidly evaded him.

There were many brave men ready to try their strength, and at their senseless call Lazarus came obediently. The Emperor was so engrossed with state affairs that he delayed receiving the visitor, and for seven days Lazarus moved among the people.

A jovial drunkard met him with a smile on his red lips. "Drink, Lazarus, drink!" he cried, "Would not Augustus laugh to see you drink!" And naked, besotted women laughed, and decked the blue hands of Lazarus with rose-leaves. But the drunkard looked into the eyes of Lazarus—and his joy ended forever. Thereafter he was always drunk. He drank no more, but was drunk all the time, shadowed by fearful dreams, instead of the joyous reveries that wine gives. Fearful dreams became the food of his broken spirit. Fearful dreams held him day and night in the mists of monstrous fantasy, and death itself was no more fearful than the apparition of its fierce precursor.

Lazarus came to a youth and his lass who loved each other and were beautiful in their love. Proudly and strongly holding in his arms his beloved one, the youth said, with gentle pity: "Look at us, Lazarus, and rejoice with us. Is there anything stronger than love?"

And Lazarus looked at them. And their whole life they continued to love one another, but their love became mournful and gloomy, even as those cypress trees over the tombs that feed their roots on the putrescence of the grave, and strive in vain in the quiet evening hour to touch the sky with their pointed tops. Hurled by fathomless life-forces into each other's arms, they mingled their kisses with tears, their joy with pain, and only succeeded in realizing the more vividly a sense of their slavery to the silent Nothing. Forever united, forever parted, they flashed like sparks, and like sparks went out in boundless darkness.

Lazarus came to a proud sage, and the sage said to him: "I already know all the horrors that you may tell me, Lazarus. With what else can you terrify me?"

Only a few moments passed before the sage realized that the knowledge of the horrible is not the horrible, and that the sight of death is not death. And he felt that in the eyes of the Infinite wisdom and folly are the same, for the Infinite knows them not. And the boundaries between knowledge and ignorance, between truth and falsehood, between top and bottom, faded and his shapeless thought was suspended in emptiness. Then he grasped his gray head in his hands and cried out insanely: "I cannot think! I cannot think!"

Thus it was that under the cool gaze of Lazarus, the man miraculously raised from the dead, all that serves to affirm life, its sense and its joys, perished. And people began to say it was dangerous to allow him to see the Emperor; that it was better to kill him and bury him secretly, and swear he had disappeared. Swords were sharpened and youths devoted to the welfare of the people announced their readiness to become assassins, when Augustus upset the cruel plans by demanding that Lazarus appear before him.

Even though Lazarus could not be kept away, it was felt that the heavy impression conveyed by his face might be somewhat softened. With that end in view expert painters, barbers and artists were secured who worked the whole night on Lazarus' head. His beard was trimmed and curled. The disagreeable and deadly bluishness of his hands and face was covered up with paint; his hands were whitened, his cheeks rouged. The disgusting wrinkles of suffering that ridged his old face were patched up and painted, and on the smooth surface, wrinkles of good-nature and laughter, and of pleasant, good-humored cheeriness, were laid on artistically with fine brushes.

Lazarus submitted indifferently to an they did with him, and soon was transformed into a stout, nice-looking old man, for all the world a quiet and good-humored grandfather of numerous grandchildren. He looked as though the smile with which he told funny stories had not left his lips, as though a quiet tenderness still lay hidden in the corner of his eyes. But the wedding-dress they did not dare to take off; and they could not change his eyes—the dark, terrible eyes from out of which stared the incomprehensible *There*.

VI

Lazarus was untouched by the magnificence of the imperial apartments. He remained stolidly indifferent, as though he saw no contrast between his ruined house at the edge of the desert and the solid, beautiful palace of stone. Under his feet the hard marble of the floor took on the semblance of the moving sands of the desert, and to his eyes the throngs of gaily dressed, haughty men were as unreal as the emptiness of the air. They looked not into his face as he passed by, fearing to come under the awful bane of his eyes; but when the sound of his heavy steps announced that he had passed, heads were lifted, and eyes examined with timid curiosity the figure of the corpulent, tall, slightly stooping old man, as he slowly passed into the heart of the imperial palace. If death itself had appeared men would not have feared it so much; for hitherto death had been known to the dead only, and to the living only, and between these two there had been no bridge. But this strange being knew death, and that knowledge of his was felt to be mysterious and cursed. "He will kill our great, divine Augustus," men cried with horror, and they hurled curses after him. Slowly and stolidly he passed them by, penetrating ever deeper into the palace.

Caesar knew already who Lazarus was, and was prepared to meet him. He was a courageous man; he felt his power was invincible, and in the fateful encounter with the man "wonderfully raised from the dead" he refused to lean on other men's weak help. Man to man, face to face, he met Lazarus.

"Do not fix your gaze on me, Lazarus," he commanded. "I have heard that your head is like the head of Medusa, and turns into stone all upon whom you look. But I should like to have a close look at you, and to talk to you before I turn into stone," he added in a spirit of playfulness that concealed his real misgivings.

Approaching him, he examined closely Lazarus' face and his strange festive clothes. Though his eyes were sharp and keen, he was deceived by the skilful counterfeit.

"Well, your appearance is not terrible, venerable sir. But all the worse for men, when the terrible takes on such a venerable and pleasant appearance. Now let us talk."

Augustus sat down, and as much by glance as by words began the discussion. "Why did you not salute me when you entered?"

Lazarus answered indifferently: "I did not know it was necessary."

"You are a Christian?"

"No."

Augustus nodded approvingly. "That is good. I do not like the Christians. They shake the tree of life, forbidding it to bear fruit, and they scatter to the wind its fragrant blossoms. But who are you?"

With some effort Lazarus answered: "I was dead."

"I heard about that. But who are you now?"

Lazarus' answer came slowly. Finally he said again, listlessly and indistinctly: "I was dead."

"Listen to me, stranger," said the Emperor sharply, giving expression to what had been in his mind before. "My empire is an empire of the living; my people are a people of the living and not of the dead. You are superfluous here. I do not know who you are, I do not know what you have seen There, but if you lie, I hate your lies, and if you tell the truth, I hate your truth. In my heart I feel the pulse of life; in my hands I feel power, and my proud thoughts, like eagles, fly through space. Behind my back, under the protection of my authority, under the shadow of the laws I have created, men live and labor and rejoice. Do you hear this divine harmony of life? Do you hear the war cry that men hurl into the face of the future, challenging it to strife?"

Augustus extended his arms reverently and solemnly cried out: "Blessed art thou, Great Divine Life!"

But Lazarus was silent, and the Emperor continued more severely: "You are not wanted here. Pitiful remnant, half devoured of death, you fill men with distress and aversion to life. Like a caterpillar on the fields, you are gnawing away at the full seed of joy, exuding the slime of despair and sorrow. Your truth is like a rusted sword in the hands of a night assassin, and I shall condemn you to death as an assassin. But first I want to look into your eyes. Mayhap only cowards fear them, and brave men are spurred on to struggle and victory. Then will you merit not death but a reward. Look at me, Lazarus."

At first it seemed to divine Augustus as if a friend were looking at him, so soft, so alluring, so gently fascinating was the gaze of Lazarus. It promised not horror but quiet rest, and the Infinite dwelt there as a fond mistress, a compassionate sister, a mother. And ever stronger grew its gentle embrace, until he felt, as it were, the breath of a mouth hungry for kisses . . . Then it seemed as if iron bones protruded in a ravenous grip, and closed upon him in an iron band; and cold nails touched his heart, and slowly, slowly sank into it.

"It pains me," said divine Augustus, growing pale; "but look, Lazarus, look!"

Ponderous gates, shutting off eternity, appeared to be slowly swinging open, and through the growing aperture poured in, coldly and calmly, the awful horror of the Infinite. Boundless Emptiness and Boundless Gloom entered like two shadows, extinguishing the sun, removing the ground from under the feet, and the cover from over the head. And the pain in his icy heart ceased.

"Look at me, look at me, Lazarus!" commanded Augustus, staggering . . .

Time ceased and the beginning of things came perilously near to the end. The throne of Augustus, so recently erected, fell to pieces, and emptiness took the place of the throne and of Augustus. Rome fell silently into ruins. A new city rose in its place, and it too was erased by emptiness. Like phantom giants, cities, kingdoms, and countries swiftly fell and disappeared into emptiness—swallowed up in the black maw of the Infinite . . .

"Cease," commanded the Emperor. Already the accent of indifference was in his voice. His arms hung powerless, and his eagle eyes flashed and were dimmed again, struggling against overwhelming darkness.

"You have killed me, Lazarus," he said drowsily.

These words of despair saved him. He thought of the people, whose shield he was destined to be, and a sharp, redeeming pang pierced his dull heart. He thought of them doomed to perish, and he was filled with anguish. First they seemed bright shadows in the gloom of the Infinite.—How terrible! Then they appeared as fragile vessels with life-agitated blood, and hearts that knew both sorrow and great joy.—And he thought of them with tenderness.

And so thinking and feeling, inclining the scales now to the side of life, now to the side of death, he slowly returned to life, to find in its suffering and joy a refuge from the gloom, emptiness and fear of the Infinite.

"No, you did not kill me, Lazarus," said he firmly. "But I will kill you. Go!"

Evening came and divine Augustus partook of food and drink with great joy. But there were moments when his raised arm would remain suspended in the air, and the light of his shining, eager eyes was dimmed. It seemed as if an icy wave of horror washed against his feet. He was vanquished but not killed, and coldly awaited his doom, like a black shadow. His nights were haunted by horror, but the bright days still brought him the joys, as well as the sorrows, of life.

Next day, by order of the Emperor, they burned out Lazarus' eyes with hot irons and sent him home. Even Augustus dared not kill him.

Lazarus returned to the desert and the desert received him with the breath of the hissing wind and the ardor of the glowing sun. Again he sat on the stone with matted beard uplifted; and two black holes, where the eyes had once been, looked dull and horrible at the sky. In the distance the Holy City surged and roared restlessly, but near him all was deserted and still. No one approached the place where Lazarus, miraculously raised from the dead, passed his last days, for his neighbors had long since abandoned their homes. His cursed knowledge, driven by the hot irons from his eyes deep into the brain, lay there in ambush; as if from ambush it might spring out upon men with a thousand unseen eyes. No one dared to look at Lazarus.

And in the evening, when the sun, swollen crimson and growing larger, bent its way toward the west, blind Lazarus slowly groped after it. He stumbled against stones and fell; corpulent and feeble, he rose heavily and walked on; and against the red curtain of sunset his dark form and outstretched arms gave him the semblance of a cross.

It happened once that he went and never returned. Thus ended the second life of Lazarus, who for three days had been in the mysterious thralldom of death and then was miraculously raised from the dead.

. . . Dead Men Working in the Cane Fields

by **W. B. Seabrook**

Having set up this story in the introduction, I have little to add beyond hearty recommendation. Along with Lafcadio Hearn, William Seabrook is notable for his sincere desire to understand the mysteries presented him: not without Western judgment, but with a willingness to consider how wrong he might be, and just how much might remain to be learned.

His pursuit of the arcane led to a lifetime of inquiry, much of it weird, some of it disturbing. Aleister Crowley is just one of the colorful characters with whom he became intimate. With that info, you may do as thou wilt.

Myself, I'm grateful for the records he left, of which ". . . Dead Men Working in the Cane Fields*" is perhaps the most influential.*

PRETTY MULATTO JULIE had taken baby Marianne to bed. Constant Polynice and I sat late before the doorway of his *caille*, talking of fire-hags, demons, werewolves, and vampires, while a full moon, rising slowly, flooded his sloping cotton fields and the dark rolling hills beyond.

Polynice was a Haitian farmer, but he was no common jungle peasant. He lived on the island of La Gonave, where I shall return to him in later chapters. He seldom went over to the Haitian mainland, but he knew what was going on in Port-au-Prince, and spoke sometimes of installing a radio.

A countryman, half peasant born and bred, he was familiar with every superstition of the mountains and the plain, yet too intelligent to believe them literally true—or at least so I gathered from his talk.

He was interested in helping me toward an understanding of the tangled Haitian folklore. It was only by chance that we came presently to a subject which—though I refused for a long time to admit it—lies in a baffling category on the ragged edge of things which are beyond either superstition or reason. He had been telling me of fire-hags who left their skins at home and set the cane fields blazing; of the vampire, a woman sometimes living, sometimes dead, who sucked the blood of children and who could be distinguished because her hair always turned an ugly red; of the werewolf—*chauché*, in creole—a man or woman who took the form of some animal, usually a dog, and went killing lambs, young goats, sometimes babies.

All this, I gathered, he considered to be pure superstition, as he told me with tolerant scorn how his friend and neighbor Osmann had one night seen a gray dog slinking with bloody jaws from his sheep-pen, and who, after having shot and exorcised and buried it, was so convinced he had killed a certain girl named Liane who was generally reputed to be a *chauché* that when he met her two days later on the path to Grande Source, he believed she was a ghost come back for vengeance, and fled howling.

As Polynice talked on, I reflected that these tales ran closely parallel not only with those of the negroes in Georgia and the Carolinas, but with the medieval folklore of white Europe. Werewolves, vampires, and demons were certainly no novelty. But I recalled one creature I had been hearing about in Haiti, which sounded exclusively local—the *zombie*.

It seemed (or so I had been assured by negroes more credulous than Polynice) that while the *zombie* came from the grave, it was neither a ghost, nor yet a person who had been raised like Lazarus from the dead. The *zombie*, they say, is a soulless human corpse, still dead, but taken from the grave and endowed by sorcery with a mechanical semblance of life—it is a dead body which is made to walk and act and move as if it were alive. People who have the power to do this go to a fresh grave, dig up the body before it has had time to rot, galvanize it into movement, and then make of it a servant or slave, occasionally for the commission of some crime, more often simply as a drudge around the habitation or the farm, setting it dull heavy tasks, and beating it like a dumb beast if it slackens.

As this was revolving in my mind, I said to Polynice: "It seems to me that these werewolves and vampires are first cousins to those we have at home, but I have never, except in Haiti, heard of anything like *zombies*. Let us talk of them for a little while. I wonder if you can tell me something of this *zombie* superstition. I should like to get at some idea of how it originated."

My rational friend Polynice was deeply astonished. He leaned over and put his hand in protest on my knee.

"Superstition? But I assure you that this of which you now speak is not a matter of superstition. Alas, these things—and other evil practices connected with the dead—exist. They exist to an extent that you whites do not dream of, though evidences are everywhere under your eyes.

"Why do you suppose that even the poorest peasants, when they can, bury their dead beneath solid tombs of masonry?

"Why do they bury them so often in their own yards, close to the doorway?

"Why, so often, do you see a tomb or grave set close beside a busy road or footpath where people are always passing?

"It is to assure the poor unhappy dead such protection as we can.

"I will take you in the morning to see the grave of my brother, who was killed in the way you know. It is over there on the little ridge when you can see clearly now in the moonlight, open space all round it, close beside the trail which everybody passes going to and from Grande Source. Through four nights we watched yonder, in the peristyle, Osmann and I, with shotguns—for at that time both my dead brother and I had bitter enemies—until we were sure the body had begun to rot.

"No, my friend, no, no. There are only too many true cases. At this very moment, in the moonlight, there are *zombies* working on this island, less than two hours' ride from my own habitation. We know about them, but we do not dare to interfere so long as our own dead are left unmolested. If you will ride with me tomorrow night, yes, I will show you dead men working in the cane fields. Close even to the cities, there are sometimes *zombies*. Perhaps you have already heard of those that were at Hasco . . ."

"What about Hasco?" I interrupted him, for in the whole of Haiti, Hasco is perhaps the last name anybody would think of connecting with either sorcery or superstition.

"The word is American-commercial-synthetic, like Nabisco, Delco, Socony. It stands for the Haitian-American Sugar Company—an immense factory plant, dominated by a huge chimney, with clanging machinery, steam whistles, freight cars. It is like a chunk of Hoboken. It lies in the eastern suburbs of Port-au-Prince, and beyond it stretch the cane fields of the Cul-de-Sac. Hasco makes rum when the sugar market is off, pays low wages, twenty or thirty cents a day, and gives steady work. It is modern big business, and it sounds it, looks it, smells it.

Such, then, was the incongruous background for the weird tale Constant Polynice now told me.

The spring of 1918 was a big cane season, and the factory, which had its own plantations, offered a bonus on the wages of new workers. Soon heads of families and villages from the mountain and the plain came trailing their ragtag little armies, men, women, children, trooping to the registration bureau and thence into the fields.

One morning an old black headman, Ti Joseph of Colombier, appeared leading a band of ragged creatures who shuffled along behind him, staring dumbly, like people walking in a daze. As Joseph lined them up for registration, they still stared, vacant-eyed like cattle, and made no reply when asked to give their names.

Joseph said they were ignorant people from the slopes of Morne-au-Diable, a roadless mountain district near the Dominican border, and that they did not understand the creole of the plains. They were frightened, he said, by the din and smoke of the great factory, but under his direction they would work hard in the fields. The farther they were sent away from the factory, from the noise and bustle of the railroad yards, the better it would be.

Better indeed, for these were not living men and women but poor unhappy *zombies* whom Joseph and his wife Croyance had dragged from their peaceful graves to slave for him in the sun—and if by chance a brother or father of the dead should see and recognize them, Joseph knew that it would be a very bad affair for him. So they were assigned to distant fields beyond the cross-roads, and camped there, keeping to themselves like any proper family or village group; but in the evening when other little companies, encamped apart as they were, gathered each around its one big common pot of savory millet or plantains, generously seasoned with dried fish and garlic, Croyance would tend *two* pots upon the fire, for as everyone knows, the *zombies* must never be permitted to taste salt or meat. So the food prepared for them was tasteless and unseasoned.

As the *zombies* toiled day after day dumbly in the sun, Joseph sometimes beat them to make them move faster, but Croyance began to pity the poor dead creatures who should be at rest—and pitied them in the evenings when she dished out their flat, tasteless *bouillie*.

Each Saturday afternoon, Joseph went to collect the wages for them all, and what division he made was no concern of Hasco, so long as the work went forward. Sometimes Joseph alone, and sometimes Croyance alone, went to Crois de Bouquet for the Saturday night *bamboche* or the Sunday cockfight, but always one of them remained with the *zombies* to prepare their food and see that they did not stray away.

Through February this continued, until Fête Dieu approached, with a Saturday-Sunday-Monday holiday for all the workers. Joseph, with his pockets full of money, went to Port-au-Prince and left Croyance behind, cautioning her as usual; and she agreed to remain and tend the *zombies*, for he promised her that at the Mardi Gras she should visit the city.

But when Sunday morning dawned, it was lonely in the fields, and her kind old woman's heart was filled with pity for the *zombies*, and she thought, "Perhaps it will cheer them a little to see the gay crowds and the processions at Croix de Bouquet, and since all the Morne-au-Diable people will have gone back to the mountain to celebrate Fête Dieu at home, no one will recognize them, and no harm can come of it." And it is the truth that Croyance also wished to see the gay procession.

So she tied a new bright-colored handkerchief around her head, aroused the *zombies* from the sleep that was scarcely different from their waking, gave them their morning bowl of cold, unsalted plantains boiled in water, which they ate dumbly uncomplaining, and set out with them for the town, single file, as the country people always walk. Croyance, in her bright kerchief, leading the nine dead men and women behind her, past the railroad crossing, where she murmured a prayer to Legba, past the great white-painted wooden Christ, who hung life-sized in the glaring sun, where she stopped to kneel and cross herself—but the poor *zombies* prayed neither to Papa Legba nor to Brother Jesus, for they were dead bodies walking, without souls or minds.

They followed her to the market square, before the church where hundreds of little thatched, open shelters, used on week days for buying and selling, were empty of trade, but crowded here and there by gossiping groups in the grateful shade.

To the shade of one of these market booths, which was still unoccupied, she led the *zombies*, and they sat like people asleep with their eyes open, staring, but seeing nothing, as the bells in the church began to ring, and the procession came from the priest's house—red-purple robes, golden crucifix held aloft, tinkling bells and swinging incense-pots, followed by little black boys in white lace robes, little black girls in starched white dresses, with shoes and stockings, from the parish school, with colored ribbons in their kinky hair, a nun beneath a big umbrella leading them.

Croyance knelt with the throng as the procession passed, and wished she might follow it across the square to the church steps, but the *zombies* just sat and stared, seeing nothing.

When noontime came, women with baskets passed to and fro in the crowd, or sat selling bonbons (which were not candy but little sweet cakes), figs (which were not figs but sweet bananas), oranges, dried herring, biscuit, cassava bread, and *clairin* poured from a bottle at a penny a glass.

As Croyance sat with her savory dried herring and biscuit baked with salt and soda, and provision of *clairin* in the tin cup by her side, she pitied the *zombies* who had worked so faithfully for Joseph in the cane fields, and who now had nothing, while all the other groups around were feasting, and as she pitied them, a woman passed, crying,

"*Tablettes! Tablettes pistaches! T'ois pour dix cobs!*"

Tablettes are a sort of candy, in shape and size like cookies, made of brown cane sugar (*rapadou*); sometimes with *pistaches*, which in Haiti are peanuts or with coriander seed.

And Croyance throught, "These *tablettes* are not salted or seasoned, they are sweet, and can do no harm to the *zombies* just this once."

So she untied the corner of her kerchief, took out a coin, a *gourdon*, the quarter of a *gourde*, and bought some of the *tablettes*, which she broke in halves and divided among the *zombies*, who began sucking and mumbling them in their mouths.

But the baker of the *tablettes* had salted the *pistache* nuts before stirring them into the *rapadou*, and as the *zombies* tasted the salt, they knew that they were dead and made a dreadful outcry and turned their faces toward the mountain.

No one dared stop them, for they were corpses walking in the sunlight, and they were themselves and all the people knew that they were corpses. And they disappeared toward the mountain.

When later they drew near their own village in the slopes of Morne-au-Diable, these dead men and women walking single file in the twilight, with no soul leading them or daring to follow, the people of their village, who were also holding *bamboche* in the market-place, saw them drawing closer, recognized among them fathers, brothers, wives, and daughters whom they had buried months before.

Most of them knew at once the truth, that these were *zombies* who had been dragged dead from their graves, but others hoped that a blessed miracle had taken place on this Fête Dieu, and rushed forward to take them in their arms and welcome them.

But the *zombies* shuffled through the market-place, recognizing neither father nor wife nor mother, and as they turned leftward up the path leading to the graveyard, a woman whose daughter was in the procession of the dead threw herself screaming before the girl's shuffling feet and begged her to stay; but the grave-cold feet of the daughter and the feet of the other dead shuffled over her and onward; and as they approached the graveyard, they began to shuffle faster and rushed among the graves, and each before his own empty grave began clawing at the stones and earth to enter it again; and as their cold hands touched the earth of their own graves, they fell and lay there, rotting carrion.

That night the fathers, son, and brothers of the *zombies*, after restoring the bodies to their graves, sent a messenger on muleback down the mountain, who returned next day with the name of Ti Joseph and with a stolen shirt of Ti Joseph's which had been worn next to his skin and was steeped in the grease-sweat of his body.

They collected silver in the village and went with the name of Ti Joseph and the shirt of Ti Joseph to a *bocor* beyond Trou Caiman, who made a deadly needle *ouanga*, a black bag *ouanga*, pierced all through with pins and needles, filled with dry goat dung, circled with cock's feathers dipped in blood.

And lest the needle *ouanga* be slow in working or be rendered weak by Joseph's counter-magic, they sent men down to the plain, who lay in wait patiently for Joseph, and one night hacked off his head with a machete . . .

When Polynice had finished this recital, I said to him, after a moment of silence, "You are not a peasant like those of the Cul-de-Sac; you are a reasonable man, or at least it seems to me you are. Now how much of that story, honestly, do you believe?"

He replied earnestly: "I did not see these special things, but there were many witnesses, and why should I not believe them when I myself have also seen *zombies*? When you also have seen them, with their faces and their eyes in which there is no life, you will not only believe in these *zombies* who should be resting in their graves, you will pity them from the bottom of your heart."

Before finally taking leave of La Gonave, I did see these "walking dead men," and I did, in a sense, believe in them and pitied them, indeed, from the bottom of my heart. It was not the next night, though Polynice, true to his promise, rode with me across the Plaine Mapou to the deserted, silent cane fields where he had hoped to show me *zombies* laboring. It was not on any night. It was in broad daylight one afternoon, when we passed that way again, on the lower trail to Picmy. Polynice reined in his horse and pointed to a rough, stony, terraced slope—on which four laborers, three men and a woman, were chopping the earth with machetes, among straggling cotton stalks, a hundred yards distant from the trail.

"Wait while I go up there," he said, excited because a chance had come to fulfill his promise. "I think it is Lamercie with the *zombies*. If I wave to you, leave your horse and come." Starting up the slope, he shouted to the woman, "It is I, Polynice," and when he waved later, I followed.

As I clambered up, Polynice was talking to the woman. She had stopped work—a big-boned, hard-faced black girl, who regarded us with surly unfriendliness. My first impression of the three supposed *zombies*, who continued dumbly at work, was that there was something about them unnatural and strange. They were plodding like brutes, like automatons. Without stooping down, I could not fully see their faces, which were bent expressionless over their work. Polynice touched one of them on the shoulder, motioned him to get up. Obediently, like an animal, he slowly stood erect—and what I saw then, coupled with what I had heard previously, or despite it, came as a rather sickening shock. The eyes were the worst. It was not my imagination. They were in truth like the eyes of a dead man, not blind, but staring, unfocused, unseeing. The whole face, for that matter, was bad enough. It was vacant, as if there was nothing behind it. It seemed not only expressionless, but incapable of expression. I had seen so much previously in Haiti that was outside ordinary normal experience that for the flash of a second I had a sickening, almost panicky lapse in which I thought, or rather felt, "Great God, maybe this stuff is really true, and if it is true, it is rather awful, for it upsets everything." By "everything" I meant the natural fixed laws and processes on which all modern human thought and actions are based. Then suddenly I remembered—and my mind seized the memory as a man sinking in water clutches a solid plank—the face of a dog I had once seen in the histological laboratory at Columbia. Its entire front brain had been removed in an experimental operation weeks before; it moved about, it was alive, but its eyes were like the eyes I now saw staring.

I recovered from my mental panic. I reached out and grasped one of the dangling hands. It was calloused, solid, human. Holding it, I said, "*Bonjour, compère.*" The *zombie* stared without responding. The black wench, Lamercie, who was their keeper, now more sullen than ever, pushed me away—"*Z'affai' nèg' pas z'affai' blanc*" (Negroes' affairs are not for whites). But I had seen enough. "Keeper" was the key to it. "Keeper" was the word that had leapt naturally into my mind as she protested, and just as naturally the *zombies* were nothing but poor, ordinary demented human beings, idiots, forced to toil in the fields.

It was a good rational explanation, but it is far from the end of this story. It satisfied me then, and I said as much to Polynice as we went down the slope. At first he did not contradict me, even said doubtfully, "Perhaps"; but as we reached the horses, before mounting, he stopped and said, "Look here, I respect your distrust of what you call superstition and your desire to find out the truth, but if what you were saying now were the whole truth, how could it be that over and over again, people who have stood by and seen their own relatives buried have, sometimes soon, sometimes months or years afterward, found those relatives working as *zombies*, and have sometimes killed the man who held them in servitude?"

"Polynice," I said, "that's just the part of it that I can't believe. The *zombies* in such cases may have may have resembled the dead persons, or even been 'doubles'—you know what doubles are, how two people resemble each other to a startling degree. But it is a fixed rule of reasoning in America that we will never accept the possibility of a thing's being 'supernatural' so long as any natural explanation, even far-fetched, seems adequate."

"Well," said he, "if you spent many years in Haiti, you would have a very hard time to fit this American reasoning into some of the things you encountered here."

As I have said, there is more to this story—and I think it is best to tell it very simply.

In all Haiti, there is no clearer scientifically trained mind, no sounder pragmatic rationalist, than Dr. Antoine Villiers. When I sat later with him in his study, surrounded by hundreds of scientific books in French, German, and English, and told him of what I had seen and of my conversations with Polynice, he said:

"My dear sir, I do not believe in miracles nor in supernatural events, and I do not want to shock your Anglo-Saxon intelligence, but this Polynice of yours, with all his superstition, may have been closer to the partial truth than you were. Understand me clearly. I do not believe that anyone has ever been raised literally from the dead—neither Lazarus, nor the daughter of Jairus, nor Jesus Christ himself—yet I am not sure, paradoxical as it might sound, that there is not something frightful, something in the nature of criminal sorcery if you like, in some cases at least, in this matter of *zombies*. I am by no means sure that some of them who now toil in the fields were not dragged from the actual graves in which they lay in their coffins, buried by their mourning families!"

"It is then something like suspended animation?" I asked.

"I will show you," he replied, "a thing which may supply the key to what you are seeking," and standing on a chair, he pulled down a paper-bound book from a top shelf. It was nothing mysterious or esoteric. It was the current official *Code Pénal* (Criminal Code) of the Republic of Haiti. He thumbed through it and pointed to a paragraph which read:

"*Article* 249. Also shall be qualified as attempted murder the employment which may be made against any person of substances which, without causing actual death, produce a lethargic coma more or less prolonged. If, after the administering of such substances, the person has been buried, the act shall be considered murder no matter what result follows."

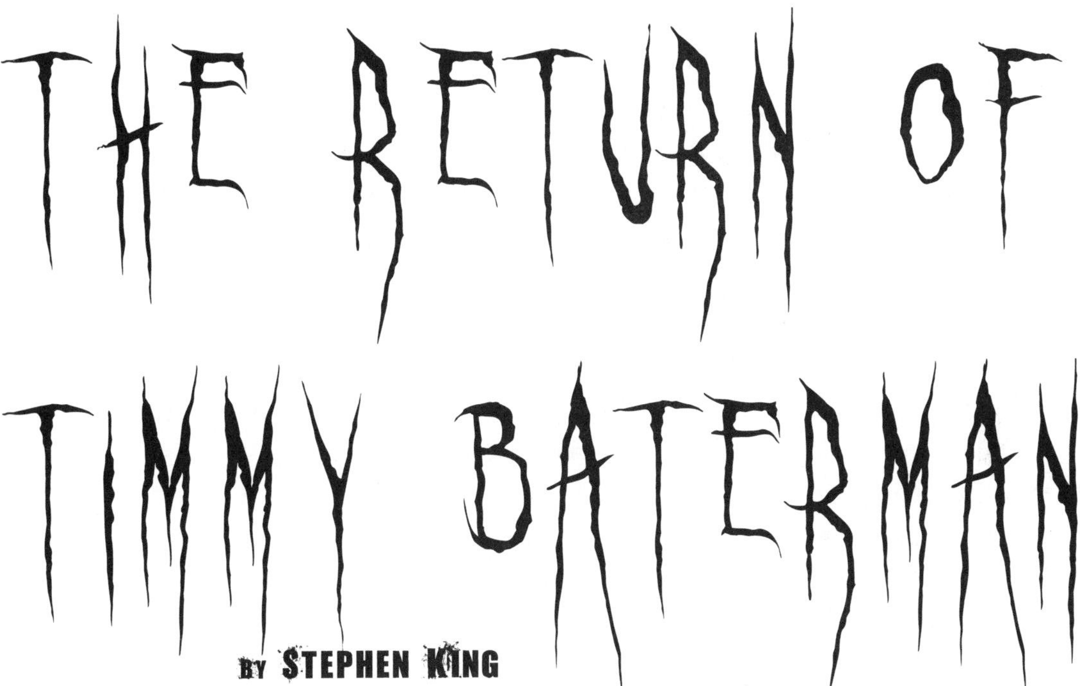

THE RETURN OF TIMMY BATERMAN

BY STEPHEN KING

Be careful what you wish for, because you just might get it.

Those words lay at the heart of many of the greatest horror stories. At their core, they are simple cautionary tales, warning us not to do that incredibly stupid thing we were just considering, lest unspeakable consequences befall us.

*"*The Return of Timmy Baterman*" is one of those greats. Like the* W. W. Jacobs *classic "*The Monkey's Paw,*" it goes out of its way to remind you that sometimes dead is better, and that some things are best left alone.*

*When "*Timmy*" first appeared—in the program book for* Crypticon II, *back in 1983—little did the* Knoxville *convention attendees know that this little beauty was just the tip of the iceberg.*

In fact, they were mere months away from the release of Pet Sematary: *a literary milestone on the order of* The Exorcist; *and, to my mind, still the most deeply disturbing, genuinely horrifying novel of* Stephen King's *long, legendary career.*

"IN THOSE DAYS—back during the war, I mean—the train still stopped in Orrington, and Bill Baterman had a funeral hack there at the loading depot to meet the freight carrying the body of his son Timmy. The coffin was unloaded by four railroad men. I was one of them. There was an army fellow on board from Graves and Registration—that was the army's wartime version of undertakers, Louis—but he never got off the train. He was sitting drunk in a boxcar that still had twelve coffins in it.

"We put Timmy into the back of a Cadillac—in those days it still wasn't uncommon to hear such things called 'hurry-up wagons' because the old days, the major concern was to get them into the ground before they rotted. Bill Baterman stood his face stony and kinda. . . .I dunno. . . .kinda dry, guess you'd say. He wept no tears. Huey Garber was driving the train that day, and he said that army fella had really had a tour for himself. Huey said they'd flown in a whole shitload of those coffins to Limestone in Presque Isle, at which point both the coffins and their keeper entrained for points south.

"The army fella comes walking up to Huey, and he takes a fifth of rye whiskey out of his uniform blouse, and he says in this soft, drawly Dixie voice, 'Well, Mr. Engineer, you're driving a mystery train today, did know that?'

"Huey shakes his head.

" 'Well, you are. At least, that's what they call funeral train down in Alabama.' Huey says the fella took a list out of his pocket and squinted at it. 'We're going to start by dropping two of those coffins off in Houlton, and then I've got one for Passadumkeag, two for Bangor, one for Derry, one for Ludlow, and so on. I feel like a fugging milkman. You want a drink?'

"Well, Huey declines the drink on the grounds the Bangor and Aroostook is pretty fussy on the subject of train drivers with rye on their breaths, and the fella from Graves and Registration don't hold it against Huey, any more than Huey holds the fact of the army fella's drunkenness against him. They even shook on her, Huey said.

"So off they go, dropping those flag-covered coffins every other stop or two. Eighteen or twenty of 'em in all. Huey said it went on all the way to Boston, and there was weeping and wailing relatives at every stop except Ludlow. . . .and at Ludlow he was treated to the sight of Bill Baterman, who, he said, looked like he was dead inside and just waiting for his soul to stink. When he got off that train, he said he woke up that army fella, and they hit some spots—fifteen or twenty—and Huey got drunker than he had ever been and went to a whore, which he'd never done in his whole life, and woke up with a set of crabs so big and mean they gave him the shivers, and he said that if this was what they called a mystery train, he never wanted to drive no mystery train again.

"Timmy's body was taken up to the Greenspan Home on Fern Street—it used to be across from where the New Franklin Laundry stands now—and two days later he was buried in Pleasantview Cemetery with full military honors.

"Well, I tell you, Louis: Missus Baterman was dead ten years then, along with the second child she tried to bring into the world, and that had a lot to do with happened. A second child might have helped to ease the pain, don't you think? A second child might have reminded old Bill that there's others that feel the pain and have to be helped through. I guess in that way, you're luckier—having another child and all, I mean. A child and a wife who are both alive and well.

"According to the letter Bill got from the lieutenant in charge of his boy's platoon, Timmy was shot down on the road to Rome on July 15, 1943. His body was shipped home two days later, and it got to Limestone on the nineteenth. It was put aboard Huey Garber's mystery train the very next day. Most of the GIs who got killed in Europe were buried in Europe, but all of the boys who went home on that train were special—Timmy had died charging a machine-gun nest, and he had won the Silver Star posthumously.

"Timmy was buried—don't hold me to this, but I think it was on July 22. It was four or five days later that Marjorie Washburn, who was the mailwoman in those days, saw Timmy walking up the road toward York's Livery Stable. Well, Margie damn near drove right off the road, and you can understand why. She went back to the post office, tossed her leather bag with all her undelivered mail still in it on George Anderson's desk, and told him she was going home and to bed right then.

" 'Margie, are you sick?' George asks. 'You are just as white as a gull's wing.'

" 'I've had the fright of my life, and I don't want to talk to you about it,' Margie Washburn says. 'I ain't going to talk to Brian about it, or my mom, or anybody. When I get up to heaven, if Jesus asks me to talk to Him about it, maybe I will. But I don't believe it.' And out she goes.

"Everybody knew Timmy was dead; there was his obituary in the Bangor Daily News and the Ellsworth American just the week before, picture and all, and half the town turned out for his funeral up to the city. And here Margie seen him, walking up the road—lurching up the road, she finally told old George Anderson—only this was twenty years later, and she was dying, and George told me it seemed to him like she wanted to tell somebody what she'd seen. George said it seemed to him like it preyed on her mind, you know.

"Pale he was, she said, and dressed in an old pair of chino pants and a faded flannel hunting shirt, although it must have been ninety degrees in the shade that day. Margie said all his hair was sticking up in the back. 'His eyes were like raisins stuck in bread dough. I saw a ghost that day, George. That's what scared me so. I never thought I'd see such a thing, but there it was.'

"Well, word got around. Pretty soon some other people saw Timmy, too. Missus Stratton—well, we called her 'missus,' but so far as anyone knew she could have been single or divorced or grass-widowed; she had a little two-room house down where the Pedersen Road joins the Hancock Road, and she had a lot of jazz records, and sometimes she'd be wilting to throw you a little party if you had a ten-dollar bill that wasn't working too hard. Well, she saw him from her porch, and she said he walked right up to the edge of the road and stopped there.

"He just stood there, she said, his hands dangling at his sides and his head pushed forward, lookin' like a boxer who's ready to eat him some canvas. She said she stood there on her porch, heart goin' like sixty, too scared to move. Then she said he turned around, and it was like watching a drunk man try to do an about-face. One leg went way out and the other foot turned, and he just about fell over. She said he looked right at her and all the strength just run out of her hands and she dropped the basket of washing she had, and the clothes fell out and got smutty all over again.

"She said his eyes…she said they looked as dead and dusty as marbles, Louis. But he saw her…and he grinned…and she said he talked to her. Asked her if she still had those records because he wouldn't mind cutting a rug with her. Maybe that very night. And Missus Stratton went back inside, and she wouldn't come out for most of a week, and by then it was over anyway.

"Lot of people saw Timmy Baterman. Many of them are dead now—Missus Stratton is, for one, and others have moved on, but there are a few old crocks like me left around who'll tell you...if you ask 'em right.

"We saw him, I tell you, walking back and forth along the Pedersen Road, a mile east of his daddy's house and a mile west. Back and forth he went, back and forth all day, and for all anyone knew, all night. Shirt untucked, pale face, hair all stuck up in spikes, fly unzipped sometimes, and this look on his face... this look..."

Jud paused to light a cigarette, then shook the match out, and looked at Louis through the haze of drifting blue smoke. And although the story was, of course, utterly mad, there was no lie in Jud's eyes.

"You know, they have these stories and these movies—I don't know if they're true—about zombies down in Haiti. In the movies they just sort of shamble along, with their dead eyes starin' straight ahead, real slow and sort of clumsy. Timmy Baterman was like that, Louis, like a zombie in a movie, but he wasn't. There was something more. There was something goin' on behind his eyes, and sometimes you could see it and sometimes you couldn't see it. Somethin' behind his eyes, Louis. I don't think that thinking is what I want to call it. I don't know what in the hell I want to call it.

"It was sly, that was one thing. Like him telling Missus Stratton he wanted to cut a rug with her. There was something goin' on in there, Louis, but I don't think it was thinking and I don't think it had much—maybe nothing at all—to do with Timmy Baterman. It was more like a...radio signal that was comin' from somewhere else. You looked at him and you thought, 'If he touches me, I'm gonna scream.' Like that.

"Back and forth he went, up and down the road, and one day after I got home from work—this must have been, oh, I'm going to say it was July 30 or so—here is George Anderson, the postmaster, don't you know, sitting on my back porch, drinking iced tea with Hannibal Benson, who was then our second selectman, and Alan Purinton, who was fire chief. Norma sat there too, but never said a thing.

"George kept rubbing the stump at the top of his right leg. Lost most of that leg working on the railroad, he did, and the stump used to bother him something fierce on those hot and muggy days. But here he was, misery or not.

" 'This has gone far enough,' George says to me. 'I got a mailwoman who won't deliver out on the Pedersen Road—that's one thing. It's starting to raise Cain with the government, and that's something else.'

" 'What do you mean, it's raising Cain with the government?' I asked.

"Hannibal said he'd had a call from the War Department. Some lieutenant named Kinsman whose job it was to sort out malicious mischief from plain old tomfoolery. 'Four or five people have written anonymous letters to the War Department,' Hannibal says, 'and this Lieutenant Kinsman is starting to get a little bit concerned. If it was just one fellow who had written one letter, they'd laugh it off. If it was just one fellow writing a whole bunch of letters, Kinsman says he'd call the state police up in Derry Barracks and tell 'em they might have a psychopath with a hate on against the Baterman family in Ludlow. But these letters all came from different people. He said you could tell that by the handwriting, name or no name, and they all say the same crazy thing—that if Timothy Baterman is dead, he makes one hell of a lively corpse walking up and down Pederson Road with his bare face hanging out.

" 'This Kinsman is going to send a fellow out or come himself if this don't settle down,' Hannibal finishes up. 'They want to know if Timmy's dead, or AWOL, or what because they don't like to think their records are all at sixes and sevens. Also they're gonna want to know who was buried in Timmy Baterman's box, if he wasn't.'

"Well, you can see what kind of a mess it was, Louis. We sat there most of an hour, drinking iced tea and talking it over. Norma asked us if we wanted sandwiches, but no one did.

"We talked it around and talked it around, and finally we decided we had to go out there to the Baterman place. I'll never forget that night, not if I live to be twice as old's I am now. It was hot, hotter than the hinges of hell, with the sun going down like a bucket of guts behind the clouds. There was none of us wanted to go, but we had to. Norma knew it before any of us. She got me inside on some pretext or other and said, 'Don't you let them dither around and put this off, Judson. You got to get this taken care of. It's an abomination.' "

Jud measured Louis evenly with his eyes.

"That was what she called it, Louis. It was her word. Abomination. And she kind of whispers in my ear, 'If anything happens, Jud, you just run. Never mind these others; they'll have to look out for themselves. You remember me and bust your hump right out of there if anything happens.'

"We drove over in Hannibal Benson's car—that son of a bitch got all the A-coupons he wanted, I don't know how. Nobody said much, but all four of us was smoking like chimblies. We was scared, Louis, just as scared as we could be. But the only one who really said anything was Alan Purinton. He says to George, 'Bill Baterman has been up to dickens in that woods north of Route 15, and I'll put my warrant to that.' Nobody answered, but I remember George noddin' his head.

"Well, we got there, and Alan knocked, but nobody answered, so we went around to the back and there the two of them were. Bill Baterman was sitting there on his back stoop with a pitcher of beer, and Timmy was at the back of the yard, just staring up at that red, bloody sun as it went down. His whole face was orange with it, like he'd been flayed alive. And Bill...he looked like the devil had gotten him after his seven years of highfalutin. He was floatin' in his clothes, and I judged he'd lost forty pounds. His eyes had gone back in their sockets until they were like little animals in a pair of caves...and his mouth kept goin tick-tick-tick on the left side."

Jud paused, seemed to consider, and then nodded imperceptibly. "Louis, he looked damned.

"Timmy looked around at us and grinned. Just seeing him grin made you want to scream. Then he turned and went back to looking at the sun go down. Bill says, 'I didn't hear you boys knock,' which was a bald-faced lie, of course, since Alan laid on that door loud enough to wake the...to wake up a deaf man.

"No one seemed like they was going to say anything, so I says, 'Bill, I heard your boy was killed over in Italy.'

"'That was a mistake,' he says, looking right at me.

" 'Was it?' I says.

" 'You see him standin right there, don't you?' he says.

" 'So who do you reckon was in that coffin you had out at Pleasantview?' Alan Purinton asks him.

" 'Be damned if I know,' Bill says, 'and be damned if I care.' He goes to get a cigarette and spills them all over the back porch, then breaks two or three trying to pick them up.

" 'Probably have to be an exhumation,' Hannibal says. 'You know that, don't you? I had a call from the goddam War Department, Bill. They are going to want to know if they buried some other mother's son under Timmy's name.'

" 'Well, what in the hell of it?' Bill says in a loud voice. 'That's nothing to me, is it? I got my boy. Timmy come home the other day. He's been shell-shocked or something. He's a little strange now, but he'll come around.'

" 'Let's quit this, Bill,' I says, and all at once I was pretty mad at him. 'If and when they dig up that army coffin, they're gonna find it dead empty, unless you went to the trouble of filling it up with rocks after you took your boy out of it, and I don't think you did. I know what happened, Hannibal and George and Alan here know what happened, and you know what happened too. You been foolin' around up in the woods, Bill, and you have caused yourself and this town a lot of trouble.'

" 'You fellas know your way out, I guess,' he says. 'I don't have to explain myself to you, or justify myself to you, or nothing. When I got that telegram, the life ran right out of me. I felt her go, just like piss down the inside of my leg. Well, I got my boy back. They had no right to take my boy. He was only seventeen. He was all I had left of his dear mother, and it was ill-fuckin'-legal. So fuck the army, and fuck the War Department, and fuck the United States of America, and fuck you boys too. I got him back. He'll come around. And that's all I got to say. Now you all just march your boots back where you came from.'

"And his mouth is tick-tick-tickin', and there's sweat, all over his forehead in big drops, and that was when I saw he was crazy. It would have driven me crazy too. Living with that...that thing."

Louis was feeling sick to his stomach. He had drunk too much beer too fast. Pretty soon it was all going to come up on him. The heavy, loaded feeling in his stomach told him it would be coming up soon.

"Well, there wasn't much else we could do. We got ready to go. Hannibal says, 'Bill, God help you.'

"Bill says, 'God never helped me. I helped myself.'

"That was when Timmy walked over to us. He even walked wrong, Louis. He walked like an old, old man. He'd put one foot high up and then bring it down and, then kind of shuffle and then lift the other one. It was like watchin' a crab walk. His hands dangled down by his legs. And when he got close enough, you could see red marks across his face on the slant, like pimples or little burns. I reckon that's where the Kraut machine gun got him. Must have damn near blowed his head off.

"And he stank of the grave. It was a black smell, like everything inside him was just lying there, spoiled. I saw Alan Purinton put a hand up to cover his nose and mouth. The stench was just awful. You almost expected to see grave maggots squirming around in his hair—"

"Stop," Louis said hoarsely. "I've heard enough."

"You ain't," Jud said. He spoke with haggard earnestness. "That's it, you ain't. And I can't even make it as bad as it was. Nobody could understand how bad it was unless they was there. He was dead, Louis. But he was alive too. And he...he...he knew things."

"Knew things?" Louis sat forward.

"Ayuh. He looked at Alan for a long time, kind of grinning—you could see his teeth, anyway—and then he spoke in this low voice; you felt like you had to strain forward to hear it. It sounded like he had gravel down in his tubes. 'Your wife is fucking that man she works with down at the drugstore, Purinton. What do you think of that? She screams when she comes. What do you think of that?'

"Alan, he kind of gasped, and you could see it had hit him. Alan's in a nursing home up in Gardener now, or was the last I heard—he must be pushing ninety. Back when all this happened, he was forty or so, and there had been some talk around about his second wife. She was his second cousin, and she had come to live with Alan and Alan's first wife, Lucy, just before the war. Well, Lucy died, and a year and a half later Alan up and married this girl. Laurine, her name was. She was no more than twenty-four when they married. And there had been some talk about her, you know. If you were a man, you might have called her ways sort of free and easy and let it go at that. But the women thought she might be loose. And maybe Alan had had a few thoughts in that direction too because he says, 'Shut up! Shut up or I'll knock you down, whatever you are!'

"'Shush now, Timmy,' Bill says, and he looks worse than ever, you know, like maybe he's going to puke or faint dead away, or do both. 'You shush, Timmy.'

"But Timmy didn't take no notice. He looks around at George Anderson and he says, 'That grandson you set such a store by is just waiting for you to die, old man. The money is all he wants, the money he thinks you got socked away in your lockbox at the Bangor Eastern Bank. That's why he makes up to you, but behind your back he makes fun of you, him and his sister. Old wooden-leg, that's what they call you,' Timmy says, and Louis, his voice—it changed. It got mean. It sounded like the way that grandson of George's would have sounded if...you know, if the things Timmy was saying was true.

"'Old wooden-leg,' Timmy says, 'and won't they shit when they find out you're poor as a church mouse because you lost it all in 1938? Won't they shit, George? Won't they just shit?'

"George, he backed away then, and his wooden leg buckled under him, and he fell back on Bill's porch and upsat his pitcher of beer, and he was as white as your undershirt, Louis.

"Bill, he gets him back on his feet somehow, and he's roarin' at his boy, 'Timmy, you stop it! You stop it!' But Timmy wouldn't. He said somethin' bad about Hannibal, and then he said something bad about me too, and by then he was...ravin', I'd say. Yeah, he was ravin', all right. Screamin'. And we started to back away, and then we started to run, draggin' George along the best we could by the arms because he'd gotten the straps and harnesses on the fake leg twisted somehow, and it was all off to one side with the shoe turned around backward and draggin' on the grass.

"The last I seen of Timmy Baterman, he was on the back lawn by the clothesline, his face all red in the settin' sun, those marks standin' out on his face, his hair all crazy and dusty somehow...and he was laughin' and screechin' over and over again 'Old wooden-leg! Old wooden leg! And the cuckold! And the whoremaster! Goodbye, gentlemen! Goodbye! Goodbye!' and then he laughed, but it was screaming, really...something inside him...screaming... and screaming...and screaming."

Jud stopped. His chest moved up and down rapidly.

"Jud," Louis said. "The thing this Timmy Baterman told you...was it true?"

"It was true," Jud muttered. "Christ! It was true. I used go to a whorehouse in Bangor betimes. Nothing many a man hasn't done, although I s'pose there are plenty that walk the straight and narrow. I just would get the urge—the compulsion, maybe—to sink it into strange flesh now and then. Or pay some woman to do the things a man can't bring himself to ask his wife to do. Men keep their gardens too, Louis. It wasn't a terrible thing, what I done, and all of that has been behind me for the last eight or nine years, and Norma would not have left me if she had known.

"But something in her would have died forever. Something dear and sweet."

Jud's eyes were red and swollen and bleary. The tears of the old are singularly unlovely, Louis thought. But when Jud groped across the table for Louis's hand, Louis took it firmly.

"He told us only the bad," he said after a moment. "Only the bad. God knows there is enough of that in any human being's life, isn't there? Two or three days later, Laurine Purinton left Ludlow for good, and folks in town who saw her before she got on the train said she was sprouting two shiners and had cotton stuffed up both bores of her pump. Alan, he would never talk about it. George died in 1950, and if he left anything to that grandson and granddaughter of his, I never heard about it. Hannibal got kicked out of office because of something that was just like what Timmy Baterman accused him of. I won't tell you exactly what it was—you don't need to know—but misappropriation of town funds for his own use comes close enough to cover it, I reckon. There was even talk of trying him on embezzlement charges, but it never came to much. Losing the post was enough punishment for him anyway; his whole life was playing the big cheese.

"But there was good in those men too. That's what I mean; that's what folks always find it so hard to remember. It was Hannibal got the fund started for the Eastern General Hospital, right before the war. Alan Puritan was one of the most generous, open-handed men I ever knew. And old George Anderson only wanted to go on running the post office forever.

"It was only the bad it wanted to talk about though. It was only the bad it wanted us to remember because it was bad...and because it knew we meant danger for it. The Timmy Baterman that went off to fight the war was a nice, ordinary kid, Louis, maybe a little dull but goodhearted. The thing we saw that night, lookin' up into that red sun...that was a monster. Maybe it was a zombie or a dybbuk or a demon. Maybe there's no name for such a thing as that, but the Micmacs would have known what it was, name or no."

"What?" Louis said numbly.

"Something that had been touched by the Wendigo," Jud said evenly. He took a deep breath, held it for a moment, let it out, and looked at his watch.

"Welladay. The hour's late, Louis. I've talked nine times as much as I meant to."

"I doubt that," Louis said. "You've been very eloquent. Tell me how it came out."

"There was a fire at the Baterman place two nights later," Jud said. "The house burned flat. Alan Purinton said there was no doubt about the fire being set. Range oil had been splashed from one end of that little house to the other. You could smell the reek of it for three days after the fire was out."

"So they both burned up."

"Oh, ayuh, they burned. But they was dead beforehand. Timmy was shot twice in the chest with a pistol Bill Baterman kept handy, an old Colt's. They found it in Bill's hand. What he'd done, or so it looked like, was to kill his boy, lay him on the bed, and then spill out that range oil. Then he sat down on his easy chair by the radio, flicked a match, and ate the barrel of that Colt .45."

"Jesus," Louis said.

"They were pretty well charred, but the county medical examiner said it looked to him like Timmy Baterman had been dead two or three weeks."

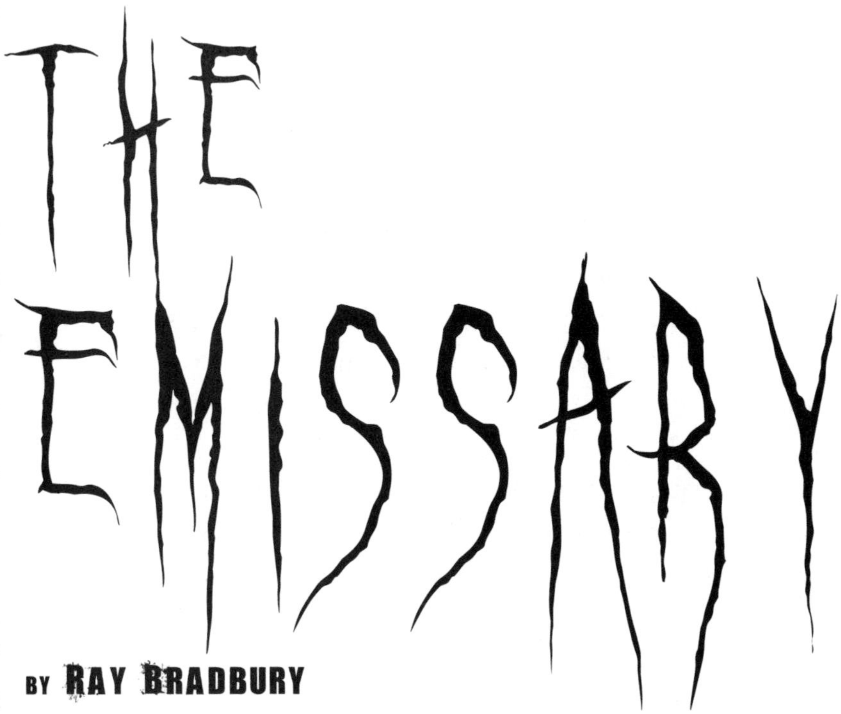

The Emissary

BY **RAY BRADBURY**

This gentle, haunting tale of a boy, his dog, and something else could only have come from the great Ray Bradbury.

I read it first, as a child, in The October Country, *which one can safely say is Bradbury's one true horror collection. Mostly known as an author of science fiction—though he has argued, and rightly, that he's a fantasist who just treats science as another stage for magic and wonder to play upon—there's always been a profound cognizance of darkness in his work.*

The October Country *is where, as a young man, he crystallized that instinctive understanding. And where I—as an even-younger man-to-be—got my first deep glimpse of a contemporary writer's ability to hit me right where I live.*

Come for the zombie. Stay for the poetry, the intimate lilt and flow of a master at work.

And be very, very nice to your dog.

MARTIN KNEW IT WAS AUTUMN AGAIN, for Dog ran into the house bringing wind and frost and a smell of apples turned to cider under trees. In dark clock-springs of hair, Dog fetched goldenrod, dust of farewell-summer, acorn-husk, hair of squirrel, feather of departed robin, sawdust from fresh-cut cordwood, and leaves like charcoals shaken from a blaze of maple trees. Dog jumped. Showers of brittle fern, blackberry vine, marsh-grass sprang over the bed where Martin shouted. No doubt, no doubt of it at all, this incredible beast was October!

"Here, boy, here!"

And Dog settled to warm Martin's body with all the bonfires and subtle burnings of the season, to fill the room with soft or heavy, wet or dry odors of far-traveling. In spring, he smelled of lilac, iris, lawn-mowered grass; in summer, ice-cream-mustached, he came pungent with firecracker, Roman candle, pinwheel, baked by the sun. But autumn! Autumn!

"Dog, what's it like outside?"

And lying there, Dog told as he always told. Lying there, Martin found autumn as in the old days before sickness bleached him white on his bed. Here was his contact, his carry-all, the quick-moving part of himself he sent with a yell to run and return, circle and scent, collect and deliver the time and texture of worlds in town, country, by creek, river, lake, down-cellar, up-attic, in closet or coal-bin. Ten dozen times a day he was gifted with sunflower seed, cinder-path, milkweed, horse-chestnut, or full flame-smell of pumpkin. Through the loomings of the universe Dog shuttled; the design was hid in his pelt. Put out your hand, it was there . . . .

"And where did you go this morning?"

But he knew without hearing where Dog had rattled down hills where autumn lay in cereal crispness, where children lay in funeral pyres, in rustling heaps, the leaf-buried but watchful dead, as Dog and the world blew by. Martin trembled his fingers, searched the thick fur, read the long journey. Through stubbled fields, over glitters of ravine creek, down marbled spread of cemetery yard, into woods. In the great season of spices and rare incense, now Martin ran through his emissary, around, about, and home!

The bedroom door opened.

"That dog of yours is in trouble again."

Mother brought in a tray of fruit salad, cocoa, and toast, her blue eyes snapping.

"Mother . . ."

"Always digging places. Dug a hole in Miss Tarkin's garden this morning. She's spittin' mad. That's the fourth hole he's dug there this week."

"Maybe he's looking for something."

"Fiddlesticks, he's too darned curious. If he doesn't behave he'll be locked up."

Martin looked at this woman as if she were a stranger. "Oh, you wouldn't do that! How would I learn anything? How would I find things out if Dog didn't tell me?"

Mom's voice was quieter. "Is that what he does—tell you things?"

"There's nothing I don't know when he goes out and around and back, *nothing* I can't find out from him!"

They both sat looking at Dog and the dry strewings of mold and seed over the quilt.

"Well, if he'll just stop digging where he shouldn't, he can run all he wants," said Mother.

"Here, boy, here!"

And Martin snapped a tin note to the dog's collar:

MY OWNER IS MARTIN SMITH—TEN YEARS OLD—SICK IN BED—VISITORS WELCOME.

Dog barked. Mother opened the downstairs door and let him out.

Martin sat listening.

Far off and away you could hear Dog run in the quiet autumn rain that was falling now. You could hear the barking-jingling fade, rise, fade again as he cut down alley, over lawn, to fetch back Mr. Holloway and the oiled metallic smell of the delicate snowflake-interiored watches he repaired in his home shop. Or maybe he would bring Mr. Jacobs, the grocer, whose clothes were rich with lettuce, celery, tomatoes, and the secret tinned and hidden smell of the red demons stamped on cans of deviled ham. Mr. Jacobs and his unseen pink-meat devils waved often from the yard below. Or Dog brought Mr. Jackson, Mrs. Gillespie, Mr. Smith, Mrs. Holmes, *any* friend or near-friend, encountered, cornered, begged, worried, and at last shepherded home for lunch, or tea-and-biscuits.

Now, listening, Martin heard Dog below, with footsteps moving in a light rain behind him. The downstairs bell rang, Mom opened the door, light voices murmured. Martin sat forward, face shining. The stair treads creaked. A young woman's voice laughed quietly. Miss Haight, of course, his teacher from school!

The bedroom door sprang open.

Martin had company.

Morning, afternoon, evening, dawn and dusk, sun and moon circled with Dog, who faithfully reported temperatures of turf and air, color of earth and tree, consistency of mist or rain, but—most important of all—brought back again and again and again—Miss Haight.

On Saturday, Sunday, and Monday she baked Martin orange-iced cupcakes, brought him library books about dinosaurs and cavemen. On Tuesday, Wednesday, and Thursday somehow he beat her at dominoes, somehow she lost at checkers, and soon, she cried, he'd defeat her handsomely at chess. On Friday, Saturday, and Sunday they talked and never stopped talking, and she was so young and laughing and handsome and her hair was a soft, shining brown like the season outside the window, and she walked clear, clean, and quick, a heartbeat warm in the bitter afternoon when he heard it. Above all, she had the secret of signs, and could read and interpret Dog and the symbols she searched out and plucked forth from his coat with her miraculous fingers. Eyes shut, softly laughing, in a gypsy's voice, she divined the world from the treasures in her hands.

And on Monday afternoon, Miss Haight was dead.

Martin sat up in bed, slowly.

"Dead?" he whispered.

Dead, said his mother, yes, dead, killed in an auto accident a mile out of town. Dead, yes, dead, which meant cold to Martin, which meant silence and whiteness and winter come long before its time. Dead, silent, cold, white. The thoughts circled round, blew down, and settled in whispers.

Martin held Dog, thinking; turned to the wall. The lady with the autumn-colored hair. The lady with the laughter that was very gentle and never made fun and the eyes that watched your mouth to see everything you ever said. The-other-half-of-autumn-lady, who told what was left untold by Dog, about the world. The heartbeat at the still center of gray afternoon. The heartbeat fading . . .

"Mom? What do they do in the graveyard, Mom, under the ground? Just lay there?"

"*Lie* there."

"Lie there? Is that *all* they do? It doesn't sound like much fun."

"For goodness sake, it's not made out to be fun."

"Why don't they jump up and run around once in a while if they get tired lying there? God's pretty silly———"

"Martin!"

"Well, you'd think He'd treat people better than to tell them to lie still for keeps. That's impossible. Nobody can do it! I tried once. Dog tries. I tell him, 'dead Dog!' He plays dead awhile, then gets sick and tired and wags his tail or opens one eye and looks at me, bored. Boy, I bet sometimes those graveyard people do the same, huh, Dog?"

Dog barked.

"Be still with that kind of talk!" said Mother.

Martin looked off into space.

"Bet that's exactly what they do," he said.

Autumn burnt the trees bare and ran Dog still farther around, fording creek, prowling graveyard as was his custom, and back in the dusk to fire off volleys of barking that shook windows wherever he turned.

In the late last days of October, Dog began to act as if the wind had changed and blew from a strange country. He stood quivering on the porch below. He whined, his eyes fixed at the empty land beyond town. He brought no visitors for Martin. He stood for hours each day, as if leashed, trembling, then shot away straight, as if someone had called. Each night he returned later, with no one following. Each night, Martin sank deeper and deeper in his pillow.

"Well, people are busy," said Mother. "They haven't time to notice the tag Dog carries. Or they mean to come visit, but forget."

But there was more to it than that. There was the fevered shining in Dog's eyes, and his whimpering tic late at night, in some private dream. His shivering in the dark, under the bed. The way he sometimes stood half the night, looking at Martin as if some great and impossible secret was his and he knew no way to tell it save by savagely thumping his tail, or turning in endless circles, never to lie down, spinning and spinning again.

On October thirtieth, Dog ran out and didn't come back at all, even when after supper Martin heard his parents call and call. The hour grew late, the streets and sidewalks stood empty, the air moved cold about the house and there was nothing, nothing.

Long after midnight, Martin lay watching the world beyond the cool, clear glass windows. Now there was not even autumn, for there was no Dog to fetch it in. There would be no winter, for who could bring the snow to melt in your hands? Father, Mother? No, not the same. They couldn't play the game with its special secrets and rules, its sounds and pantomimes. No more seasons. No more time. The go-between, the emissary, was lost to the wild throngings of civilization, poisoned, stolen, hit by a car, left somewhere in a culvert. . . .

Sobbing, Martin turned his face to his pillow. The world was a picture under glass, untouchable. The world was dead.

Martin twisted in bed and in three days the last Hallowe'en pumpkins were rotting in trash cans, papier-mache skulls and witches were burnt on bonfires, and ghosts were stacked on shelves with other linens until next year.

To Martin, Hallowe'en had been nothing more than one evening when tin horns cried off in the cold autumn stars, children blew like goblin leaves along the flinty walks, flinging their heads, or cabbages, at porches, soap-writing names or similar magic symbols on icy windows. All of it as distant, unfathomable, and nightmarish as a puppet show seen from so many miles away that there is no sound or meaning.

For three days in November, Martin watched alternate light and shadow sift across his ceiling. The fire-pageant was over forever; autumn lay in cold ashes. Martin sank deeper, yet deeper in white marble layers of bed, motionless, listening always listening. . . .

Friday evening, his parents kissed him good-night and walked out of the house into the hushed cathedral weather toward a motion-picture show. Miss Tarkins from next door stayed on in the parlor below until Martin called down he was sleepy, then took her knitting off home.

In silence, Martin lay following the great move of stars down a clear and moonlit sky, remembering nights such as this when he'd spanned the town with Dog ahead, behind, around about, tracking the green-plush ravine, lapping slumbrous streams gone milky with the fullness of the moon, leaping cemetery tombstones while whispering the marble names; on, quickly on, through shaved meadows where the only motion was the off-on quivering of stars, to streets where shadows would not stand aside for you but crowded all the sidewalks for mile on mile. Run now run! chasing, being chased by bitter smoke, fog, mist, wind, ghost of mind, fright of memory; home, safe, sound, snug-warm, asleep. . . .

Nine o'clock.

Chime. The drowsy clock in the deep stairwell below. Chime.

Dog, come home, and run the world with you. Dog, bring a thistle with frost on it, or bring nothing else but the wind. Dog, where *are* you? Oh, listen, now, I'll call.

Martin held his breath.

Way off somewhere—a sound.

Martin rose up, trembling.

There, again—the sound.

So small a sound, like a sharp needle-point brushing the sky long miles and many miles away.

The dreamy echo of a dog—barking.

The sound of a dog crossing fields and farms, dirt roads and rabbit paths, running, running, letting out great barks of steam, cracking the night. The sound of a circling dog which came and went, lifted and faded, opened up, shut in, moved forward, went back, as if the animal were kept by someone on a fantastically long chain. As if the dog were running and someone whistled under the chestnut trees, in mold-shadow, tar-shadow, moon-shadow, walking, and the dog circled back and sprang out again toward home.

Dog! Martin thought, oh Dog, come home, boy! Listen, oh, listen, where you *been*? Come on, boy, make tracks!

Five, ten, fifteen minutes; near, very near, the bark, the sound. Martin cried out, thrust his feet from the bed, leaned to the window. Dog! Listen, boy! Dog! Dog! He said it over and over. Dog! Dog! Wicked Dog, run off and gone all these days! Bad Dog, good Dog, home, boy, hurry, and bring what you can!

Near now, near, up the street, barking, to knock clapboard housefronts with sound, whirl iron cocks on rooftops in the moon, firing off volleys—Dog! now at the door below. . . .

Martin shivered.

Should he run—let Dog in, or wait for Mom and Dad? Wait? Oh, God, wait? But what if Dog ran off again? No, he'd go down, snatch the door wide, yell, grab Dog in, and run upstairs so fast, laughing, crying, holding tight, that . . .

Dog stopped barking.

Hey! Martin almost broke the window, jerking to it. Silence. As if someone had told Dog to hush now, hush, hush.

A full minute passed. Martin clenched his fists.

Below, a faint whimpering.

Then, slowly, the downstairs front door opened. Someone was kind enough to have opened the door for Dog. Of course! Dog had brought Mr. Jacobs or Mr. Gillespie or Miss Tarkins, or . . .

The downstairs door shut.

Dog raced upstairs, whining, flung himself on the bed.

"Dog, Dog, where've you *been*, what've you *done!* Dog, Dog!"

And he crushed Dog hard and long to himself, weeping. Dog, Dog. He laughed and shouted. Dog! But after a moment he stopped laughing and crying, suddenly.

He pulled back away. He held the animal and looked at him, eyes widening.

The odor coming from Dog was different.

It was a smell of strange earth. It was a smell of night within night, the smell of digging down deep in shadow through earth that had lain cheek by jowl with things that were long hidden and decayed. A stinking and rancid soil fell away in clods of dissolution from Dog's muzzle and paws. He had dug deep. He had dug very deep indeed. That *was* it, wasn't it? wasn't it? *wasn't* it!

What kind of message was this from Dog? What could such a message mean? The stench—the ripe and awful cemetery earth.

Dog was a bad dog, digging where he shouldn't. Dog was a good dog, always making friends. Dog loved people. Dog brought them home.

And now, moving up the dark hall stairs, at intervals, came the sound of feet, one foot dragged after the other, painfully, slowly, slowly, slowly.

Dog shivered. A rain of strange night earth fell seething on the bed.

Dog turned.

The bedroom door whispered in.

Martin had company.

A Case of the Stubborns

BY **ROBERT BLOCH**

Along with Dr. Seuss, Edgar Allan Poe, and Ray Bradbury, Robert Bloch was one of my easliest literary heroes. Best known for the extremely short novel Psycho, *from which Hitchcock's film was drawn, he was also responsible for dozens of crisp, crafty, jolting short stories, frequently punctuated with some of the snappiest punchline endings in the history of popular storytelling.*

Although his zomboid forays range from old-fashioned voodoo ("Mother of Serpents") to far more modern iterations ("Maternal Instinct"), this is my personal favorite.

"A Case of the Stubborns" is classic Bloch: so funny, so succinct, so rife with awful implications that not another word is needed. Your helpless mind will do the rest.

THE MORNING AFTER HE DIED, Grandpa come downstairs for breakfast.

It kind of took us by surprise.

Ma looked at Pa, Pa looked at little sister Susie, and Susie looked at me. Then we all just set there looking at Grandpa.

"What's the matter?" he said. "Why you all staring at me like that?"

Nobody said, but I knowed the reason. Only been last night since all of us stood by his bedside when he was took by his attack and passed away right in front of our very eyes. But here he was, up and dressed and feisty as ever.

"What's for breakfast?" he said.

Ma sort of gulped. "Don't tell me you fixing to eat?"

"Course I am. I'm nigh starved."

Ma looked at Pa, but he just rolled his eyes. Then she went and hefted the skillet from the stove and dumped some eggs on a plate.

"That's more like it," Grandpa told her. "But don't I smell sausages?"

Ma got Grandpa some sausage. The way he dug into it, they sure was nothing wrong with his appetite.

After he started on seconds, Grandpa took heed of us staring at him again.

"How come nobody else is eating?" he asked.

"We ain't hungry," Pa said. And that was the gospel truth.

"Man's got to eat to keep up his strenth," Grandpa told him. "Which reminds me—ain't you gonna be late at the mill?"

"Don't figure on working today," Pa said.

Grandpa squinted at him. "You all fancied up this morning. Shave and a shirt, just like Sunday. You expecting company?"

Ma was looking out the kitchen window, and she give Grandpa a nod. "Yes indeedy. Here he comes now."

Sure enough, we could see ol' Bixbee hotfooting up the walk.

Ma went through the parlor to the front door—meaning to head him off, I reckon—but he fooled her and came around the back way. Pa got to the kitchen door too late, on account of Bixbee already had it and his mouth open at the same time.

"Morning, Jethro," he said, in that treacle-and-molasses voice of his. "And a sad grievous morning it is, too! I purely hate disturbing you so early on this sorrowful occasion, but it looks like today's another scorcher." He pulled out a tape-measure. "Best if I got the measurements so's to get on with the arrangements. Heat like this, the sooner we get everything boxed and squared away the better, if you take my meaning—"

"Sorry," said Pa, blocking the doorway so ol' Bixbee couldn't peek inside. "Needs be you come back later."

"How much later?"

"Can't say for sure. We ain't rightly made up our minds as yet."

"Well, don't dilly-dally too long," Bixbee said. "I'm liable to run short of ice."

Then Pa shut the door on him and he took off. When Ma come back from the parlor, Pa made a sign for her to keep her gap shut, but of course that didn't stop Grandpa.

"What was that all about?" he asked.

"Purely a social call."

"Since when?" Grandpa looked suspicious. "Ol' Bixbee ain't nobody's friend—him with his high-toned airs! Calls hisself a Southern planter. Shucks, he ain't nothing but an undertaker."

"That's right, Grandpa," said sister Susie. "He come to fit you for your coffin."

"Coffin?" Grandpa reared up in his seat like a hog caught in a bobwire fence. "What in bo-diddley blazes do I need with a coffin?"

"Because you're dead."

Just like that she come out with it. Ma and Pa was both ready to take after her but Grandpa laughed fit to bust.

"Holy hen-tracks, child—what on earth give you an idee like that?"

Pa moved in on Susie, taking off his belt, but Ma shook her head. Then she nodded to Grandpa.

"It's true. You passed on last night. Don't you recollect?"

"Ain't nothing wrong with my memory," Grandpa told her. "I had me one of my spells, is all."

Ma fetched a sigh. "Wasn't just no spell this time."

"A fit, mebbe?"

"More'n that. You was took so bad, Pa had to drag Doc Snodgrass out of his office—busted up the game right in the middle of a three-dollar pot. Didn't do no good, though. By the time he got here you was gone."

"But I ain't gone! I'm here."

Pa spoke up. "Now don't git up on your high horse, Grandpa. We all saw you. We're witnesses."

"Witnesses?" Grandpa hiked his galluses like he always did when he got riled. "What kind of talk is that? You aim to hold a jury-trial to decide if I'm alive or dead?"

"But Grandpa—"

"Save your sass, sonny." Grandpa stood up. "Ain't nobody got a right to put me six feet under 'thout my say-so."

"Where you off to?" Ma asked.

"Where I go evvy morning," Grandpa said. "Gonna set on the front porch and watch the sights."

Durned if he didn't do just that, leaving us behind in the kitchen.

"Wouldn't that frost you?" Ma said. She crooked a finger at the stove. "Here I went and pulled up half the greens in the garden, just planning my spread for after the funeral. I already told folks we'd be serving possum-stew. What will the neighbors think?"

"Don't you go fret now," Pa said. "Mebbe he ain't dead after all."

Ma made a face. "We know different. He's just being persnickety." She nudged at Pa. "Only one thing to do. You go fetch Doc Snodgrass. Tell him he'd best sashay over here right quick and settle this matter once and for all."

"Reckon so," Pa said, and went out the back way, Ma looked at me and sister Susie.

"You kids go out on the porch and keep Grandpa company. See that he stays put 'til the Doc gets here."

"Yessum," said Susie, and we traipsed out of there.

Sure enough, Grandpa set in his rocker, big as life, squinting at cars over the road and watching the drivers cuss when they tried to steer around our hogs.

"Lookee here!" he said, pointing. "See that fat feller in the Hupmobile? He came barreling down the road like a bat outta hell—must of been doing thirty mile an hour. 'Fore he could stop, ol' Bessie poked out of the weeds right in front of him and run that car clean into the ditch. I swear I never seen anything so comical in all my life!"

Susie shook her head. "But you ain't alive, Grandpa."

"Now don't you start in on that again, hear!" Grandpa looked at her, disgusted, and Susie shut up.

Right then Doc Snodgrass come driving up front in his big Essex and parked alongside ol' Bessie's pork-butt. Doc and Pa got out and moseyed up to the porch. They was jawing away something fierce and I could see Doc shaking his head like he purely disbelieved what Pa was telling him.

Then Doc noticed Grandpa setting there, and he stopped cold in his tracks. His eyes bugged out.

"Jumping Jehosephat!" he said to Grandpa. "What you doing here?"

"What's it look like?" Grandpa told him. "Can't a man set on his own front porch and rockify in peace?"

"Rest in peace, that's what you should be doing," said Doc. "When I examined you last night you were deader'n a doornail!"

"And you were drunker'n a coot, I reckon," Grandpa said.

Pa give Doc a nod. "What'd I tell you?"

Doc paid him no heed. He come up to Grandpa, "Mebbe I was a wee bit mistaken," he said. "Mind if I examine you now?"

"Fire away." Grandpa grinned. "I got all the time in the world."

So Doc opened up his little black bag and set about his business. First off he plugged a stethyscope in his ears and tapped Grandpa's chest. He listened, and then his hands begun to shake.

"I don't hear nothing," he said.

" 'What do you expect to hear—the Grand Ol' Opry?"

"This here's no time for funning," Doc told him. "Suppose I tell you your heart's stopped beating?"

"Suppose I tell you your stethyscope's busted?"

Doc begun to break out in a sweat. He fetched out a mirror and held it up to Grandpa's mouth. Then his hands got to shaking worse than ever.

"See this?" he said. "The mirror's clear. Means you got no breath left in your body."

Grandpa shook his head. "Try it on yourself. You got a breath on you would knock a mule over at twenty paces."

"Mebbe this'll change your tune." Doc reached in his pocket and pulled out a piece of paper. "See for yourself."

"What is it?"

"Your death certificate." Doc jabbed his finger down. "Just you read what it says on this line. 'Cause of death—card-yak arrest.' That's medical for heart attack. And this here's a legal paper. It'll stand up in court."

"So will I, if you want to drag the law into this," Grandpa told him. "Be a pretty sight, too—you standing on one side with your damfool piece of paper and me standing on the other! Now, which do you think the judge is going to believe?"

Doc's eyes bugged out again. He tried to stuff the paper into his pocket, but his hands shook so bad he almost didn't make it.

"What's wrong with you?" Pa asked.

"I feel poorly," Doc said. "Got to get back to my office and lie down for a spell."

He picked up his bag and headed for his car, not looking back.

"Don't lie down too long," Grandpa called. "Somebody's liable to write out a paper saying you died of a hangover."

When lunchtime come around nobody was hungry. Nobody but Grandpa, that is.

He set down at the table and put away black-eyed peas, hominy grits, a double helping of chitlins, and two big slabs of rhubarb pie with gravy.

Ma was the kind who liked seeing folks enjoy her vittles, but she didn't look kindly on Grandpa's appetite. After he finished and went back on the porch she stacked the plates on the drainboard and told us kids to clean up. Then she went into the bedroom and come out with her shawl and pocketbook.

"What you all dressed up about?" Pa said.

"I'm going to church."

"But this here's only Thursday."

"Can't wait no longer," Ma told him. "It's been hot all forenoon and looking to get hotter. I seen you wrinkle up your nose whilst Grandpa was in here for lunch."

Pa sort of shrugged. "Figgered the chitlins was mebbe a little bit spoiled, is all."

"Weren't nothing of the sort," Ma said. "If you take my meaning."

"What you fixing to do?"

"Only thing a body can do. I'm putting evvything in the hands of the Lord."

And off she skedaddled, leaving sister Susie and me to scour the dishes whilst Pa went out back, looking powerful troubled. I spied him through the window, slopping the hogs, but you could tell his heart wasn't in it.

Susie and me, we went out to keep tabs on Grandpa.

Ma was right about the weather heating up. That porch was like a bake-oven in the devil's own kitchen. Grandpa didn't seem to pay it any heed, but I did. Couldn't help but notice Grandpa was getting ripe.

"Look at them flies buzzing 'round him," Susie said.

"Hush up, sister. Mind your manners."

But sure enough, them old blueflies buzzed so loud we could hardly hear Grandpa speak. "Hi, young 'uns," he said. "Come visit a spell."

"Sun's too hot for setting," Susie told him.

"Not so's I can notice," He weren't even working up a sweat.

"What about all them blueflies?"

"Don't bother me none." Big ol' fly landed right on Grandpa's nose and he didn't even twitch.

Susie begun to look scared. "He's dead for sure," she said.

"Speak up, child," Grandpa said. "Ain't polite to go mumbling your elders."

Just then he spotted Ma marching up the road. Hot as it was, she come along lickety-split, with the Reverend Peabody in tow. He was huffing and puffing, but she never slowed until they fetched up alongside the front porch.

"Howdy, Reverend," Grandpa sung out.

Reverend Peabody blinked and opened his mouth, but no words come out.

"What's the matter?" Grandpa said. "Cat got your tongue?"

The Reverend got a kind of sick grin on his face, like a skunk eating bumblebees.

"Reckon I know how you feel," Grandpa told him. "Sun makes a feller's throat parch up." He looked at Ma. "Addie, whyn't you go fetch the Reverend a little refreshment?"

Ma went in the house.

"Well now, Rev," said Grandpa. "Rest your britches and be sociable."

The Reverend swallowed hard. "This here's not exactly a social call."

"Then what you come dragging all the way over here for?"

The Reverend swallowed again. "After what Addie and Doc told me, I just had to see for myself." He looked at the flies buzzing around Grandpa. "Now I wish I'd just took their word on it."

"Meaning what?"

"Meaning a man in your condition's got no right to be asking questions. When the good Lord calls, you're supposed to answer."

"I ain't heard nobody calling," Grandpa said. "Course my hearing's not what it used to be."

"So Doc says. That's why you don't notice your heart's not beating."

"Onny natural for it to slow down a piece. I'm pushing ninety."

"Did you ever stop to think that ninety might be pushing back? You lived a mighty long stretch, Grandpa. Don't you reckon mebbe it's time to lie down and call it quits? Remember what the Good Book says—the Lord giveth, and the Lord taketh away."

Grandpa got that feisty look on his face. "Well, he ain't gonna taketh away me."

Reverend Peabody dug into his jeans for a bandana and wiped his forehead. "You got no cause to fear. It's a mighty rewarding experience. No more sorrow, no more care, all your burdens laid to rest. Not to mention getting out of this hot sun."

"Can't hardly feel it." Grandpa touched his whiskers. "Can't hardly feel anything."

The Reverend give him a look. "Hands getting stiff?"

Grandpa nodded. "I'm stiff all over."

"Just like I thought. You know what that means? Rigor mortis is setting in."

"Ain't never heard tell of anybody named Rigger Morris," Grandpa said. "I got me a touch of the rheumatism, is all."

The Reverend wiped his forehead again. "You sure want a heap of convincing," he said. "Won't take the word of a medical doctor, won't take the word of the Lord. You're the contrariest old coot I ever did see."

"Reckon it's my nature," Grandpa told him. "But I ain't unreasonable. All I'm asking for is proof. Like the feller says, I'm from Missouri. You got to show me."

The Reverend tucked away his bandana. It was sopping wet anyhow, wouldn't do him a lick of good. He heaved a big sigh and stared Grandpa right in the eye.

"Some things we just got to take on faith," he said. "Like you setting here when by rights you should be six feet under the daisies. If I can believe that, why can't you believe me? I'm telling you the mortal truth when I say you got no call to fuss. Mebbe the notion of lying in the grave don't rightly hold much appeal for you. Well, I can go along with that. But one thing's for sure. Ashes to ashes, dust to dust—that's just a saying. You needn't trouble yourself about spending eternity in the grave. Whilst your remains rest peaceful in the boneyard, your soul is on the wing. Flying straight up, yesiree, straight into the arms of the Lord! And what a great day it's fixing to be—you free as a bird and scooting around with them heavenly hosts on high, singing the praises of the Almighty and twanging away like all git-out on your genuine eighteen carats solid golden harp—"

"I ain't never been much for music," Grandpa said. "And I get dizzy just standing on a ladder to shingle the privy." He shook his head. "Tell you what—you think heaven is such a hellfired good proposition, why don't you go there yourself?"

Just then Ma come back out. "We're fresh out of lemonade," she said. "All's I could find was a jug. I know your feeling about such things, Reverend, but—"

"Praise the Lord!" The Reverend snatched the jug out of her hand, hefted it up, and took a mighty swallow.

"You're a good woman," he told Ma. "And I'm much beholden to you." Then he started down the path for the road, moving fast.

"Here, now!" Ma called after him. "What you aim to do about Grandpa?"

"Have no fear," the Reverend said. "We must put our trust now in the power of prayer."

He disappeared down the road, stirring dust.

"Danged if he didn't take the jug!" Grandpa mumbled. "You ask me, the onny power he trusts is in that corn-likker."

Ma give him a look. Then she bust out crying and run into the house.

"Now, what got into her?" Grandpa said.

"Never you mind," I told him. "Susie, you stay here and whisk those flies off Grandpa. I got things to attend to."

And I did.

Even before I went inside I had my mind set. I couldn't hold still to see Ma bawling that way. She was standing in the kitchen hanging on to Pa, saying, "What can we do? What can we do?"

Pa patted her shoulder. "There now, Addie, don't you go carrying on. It can't last forever."

"Nor can we," Ma said. "If Grandpa don't come to his senses, one of these mornings we'll go downstairs and serve up breakfast to a skeleton. And what do you think the neighbors will say when they see a bag of bones setting out there on my nice front porch? It's plumb embarrassing, that's what it is!"

"Never you mind, Ma," I said. "I got an idea."

Ma stopped crying. "What kind of idea?"

"I'm fixing to take me a hike over to Spooky Hollow."

"Spooky Hollow?" Ma turned so pale you couldn't even see her freckles. "Oh, no, boy—"

"Help is where you find it," I said. "And I reckon we got no choice."

Pa took a deep breath. "Ain't you afeard?"

"Not in daylight," I told him. "Now don't you fret. I'll be back afore dark."

Then I scooted out the back door.

I went over the fence and hightailed it along the back forty to the crick, stopping just long enough to dig up my piggy-bank from where it was stashed in the weeds alongside the rocks. After that I waded across the water and headed for tall timber.

Once I got into the piney woods I slowed down a smidge to get my bearings. Weren't no path to follow, because nobody never made one. Folks tended to stay clear of there, even in daytimes—it was just too dark and too lonesome. Never saw no small critters in the brush, and even the birds kep' shut of this place.

But I knowed where to go. All's I had to do was top the ridge, then move straight on down. Right smack at the bottom, in the deepest, darkest, lonesomest spot of all, was Spooky Hollow.

In Spooky Hollow was the cave.

And in the cave was the Conjure Lady.

Leastwise I reckoned she was there. But when I come tippy-toeing down to the big black hole in the rocks I didn't see a mortal soul, just the shadows bunching up on me from all around.

It sure was spooky, and no mistake. I tried not to pay any heed to the way my feet was itching. They wanted to turn and run, but I wasn't about to be put off.

After a bit I started to sing out. "Anybody home? You got company."

"Who?"

"It's me—Jody Tolliver."

"Whoooo?"

I was wrong about the birds, because now when I looked up I could see the big screech-owl glaring at me from a branch over yonder near the cave.

And when I looked down again, there she was—the Conjure Lady, peeking out at me from the hole between the rocks.

It was the first time I ever laid eyes on her, but it couldn't be no one else. She was a teensy rail-thin chickabiddy in a linsey-woolsey dress, and the face under her poke-bonnet was black as a lump of coal.

Shucks, I says to myself, there ain't nothing to be afeard of—she's just a little ol' lady, is all.

Then she stared up at me and I saw her eyes. They was lots bigger than the screech-owl's, and twice as glarey.

My feet begun to itch something fierce, but I stared back. "Howdy, Conjure Lady," I said.

"Whoooo?" said the screech-owl.

"It's young Tolliver," the Conjure Lady told him. "What's the matter, you got wax in your ears? Now go on about your business, you hear?"

The screech-owl give her a dirty look and took off. Then the Conjure Lady come out into the open.

"Pay no heed to Ambrose," she said. "He ain't rightly used to company. All's he ever sees is me and the bats."

"What bats?"

"The bats in the cave." The Conjure Lady smoothed down her dress. "I beg pardon for not asking you in, but the place is purely a mess. Been meaning to tidy it up, but what with one thing and another—first that dadblamed World War and then this dadgummed Prohibition—I just ain't got round to it yet."

"Never you mind," I said, polite-like. "I come on business."

"Reckoned you did."

"Brought you a pretty, too." I give it to her.

"What is it?"

"My piggy-bank."

"Thank you kindly," said the Conjure Lady.

"Go ahead, bust it open," I told her.

She whammed it down on a rock and the piggy-bank broke, spilling out money all over the place. She scrabbbled it up right quick.

"Been putting aside my cash earnings for nigh onto two years now," I said. "How much is they?"

"Eighty-seven cents, a Confederate two-bits piece, and this here button." She kind of grinned. "Sure is a purty one, too! What's it say on there?"

"Keep Cool With Coolidge."

"Well, ain't that a caution." The Conjure Lady slid the money into her pocket and pinned the button atop her dress. "Now, son—purty is as purty does, like the saying goes. So what can I do for you?"

"It's about my Grandpa," I said. "Grandpa Titus Tolliver."

"Titus Tolliver? Why, I reckon I know him! Use to run a still up in the toolies back of the crick. Fine figure of a man with a big black beard, he is."

"Is turns to was," I told her. "Now he's all dried up with the rheumatiz. Can't rightly see too good and can't hear for sour apples."

"Sure is a crying shame!" the Conjure Lady said. "But sooner or later we all get to feeling poorly. And when you gotta go, you gotta go."

"That's the hitch of it. He won't go."

"Meaning he's bound-up?"

"Meaning he's dead."

The Conjure Lady give me a hard look. "Do tell," she said.

So I told. Told her the whole kit and kaboodle, right from the git-go.

She heard me out, not saying a word. And when I finished up she just stared at me until I was fixing to jump out of my skin.

"I reckon you mightn't believe me," I said. "But it's the gospel truth."

The Conjure Lady shook her head. "I believe you, son. Like I say, I knowed your Grandpappy from the long-ago. He was plumb set in his ways then, and I take it he still is. Sounds to me like he's got a bad case of the stubborns."

"Could be," I said. "But there's nary a thing we can do about it, nor the Doc or the Reverend either."

The Conjure Lady wrinkled up her nose. "What you 'spect from them two? They don't know grit from granola."

"Mebbe so. But that leaves us betwixt a rock and a hard place—'less you can help."

"Let me think on it a piece."

The Conjure Lady pulled a corncob out of her pocket and fired up. I don't know what brand she smoked, but it smelled something fierce. I begun to get itchy again—not just in the feet but all over. The woods was darker now, and a kind of cold wind come wailing down between the trees, making the leaves whisper to themselves.

"Got to be some way," I said. "A charm, mebbe, or a spell."

She shook her head. "Them's ol'-fashioned. Now this here's one of them newfangled mental things, so we got to use newfangled idees. Your Grandpa don't need hex nor hoodoo. Like he says, he's from Missouri. He got to be showed, is all."

"Showed what?"

The Conjure Lady let out a cackle. "I got it!" She give me a wink. "Sure 'nough, the very thing! Now just you hold your water—I won't be a moment." And she scooted back into the cave.

I stood there, feeling the wind whooshing down the back of my neck and listening to the leaves that was like voices whispering things I didn't want to hear too good.

Then she come out again, holding something in her hand.

"Take this," she said.

"What is it?"

She told me what it was, and then she told me what to do with it.

"You really reckon this'll work?"

"It's the onny chance."

So I stuck it in my britches' pocket and she give me a little poke. "Now sonny, you best hurry and git home afore supper."

Nobody had to ask me twice—not with that chill wind moaning and groaning in the trees, and the dark creeping and crawling all around me.

I give her my much-obliged and lit out, leaving the Conjure Lady standing in front of the cave. Last I saw of her she was polishing her Coolidge button with a hunk of poison oak.

Then I was tearing through the woods, up the hill to the ridge and over. By the time I got to the clearing it was pitch-dark, and when I waded the crick I could see the moonlight wiggling on the water. Hawks on the hover went flippy-flapping over the back forty but I didn't stop to heed. I made a beeline for the fence, up and over, then into the yard and through the back door.

Ma was standing at the stove holding a pot whilst Pa ladled up the soup. They looked downright pleasured to see me.

"Thank the Lord!" Ma said. "I was just fixing to send Pa after you."

"I come quick as I could."

"And none too soon," Pa told me. "We like to go clean out'n our heads, what with the ruckus and all."

"What kind of ruckus?"

"First off, Mis Francy. Folks in town told her about Grandpa passing on, so she done the neighborly thing—mixed up a mess of stew to ease our appeytite in time of sorrow. She come lollygagging up the walk, all rigged out in her Sunday go-to-meeting clothes, toting the bowl under her arm and looking like lard wouldn't melt in her mouth. Along about then she caught sight of Grandpa setting there on the porch, kind of smiling at her through the flies.

"Well, up went the bowl and down come the whole shebang. Looked like it was raining stew-greens over that fancy Sears and Roebuck dress. And then she turned and headed for kingdom come, letting out a whoop that'd peel the paint off a privy wall."

"That's sorrowful," I said.

"Save your grieving for worse," Pa told me. "Next thing you know, Bixbee showed up, honking his horn. Wouldn't come nigh Grandpa, nosiree—I had to traipse clear down to where he set in the hearse."

"What'd he want?"

"Said he'd come for the remains. And if we didn't cough them up right fast, he was aiming to take a trip over to the county seat first thing tomorrow morning to get hisself a injection."

"Injunction," Ma said, looking like she was ready to bust out with the bawls again. "Said it was a scandal and a shame to let Grandpa set around like this. What with the sun and the flies and all, he was fixing to have the Board of Health put us under quar-and-tine."

"What did Grandpa say?" I asked.

"Nary a peep. Ol' Bixbee gunned his hearse out of here and Grandpa kep' right on rocking with Susie. She come in 'bout half hour ago, when the sun went down—says he's getting stiff as a board but won't pay it no heed. Just keeps asking what's to eat."

"That's good," I said. "On account of I got the very thing. The Conjure Lady give it to me for his supper."

"What is it—pizen?" Pa looked worried. "You know I'm a God-fearing man and I don't hold with such doings. 'Sides, how you 'spect to pizen him if he's already dead?"

"Ain't nothing of the sort," I said. "This here's what she sent."

And I pulled it out of my britches pocket and showed it to them.

"Now what in the name of kingdom come is that?" Ma asked.

I told her what it was, and what to do with it.

"Ain't never heard tell of such foolishness in all my born days!" Ma told me.

Pa looked troubled in his mind. "I knowed I shouldn't have let you go down to Spooky Hollow. Conjure Lady must be short of her marbles, putting you up to a thing like that."

"Reckon she knows what she's doing," I said. "'Sides, I give all my savings for this here—eighty-seven cents, a Confederate quarter, and my Coolidge button."

"Never you mind about no Coolidge button," Pa said. "I swiped it off'n a Yankee, anyway—one of them revenooers." He scratched his chin. "But hard money's something else. Mebbe we best give this notion a try."

"Now, Pa—" Ma said.

"You got any better plan?" Pa shook his head. "Way I see it, what with the Board of Health set to come a-snapping at our heels tomorrow, we got to take a chance."

Ma fetched a sigh that come clean up from her shoes, or would of if she'd been wearing any.

"All right, Jody," she told me. "You just put it out like the Conjure Lady said. Pa, you go fetch Susie and Grandpa. I'm about to dish up."

"You sure this'll do the trick?" Pa asked, looking at what I had in my hand.

"It better," I said. "It's all we got."

So Pa went out and I headed for the table, to do what the Conjure Lady had in mind.

Then Pa come back with sister Susie.

"Where's Grandpa?" Ma asked.

"Moving slow," Susie said. "Must be that Rigger Morris."

"No such thing." Grandpa come through the doorway, walking like a cockroach on a hot griddle. "I'm just a wee mite stiff."

"Stiff as a four-by-four board," Pa told him. "Upstairs in bed, that's where you ought to be, with a lily in your hand."

"Now don't start on that again," Grandpa said. "I told you I ain't dead so many times I'm blue in the face."

"You sure are," said sister Susie. "Ain't never seen nobody look any bluer."

And he was that—blue and bloated, kind of—but he paid it no heed. I recollected what Ma said about mebbe having to put up with a skeleton at mealtime, and I sure yearned for the Conjure Lady's notion to work. It plumb had to, because Grandpa was getting deader by the minute.

But you wouldn't think so when he caught sight of the vittles on the table. He just stirred his stumps right over to his chair and plunked down.

"Well, now," Grandpa said. "You done yourself proud tonight, Addie. This here's my favorite—collards and catfish heads!"

He was all set to take a swipe at the platter when he up and noticed what was setting next to his plate.

"Great day in the morning!" he hollered. "What in tarnation's this?"

"Ain't nothing but a napkin," I said.

"But it's black!" Grandpa blinked. "Who ever heard tell of a black napkin?"

Pa looked at Ma. "We figger this here's kind of a special occasion," he said. "If you take my meaning—"

Grandpa fetched a snort. "Consarn you and your meaning! A black napkin? Never you fear, I know what you're hinting around at, but it ain't a-gonna work—nosiree, bub!"

And he filled his plate and dug in.

The rest of us just set there staring, first at Grandpa, then at each other.

"What'd I tell you?" Pa said to me, disgusted-like.

I shook my head. "Wait a spell."

"Better grab whilst you can git," Grandpa said. "I aim to eat me up a storm."

And he did. His arms was stiff and his fingers scarce had enough curl left to hold a fork and his jaw-muscles worked extra hard—but he went right on eating. And talking.

"Dead, am I? Ain't never seen the day a body'd say a thing like that to me before, let alone kinfolk! Now could be I'm tolerable stubborn, but that don't signify I'm mean. I ain't about to make trouble for anyone, least of all my own flesh and blood. If I was truly dead and knowed it for a fact—why, I'd be the first one to go right upstairs to my room and lie down forever. But you got to show me proof 'fore I do. That's the pure and simple of it—let me see some proof!"

"Grandpa," I said.

"What's the matter, sonny?"

"Begging your pardon, but you got collards dribbling all over your chin."

Grandpa put down his fork. "So they is. I thank you kindly."

And before he rightly knowed what he was doing, Grandpa wiped his mouth on the napkin.

When he finished he looked down at it. He looked once and he looked twice. Then he just set the napkin down gentle-like, stood up from the table, and headed straight for the stairs.

"Goodbye all," he said.

We heard him go clumping up the steps and down the hall into his room and we heard the mattress sag when he laid down on his bed.

Then everything was quiet.

After a while Pa pushed his chair back and went upstairs. Nobody said a word until he come down again.

"Well?" Ma looked at him.

"Ain't nothing more to worry about," Pa said. "He's laid down his burden at last. Gone to glory, amen."

"Praise be!" Ma said. Then she looked at me and crooked a finger at the napkin. "Best get rid of that."

I went round and picked it up. Sister Susie give me a funny look. "Ain't nobody fixing to tell me what happened?" she asked.

I didn't answer—just toted the napkin out and dropped it deep down in the crick. Weren't no sense telling anybody the how of it, but the Conjure Lady had the right notion after all. She knowed Grandpa'd get his proof—just as soon as he wiped his mouth.

Ain't nothing like a black napkin to show up a little ol' white maggot.

BY **THEODORE STURGEON**

Rarely has the innocence of waking up dead been portrayed more beautifully than in the following story.

Sympathy with the monster is one of horror's oldest and most rewarding strategies. Think Frankenstein's monster, who—if not a zombie proper—was at least a makeshift and godforsaken quilt of corpses, forced to helplessly wander through a landscape of hate, fear, and woeful incomprehension.

Ted Sturgeon was one of those writers who—in the '60s New Wave of speculative fiction—most successfully carved new neural pathways through the brainscape of popular lit.

And with "It," he created a kindred spirit to "The Heep" and other malformed monsters of the era. But in keeping with the renegade brilliance that was his trademark, he infused it with the purest sort of curiosity.

Making it oddly loveable, as well as exceedingly dangerous.

IT WALKED IN THE WOODS.

It was never born. It existed. Under the pine needles the fires burn, deep and smokeless in the mold. In heat and in darkness and decay there is growth. There is life and there is growth. It grew, but it was not alive. It walked unbreathing through the woods, and thought and saw and was hideous and strong, and it was not born and it did not live. It grew and moved about without living.

It crawled out of the darkness and hot damp mold into the cool of a morning. It was huge. It was lumped and crusted with its own hateful substances, and pieces of it dropped off as it went its way, dropped off and lay writhing, and stilled, and sank putrescent into the forest loam.

It had no mercy, no laughter, no beauty. It had strength and great intelligence. And—perhaps it could not be destroyed. It crawled out of its mound in the wood and lay pulsing in the sunlight for a long moment. Patches of it shone wetly in the golden glow, parts of it were nubbled and flaked. And whose dead bones had given it the form of a man?

It scrabbled painfully with its half-formed hands, beating the ground and the bole of a tree. It rolled and lifted itself up on its crumbling elbows, and it tore up a great handful of herbs and shredded them against its chest, and it paused and gazed at the gray-green juices with intelligent calm. It wavered to its feet, and seized a young sapling and destroyed it, folding the slender trunk back on itself again and again, watching attentively the useless, fibered splinters. And it snatched up a fear-frozen field creature, crushing it slowly, letting blood and pulpy flesh and fur ooze from between its fingers, run down and rot on the forearms.

It began searching.

Kimbo drifted through the tall grasses like a puff of dust, his bushy tail curled tightly over his back and his long jaws agape. He ran with an easy lope, loving his freedom and the power of his flanks and furry shoulders. His tongue lolled listlessly over his lips. His lips were black and serrated, and each tiny pointed liplet swayed with his doggy gallop. Kimbo was all dog, all healthy animal.

He leaped high over a boulder and landed with a startled yelp as a longeared cony shot from its hiding place under the rock. Kimbo hurtled after it, grunting with each great thrust of his legs. The rabbit bounced just ahead of him, keeping its distance, its ears flattened on its curving back and its little legs nibbling away at distance hungrily. It stopped, and Kimbo pounced, and the rabbit shot away at a tangent and popped into a hollow log. Kimbo yelped again and rushed snuffling at the log, and knowing his failure, curvetted but once around the stump and ran on into the forest. The thing watched from the wood raised its crusted arms and waited for Kimbo.

Kimbo sensed it there, standing dead-still by the path. To him it was a bulk which smelled of carrion not fit to roll in, and he snuffled distastefully and ran to pass it.

The thing let him come abreast and dropped a heavy twisted fist on him. Kimbo saw it coming and curled up tight as he ran, and the hand clipped stunningly on his rump, sending him rolling and yipping down the slope. Kimbo straddled to his feet, shook his head, shook his body with a deep growl, came back to the silent thing with green murder in his eyes. He walked stiffly, straight-legged, his tail as low as his lowered head and a ruff of fury round his neck. The thing raised its arms again, waited.

Kimbo slowed, then flipped himself through the air at the monster's throat. His jaws closed on it; his teeth clicked together through a mass of filth, and he fell choking and snarling at its feet. The thing leaned down and struck twice, and after the dog's back was broken, it sat beside him and began to tear him apart.

"Be back in an hour or so," said Alton Drew, picking up his rifle from the corner behind the wood box. His brother laughed.

"Old Kimbo 'bout runs your life, Alton," he said.

"Ah, I know the ol' devil," said Alton. "When I whistle for him for half an hour and he don't show up, he's in a jam or he's treed something wuth shootin' at. The ol' son of a gun calls me by not answerin'."

Cory Drew shoved a full glass of milk over to his nine-year-old daughter and smiled. "You think as much o' that houn'-dog o' yours as I do of Babe here."

Babe slid off her chair and ran to her uncle. "Gonna catch me the bad fella,

Uncle Alton?" she shrilled. The "bad fella" was Cory's invention—the one who lurked in corners ready to pounce on little girls who chased the chickens and played around mowing machines and hurled green apples with a powerful young arm at the sides of the hogs, to hear the synchronized thud and grunt; little girls who swore with an Austrian accent like an ex-hired man they had had; who dug caves in haystacks till they tipped over, and kept pet crawfish in tomorrow's milk cans, and rode work horses to a lather in the night pasture.

"Get back here and keep away from Uncle Alton's gun!" said Cory. "If you see the bad fella, Alton, chase him back here. He has a date with Babe here for that stunt of hers last night." The preceding evening, Babe had kindheartedly poured pepper on the cows' salt block.

"Don't worry, kiddo," grinned her uncle, "I'll bring you the bad fella's hide if he don't get me first."

Alton Drew walked up the path toward the wood, thinking about Babe. She was a phenomenon—a pampered farm child. Ah well—she had to be. They'd both loved Clissa Drew, and she'd married Cory, and they had to love Clissa's child. Funny thing, love. Alton was a man's man, and thought things out that way; and his reaction to love was a strong and frightened one. He knew what love was because he felt it still for his brother's wife and would feel it as long as he lived for Babe. It led him through his life, and yet he embarrassed himself by thinking of it. Loving a dog was an easy thing, because you and the old devil could love one another completely without talking about it. The smell of gun smoke and wet fur in the rain were perfume enough for Alton Drew, a grunt of satisfaction and the scream of something hunted and hit were poetry enough. They weren't like love for a human, that choked his throat so he could not say words he could not have thought of anyway. So Alton loved his dog Kimbo and his Winchester for all to see, and let his love for his brother's women, Clissa and Babe, eat at him quietly and unmentioned.

His quick eyes saw the fresh indentations in the soft earth behind the boulder, which showed where Kimbo had turned and leaped with a single surge, chasing the rabbit. Ignoring the tracks, he looked for the nearest place where a rabbit might hide, and strolled over to the stump. Kimbo had been there, he saw, and had been there too late. "You're an ol' fool," muttered Alton. "Y' can't catch a cony by chasin' it. You want to cross him up some way." He gave a peculiar trilling whistle, sure that Kimbo was digging frantically under some nearby stump for a rabbit that was three counties away by now. No answer. A little puzzled, Alton went back to the path. "He never done this before," he said softly.

He cocked his .32-40 and cradled it. At the county fair someone had once said of Alton Drew that he could shoot at a handful of corn and peas thrown in the air and hit only the corn. Once he split a bullet on the blade of a knife and put two candles out. He had no need to fear anything that could be shot at. That's what he believed.

The thing in the woods looked curiously down at what it had done to Kimbo, and tried to moan the way Kimbo had before he died. It stood a minute storing away facts in its foul, unemotional mind. Blood was warm. The sunlight was warm. Things that moved and bore fur had a muscle to force the thick liquid through tiny tubes in their bodies. The liquid coagulated after a time. The liquid on rooted green things was thinner and the loss of a limb did not mean loss of life. It was very interesting, but the thing, the mold with a mind, was not pleased. Neither was it displeased. Its accidental urge was a thirst for knowledge, and it was only—interested.

It was growing late, and the sun reddened and rested awhile on the hilly horizon, teaching the clouds to be inverted flames. The thing threw up its head suddenly, noticing the dusk. Night was ever a strange thing, even for those of us who have known it in life. It would have been frightening for the monster had it been capable of fright, but it could only be curious; it could only reason from what it had observed.

What was happening? It was getting harder to see. Why? It threw its shapeless head from side to side. It was true—things were dim, and growing dimmer. Things were changing shape, taking on a new and darker color. What did the creatures it had crushed and torn apart see? How did they see? The larger one, the one that had attacked, had used two organs in its head. That must have been it, because after the thing had torn off two of the dog's legs it had struck at the hairy muzzle; and the dog, seeing the blow coming, had dropped folds of skin over the organs—closed its eyes. Ergo, the dog saw with its eyes. But then after the dog was dead, and its body still, repeated blows had had no effect on the eyes. They remained open and staring. The logical conclusion was, then, that a being that had ceased to live and breathe and move about lost the use of its eyes. It must be that to lose sight was, conversely, to die. Dead things did not walk about. They lay down and did not move. Therefore the thing in the wood concluded that it must be dead, and so it lay down by the path, not far away from Kimbo's scattered body, lay down and believed itself dead.

Alton Drew came up through the dusk to the wood. He was frankly worried. He whistled again, and then called, and there was still no response, and he said again, "The ol' fleabus never done this before," and shook his heavy head. It was past milking time, and Cory would need him. "Kimbo!" he roared. The cry echoed through the shadows, and Alton flipped on the safety catch of his rifle and put the butt on the ground beside the path. Leaning on it, he took off his cap and scratched the back of his head, wondering. The rifle butt sank into what he thought was soft earth; he staggered and stepped into the chest of the thing that lay beside the path. His foot went up to the ankle in its yielding rottenness, and he swore and jumped back.

"*Whew!* Somp'n sure dead as hell there! Ugh!" He swabbed at his boot with a handful of leaves while the monster lay in the growing blackness with the edges of the deep footprint in its chest sliding into it, filling it up. It lay there regarding him dimly out of its muddy eyes, thinking it was dead because of the darkness, watching the articulation of Alton Drew's joints, wondering at this new uncautious creature.

Alton cleaned the butt of his gun with more leaves and went on up the path, whistling anxiously for Kimbo.

Clissa Drew stood in the door of the milk shed, very lovely in red-checked gingham and a blue apron. Her hair was clean yellow, parted in the middle and stretched tautly back to a heavy braided knot. "Cory! Alton!" she called a little sharply.

"Well?" Cory responded gruffly from the barn, where he was stripping off the Ayrshire. The dwindling streams of milk plopped pleasantly into the froth of a full pail.

"I've called and called," said Clissa. "Supper's cold, and Babe won't eat until you come. Why—where's Alton?"

Cory grunted, heaved the stool out of the way, threw over the stanchion lock and slapped the Ayrshire on the rump. The cow backed and filled like a towboat, clattered down the line and out into the barnyard. "Ain't back yet."

"Not back?" Clissa came in and stood beside him as he sat by the next cow, put his forehead against the warm flank. "But, Cory, he said he'd—"

"Yeh, yeh, I know. He said he'd be back fer the milkin'. I heard him. Well, he ain't."

"And you have to— Oh, Cory, I'll help you finish up. Alton would be back if he could. Maybe he's—"

"Maybe he's treed a blue jay," snapped her husband. "Him an' that damn dog." He gestured hugely with one hand while the other went on milking. "I got twenty-six head o' cows to milk. I got pigs to feed an' chickens to put to bed. I got to toss hay for the mare and turn the team out. I got harness to mend and a wire down in the night pasture. I got wood to split an' carry." He milked for a moment in silence, chewing on his lip. Clissa stood twisting her hands together, trying to think of something to stem the tide. It wasn't the first time Alton's hunting had interfered with the chores. "So I got to go ahead with it. I can't interfere with Alton's spoorin'. Every damn time that hound o' his smells out a squirrel I go without my supper. I'm gettin' sick and—"

"Oh, I'll help you!" said Clissa. She was thinking of the spring, when Kimbo had held four hundred pounds of raging black bear at bay until Alton could put a bullet in its brain, the time Babe had found a bearcub and started to carry it home, and had fallen into a freshet, cutting her head. You can't hate a dog that has saved your child for you, she thought.

"You'll do nothin' of the kind!" Cory growled. "Get back to the house. You'll find work enough there. I'll be along when I can. Dammit, Clissa, don't cry! I didn't mean to— Oh, shucks!" He got up and put his arms around her. "'I'm wrought up," he said. "Go on now. I'd no call to speak that way to you. I'm sorry.

Go back to Babe. I'll put a stop to this for good tonight. I've had enough. There's work here for four farmers an' all we've got is me an' that . . . that huntsman.

"Go on now, Clissa."

"All right," she said into his shoulder. "But, Cory, hear him out first when he comes back. He might be unable to come back. He might be unable to come back this time. Maybe he . . . he—"

"Ain't nothin' kin hurt my brother that a bullet will hit. He can take care of himself. He's got no excuse good enough this time. Go on, now. Make the kid eat."

Clissa went back to the house, her young face furrowed. If Cory quarreled with Alton now and drove him away, what with the drought and the creamery about to close and all, they just couldn't manage. Hiring a man was out of the question. Cory'd have to work himself to death, and he just wouldn't be able to make it. No one man could. She sighed and went into the house. It was seven o'clock, and the milking not done yet. Oh, why did Alton have to—

Babe was in bed at nine when Clissa heard Cory in the shed, slinging the wire cutters into a corner. "Alton back yet?" they both said at once as Cory stepped into the kitchen; and as she shook her head he clumped over to the stove, and lifting a lid, spat into the coals. "Come to bed," he said.

She laid down her stitching and looked at his broad back. He was twenty-eight, and he walked and acted like a man ten years older, and looked like a man five years younger. "I'll be up in a while," Clissa said.

Cory glanced at the corner behind the wood box where Alton's rifle usually stood, then made an unspellable, disgusted sound and sat down to take off his heavy muddy shoes.

"It's after nine," Clissa volunteered timidly. Cory said nothing, reaching for house slippers.

"Cory, you're not going to—"

"Not going to what?"

"Oh, nothing. I just thought that maybe Alton—"

"Alton!" Cory flared. "The dog goes hunting field mice. Alton goes hunting the dog. Now you want me to go hunting Alton. That's what you want?"

"I just— He was never this late before."

"I won't do it! Go out lookin' for him at nine o'clock in the night? I'll be damned! He has no call to use us so, Clissa."

Clissa said nothing. She went to the stove, peered into the wash boiler, set it aside at the back of the range. When she turned around, Cory had his shoes and coat on again.

"I knew you'd go," she said. Her voice smiled though she did not.

"I'll be back durned soon," said Cory. "I don't reckon he's strayed far. It is late. I ain't feared for him, but—" He broke his 12-gauge shotgun, looked through the barrels, slipped two shells in the breech and a box of them into his pocket. "Don't wait up," he said over his shoulder as he went out.

"I won't," Clissa replied to the closed door, and went back to her stitching by the lamp.

The path up the slope to the wood was very dark when Cory went up it, peering and calling. The air was chill and quiet, and a fetid odor of mold hung in it. Cory blew the taste of it out through impatient nostrils, drew it in again with the next breath, and swore. "Nonsense," he muttered. "Houn' dawg. Huntin', at ten in th' night, too. Alton!" he bellowed. "Alton Drew!" Echoes answered him, and he entered the wood. The huddled thing he passed in the dark heard him and felt the vibrations of his footsteps and did not move because it thought it was dead.

Cory strode on, looking around and ahead and not down since his feet knew the path.

"Alton!"

"That you, Cory?"

Cory Drew froze. That corner of the wood was thickly set and as dark as a burial vault. The voice he heard was choked, quiet, penetrating.

"Alton?"

"I found Kimbo, Cory."

"Where the hell have you been?" shouted Cory furiously. He disliked this pitch-darkness; he was afraid at the tense hopelessness of Alton's voice, and he mistrusted his ability to stay angry at his brother.

"I called him, Cory. I whistled at him, an' the ol' devil didn't answer."

"I can say the same for you, you . . . you louse. Why weren't you to milkin'? Where are you? You caught in a trap?"

"The houn' never missed answerin' me before, you know," said the tight, monotonous voice from the darkness.

"Alton! What the devil's the matter with you? What do I care if your mutt didn't answer? Where—"

"I guess because he ain't never died before," said Alton, refusing to be interrupted.

"You *what?*" Cory clicked his lips together twice and then said, "Alton, you turned crazy? What's that you say?"

"Kimbo's dead."

"Kim . . . oh! Oh!" Cory was seeing that picture again in his mind—Babe sprawled unconscious in the freshet, and Kimbo ragging and snapping against a monster bear, holding her back until Alton could get there. "What happened, Alton?" he asked more quietly.

"I aim to find out. Someone tore him up."

"*Tore him up?*"

"There ain't a bit of him left tacked together, Cory. Every damn joint in his body tore apart. Guts out of him."

"Good God! Bear, you reckon?"

"No bear, nor nothin' on four legs. He's all here. None of him's been et. Whoever done it just killed him an'—tore him up."

"Good God!" Cory said again. "Who could've—" There was a long silence, then. "Come 'long home," he said almost gently. "There's no call for you to set up by him all night."

"I'll set. I aim to be here at sunup, an' I'm goin' to start trackin', an' I'm goin' to keep trackin' till I find the one done this job on Kimbo."

"You're drunk or crazy, Alton."

"I ain't drunk. You can think what you like about the rest of it. I'm stickin' here."

"We got a farm back yonder. Remember? I ain't going to milk twenty-six head o' cows again in the mornin' like I did jest now, Alton."

"Somebody's got to. I can't be there. I guess you'll just have to, Cory."

“You dirty scum!” Cory screamed. “You’ll come back with me now or I’ll know why!”

Alton’s voice was still tight, half-sleepy. “Don’t you come no nearer, bud.”

Cory kept moving toward Alton’s voice.

“I said”—the voice was very quiet now—”*stop where you are.*” Cory kept coming. A sharp click told of the release of the .32-40’s safety. Cory stopped.

“You got your gun on me, Alton?” Cory whispered.

“Thass right, bud. You ain’t a-trompin’ up these tracks for me. I need ’em at sunup.”

A full minute passed, and the only sound in the blackness was that of Cory’s pained breathing. Finally:

“I got my gun, too, Alton. Come home.”

“You can’t see to shoot me.”

“We’re even on that.”

“We ain’t. I know just where you stand, Cory. I been here four hours.”

“My gun scatters.”

“My gun kills.”

Without another word Cory Drew turned on his heel and stamped back to the farm.

Black and liquidescent it lay in the blackness, not alive, not understanding death, believing itself dead. Things that were alive saw and moved about. Things that were not alive could do neither. It rested its muddy gaze on the line of trees at the crest of the rise, and deep within it thoughts trickled wetly. It lay huddled, dividing its new-found facts, dissecting them as it had dissected live things when there was light, comparing, concluding, pigeonholing.

The trees at the top of the slope could just be seen, as their trunks were a fraction of a shade lighter than the dark sky behind them. At length they, too, disappeared, and for a moment sky and trees were a monotone. The thing knew it was dead now, and like many a being before it, it wondered how long it must stay like this. And then the sky beyond the trees grew a little lighter. That was a manifestly impossible occurrence, thought the thing, but it could see it and it must be so. Did dead things live again? That was curious. What about dismembered dead things? It would wait and see.

The sun came hand over hand up a beam of light. A bird somewhere made a high yawning peep, and as an owl killed a shrew, a skunk pounced on another, so that the night shift deaths and those of the day could go on without cessation. Two flowers nodded archly to each other, comparing their pretty clothes. A dragonfly nymph decided it was tired of looking serious and cracked its back open, to crawl out and dry gauzily. The first golden ray sheared down between the trees, through the grasses, passed over the mass in the shadowed bushes. "I am alive again," thought the thing that could not possibly live. "I am alive, for I see clearly." It stood up on its thick legs, up into the golden glow. In a little while the wet flakes that had grown during the night dried in the sun, and when it took its first steps, they cracked off and a small shower of them fell away. It walked up the slope to find Kimbo, to see if he, too, were alive again.

Babe let the sun come into her room by opening her eyes. Uncle Alton was gone—that was the first thing that ran through her head. Dad had come home last night and had shouted at mother for an hour. Alton was plumb crazy. He'd turned a gun on his own brother. If Alton ever came ten feet into Cory's land, Cory would fill him so full of holes he'd look like a tumbleweed. Alton was lazy, shiftless, selfish, and one or two other things of questionable taste but undoubted vividness. Babe knew her father. Uncle Alton would never be safe in this county.

She bounced out of bed in the enviable way of the very young, and ran to the window. Cory was trudging down to the night pasture with two bridles over his arm, to get the team. There were kitchen noises from downstairs.

Babe ducked her head in the washbowl and shook off the water like a terrier before she toweled. Trailing clean shirt and dungarees, she went to the head of the stairs, slid into the shirt, and began her morning ritual with the trousers. One step down was a step through the right leg. One more, and she was into the left. Then, bouncing step by step on both feet, buttoning one button per step, she reached the bottom fully dressed and ran into the kitchen.

"Didn't Uncle Alton come back a-tall, Mum?"

"Morning, Babe. No, dear." Clissa was too quiet, smiling too much, Babe thought shrewdly. Wasn't happy.

"Where'd he go, Mum?"

"We don't know, Babe. Sit down and eat your breakfast."

"What's a misbegotten, Mum?" the Babe asked suddenly. Her mother nearly dropped the dish she was drying. "Babe! You must never say that again!"

"Oh. Well, why is Uncle Alton, then?"

"Why is he what?"

Babe's mouth muscled around an outsize spoonful of oatmeal. "A misbe—"

"Babe!"

"All right, Mum," said Babe with her mouth full. "Well, why?"

"I told Cory not to shout last night," Clissa said half to herself.

"Well, whatever it means, he isn't," said Babe with finality. "Did he go hunting again?"

"He went to look for Kimbo, darling."

"Kimbo? Oh Mummy, is Kimbo gone, too? Didn't he come back either?"

"No dear. Oh, please, Babe, stop asking questions!"

"All right. Where do you think they went?"

"Into the north woods. Be quiet."

Babe gulped away at her breakfast. An idea struck her; and as she thought of it she ate slower and slower, and cast more and more glances at her mother from under the lashes of her tilted eyes. It would be awful if Daddy did anything to Uncle Alton. Someone ought to warn him.

Babe was halfway to the woods when Alton's .32-40 sent echoes giggling up and down the valley.

Cory was in the south thirty, riding a cultivator and cussing at the team of grays when he heard the gun. "Hoa," he called to the horses, and sat a moment to listen to the sound. "One-two-three. Four," he counted. "Saw someone, blasted away at him. Had a chance to take aim and give him another, careful. My God!" He threw up the cultivator points and steered the team into the shade of three oaks. He hobbled the gelding with swift tosses of a spare strap, and headed for the woods. "Alton a killer," he murmured, and doubled back to the house for his gun. Clissa was standing just outside the door.

"Get shells!" he snapped and flung into the house. Clissa folllowed him. He was strapping his hunting knife on before she could get a box off the shelf. "Cory—"

"Hear that gun, did you? Alton's off his nut. He don't waste lead. He shot at someone just then, and he wasn't fixin' to shoot pa'tridges when I saw him last. He was out to get a man. Gimme my gun."

"Cory, Babe—"

"You keep her here. Oh, God, this is a helluva mess. I can't stand much more." Cory ran out the door.

Clissa caught his arm: "Cory I'm trying to tell you. Babe isn't here. I've called, and she isn't here."

Cory's heavy, young-old face tautened. "Babe— Where did you last see her?"

"Breakfast." Clissa was crying now.

"She say where she was going?"

"No. She asked a lot of questions about Alton and where he'd gone."

"Did you say?"

Clissa's eyes widened, and she nodded, biting the back of her hand.

"You shouldn't ha' done that, Clissa," he gritted, and ran toward the woods. Clissa stood looking after him, and in that moment she could have killed herself.

Cory ran with his head up, straining with his legs and lungs and eyes at the long path. He puffed up the slope to the woods, agonized for breath after the forty-five minutes' heavy going. He couldn't even notice the damp smell of mold in the air.

He caught a movement in a thicket to his right, and dropped. Struggling to keep his breath, he crept forward until he could see clearly. There was something in there, all right. Something black, keeping still. Cory relaxed his legs and torso completely to make it easier for his heart to pump some strength back into them, and slowly raised the 12-gauge until it bore on the thing hidden in the thicket.

"Come out!" Cory said when he could speak.

Nothing happened.

"Come out or by God I'll shoot!" rasped Cory.

There was a long moment of silence, and his finger tightened on the trigger.

"You asked for it," he said, and as he fired the thing leaped sideways into the open, screaming.

It was a thin little man dressed in sepulchral black, and bearing the rosiest baby-face Cory had ever seen. The face was twisted with fright and pain. The man scrambled to his feet and hopped up and down saying over and over, "Oh, my hand. Don't shoot again! Oh, my hand. Don't shoot again!" He stopped after a bit, when Cory had climbed to his feet, and he regarded the farmer out of sad china-blue eyes. "You shot me," he said reproachfully, holding up a little bloody hand. "Oh, my goodness."

Cory said, "Now, who the hell are you?"

The man immediately became hysterical, mouthing such a flood of broken sentences that Cory stepped back a pace and half raised his gun in self-defense. It seemed to consist mostly of "I lost my papers," and "I didn't do it," and "It was horrible. Horrible. Horrible," and "The dead man," and "Oh, don't shoot again."

Cory tried twice to ask him a question, and then he stepped over and knocked the man down. He lay on the ground writhing and moaning and blubbering and putting his bloody hand to his mouth where Cory had hit him.

"Now what's going on around here?"

The man rolled over and sat up. "I didn't do it!" he sobbed. "I didn't I was walking along and I heard the gun and I heard some swearing and an awful scream and I went over there and peeped and I saw the dead man and I ran away and you came and I hid and you shot me and—"

"*Shut up!*" The man did, as if a switch had been thrown. "Now," said Cory, pointing along the path, "you say there's a dead man up there?"

The man nodded and began crying in earnest. Cory helped him up. "Follow this path back to my farmhouse," he said. "Tell my wife to fix up your hand. *Don't* tell her anything else. And wait there until I come. Hear?"

"Yes. Thank you. Oh, thank you. *Snff.*"

"Go on now." Cory gave him a gentle shove in the right direction and went alone, in cold fear, up the path to the spot where he had found Alton the night before.

He found him here now, too, and Kimbo. Kimbo and Alton had spent several years together in the deepest friendship; they had hunted and fought and slept together, and the lives they owed each other were finished now. They were dead together.

It was terrible that they died the same way. Cory Drew was a strong man, but he gasped and fainted dead away when he saw what the thing of the mold had done to his brother and his brother's dog.

The little man in black hurried down the path, whimpering and holding his injured hand as if he rather wished he could limp with it. After a while the whimper faded away, and the hurried stride changed to a walk as the gibbering terror of the last hour receded. He drew two deep breaths, said: "My goodness!" and felt almost normal. He bound a linen handkerchief around his wrist, but the hand kept bleeding. He tried the elbow, and that made it hurt. So he stuffed the handkerchief back in his pocket and simply waved the hand stupidly in the air until the blood clotted. He did not see the great moist horror that clumped along behind him, although his nostrils crinkled with its foulness.

The monster had three holes close together on its chest, and one hole in the middle of its slimy forehead. It had three close-set pits in its back and one on the back of its head. These marks were where Alton Drew's bullets had struck and passed through. Half of the monster's shapeless face was sloughed away, and there was a deep indentation on its shoulder. This was what Alton Drew's gun butt had done after he clubbed it and struck at the thing that would not lie down after he put his four bullets through it. When these things happened the monster was not hurt or angry. It only wondered why Alton Drew acted that way. Now it followed the little man without hurrying at all, matching his stride step by step and dropping little particles of muck behind it.

The little man went on out of the wood and stood with his back against a big tree at the forest's edge, and he thought. Enough had happened to him here. What good would it do to stay and face a horrible murder inquest, just to continue this silly, vague search? There was supposed to be the ruin of an old, old hunting lodge deep in this wood somewhere, and perhaps it would hold the evidence he wanted. But it was a vague report—vague enough to be forgotten without regret. It would be the height of foolishness to stay for all the hick-town red tape that would follow that ghastly affair back in the wood. Ergo, it would be ridiculous to follow that farmer's advice, to go to his house and wait for him. He would go back to town.

The monster was leaning against the other side of the big tree.

The little man snuffled disgustedly at a sudden overpowering odor of rot. He reached for his handkerchief, fumbled and dropped it. As he bent to pick it up, the monster's arm *whuffed* heavily in the air where his head had been—a blow that would certainly have removed that baby-faced protuberance. The man stood up and would have put the handkerchief to his nose had it not been so bloody. The creature behind the tree lifted its arm again just as the little man tossed the handkerchief away and stepped out into the field, heading across country to the distant highway that would take him back to town. The monster pounced on the handkerchief, picked it up, studied it, tore it across several times and inspected the tattered edges. Then it gazed vacantly at the disappearing figure of the little man, and, finding him no longer interesting, turned back into the woods.

Babe broke into a trot at the sound of the shots. It was important to warn Uncle Alton about what her father had said, but it was more interesting to find out what he had bagged. Oh, he'd bagged it, all right. Uncle Alton never fired without killing. This was about the first time she had ever heard him blast away like that. Must be a bear, she thought excitedly, tripping over a root, sprawling, rolling to her feet again, without noticing the tumble. She'd love to have another bearskin in her room. Where would she put it? Maybe they could line it and she could have it for a blanket. Uncle Alton could sit on it and read to her in the evening— Oh, no. No. Not with this trouble between him and Dad. Oh, if she could only do something! She tried to run faster, worried and anticipating, but she was out of breath and went more slowly instead.

At the top of the rise by the edge of the woods she stopped and looked back. Far down in the valley lay the south thirty. She scanned it carefully, looking for her father. The new furrows and the old were sharply defined, and her keen eyes saw immediately that Cory had left the line with the cultivator and had angled the team over to the shade trees without finishing his row. That wasn't like him. She could see the team now, and Cory's pale-blue denim was nowhere in sight. She giggled lightly to herself as she thought of the way she would fool her father. And the little sound of laughter drowned out, for her, the sound of Alton's hoarse dying scream.

She reached and crossed the path and slid through the brush beside it. The shots came from up around here somewhere. She stopped and listened several times, and then suddenly heard something coming toward her, fast. She ducked under cover, terrified, and a little baby-faced man in black, his blue eyes wide with horror, crashed blindly past her, the leather case he carried catching on the branches. It spun a moment and then fell right in front of her. The man never missed it.

Babe lay there for a long moment and then picked up the case and faded into the woods. Things were happening too fast for her. She wanted Uncle Alton, but she dared not call. She stopped again and strained her ears. Back toward the edge of the wood she heard her father's voice, and another's—probably the man who had dropped the briefcase. She dared not go over there. Filled with enjoyable terror, she thought hard, then snapped her fingers in triumph. She and Alton had played Injun many times up here; they had a whole repertoire of secret signals. She had practiced birdcalls until she knew them better than the birds themselves. What would it be? Ah—blue jay. She threw back her head and by some youthful alchemy produced a nerve-shattering screech that would have done justice to any jay that ever flew. She repeated it, and then twice more.

The response was immediate—the call of a blue jay, four times, spaced two and two. Babe nodded to herself happily. That was the signal that they were to meet immediately at The Place. The Place was a hide-out that he had discovered and shared with her, and not another soul knew of it; an angle of rock beside a stream not far away. It wasn't exactly a cave, but almost. Enough so to be entrancing. Babe trotted happily away toward the brook. She had just known that Uncle Alton would remember the call of the blue jay, and what it meant.

In the tree that arched over Alton's scattered body perched a large jay bird, preening itself and shining in the sun. Quite unconscious of the presence of death, hardly noticing the Babe's realistic cry, it screamed again four times, two and two.

It took Cory more than a moment to recover himself from what he had seen. He turned away from it and leaned weakly against a pine, panting. Alton. That was Alton lying there, in—parts.

"God! God, God, God—"

Gradually his strength returned, and he forced himself to turn again. Stepping carefully, he bent and picked up the .32-40. Its barrel was bright and clean, but the butt and stock were smeared with some kind of stinking rottenness. Where had he seen the stuff before? Somewhere—no matter. He cleaned it off absently, throwing the befouled bandanna away afterward. Through his mind ran Alton's words—was that only last night?—"*I'm goin' to start trackin'. An' I'm goin' to keep trackin' till I find the one done this job on Kimbo.*"

Cory searched shrinkingly until he found Alton's box of shells. The box was wet and sticky. That made it—better, somehow. A bullet wet with Alton's blood was the right thing to use. He went away a short distance, circled around till he found heavy footprints, then came back.

"I'm a-trackin' for you, bud," he whispered thickly, and began. Through the brush he followed its wavering spoor, amazed at the amount of filthy mold about, gradually associating it with the thing that had killed his brother. There was nothing in the world for him any more but hate and doggedness. Cursing himself for not getting Alton home last night, he followed the tracks to the edge of the woods. They led him to a big tree there, and there he saw something else—the footprints of the little city man. Nearby lay some tattered scraps of linen, and—what was that?

Another set of prints—small ones. Small, stub-toed ones.

"Babe!"

No answer. The wind sighed. Somewhere a blue jay called.

Babe stopped and turned when she heard her father's voice, faint with distance, piercing.

"Listen at him holler," she crooned delightedly. "Gee, he sounds mad." She sent a jay bird's call disrespectfully back to him and hurried to The Place.

It consisted of a mammoth boulder beside the brook. Some upheaval in the glacial age had cleft it, cutting out a huge V-shaped chunk. The widest part of the cleft was at the water's edge, and the narrowest was hidden by bushes. It made a little ceilingless room, rough and uneven and full of pot-holes and cavelets inside, and yet with quite a level floor. The open end was at the water's edge.

Babe parted the bushes and peered down the cleft.

"Uncle Alton!" she called softly. There was no answer. Oh, well, he'd be along. She scrambled in and slid down to the floor.

She loved it here. It was shaded and cool, and the chattering stream filled it with shifting golden lights and laughing gurgles. She called again, on principle, and then perched on an outcropping to wait. It was only then she realized that she still carried the little man's briefcase.

She turned it over a couple of times and then opened it. It was divided in the middle by a leather wall. On one side were a few papers in a large yellow envelope, and on the other some sandwiches, a candy bar, and an apple. With a youngster's complacent acceptance of manna from heaven, Babe fell to. She saved one sandwich for Alton, mainly because she didn't like its highly spiced bologna. The rest made quite a feast.

She was a little worried when Alton hadn't arrived, even after she had consumed the apple core. She got up and tried to skim some flat pebbles across the roiling brook, and she stood on her hands, and she tried to think of a story to tell herself, and she tried just waiting. Finally, in desperation, she turned again to the briefcase, took out the papers, curled up by the rocky wall and began to read them. It was something to do, anyway.

There was an old newspaper clipping that told about strange wills that people had left. An old lady had once left a lot of money to whoever would make the trip from the Earth to the Moon and back. Another had financed a home for cats whose masters and mistresses had died. A man left thousands of dollars to the first man who could solve a certain mathematical problem and prove his solution. But one item was blue-penciled. It was:

> One of the strangest of wills still in force is that of Thaddeus M. Kirk, who died in 1920. It appears that he built an elaborate mausoleum with burial vaults for all the remains of his family. He collected and removed caskets from all over the country to fill the designated niches. Kirk was the last of his line; there were no relatives when he died. His will stated that the mausoleum was to be kept in repair permanently, and that a certain sum was to be set aside as a reward for whoever who could produce the body of his grandfather, Roger Kirk, whose niche is still empty. Anyone finding this body is eligible to receive a substantial fortune.

Babe yawned vaguely over this, but kept on reading because there was nothing else to do. Next was a thick sheet of business correspondence, bearing the letterhead of a firm of lawyers. The body of it ran:

> In regard to your query regarding the will of Thaddeus Kirk, we are authorized to state that his grandfather was a man about five feet, five inches, whose left arm had been broken and who had a triangular silver plate set into his skull. There is no information as to the whereabouts of his death. He disappeared and was declared legally dead after the lapse of fourteen years.
>
> The amount of the reward as stated in the will, plus accrued interest, now amounts to a fraction over sixty-two thousand dollars. This will be paid to anyone who produces the remains, providing that said remains answer descriptions kept in our private files.

There was more, but Babe was bored. She went on to the little black notebook. There was nothing in it but penciled and highly abbreviated records of visits to libraries; quotations from books with titles like "History of Angelina and Tyler Counties" and "Kirk Family History." Babe threw that aside, too. Where could Uncle Alton be?

She began to sing tunelessly, "Tumalumalum tum, ta ta ta," pretending to dance a minuet with flowing skirts like a girl she had seen in the movies. A rustle of the bushes at the entrance to The Place stopped her. She peeped upward, saw them being thrust aside. Quickly she ran to a tiny cul-de-sac in the rock wall, just big enough for her to hide in. She giggled at the thought of how surprised Uncle Alton would be when she jumped out at him.

She heard the newcomer come shuffling down the steep slope of the crevice and land heavily on the floor. There was something about the sound— What was it? It occurred to her that though it was a hard job for a big man like Uncle Alton to get through the little opening in the bushes, she could hear no heavy breathing. She heard no breathing at all!

Babe peeped out into the main cave and squealed in utmost horror. Standing there was, not Uncle Alton, but a massive caricature of a man: a huge thing like an irregular mud doll, clumsily made. It quivered and parts of it glistened and parts of it were dried and crumbly. Half of the lower left part of its face was gone, giving it a lopsided look. It had no perceptible mouth or nose, and its eyes were crooked, one higher than the other, both a dingy brown with no whites at all. It stood quite still looking at her, its only movement a steady unalive quivering.

It wondered about the queer little noise Babe had made.

Babe crept far back against a little pocket of stone, her brain running round and round in tiny circles of agony. She opened her mouth to cry out, and could not. Her eyes bulged and her face flamed with the strangling effort, and the two golden ropes of her braided hair twitched and twitched as she hunted hopelessly for a way out. If only she were out in the open—or in the wedge-shaped half-cave where the thing was—or home in bed!

The thing clumped toward her, expressionless, moving with a slow inevitability that was the sheer crux of horror. Babe lay wide-eyed and frozen, mounting pressure of terror stilling her lungs, making her heart shake the whole world. The monster came to the mouth of the little pocket, tried to walk to her and was stopped by the sides. It was such a narrow little fissure, and it was all Babe could do to get in. The thing from the wood stood straining against the rock at its shoulders, pressing harder and harder to get to Babe. She sat up slowly, so near to the thing that its odor was almost thick enough to see, and a wild hope burst through her voiceless fear. It couldn't get in! It couldn't get in because it was too big!

The substance of its feet spread slowly under the tremendous strain and at its shoulder appeared a slight crack. It widened as the monster unfeelingly crushed itself against the rock, and suddenly a large piece of the shoulder came away and the being twisted slushily three feet farther in. It lay quietly with its muddy eyes fixed on her, and then brought one thick arm up over its head and reached.

Babe scrambled in the inch farther she had believed impossible, and the filthy clubbed hand stroked down her back, leaving a trail of muck on the blue denim of the shirt she wore. The monster surged suddenly and, lying full length now, gained that last precious inch. A black hand seized one of her braids, and for Babe the lights went out.

When she came to, she was dangling by her hair from that same crusted paw. The thing held her high, so that her face and its featureless head were not more than a foot apart. It gazed at her with a mild curiosity in its eyes, and it swung her slowly back and forth. The agony of her pulled hair did what fear could not do—gave her a voice. She screamed. She opened her mouth and puffed up her powerful young lungs, and she sounded off. She held her throat in the position of the first scream, and her chest labored and pumped more air through the frozen throat. Shrill and monotonous and infinitely piercing, her screams.

The thing did not mind. It held her as she was, and watched. When it had learned all it could from this phenomenon, it dropped her jarringly, and looked around the half-cave, ignoring the stunned and huddled Babe. It reached over and picked up the leather briefcase and tore it twice across as if it were tissue. It saw the sandwich Babe had left, picked it up, crushed it, dropped it.

Babe opened her eyes, saw that she was free, and just as the thing turned back to her she dove between its legs and out into the shallow pool in front of the rock, paddled across and hit the other bank screaming. A vicious little light of fury burned in her; she picked up a grapefruit-sized stone and hurled it with all her frenzied might. It flew low and fast, and struck squashily on the monster's ankle. The thing was just taking a step toward the water; the stone caught it off balance, and its unpracticed equilibrium could not save it. It tottered for a long, silent moment at the edge and then splashed into the stream. Without a second look Babe ran shrieking away.

Cory Drew was following the little gobs of mold that somehow indicated the path of the murderer, and he was nearby when he first heard her scream. He broke into a run, dropping his shotgun and holding the .32-40 ready to fire. He ran with such deadly panic in his heart that he ran right past the huge cleft rock and was a hundred yards past it before she burst out through the pool and ran up the bank. He had to run hard and fast to catch her, because anything behind her was that faceless horror in the cave, and she was living for the one idea of getting away from there. He caught her in his arms and swung her to him, and she screamed on and on and on.

Babe didn't see Cory at all, even when he held her and quieted her.

The monster lay in the water. It neither liked nor disliked this new element. It rested on the bottom, its massive head a foot beneath the surface, and it curiously considered the facts it had garnered. There was the little humming noise of Babe's voice that sent the monster questing into the cave. There was the black material of the briefcase that resisted so much more than green things when he tore it. There was the little two-legged one who sang and brought him near, and who screamed when he came. There was this new cold moving thing he had fallen into. It was washing his body away. That had never happened before. That was interesting. The monster decided to stay and observe this new thing. It felt no urge to save itself; it could only be curious.

The brook came laughing down out of its spring, ran down from its source beckoning to the sunbeams and embracing freshets and helpful brooklets. It shouted and played with streaming little roots, and nudged the minnows and pollywogs about in its tiny backwaters. It was a happy brook. When it came to the pool by the cloven rock it found the monster there, and plucked at it. It soaked the foul substances and smoothed and melted the molds, and the waters below the thing eddied darkly with its diluted matter. It was a thorough brook. It washed all it touched, persistently. Where it found filth, it removed filth; if there were layer on layer of foulness, then layer by foul layer it was removed. It was a good brook. It did not mind the poison of the monster, but took it up and thinned it and spread it in little rings round rocks downstream, and let it drift to the rootlets of water plants, that they might grow greener and lovelier. And the monster melted.

"I am smaller," the thing thought. "That is interesting. I could not move now. And now this part of me which thinks is going, too. It will stop in just a moment, and drift away with the rest of the body. It will stop thinking and I will stop being, and that, too, is a very interesting thing."

So the monster melted and dirtied the water, and water was clean again, washing and washing the skeleton that the monster had left. It was not very big, and there was a badly healed knot on the left arm. The sunlight flickered on the triangular silver plate set into the pale skull, and the skeleton was very clean now. The brook laughed about it for an age.

They found the skeleton, six grimlipped men who came to find a killer. No one had believed Babe, when she told her story days later. It had to be days later because Babe had screamed for seven hours without stopping, and had lain like a dead child for a day. No one believed her at all, because her story was all about the bad fella, and they knew that the bad fella was simply a thing that her father had made up to frighten her with. But it was through her that the skeleton was found, and so the men at the bank sent a check to the Drews for more money than they had ever dreamed about. It was old Roger Kirk, sure enough, that skeleton, though it was found five miles from where he had died and sank into the forest floor where the hot molds builded around his skeleton and emerged—a monster.

So the Drews had a new barn and fine new livestock and they hired four men. But they didn't have Alton. And they didn't have Kimbo. And Babe screams at night and has grown very thin.

Lie Still, Sleep Becalmed

by Steve Duffy

Maritime zombies hold a unique position for me. Perhaps because I harbor a fear of deep waters, and what might possibly lie beneath them. Perhaps because they hark back to the stories I read as a kid: adventurous tales of pirates and sailors and nautical mishaps far away from dry land.

Whatever the case, Steve Duffy's "Lie Still, Sleep Becalmed" stirred up a whole lot of ghosts for me.

It's a modern story told in an old-fashioned way, or perhaps vice versa. Maybe it's just the excellent weed that's confusing me, as it does the great protagonists herein.

But I swear to God, few recent stories have thrown me so thoroughly back to the sweaty excitement I felt as a kid when suddenly confronted with the notion that reading could be fun. And more than fun: a strange rite of passage into a world far deeper and creepier than officially let on to. A world that I was entering with every word I read.

I'm gonna go out on a limb here, and proclaim this piece a modern classic: just chaste enough to recommend to the kids, and just profound enough to forever haunt the parents who might take the quality time to read it to 'em.

IT WAS A NIGHT TRIP, and the thing to remember is: noone's looking for surprises on a night trip. You ride at anchor, out where it's nice and quiet; kick back, chill out, talk rubbish till sunup. No surprises.

Back when Danny had the *Katie Mae*, we often used to take her out of Beuno's Cove at ten, eleven p.m., and head for the banks off Puffin Island, near the south-east tip of Anglesey; *we* being Danny, who owned the boat, Jack, who crewed on a regular basis, and me. Jack was a great big grinning party-monster who'd do anything for anyone; anything, that is, except resist temptation when it offered itself, as it seemed to on a regular basis. Any other owner but Danny would probably have sacked him, no matter how good he was with boats: the reason Danny didn't would never have been clear to an outsider, really. Claire, who was always quick to pick up on that sort of thing, reckoned that Jack—Mr. Happy-go-Lucky—represented something that Danny—Mr. Plodder—had probably always dreamed of being himself, but had never quite worked up the nerve to go for. It was a classic case of vicarious wish-fulfillment, apparently.

"And I'll tell you something else about Danny," she'd added, "I bet once you get past that Big-I-Am act he puts on, it's Jack who does all the graft—am I right? It's the same with you: if you didn't sort out all his tax returns and VAT for him, they'd probably have taken that boat off him by now. He likes to think he's running the show, but he'd be sunk without the pair of you. It's quite funny, really." I remember her whispering all this in my ear as we watched Jack and Danny playing pool in the basement bar of the Toad Hall, not long after we'd first started dating.

That was the summer of '95: on dry land it was banging, hammering heatwave all the way, long sundrenched days and sticky muggy night-times. Out at sea, though, you got the breeze, cool and wonderful, and whenever the next day's bookings sheet was blank Danny needed little enough persuading to pick up a tray or two of Red Stripe and take the *Katie Mae* out for the night. Jack would turn up with a bag of Bangor hydroponic and we'd make the run out to the fishing banks west of the Conwy estuary; we'd lie out on the deck drinking, smoking, chatting about nothing in particular, or maybe go below to pursue the Great and Never-Ending Backgammon Marathon, in which stupendous, entirely fictional sums of money would change hands over the course of a season's fishing. Good times, easy, untroubled; I look back now and think how sweet we had it then.

One night in early August Claire said she wanted to go out with us. I can't really say why I was resistant to the idea. Part of it, if I'm honest, was probably to do with keeping her well away from Jack until I was a bit more confident in the relationship. Remember I told you about Jack and temptation? Well, if I'd gone on to mention me and insecurity, that would've given you the whole of the picture. Over and above that . . . I honestly don't know. Nothing like a premonition, nothing that dramatic or well-defined. Just the feeling, somewhere under my scalp, that things might be on the cusp; might be changing, one way or another, and changing irrevocably. The fact was I always made an excuse, put her off; until that particular night when it had all the potential to turn into an argument, which would have been our first. Fine, I said, yeah, come along, no problem.

It had been another scorcher. Walking down the hill to the harbor you could feel the pavement underfoot giving out the last of the day's heat to the baking breathless night; under the cotton of her tee-shirt the small of Claire's back was slick with sweat where my hand rested. Danny was waiting for us on the *Katie Mae*, and Jack came by soon after; he'd been away for the weekend at a festival, got back only that morning, slept till nine p.m., and now here he was ready for action again, invincible. It was just eleven thirty when we fired up the engine and cast off; I remember Claire squeezed my hand in excitement.

The last of the sunset was gone out of the sky, and it was very dark, very quiet, a still, calm night with just a sliver of the waning moon swinging round behind the headland. The beacon winked one, two, three as we eased out beyond the end of the breakwater, Claire and I sitting out on the foredeck, Danny and Jack in the wheelhouse. As always when we were putting out on a night trip, I felt that little kick of expectation: I'd get it in the daytime, too, but at night particularly. There was a magic to it, some song of the sea, pitched between shanties and sirens. "It's the ocean, innit?" Jack once said; "you never know what it's going to throw at you," and soon enough I learned this to be true. Tongue in cheek, I told the same thing to Claire as we rounded the Trwyn y Ddraig and pulled away from the coast. "Listen, I don't care what it throws at me," she said, arching like a cat in the first stirrings of a sea-breeze, "just so long as it's this temperature or below. Oh, that's good. That's the coolest I've been all day." She stretched out on the foredeck, head propped up in my lap as I sat cross-legged behind her, absently ruffling her hair with my fingers.

At this stage you probably need to know a bit about the layout of the boat. The *Katie Mae* was thirteen meters stem-to-stern, pretty roomy for a standard fishing vessel, with reasonably poky diesels (in need of an overhaul, but fine so long as you didn't try and race them straight from cold). The wheelhouse was amidships, the center of the boat; behind that, on the aft deck, were the gear lockers, the bilge pump, the engine hatch. Up towards the stem, there was the foredeck and the Samson post. In the wheelhouse we had VHF ship-to-shore, GPS, radar, and also the "fish-finder," the sonar that not only showed the sea-bottom but tracked the shoals. Down below, bench seats followed the shape of the hull for'ard of the wheelhouse above, curving with the prow around a drop-down table where we kept the beer and the backgammon set. Hurricane lights hung from the bulkheads between the portholes, posters of mermaids were tacked up on the ceiling: all snug as a bug in a rug. And outside, where Claire and I were, you had the best air-conditioning in all North Wales, entirely free and gratis.

Claire snuggled her head in my lap, enjoying the cool breeze of our passage. "This is nice," she said, letting the last word stretch to its full extent. "Just like you to keep it all to yourself—typical greedy pig bloke."

I dodged her playful backward punches, one for every slur. "Keep what to myself? A bunch of sweaty geezers sitting round getting smashed and talking garbage all night? You should've said—I'd have taken you down the rugby club, back in town."

"Getting smashed and talking garbage? Is that all there is to it? It's got to be a bit more cerebral than that, surely—big smart boys like you, university types and all?"

"You'd think so, wouldn't you?" Danny had joined us on the foredeck. "Well, you'd be wrong. No culture on this here tub."

"If it's culture you want," I pointed out, moving over to make room, "I believe P&O do some very nice cruises this time of year."

"Do you want the guided tour then, Claire?" Danny settled himself alongside us. That's Llandudno—see the lights round the West Shore?—and that's the marina at Deganwy over there."

Not to be outdone, I chipped in my own bit of local color. "This stretch here is where the lost land of Helig used to be, before the sea came in and covered it all."

"Helig ap Glannog, aye," Danny amplified in his amusingly nit-picking way, at pains to remind Claire just who was the captain on this boat, and who was the guy who helped out now and then. Danny's dad had fished these waters since the 1940s; he'd been delighted when his eldest dropped out of Bangor Uni and picked up a charter boat of his own. Since then, Danny had been busy proving Jack's adage that you could take the boy out of university, but you couldn't take university out of the boy: it was just a way he had. You couldn't let it get to you.

"Helig ap what?" Claire seemed slightly amused herself—remember, I told you she'd already got Danny figured out.

"Way back," Danny explained, "sixth century AD. There was a curse on the family, and a big tide came and covered all their lands, and everybody died except for one harpist on the hill there crying woe is me, woe is me, some shit or other. And nowadays hardly anyone moors a boat out there—"

"Except for Danny," I chipped in, "because he's big and hard and don't take no shit from no-one, innit, Danny lad?" He tried to punch me in a painful place, but I rolled over just in time. "Who's steering this tub, anyway?"

"Jack," said Danny, waiting till I'd resumed my former position before trying, and failing once more, to hit me where it hurt. "We'll keep going for a bit," he went on, ignoring my stifled laughter, "till we're out of everyone's way. Then we'll drop anchor and get down to business." He rubbed his hands together in anticipation of the night's entertainment. "So, do you play backgammon then, Claire?"

Claire smiled sweetly, her blonde hair blowing back into my face. "Well, I know the moves," she said, and nudged me surreptitiously.

*

Several hours later, Claire owned, in theory at least, the *Katie Mae*, the papers on Danny's house and fifty per cent of both Jack's and mine earnings through to the year 2015. Down below Danny and Jack were skinning up and arguing over who was most in debt to who; Claire and I were up in the wheelhouse, enjoying a little quality relationship time with the lights out.

"Mmmm," she said, into my left ear. "That was easy enough."

"What?" I said. "Me? I'm dead easy, me. You should know that by now."

"Oh, I do," she said, "I do. No—I meant those two downstairs."

"*Down below*," I reminded her, in Danny's pedantic voice. "What—you mean you get up to this sort of thing with those two as well? I'm crushed."

She chuckled, and moved her hand a little. "There—is that better? Didn't mean to crush you. Are they always that dozy?"

"Well, you had an unfair advantage."

"What?"

"You were distracting them all the time."

"Me? What was I doing?"

"Nothing," I said, burying my face in her neck. "You were just making the most of your natural advantages: this, and this, and this . . ."

"Mmmm . . . ooh. What's that?"

"You mean you don't know what *that* is? Here, let me show you—"

"Not that." Firmly, she brushed the possibility aside. "That thing behind you. It's beeping."

"Beeping . . . ?" I disengaged myself awkwardly and looked around. "Oh, that. That's the fish-finder. Didn't think it was me."

"The whatter?"

"Fish-finder: it's sonar, like in the movies, ping-ping, ping-ping? It shows you the sea-bed underneath the vessel—down here, look—and then where the shoals are. Look, there's something: that blob there, coming up now."

"So is that fish, then?" There was another ping. The target was rising, moving closer to the boat, so far as I could tell. Or it could have been the boat was sinking, I wasn't an expert.

"Must be, I suppose. Hang on, Jack knows this kit better than I do—Jack?"

Jack's grinning head popped up from below: the original Jack-in-the-box. "Aye, aye, mateys—here you go, I've done up a little dragon each for you, all classy-like." He swarmed up the short companionway to join us in the wheelhouse. "Hell's teeth, now, what's this?" He flipped a switch up and down on the fish-finder. "Have you been pressing buttons again, Billy-thick-lad? Bloody cabin boys, Claire, I tell you—"

I dug him in the ribs, and we wrestled amiably for a moment. "It's nothing to do with me, that—I never touched it. It just went off."

"I see. Big boy done it and ran off, is that it?" He smiled at Claire. "No, you're in the clear for once. I'll tell you who'll have left this on—bloody Captain Birdseye down there. You can't trust him to do anything properly: that right, Will?"

From down below came a smothered counter-accusation: Jack showed it his middle finger and grinned again, even more roguishly. I put an arm around Claire, just so's Jack didn't get carried away. "Claire wants to know is that a shoal or what?"

"Let's have a butcher's . . . what, that there? No, that's not a shoal." He bent over the screen. In its faint green glow he looked a little perplexed. "Too small, see? And it's right up on the surface, practically—I don't know what that is. Sometimes you get seals round Puffin Island, off the Orme even . . . I dunno. It might be a seal, I suppose." He glanced up, through the cabin window. "There isn't any moon, worse luck, but if we look over, lemme see . . . *that* way"—he pointed out on the starboard side—"we might be able to see something, if we get out on deck and stay quiet-like."

Which we did, joined by Danny, who'd just appeared from below decks with more beer; and perhaps I should mention at this point that Claire and I had only had a couple of cans each by that time. I'd been hitting on the majority of the joints as they went round, Claire hadn't, but we were both completely on the case so far as our shared perceptions went. Given what happened over the next hour or so, it's important you know that.

Out on the aft deck, Jack explained to Danny what we'd seen on the fishfinder. We were all of us whispering, in case we scared the seal; we were still expecting seals at this point. Danny nodded, and pottered over behind the wheelhouse on the port side. Claire cupped her hand around my ear and whispered, "What's he up to?" At that time I didn't know. Soon enough it would become clear.

The three of us on the aft deck—Jack, Claire, and I—gazed out over the waves. It was difficult to make much out on the surface, even with the light in the wheelhouse switched off and our eyes accustomed to the darkness. Away off in the far distance was a glitter of shore-lights: Anglesey to the north-west, Penhirion and the mainland south-west. Between the lights on land and where we lay at anchor was mile after mile of still dark ocean. The green navigation light danced on the tops of the soft sluicing wavelets near the hull; all the rest was a vast murky undulation, slop and ebb, slop and ebb, featureless, unknowable.

Suddenly light sprang out from the *Katie Mae*, swinging through the darkness, settling on the waves in a rough rippling ellipse. I jumped a little, tightened my grip on Claire, looked 'round: there was Danny, all but invisible behind the spotlight on the wheelhouse roof, directing the strong beam through and beyond us to light up the slow dark waves. "Shit," swore Jack under his breath, then, louder, hissing: "Turn it off, man, you'll frighten it away! Bastard's left his nav-lights on as it is," he added *sotto voce*.

"I thought you wanted to see!" Danny sounded a bit smashed already. Claire looked at me, and I read the same judgement in her eyes. The harsh light from the *Katie Mae*'s spot made her look even paler than usual; almost translucent.

"We *do*, but we're not gonna see anythin' if you frighten it away, you knob! Turn it off and come back here—no—wait a minute . . ." Jack's voice trailed off, and I turned back to the water, trying to see what he'd seen. If anything, the spotlight made it harder; it was total illumination or total blackout, vivid purple afterimages blooming on your retinas whenever you looked outside its magic circle. I squinted, tried to shield my eyes. Beside me Jack was doing the same thing. "Hold it steady, over there—look—what's that?"

A slumped low shape in the black water. Dull and dark, the waves washing over it as it dipped and rose on a tranquil tide; then Claire gasped and dug her fingers into my arm as a slight swell lifted it far enough out of the water for us to see a gleam of white. A face, all tangled round with lank dark strands like seaweed.

Jack had seen it too. "Christ almighty," he breathed; then to Danny: "Hold it! Hold it there!"

"What?" shouted Danny.

"Look where you're pointing it, man! Forget about the bloody seal—there's someone in the water!" Abruptly Jack was gone from beside me, over to the aft lockers, flinging them open one after another. His voice came back on the quiet night air as Claire and I clung to each other and watched the body floating towards us in the spotlight: ". . . find anything on this *bastard* boat . . ." Then he was back, a long boathook under his arm like a jousting lance. "Right," he called to Danny: "Listen up. Claire's gonna come up and get that light, okay?" He glanced at Claire; she nodded. He smiled briefly at her and resumed: "You get down here and give Will a hand. I'm gonna hook him when he gets close enough in, then you two'll have to pull him up."

And we did just that: Danny and I knelt down in the scuppers, braced against the capstans while Jack leaned perilously far out from the side, one hand grasping the side of the boat, the other waving the boathook back and forth till the waterlogged shape drifted within reach. All the way in, until it was so close to the boat the spotlight wouldn't go far enough down on its mount, Claire never wavered: she knelt on the wheelhouse roof and trained the light dead straight on the bobbing body in the waves. Danny had got a torch from somewhere, and that gave us light enough for the last part of the job.

Jack's hook snagged in the clothing of the body; he hauled it in like a fish on a gaff, and Danny and I managed to get a grasp underneath its arms. Together we dragged it out of the water and up on to deck, where it plopped down as if on a fishmonger's slab, a cold dead weight of waterlogged clothing and wrinkled flesh.

I think we all thought at that time it was a dead man. It had been lying, after all, face down in the water; it was clammy cold to the touch; and we hadn't felt anything like a heartbeat as we heaved it aboard. The three of us stood around it as the saltwater drained off into the scuppers; no-one quite knew what to say, or do. A hand touched my shoulder, and I nearly jumped off the side; Claire had come down from the roof of the wheelhouse and was standing behind me. "Jesus," I muttered fretfully, and she squeezed my arm remorsefully, peering around me at the body on the deck. "Sorry," she whispered; then, quite unexpectedly, she buried her face in my shoulder. "Has anyone looked to see . . ." she began, and couldn't finish. Danny just looked at me, his tanned, weather-roughened face as pale as Claire's; it was left to Jack, as ever, to take care of the practicalities. "She's right," he said, grimacing; "suppose we'd better have a look who he is and that. Do us a favor, Danny boy; get that flashlight down here, will you?"

He knelt on the deck, and gently turned the body over by its shoulders. What we'd thought was seaweed around the head we could see now were long, damp locks of hair: Danny brushed them away from the face, a thing I doubt I could have done myself right then. He wiped his hand several times on the leg of his jeans, and straightened up a little. We could all see the face now: it was a man in his early twenties, unshaven, startlingly pallid. "Shit," Danny said, and the torch he was holding wobbled for a moment. "Just look at his face a minute, Jack . . ."

"I'm *looking* at his face." Jack sounded stressed. "What the fuck d'you think I'm *doing* down here—" and then he drew in his breath sharply.

"It's him, isn't it?" Like the beam from the flashlight, Danny's voice was wavering slightly. "That lad we were talking to in the Liverpool Arms on Regatta Day that time, what's his name . . ."

"Andy." There was a slight roughness, a catch, to Jack's voice. "Andy something or other; crews on that boat out of Bangor these days, doesn't he? Andy, Andy . . . Christ, I must be going senile in my old age." He slapped the side of his head, and Claire jumped a little at the sudden noise in the midst of all that illimitable stillness. "Andy Farlowe, that's it. His old feller used to have a fishing boat in Conwy harbor; he's retired now, lives up Gyffin somewhere. Christ. I'll have to go 'round, I suppose, tell him what's happened—"

"*Wait.*" Claire's nails dug into my arm. "Wait. Look at him, Will."

"What?" I looked at her instead; she was staring fixedly at the body, her mouth slightly open. "*What?*" I asked her again, and she whispered it, no more, so quiet you would have missed it in the normal run of things: "He's *moving. . . .*"

I was going to say, impossible, you're imagining it; but now as I looked I could see the limbs twitch, just a little. The hands clenched, unclenched, the head moved ever so slightly from side to side. It—he—gulped a little, and his jaw sagged open. A little trickle of seawater came out in a splutter. All at once his eyelids opened, and the eyes rolled back from up inside his head. He blinked once or twice, and seemed to be trying to speak.

Jack was down with him in a shot, finger probing the airway for obstructions, ear pressed to his mouth to gauge the breathing. "Fuck," he said, looking up as if unable to believe what he was seeing or feeling: "He's still alive, you know."

Not only that: within a few minutes he was conscious, talking, the lot. With Jack and Danny helping him we got him on his feet and down below decks, where Danny had the best part of a bottle of rum held against emergencies, like when we ran out of lager. He coughed and spluttered a bit, but it seemed to do the trick; he looked round at us, shook his head and cleared his throat. "Who are you lot, then?" he croaked. We all burst out laughing, I think from sheer relief as much as anything.

He couldn't say how long he'd been in the water: "I must've been spark out of it," was all he could manage. "You were that," said Jack, one arm round his shoulders in a bracing grapple. His attitude to the younger man seemed almost fatherly, most un-Jacklike: it was altogether more responsibility than I could remember him showing towards anything or anyone before.

"How about the boat?" asked Danny, and it suddenly occurred to all of us: how had he got out there in the first place? We looked at him: he closed his eyes briefly, as if trying to remember. "We gone out . . ." he began, and paused. Jack nodded encouragingly. "We gone out in the evening . . . in the straits past Beaumaris . . ." Every word seemed to be an effort; not so much physically, though he still looked very weak, but an effort of remembrance. It was like watching someone being asked to remember what he did on his birthday when he was seven.

"What happened, Andy? Did you fall overboard, or did the boat go down?" Danny seemed anxious to clear up the technicalities of it all.

"I was out on deck," Andy said slowly. He pushed his lank black mane of hair back, looked round helplessly for words. "It was . . . it was cold." Jack nodded, as if Andy had just given him the temperature down to the nearest degree centigrade; Andy hardly noticed. "In the water. It was cold." He shivered a little, and Claire said, "Have you got any spare clothes on board? We should get him out of those; he'll be freezing. He's probably in shock already: we should get him warm. Get some blankets round him as well if you've got them."

Jack sprang to it. "Shit, why didn't I think of that—see that locker under the seats there, Claire? You have a look in there; that's blankets. I think I've got a few things, sweaters and that, in there too, have I?"

Claire rummaged down in the locker, came up with a thick fisherman's sweater and a couple of blankets. "Right, mate," Jack rapped out a little paradiddle on the table-top. "Get you into these, shall we? Danny—let's have the engines on and home James, what about it?"

"Yeah . . ." Danny was a little slower to react; he was staring at Andy as if he was having trouble taking it all in. At first I put it down to him still being a bit smashed; I'd have thought what had happened in the last ten minutes would have sobered anyone up, but it all depended on what sort of state he'd been in in the first place—he was always a pig when it came to spliff. "Yeah: You come up too, Will. Get on the ship-to-shore, just in case, let them know there might be a problem with the . . . with the . . . what is it, Jack?"

"*Wanderley*." This over his shoulder as he turned the balled-up sweater right way out. "Better get on to them; nice one, Danny boy."

"The *Wanderley*, out of Bangor. Okay?" With one long last look at Andy, he turned and went up the companionway to the wheelhouse. I went to follow him; stopped, and said irresolutely, "Claire?" She looked up at me, reached instinctively for my hand.

"Never mind Claire—it's crowded enough in here." This from up in the wheelhouse. "Get up here, Will, I need you."

"You can give us a hand, Claire," said Jack, "give our boy here the once-over." He nudged Andy. "How about that for luck, eh, Andy lad? Floating in the water all night, and the first boat to come along's got a posh lady doctor on it!"

"I'm not a doctor, Jack," Claire told him patiently, correcting this mistake for no more than the third or fourth time that night. "I work at the hospital; I'm a junior pharmacist."

"Well, it's all the same, innit?" Jack wasn't listening. He smoothed the last of the folds out of the sweater, turned to face us with a determinedly bright smile. "You've done all the first aid and that, haven't you?"

"I might not have been paying attention, though," Claire said, in an uncharacteristically small girly-voice; but she knew she was beaten. Better women than her had been powerless in the grip of a full-on Jack attack. I squeezed her hand and turned to go up the companionway. She held on to it for a moment longer than I thought she would; I glanced back, and she was looking at me, her violet eyes dark and smudgy-looking in the lamplight. I raised an eyebrow, *what*? She bit at her lower lip, shook her head slightly, *nothing*, and gave my hand one last squeeze. I squeezed back, and smiled encouragingly. "See you later," I said, and Jack, overhearing me, said "Yeah, yeah, get up there Will man."

Beside him on the bench, Andy looked up, silhouetted in the lantern light, running a hand through his sopping merman's mane. He did seem to be in some sort of shock; bewildered by it all, withdrawn almost, as if part of him was still floating out in the water, in the long night reaches where no boats carne. He tried to smile; I smiled back, then trotted up the short companionway to join Danny in the wheelhouse.

"About time, Will," He sounded edgy, about half a beat off a full-scale Danny fluster. "Ship-to-shore, there: get a move on."

There was a limit to how much I could stand of Danny playing Captain Bligh, but this was not the time to bring it up. I said nothing, and flipped the switch on the radio. Nothing. I tried again: still nothing. "VHF's down," I said in a neutral tone, hoping Danny wouldn't take it the wrong way.

He did, of course. "*Down?* It can't be *down*, no way, I had it up and running this afternoon. Here—" He pushed past me in the constricted space. "It's simple, look. On, off . . ." He did exactly what I'd done: joggled the switch a few times. No gray-yellow glow on the LED frequency readout; no power-up, no nothing. Danny swore, and tried the other great standby of the non-technical layman, slapping the top of the set. The handset fell off its rest and dangled on its cord; besides that, nothing. That was Danny finished, then. "Bollocks," he muttered under his breath. "Bollocks, bollocks, bollocks . . ." He seemed disproportionately panicky, I thought. After all, it wasn't the first thing that had ever gone wrong on his old tub of a charter boat: most of the equipment was second-hand or obsolete, or both, and something or other was always conking out on us. So how come he was so hyper now? He shouted down the companionway: "Jack?"

"What?"

"Ship-to-shore's out."

"Out? What you mean, out? Channel eight for comms, channel sixteen for emergencies. Have I got to do everything on this poxy boat?"

"It's not coming on." Panic rose in Danny's voice, sending it high and querulous.

Silence for a second down below decks. Then, Jack's exasperated head thrust up the companionway: "Is it the batteries?"

Quickly I tried all the rest of the gear. The fish-finder, our newest piece of kit, ran off its own nickel-cadmiums, but everything else came off the main batteries, and it was all down, no power on board the whole of the *Katie Mae*. "Oh, brilliant," I said under my breath.

"There's no juice," Danny told Jack, who had watched me all the way round the wheelhouse and didn't need telling.

"What you think I am, Blind Pew? I can bloody see there's no juice—get your arse down that engine hatch and find out *why* there's no juice, Danny. Make yourself useful for once, 'stead of standing round giving other people orders."

That last bit didn't go down too well, but Jack had already vanished back below. Danny stood a moment by the wheel, breathing heavily, then barged past me out on deck. The engine hatch was in the stern: I could hear Danny swearing as he banged it open and clattered down the short ladder. A few seconds later, Jack came swarming up the companionway and out on to the aft deck. "Bloody typical," I heard him mutter, before he let himself down through the hatch to see what he could do.

I stood in the dark wheelhouse and tried to work out our options in this, our newly powerless state. Down below decks there were the hurricane lamps, and right now they were the only light we had, apart from Danny's flashlight. I looked at the inert console: without electricity, the head-up radar wouldn't work, and more to the point, neither would the ship-to-shore VHF radio. Most worryingly of all, we could forget about the electric starter motor for the diesels; and without the diesels, we were going nowhere in a hurry. True, we might be able to start them using the auxiliary power supply, but we'd had trouble with that before when the main batteries had run down flat—which they had a habit of doing. It had been one of the things Danny had been meaning to get around to, for which read: one of the things he was going to get Jack to do for him.

At least there was the fish-finder, I thought sarcastically. That was still doing a grand job there on the side of the console, beeping away occasionally, mapping out the gently shelving bottom below the boat. Here and there on the display stray sonar returns stirred lethargically; if we'd been on a charter the punters would have been wetting themselves in anticipation of a big haul. My attention was distracted from the slow drifts and patterns on the electronic screen by Claire coming up the companionway.

"All right?" I smiled, to show her that everything was okay, just a few minor hiccups here, absolutely no-problemo. The dauntless crew of the *Katie Mae* coping with an emergency, just watch 'em go. "How's Andy?"

She didn't answer me straightaway. "Danny's gone to sort the batteries out," I explained, assuming she was worried about the power being out; then I looked at her more closely, and realized it was something more than that. She was shaking from head to toe—quite literally shaking, gooseflesh standing out on her bare skin.

I was ashamed of myself. It had been a long fifteen minutes or so since we'd first had an inkling of something floating out there in the water: we'd all been through the mill a bit, emotionally speaking. No wonder Claire was still a bit freaked. I put my arms around her, but she didn't stop shivering. "What's the matter?" I muttered into her soft-smelling hair. "No need to worry now. It's all right."

She put her hands on my biceps and held me slightly away from her. "No it's not, Will," she whispered urgently. "It's not all right—you don't know the half of it."

"What is it?" I could tell it was bad from the intensity of her response. "Why are you shaking like that?"

A huge reflexive tremor shook her all over. "It's down there." She indicated the short companionway with a glance. "It's . . . it's *cold*. Don't you feel it?"

Now she mentioned it, I did. It was pleasantly cool in the wheelhouse, but standing at the top of the companionway was like being in front of an open walk-in fridge. "It's water-level down there," I explained, less than sure of my own explanation: "the water's always a few degrees colder than the ambient air temperature."

"It's not that." Claire shook her head vehemently, lips pursed. I had the feeling she knew very well what she wanted to say, but couldn't quite bring herself to say it: it was like watching someone with a stutter trying to spit it out. "It's . . ." she glanced back down the steps: "it's him." She hissed the last word, lips almost touching my ear.

"What do you mean?" I was whispering, too.

Again she glanced down below; shook her head. "Not here," she said, and practically manhandled me backwards out of the wheelhouse: I had to brace my foot against the gutters to avoid going overboard. From aft came the clashing sounds of metal on metal, and of Jack and Danny arguing down the engine hatch. Claire and I went and knelt down on the foredeck, face-on to each other, knees touching.

"Should we be out here?" I wanted to know. "I don't think we ought to leave Andy on his own."

Claire took a deep breath. "Listen," she said, "that's the trouble. I've been down there with him just now, and there's something not right."

And here we were with the radio down, I thought. Brilliant. "How do you mean? Is he injured? Has he gone into shock or something?"

"Worse than that," she said, and my heart sank. "Didn't you feel anything down there?"

I looked at her, trying to work out what she was getting at. "Feel anything? Like what? I don't know: I was still a bit hyper from getting him out of the water and all that, you know?"

Claire frowned. "You were sat the other side of the table from him, weren't you?" I nodded. "So you couldn't—p" A seagull swooped low over the boat sounding its harsh staccato alarm cry, a flash in the darkness over our heads. Claire jumped; if I hadn't been holding on to her she'd have probably gone over the side. She held on to me for a moment or two, then tried to tell it another way. "Listen. When you and Danny went up Jack was fussing round him like an old mother hen. He got him to take his clothes off and put dry ones on, towel himself off and what have you. I picked up the wet clothes; I was going to put them in one of the lockers, but I didn't like to—the touch of them . . ." She paused, controlled herself and carried on. "They were corning apart, Will; they were rotting away."

I didn't know what to say. "We were grabbing on to his clothes when we were trying to fish him out. I think we tore a few of the seams . . ."

"I didn't say *torn*," she said; "they were rotten, Will. Like they'd been in the water . . . I don't know. A long time."

"How long?" The voice behind me made me flinch. Danny had crept up on me again. I wished people would stop doing that; it had been a long night already, and I was getting edgy. Claire looked up. I could see the whites of her wide round eyes.

"The fabric was . . . disintegrating," she said "A long time." Danny nodded. He seemed to be about to say something, but Claire went on:

"And that's not all. Jack got me to look him over, see if he was injured at all." Again the full-body reflex tremble. "It was like touching dead meat: he didn't have any warmth in him whatsoever. What his core temperature would have been . . . I was shivering just touching him, *but he wasn't*." She glanced between the two of us, to make sure we registered her emphasis. "He wasn't shivering, the way you would be if you'd been hauled out of the water in the middle of the night. He never shivered, not once. He was just sitting on the bench, looking at us . . ." She started to shake again, and I tightened the grip of my arm around her. She squeezed it gratefully, and continued:

"Then Jack followed you up into the cabin thing, and I was left down there with him." She clutched at both her shoulders, arms crossed tightly across her chest. "He hadn't put the dry clothes on or anything; he was just looking around, as if—as if he'd never seen anything quite like that before, you know? As if there was something he couldn't get his head around; like when you're in a dream, and the details are just, I don't know, *out* . . . wrong somehow. And everything's slowed down, and your reactions are like, you're trying to move, but everything's going like *this*—" She mimicked slow-motion, moving her head laboriously from side to side.

Yes, I thought, that was it; Claire had put her finger on it. I could see it now, the way he'd looked with a stupefied sort of incomprehension from one to the other of us as we'd gathered round him down below; the way he'd gazed at the lanterns hanging from the bulkheads, at the pictures of mermaids on the ceiling up above. Beside us on the deck Danny was nodding; he'd recognized it, too.

"So," Claire resumed: "I said to him, come on, better get these dry clothes on, or you'll catch your death. And he just; he looked round at me, and he nodded, but it was as if he couldn't really work out what I was asking him to do. I thought he might've taken a knock to the head or something, maybe he was still concussed, so I said, here, I'll help you, and I went over to him and sort of got his arms up above his head, you know, like when you're trying to put a sweater on a little kid?

"I was trying not to touch him too much, 'cos—" she looked at me, and I nodded *yeah, go on*— "and I got the dry sweater and slipped it over his head, and then . . ." She started shivering again, her voice suddenly tremulous. "And then I felt the back of his head, and there was all his hair, you know, all long and wet, and underneath it—" the words came out all in a rush—"underneath it there was this big dent in the back of his head, it was huge, like the size of my fist, and it was like the whole back of his head had been caved in, and you could feel the edges of the bones grinding together." She wrung at my arm, as if to make my own bones grind. "And I snatched my hand away, and I thought there'd be blood, but there wasn't any blood, and he just kept on looking at me, like he didn't understand . . ." She was crying by now, and I hugged her, as much to stop myself from shaking as to stop her.

Danny was still nodding his head. "I was trying to tell Jack down the engine hatch just now," he said slowly, and if he'd been drunk or stoned before, he sounded dead straight now. Scared out of his wits, but straight. "I heard something about a lad going missing off one of the Bangor boats—I couldn't think of the name, though. It might have been the *Wanderley*." He stopped.

"When did you hear that?" It didn't sound like my voice; it sounded like the voice of someone much younger and much, much more nervous.

". . . Two or three days back," said Danny miserably, and none of us said anything for a minute or two there on the foredeck. Eventually I broke the silence.

"He can't . . . that can't be him. No way."

"You didn't touch his skin," said Claire stubbornly. "I did. He's been out the water fifteen minutes now, and he still hasn't got *any* body heat. That's not natural. Even in the middle of winter that wouldn't be natural. It's summer, a hot summer night. And he's freezing."

"You saw him," was all Danny said to me. "You saw what he was like."

"So he's still cold—so he's a bit out of it still—so what?" I was only resisting for fear of what might follow, because even to admit the possibility of what

Claire and Danny were suggesting would be to kiss goodbye to anything resembling sanity, or safety. "He can't get warm. It doesn't make him a fucking zombie." Well, the word was out now.

Danny was shaking his head. "You don't last three days in the water, Will. If he went off that boat Saturday night, he'd've been dead for Sunday. Sunday at the latest—and even then he still wouldn't've been lying 'round waiting for us to come by. The coastguards would've been crawling all over this stretch, and the choppers from RAF Valley: they'd have got him if he'd been floating on top of the water, man . . . what is it?"

My mouth must have been open; it's a bad habit I have. I was thinking about back before in the wheelhouse, when Claire and I had been necking, and she'd asked me what was that thing going beep. The fish-finder, I'd said; and now I remembered it, that large echo we'd all thought was a seal. By the time we asked Jack, it was already up on the surface; but before that—I swallowed. Before that, it had been rising, slowly, from off the sea-bed. That's what corpses do, after a day or so. The gases balance out the dead weight, and they rise . . .

"*What?*" We were all extremely nervous now, Danny as much as anyone. "Spit it out, for Christ's sake."

"This is the Llys Helig stretch, isn't it?" My voice was steady, just. "We were talking about it, just before. What was it your dad used to say about this stretch?"

Danny was nodding before I'd finished. Clearly he'd been thinking along the same lines. "It was all along the banks here." He gestured out across the waves. "All the old fishermen; they said the sea was twitchy from here out to Puffin Island." Twitchy; that had been it. Strange word to use. "They said . . . they said it would spit out its drowned." He glanced back towards the wheelhouse unhappily.

"Yeah," I said, looking straight at Claire. I was going to tell her she was right, if I could find the bottle to come out with it, but in the end I just nodded. She didn't say anything; but she put a hand to my face and I held it, very tight.

"What are we gonna *do*—" began Danny, but then Jack shouted from down the engine hatch, "Oy! Knobber! *Hand* down here? Jesus . . ."

"Okay," I said, deciding I'd be the grown-up on this boat. "Look, whatever we do, we've got to get moving again. You go and get those diesels started up, Danny."

He was half-way over to the hatch before he remembered who was supposed to be playing captain. "What about you two? What are you going to do?"

"We're going to take care of the other thing," I said. In all my years on boats I'd never been seasick; but I came close to it then, thinking about what the two of us would have to do next.

Claire and I talked it over for five minutes or so. It wasn't that we disagreed on the crux of it—I think part of her had sensed the truth about Andy almost from the start, and I was all the way convinced by now—but she wasn't happy with what I proposed doing about it.

"It's murder," she said, and I said, "How can it be? He's dead already." Saying it like that was awful; as bad as touching him would have been, knowing what we knew now, as bad as the thought that what you'd touch was . . . not alive, not in any way that you could recognize. But something in her balked at doing the necessary thing. I tried to argue my case, to convince her, but the trouble was, what I wanted to do had nothing with reason or logic. It was as instinctive as treading in something and wiping your foot clean; as brushing a fly off your food.

But she knew that as well, every bit as much as I did. More so, because she'd been down in the cabin with him, had laid hands on his bare skin and felt . . . what she'd felt. I think those scruples we were both wrestling with were actually something more like nostalgia, a longing for the last few remnants of the everyday shape of things. Maybe in situations like that, you'll hang on to anything that says, this isn't happening, everything is perfectly normal, you can't seriously be going to do this . . .

But we were going to do it, because it had to be done. We couldn't have taken *that* back to harbor with us—we couldn't have walked him off the boat, taken him back to his dad in Conwy and said, look, here he is, here's your lad

Andy back safe and sound. That would have been a hundred times crueller than what we were about to do now. So yes, I felt bad; but it was the lesser of two evils. I was completely sure of that, just as sure as I was that come the daylight, I would probably feel like the shittiest, most cowardly assassin in all creation. But it was hours yet till the daylight, and below decks we had a dead man who didn't know he was dead yet. So I went into the wheelhouse, stood at the top of the companionway and called "Andy?" The first time it got swallowed up in a sort of gag reflex; I gulped, and called out again, "Andy?"

No answer from below decks; just the slow pinging of the fish-finder. This was what I'd been afraid of. Gingerly, I grabbed the woodwork of the companionway hatch, and lowered myself into the space below decks. I was ready to spring back if anything happened; what, I didn't know. But I knew that I didn't want to do this; didn't want to look now into the lantern light and see—

He was sitting just as we'd left him. The sweater Claire had tried to put on him was ruched up around his chest; he had one arm still caught in the arm-hole, and I think it was that—something as banal and stupid as that—that finally convinced me, if I'd really needed convincing. A child could have poked his arm through that sleeve—*would* have done it, out of pure reflex; but Andy hadn't.

I stepped down, till there was just the table between us. "Andy?" I said again, and he looked up. I was already making to look away, but I couldn't help it, our eyes met. His eyes were so black, so empty; how could I have looked into them and thought him alive?

I'd meant to say something else, but what came out was, "You all right?" It was crazy enough on the face of it, but what would have been normal? He nodded; I could see him nodding, as I stared down at my feet. "Cold," he said; that was all. Then, out of nowhere, I found myself saying, "Come on: let's get your arm through there."

Considering what I had in mind, seemed like the height of hypocrisy; but I think it was a kinder instinct than I gave myself credit for at the time. Steeling myself, still not looking him straight in the face, I reached across and lifted the folding table up. I stretched out the wool of the jumper with one hand and slipped the other into the sleeve. Feeling around inside, my fingers touched his: he was making no attempt to reach through and hold on, which was probably just as well. Cold? More than cold; it was as if he'd never been warm, as if he'd lain on that ocean bed for as long as the sea had lain on the land. Fighting to keep my guts down, I dragged his arm through and let go the jumper. Released, his arm fell back down by his side; dead weight.

Doing that helped me with what came next, with the physical side of it at least. "Right," I said, in a ghastly pretense at practicality; "let's get you up on deck, shall we?" He looked up blankly. I had to look, had to make sure he was going to do it. Those eyes: I couldn't afford to look into them for too long. God knows what I would have seen in there; or what he might have seen in mine, perhaps. "Come on," I said, turned part-way away from him. "They're waiting for you up on deck."

In the end I had to help him to his feet. He was like a machine running down, almost; I hate to think what would have happened if we'd actually tried to take him back to dry land. Even through the layer of wool I could feel a dreadful pulpiness everywhere that wasn't bone. Again the gag came in my throat; I clamped my jaw shut and took him under one arm, and he came up unresisting, balanced precariously in his squelching shoes. A little puddle of rank seawater had collected around his feet. The smell—I was close enough to get the smell now, but I don't want to talk about it. I dream about it, sometimes, on bad sweating nights in the hot midsummer.

I motioned him ahead. Obediently, he stepped forward, and as he passed me I saw the horrible indentation in the back of his skull. The hair which had covered it before had flattened now, and the concave dent was all too clearly visible. No-one could have taken a wound like that and survived. Just before I looked away, the bile rising in my throat, I thought I saw something in there; something white and wriggling. I came very near to losing it entirely in that moment.

If he'd needed help getting up the companionway, I would've had to have called Danny through—there was no way I could have touched him, not after seeing that wound in the back of his head. As it was, he put one foot on the steps, then, after what seemed ages, the next, and trudged up into the wheelhouse. I tried to focus on the normal things: on the feel of the wooden rail as

I stepped up behind him into the wheelhouse; on the brass plaque that said *Katie Mae*, there beside the wheel; on the ping of the fish-finder in the silence. As Andy paused, silhouetted against the dim starlight of outside, waiting for me to tell him what to do next, I took several deep breaths. "Now?" I said, and waited for Claire's voice.

"Now," she said, a small voice from out of the darkness, and I ran forwards with both arms straight out in front of me. Andy was in the act of turning 'round, and I just glimpsed his eyes; there was a greenish phosphorescence to them in the dark, and Claire said later that I screamed out loud as my hands made contact with his shoulder-blades.

He was standing in the wheelhouse doorway. Ahead of him was just the narrow stretch of deck that linked fore and aft, and then the low side of the boat. Claire was crouching beneath the level of the wheelhouse door; on my signal she'd straightened up on to her hands and knees as I came up on Andy from behind. My push sent him careening forwards; he flipped straight over Claire's upthrust back and out over the side of the boat. There was a solid, crunching impact as he hit the water; Claire was up off her knees and into my arms as the cold spray drenched the pair of us.

"What the *fuck*?" It was Jack. He was standing in the engine hatch; clearly he couldn't believe what he'd just seen. "You stupid bloody—what the *fuck*, man?" He clambered up through the hatch and started towards us. Claire tried to get in his way, but he pushed her angrily to one side; she went sprawling into the wheelhouse. Jack squared up to me, fists clenched: no matter how smoothly it had gone with Andy, I saw I was in for at least one fight that evening. He swung away, cursing, and dropped to his knees; I realized he was scrabbling around down in the gutters for the boat-hook he'd used earlier, so that he could fish Andy out of the water a second time.

I was backing round on to the foredeck, trying to think what to do, how to explain it to him, when several things happened more or less simultaneously.

The spotlight on top of the wheelhouse glowed dully for a moment, then blinked sharply back into life; it caught Jack in the act of rising from his knees, boathook in one hand, the other shielding his squinting eyes as the beam shone full into his face. Danny's voice rose above the engine sound: "Got you, you bastard! Batteries up and *running*!" And in the wheelhouse, Claire was shouting: "Will? *Will*!"

Heedless of Jack, who by then was down on his knees plunging the boat-hook into the black water, I pushed past and into the wheelhouse. "What? What is it?"

Fist up to her mouth, Claire just stood there, unable to speak. Then she pointed at the console. The fish-finder was beeping still, more frequently than before, more insistently. I looked at the traces on screen and my mouth went dry.

Down underneath the *Katie Mae*, fathoms down in the dark and cold, big sluggish blips were rising; detaching themselves from the sea-bed, drifting up towards the surface. I didn't need Jack to interpret them for me this time; I recognized them all too well. Before, we'd thought they were seals. Now, we knew better.

". . . Stay here," I managed to get out. Claire nodded, and I turned back to the doorway of the wheelhouse. There was Jack, bending over the side of the boat, his back to us. The stretch of water beyond him was brightly illuminated by our spotlight, still pointing where Claire had left it earlier. One look was all I needed. I grabbed Jack by the shoulder: he'd managed to hook a shapeless mass in the water, and was struggling to bring it in to the side of the boat. "Jack, Jack," I croaked in his ear; "wait, no, look out there . . ."

He pushed me away with a curse, went on trying to raise up the body in the water. I thumped his back, hard, and he swung round, ready to hit me. "Fucking look," I hissed, and almost despite himself he turned round.

There they were, caught by the spotlight on the still surface; bodies, rising up out of the sea. Five or six just in that bright ellipse of light; how many others, out there in the dark where we couldn't see? I'd counted at least a dozen on the fish-finder; there might be more by now. A low, unspeakably nasty sound carne back to us over the waves, somewhere between a hiss and a gurgle. At the same time a stink hit us from off the water, like nothing I'd smelled before nor want to ever again. Jack turned back to me, round-eyed, horrified; opened his mouth to say something. Then it happened.

A hand came up and grasped the boathook. It nearly pulled Jack in; quickly he steadied himself, clutching at me and letting go his grip on the wooden shaft. The thing that had grabbed it—the thing Jack had thought was Andy—disappeared under the waves again, taking the boathook down with it, then bobbed back up to the surface. Whatever it was, it had been down there far longer than Andy had. Most of what had once made it human was rotted away; what was left was vile beyond my capacity to describe. It rested there on the swell awhile, goggling up at us as we stood petrified on the deck. Then, without warning, it swung the boathook up out of the water.

The metal hook ripped a long hole in Jack's tee-shirt. Within seconds, the whole of his chest was slick with blood. He staggered back, and the hook caught on the belt of his jeans. It nearly dragged him into the water, but I grabbed him just in time. He was screaming, wordlessly, incoherently. So was I; but I held on tight, arms round his body, feet braced against the scuppers, straining backwards with all my might.

I managed to call out Danny's name. I felt him grab on to me from behind and yelled as loudly as I could, "Pull!" We both strained away, and then all of a sudden the pressure was off and we all three of us went sprawling backwards, me on top of Danny, Jack across both of us. We disentangled ourselves, and Jack pulled clear the boathook from his belt. Before he flung the whole thing as far away as he could, we had just enough time to see the hand and lower part of an arm that still clung to the other end.

Meanwhile Danny had seen what was happening out on the water, the bodies coming to the surface all around. From the look on his face I knew he was going to lose it unless I did something drastic, so without thinking I spun him round and practically threw him into the wheelhouse. "Get us out of here," I told him, and turned back to where Jack was kneeling on the deck. There was blood all over him, and over me too where I'd held on to him: I knelt down alongside him to see how badly he was hurt, but he pushed me away. I knew it was because of what Claire and I had done to Andy, but there was no time for that now. I looked round for something I could use to defend the boat with, yelling over my shoulder, "Danny! Move it!"

A throaty grumble came from aft as the diesels turned over, choked momentarily, then caught. "Get us out," I shouted, as there came a clang from the foredeck. I clambered up around the wheelhouse, spinning the spotlight around to face for'ard as I went. There was the boathook that Jack had thrown away, snagged this time on the prow. Something was using it to clamber up and over the rail: without thinking I ran towards it and kicked out hard. My foot sank partway into a soft crunching mass; the momentum almost sent me spinning over, but I managed to steady myself on the Samson post as the thing splashed backwards into the water. There was something on my foot, some reeking slimy filth or other—I was scraping it frenziedly against one of the cleats, trying to get the worst of it off, when I became aware of Danny hammering the glass windscreen of the wheelhouse.

He was yelling something about "haul it in": I didn't understand what he was saying at first, but then I realized. We were still riding at anchor; Danny had revved the engines to loosen the anchor from its lodgement on the sea-bed, but before we could open up the throttle and head for clear water it needed to be winched all the way back in.

I edged back round the side of the wheelhouse, with no time to stop for Claire as she pressed her face to the glass, her lips forming words I couldn't hear. Below me, down in the water, things were moving up against the side of the boat. We had to get clear.

The capstan was on the starboard side, by the door to the wheelhouse. I gave a tug at the anchor-rope: it wouldn't shift. "Again," I called up to Danny in the wheelhouse; he engaged reverse thrust again, and the rope creaked, then gave a little as the anchor cleared the sea-bed. I threw the switch that turned on the electric motor of the capstan, but just at that moment there came a vicious tug on the rope. Sparks flashed beneath the motor housing, and an acrid gout of smoke rose from the capstan-head; I tried it again, and again, but the motor had burned out. Frantically, I tried to use the hand-bars to winch up the anchor, but the whole thing seemed to be fused solid. "Jack," I shouted; he looked up from where he lay cradling his stomach, saw the problem, and struggled over to help.

Five fathoms, maybe six; that's thirty-six feet of rope first, then chain, and a heavy iron anchor at the end of it. It took Jack and I all the strength we could muster to raise it, arm over arm, winding the slack around the useless capstan-head. It wasn't the first time we'd had to haul up an anchor manually, but it seemed far heavier now than it ever had before, impossibly heavy, and when we'd got it almost all the way up, as far as the ten foot or so of chain before the anchor itself, I looked over the side to see if we were still snagged on anything.

Have patience with me now, because I have to tell this a certain way. In the village where I used to live as a child, near Diss in Norfolk, there was a pool out in the fields which was absolutely stiff with rudd, a freshwater fish related to the roach. We used to tie a piece of string around a fivepenny loaf and throw it in, and then we'd watch the water boil as we pulled on the string to bring the bread back up, the whole thing completely covered in a huge squirming feeding-cluster of rudd. That scene, that image, was what I thought of as I peered over the side of the *Katie Mae* and saw the anchor just below the surface.

Clustered round the anchor, hanging on to it in a crawling hideous mass, were maybe six or seven of the bodies; dragged up from the oozing deep, these, up from long years of slow decay down where the sun's warmth and light never penetrates, there on the chilly bottom. Green phosphorescent eyes stared back at me, and a billow of putrescence erupted in bubbles on to the surface. I dropped the anchor chain as if it had been electrified, and the gruesome mass sank back a foot or two into the water.

"Hang on!" Jack grabbed at the chain quickly before the lot went down again. "Keep it tight!" Out of his pocket he pulled a hunting-knife; I didn't get what he meant to do with it until he began to saw at the anchor-rope above the chain where it was wound round the capstan. Understanding at last, I pulled on the chain to keep the line taut. All the while, I was hearing things: sounds of splashing and gulping from over the side where the anchor was banging against the hull, and that awful gurgling hiss rising off the water again. Out of nowhere, words came into my head: *the voices of all the drowned . . .*

I didn't dare look down there; only when Jack sawed through the last strands of the rope and the freed chain rattled over the side did I risk one quick glance over, just in time to see the anchor with its cluster of bodies receding into the deep. Hands clutched vainly up towards the surface, and those greenish eyes blinked out into cold fathoms of blackness.

Sick to my stomach with fear and disgust, I turned away to where Jack was clambering to his feet. I tried to help him up, but he brushed my hand away and went foraging instead through the storage box where we'd formerly kept the anchor and its chain. He came up with an old length of chain about four feet long; he took a couple of turns around his fist, and swung the rest around. "You take the for'ard," he said, wincing as he held his wounded stomach; "I'll get the aft. Get something from in here—" he kicked the storage box—"and use the spotlight if you can, so's we can see what we're up against. Danny!" He roared the last word in the direction of the wheelhouse. "What's with the fucking hold-up? They're all around us, man: Will and me can't keep 'em off forever, you know!"

The boat was hardly moving in the water. From aft came the sound of spluttering, overstressed engines; Jack swore and looked at me narrowly. "You just keep your eyes peeled back here," was all he said; he tossed me the length of chain and stumbled off into the wheelhouse to get the *Katie Mae* moving again. Around us in the water, the shapes multiplied: there must have been twenty of them now, more maybe. Drawn by God knows what—the promise of dry land, perhaps, or some primal impulse more atavistic, more terrible than that—they were converging on the boat. And all I had was a four-foot length of chain to keep them off.

Maybe not all: suddenly there was the beam of the spotlight shining on to the aft deck, picking out the white painted railings, the glimmer of the sea beyond and below. I heard Claire's voice: "Over that way, Will;" the beam swung round, then steadied on a ghastly greenish arm slung over the port side.

I swung the chain at it. It cut a rent along the length of the arm, laid bare the glint of white bone, but the fingers didn't relinquish their grip. A head and shoulders hoisted up above the side of the boat. I gave it another swing of the chain, and this time the contact was good. It toppled upside-down, its head in the water, its feet caught up in the tire buffers slung around the hull, and with a few more slashes I managed to dislodge it entirely. But by then Claire was screaming, "Behind you, behind you," and when I turned round another of the creatures was already halfway over the aft rail. Again I let fly, but not strongly or viciously enough. The chain only wrapped around its arm: it caught hold of the links, and began tugging me in towards it. Repulsed, I let go immediately; the thing teetered there a moment, then the engines kicked in at last. It was caught off balance and fell backwards: a horrible splintering noise and a shiver that went clean through the boat told me it had hit the propeller.

We began to pick up speed, pulling away from the writhing mass of bodies on the surface, but there were still a dozen or more of the things hanging on to the side of the boat, arms twined in the tire buffers, hands clutching on to the railings, hammering at the clanging echoing hull. If we slowed down, they would try again to get up on board. We had to shift them somehow. I was leaning over the side, whacking away with a wrench from down the engine hatch, when Jack appeared at my side. The blood had dried black all down him, and he looked like he should have been in a hospital bed; instead, he was sloshing diesel oil from a big jerrycan over the side of the boat and on to the clinging bodies. "What you doing?" was all I could get out between panting.

"Kill or cure," he said grimly, edging all along the side of the boat emptying out the diesel on to the creatures that hung leechlike to the hull. In a minute he was back round to my other side. He dumped the jerrycan straight down onto the head of one of the things, sending it sinking beneath the waves, then reached in his pocket and brought out his cherished old brass Zippo with the engraved marijuana leaf. With just a trace of his usual flamboyance, he flicked open the top and ran the wheel quickly along the seam of his bloodied jeans, down, then up, like a gunslinger's quick-draw. The flint struck and the flame sparked bright, first time every time; Jack held it aloft for a second, then dropped it over the side.

I snapped my head back just in time, feeling my eyebrows singe and shrivel in the sudden blast of heat. Immediately, flames sprang up all along the waterline, lighting up the ocean all around us a vivid orange. For a little while we could see every detail of the things in the water; how they writhed and bubbled in the flame, how their mouths opened and closed, how they charred and blackened as the fire licked up the hull, blistering the paintwork, setting light to the tire-buffers. I heard a hissing indrawn breath from Jack beside me, thought for a moment *oh no, he's fucked up, he's got it wrong with the diesel, the ship's going up*, and then I saw where he was looking down in the water. One of the burning bodies was Andy's: arm upraised, face still recognizable amidst the flames, it slowly rolled off the side and was lost in our wake, along with the rest of the corpses of the drowned.

It was already brightening in the east as we brought the *Katie Mae* back into harbor. All her sides were scorched and black and battered, and we her crew were similarly scarred, though in ways less obvious and maybe less repairable with a sanding-off and a fresh lick of paint. Jack had refused our help with his stomach wound on the way back; he'd sat out on the aft deck hugged into a fetal tuck, not talking to anyone, not looking anywhere except backwards at our lengthening wake. Claire and I sat squeezed up on the wheelhouse bench behind Danny, who stood at the wheel staring for'ard all the way home to Beuno's Cove. We didn't try talking to each other; really, what was there to say?

When we came alongside, Jack scrambled up on to the quayside to tie us up. He stood looking back at the boat for a second, silhouetted above us in the predawn light, then without saying anything he turned away. I glanced back at Danny and saw he was crying. Perhaps I should have done something, I don't know what, but Claire took my hand and more or less dragged me up on to the quay. We left him there on the deck; I wanted to say, are you going to be okay, but perhaps Claire was right. It was the last time I ever set foot on the *Katie Mae*.

Back home Claire ran straight upstairs and turned the shower on. I went up after about twenty minutes and she was squatting in a corner of the stall with the hot water running cold, arms wound about her knees, sobbing uncontrollably. What could I do? I got in there and fetched her out, got her dry, got her warm; but I couldn't stop her shivering, not until she finally fell asleep on the bed, hours later, after we'd tried and failed to talk through the events of the night just gone. We tried several times again, in the days and weeks that followed, but it never came to anything; we felt the way murderers must feel, and so, I suppose, did Jack, because not long after he moved away, and no-one ever saw him again, not Claire or me, not even Danny.

Back to that first morning, though, the morning after. I stayed with Claire for a while till I was sure she was properly asleep, then I eased off the bed and went downstairs. There was a book I'd borrowed from Danny's old man, a collection of maritime myths and legends of North Wales: I went through it and found the entry for Llys Helig. A curse had been laid on Helig's family and their lands, vengeance for old wrongs, a whispering voice coming out of nowhere heard all around the great halls and gardens of Llys Helig prophesying doom on his grandsons and great-grandsons, and one day the floodwaters came and washed over everything. And ever since, said the legend, the drowned have never rested easy in that stretch. As if. I preferred Danny's dad's unvarnished version myself: that the sea was just twitchy out there, no more, no less. Nothing you could explain away with spells and whispers and fairy tales, a condition no story would cover; just a state of things, something you knew about and left well alone, if you knew what was good for you.

But there was something else; something that had been at the back of my mind ever since I'd first heard those hisses and gurgles out on the waves. I didn't have nearly as many books then as I have now, but it still took me the best part of half an hour to lay my hands on it: Dylan Thomas' *Selected Poems*. And I read there the poem, the one I'd half-remembered:

Under the mile off moon we trembled listening
To the sea sound flowing like blood from the loud wound
And when the salt sheet broke in a storm of singing
The voices of all the drowned swam on the wind

Upstairs Claire moaned a little in her sleep. I got up, climbed the creaky stairs as quietly as I could, and eased myself on to the bed beside her. The curtains were pulled to, and the little bedroom under the eaves was getting stuffy in the full heat of the day. The paperback was still in my other hand, finger marking my place, and I read from it again:

We heard the sea sound sing, we saw the salt sheet tell
Lie still, sleep becalmed, hide the mouth in the throat
Or we shall obey, and ride with you through the drowned.

I shivered, and beside me Claire shivered too, as if in unconscious sympathy. The sun was hot and strong through the bright yellow curtains, but I felt as if I'd never be warm again.

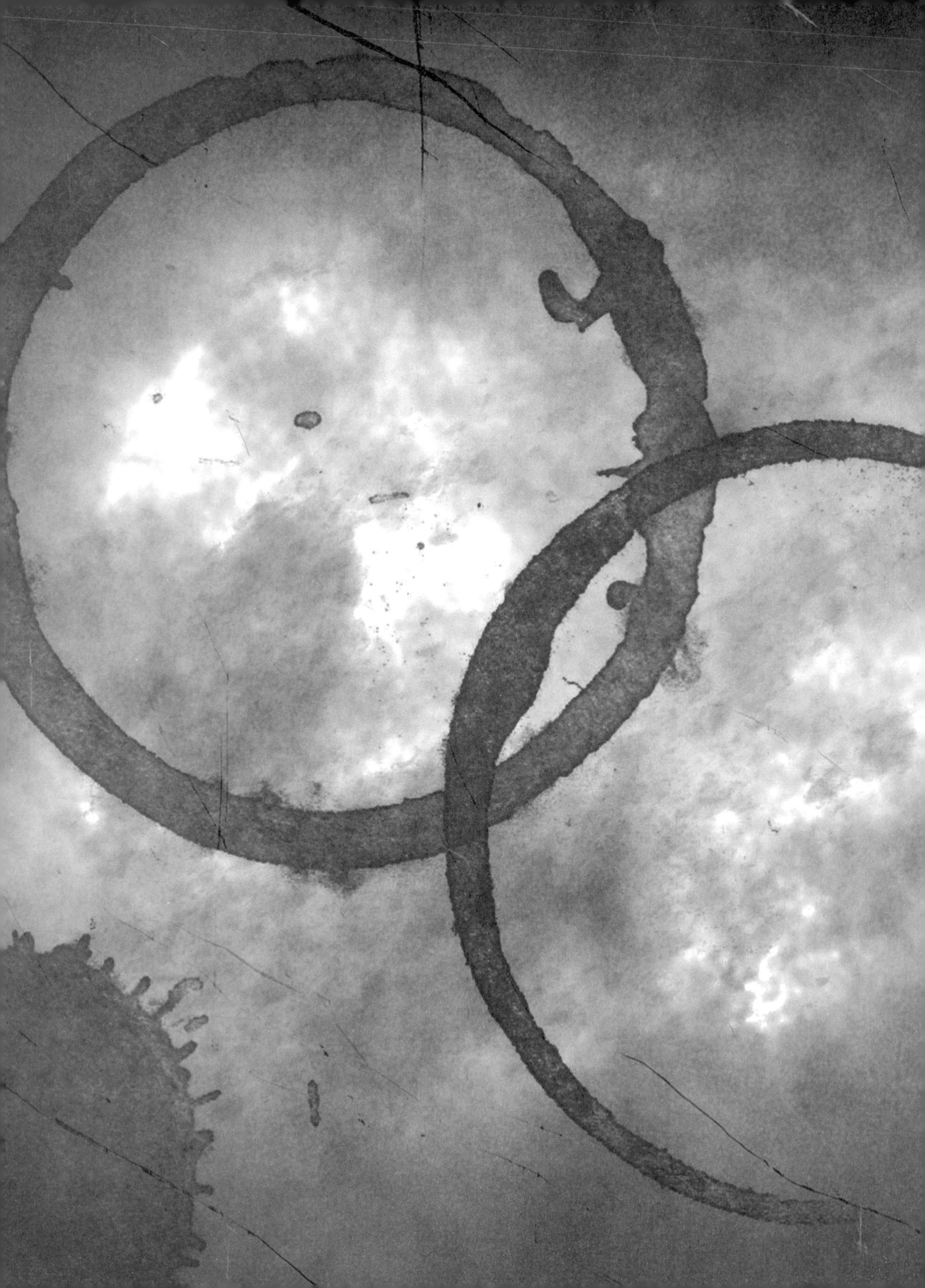

If there's one thing I love, it's a full-frontal assault. But there's definitely something to be said for stealth: sidling in sideways, your prey distracted by a smile, sneaking up from every direction until they don't even know what hit 'em.

This helps explain the appeal of the astonishing Neil Gaiman, a guy who never saw an oddball angle of attack he couldn't deploy for maximum impact. He's one of the sneakiest, smartest, most charming authors on the contemporary block.

But the greatest tool in his arsenal is that he's just such a pleasure to read. He makes you want to go with him, wherever he may lead. And this skill is on full display in "Bitter Grounds"*, a tricky little bastard that winds around and around, leaves you hanging, then begs you to dig back into the tangled web it weaves.*

The more I think about it, the more I like it. Which was certainly his intent.

I hope you fall for it, too.

1

"COME BACK EARLY OR NEVER COME"

In every way that counted, I was dead. Inside somewhere maybe I was screaming and weeping and howling like an animal, but that was another person deep inside, another person who had no access to the face and lips and mouth and head, so on the surface I just shrugged and smiled and kept moving. If I could have physically passed away, just let it all go, like that, without doing anything, stepped out of life as easily as walking through a door, I would have. But I was going to sleep at night and waking in the morning, disappointed to be there and resigned to existence.

Sometimes I telephoned her. I let the phone ring once, maybe even twice before I hung up.

The me who was screaming was so far inside nobody knew he was even there at all. Even I forgot that he was there, until one day I got into the car—I had to go to the store, I had decided, to bring back some apples—and I went past the store that sold apples and I kept driving, and driving. I was going south, and west, because if I went north or east I would run out of world too soon.

A couple of hours down the highway my cell phone started to ring. I wound down the window and threw the cell phone out. I wondered who would find it, whether they would answer the phone and find themselves gifted with life.

When I stopped for gas I took all the cash I could on every card I had. I did the same for the next couple of days, ATM by ATM, until the cards stopped working.

The first two nights I slept in the car.

I was halfway through Tennessee when I realized I needed a bath badly enough to pay for it. I checked into a motel, stretched out in the bath, and slept in it until the water got cold and woke me. I shaved with a motel courtesy kit plastic razor and a sachet of foam. Then I stumbled to the bed, and I slept.

Awoke at 4:00 A.M., and knew it was time to get back on the road.

I went down to the lobby.

There was a man standing at the front desk when I got there: silver-gray hair although I guessed he was still in his thirties, if only just, thin lips, good suit rumpled, saying, "I *ordered* that cab an *hour* ago. One *hour* ago." He tapped the desk with his wallet as he spoke, the beats emphasizing his words.

The night manager shrugged. "I'll call again," he said. "But if they don't have the car, they can't send it." He dialed a phone number, said, "This is the Night's Out Inn front desk . . . . Yeah, I told him . . . . Yeah, I told him."

"Hey," I said. "I'm not a cab, but I'm in no hurry. You need a ride somewhere?"

For a moment the man looked at me like I was crazy, and for a moment there was fear in his eyes. Then he looked at me like I'd been sent from Heaven. "You know, by God, I do," he said.

"You tell me where to go," I said. "I'll take you there. Like I said, I'm in no hurry."

"Give me that phone," said the silver-gray man to the night clerk. He took the handset and said, "You can *cancel* your cab, because God just sent me a Good Samaritan. People come into your life for a reason. That's right. And I want you to think about that."

He picked up his briefcase—like me he had no luggage—and together we went out to the parking lot.

We drove through the dark. He'd check a hand-drawn map on his lap, with a flashlight attached to his key ring; then he'd say, "Left here," or "This way."

"It's good of you," he said.

"No problem. I have time."

"I appreciate it. You know, this has that pristine urban-legend quality, driving down country roads with a mysterious Samaritan. A Phantom Hitchhiker story. After I get to my destination, I'll describe you to a friend, and they'll tell me you died ten years ago, and still go round giving people rides."

"Be a good way to meet people."

He chuckled. "What do you do?"

"Guess you could say I'm between jobs," I said. "You?"

"I'm an anthropology professor." Pause. "I guess I should have introduced myself. Teach at a Christian college. People don't believe we teach anthropology at Christian colleges, but we do. Some of us."

"I believe you."

Another pause. "My car broke down. I got a ride to the motel from the highway patrol, as they said there was no tow truck going to be there until morning. Got two hours of sleep. Then the highway patrol called my hotel room. Tow truck's on the way. I got to be there when they arrive. Can you believe that? I'm not there, they won't touch it. Just drive away. Called a cab. Never came. Hope we get there before the tow truck."

"I'll do my best."

"I guess I should have taken a plane. It's not that I'm scared of flying. But I cashed in the ticket; I'm on my way to New Orleans. Hour's flight, four hundred and forty dollars. Day's drive, thirty dollars. That's four hundred and ten dollars spending money, and I don't have to account for it to anybody. Spent fifty dollars on the motel room, but that's just the way these things go. Academic conference. My first. Faculty doesn't believe in them. But things change. I'm looking forward to it. Anthropologists from all over the world." He named several, names that meant nothing to me. "I'm presenting a paper on the Haitian coffee girls."

"They grow it, or drink it?"

"Neither. They sold it, door to door in Port-au-Prince, early in the morning, in the early years of the century."

It was starting to get light, now.

"People thought they were zombies," he said. "You know. The walking dead. I think it's a right turn here."

"Were they? Zombies?"

He seemed very pleased to have been asked. "Well, anthropologically, there are several schools of thought about zombies. It's not as cut-and-dried as popularist works like *The Serpent and the Rainbow* would make it appear. First we have to define our terms: are we talking folk belief, or zombie dust, or the walking dead?"

"I don't know," I said. I was pretty sure *The Serpent and the Rainbow* was a horror movie.

"They were children, little girls, five to ten years old, who went door-to-door through Port-au-Prince selling the chicory coffee mixture. Just about this time of day, before the sun was up. They belonged to one old woman. Hang a left just before we go into the next turn. When she died, the girls vanished. That's what the books tell you."

"And what do you believe?" I asked.

"That's my car," he said, with relief in his voice. It was a red Honda Accord, on the side of the road. There was a tow truck beside it, lights flashing, a man beside the tow truck smoking a cigarette. We pulled up behind the tow truck.

The anthropologist had the door of the car opened before I'd stopped; he grabbed his briefcase and was out of the car.

"Was giving you another five minutes, then I was going to take off," said the tow-truck driver. He dropped his cigarette into a puddle on the tarmac. "Okay, I'll need your triple-A card, and a credit card."

The man reached for his wallet. He looked puzzled. He put his hands in his pockets. He said, "My wallet." He came back to my car, opened the passenger-side door and leaned back inside. I turned on the light. He patted the empty seat. "My wallet," he said again. His voice was plaintive and hurt.

"You had it back in the motel," I reminded him. "You were holding it. It was in your hand."

He said, "God *damn* it. God fucking *damn* it to hell."

"Everything okay there?" called the tow-truck driver.

"Okay," said the anthropologist to me, urgently. "This is what we'll do. You drive back to the motel. I must have left the wallet on the desk. Bring it back here. I'll keep him happy until then. Five minutes, it'll take you five minutes." He must have seen the expression on my face. He said, "Remember. People come into your life for a reason."

I shrugged, irritated to have been sucked into someone else's story.

Then he shut the car door and gave me a thumbs-up.

I wished I could just have driven away and abandoned him, but it was too late, I was driving to the hotel. The night clerk gave me the wallet, which he had noticed on the counter, he told me, moments after we left.

I opened the wallet. The credit cards were all in the name of Jackson Anderton.

It took me half an hour to find my way back, as the sky grayed into full dawn. The tow truck was gone. The rear window of the red Honda Accord was broken, and the driver's-side door hung open. I wondered if it was a different car, if I had driven the wrong way to the wrong place; but there were the tow-truck driver's cigarette stubs, crushed on the road, and in the ditch nearby I found a gaping briefcase, empty, and beside it, a manila folder containing a fifteen-page typescript, a prepaid hotel reservation at a Marriott in New Orleans in the name of Jackson Anderton, and a packet of three condoms, ribbed for extra pleasure.

On the title page of the typescript was printed:

> *This was the way Zombies are spoken of: They are the bodies without souls. The living dead. Once they were dead, and after that they were called back to life again.*
>
> Hurston, *Tell My Horse*

I took the manila folder, but left the briefcase where it was. I drove south under a pearl-colored sky.

People come into your life for a reason. Right.

I could not find a radio station that would hold its signal. Eventually I pressed the scan button on the radio and just left it on, left it scanning from channel to channel in a relentless quest for signal, scurrying from gospel to oldies to Bible talk to sex talk to country, three seconds a station with plenty of white noise in between.

. . . Lazarus, who was dead, you make no mistake about that, he was dead, and Jesus brought him back to show us—I say to show us . . .

. . . what I call a Chinese dragon. Can I say this on the air? Just as you, y'know get your rocks off, you whomp her round the backatha head, it all spurts outta her nose. I damn near laugh my ass off . . .

. . . If you come home tonight I'll be waiting in the darkness for my woman with my bottle and my gun . . .

. . . When Jesus says will you be there, will you be there? No *man knows the day or the hour, so will you be there . . .*

. . . president unveiled an initiative today . . .

. . . fresh-brewed in the morning. For you, for me. For every day. Because every day is freshly ground . . .

Over and over. It washed over me, driving through the day, on the back roads. Just driving and driving.

They become more personable as you head south, the people. You sit in a diner, and along with your coffee and your food, they bring you comments, questions, smiles, and nods.

It was evening, and I was eating fried chicken and collard greens and hush puppies, and a waitress smiled at me. The food seemed tasteless, but I guessed that might have been my problem, not theirs.

I nodded at her politely, which she took as an invitation to come over and refill my coffee cup. The coffee was bitter, which I liked. At least it tasted of something.

"Looking at you," she said, "I would guess that you are a professional man. May I enquire as to your profession?" That was what she said, word for word.

"Indeed you may," I said, feeling almost possessed by something, and affably pompous, like W. C. Fields or the Nutty Professor (the fat one, not the Jerry Lewis one, although I am actually within pounds of the optimum weight for my height). "I happen to be . . . an anthropologist, on my way to a conference in New Orleans, where I shall confer, consult, and otherwise hobnob with my fellow anthropologists."

"I knew it," she said. "Just looking at you. I had you figured for a professor. Or a dentist, maybe."

She smiled at me one more time. I thought about stopping forever in that little town, eating in that diner every morning and every night. Drinking their bitter coffee and having her smile at me until I ran out of coffee and money and days.

Then I left her a good tip, and went south and west.

2
"TONGUE BROUGHT ME HERE"

There were no hotel rooms in New Orleans, or anywhere in the New Orleans sprawl. A jazz festival had eaten them, everyone. It was too hot to sleep in my car, and even if I'd cranked a window and been prepared to suffer the heat, I felt unsafe. New Orleans is a real place, which is more than I can say about most of the cities I've lived in, but it's not a safe place, not a friendly one.

I stank, and itched. I wanted to bathe, and to sleep, and for the world to stop moving past me.

I drove from fleabag motel to fleabag motel, and then, at the last, as I had always known I would, I drove into the parking lot of the downtown Marriott on Canal Street. At least I knew they had one free room. I had a voucher for it in the manila folder.

"I need a room," I said to one of the women behind the counter.

She barely looked at me. "All rooms are taken," she said. "We won't have anything until Tuesday."

I needed to shave, and to shower, and to rest. *What's the worst she can say?* I thought. *I'm sorry, you've already checked in?*

"I have a room, prepaid by my university. The name's Anderton."

She nodded, tapped a keyboard, said "Jackson?" then gave me a key to my room, and I initialed the room rate. She pointed me to the elevators.

A short man with a ponytail, and a dark, hawkish face dusted with stubble, cleared his throat as we stood beside the elevators. "You're the Anderton from Hopewell," he said. "We were neighbors in the *Journal of Anthropological Heresies.*" He wore a white T-shirt that said "Anthropologists Do It While Being Lied To."

"We were?"

"We were. I'm Campbell Lakh. University of Norwood and Streatham. Formerly North Croydon Polytechnic. England. I wrote the paper about Icelandic spirit walkers and fetches."

"Good to meet you," I said, and shook his hand. "You don't have a London accent."

"I'm a Brummie," he said. "From Birmingham," he added. "Never seen you at one of these things before."

"It's my first conference," I told him.

"Then you stick with me," he said. "I'll see you're all right. I remember my first one of these conferences, I was scared shitless I'd do something stupid the entire time. We'll stop on the mezzanine, get our stuff, then get cleaned up. There must have been a hundred babies on my plane over, IsweartoGod. They took it in shifts to scream, shit, and puke, though. Never fewer than ten of them screaming at a time."

We stopped on the mezzanine, collected our badges and programs. "Don't forget to sign up for the ghost walk," said the smiling woman behind the table. "Ghost walks of Old New Orleans each night, limited to fifteen people in each party, so sign up fast."

I bathed, and washed my clothes out in the basin, then hung them up in the bathroom to dry.

I sat naked on the bed, and examined the papers that had been in Anderton's briefcase. I skimmed through the paper he had intended to present, without taking in the content.

On the clean back of page five he had written, in a tight, mostly legible scrawl, *In a perfect perfect world you could fuck people without giving them a piece of your heart. And every glittering kiss and every touch of flesh is another shard of heart you'll never see again. Until walking (waking? calling?) on your own is unsupportable.*

When my clothes were pretty much dry I put them back on and went down to the lobby bar. Campbell was already there. He was drinking a gin and tonic with a gin and tonic on the side.

He had out a copy of the conference program, and had circled each of the talks and papers he wanted to see. ("Rule one, if it's before midday, fuck it unless you're the one doing it," he explained.) He showed me my talk, circled in pencil.

"I've never done this before," I told him. "Presented a paper at a conference."

"It's a piece of piss, Jackson," he said. "Piece of piss. You know what I do?"

"No," I said.

"I just get up and read the paper. Then people ask questions, and I just bullshit," he said. "Actively bullshit, as opposed to passively. That's the best bit. Just bullshitting. Piece of utter piss."

"I'm not really good at, um, bullshitting," I said. "Too honest."

"Then nod, and tell them that that's a really perceptive question, and that it's addressed at length in the longer version of the paper, of which the one you are reading is an edited abstract. If you get some nut job giving you a really difficult time about something you got wrong, just get huffy and say that it's not about what's fashionable to believe, it's about the truth."

"Does that work?"

"Christ yes. I gave a paper a few years back about the origins of the Thuggee sects in Persian military troops. It's why you could get Hindus and Muslims equally becoming Thuggee, you see—the Kali worship was tacked on later. It would have begun as some sort of Manichaean secret society—"

"Still spouting that nonsense?" She was a tall, pale woman with a shock of white hair, wearing clothes that looked both aggressively, studiedly Bohemian and far too warm for the climate. I could imagine her riding a bicycle, the kind with a wicker basket in the front.

"Spouting it? I'm writing a fucking book about it," said the Englishman. "So, what I want to know is, who's coming with me to the French Quarter to taste all that New Orleans can offer?"

"I'll pass," said the woman, unsmiling. "Who's your friend?"

"This is Jackson Anderton, from Hopewell College."

"The Zombie Coffee Girls paper?" She smiled. "I saw it in the program. Quite fascinating. Yet another thing we owe Zora, eh?"

"Along with *The Great Gatsby*," I said.

"Hurston knew F. Scott Fitzgerald?" said the bicycle woman. "I did not know that. We forget how small the New York literary world was back then, and how the color bar was often lifted for a genius."

The Englishman snorted. "Lifted? Only under sufferance. The woman died in penury as a cleaner in Florida. Nobody knew she'd written any of the stuff she wrote, let alone that she'd worked with Fitzgerald on *The Great Gatsby.* It's pathetic, Margaret."

"Posterity has a way of taking these things into account," said the tall woman. She walked away.

Campbell stared after her. "When I grow up," he said, "I want to be her."

"Why?"

He looked at me. "Yeah, that's the attitude. You're right. Some of us write the best-sellers; some of us read them. Some of us get the prizes; some of us don't. What's important is being human, isn't it? It's how good a person you are. Being alive."

He patted me on the arm.

"Come on. Interesting anthropological phenomenon I've read about on the Internet I shall point out to you tonight, of the kind you probably don't see back in Dead Rat, Kentucky. Id est, women who would, under normal circumstances, not show their tits for a hundred quid, who will be only too pleased to get 'em out for the crowd for some cheap plastic beads."

"Universal trading medium," I said. "Beads."

"Fuck," he said. "There's a paper in that. Come on. You ever had a Jell-O shot, Jackson?"

"No."

"Me neither. Bet they'll be disgusting. Let's go and see."

We paid for our drinks. I had to remind him to tip.

"By the way," I said. "F. Scott Fitzgerald. What was his wife's name?"

"Zelda? What about her?"

"Nothing," I said.

Zelda. Zora. Whatever. We went out.

3

"NOTHING LIKE SOMETHING HAPPENS ANYWHERE"

Midnight, give or take. We were in a bar on Bourbon Street, me and the English anthropology prof, and he started buying drinks—real drinks, this place didn't do Jell-O shots—for a couple of dark-haired women at the bar. They looked so similar they might have been sisters. One wore a red ribbon in her hair; the other wore a white ribbon. Gauguin might have painted them, only he would have painted them bare-breasted, and without the silver mouse-skull earrings. They laughed a lot.

We had seen a small party of academics walk past the bar at one point, being led by a guide with a black umbrella. I pointed them out to Campbell.

The woman with the red ribbon raised an eyebrow. "They go on the Haunted History tours, looking for ghosts. You want to say, 'Dude, this is where the ghosts come; this is where the dead stay.' Easier to go looking for the living."

"You saying the tourists are *alive*?" said the other, mock concern on her face.

"When they *get* here," said the first, and they both laughed at that.

They laughed a lot.

The one with the white ribbon laughed at everything Campbell said. She would tell him, "Say 'fuck' again," and he would say it, and she would say "Fook! Fook!" trying to copy him. And he'd say, "It's not *fook*, it's *fuck*," and she couldn't hear the difference, and would laugh some more.

After two drinks, maybe three, he took her by the hand and walked her into the back of the bar, where music was playing, and it was dark, and there were a couple of people already, if not dancing, then moving against each other.

I stayed where I was, beside the woman with the red ribbon in her hair.

She said, "So you're in the record company, too?"

I nodded. It was what Campbell had told them we did. "I hate telling people I'm a fucking academic," he had said reasonably, when they were in the ladies' room. Instead he had told them that he had discovered Oasis.

"How about you? What do you do in the world?"

She said, "I'm a priestess of Santeria. Me, I got it all in my blood; my papa was Brazilian, my momma was Irish-Cherokee. In Brazil, everybody makes love with everybody and they have the best little brown babies. Everybody got black slave blood; everybody got Indian blood; my pappa even got some

Japanese blood. His brother, my uncle, he looks Japanese. My pappa, he just a good-looking man. People think it was my pappa I got the Santeria from, but no, it was my grandmomma—said she was Cherokee, but I had her figgered for mostly high yaller when I saw the old photographs. When I was three I was talking to dead folks. When I was five I watched a huge black dog, size of a Harley-Davidson, walking behind a man in the street; no one could see it but me. When I told my mom, she told my grandmomma, they said, 'She's got to know; she's got to learn.' There was people to teach me, even as a little girl.

"I was never afraid of dead folk. You know that? They never hurt you. So many things in this town can hurt you, but the dead don't hurt you. Living people hurt you. They hurt you so bad."

I shrugged.

"This is a town where people sleep with each other, you know. We make love to each other. It's something we do to show we're still alive."

I wondered if this was a come-on. It did not seem to be.

She said, "You hungry?"

"A little," I said.

She said, "I know a place near here they got the best bowl of gumbo in New Orleans. Come on."

I said, "I hear it's a town where you're best off not walking on your own at night."

"That's right," she said. "But you'll have me with you. You're safe, with me with you."

Out on the street, college girls were flashing their breasts to the crowds on the balconies. For every glimpse of nipple the onlookers would cheer and throw plastic beads. I had known the red-ribbon woman's name earlier in the evening, but now it had evaporated.

"Used to be they only did this shit at Mardi Gras," she said. "Now the tourists expect it, so it's just tourists doing it for the tourists. The locals don't care. When you need to piss," she added, "you tell me."

"Okay. Why?"

"Because most tourists who get rolled, get rolled when they go into the alleys to relieve themselves. Wake up an hour later in Pirates' Alley with a sore head and an empty wallet."

"I'll bear that in mind."

She pointed to an alley as we passed it, foggy and deserted. "Don't go there," she said.

The place we wound up in was a bar with tables. A TV on above the bar showed *The Tonight Show* with the sound off and subtitles on, although the subtitles kept scrambling into numbers and fractions. We ordered the gumbo; a bowl each.

I was expecting more from the best gumbo in New Orleans. It was almost tasteless. Still, I spooned it down, knowing that I needed food, that I had nothing to eat that day.

Three men came into the bar. One sidled; one strutted; one shambled. The sidler was dressed like a Victorian undertaker, high top hat and all. His skin was fish-belly pale; his hair was long and stringy; his beard was long and threaded with silver beads. The strutter was dressed in a long black leather coat, dark clothes underneath. His skin was very black. The last one, the shambler, hung back, waiting by the door. I could not see much of his face, nor decode his race: what I could see of his skin was a dirty gray. His lank hair hung over his face. He made my skin crawl.

The first two men made straight to our table, and I was, momentarily, scared for my skin, but they paid no attention to me. They looked at the woman with the red ribbon, and both of the men kissed her on the cheek. They asked about friends they had not seen, about who did what to whom in which bar and why. They reminded me of the fox and the cat from *Pinocchio*.

"What happened to your pretty girlfriend?" the woman asked the black man.

He smiled, without humor. "She put a squirrel tail on my family tomb."

She pursed her lips. "Then you better off without her."

"That's what I say."

I glanced over at the one who gave me the creeps. He was a filthy thing, junkie thin, gray-lipped. His eyes were downcast. He barely moved. I wondered what the three men were doing together: the fox and the cat and the ghost.

Then the white man took the woman's hand and pressed it to his lips, bowed to her, raised a hand to me in a mock salute, and the three of them were gone.

"Friends of yours?"

"Bad people," she said. "Macumba. Not friends of anybody."

"What was up with the guy by the door? Is he sick?"

She hesitated; then she shook her head. "Not really. I'll tell you when you're ready."

"Tell me now."

On the TV, Jay Leno was talking to a thin blond woman, IT&S NOT .UST THE MOVIE, said the caption. SO H.VE SS YOU SEEN THE AC ION F!GURE? He picked up a small toy from his desk, pretended to check under its skirt to make sure it was anatomically correct, [LAUGHTER], said the caption.

She finished her bowl of gumbo, licked the spoon with a red, red tongue, and put it down in the bowl. "A lot of kids they come to New Orleans. Some of them read Anne Rice books and figure they learn about being vampires here. Some of them have abusive parents; some are just bored. Like stray kittens living in drains, they come here. They found a whole new breed of cat living in a drain in New Orleans, you know that?"

"No."

SLAUGHTER S] said the caption, but Jay was still grinning, and *The Tonight Show* went to a car commercial.

"He was one of the street kids, only he had a place to crash at night. Good kid. Hitchhiked from LA to New Orleans. Wanted to be left alone to smoke a little weed, listen to his Doors cassettes, study up on chaos magick and read the complete works of Aleister Crowley. Also get his dick sucked. He wasn't particular about who did it. Bright eyes and bushy tail."

"Hey," I said. "That was Campbell. Going past. Out there."

"Campbell?"

"My friend."

"The record producer?" She smiled as she said it, and I thought, *She knows. She knows he was lying. She knows what he is.*

I put down a twenty and a ten on the table, and we went out onto the street, to find him, but he was already gone. "I thought he was with your sister," I told her.

"No sister," she said. "No sister. Only me. Only me."

We turned a comer and were engulfed by a crowd of noisy tourists, like a sudden breaker crashing onto the shore. Then, as fast as they had come, they were gone, leaving only a handful of people behind them. A teenaged girl was throwing up in a gutter, a young man nervously standing near her, holding her purse and a plastic cup half-full of booze.

The woman with the red ribbon in her hair was gone. I wished I had made a note of her name, or the name of the bar in which I'd met her.

I had intended to leave that night, to take the interstate west to Houston and from there to Mexico, but I was tired and two-thirds drunk, and instead I went back to my room. When the morning came I was still in the Marriott. Everything I had worn the night before smelled of perfume and rot.

I put on my T-shirt and pants, went down to the hotel gift shop, picked out a couple more T-shirts and a pair of shorts. The tall woman, the one without the bicycle, was in there, buying some Alka-Seltzer.

She said, "They've moved your presentation. It's now in the Audubon Room, in about twenty minutes. You might want to clean your teeth first. Your best friends won't tell you, but I hardly know you, Mister Anderton, so I don't mind telling you at all."

I added a traveling toothbrush and toothpaste to the stuff I was buying. Adding to my possessions, though, troubled me. I felt I should be shedding them. I needed to be transparent, to have nothing.

I went up to the room, cleaned my teeth, put on the jazz festival T-shirt. And then, because I had no choice in the matter; or because I was doomed to confer, consult, and otherwise hobnob; or because I was pretty certain Campbell would be in the audience and I wanted to say good-bye to him before I drove away, I picked up the typescript and went down to the

Audubon Room, where fifteen people were waiting. Campbell was not one of them.

I was not scared. I said hello, and I looked at the top of page one.

It began with another quote from Zora Neale Hurston:

Big Zombies who come in the night to do malice are talked about. Also the little girl Zombies who are sent out by their owners in the dark dawn to sell little packets of roasted coffee. Before sun-up their cries of "Café grille" can be heard from dark places in the streets and one can only see them if one calls out for the seller to come with the goods. Then the little dead one makes herself visible and mounts the steps.

Anderton continued on from there, with quotations from Hurston's contemporaries and several extracts from old interviews with older Haitians, the man's paper leaping, as far as I was able to tell, from conclusion to conclusion, spinning fancies into guesses and suppositions and weaving those into fact.

Halfway through, Margaret, the tall woman without the bicycle, came in and simply stared at me. I thought, *She knows I'm not him. She knows.* I kept reading though. What else could I do? At the end, I asked for questions.

Somebody asked me about Zora Neale Hurston's research practices. I said that was a very good question, which was addressed at greater length in the finished paper, of which what I had read was essentially an edited abstract.

Someone else—a short, plump woman—stood up and announced that the zombie girls could not have existed: zombie drugs and powders numbed you, induced deathlike trances, but still worked fundamentally on belief—the belief that you were now one of the dead, and had no will of your own. How she asked, could a child of four or five be induced to believe such a thing? No. The coffee girls were, she said, one with the Indian rope trick, just another of the urban legends of the past.

Personally I agreed with her, but I nodded and said that her points were well made and well taken, and that from my perspective—which was, I hoped, genuinely anthropological perspective—what mattered was not whether it was easy to believe, but, much more importantly, if it was the truth.

They applauded, and afterward a man with a beard asked me whether I might be able to get a copy of the paper for a journal he edited. It occurred to me that it was a good thing that I had come to New Orleans, that Anderton's career would not be harmed by his absence from the conference.

The plump woman, whose badge said her name was Shanelle Gravely-Kin was waiting for me at the door. She said, "I really enjoyed that. I don't want you to think that I didn't."

Campbell didn't turn up for his presentation. Nobody ever saw him again.

Margaret introduced me to someone from New York and mentioned that Zora Neale Hurston had worked on *The Great Gatsby*. The man said yes, that was pretty common knowledge these days. I wondered if she had called the police, but she seemed friendly enough. I was starting to stress, I realized. I wished I had not thrown away my cell phone.

Shanelle Gravely-King and I had an early dinner in the hotel, at the beginning of which I said, "Oh, let's not talk shop." And she agreed that only the very dull talked shop at the table, so we talked about rock bands we had seen live, fictional methods of slowing the decomposition of a human body, and about her partner, who was a woman older than she was and who owned a restaurant, and then we went up to my room. She smelled of baby powder and jasmine, and her naked skin was clammy against mine.

Over the next couple of hours I used two of the three condoms. She was sleeping by the time I returned from the bathroom, and I climbed into the bed next to her. I thought about the words Anderton had written, hand-scrawled on the back of a page of the typescript, and I wanted to check them, but I fell asleep, a soft-fleshed jasmine-scented woman pressing close to me.

After midnight, I woke from a dream, and a woman's voice was whispering in the darkness.

She said, "So he came into town, with his Doors cassettes and his Crowley books, and his handwritten list of the secret URLs for chaos magick on the Web, and everything was good. He even got a few disciples, runaways like him, and he got his dick sucked whenever he wanted, and the world was good.

"And then he started to believe his own press. He thought he was the real thing. That he was the dude. He thought he was a big mean tiger-cat, not a little kitten. So he dug up . . . something . . . someone else wanted.

"He thought the something he dug up would look after him. Silly boy. And that night, he's sitting in Jackson Square, talking to the Tarot readers, telling them about Jim Morrison and the cabala, and someone taps him on the shoulder, and he turns, and someone blows powder into his face, and he breathes it in.

"Not all of it. And he is going to do something about it, when he realizes there's nothing to be done, because he's all paralyzed. There's fugu fish and toad skin and ground bone and everything else in that powder, and he's breathed it in.

"They take him down to emergency, where they don't do much for him, figuring him for a street rat with a drug problem, and by the next day he can move again, although it's two, three days until he can speak.

"Trouble is, he needs it. He wants it. He knows there's some big secret in the zombie powder, and he was almost there. Some people say they mixed heroin with it, some shit like that, but they didn't even need to do that. He wants it.

"And they told him they wouldn't sell it to him. But if he did jobs for them, they'd give him a little zombie powder, to smoke, to sniff, to rub on his gums, to swallow. Sometimes they'd give him nasty jobs to do no one else wanted. Sometimes they'd just humiliate him because they could—make him eat dog shit from the gutter, maybe. Kill for them, maybe. Anything but die. All skin and bones. He'd do anything for his zombie powder.

"And he still thinks, in the little bit of his head that's still him, that he's not a zombie. That he's not dead, that there's a threshold he hasn't stepped over. But he crossed it long time ago."

I reached out a hand, and touched her. Her body was hard, and slim, and lithe, and her breasts felt like breasts that Gauguin might have painted. Her mouth, in the darkness, was soft and warm against mine.

People come into your life for a reason.

4

"THOSE PEOPLE OUGHT TO KNOW WHO WE ARE AND TELL THAT WE ARE HERE"

When I woke, it was still almost dark, and the room was silent. I turned on the light, looked on the pillow for a ribbon, white or red, or for a mouse-skull earring, but there was nothing to show that there had ever been anyone in the bed that night but me.

I got out of bed and pulled open the drapes, looked out of the window. The sky was graying in the east.

I thought about moving south, about continuing to run, continuing to pretend I was alive. But it was, I knew now, much too late for that. There are doors, after all, between the living and the dead, and they swing in both directions.

I had come as far as I could.

There was a faint *tap-tapping* on the hotel-room door. I pulled on my pants and the T-shirt I had set out in, and barefoot, I pulled the door open.

The coffee girl was waiting for me.

Everything beyond the door was touched with light, an open, wonderful predawn light, and I heard the sound of birds calling on the morning air. The street was on a hill, and the houses facing me were little more than shanties. There was mist in the air, low to the ground, curling like something from an old black-and-white film, but it would be gone by noon.

The girl was thin and small; she did not appear to be more than six years old. Her eyes were cobwebbed with what might have been cataracts; her skin was as gray as it had once been brown. She was holding a white hotel cup out to me, holding it carefully, with one small hand on the handle, one hand beneath the saucer. It was half filled with a steaming mud-colored liquid.

I bent to take it from her, and I sipped it. It was a very bitter drink, and it was hot, and it woke me the rest of the way.

I said, "Thank you."

Someone, somewhere, was calling my name. The girl waited, patiently, while I finished the coffee. I put the cup down on the carpet; then I put out my hand and touched her shoulder. She reached up her hand, spread her small gray fingers, and took hold of mine. She knew I was with her. Wherever we were headed now, we were going there together.

I remembered something somebody had once said to me. "It's okay. Every day is freshly ground," I told her.

The coffee girl's expression did not change, but she nodded, as if she had heard me, and gave my arm an impatient tug. She held my hand tight with her cold, cold fingers, and we walked, finally, side by side into the misty dawn.

SEA OAK

BY **GEORGE SAUNDERS**

Zombie fiction is largely perceived as a lowbrow affair. And though many fine writers from other genre hinterlands have dipped their toes in, to great effect, it's passing rare for bona fide literary author to seriously, unashamedly immerse themselves in its dank baptismal waters.

That's one of the many reasons why "Sea Oak" *by* George Saunders *is such a remarkable addition to this book—and the richness of zombie lore.*

Suffice it to say that there's no sense of slumming in this bawdy, brilliant back-from-the-dead advisory notice. Like many of the best zombie tales, it's a cautionary one; but it warns less against being torn apart than against being worn down by dumbass entropy and squalor.

I would like to thank the New Yorker *for letting us borrow one of its stars, and the* Barcelona Review *for recognizing that sometimes zombie literature is literature, too.*

Prepare to laugh and wince out loud.

The *written word isn't dead.*

It just smells funny.

AT SIX MR. FRENDT COMES ON THE P.A. and shouts, "Welcome to Joysticks!" Then he announces Shirts Off. We take off our flight jackets and fold them up. We take off our shirts and fold them up. Our scarves we leave on. Thomas Kirster's our beautiful boy. He's got long muscles and bright-blue eyes. The minute his shirt comes off two fat ladies hustle up the aisle and stick some money in his pants and ask will he be their Pilot. He says sure. He brings their salads. He brings their soups. My phone rings and the caller tells me to come see her in the Spitfire mock-up. Does she want me to be her Pilot? I'm hoping. Inside the Spitfire is Margie, who says she's been diagnosed with Chronic Shyness Syndrome, then hands me an Instamatic and offers me ten bucks for a close-up of Thomas's tush.

Do I do it? Yes I do.

It could be worse. It is worse for Lloyd Betts. Lately he's put on weight and his hair's gone thin. He doesn't get a call all shift and waits zero tables and winds up sitting on the P-51 wing, playing solitaire in a hunched-over position that gives him big gut rolls.

I Pilot six tables and make forty dollars in tips plus five an hour in salary.

After closing we sit on the floor for Debriefing. "There are times," Mr. Frendt says, "when one must move gracefully to the next station in life, like for example certain women in Africa or Brazil, I forget which, who either color their faces or don some kind of distinctive headdress upon achieving menopause. Are you with me? One of our ranks must now leave us. No one is an island in terms of being thought cute forever, and so today we must say good-bye to our friend Lloyd. Lloyd, stand up so we can say good-bye to you. I'm sorry. We are all so very sorry."

"Oh God," says Lloyd. "Let this not be true."

But it's true. Lloyd's finished. We give him a round of applause, and Frendt gives him a Farewell Pen and the contents of his locker in a trash bag and out he goes. Poor Lloyd. He's got a wife and two kids and a sad little duplex on Self-Storage Parkway.

"It's been a pleasure!" he shouts desperately from the doorway, trying not to burn any bridges.

What a stressful workplace. The minute your Cute Rating drops you're a goner. Guests rank us as Knockout, Honeypie, Adequate, or Stinker. Not that I'm complaining. At least I'm working. At least I'm not a Stinker like Lloyd.

I'm a solid Honeypie/Adequate, heading home with forty bucks cash.

At Sea Oak there's no sea and no oak, just a hundred subsidized apartments and a rear view of FedEx. Min and Jade are feeding their babies while watching *How My Child Died Violently*. Min's my sister. Jade's our cousin. *How My Child Died Violently* is hosted by Matt Merton, a six-foot-five blond who's always giving the parents shoulder rubs and telling them they've been sainted by pain. Today's show features a ten-year-old who killed a five-year-old for refusing to join his gang. The ten-year-old strangled the five-year-old with a jump rope, filled his mouth with baseball cards, then locked himself in the bathroom and wouldn't come out until his parents agreed to take him to FunTimeZone, where he confessed, then dove screaming into a mesh cage full of plastic balls. The audience is shrieking threats at the parents of the killer while the parents of the victim urge restraint and forgiveness to such an extent that finally the audience starts shrieking threats at them too. Then it's a commercial. Min and Jade put down the babies and light cigarettes and pace the room while studying aloud for their GEDs. It doesn't look good. Jade says "regicide" is a virus. Min locates Biafra one planet from Saturn. I offer to help and they start yelling at me for condescending.

"You're lucky, man!" my sister says. "You did high school. You got your frigging diploma. We don't. That's why we have to do this GED shit. If we had our diplomas we could just watch TV and not be all distracted."

"Really," says Jade. "Now shut it, chick! We got to study. Show's almost on."

They debate how many sides a triangle has. They agree that Churchill was in opera. Matt Merton comes back and explains that last week's show on suicide, in which the parents watched a reenactment of their son's suicide, was a healing process for the parents, then shows a video of the parents admitting it was a healing process.

My sister's baby is Troy. Jade's baby is Mac. They crawl off into the kitchen and Troy gets his finger caught in the heat vent. Min rushes over and starts pulling.

"Jesus freaking Christ!" screams Jade. "Watch it! Stop yanking on him and get the freaking Vaseline. You're going to give him a really long arm, man!"

Troy starts crying. Mac starts crying. I go over and free Troy no problem. Meanwhile Jade and Min get in a slap fight and nearly knock over the TV.

"Yo, chick!" Min shouts at the top of her lungs. "I'm sure you're slapping me? And then you knock over the freaking TV? Don't you care?"

"I care!" Jade shouts back. "You're the slut who nearly pulled off her own kid's finger for no freaking reason, man!"

Just then Aunt Bernie comes in from DrugTown in her DrugTown cap and hobbles over and picks up Troy and everything calms way down.

"No need to fuss, little man," she says. "Everything's fine. Everything's just hunky-dory."

"Hunky-dory," says Min, and gives Jade one last pinch.

Aunt Bernie's a peacemaker. She doesn't like trouble. Once this guy backed over her foot at FoodKing and she walked home with ten broken bones. She never got married, because Grandpa needed her to keep house after Grandma died. Then he died and left all his money to a woman none of us had ever heard of, and Aunt Bernie started in at DrugTown. But she's not bitter. Sometimes she's so nonbitter it gets on my nerves. When I say Sea Oak's a pit she says she's just glad to have a roof over her head. When I say I'm tired of being broke she says Grandpa once gave her pencils for Christmas and she was so thrilled she sat around sketching horses all day on the backs of used envelopes. Once I asked was she sorry she never had kids and she said no, not at all, and besides, weren't we were her kids?

And I said yes we were.

But of course we're not.

For dinner it's beanie-wienies. For dessert it's ice cream with freezer burn.

"What a nice day we've had." Aunt Bernie says once we've got the babies in bed.

"Man, what an optometrist," says Jade.

*

Next day is Thursday, which means a visit from Ed Anders from the Board of Health. He's in charge of ensuring that our penises never show. Also that we don't kiss anyone. None of us ever kisses anyone or shows his penis except Sonny Vance, who does both, because he's saving up to buy a FaxIt franchise. As for our Penile Simulators, yes, we can show them, we can let them stick out the top of our pants, we can even periodically dampen our tight pants with spray bottles so our Simulators really contour, but our real penises, no, those have to stay inside our hot uncomfortable oversized Simulators.

"Sorry fellas, hi fellas," Anders says as he comes wearily in. "Please know I don't like this any better than you do. I went to school to learn how to inspect meat, but this certainly wasn't what I had in mind. Ha ha!"

He orders a Lindbergh Enchilada and eats it cautiously, as if it's alive and he's afraid of waking it. Sonny Vance is serving soup to a table of hairstylists on a bender and for a twenty shoots them a quick look at his unit.

Just then Anders glances up from his Lindbergh.

"Oh for crying out loud," he says, and writes up a Shutdown and we all get sent home early. Which is bad. Every dollar counts. Lately I've been sneaking toilet paper home in my briefcase. I can fit three rolls in. By the time I get home they're usually flat and don't work so great on the roller but still it saves a few bucks.

I clock out and cut through the strip of forest behind FedEx. Very pretty. A raccoon scurries over a fallen oak and starts nibbling at a rusty bike. As I come out of the woods I hear a shot. At least I think it's a shot. It could be a backfire. But no, it's a shot, because then there's another one, and some kids sprint across the courtyard yelling that Big Scary Dawgz rule.

I run home. Min and Jade and Aunt Bernie and the babies are huddled behind the couch. Apparently they had the babies outside when the shooting started. Troy's walker got hit. Luckily he wasn't in it. It's supposed to look like a duck but now the beak's missing.

"Man, fuck this shit!" Min shouts.

"Freak this crap you mean," says Jade. "You want them growing up with shit-mouths like us? Crap-mouths I mean?"

"I just want them growing up, period," says Min.

"Boo-hoo, Miss Dramatic," says Jade.

"Fuck off, Miss Ho," shouts Min.

"I mean it, jagoff, I'm not kidding," shouts Jade, and punches Min in the arm.

"Girls, for crying out loud!" says Aunt Bernie. "We should be thankful. At least we got a home. And at least none of them bullets actually hit nobody."

"No offense, Bernie?" says Min. "But you call this a freaking home?"

Sea Oak's not safe. There's an ad hoc crackhouse in the laundry room and last week Min found some brass knuckles in the kiddie pool. If I had my way I'd move everybody up to Canada. It's nice there. Very polite. We went for a weekend last fall and got a flat tire and these two farmers with bright-red faces insisted on fixing it, then springing for dinner, then starting a college fund for the babies. They sent us the stock certificates a week later, along with a photo of all of us eating cobbler at a diner. But moving to Canada takes bucks. Dad's dead and left us nada and Ma now lives with Freddie, who doesn't like us, plus he's not exactly rich himself. He does phone polls. This month he's asking divorced women how often they backslide and sleep with their exes. He gets ten bucks for every completed poll.

So not lucrative, and Canada's a moot point.

I go out and find the beak of Troy's duck and fix it with Elmer's.

"Actually you know what?" says Aunt Bernie. "I think that looks even more like a real duck now. Because some-times their beaks are cracked? I seen one like that down-town."

"Oh my God," says Min. "The kid's duck gets shot in the face and she says we're lucky."

"Well, we are lucky," says Bernie.

"Somebody's beak is cracked," says Jade.

"You know what I do if something bad happens?" Bernie says. "I don't think about it. Don't take it so serious. It ain't the end of the world. That's what I do. That's what I always done. That's how I got where I am."

My feeling is, Bernie, I love you, but where are you? You work at DrugTown for minimum. You're sixty and own nothing. You were basically a slave to your father and never had a date in your life.

"I mean, complain if you want," she says. "But I think we're doing pretty darn good for ourselves."

"Oh, we're doing great," says Min, and pulls Troy out from behind the couch and brushes some duck shards off his sleeper.

Joysticks reopens on Friday. It's a madhouse. They've got the fog on. A bridge club offers me fifteen bucks to oil-wrestle Mel Turner. So I oil-wrestle Mel Turner. They offer me twenty bucks to feed them chicken wings from my hand. So I feed them chicken wings from my hand. The afternoon flies by. Then the evening. At nine the bridge club leaves and I get a sorority. They sing intelligent nasty songs and grope my Simulator and say they'll never be able to look their boyfriends' meager genitalia in the eye again. Then Mr. Frendt comes over and says phone. It's Min. She sounds crazy. Four times in a row she shrieks get home. When I tell her calm down, she hangs up. I call back and no one answers. No biggie. Min's prone to panic. Probably one of the babies is puky. Luckily I'm on FlexTime.

"I'll be back," I say to Mr. Frendt.

"I look forward to it," he says.

I jog across the marsh and through FedEx. Up on the hill there's a light from the last remaining farm. Sometimes we take the boys to the adjacent car wash to look at the cow. Tonight however the cow is elsewhere.

At home Min and Jade are hopping up and down in front of Aunt Bernie, who's sitting very very still at one end of the couch.

"Keep the babies out!" shrieks Min. "I don't want them seeing something dead!"

"Shut up, man!" shrieks Jade. "Don't call her something dead!"

She squats down and pinches Aunt Bernie's cheek.

"Aunt Bernie?" she shrieks. "Fuck!"

"We already tried that like twice, chick!" shrieks Min. "Why are you doing that shit again? Touch her neck and see if you can feel that beating thing!"

“Shit shit shit!” shrieks Jade.

I call 911 and the paramedics come out and work hard for twenty minutes, then give up and say they’re sorry and it looks like she’s been dead most of the afternoon. The apartment’s a mess. Her money drawer’s empty and her family photos are in the bathtub.

“Not a mark on her,” says a cop.

“I suspect she died of fright,” says another. “Fright of the intruder?”

“My guess is yes,” says a paramedic.

“Oh God,” says Jade. “God, God, God.”

I sit down beside Bernie. I think: I am so sorry. I’m sorry I wasn’t here when it happened and sorry you never had any fun in your life and sorry I wasn’t rich enough to move you somewhere safe. I remember when she was young and wore pink stretch pants and made us paper chains out of DrugTown receipts while singing “Froggie Went A-Courting.” All her life she worked hard. She never hurt anybody. And now this.

Scared to death in a crappy apartment.

Min puts the babies in the kitchen but they keep crawling out. Aunt Bernie’s in a shroud on this sort of dolly and on the couch are a bunch of forms to sign.

We call Ma and Freddie. We got their machine.

“Ma, pick up!” says Min. “Something bad happened! Ma, please freaking pick up!”

But nobody picks up.

So we leave a message.

Lobton’s Funeral Parlor is just a regular house on a regular street. Inside there’s a rack of brochures with titles like “Why Does My Loved One Appear Somewhat Larger?” Lobton looks healthy. Maybe too healthy. He’s wearing a yellow golf shirt and his biceps keep involuntarily flexing. Every now and then he touches his delts as if to confirm they’re still big as softballs.

“Such a sad thing,” he says.

“How much?” asks Jade. “I mean, like for basic. Not superfancy.”

“But not crappy either,” says Min. “Our aunt was the best.”

"What price range were you considering?" says Lobton, cracking his knuckles. We tell him and his eyebrows go up and he leads us to something that looks like a moving box.

"Prior to usage we'll moisture-proof this with a spray lacquer," he says. "Makes it look quite woodlike."

"That's all we can get?" says Jade. "Cardboard?"

"I'm actually offering you a slight break already," he says, and does a kind of push-up against the wall. "On account of the tragic circumstances. This is Sierra Sunset. Not exactly cardboard. More of a fiberboard. "

"I don't know," says Min. "Seems pretty gyppy."

"Can we think about it?" says Ma.

"Absolutely," says Lobton. "Last time I checked this was still America."

I step over and take a closer look. There are staples where Aunt Bernie's spine would be. Down at the foot there's some writing about Folding Tab A into Slot B.

"No freaking way," says Jade. "Work your whole life and end up in a Mayflower box? I doubt it. "

We've got zip in savings. We sit at a desk and Lobton does what he calls a Credit Calc. If we pay it out monthly for seven years we can afford the Amber Mist, which includes a double-thick balsa box and two coats of lacquer and a one-hour wake.

"But seven years, jeez," says Ma.

"We got to get her the good one," says Min. "She never had anything nice in her life."

So Amber Mist it is.

We bury her at St. Leo's, on the hill up near BastCo. Her part of the graveyard's pretty plain. No angels, no little rock houses, no flowers, just a bunch of flat stones like parking bumpers and here and there a Styrofoam cup. Father Brian says a prayer and then one of us is supposed to talk. But what's there to say? She never had a life. Never married, no kids, work work work. Did she ever go on a cruise? All her life it was buses. Buses buses buses. Once she went with Ma on a bus to Quigley, Kansas, to gamble and shop at an outlet mall. Someone broke into her room and stole her clothes and took a dump in her suitcase while they were at the Roy Clark show. That was it. That was the extent of her tourism. After that it was DrugTown, night and day. After fifteen years as Cashier she got demoted to Greeter. People would ask where the cold remedies were and she'd point to some big letters on the wall that said Cold Remedies.

Freddie, Ma's boyfriend, steps up and says he didn't know her very long but she was an awful nice lady and left behind a lot of love, etc., etc., blah blah blah. While it's true she didn't do much in her life, still she was very dear to those of us who knew her and never made a stink about anything but was always content with whatever happened to her, etc., etc., blah blah blah.

Then it's over and we're supposed to go away.

"We gotta come out here like every week," says Jade.

"I know I will," says Min.

"What, like I won't?" says Jade. "She was so freaking nice."

"I'm sure you swear at a grave," says Min.

"Since when is freak a swear, chick?" says Jade.

"Girls," says Ma.

"I hope I did okay in what I said about her," says Freddie in his full-of-crap way, smelling bad of English Navy. "Actually I sort of surprised myself."

"Bye-bye, Aunt Bernie," says Min.

"Bye-bye, Bern," says Jade.

"Oh my dear sister," says Ma.

I scrunch my eyes tight and try to picture her happy, laughing, poking me in the ribs. But all I can see is her terrified on the couch. It's awful. Out there, somewhere, is whoever did it. Someone came in our house, scared her to death, watched her die, went through our stuff, stole her money. Someone who's still living, someone who right now might be having a piece of pie or running an errand or scratching his ass, someone who, if he wanted to, could drive west for three days or whatever and sit in the sun by the ocean.

We stand a few minutes with heads down and hands folded.

Afterward Freddie takes us to Trabanti's for lunch. Last year Trabanti died and three Vietnamese families went in together and bought the place, and it still serves pasta and pizza and the big oil of Trabanti is still on the wall but now from the kitchen comes this very pretty Vietnamese music and the food is somehow better.

Freddie proposes a toast. Min says remember how Bernie always called lunch dinner and dinner supper? Jade says remember how when her jaw clicked she'd say she needed oil?

"She was a excellent lady," says Freddie.

"I already miss her so bad," says Ma.

"I'd like to kill that fuck that killed her," says Min.

"How about let's don't say fuck at lunch," says Ma.

"It's just a word, Ma, right?" says Min. "Like pluck is just a word? You don't mind if I say pluck? Pluck pluck pluck?"

"Well, shit's just a word too," says Freddie. "But we don't say it at lunch."

"Same with puke," says Ma.

"Shit puke, shit puke," says Min.

The waiter clears his throat. Ma glares at Min.

"I love you girls' manners," Ma says.

"Especially at a funeral," says Freddie.

"This ain't a funeral," says Min.

"The question in my mind is what you kids are gonna do now" says Freddie. "Because I consider this whole thing a wake-up call, meaning it's time for you to pull yourselfs up by the bootstraps like I done and get out of that dangerous craphole you're living at."

"Mr. Phone Poll speaks," says Min.

"Anyways it ain't that dangerous," says Jade.

"A woman gets killed and it ain't that dangerous?" says Freddie.

"All's we need is a dead bolt and a eyehole," says Min.

"What's a bootstrap," says Jade.

"It's like a strap on a boot, you doof," says Min.

"Plus where we gonna go?" says Min. "Can we move in with you guys?"

"I personally would love that and you know that," says Freddie. "But who would not love that is our landlord."

"I think what Freddie's saying is it's time for you girls to get jobs," says Ma.

"Yeah right, Ma," says Min. "After what happened last time?"

When I first moved in, Jade and Min were working the info booth at HardwareNiche. Then one day we picked the babies up at day care and found Troy sitting naked on top of the washer and Mac in the yard being nipped by a Pekingese and the day-care lady sloshed and playing KillerBirds on Nintendo.

So that was that. No more HardwareNiche.

"Maybe one could work, one could baby-sit?" says Ma.

"I don't see why I should have to work so she can stay home with her baby," says Min.

"And I don't see why I should have to work so she can stay home with her baby," says Jade.

"It's like a freaking veece versa," says Min.

"Let me tell you something," says Freddie. "Something about this country. Anybody can do anything. But first they gotta try. And you guys ain't. Two don't work and one strips naked? I don't consider that trying. You kids make squat. And therefore you live in a dangerous craphole. And what happens in a dangerous craphole? Bad tragic shit. It's the freaking American way—you start out in a dangerous craphole and work hard so you can someday move up to a somewhat less dangerous craphole. And finally maybe you get a mansion. But at this rate you ain't even gonna make it to the somewhat less dangerous craphole."

"Like you live in a mansion," says Jade.

"I do not claim to live in no mansion," says Freddie. "But then again I do not live in no slum. The other thing I also do not do is strip naked."

"Thank God for small favors," says Min.

"Anyways he's never actually naked," says Jade.

Which is true. I always have on at least a T-back.

"No wonder we never take these kids out to a nice lunch," says Freddie.

"I do not even consider this a nice lunch," says Min.

*

For dinner Jade microwaves some Stars-n-Flags. They're addictive. They put sugar in the sauce and sugar in the meat nuggets. I think also caffeine. Someone told me the brown streaks in the Flags are caffeine. We have like five bowls each.

After dinner the babies get fussy and Min puts a mush of ice cream and Hershey's syrup in their bottles and we watch *The Worst That Could Happen*, a half-hour of computer simulations of tragedies that have never actually occurred but theoretically could. A kid gets hit by a train and flies into a zoo, where he's eaten by wolves. A man cuts his hand off chopping wood and while wandering around screaming for help is picked up by a tornado and dropped on a preschool during recess and lands on a pregnant teacher.

"I miss Bernie so bad," says Min.

"Me too," Jade says sadly.

The babies start howling for more ice cream.

"That is so cute," says Jade. "They're like, *Give it the fuck up!*"

"We'll give it the fuck up, sweeties, don't worry," says Min. "We didn't forget about you."

Then the phone rings. It's Father Brian. He sounds weird. He says he's sorry to bother us so late. But something strange has happened. Something bad. Something sort of, you know, unspeakable. Am I sitting? I'm not but I say I am.

Apparently someone has defaced Bernie's grave.

My first thought is there's no stone. It's just grass. How do you deface grass? What did they do, pee on the grass on the grave? But Father's nearly in tears.

So I call Ma and Freddie and tell them to meet us, and we get the babies up and load them into the K-car.

"Deface," says Jade on the way over. "What does that mean, deface?"

"It means like fucked up," says Min.

"But how?" says Jade. "I mean, like what did they do?"

"We don't know, dumbass," says Min. "That's why we're going there."

"And why?" says Jade. "Why would someone do that?"

"Check out Miss Shreelock Holmes," says Min. "Someone done that because someone is a asshole."

"Someone is a big-time asshole," says Jade.

Father Brian meets us at the gate with a flashlight and a golf cart.

"When I saw this," he says." I literally sat down in astonishment. Nothing like this has ever happened here. I am so sorry. You seem like nice people."

We're too heavy and the wheels spin as we climb the hill, so I get out and jog alongside.

"Okay, folks, brace yourselves," Father says, and shuts off the engine.

Where the grave used to be is just a hole. Inside the hole is the Amber Mist, with the top missing. Inside the Amber Mist is nothing. No Aunt Bernie.

"At least you folks have retained your feet," says Father Brian. "I'm telling you I literally sat right down. I sat right down on that pile of dirt. I dropped as if shot. See that mark? That's where I sat."

On the pile of grave dirt is a butt-shaped mark.

The cops show up and one climbs down in the hole with a tape measure and a camera. After three or four flashes he climbs out and hands Ma a pair of blue pumps.

"Her little shoes," says Ma. "Oh my God."

"Are those them?" says Jade.

"Those are them," says Min.

"I am freaking out," says Jade.

"I am totally freaking out," says Min.

"I'm gonna sit," says Ma, and drops into the golf cart.

"What I don't get is who'd want her?" says Min.

"She was just this lady," says Jade.

"Typically it's teens?" one cop says. "Typically we find the loved one nearby? Once we found the loved one nearby with, you know, a cigarette between its lips, wearing a sombrero? These kids today got a lot more nerve than we ever did. I never would've dreamed of digging up a dead corpse when I was a teen. You might tip over a stone, sure, you might spray-paint something on a crypt, you might, you know, give a wino a hotfoot."

"But this, jeez," says Freddie. "This is a entirely different ballgame."

"Boy howdy," says the cop, and we all look down at the shoes in Ma's hands.

Next day I go back to work. I don't feel like it but we need the money. The grass is wet and it's hard getting across the ravine in my dress shoes. The soles are slick. Plus they're too tight. Several times I fall forward on my briefcase. Inside the briefcase are my T-backs and a thing of mousse.

Right off the bat I get a tableful of MediBen women seated under a banner saying Best of Luck, Beatrice, No Hard Feelings. I take off my shirt and serve their salads. I take off my flight pants and serve their soups. One drops a dollar on the floor and tells me feel free to pick it up.

I pick it up.

"Not like that, not like that," she says. "Face the other way, so when you bend we can see your crack."

I've done this about a million times, but somehow I can't do it now.

I look at her. She looks at me.

"What?" she says. "I'm not allowed to say that? I thought that was the whole point."

"That is the whole point, Phyllis," says another lady. "You stand your ground."

"Look;" Phyllis says. "Either bend how I say or give back the dollar. I think that's fair."

"You go, girl," says her friend.

I give back the dollar. I return to the Locker Area and sit awhile. For the first time ever, I'm voted Stinker. There are thirteen women at the MediBen table and they all vote me Stinker. Do the MediBen women know my situation? Would they vote me Stinker if they did? But what am I supposed to do, go out and say, Please ladies, my aunt just died, plus her body's missing?

Mr. Frendt pulls me aside.

"Perhaps you need to go home," he says. "I'm sorry for your loss. But I'd like to encourage you not to behave like one of those Comanche ladies who bite off their index fingers when a loved one dies. Grief is good, grief is fine, but too much grief, as we all know, is excessive. If your aunt's death has filled your mouth with too many bitten-off fingers, for crying out loud, take a week off, only don't take it out on our Guests, they didn't kill your dang aunt."

But I can't afford to take a week off. I can't even afford to take a few days off.

"We really need the money," I say.

"Is that my problem?" he says. "Am I supposed to let you dance without vigor just because you need the money? Why don't I put an ad in the paper for all sad people who need money? All the town's sad could come here and strip. Good-bye. Come back when you feel halfway normal."

From the pay phone I call home to see if they need anything from the FoodSoQuik.

"Just come home," Min says stiffly. "Just come straight home."

"What is it?" I say.

"Come home," she says.

Maybe someone's found the body. I imagine Bernie naked, Bernie chopped in two, Bernie posed on a bus bench. I hope and pray that something only mildly bad's been done to her, something we can live with.

At home the door's wide open. Min and Jade are sitting very still on the couch, babies in their laps, staring at the rocking chair, and in the rocking chair is Bernie. Bernie's body.

Same perm, same glasses, same blue dress we buried her in.

What's it doing here? Who could be so cruel? And what are we supposed to do with it?

Then she turns her head and looks at me.

"Sit the fuck down," she says.

In life she never swore.

I sit. Min squeezes and releases my hand, squeezes and releases, squeezes and releases.

"You, mister," Bernie says to me, "are going to start showing your cock. You'll show it and show it. You go up to a lady, if she wants to see it, if she'll pay to see it, I'll make a thumbprint on the forehead. You see the thumbprint, you ask. I'll try to get you five a day, at twenty bucks a pop. So a hundred bucks a day. Seven hundred a week. And that's cash, so no taxes. No withholding. See? That's the beauty of it."

She's got dirt in her hair and dirt in her teeth and her hair is a mess and her tongue when it darts out to lick her lips is black.

"You, Jade," she says. "Tomorrow you start work. Andersen Labels, Fifth and Rivera. Dress up when you go. Wear something nice. Show a little leg. And don't chomp your gum. Ask for Len. At the end of the month, we take the money you made and the cock money and get a new place. Somewhere safe. That's part one of Phase One. You, Min. You baby-sit. Plus you quit smoking. Plus you learn how to cook. No more food out of cans. We gotta eat right to look our best. Because I am getting me so many lovers. Maybe you kids don't know this but I died a freaking virgin. No babies, no lovers. Nothing went in, nothing came out. Ha ha! Dry as a bone, completely wasted, this pretty little thing God gave me between my legs. Well I am going to have lovers now, you fucks! Like in the movies, big shoulders and all, and a summer house, and nice trips, and in the morning in my room a big vase of flowers, and I'm going to get my nipples hard standing in the breeze from the ocean, eating shrimp from a cup, you sons of bitches, while my lover watches me from the veranda, his big shoulders shining, all hard for me, that's one damn thing I will guarantee you kids! Ha ha! You think I'm joking? I ain't freaking joking. I never got nothing! My life was shit! I was never even up in a freaking plane. But that was that life and this is this life. My new life. Cover me up now! With a blanket. I need my beauty rest. Tell anyone I'm here, you all die. Plus they die. Whoever you tell, they die. I kill them with my mind. I can do that. I am very freaking strong now. I got powers! So no visitors. I don't exactly look my best. You got it? You all got it?"

We nod. I go for a blanket. Her hands and feet are shaking and she's grinding her teeth and one falls out.

"Put it over me, you fuck, all the way over!" she screams, and I put it over her.

We sneak off with the babies and whisper in the kitchen.

"It looks like her," says Min.

"It is her," I say.

"It is and it ain't," says Jade.

"We better do what she says," Min says.

"No shit," Jade says.

All night she sits in the rocker under the blanket, shaking and swearing.

All night we sit in Min's bed, fully dressed, holding hands.

"See how strong I am!" she shouts around midnight, and there's a cracking sound, and when I go out the door's been torn off the microwave but she's still sitting in the chair.

In the morning she's still there, shaking and swearing.

"Take the blanket off!" she screams. "It's time to get this show on the road."

I take the blanket off. The smell is not good. One ear is now in her lap. She keeps absentmindedly sticking it back on her head.

"You, Jade!" she shouts. "Get dressed. Go get that job. When you meet Len, bend forward a little. Let him see down your top. Give him some hope. He's a sicko, but we need him. You, Min! Make breakfast. Something homemade. Like biscuits."

"Why don't you make it with your powers?" says Min.

"Don't be a smartass!" screams Bernie. "You see what I did to that microwave?"

"I don't know how to make freaking biscuits," Min wails.

"You know how to read, right?" Bernie shouts. "You ever heard of a recipe? You ever been in the grave? It sucks so bad! You regret all the things you never did. You little bitches are gonna have a very bad time in the grave unless you get on the stick, believe me! Turn down the thermostat! Make it cold. I like cold. Something's off with my body. I don't feel right."

I turn down the thermostat. She looks at me.

"Go show your cock!" she shouts. "That is the first part of Phase One. After we get the new place, that's the end of the first part of Phase Two. You'll still show your cock, but only three days a week. Because you'll start community college. Pre-law. Pre-law is best. You'll be a whiz. You ain't dumb. And Jade'll work weekends to make up for the decrease in cock money. See? See how that works? Now get out of here. What are you gonna do?"

"Show my cock?" I say.

"Show your cock, that's right," she says, and brushes back her hair with her hand, and a huge wad comes out, leaving her almost bald on one side.

"Oh God," says Min. "You know what? No way me and the babies are staying here alone."

"You ain't alone," says Bernie. "I'm here."

"Please don't go," Min says to me.

"Oh, stop it," Bernie says, and the door flies open and I feel a sort of invisible fist punching me in the back.

Outside it's sunny. A regular day. A guy's changing his oil. The clouds are regular clouds and the sun's the regular sun and the only nonregular thing is that my clothes smell like Bernie, a combo of wet cellar and rotten bacon.

Work goes well. I manage to keep smiling and hide my shaking hands, and my midshift rating is Honeypie. After lunch this older woman comes up and says I look so much like a real Pilot she can hardly stand it.

On her head is a thumbprint. Like Ash Wednesday, only sort of glowing.

I don't know what to do. Do I just come out and ask if she wants to see my cock? What if she says no? What if I get caught? What if I show her and she doesn't think it's worth twenty bucks?

Then she asks if I'll surprise her best friend with a birthday table dance. She points out her friend. A pretty girl, no thumbprint. Looks somehow familiar.

We start over and at about twenty feet I realize it's Angela.

Angela Silveri.

We dated senior year. Then Dad died and Ma had to take a job at Patty-Melt Depot. From all the grease Ma got a bad rash and could barely wear a blouse. Plus Min was running wild. So Angela would come over and there'd be Min getting high under a tarp on the carport and Ma sitting in her bra on a kitchen stool with a fan pointed at her gut. Angela had dreams. She had plans. In her notebook she pasted a picture of an office from the J. C. Penney catalogue and under it wrote, *My (someday?) office.* Once we saw this black Porsche and she said very nice but make hers red. The last straw was Ed Edwards, a big drunk, one of Dad's cousins. Things got so bad Ma rented him the utility room. One night Angela and I were making out on the couch late when Ed came in soused and started peeing in the dishwasher.

What could I say? He's only barely related to me? He hardly ever does that?

Angela's eyes were like these little pies.

I walked her home, got no kiss, came back, cleaned up the dishwasher as best I could. A few days later I got my class ring in the mail and a copy of *The Prophet.*

You will always be my first love, she'd written inside. *But now my path converges to a higher ground. Be well always. Walk in joy Please don't think me cruel, it's lust that I want so much in terms of accomplishment, plus I couldn't believe that guy peed right on your dishes.*

No way am I table dancing for Angela Silveri. No way am I asking Angela Silveri's friend if she wants to see my cock. No way am I hanging around here so Angela can see me in my flight jacket and T-backs and wonder to herself how I went so wrong etc., etc.

I hide in the kitchen until my shift is done, then walk home very, very slowly because I'm afraid of what Bernie's going to do to me when I get there.

Min meets me at the door. She's got flour all over her blouse and it looks like she's been crying.

"I can't take any more of this," she says. "She's like falling apart. I mean shit's falling off her. Plus she made me bake a freaking pie."

On the table is a very lumpy pie. One of Bernie's arms is now disconnected and lying across her lap.

"What are you thinking of!" she shouts. "You didn't show your cock even once? You think it's easy making those thumbprints? You try it, smartass! Do you or do you not know the plan? You gotta get us out of here! And to get us out, you gotta use what you got. And you ain't got much. A nice face. And a decent unit. Not huge, but shaped nice."

"Bernie, God," says Min.

"What, Miss Priss?" shouts Bernie, and slams the severed arm down hard on her lap, and her other ear falls off.

"I'm sorry, but this is too fucking sickening," says Min. "I'm going out."

"What's sickening?" says Bernie. "Are you saying I'm sickening? Well, I think you're sickening. So many wonderful things in life and where's your mind? You think with your lazy ass. Whatever life hands you, you take. You're not going anywhere. You're staying home and studying."

"I'm what?" says Min. "Studying what? I ain't studying. Chick comes into my house and starts ordering me to study? I freaking doubt it."

"You don't know nothing!" Bernie says. "What fun is life when you don't know nothing? You can't find your own town on the map. You can't name a single president. When we go to Rome you won't know nothing about the history. You're going to study the World Book. Do we still have those World Books?"

"Yeah right," says Min. "We're going to Rome."

"We'll go to Rome when he's a lawyer," says Bernie.

"Dream on, chick," says Min. "And we'll go to Mars when I'm a stockbreaker."

"Don't you dare make fun of me!" Bernie shouts, and our only vase goes flying across the room and nearly nails Min in the head.

"She's been like this all day," says Min.

"Like what?" shouts Bernie. "We had a perfectly nice day."

"She made me help her try on my bras," says Min.

"I never had a nice sexy bra," says Bernie.

"And now mine are all ruined," says Min. "They got this sort of goo on them."

"You ungrateful shit!" shouts Bernie. "Do you know what I'm doing for you? I'm saving your boy. And you got the nerve to say I made goo on your bras! Troy's gonna get caught in a crossfire in the courtyard. In September. September eighteenth. He's gonna get thrown off his little trike. With one leg twisted under him and blood pouring out of his ear. It's a freaking prophecy. You know that word? It means prediction. You know that word? You think I'm bullshitting? Well I ain't bullshitting. I got the power. Watch this: All day Jade sat licking labels at a desk by a window. Her boss bought everybody subs for lunch. She's bringing some home in a green bag."

"That ain't true about Troy, is it?" says Min. "Is it? I don't believe it."

"Turn on the TV!" Bernie shouts. "Give me the changer."

I turn on the TV. I give her the changer. She puts on *Nathan's Body Shop.* Nathan says washboard abs drive the women wild. Then there's a close-up of his washboard abs.

"Oh yes," says Bernie. "Them are for me. I'd like to give those a lick. A lick and a pinch. I'd like to sort of straddle those things."

Just then Jade comes through the door with a big green bag.

"Oh God," says Min.

"Told you so!" says Bernie, and pokes Min in the ribs. "Ha ha! I really got the power!"

"I don't get it," Min says, all desperate. "What happens? Please. What happens to him? You better freaking tell me."

"I already told you," Bernie says. "He'll fly about fifteen feet and live about three minutes."

"Bernie, God," Min says, and starts to cry. "You used to be so nice."

"I'm still so nice," says Bernie, and bites into a sub and takes off the tip of her finger and starts chewing it up.

Just after dawn she shouts out my name.

"Take the blanket off," she says. "I ain't feeling so good."

I take the blanket off. She's basically just this pile of parts: both arms in her lap, head on the arms, heel of one foot touching the heel of the other, all of it sort of wrapped up in her dress.

"Get me a washcloth," she says." Do I got a fever? I feel like I got a fever. Oh, I knew it was too good to be true. But okay. New plan. New plan. I'm changing the first part of Phase One. If you see two thumbprints, that means the lady'll screw you for cash. We're in a fix here. We gotta speed this up. There ain't gonna be nothing left of me. Who's gonna be my lover now?"

The doorbell rings.

"Son of a bitch," Bernie snarls.

It's Father Brian with a box of doughnuts. I step out quick and close the door behind me. He says he's just checking in. Perhaps we'd like to talk? Perhaps we're feeling some residual anger about Bernie's situation? Which would of course be completely understandable. Once when he was a young priest someone broke in and drew a mustache on the Virgin Mary with a permanent marker, and for weeks he was tortured by visions of bending back the finger of the vandal until he or she burst into tears of apology.

"I knew that wasn't appropriate," he says. "I knew that by indulging in that fantasy I was honoring violence. And yet it gave me pleasure. I also thought of catching them in the act and boinking them in the head with a rock. I also thought of jumping up and down on their backs until something in their spinal column cracked. Actually I had about a million ideas. But you know what I did instead? I scrubbed and scrubbed our Holy Mother, and soon she was as good as new. Her statue, I mean. She herself of course is always good as new. "

From inside comes the sound of breaking glass. Breaking glass and then something heavy falling, and Jade yelling and Min yelling and the babies crying.

"Oops, I guess?" he says. "I've come at a bad time? Look, all I'm trying to do is urge you, if at all possible, to forgive the perpetrators, as I forgave the perpetrator that drew on my Virgin Mary. The thing lost, after all, is only your aunt's body, and what is essential, I assure you, is elsewhere, being well taken care of."

I nod. I smile. I say thanks for stopping by. I take the doughnuts and go back inside.

The TV's broke and the refrigerator's tipped over and Bernie's parts are strewn across the living room like she's been shot out of a cannon.

"She tried to get up," says Jade.

"I don't know where the hell she thought she was going," says Min.

"Come here," the head says to me, and I squat down. "That's it for me. I'm fucked. As per usual. Always the bridesmaid, never the bride. Although come to think of it I was never even the freaking bridesmaid. Look, show your cock. It's the shortest line between two points. The world ain't giving away nice lives. You got a trust fund? You a genius? Show your cock. It's what you got. And remember: Troy in September. On his trike. One leg twisted. Don't forget. And also. Don't remember me like this. Remember me like how I was that night we all went to Red Lobster and I had that new perm. Ah Christ. At least buy me a stone."

I rub her shoulder, which is next to her foot.

"We loved you," I say.

"Why do some people get everything and I got nothing?" she says. "Why? Why was that?"

"I don't know," I say.

"Show your cock," she says, and dies again.

We stand there looking down at the pile of parts. Mac crawls toward it and Min moves him back with her foot.

"This is too freaking much," says Jade, and starts crying.

"What do we do now?" says Min.

"Call the cops," Jade says.

"And say what?" says Min.

We think about this awhile.

I get a Hefty bag. I get my winter gloves.

"I ain't watching," says Jade.

"I ain't watching either," says Min, and they take the babies into the bedroom.

I close my eyes and wrap Bernie up in the Hefty bag and twistie-tie the bag shut and lug it out to the trunk of the K-car. I throw in a shovel. I drive up to St. Leo's. I lower the bag into the hole using a bungee cord, then fill the hole back in.

Down in the city are the nice houses and the so-so houses and the lovers making out in dark yards and the babies crying for their moms, and I wonder if, other than Jesus, this has ever happened before. Maybe it happens all the time. Maybe there's angry dead all over, hiding in rooms, covered with blankets, bossing around their scared, embarrassed relatives. Because how would we know?

I for sure don't plan on broadcasting this.

I smooth over the dirt and say a quick prayer: If it was wrong for her to come back, forgive her, she never got beans in this life, plus she was trying to help us.

At the car I think of an additional prayer: But please don't let her come back again.

When I get home the babies are asleep and Jade and Min are watching a phone-sex infomercial, three girls in leatherjumpsuits eating bananas in Slo-mo while across the screen runs a constant disclaimer: "Not Necessarily the Girls Who Man the Phones! Not Necessarily the Girls Who Man the Phones!"

"Them chicks seem to really be enjoying those bananas," says Min in a thin little voice.

"I like them jumpsuits though," says Jade.

"Yeah them jumpsuits look decent," says Min.

Then they look up at me. I've never seen them so sad and beat and sick.

"It's done," I say.

Then we hug and cry and promise never to forget Bernie the way she really was, and I use some Resolve on the rug and they go do some reading in their World Books.

Next day I go in early. I don't see a single thumbprint. But it doesn't matter. I get with Sonny Vance and he tells me how to do it. First you ask the woman would she like a private tour. Then you show her the fake P-40, the Gallery of Historical Aces, the shower stall where we get oiled up, etc., etc. and then in the hall near the rest room you ask if there's anything else she'd like to see. It's sleazy. It's gross. But when I do it I think of September. September and Troy in the crossfire, his little leg bent under him etc., etc.

Most say no but quite a few say yes.

I've got a place picked out at a complex called Swan's Glen. They've never had a shooting or a knifing and the public school is great and every Saturday they have a nature walk for kids behind the clubhouse.

For every hundred bucks I make, I set aside five for Bernie's stone.

What do you write on something like that? Life Passed Her By? Died Disappointed? Came Back to Life but Fell Apart? All true, but too sad, and no way I'm writing any of those.

Bernie Kowalski, it's going to say: Beloved Aunt.

Sometimes she comes to me in dreams. She never looks good. Sometimes she's wearing a dirty smock. Once she had on handcuffs. Once she was naked and dirty and this mean cat was clawing its way up her front. But every time it's the same thing.

"Some people get everything and I got nothing," she says. "Why? Why did that happen?"

Every time I say I don't know.

And I don't.

ome in
WE'RE
OPE

The Late Shift

by Dennis Etchison

When I first entered the horror scene—at the dawn of the 1980s—it was common knowledge amongst the cognoscenti that Dennis Etchison was one of the best we had.

Simultaneously, there was much talk—some by Etchison himself—that he wasn't really a horror writer at all. That he had fallen into the genre by default, when it became clear that his biggest, most appreciative audience was made up of horror readers.

The Late Shift *is a case in point: a mordant slice of L.A. neorealism with an unerring nose for the whiff of decay. Is it literary fiction just a shade too dark to be embraced by literary fiction proper? Or is it just extremely well-written horror?*

The answer, of course, is both. And we are all the richer for it.

THEY WERE DRIVING BACK from a midnight screening of *The Texas Chainsaw Massacre* ("Who will survive and what will be left of them?") when one of them decided they should make the Stop 'N Start Market on the way home. Macklin couldn't be sure later who said it first, and it didn't really matter, for there was the all-night logo, its bright colors cutting through the fog before they had reached 26th Street, and as soon as he saw it Macklin moved over close to the curb and began coasting toward the only sign of life anywhere in town at a quarter to two in the morning.

They passed through the electric eye at the door, rubbing their faces in the sudden cold light. Macklin peeled off toward the news rack, feeling like a newborn before the LeBoyer Method. He reached into a row of well-thumbed magazines, but they were all chopper, custom car, detective and stroke books, as far as he could see.

"Please, please, sorry, thank you," the night clerk was saying.

"No, no," said a woman's voice, "can't you hear? I want that box, *that* one."

"Please, please," said the night man again.

Macklin glanced up.

A couple of guys were waiting in line behind her, next to the styrofoam ice chests. One of them cleared his throat and moved his feet.

The woman was trying to give back a small, oblong carton, but the clerk didn't seem to understand. He picked up the box, turned to the shelf, back to her again.

Then Macklin saw what it was: a package of one dozen prophylactics from behind the counter, back where they kept the cough syrup and airplane glue and film. That was all she wanted—a pack of Polaroid SX-70 Land Film.

Macklin wandered to the back of the store.

"How's it coming, Whitey?"

"I got the Beer Nuts," said Whitey, "and the Jiffy Pop, but I can't find any Olde English 800." He rummaged through the refrigerated case.

"Then get Schlitz Malt Liquor," said Macklin. "That ought to do the job." He jerked his head at the counter. "Hey, did you catch that action up there?"

"What's that?"

Two more guys hurried in, heading for the wine display. "Never mind.

Look, why don't you just take this stuff up there and get a place in line? I'll find us some Schlitz or something. Go on, they won't sell it to us after two o'clock."

He finally found a six-pack hidden behind some bottles, then picked up a quart of milk and a half-dozen eggs. When he got to the counter, the woman had already given up and gone home. The next man in line asked for cigarettes and beef jerky. Somehow the clerk managed to ring it up; the electronic register and UPC Code lines helped him a lot.

"Did you get a load of that one?" said Whitey. "Well, I'll be gonged. Old Juano's sure hit the skids, huh? The pits. They should have stood him in an aquarium."

"Who?"

"Juano. It *is* him, right? Take another look." Whitey pretended to study the ceiling.

Macklin stared at the clerk. Slicked-back hair, dyed and greasy and parted in the middle, a phony Hitler moustache, thrift shop clothes that didn't fit. And his skin didn't look right somehow, like he was wearing makeup over a face that hadn't seen the light of day in ages. But Whitey was right. It was Juano. He had waited on Macklin too many times at that little Mexican restaurant over in East L.A., Mama Something's. Yes, that was it, Mama Carnita's on Whittier Boulevard. Macklin and his friends, including Whitey, had eaten there maybe fifty or a hundred times, back when they were taking classes at Cal State. It was Juano for sure.

Whitey set his things on the counter. "How's it going, man?" he said.

"Thank you," said Juana.

Macklin laid out the rest and reached for his money. The milk made a lumpy sound when he let go of it. He gave the carton a shake. "Forget this," he said. "It's gone sour." Then, "Haven't seen you around, old buddy. Juano, wasn't it?"

"Sorry. Sorry," said Juano. He sounded dazed, like a sleepwalker.

Whitey wouldn't give up. "Hey, they still make that good *menudo* over there?" He dug in his jeans for change. "God, I could eat about a gallon of it right now, I bet."

They were both waiting. The seconds ticked by. A radio in the store was playing an old '60's song. *Light My Fire*, Macklin thought. The Doors. "You remember me, don't you? Jim Macklin." He held out his hand. "And my trusted Indian companion, Whitey? He used to come in there with me on Tuesdays and Thursdays."

The clerk dragged his feet to the register, then turned back, turned again. His eyes were half-closed. "Sorry," he said. "Sorry. Please."

Macklin tossed down the bills, and Whitey counted his coins and slapped them onto the counter top. "Thanks," said Whitey, his upper lip curling back. He hooked a thumb in the direction of the door. "Come on. This place gives me the creeps."

As he left, Macklin caught a whiff of Juano or whoever he was. The scent was sickeningly sweet, like a gilded lily. His hair? Macklin felt a cold draft blow through his chest, and shuddered; the air conditioning, he thought.

At the door, Whitey spun around and glared.

"So what," said Macklin. "Let's go."

"What time does Tube City here close?"

"Never. Forget it." He touched his friend's arm.

"The hell I will," said Whitey. "I'm coming back when they change fucking shifts. About six o'clock, right? I'm going to be standing right there in the parking lot when he walks out. That son of a bitch still owes me twenty bucks."

"Please," muttered the man behind the counter, his eyes fixed on nothing. "Please. Sorry. Thank you."

The call came around ten. At first he thought it was a gag; he propped his eyelids up and peeked around the apartment, half-expecting to find Whitey still there, curled up asleep among the loaded ashtrays and pinched beer cans. But it was no joke.

"Okay, okay, I'll be right there," he grumbled, not yet comprehending, and hung up the phone.

St. John's Hospital on 14th. In the lobby, families milled about, dressed as if on their way to church, watching the elevators and waiting obediently for the clock to signal the start of visiting hours. Business hours, thought Macklin. He got the room number from the desk and went on up.

A police officer stood stiffly in the hall, taking notes on an accident report form. Macklin got the story from him and from an irritatingly healthy-looking doctor—the official story—and found himself, against his will, believing in it. In some of it.

His friend had been in an accident, sometime after dawn. His friend's car, the old VW, had gone over an embankment, not far from the Arroyo Seco. His friend had been found near the wreckage, covered with blood and reeking of alcohol. His friend had been drunk.

"Let's see here now, Any living relatives?" asked the officer. "All we could get out of him was your name. He was in a pretty bad state of shock, they tell me."

"No relatives," said Macklin. "Maybe back on the reservation. I don't know. I'm not even sure where the—"

A long, angry rumble of thunder sounded outside the windows. A steely light reflected off the clouds and filtered into the corridor. It mixed with the fluorescents in the ceiling, rendering the hospital interior a hard-edged, silvery gray. The faces of the policeman and the passing nurses took on a shaded, unnatural cast.

It made no sense. Whitey couldn't have been that drunk when he left Macklin's apartment. Of course he did not actually remember his friend leaving. But Whitey was going to the Stop 'N Start if he was going anywhere, not halfway across the county to—where? Arroyo Seco? It was crazy.

"Did you say there was liquor in the car?"

"Afraid so. We found an empty fifth of Jack Daniels wedged between the seats. "

But Macklin knew he didn't keep anything hard at his place, and neither did Whitey, he was sure. Where was he supposed to have gotten it, with every liquor counter in the state shut down for the night?

And then it hit him. Whitey never, but never drank sour mash whiskey. In fact, Whitey never drank anything stronger than beer, anytime, anyplace. Because he couldn't. It was supposed to have something to do with his liver, as it did with other Amerinds. He just didn't haye the right enzymes.

Macklin waited for the uniforms and coats to move away, then ducked inside.

"Whitey," he said slowly.

For there he was, set up against firm pillows, the upper torso and most of the hand bandaged. The arms were bare, except for an ID bracelet and an odd pattern of zigzag lines from wrist to shoulder. The lines seemed to have been painted by an unsteady hand, using a pale gray dye of some kind.

"Call me by my name," said Whitey groggily. "It's White Feather."

He was probably shot full of painkillers. But at least he was okay. Wasn't he? "So what's with the war paint, old buddy?"

"I saw the Death Angel last night."

Macklin faltered. "I—I hear you're getting out of here real soon," he tried. "You know, yon almost had me worried there. But I reckon you're just not ready for the bone orchard yet."

"Did you hear what I said?"

"What? Uh, yeah. Yes." What had they shot him up with? Macklin cleared his throat and met his friend's eyes, which were focused beyond him. "What was it, a dream?"

"A dream," said Whitey. The eyes were glazed, burned out.

What happened? Whitey, he thought. Whitey. "You put that war paint on yourself?" he said gently.

"It's pHisoHex," said Whitey, "mixed with lead pencil. I put it on, the nurse washes it off, I put it on again."

"I see." He didn't, but went on. "So tell me what happened, partner. I couldn't get much out of the doctor."

The mouth smiled humorlessly, the lips cracking back from the teeth. "It was Juano," said Whitey. He started to laugh bitterly. He touched his ribs and stopped himself.

Macklin nodded, trying to get the drift. "Did you tell that to the cop out there?"

"Sure. Cops always believe a drunken Indian. Didn't you know that?"

"Look. I'll take care of Juano. Don't worry."

Whitey laughed suddenly in a high voice that Macklin had never heard before. "*He-he-he!* What are you going to do, kill him?"

"I don't know," he said, trying to think in spite of the clattering in the hall.

"They make a living from death, you know," said Whitey.

Just then a nurse swept into the room, pulling a cart behind her.

"How did you get in here?" she demanded.

"I'm just having a conversation with my friend here."

"Well, you'll have to leave. He's scheduled for surgery this afternoon. "

"Do you know about the Trial of the Dead?" asked Whitey.

"Shh, now," said the nurse. "You can talk to your friend as long as you want to, later."

"I want to know," said Whitey, as she prepared a syringe.

"What is it we want to know, now?" she said, preoccupied. "What dead? Where?"

"Where?" repeated Whitey. "Why, here, of course. The dead are here. Aren't they." It was a statement. "Tell me something. What do you do with them?"

"Now what nonsense . . . ?" The nurse swabbed his arm, clucking at the ritual lines on the skin.

"I'm asking you a question," said Whitey.

"Look, I'll be outside," said Macklin, "okay?"

"This is for you, too," said Whitey. "I want you to hear. Now if you'll just tell us, Miss Nurse. What do you do with the people who die in here?"

"Would you please—"

"I can't hear you." Whitey drew his arm away from her.

She sighed. "We take them downstairs. Really, this is most . . ."

But Whitey kept looking at her, nailing her with those expressionless eyes.

"Oh, the remains are tagged and kept in cold storage," she said, humoring him. "Until arrangements can be made with the family for services. There now, can we—?"

"But what happens? Between the time they become 'remains' and the services? How long is that? A couple of days? Three?"

She lost patience and plunged the needle into the arm.

"Listen," said Macklin, "I'll be around if you need me. And hey, buddy," he added, "we're going to have everything all set up for you when this is over. You'll see. A party, I swear. I can go and get them to send up a TV right now, at least."

"Like a bicycle for a fish," said Whitey.

Macklin attempted a laugh. "You take it easy, now."

And then he heard it again, that high, strange voice. "*He-he-he! tamunka sni kun.*"

Macklin needed suddenly to be out of there.

"Jim."

"What?"

"I was wrong about something last night."

"Yeah?"

"Sure was. That place wasn't Tube City. This is. *He-he-he!*"

That's funny, thought Macklin, like an open grave. He walked out. The last thing he saw was the nurse bending over Whitey, drawing her syringe of blood like an old-fashioned phlebotomist.

All he could find out that afternoon was that the operation wasn't critical, and that there would be additional X-rays, tests, and a period of "observation," though when pressed for details the hospital remained predictably vague no matter how he put the questions.

Instead of killing time, he made for the Stop 'N Start.

He stood around until the store was more or less empty, then approached the counter. The manager, whom Macklin knew slightly, was working the register himself.

Raphael stonewalled Macklin at the first mention of Juano; his beady eyes receded into glacial ignorance. No, the night man was named Dom or Don; he mumbled so that Macklin couldn't be sure. No, Don (or Dom) had been working here for six, seven months; no, no, no.

Until Macklin came up with the magic word: police.

After a few minutes of bobbing and weaving, it started to come out. Raphe sounded almost scared, yet relieved to be able to talk about it to someone, even to Macklin.

"They bring me these guys, my friend," whispered Raphe. "I don't got nothing to do with it, believe me.

"The way it seems to me, it's company policy for all the stores, not just me. Sometimes they call and say to lay off my regular boy, you know, on the graveyard shift. 'Specially when there's been a lot of holdups. Hell, that's right by me. I don't want Dom shot up. He's my best man!

"See, I put the hours down on Dom's pay so it comes out right with the taxes, but he has to kick it back. It don't even go on his check. Then the district office, they got to pay the outfit that supplies these guys, only they don't give 'em the regular wage. I don't know if they're wetbacks or what. I hear they only get maybe $1.25 an hour, or at least the outfit that brings 'em in does, so the office is making money. You know how many stores, how many shift that adds up to?

"Myself, I'm damn glad they only use 'em after dark, late, when things can get hairy for an all-night man. It's the way they look. But you already seen one, this Juano-Whatever. So you know. Right? You know something else, my friend? They *all* look messed up."

Macklin noticed goose bumps forming on Raphe's arms.

"*But I don't personally know nothing about it.*"

They, thought Macklin, poised outside the Stop 'N Start. Sure enough, like clockwork They had brought Juano to work at midnight. Right on schedule. With raw, burning eyes he had watched Them do something to Juano's shirt front and then point him at the door and let go. What did They do, wind him up? But They would be back. Macklin was sure of that. They, whoever They were. The Paranoid They.

Well, he was sure as hell going to find out who They were now.

He popped another Dexamyl and swallowed dry until it stayed down.

Threats didn't work any better than questions with Juano himself. Macklin had had to learn that the hard way. The guy was so sublimely creepy it was all he could do to swivel back and forth between register and counter, slithering a hyaline hand over the change machine in the face of the most outraged customers, like Macklin, giving out with only the same pathetic, wheezing *please, please, sorry, thank you*, like a stretched cassette tape on its last loop.

Which had sent Macklin back to the car with exactly no options, nothing to do that might jar the nightmare loose except to pound the steering wheel and curse and dream redder and redder dreams of revenge. He had burned rubber between the parking lot and Sweeney Todd's Pub, turning over two pints of John Courage and a shot of Irish whiskey before he could think clearly enough to waste another dime calling the hospital, or even to look at his watch.

At six o'clock They would be back for Juano. And then. He would. Find out.

Two or three hours in the all-night movie theatre downtown, merging with the shadows on the tattered screen. The popcorn girl wiping stains off her uniform. The ticket girl staring through him, and again when he left. Something about her. He tried to think. Something about the people who work night owl shifts anywhere. He remembered faces down the years. It didn't matter what they looked like. The nightwalkers, insomniacs, addicts, those without money for a cheap hotel, they would always come back to the only game in town. They had no choice. It didn't matter that the ticket girl was messed up. It didn't matter that Juano was messed up. Why should it?

A blue van glided into the lot.

The Stop 'N Start sign dimmed, paling against the coming morning. The van braked. A man in rumpled clothes climbed out. There was a second figure in the front seat. The driver unlocked the back doors, silencing the birds that were gathering in the trees. Then he entered the store.

Macklin watched. Juano was led out. The a.m. relief man stood by, shaking his head.

Macklin hesitated. He wanted Juano, but what could he do now? What the hell had he been waiting for, exactly? There was still something else, something else . . . It was like the glimpse of a shape under a sheet in a busy corridor. You didn't know what it was at first, but it was there; you knew what it might be, but you couldn't be sure, not until you got close and stayed next to it long enough to be able to read its true form.

The driver helped Juano into the van. He locked the doors, started the engine and drove away.

Macklin, his lights out, followed.

He stayed with the van as it snaked a path across the city, nearer and nearer the foothills. The sides were unmarked, but he figured it must operate like one of those minibus porta-maid services he had seen leaving Malibu and Bel-Air late in the afternoon, or like the loads of kids trucked in to push magazine subscriptions and phony charities in the neighborhoods near where he lived.

The sky was still black, beginning to turn to slate close to the horizon. Once they passed a garbage collector already on his rounds. Macklin kept his distance.

They led him finally to a street that dead-ended at a construction site. Macklin idled by the corner, then saw the van turn back.

He let them pass, cruised to the end and made a slow turn.

Then he saw the van returning.

He pretended to park. He looked up.

They had stopped the van crosswise in front of him, blocking his passage.

The man in rumpled clothes jumped out and opened Macklin's door.

Macklin started to get out but was pushed back.

"You think you're a big enough man to be trailing people around?"

Macklin tried to penetrate the beam of the flashlight. "I saw my old friend Juano get into your truck," he began. "Didn't get a chance to talk to him. Thought I might as well follow him home and see what he's been up to."

The other man got out of the front seat of the van. He was younger, delicate-boned. He stood on one side, listening.

"I saw him get in," said Macklin, "back at the Stop 'N Start on Pica?" He groped under the seat for the tire iron. "I was driving by and—"

"Get out."

"What?"

"We saw you. Out of the car."

He shrugged and swung his legs around, lifting the iron behind him as he stood.

The younger man motioned with his head and the driver yanked Macklin forward by the shirt, kicking the door closed on Macklin's arm at the same time. He let out a yell as the tire iron clanged to the pavement.

"Another accident?" suggested the younger man.

"Too messy, after the one yesterday. Come on, pal, you're going to get to see your friend."

Macklin hunched over in pain. One of them jerked his bad arm up and he screamed. Over it all he felt a needle jab him high, in the armpit, and then he was falling.

The van was bumping along on the freeway when he came out of it. With his good hand he pawed his face, trying to clear his vision. His other arm didn't hurt, but it wouldn't move when he wanted it to.

He was sprawled on his back. He felt a wheel humming under him, below the tirewell. And there were the others. They were sitting up. One was Juano.

He was aware of a stink, sickeningly sweet, but with an overlay he remembered from his high school lab days but couldn't quite place. It sliced into his nostrils.

He didn't recognize the others. Pasty faces. Heads thrown forward, arms distended strangely with the wrists jutting out from the coat sleeves.

"Give me a hand," he said, not really expecting it.

He strained to sit up. He could make out the backs of two heads in the cab, on the other side of the grid.

He dropped his voice to a whisper. "Hey. Can you guys understand me?"

"Let us rest," someone said weakly.

He rose too quickly and his equilibrium failed. He had been shot up with something strong enough to knock him out, but it was probably the Dexamyl that had kept his mind from leaving his body completely. The van yawed, descending an off ramp, and he began to drift. He heard voices. They slipped in and out of his consciousness like fish in darkness, moving between his ears in blurred levels he could not always identify.

"There's still room at the cross." That was the younger, small-boned man, he was almost sure.

"Oh, I've been interested in Jesus for a long time, but I never could get a handle on him . . ."

"Well, beware the wrath to come. You really should, you know."

He put his head back and became one with a dark dream. There was something he wanted to remember. He did not want to remember it. He turned his mind to doggerel, to the old song. *The time to hesitate is through,* he thought. *No time to wallow in the mire. Try now we can only lose! And our love become a funeral pyre.* The van bumped to a halt. His head bounced off steel.

The door opened. He watched it. It seemed to take forever.

Through slitted eyes: a man in a uniform that barely fit, hobbling his way to the back of the van, supported by the two of them. A line of gasoline pumps and a sign that read WE NEVER CLOSE—NEVER UNDERSOLD. The letters breathed. Before they let go of him, the one with rumpled clothes unbuttoned the attendant's shirt and stabbed a hypodermic into the chest, close to the heart and next to a strap that ran under the arms. The needle darted and flashed dully in the wan morning light.

"This one needs a booster," said the driver, or maybe it was the other one. Their voices ran together. "Just make sure you don't give him the same stuff you gave old Juano's sweetheart there. I want them to walk in on their own hind legs." "You think I want to carry 'em?" "We've done it before, brother. Yesterday, for instance." At that Macklin let his eyelids down the rest of the way, and then he was drifting again.

The wheels drummed under him.

"How much longer?" "Soon now. Soon."

These voices weak, like a folding and unfolding of paper.

Brakes grabbed. The doors opened again. A thin light played over Macklin's lids, forcing them up.

He had another moment of clarity; they were becoming more frequent now. He blinked and felt pain. This time the van was parked between low hills. Two men in Western costumes passed by, one of them leading a horse. The driver stopped a group of figures in togas. He seemed to be asking for directions.

Behind them, a castle lay in ruins. Part of a castle. And over to the side Macklin identified a church steeple, the corner of a turn-of-the-century street, a mock-up of a rocket launching pad and an old brick schoolhouse. Under the flat sky they receded into intersections of angles and vistas which teetered almost imperceptibly, ready to topple.

The driver and the other one set a stretcher on the tailgate. On the litter was a long, crumpled shape, sheeted and encased in a plastic bag. They sloughed it inside and started to secure the doors.

"You got the pacemaker back, I hope." "Stunt director said it's in the body bag." "It better be. Or it's our ass in a sling. *Your* ass. How'd he get so racked up, anyway?" "Ran him over a cliff in a sports car. Or no, maybe this one was the head-on they staged for, you know, that new cop series. That's what they want now, realism. Good thing he's a cremation—ain't no way Kelly or Dee's gonna get this one pretty again by tomorrow." "That's why, man. That's why they picked him. Ashes don't need makeup."

The van started up.

"Going home," someone said weakly.

"Yes . . ."

Macklin was awake now. Crouching by the bag, he scanned the faces, Juano's and the others'. The eyes were staring, fixed on a point as untouchable as the thinnest of plasma membranes, and quite unreadable.

He crawled over next to the one from the self-service gas station. The shirt hung open like folds of skin. He saw the silver box strapped to the flabby chest, directly over the heart. Pacemaker? he thought wildly.

He knelt and put his ear to the box.

He heard a humming, like an electric wristwatch.

What for? To keep the blood pumping just enough so the tissues don't rigor mortis and decay? For God's sake, for how much longer?

He remembered Whitey and the nurse. "*What happens? Between the time they become 'remains' and the services? How long is that? A couple of days? Three?*"

A wave of nausea broke inside him. When he gazed at them again the faces were wavering, because his eyes were filled with tears.

"Where are we?" he asked.

"I wish you could be here," said the gas station attendant.

"And where is that?"

"We have all been here before," said another voice.

"Going home," said another.

Yes, he thought, understanding. Soon you will have your rest; soon you will no longer be objects, commodities. You will be honored and grieved for and your personhood given back, and then you will at last rest in peace. It is not for nothing that you have labored so long and so patiently. You will see, all of you. Soon.

He wanted to tell them, but he couldn't. He hoped they already knew.

The van lurched and slowed. The hand brake ratcheted.

He lay down and closed his eyes.

He heard the door creak back.

"Let's go."

The driver began to herd the bodies out. There was the sound of heavy, dragging feet, and from outside the smell of fresh-cut grass and roses.

"What about this one?" said the driver, kicking Macklin's shoe.

"Oh, he'll do his 48-hours' service, don't worry. It's called utilizing your resources."

"Tell me about it. When do we get the Indian?"

"Soon as St. John's certificates him. He's overdue. The crash was sloppy."

"This one won't be. But first Dee'll want him to talk, what he knows and who he told. Two doggers in two days is too much. Then we'll probably run him back to his car and do it. And phone it in, so St. John's gets him. Even if it's DOA. Clean as hammered shit. Grab the other end."

He felt the body bag sliding against his leg. Grunting, they hauled it out and hefted it toward—where?

He opened his eyes. He hesitated only a second, to take a deep breath.

Then he was out of the van and running.

Gravel kicked up under his feet. He heard curses and metal slamming. He just kept his head down and his legs pumping. Once he twisted around and saw a man scurrying after him. The driver paused by the mortuary building and shouted. But Macklin kept moving.

He stayed on the path as long as he dared. It led him past mossy trees and bird-stained statues. Then he jumped and cut across a carpet of matted leaves and into a glade. He passed a gate that spelled DRY LAWN CEMETERY in old iron, kept running until he spotted a break in the fence where it sloped by the edge of the grounds. He tore through huge, dusty ivy and skidded down, down. And then he was on a sidewalk.

Cars revved at a wide intersection, impatient to get to work. He heard coughing and footsteps, but it was only a bus stop at the middle of the block. The air brakes of a commuter special hissed and squealed. A clutch of grim people rose from the bench and filed aboard like sleepwalkers.

He ran for it, but the doors flapped shut and the bus roared on.

More people at the corner, stepping blindly between each other. He hurried and merged with them.

Dry cleaners, laundromat, hamburger stand, parking lot, gas station, all closed. But there was a telephone at the gas station.

He ran against the light. He sealed the booth behind him and nearly collapsed against the glass.

He rattled money into the phone, dialed Operator and called for the police.

The air was close in the booth. He smelled hair tonic. Sweat swelled out of his pores and glazed his skin. Somewhere a radio was playing.

A sergeant punched onto the line. Macklin yelled for them to come and get him. Where was he? He looked around frantically, but there were no street signs. Only a newspaper rack chained to a post. NONE OF THE DEAD HAS BEEN IDENTIFIED, read the headline.

His throat tightened, his voice racing. "None of the dead has been identified," he said, practically babbling.

Silence.

So he went ahead, pouring it out about a van and a hospital and a man in rumpled clothes who shot guys up with some kind of super-adrenalin and electric pacemakers and nightclerks and crash tests. He struggled to get it all out before it was too late. A part of him heard what he was saying and wondered if he had lost his mind.

"Who will bury them?" he cried. "What kind of monsters—"

The line clicked off.

He hung onto the phone. His eyes were swimming with sweat. He was aware of his heart and counted the beats, while the moisture from his breath condensed on the glass.

He dropped another coin into the box.

"Good morning, St. John's, may I help you?"

He couldn't remember the room number. He described the man, the accident, the date. Sixth floor, yes, that was right. He kept talking until she got it.

There was a pause. Hold.

He waited.

"Sir?"

He didn't say anything. It was as if he had no words left.

"I'm terribly sorry . . ."

He felt the blood drain from him. His fingers were cold and numb.

". . . But I'm afraid the surgery wasn't successful. The party did not recover. If you wish I'll connect you with—"

"The party's name was White Feather," he said mechanically. The receiver fell and dangled, swinging like the pendulum of a clock.

He braced his legs against the sides of the booth. After what seemed like a very long time he found himself reaching reflexively for his cigarettes. He took one from the crushed pack, straightened it and hung it on his lips.

On the other side of the frosted glass, featureless shapes lumbered by on the boulevard. He watched them for a while.

He picked up a book of matches from the floor, lit two together and held them close to the glass. The flame burned a clear spot through the moisture.

Try to set the night on fire, he thought stupidly, repeating the words until they and any others he could think of lost meaning.

The fire started to burn his fingers. He hardly felt it. He ignited the matchbook cover, too, turning it over and over. He wondered if there was anything else that would burn, anything and everything. He squeezed his eyelids together. When he opened them, he was looking down at his own clothing.

He peered out through the clear spot in the glass.

Outside, the outline fuzzy and distorted but quite unmistakable, was a blue van. It was waiting at the curb.

BY **S. G. BROWNE**

S. G. Browne *is the author of* Breathers, *a wildly popular and playful first novel about a young man's search for love, truth, meaning, and basic civil rights in a world with no place in its heart for the undead.*

Alternately sweet, sad, and snarky in tone, it may come as a surprise that Breathers *is not shy as regards matters of people-eating and sudden, violent limblessness.*

All of these qualities are sparklingly evident in "A Zombie's Lament," *the short story that inspired and provoked the novel. Reading it, it's clear why he had to write the book. And why* Breathers *has been met with such a warm and loyal following.*

So sit back and let Andy—the Holden Caulfield *of zombiedom—tell you all about how completely undeath sucks. And forgive him the misplaced notion that* George Romero*—one of film's great outsiders—is somehow part of the Hollywood system. When the connection is made, it's a true underdog revelation. And a kick-start into the emancipation to come.*

FOR THE DEAD, EVERYTHING'S PRETTY EASY. They have no responsibilities, no plans to make, no one to take care of, and no one gives them any grief—unless, of course, they end up in hell, but that opens a whole can of metaphysical worms I don't even want to begin to get into.

The *undead*, however, have more grief to deal with than southern blacks in the 1950's. Talk about civil rights issues. We can't vote, get a driver's license, or attend public schools. We're not allowed in movie theaters or any other dark, public venue where we might bite or devour a Breather. No one will hire us, we can't apply for unemployment, and we can't find a decent place to live. Even homeless shelters turn us away.

When you die, your social security number gets "retired," which isn't a problem if you stay dead. But if you come back, become a zombie due to some genetic abnormality or because you consumed too much fast food while you were alive, well then, you're pretty much screwed. Your social security number is gone and you can't get it back. And since the undead aren't considered human beings, even by Breathers who don't belong to organized religions, the chances of getting another social security number are about as good as a town in Wyoming electing a gay sheriff.

Of course, without a social security number, you can't get a job, apply for federal or state benefits, or get financial aid to go to school. And if you think your family is willing to take you in and give you shelter and return whatever inheritance you might have left, forget about it. Breathers get pretty pissed off when the dead come back.

I don't really understand it. I mean, it's not like we're any different than we were before we died. We crave security, companionship, and love. We laugh and cry and feel emotional pain. We enjoy listening to Elvis Presley and watching public television. Sure, there's the whole eating of human flesh stigma, but that's so George Romero. Outside of Hollywood, the undead typically don't eat the living—except for a growing minority of zombies who give the rest of us a bad name. After all, just because some Asians don't know how to drive doesn't mean they're all bad drivers. Okay. Bad example. But you get my point. Breathers are going to believe what they want to believe, even if they're family.

My parents weren't too happy when I showed up on their front porch, stinking of wet, worm-infested earth and formaldehyde deodorant. That's one of the biggest problems about coming back from the dead. The smell never quite goes away. I've taken dozens of showers and even soaked in a tub filled with disinfectant, but I still smell like I crawled out of a compost bin and washed my hair with ammonia.

Of course, the stench wasn't what initially set my parents off. I can't say I know what they went through, but I can imagine what it must have been like to see their thirty-two-year-old son come walking up to the front door, wearing the suit they'd buried him in. And that doesn't begin to address my physical condition. I didn't exactly die of natural causes.

I spent about a week on my parents' front porch before my dad finally came out and spoke to me, asked me what I wanted. I tried to answer, but the words came out in a croak and a screech. Apparently, my vocal cords were damaged in the accident, which would explain the stitches across my throat.

I've tried to learn sign language, but the cognitive functions just aren't there and it's kind of hard to sign with just one hand. The mortician did a good job of stitching me up, but he didn't bother fixing my left arm, which was pretty much mangled from the shoulder to the elbow. At least he managed to stitch my ear back in place.

I don't remember much about what happened after I died. I didn't see any bright light or hear any ethereal voices, but then this isn't exactly heaven, is it? I just remember the accident and then darkness, endless and close, like a membrane. The next thing I knew, I was walking along the shoulder of Old San Jose Road in the morning, wondering what day it was and where I was coming from and why my left arm didn't work. Then a pick-up truck drove past and a rotten tomato exploded against the side of my face. Two teenage kids were riding in the back of the truck. One of them had his pants around his ankles and his bare ass pointed my way while the second kid threw another tomato at me and yelled:

"Go back to your grave, you freak!"

At first I thought they were just being kids—causing mischief, raising hell, throwing rotten tomatoes at people for kicks. Denial is one of the first hurdles zombies have to overcome. Then I passed Bill's Groceries and caught a glimpse of myself in the front window. As I stood and stared at my reflection, a six-year-old girl who walked out the door dropped her frozen fudge bar when she saw me and ran off screaming.

It took me a while to come to terms with what had happened to me. What I was. I still have trouble with it. It's a big adjustment, harder than you might imagine. After all, I still have the same basic hopes and desires I had when I was alive, but now they're unattainable. I may as well wish for wings.

Some nights, I still hear my father's voice, shaky and high-pitched, as he approached me that first time on the porch.

What . . . what do you want, Andy?

To be honest, I don't know what I want. I know what I'd like—I'd like to have my life back, to be married again and sitting on the couch in the family room with my wife and daughter, watching a movie while our two cats chase each other around the house. But my wife didn't survive the accident, either, and she's still buried out in the cemetery. I don't know why I came back and she didn't. Maybe it has something to do with genetics. Or fate. Or the universe's twisted sense of humor. Whatever the reason, I miss her. Even though my heart has stopped beating, it still aches.

As if things weren't bad enough, I can't even go out to visit Sara's grave until after the cemetery closes because the mourners freak out. I understand why Breathers don't want the undead at the cemetery during the day, but I don't like having to go there at night. It's so dark and creepy. And there are sounds, things I hear that don't seem natural. I know I'm supposed to be the one everyone's afraid of, but I still get scared. Especially at night.

After the accident, my daughter went to live with my wife's sister. I think about Annie all the time—what she's up to, who her friends are, how she's doing in school. I used to call every day, hoping to hear her voice answer the phone, but then her aunt and uncle got an unlisted number and moved out of state.

As much as I'd like to visit her, I don't think it'd be a good idea, even if I knew where she lived. I don't want her to remember me this way. And I don't think she'd exactly want to take me to any father/daughter picnics. Show and tell, maybe.

Still, I wish I could see her just one more time, tell her how much I love her, how much I miss her, but I've pretty much given up any hope of that. I've pretty much given up any hope of anything. It's just not the way I envisioned spending my life, or my death, or whatever you call this. Mostly I just sit in my parents' attic, staring at the walls and out the ventilation panel, wondering what I'm going to do. I can't get a job, I can't go to school, I can't hang out at The Aptos Club or shoot pool at Fast Eddie's or visit any of the other places I used to haunt. My parents let me stay in the attic, but they avoid me, and none of my old friends want anything to do with me. Sure, there's other zombies I can hang out with—more than a dozen live in the county—but it's not the same.

After a while, I get bored, like a dog left alone in the house who starts chewing on things in frustration—shoes, couches, pillows. And like a dog, I'm starting to feel anxious and frustrated. Except I don't think I'm going to be satisfied with chewing on pillows.

I've joined a support group, the local chapter of UA—Undead Anonymous. I think we need to come up with a new name. After all, when you're undead, you're about as anonymous as a transvestite with a five o'clock shadow, but I guess I shouldn't complain. At least we don't get any support group imposters crashing our meetings, trying to pick up on vulnerable women. That would be sick. Interesting, but sick.

I've met some nice zombies in the meetings. I mean *survivors*. That's what the UA handbook says we're supposed to refer to each other and ourselves as. *Survivors*. It's supposed to make us feel better about ourselves, less estranged from society. More human. Most of us think it's just a bunch of semantic bullshit. As far as Breathers are concerned, we're no more human than dogs or cats. And we don't have the same rights as animals. Since we're dead, any crimes committed against us are misdemeanors at worst. Most of the time, they're not even considered crimes. If you've never known someone who had his arms torn out of his sockets by a gang of drunks who then slapped him repeatedly in the face with his own hands, then you probably wouldn't understand.

A few of us have been getting together outside of the group and talking about what we can do to protect ourselves. At first we stuck to the basics—

using the buddy system, having a curfew, carrying mace. Lately, however, we've been broaching issues considered taboo in the support group.

One of the members, a forty-seven-year-old truck driver named Carl, managed to get a copy of the original *Night of the Living Dead*. Rita, a twenty-two-year-old suicide victim, posed as a Breather to get a hotel room with a VCR where we could watch the movie. Bracelets and jewelry hid Rita's scars pretty well. Add sunglasses, a little make-up, a couple bottles of cheap perfume, and a horny desk clerk with bad vision, and we were good to go.

I'd never seen the film while I was alive, was never drawn to zombie or slasher fare, but I found the film fascinating. Not from a film-making standpoint—plot, story, direction, acting, all that artsy crap. I'm talking about something more spiritual, a moment of clarity, an epiphany about my own existence. And I don't think I was the only one who felt it.

I know we're not supposed to perpetuate the stereotype of the undead, or living dead, whatever you want to call us. UA preaches restraint at all times. And God knows I'm the last one who thought I'd consider doing this. I was a vegetarian, for Christ's sake. But what else am I supposed to do? When I get lonely I get bored. When I get bored, I get anxious. When I get anxious, I get frustrated. And when I get frustrated, I want to chew on things.

I just hope my parents understand.

BEST SERVED COLD

BY **JUSTINE MUSK**

If Justine Musk were a singer/songwriter, her seat at the table would likely be somewhere between Joni Mitchell and Aimee Mann. She is a meticulous observer of the human condition; her personal journey has allowed her rarified glimpses of the Powers-That-Be, behind the scenes, which she elucidates with both great discretion and power, not to mention remarkable wit.

"Best Served Cold"—written specifically for this volume—builds a wonderful bridge between old zombies and new, using issues of class and unbridled privilege to pave the way for the pettiest zombie apocalypse imaginable. Wouldn't be at all surprised if it actually happens that way.

That's why we call them cautionary tales.

LOCKING THE GIRL IN THE CLOSET SOUNDED BAD, Thad knew, but it's not like it was a cramped little coffin of a closet, or even what a typical person thought of when a typical person thought "closet:" it was a freaking room, lined with his three thousand dollar suits and five hundred dollar custom shirts, also his more casual wear, his organic cotton and denim and cashmere, also his rows on rows of Ferragamo shoes, his cowboy boots, his sneaks. There was a rack just for all his leather jackets, because a person could never have too many leather jackets, and push them aside and you'd find his built-in safe, where he kept some cash and a few prized video tapes and a stash of cocaine that would make Scarface proud.

He was taking the girl on a tour of the house, separating her from the little herd of friends she'd come with. He wasn't exactly sure when they had arrived. Navaid had sent them, knowing how reluctant Thad was to step out of the house ever since he'd walked in on a burglary, been tied up naked and thrown in the back of a car and dumped at the bottom of the hill, where he'd had to hop across the road at 2 A.M. and pound on the door of the Bel Air Security guardhouse. The delivery of attractive females was a service Navaid provided for a few select friends: he owned the club Tasty, and he would round up cute girls and put them on a shuttle bus and send them to a house in the hills for a private party. They weren't prostitutes or anything, just sweet young things from the Valley or the O.C. who wanted the buzz of being around wealth and fame—even if it was B-level fame, or notoriety, as in Thad's case. Thad did remember checking their driver's licenses before allowing them into his private residence, he had to be mindful of such things now, and besides, it was a good excuse to turn away the fat-for-LA one and the one with the sour look on her face. This girl—her name was Andrea—was an actress or model of some kind (big surprise, in this town) but had a classy look to her, which he liked, and she was a little bit more archaeological than what he usually went for, she was at least twenty-five, and he liked that too, at least once in a while.

So. Up the curving staircase and through the hall, here's the bathroom with the dark Italian marble, the Jacuzzi nestled against the corner windows overlooking the drop of Bel Air valley below—oh look at the hawk surfing the treetops, nature is so wonderful—and into the bedroom with the big platform bed right in the center heaped with zebra-print pillows—oh look at the African masks on the walls, African art is so wonderful—and then, see this amazing closet, and he guided her inside and went to his safe and chopped up some lines on the back of a framed Picasso drawing that someone, not him, had set on the center island for precisely this purpose, and then they were making out. When he had his tongue in her mouth and his hand on her breast he realized she was yielding and open and he could fuck her right here right now. Which wasn't exactly what he'd been intending but he'd been chubby and shy as a kid, the son that his father had labeled a loser, and so the fact that he was now that guy who had girls practically throwing blowjobs at him, assuming of course that a blowjob was a thing you could throw, which it wasn't, never ceased to amaze him. Not that he would admit that to anybody. But somehow it made it impossible to ever turn down the opportunity for sex, assuming the girl was even remotely attractive, because saying no to sex was all broken mirrors and black cats and the number 666. It didn't matter if it was good, or if he was good, if he was too coked up to perform the deed for long or even at all. So long as sex was on offer, all was right with the world, that horrible personal catastrophe he always sensed dangling over his head like the sword of Damocles prevented yet again from plunging down into his skull. All thanks to the magical ritualistic power of fucking.

So they were getting it on and he had just slipped his fingers inside the white lace of her panties when something tossed itself against the closet door, yipping and scrabbling, and he cursed into the girl's neck.

"What is that?" she said. Andrea, her name was Andrea, he wasn't some sleazebag who couldn't even remember a chick's name. Most of them, anyway. "Is that a dog?"

"No," he said, "it's a ferret."

"It's a ferret?"

"It's a platypus, it's an aardvark, it's one of those hairless creepy cats, of *course* it's a canine, it's the highly annoying little canine that belongs to the female personage who calls herself my girlfriend so would you hunker here for a few minutes between Mr. Gucci and Mr. Paul Smith and save us some drama? It's appreciated," and he shoved her away from him—but it was a gentle shove, more of a push, not really a push so much as a nudge—and opened the door and scooped up the barking creature with one arm and shut and locked the closet door with the other. He didn't have locks on all his doors, he wasn't paranoid, just the places where he tended to keep certain possessions that society in all its underwhelming wisdom liked to label "illegal."

Then Kimmie was in his face, taking the dog from him and nuzzling—hell, practically *chewing* on the creature's neck, "You're so yummy, I could eat you up,"—and telling him that the girl's friends were downstairs and of course they didn't know the gate code that would release them from the property. He said, "You mean they're still here?" and she said, "Where were they supposed to go?" and he had no answer for that.

As he pressed the numbers of the gate code into the device beside his front door—he refused to give his code to anybody, despite the inconvenience it tended to cause him—something struck him as wrong. He couldn't figure out what it was, but it burrowed beneath the skin of his soul—if you believed in souls, which he sort of mostly did—and remained there. "Thaddy?" Kimmie said, and she came up to him, and something she saw in his face or his body language made her wrap her arms around him. She smelled like vanilla. She was a cleancut, fresh-faced nineteen-year-old from some nothing place in one of the flyover states, where he had never been and knew he'd never go. "Thaddy, baby, what's wrong?"

"Nothing," he said. He couldn't possibly explain it. Just this empty feeling that washed over him, triggered by something—something—that he could never quite figure out but knew he would later, probably, at some point, when it would crash him low and blue all over again.

It was almost eleven am. He hadn't really slept since the night before the night before and was giving a dinner party in some number of hours. He asked Kimmie to lie down with him for a while, just to hold him, and she liked that. It made her think he had a sensitive streak somewhere deep inside him. Somewhere really really deep. He lay there on the wide slouchy leather couch in the living room, feeling the warmth of her lanky-limbed nineteen-year-old body, and he waited to feel okay again. His eyes wide, his mind racing.

At one point she said, "Do you want to talk about it?"

She meant the thing that had happened to him. The incident. The burglary. The tied-up naked romp along the bottom of Bel Air Road.

He felt again the cold steel press of the barrel at his temple, the rasp of the rope around his wrists and ankles. "No," he said.

Somehow time passed. The drycleaning came—his gray Paul Smith suit—which reminded him that a shower and change of clothes was in order. Why not wear the suit? He kept on his rumpled white t-shirt, his Converse sneakers. For that decadent, cracked-out look. Something was nagging at him. Something he'd forgotten about, but Thad was used to forgetting things, he did it all the time. Kimmie went away and came back again, the little dog dancing at her heels. The chef arrived, the servers, one of them so good-looking he could be a male model in an underwear ad, proving once again that some of the most beautiful people in this town were serving the food and drink. The house filled with the smell of roasting flesh. Something was still nagging at him, but he took some business calls and did more lines and the underwear model put a glass of Opus One in his hand. Then his guests arrived.

Conversation buzzed. The fresh human presences streaming through the door made him feel better, more relaxed, or at least as relaxed as it was possible for him to be. It was a good mix, he thought. The Hollywood types you would expect—an agent, an independent film producer—but there was also some kind of Internet dude. Rayne Betancourt was there, the socialite who'd gotten famous for being best friends with a socialite famous for being famous. The camera crew from her reality show—*When It Raynes It Pours*—came up behind her, like faithful Sherpas, and everybody pretended to ignore them while greeting Rayne with extra doses of enthusiasm to get the cameras swinging in their direction. There were a couple of wives or girlfriends, whose names nobody would remember (except Thad) and who would spend the evening chatting quietly with each other or listening to the men. And Z was there. His real name was Zachariah Fields, and he'd been composing and producing music for longer than Thad was alive. He was so famous he rarely ventured out of his house. The world came to him, usually in a limousine or town car. He was Thad's neighbor, or, more accurately, several of Thad's neighbors, since he owned three of the five properties on the gated Bel Air cul-de-sac in which

Thad had been living for close to six years now. "Baby," Z said, in his booming, throaty voice, "hey baby," and he pulled Thad into his trademark bear hug, both men competing to see who could slap backs the hardest.

Kimmie went in and out of his vision, the little dog at her heels, hard to say which of them was cuter. "The chef," she reported, "is looking kind of greenish. You think he might be sick? Should he be, like, handling our food and stuff?"

"What?"

"The chef."

"Who?"

"The chef."

"Stop talking to me," Thad said, and wandered into the bathroom. He did another bump off the glass of a handheld mirror and wandered back out.

And then suddenly they were at the table, a grand oak affair that had been especially designed for Thad's dining room. A raised planter ran down the center and sprouted grass. It was the one act by his interior designer that Thad tended to seriously question. The guests peered at each other over the little green stalks. Thad heard himself talking and his guests laughing appreciatively and then suddenly they were halfway through the fish dish. The fish was dry, which struck Thad as pretty damn careless for a chef this expensive, this new chef he was trying out for the first time because someone had recommended the chef to someone who had recommended the chef to Thad, but no one seemed to really mind about the fish and Thad didn't have much appetite anyway.

He realized that Rayne was talking to him. Apparently she had asked him a question because she seemed to be expecting an answer. Then a crew member stepped up to Rayne and whispered in her ear. Rayne stood, and there was some happy male ogling as she and the crewperson fiddled with the mike pack taped above the low rise of her jeans. Then Rayne sat down and said, as if she was saying it for the first time, which Thad suspected she was not, "You and Sabine are friends now, right?"

"You know Sabine?" someone said.

Sabine was one of his ex-girlfriends.

"Not really." Rayne waved a hand. "But we move in some of the same circles."

"The beautiful people circles," someone said.

"Those are small circles."

"Unfortunately so."

Sabine. with the flowing red hair that had first caught Thad's eye, because he hadn't done a redhead in a long time, and the sharp green eyes that had become maybe a little too sharp for his liking. Sabine, with her cultivated air of mystery and all those charms and amulets and shit. There was this thing that had happened, this incident concerning a certain video that had somehow found its way onto the web, a video featuring Sabine in rather a range of compromising positions, and she appeared to be less than happy about this. She also appeared to blame Thad.

Thad said, "Friend? How would you define 'friend'? If you define 'friend' as somebody with whom you generate consistent mutual positive regard then I would say 'no.'" This sounded somewhat more polite than: I *hate that bitch.* "I would definitely say no. No. So in other words—no."

"She said she sent you something. Special delivery."

Which is when he remembered the girl in his closet.

"Shit," he half-hollered, and pushed back his chair.

"Thaddy?"

"Right back!" he yelled over his shoulder. "Don't go anywhere!"

He took the stairs two at a time. What had he been thinking? No, what had that *girl* been thinking, and why the hell hadn't she done anything—screamed, pounded, thrown shoes at the door—to attract his attention to the fact that she had been locked in the fucking closet for hours and hours? What kind of idiot was she, and more importantly, was she going to sue him? Did she have legitimate cause? He made a mental note to ask his lawyer.

But as he wound through his darkened bedroom to the closet these initial questions subsided as another rose up to replace them: Was she okay? Could she have O.D.'d—not on anything he'd given her, of course not—but something she maybe took before she got to his house, maybe Navaid had given her? He cursed Navaid. He would have to speak to Navaid.

Because how would that look, if there was a dead girl in his—

He yanked open the door.

Silence.

Shadows.

His shirts and pants, his jackets, his shoes, formed vague jumbled shapes in the near-darkness.

He heard, then, a soft scrape, a rustle from the far corner.

Heard an intake of breath, then a low grunting exhale.

She was alive. Thank Christ.

"You're alive!" he yelped. "Thank Christ!"

He actually felt weak in the knees.

Except wait.

Should her breathing sound quite so . . . quite so . . . bubbly? Like she was dragging air through her own . . . through . . . was "blood" the word he wanted? No. Not. Surely not. And why, exactly, was he continuing to stand in the goddamn dark? What was wrong with him—besides that he hadn't slept in days, was sort of afraid to leave his own house since the whole burglary incident less than a month ago, and the drugs?

He reached for the wall switch.

She was on the floor by his wool-and-cashmere overcoat—a shame he could rarely wear that in LA, *such* a gorgeous coat—her miniskirt hiked up her thighs, her legs splayed across the carpet in a way that seemed . . . uncomfortable. Her head was hanging down, long blonde hair falling over her face.

And again, that breathing: the long, bubbling inhale, the thick grunting exhale.

He said, "Uh, sweetie? Sweetheart? You okay there?"

He noticed her hands clawing at the carpet: the fingers rigid, the skin an odd, marbled white.

"I'm . . ." Thad said.

She lifted her head.

". . . sorry about this," Thad muttered.

Through the lanks of tangled hair, he could see her eyes. The gaping whites of her eyes. Her face was contorted, her lipstick-smeared lips pulled in a weird rictus grin.

She was whispering something, as she began to drag herself toward him.

"Nice . . . nice girl," Thad said. "Good little girl."

She wasn't whispering actual words. It was gibberish, like she was speaking in tongues or something. He wished at the very least that she would shut up. This wasn't really happening to him. He'd had much the same feeling when he'd walked in on the burglary. There'd been a moment when he could have bolted back out through the front door, except everything had gone flat and surreal, like he'd been dropped into a television show. Except it hadn't been a show, any more than this was, and the knowledge busted through him just as the girl got on her hands and knees and seemed to be gathering herself, pulling in that ragged, bubbling breath, and he saw the discoloration in her cheeks and throat and cleavage and realized she was rotting, that the smell in the closet was the smell of rotting flesh.

She launched herself at him, head down, blonde hair flying.

Thad stepped back. He shut the door just as her face came so close he could see the pupils roiling in the great dead white of her eyes.

There was a heavy thumping sound as she slammed against the door and again as she dropped to the ground.

Thad stood there.

He listened.

Nothing. No sound.

He opened the door just a crack and peered inside. Saw the girl's limp form on the floor. She wasn't whispering anything anymore. He might have thought she was dead, except for the wretched thing that was her breathing. Before he could think about what he was doing, he leaped over her. Two strides and he was at his safe, hands shaking as he worked out the combination, then he was grabbing the vials, the bag of cocaine, shoving them in the pockets of his jacket. Then he was vaulting over the girl, and did he maybe feel her fingers brush his pant leg, hear again that hoarse senseless whisper or was it his imagination, as if it even mattered, just shut the door and backpedal, stumbling, watching the door, as if she was about to tear through it like the Terminator or something.

Thad sat down on the bed. He did some thinking. He did more coke. He did more thinking. Then he went back downstairs.

It seemed best to give it to them straight.

"There's a zombie in my closet," Thad said.

He picked up the linen napkin and unfolded it across his lap.

His guests were looking at him. The grass was sticking up along the center length of the dining room table. He really needed to talk to his interior designer about that. Fucking grass. His guests were still looking at him. He felt the need to keep on talking. "This girl, she's been in my closet for many hours," he babbled, "and I just went upstairs to let her out, right, except she was on the floor in this really weird position and she looked up at me like this—" He contorted his own face to demonstrate. "—and then she came at me like this—" He got out of his chair to show them, then sat down again and picked up his napkin from where it had fallen on the floor. "—and I realized that somehow between the time she got locked in there and now, she turned into this *really annoying* zombie. Anybody have any thoughts on this?"

He looked around the table.

Eyes met his for the briefest moments before sliding away. There was a silence, interrupted only by the shuffling of one of the servers and the sliding of ice in the pitcher as he went around refilling water glasses. He missed his aim with one, water splashing and dripping off the edge of the table, but no one except Thad seemed to notice. There was a loud thunk as a camera man dropped his camera. He picked it up with a sheepish grin on his face. It was a strange kind of grin, Thad thought. Kind of frozen.

"Baby," said Z, his voice booming the length of the room. He slapped his hands together. "A zombie! That's wonderful!"

"It isn't," Thad said. "It really isn't."

"You always surprise me, Thad," Z went on. "I said to myself—didn't I, honey—" turning to the raven-haired woman next to him "—I said to myself, 'What surprises will Thad have in store for us tonight?' There's always something! Usually it's some little honey slashing your tires or throwing wine in your face, but this—this is priceless."

"I'm not joking," Thad said. "There is a zombie in my closet."

Another silence.

His guests looked at him, looked at each other, looked at him again.

"Thad," Kimmie said tentatively, "are you okay? You've been under so much stress and—you're still recovering from the, from the, you know, the incident—and you've been partying kind of hard, and—"

"Zombie!" Thad said, and slammed his fist on the table. Silverware jumped and clattered.

He became aware of the server maneuvering behind him. It was the underwear model. One long thin arm extended with the water pitcher, and Thad noticed the red paper wristband. It had *Tasty* printed all over it. It was one of those VIP things that Navaid gave out at his club. Thad also noticed the bluish-white tinge to the skin, and the way it seemed to just drape off the bone. He rocked back in his chair and glanced up at the man. The server's eyes seemed dull, but that could be from the banality of the task at hand, or maybe his customary expression. Still, Thad could feel his mind struggling to make a connection, one he felt he should probably share with his guests.

But voices were floating around the table, distracting him. ". . . if there really is a girl, and she's sick or something, maybe we should get her to a doctor."

"She doesn't need a doctor," Thad said. "She would eat the doctor."

"Thaddy, why is there a girl in your closet?"

"Zombies aren't sexy like vampires. Would you ever want to fuck a zombie?"

"Of course not. Zombies are the walking undead."

"But so are vampires."

"Actually," said the agent, who tended to be a bit of a know-it-all, "real zombies don't technically qualify as the undead. What appears to be death is actually a brief coma. They seem to be rising from the dead—'reanimating' if you will—when really they're only waking up."

"I thought it was some kind of voodoo thing. Haitian zombie powder."

"Like protein powder. Only not."

"Thaddy, why is there a girl in your closet?"

"That was the old zombie," the agent's boyfriend, who was a manager, informed them. He sipped his wine. "Now there's the new zombie."

"I get it. Like the old face. But now there's the new face."

"And by the time I'm old enough to need it, we'll have the new new face."

"They'd better hurry up. You're almost twenty-eight. Sweetie, don't throw the bread at me. I said don't throw—"

"There's this absolutely fabulous urban legend going around—one of my writers and I jumped all over it, fleshed out a treatment that sold to Warner just this morning—"

There were murmured congratulations, a few of which might have been sincere.

"—about a drug. It was supposed to be this new fabulous club drug, right, keep you up all night, keep you moving. Like Ecstasy, only better—"

"I never got the whole E thing. Coke is so much better."

"It's a generational thing."

"Thaddy—?"

"It is not a generational thing! Everybody does coke!"

"I never do coke."

"You're such a liar. That's one of the two big lies that women at the clubs will always tell you. 'I never do coke.'"

"What's the other one?"

"It—"

"It's like cocaine invents other people just for you, so you can go to their parties and talk about yourself."

"Some genius was developing it in his parents' basement in Palo Alto—"

"I lived in Palo Alto during the dot com boom. God, the parking. You could never find parking. And then I could never remember *where* I parked, so I'd end up wandering the streets, like some homeless, carless person."

"Or a pedestrian."

"Only what he came up with instead was this substance that had some highly questionable side effects—"

"Thaddy—?"

"Once it gets into your blood it acts like a virus, a kind of flesh-eating virus," the manager said, "that infects your skin, your muscles and your brain. It is also contagious. You understand? You can slip this thing to someone—"

"Zombie roofie!"

"—infect them, and then watch that infection spread in a very short time."

"My kid's birthday party is going to have a zombie theme."

"You want to turn your kids into zombies?"

"No. I said a zombie *theme*."

"I want to turn his kids into zombies."

"Thaddy, honey—?"

"But he thought hey, I've got this thing, maybe I can sell it to the military. You know, for biological warfare or something—"

"It's like the swine flu. Only not."

"So he goes to a friend of the family for advice, and the friend knows someone who knows someone, and so to make a long story short this drug ends up in the hands of a profoundly well-heeled, connected and . . . esoteric . . . few—"

"Thad—"

"At least it wasn't the Scientologists."

"Or the gay mafia."

"I *like* the gay mafia."

"—who start experimenting with it for their own personal use. And that," the manager said triumphantly, "is where our screenplay begins."

"You're saying this is an urban legend? 'Cause that is news to me—"

"It's just starting to get passed around. Actors, mostly. You know how *they* are. But like I said, we jumped on it."

"How much did the treatment sell for?"

"A lot," the agent said, and he and his boyfriend exchanged smug little smiles.

A pounding from upstairs.

Repeated thumps so strong and loud that Thad imagined he could hear—or maybe he actually could, his senses seemed so heightened—the closet door rattling in its frame.

"That's her," he said. "I guess she wants out."

Thad arranged two lines of cocaine beside his plate, lowered his nostrils and hoovered it all off the tablecloth. As the pounding sounded again, he sniffed and rubbed his nose and tipped his head back. He blinked repeatedly. The light from the chandelier was rather dazzling.

". . . don' t know what's going on," someone was muttering, "but somebody should maybe do something."

"Oh, hell, I'll do it," Thad said. He got up, misjudging the distance between chair and table, and banged his knee. "I'm the host. It falls to me."

"Thaddy? Why is there a girl in your closet?"

He loped up the stairs, ducked into the bathroom and shut the door. He dug his cell phone from his pocket. *Why is there a girl in your closet?* Why, indeed? It seemed to Thad an excellent question. Before that girl, Andrea, had somehow gotten herself into the closet, she had gotten herself into his house, and how exactly had that transpired? *Special delivery.*

He called Sabine's number. He was good with girls' numbers, just like he was good with their names. Most of them, anyway.

He got voicemail. He left a message that he thought was admirably succinct. He put some cocaine on the edge of his credit card, lifted it to his nostrils, snorted. Which was when he noticed the silence.

The pounding had stopped.

Footsteps in the hall beyond the bathroom door.

Shuffling, dragging footsteps.

Thad was no idiot. He knew who *that* was.

And it occurred to Thad that possibly, very possibly, in his rush to get away from the zombie girl—and possibly to do another line of coke—he had forgotten to lock the closet door.

He said, "Oh shit."

He considered the situation.

Tried to consider the situation. He was aware that the level of his thinking was not at its finest. In fact, it seemed to be getting fuzzier by the minute. He *felt* surprisingly good, though. Strong. Invincible. And a little hungry. Although his knee hurt from where he'd banged it against the coffee table. He hitched up his pant leg. The bruise was bigger than he would have expected, a splotch of blue-black spreading just beneath his kneecap. But he had to focus. The problem was not the bruise on his leg. The problem was the zombie currently on its way downstairs to greet his dinner guests.

And yet.

He was still sharp enough to know what he was *not* hearing.

He was *not* hearing screams and sounds of mayhem.

Somehow another minute passed. Then he splashed water on his face. He examined his bloodshot eyes in the mirror. He wasn't maybe *looking* all that great. Who could blame him, there was a fucking *zombie* in his house.

Except . . .

From downstairs, he heard conversation, even laughter.

Was it possible he'd gotten it wrong? Maybe the zombie stuff was all in his head? Or someone was playing a joke? Or it was a stunt they were pulling for Rayne's reality show, because Rayne's tits just weren't entertaining enough?

Determined to get to the bottom of this, Thad stalked out of the bathroom and returned to the dining room.

"Where is it?" he demanded. "Did a zombie pass by here?"

"Thad," Kimmie said gently, "sit down. Take it easy."

She came up beside him, took his arm and tugged him toward his chair. He shook her off. "The zombie," he said again. "Where is it?"

"Thaddy! There's just some girl who's, like, really sick, and seriously about to upchuck, and you are *embarrassing* me." Her voice was a hiss. "Why was she in your closet, Thad?"

"Ashley and Jessica took her into the bathroom," Z announced. "Jesus lord in heaven, Thad my man, what did you *do* to that little honey?"

Thad pulled in breath and tipped his head back. He addressed the ceiling. "She's a fucking zombie."

"Sit," Kimmie snapped, and her voice was so authoritative, so unlike her usual kitten self, that Thad found himself abruptly sitting.

It appeared that dessert had been served. It was molten chocolate cake. The hunger stirred again, deep inside him, sending a strange rippling sensation through his gut and groin. His guests were talking, maybe they were even talking to him, but their words had turned into a strange kind of gibberish. His entire being was focused on the cake. Attuned to the cake. He was one with the cake. He picked up his fork, and dropped it, and picked it up again. A little hard to hold this fork in his fingers, something was obviously wrong with it, he'd have to speak to somebody about that, but in the meantime he could manage. He sent the edge of the fork slicing down through the dessert and dark viscous liquid oozed over the cake and pooled onto the plate. Voices moved up and down the table and got a little louder, a little agitated. Someone might have given a little shriek, Thad wasn't entirely sure, he was so intent on the sauce in his mouth, the thick salty satisfaction of it. It wasn't like any chocolate sauce he'd ever had, there was a coppery aftertaste to it, but it was . . . *good.*

The cake, too, had a kind of . . . meatiness . . . to it, but it was also . . . *good.* He ate all the cake and lifted the plate and licked off all the sauce. He noticed the sauce on his fingers and hands and licked that off too. The hunger churned and boiled inside him. It seemed to have deepened. The cake was not enough to satisfy. He wanted more.

"Thad."

More.

Kimmie's face swam in front of him. There was a trembling in her voice. "Is this a joke?"

"What?"

"The cake," she said.

"What?"

"The cake," she was yelling now, "the cake, the cake! Is this a joke?"

His gaze shifted beyond her to the other faces at the table. But they had all gone kind of blurred, were overlapping with one another, he could no longer pick them apart and didn't care. He felt a vibrating in his pocket. His cell.

"Stop talking to me," he said to Kimmie. His tongue felt like a dead fish inside his mouth, but the words were clear enough. "Excuse me," he said to the blurred, meaty-smelling mass that ranged around the table, "I need to take this."

Raised chatter behind him. He tuned it out, because for some reason it was taking an unusual amount of concentration just to put one foot in front of the other. He didn't think he could manage the stairs so he headed for the study at the back. On the way he passed a bathroom. There were sounds from inside. Now these sounds, unlike the babble at the table, were interesting to him. They were wet, crunching, ripping sounds. He flung his hand against the door and when no one answered he said, "Hello?" The door wasn't locked. He pushed it a little bit open and peered inside.

The zombie girl was crouched on the floor. Bits of gray matter clung to her lips. There was blood on her chin and her clothes and the floor and the walls. Sprawled in front of her were two of his female guests. He couldn't put names to them because the faces were mutilated beyond recognition. The zombie girl reached for one of the bodies and appeared to be doing something to the spinal cord. Then she lifted her head and looked toward Thad. She was chewing loudly.

Thad closed the door.

He went into the study. He pressed the phone to his ear.

"I want to make sure I understand this," Sabine was saying. "You think I sent you some kind of . . . clubgirl zombie?"

"I think . . ." Fighting to form his mouth around the words. "I think . . . I just want to know." Indeed, his only reason at this point seemed to be sheer curiosity. Maybe because he was so tired. He could hear—and it see be coming from very far away—some kind of ruckus coming from th tion of the dining room. "Just want to know," Thad said again. It came wannaknow. "Yes or no?" Yezzzorno?

Sabine was laughing. The sound hurt his eardrums. He held th away from his head, waited a moment, pressed it back to his ear. She laughing, but now there was a wild, hysterical ring to it.

"I didn't send you the girl. I sent you the chef."

"The chef," he said blankly.

"And the servers. And Rayne's new camera crew. I did not send you that girl. She got infected all on her own. You got her all on your own. Fuck it, I should have known it would turn out like this! You're soooo predictable."

He had nothing to say.

"But you know what this means, Thad? *It means it's spreading.* That was not supposed to happen. That was not in the *plan*, okay? This could be the end of the fucking world, *and all because you're an asshole.*"

Thad tried to say, "I'm not the one who—" but his mouth couldn't do it, and then she hung up the phone.

Elsewhere in the house, someone was screaming. He heard pounding footsteps, thumping, more screaming. Something crashed and splintered. A dog was yipping right outside his door, then there was a kind of squashing sound and the dog wasn't barking anymore. He was so tired. A man was yelling, his voice starting out low and spiraling up through the octaves into some unrecognizable high-pitched keening and then he, too, wasn't barking anymore. Thad thought he should probably take a nap. The cacophony outside the door was only growing, getting on his nerves, so he turned on the stereo and turned up the volume. Hits from the '80s. Duran Duran was singing about girls on film.

He lay down on the floor, the white shag rug, and closed his eyes.

As he drifted off he thought again of the girl. Andrea. He remembered, now, what had bothered him when he let her so-called friends out of the house: none of them had asked after her. They had abandoned her to him, a stranger with a notorious reputation, the date-rape scandals, the thing with the underage girl. Maybe they had noticed something wrong with her. Maybe she had creeped them out. Maybe they had known her for all of three hours. But it didn't seem like the right thing to do. It was an unusual thought for him to have. It seemed connected somehow to his memory of being locked inside the foul-smelling trunk of the car, bound and gagged and convinced he was about to die alone, with no one who would remember him for long, or care. The thought flickered like a candle flame and went out. And now he was back in the closet with the girl, breath mint taste of her mouth and tongue, the faint tang of tequila, and the cigarette smoke in her hair. And maybe there had been something strange about her, the limp, sluggish weight of her, but he hadn't paid much attention at the time. What he had noticed was the feel of the breast in his hand, the firmness of her thighs, the roundness of that ass, and it was all melting into the others, so many others, sweet young yummy flesh, the warmth and musk and tenderness that he believed could somehow save him, sucking it all up between his teeth, bodies writhing and opening beneath him, and he plunged inside one after the other after the other, and somehow it wasn't enough, not yet, he needed more, he was digging himself into their flesh, he was opening them up, he was cracking their bones to get at their marrow. He was burying himself alive in blood and meat and bone and hungry, so hungry, so hungry—

He opened his eyes.

The world had gone all jittery. Shapes and colors came in at him at weird angles. But he could smell the spilled blood and chunks of meat scattered through the rest of the house and that was all the direction he needed. He stood up. He took a moment to orient himself as best he could.

Then shambled out to see what the others had left it.

PART TWO:

POST EMANCIPATION

80
100
60
MPH
120
40
140
20
160
0
180
15118962

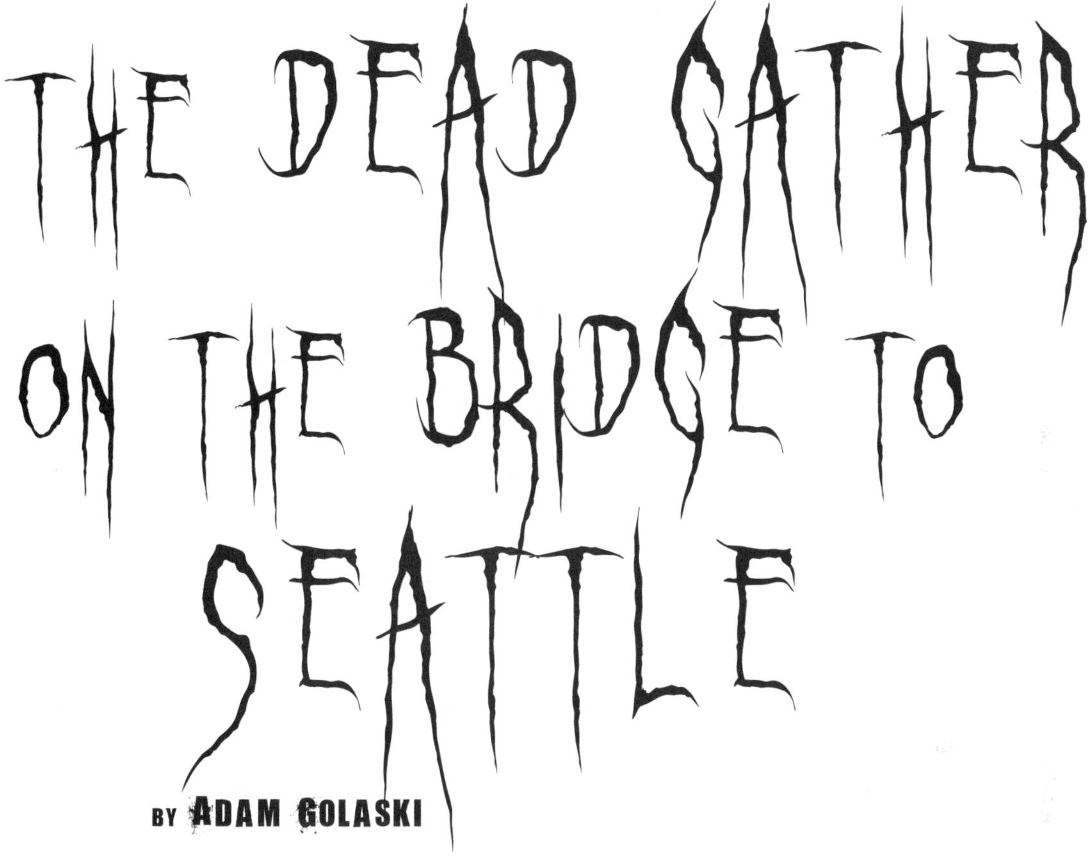

THE DEAD GATHER ON THE BRIDGE TO SEATTLE

BY ADAM GOLASKI

Adam Golaski is the only author in this book I had never heard of before, though his work in the small press—as editor of New Genre *magazine, and publisher of* Film Forum Press*—make him less unknown than I'd originally thought. (He refers to himself to teetering on the cusp of "slightly known.")*

That said: this is the one story in the book that came out of seeming nowhere and blew me away with its stark, frightening voice and unsettlingly original take on "our hero": the guy you're inclined to be rooting for.

If there's one thing I know, it's a great zombie story.

I suspect that George Romero would be proud.

THE RACCOON WASN'T EATING GARBAGE—the can hadn't been knocked over—it was eating another raccoon. From across the yard, Roger could see that the raccoon's little mouth glimmered with gore. Roger unlocked the trunk of his car, unzipped a narrow case and removed a shotgun. He looked for the raccoon with his flashlight—it was no longer standing above its cannibalized mate. He jumped when the light fell on the raccoon—large as a dog and shambling toward him. Roger called out, once, a single profanity eaten up by the surrounding woods. The raccoon wasn't startled, didn't draw back or run as any raccoon would when confronted by a man. Roger cursed again and shot the raccoon. It burst open, as if rotten.

The phone in Roger's mobile home rang.

Roger dashed up the back step into the kitchen where he'd left the portable. He glanced at the wall clock—a little past eleven—then at the caller I.D.—his sister Vivienne. "Viv," he said. "Oh, hello, Martin," he said. "Is everything all right?" he asked. He said, "Fine. Martin, what's this about?" Roger set the shotgun down on the kitchen table. He picked up a pizza crust left from his dinner. He took a bite. "She's sick?" He tossed the crust down. "How long have you been at the hospital?" The light above the table dimmed. "I don't know what I can do." Roger pushed the kitchen door shut. "It's fifteen hours," he said. "She asked?" Roger looked again at the wall clock. "I'll leave in a few hours." "No? OK. I'll be on the road in an hour. Still, I won't be there until tomorrow evening." "Five o'clock. I'll call from the road." "Yes," Roger said, "I'll call."

Roger stared at the shotgun on the table; he let his eyes un-focus over the dull gleam it gave. He thought about the raccoon, and of how sick it must have been, and of how it sickened him. He tried to recall what had woken him. The phone wasn't what'd woken him, neither the raccoon—he was surely accustomed to the noise animals made during the night. The prospect of the drive did not appeal to him, but for Vivienne to ask him to make the trip, all the way from Decker, from Montana to Washington, to Seattle, was extraordinary.

With the cell phone he'd been given by his employer, he called Peter and asked him to cover his route. Peter said he was feeling ill and didn't think he could do it; Roger pressed and Peter agreed. Roger said, "I'll leave the keys to the truck and the freezers on the driver's seat." Roger went out, carrying his shotgun and a ring of keys. He returned the shotgun to the case in the trunk of his car. He checked the freezers—three freestanding units. He unlocked the generator shed and topped off the fuel. He added gas to the truck's tank, too, and placed the keys on the driver's seat. After he'd shut the door to the cab, he reopened the door and took the key for the padlocked generator shed off the ring. The time was just before midnight. He set his alarm clock for one AM, and lay down.

Roger slept, but hardly.

He called his boss: "I won't be able to make the deliveries this morning," he said.

His boss said, "You can't call in sick."

"Peter's covering the route."

"Pete's only been out with you once or twice. You can't have the morning off."

"Don't hand me that, Harry. You can help Peter if he gets lost."

"You can't just call in like this."

"Harry, I haven't taken a day off in the two years I've worked for you. I've covered for everyone, I've even covered for you. Peter will do the route. He'll do it tomorrow too. I'll pay him out of my check so don't worry about payroll."

"Okay, okay. What's this about, anyhow?"

"Personal."

"Are you all right?"

"I'm okay."

"Is there anything I can do?"

"No, but thanks. I have to go."

The sky brimmed with stars. A shooting star, another. A bright, raspberry cloud of light flickered in the sky. Roger squinted at the cloud, perplexed by the sight—not Northern Lights, he didn't think. An animal moved behind the trees that bordered Roger's yard.

Roger filled a thermos with coffee. He hadn't been away since he'd first moved out to Decker. He locked the windows and behind himself the front door. The leaves of the big cottonwood rustled; a sound like a brook. Stars fell, one after another: a shower. Roger had never seen a shower so full, and would've stopped to watch, had he the time. The grass and the trees were black. The car turned over smoothly; the gas tank was full, the oil clean, tire pressure good. Roger kept his car neat. On the passenger seat were a handful of CDs, all gifts from Vivienne. Vivienne was the only family who kept in touch with Roger since his move. He drove off his property, onto the dirt road that began his daily delivery route. In an hour, Roger would be on the highway, headed away from his customers, away from Decker. With enough coffee, he thought, and some No Doze he'd buy at the gas station in Lodge Grass, he might not have to sleep.

Roger's car was all he'd kept from his former life. The car didn't belong in Decker, and he rarely drove it, a black Saab sedan, a forty-thousand dollar car purchased when forty-thousand wasn't a whole lot of money for Roger to spend on a car or on anything else. When he left San Francisco, he decided to keep the car because it was solid. A powerful engine, four-wheel drive, and black.

The roof of his car reflected the stars. Roger picked up 314.

Spread out, sixty miles north, a little south of the Yellowstone River, were the foundations of fur trading posts. Crumbled dust foundations. To the west of Custer is Junction, which was no more a town but a graveyard, left to its own except for dinosaur bones. Buffalo grazed the plains. Roger drove through the Wolf Mountains with his stereo off. What was dead in those mountains lay still; the wolves ate their kill. Long stretches of 314 were unpaved. Roger's high beams bounced and blurred ahead of his car. Rodents scurried to the sides of the road. He drove as fast as the road permitted, steering wheel firmly gripped as the irregular road wrenched the car right and left, toward black trees and boulders. The Rosebud battlefield, the little rivers.

Lodge Grass, *greasy grass*, the first full-service gas station on Roger's route. The needle still at full, Roger topped off the gas. Two truckers stood mesmerized by the meteor shower, ball caps tilted back on their foreheads. Roger bought No Doze and poured water into a little cone. The clerk said, "There's stars falling all over the North. The radio says it's something special." Roger nodded, waited for the clerk to count his change. As Roger broke open the box of No Doze, a news item caught his attention: a man presumed dead, and in that state for some hours, was revived. A good omen, Roger thought. At the gas station, Roger had a brief window of cell phone reception, so he dialed Martin.

"I'm on the road," Roger said. "I'm calling so you'll have my cell number." Roger said, "I should go," but before he ended the call he asked, "How's Vivienne?" Bad, was the answer. "Do the doctors know what it is?" Roger asked. Only that it's an infection.

From Lodge Grass: Rt. 90 all the way to Seattle. The highway was empty. Roger kept his high beams on and an eye out for deer and bighorn sheep, apt to simply *be* in the road. Roger watched for their eyes. He passed Garryowen, Crow Agency, and Hardin. Billings would soon emerge as a cluster of light. South of Billings, opposite Boothill Cemetery, near The Place of Skulls, was Sacrifice Cliff, where two Crow rode on the back of a single white horse, a horse blindfolded so it could be made to ride off a cliff. Two young Crow returned from a hunt to find their tribe dead by smallpox. They mourned, singing, yelling, clutching one another on the back of a blindfolded white horse. *The place where the white horse went down.* A blind horse, snuffing, kicking dust, led by two anguished Crow off the edge of a cliff.

The city of Billings was electric lights and dark industrial shapes, all set in a cup of mountains and rim rocks. The traffic around Roger grew heavier. Trucks, mostly. Roger wanted a real breakfast, but knew he couldn't spare the time. He'd stop in Billings, though, relieve himself and buy an egg and sausage sandwich from a gas station.

All along the highway were parked cars. People had driven out of Billings to get a better look at the star shower, still in full. The sky carried an aura, a hint of color, a haze of red.

When Roger moved to San Francisco, five years before, Vivienne came with. The realtor who sold Roger his home assumed Vivienne was Roger's girlfriend, and was visibly relieved when Roger corrected her: "She's my little sister." Vivienne's room in Roger's house—the guest room—was small but sunny and featured floor-to-ceiling, built-in bookcases. Vivienne bought books with Roger's money and quickly filled those shelves. Roger's room was large and always felt empty, except on the nights when Vivienne, afraid or drunk or sad would sleep in Roger's room, curled into the green leather chair set beside the fireplace.

Roger exited the highway for the first gas station he saw with its lights on and topped off the Saab's tank. He liked the needle at full. He washed the car's windows and lights. He borrowed a key for the restroom in back, where he washed his hands and face as well as he could with the soap-grit provided. The paper towel dispenser was empty, so he dried himself with his un-tucked shirt. Inside the mart he found a sausage sandwich, which he heated in the microwave and ate while he picked up a glass jar of peanuts, several tall bottles of water, and two apple juices. The clock above the microwave read 2:17. He added elk jerky and crackers to his purchases.

Outside, a man stood by the pumps, lit by fluorescent bulbs peppered with moths and flies. He leaned over and removed the cap from a bright red gas can—Roger heard the ping of a spring-release. A star fell, died behind the mountains; the star shower was over. Another man, wearing a John Deere cap, emerged from shadow, from behind the last pump. Something in the way he walked—the angle at which he held his head—struck Roger as off. Roger put his groceries down on the roof of his car and took a step toward the pumps. The man with the gas can, bent over, pumping gas, touched the bill of his hat, acknowledging Roger. Roger nodded, took another step toward the pumps. John Deere moved like a man short on sleep, someone just up from the thick of a dream.

"Evening," Roger said to the man with the gas can, but with an eye on John Deere.

The man with the gas can released the pump trigger, stood and replied, "Morning, more like it." The man with the gas can then heard what Roger heard, a sickly sound, a rale, something unhealthy between breath.

John Deere fell upon the man with the gas can. Roger ran toward the two men; the man with the gas can yelled out in pain; Roger hit John Deere hard with his shoulder. John Deere's head hit hard against a pump, then hit the ground with a sound like a soggy sponge thrown against a tile floor. The man with the gas can started to complain—"son of a bitch bit"—but stopped when he got a look at John Deere.

The side of John Deere's head had collapsed, as if the skull was ceramic, as if there had been nothing inside—but, splattered against the pump was blood and tissue, a shivering jelly.

The man with the gas can vomited. Roger watched: The man wasn't vomiting because of the gross corpse; he was sick, abruptly, violently ill. The man said, gasping and bewildered, "He bit me," and held out his arm. Roger jogged to the gas mart, opened the door and shouted to the clerk, "There's a man sick out there." The clerk glanced at one of the monitors behind the counter—two men, and both looked to be in bad shape. The clerk couldn't quite comprehend what he was seeing and began to ask, but Roger was gone. He wouldn't wait anymore. He didn't have time to get involved. He put his groceries on the passenger seat of his car and drove. Without the stars flashing across the sky, the night was very dark indeed.

Roger drove out of Billings. Though the star shower was over, cars were still parked alongside the highway. A pickup with its doors open wide offered a glimpse of a woman awkwardly asleep on the front seat. People wandered on the median: the headlights of stationary cars lit up men and women who appeared lost—at least, uncertain. Strange sights.

A car pulled onto the highway toward Billings. With his rear-view mirror, Roger watched the car drift from lane to lane. Perhaps a few six packs brought along for star gazing. Or sick. Roger let his mind go to worry: his sister had once been quite needy, but since Roger had left, she'd pulled herself together. To ask Roger to come and see her, well, she must really be sick. Roger put this out of his mind.

He considered the possibility that the police would connect Roger with the incident at the Billings gas station—as Roger was indeed connected. Perhaps the clerk would say something suggestive, "He was in an awful hurry to get out of here," or the police would watch video and see Roger kill John Deere. Roger admitted that to himself: He did kill John Deere, though, he added—and this he said aloud, "His head shouldn't've been like that." Roger felt a nervous-sick, took a swig of water, pressed the gas pedal, and brought the speedometer's needle to 90. If the police came, Roger would probably stop. But he didn't want to think about it anymore so he didn't. He didn't allow himself to think about the incident.

Two years ago, during Roger's first month on the job in Decker, at the warehouse where frozen food was loaded onto the truck Roger drove, enormous cuts of meat but also meals in boxes, vegetables and microwavable burritos, there had been a terrible accident. A truck driver named Davis, a fork lift, a crate, and a cracked palette. Roger heard wood split, a shout, a scream. A crate—three-hundred pounds of frozen food—had crushed Davis's gut and abdomen. Davis's legs lay separate from his body, pumping ever-weaker gasps of blood. Roger knelt beside Davis; Davis was alive; he whimpered and gripped Roger's hand. Davis wept, whimpered and begged. Davis cried because he knew he was dead. Roger had never seen anything so horrible and he muttered, "This is the most horrible thing I've ever seen," but he thought: "I can bear it."

As Roger drove past the Laurel exit, he turned on the radio, let it scan through the empty stations, numbers flicking from one end of the dial to the other without a word or a note, FM and AM—not too unusual, but—a little unusual. A tractor-trailer rushed past, rocking the Saab in its wake. Roger slowed his car, down to 85, and shook his head at the truck driver. Too dark to drive like that. He reached for a CD. Without looking to see which of his sister's mixes he'd picked up, he opened the case, popped out the CD, and slipped it into the player. When he and Vivienne lived together in his San Francisco apartment, he often came home from work to find his sister getting ready for a night out, music loud, sometimes with a girlfriend, both checking their makeup, both dancing, both teasing Roger for his suits. Roger hadn't minded. He liked to see his sister happy. He turned off the music.

On the road ahead, two. little. lights.

Roger hit the brakes hard, glanced at his rear-view mirror—he was alone on the highway. The tires held the road, his belt held him: he did not hit the bighorn sheep that lay in the road. He'd seen the animal's eyes, made gold by his headlights. The sheep's hip was crushed, its hind legs bend, hooves in the air. With its forelegs, the sheep dragged itself toward the car.

That the animal had been hit (very likely by the truck that had passed Roger a few miles back) did not trouble Roger much; certainly, he would not have gotten out of his car to stare if that had been the whole story. Roger was troubled because the animal was calm. There was no fear in its expression, no struggle in its movement. He'd seen animals similarly injured, mostly deer, and always they had looked terrified.

He let the sheep get quite close before he snapped out of his uncomfortable reverie *it's as if it's dead* and got back into his car.

A sign for Red Lodge distracted Roger; he recalled the only fact he knew about the area, that in 1943, the Smith Mine exploded, killing seventy-four miners. He thought of the sheep again, and he wished he'd shot it. Not to free it from its misery, but because it was horrible. In San Francisco, there were bad periods with Vivienne. He thought of the night he'd woken to find her standing in his bedroom doorway. He'd waited for her to say something, but she'd stood without moving, dressed in a pair of his pajamas, for long minutes—he'd glanced at his clock—3:07, 3:08, 3:09, etc.—until 3:20. He'd gotten out of bed, had put his hands on her shoulders and looked into her face. The illusion that she had no eyes was shockingly vivid, even now, as Roger drove I-90 toward western Montana, toward Seattle where Vivienne lived and was now sick in a hospital. She'd had eyes, of course, dull, blank, surrounded by puffy, gray skin. The illusion had disturbed Roger, but he blurted a cry when drool had dribbled from her lower lip, a great elastic strand. "Vivienne," he'd said. She'd closed her eyes, reopened them—eyes alive again—and she'd said, "What it is, Roger?" When Roger hadn't answered, she'd laughed and returned to the guest room. Some weeks, she'd done that every night. A few nights had been worse and once she'd screamed so much a neighbor had called the police (Roger had been glad when they'd shown up, banging on the door, if only so he could show Vivienne—asleep by the time they arrived, of course—to someone else, so that someone else could say, "She looks fine to me").

Roger drove slow for a few miles. A group of bighorn sheep, clustered at the side of the road, appeared to be normal. He brought the Saab back up to 85, drove fast past Greycliff, Springdale, McLeod, and Livingston. Just outside of Bozeman, a car merged onto the highway. Its left taillight flickered, a loose wire, a red wink in the dark. The car exited, turned sharply onto an unmarked dirt road. Roger was once more alone on the road. The sky became silver blue. Roger ate elk jerky and peanuts. He'd been on the road for six hours. He tried the radio again.

A few miles from Main Street, Bozeman, in a trailer park, a teenaged boy, sixteen, woke up. His girlfriend, Dorie, was asleep beside him. His mind felt smoke-filled, vague; his skin stung and was slick and gritty. The night before—generic smokes, beer, and finally—finally!—sex, though stupid, frightening sex—Dorie yelped with pain and his orgasm came too quick and all over her thigh, and when she'd looked at the mess she'd said it was, "Absolutely disgusting." But he was not hungover sick, not embarrassed or guilty sick. "Dorie," he said, just before his eyes rolled up and he felt his brain shift, slip inside his skull, felt things liquefy.

Thought—as he'd known it—was gone from his head. He pawed at Dorie's body, curious, her neck and her face, and skin came loose as he did. He ate a little bit of Dorie, but quickly lost the thread of what he was doing, wandered away from Dorie, into town.

Outside, the grassy mountains were white, their snow-covered peaks gray. The sky was empty. The teenaged boy was not alone in the park. Others walked sluggishly from their trailers. They had no interest in each other.

Roger was nearly to Bozeman. He dialed Martin's number: The news broadcast he'd found had been hysterical. "Martin, it's Roger." Alongside the highway were parked cars. "Martin, calm down." A man stood by a car, his hand up, a weak wave, but there was something so totally wrong in the way he waved. "Shut up, Martin. Shut up. How's my sister?" Roger clenched his teeth. "You stay there with her. You tell her I'm just eight hours away." Roger pulled the wheel to the left, let his cell phone drop to the floor, just missed hitting a car stopped in the middle of the highway. "Damn it!" he shouted. He reached for the phone and said, "Martin, what's going on?" but the call was lost.

Roger kept his radio off, to focus on driving. More people had parked their cars on the highway. A motorcycle lay on its side. A man and a woman were hugging. Roger slowed to 45. He hoped the traffic—if it could be called traffic—would clear once he was past Bozeman. Eight hours away. Roger wanted to be with his sister *now*, not in eight hours. He felt ridiculous and angry for leaving her. He reminded himself that he had his reasons and thus cleared his head. Had Roger turned on his radio, had Roger's antenna picked up a signal, he would have heard the news that a connection was being made to a worldwide star shower and several new diseases, or one disease with a variety of possible outcomes, a disease that affected not just people but mammals of all sorts. There was a warning about dogs and a story about a horse that tore off the leg of a little girl.

But Roger didn't hear the news, he drove in relative silence, cautiously until the traffic did clear up, just past Bozeman. He accelerated, brought the car up to 85, spied the green dinosaur logo of a Sinclair, and decided to stop in Belgrade to fuel up. He was more than a quarter down, and he didn't like that.

The gas station appeared unattended, but the pumps were on, so Roger filled up. As he stood by his car, he watched the window of the gas attendant's shack. A flicker on the glass; not someone in the station, headlights. The car weaved, and for a sick moment Roger was sure it would crash into the tanks, until it jerked away, tumbled down a dirt path, the gated entrance to a ranch, the gate wide. The pump clicked off. "Hello!" Roger shouted. He screwed on the cap, took half a dozen steps toward the shack, stopped and cried out again. He walked back to the car, opened the trunk, contemplated his shotgun for a moment, picked up a tire iron and a flashlight instead.

He did not go into the shack. He shouted once more, saw the glass door rattle against his voice, shined the light into the room. A few racks of maps were tumbled over. A coffee pot was smashed on the floor. He couldn't see over the counter. "This'll be on Sinclair," he thought, until he heard breathing, ragged like he'd heard before, in Billings, from the John Deere man.

"I'd like to pay for my gas," Roger said to the attendant, who'd come around the corner of the shack. Roger kept the beam of his light low on the man.

"I said I'd like to pay." He raised the beam up, from crotch to chest, chest to face—

When the light hit the attendant's face the attendant screamed—squealed, really, a wet, porcine cry. The attendant raised his hands up, presumably to block the light but didn't actually cover his eyes, only held his hands up, on either side of his face.

The left side of the attendant's face showed bone, had the look of something chewed and raw.

Roger moved toward his car, tire iron raised and ready, but he attendant did not move, only screamed. Roger wanted to smash the attendant's face, to shut him up, to feel his head turn to mush at the end of the iron, but he saw no practical reason to do so, and so got into his car, and drove onto the road that led back to 90 West. The attendant squealed and squealed, hands up, tongue circling chapped lips, round and round, well after Roger was miles gone, past Churchill and Amsterdam, past Manhattan, fast approaching Three Forks. There, between Manhattan and Three Forks, Roger calmed enough to pull the car to the side of the road, found the presence of mind to get out of the car—tire iron firmly in hand—and retrieve his shotgun and the boxes of shells from the trunk. Once these comforts were on the back seat, Roger checked to see if he was close enough to Butte to get any reception on his phone.

"Martin, it's Roger," he said. He looked around: beyond his headlights there were only black shapes and much nothing in between. "Martin, what the hell is going on?" Behind Martin's voice the clatter of wheeled, metal furniture, the flash of brushed steel. "You're moving her where?" Vivienne was being moved upstairs, Martin said, because, ". . . more secure." Roger shouted—he didn't realize he was shouting, the noise from Seattle so loud, "Why secure?" Roger remembered Vivienne violent, coming home to find the glass-top coffee table shattered, Vivienne a mess on the floor, that vacant stare. "Is it Viv?" he asked. Martin shouted back, a "No," but wasn't speaking to Roger. Martin's voice lowered said something like "another patience," and the call died. Roger redialed, hung up—the road again, he needed to be *there*.

He thought he'd heard police sirens more than once, checked his mirrors, but all the way to Butte there was no one else on the road, and even for Montana, even so early in the morning, this wasn't normal. Roger scanned through the radio stations—near Butte there'd be something. He picked up a top 40 station, all preprogrammed, even the DJ, but otherwise there was nothing. Roger opted for silence.

Off the highway, down in Butte, men crawled along the jet-black slag walls, moved over the walls on all fours. A woman walked from a bar to the wall. Her walk was straight-backed, rigid. She grabbed a man from the wall, plucked him from the wall by his foot, dropped onto him, her knees snapped a rib, and she took a bite of the man's cheek. He did not struggle. He moved as if he were still crawling on the wall. A young mother, her child strapped into the backseat of her car, an '81 Rabbit Volkswagen, swerved onto Harrison Avenue, toward I-90. She'd never catch up to Roger, but she'd follow, miles behind, all the way to Seattle.

Behind her, Our Lady of the Rockies, a statue of Mary, mother of Jesus, ninety feet tall, usually brilliant white and lit by floods at night, was dark; all the flood lights were shattered. Mary was a dim shade, her face blank.

The sky, for the first few hours of Roger's drive, had been distracting with stars and with lights falling to Earth. Then the sky went dead, exhausted, and for hours was gray-black, pasty, murky. At 5:13 A.M., the sky got purple and clouds stretched low were visible and the mountains, too, vivid. The shadows of pines and rippled rock cast deep black lines. Roger had made good time—by driving between 85 and 95 most of the trip—yet he felt late, felt an anxious grip on his stomach and groin. All around were cars, most pulled over, like the sightseers' cars back in Billings. By 5:45, the sky was a deep pink.

And ahead, a car—for an instant Roger was sure the car was moving—maybe slow—but as he approached—fast—he saw that the car was stopped and that its front end was just off the road and touching the front end of another car. He jammed the brakes. He thought, I *don't have time to see if anyone's okay*, and, I *don 't care*. Roger sat behind the wheel, finger on the door-lock, engine clicking, ignition off. 5:49 A.M—still ten hours to drive—the clock went dark, came back to light, blinking 6:00 A.M. "Close enough," Roger muttered, and without another thought he stepped out the car, shotgun in hand.

"Is anyone here?"

No response. The sky was empty, growing gorgeously pink, hints of a clear blue sky appearing up high, well above the mountains. A bull, a small shape near the tree line to Roger's left, walked toward the road, something about its gait unhealthy—and Roger heard the sound of gristle, chewed. For a moment he thought it was the crackle of a fire, and carefully examined the cars—the cars were fine, a little dent where the bumpers kissed, it looked to Roger as if the cars had slowly rolled into each other. He walked around the cars—glanced at the bull as he did so and saw that it was closer and that its flank was smeared with mud. The chewing sound grew loud and Roger caught a whiff of something foul, feces. Not the sweet smell of manure; more acrid.

On the other side of the stopped cars was a man wearing nothing but black dress socks. His pale skin was covered with excrement and dirt and blood. His face was buried in the stomach of a still living deer. The deer strained to keep its head off the pavement, its legs kicked. The man was holding the deer down—his strength—

"Stop," Roger said.

The man jerked his shoulders, pulled his head up out of the deer's gut, then released the deer—it struggled to move, but its viscera was spread around the naked man's knees, the deer, falling out of itself. Roger shot the deer in the head; it gave a great kick which broke open the naked man's head—

and a woman sat up in one of the cars and thrashed around, maybe an epileptic—

her head hit the dash and broke apart like glass, its contents, thick liquid.

The naked man, flailing, attempting to keep upright, reached for Roger, clawed at Roger's pant leg. That was when Roger began to think of those people—the John Deere man, the gas attendant, the woman in the car, and the naked man—as dead. Clearly they were not without animation, but they were not alive. Roger shot the naked man.

The bull was now at the side of the road. It's flank was not mud covered but an open wound—a great, wet hole—and Roger knew that it too was dead, that the dead were not just people but animals, too—*the raccoon*—and this gave Roger a terrible, lonely feeling—desperate. From now on, he would only stop for gas. The bull bellowed. Roger got into his car and drove away.

In no time at all, Roger drove past Anaconda, where the dead were lost in the Washoe Theater, confused by the golden deer painted on the theater's curtain, by the copper fixtures that dimly shone, by the rams' heads carved into the ceiling. Those still alive in Anaconda—a dog and a brother and sister, hid from their mother, who knew where her children were, but could not remember how to open door to the basement.

There are stretches on 90 through Montana where the mountains are far from the road—always in view, but distant. Once far enough west, the mountains move in, the road curves up and among them. Snow drifts in May. When Roger saw the opportunity to fuel up, he did. Gas pumps were rarely manned and were often old—no slot to swipe a card. This worked. If a station looked disorderly or dark, Roger fueled up and left, no worries. He would have welcomed the sight of a police cruiser in his rearview. Once, a car passed, headed east, the back piled with household belongings, and two girls huddled together in the backseat. The driver's expression a warning: the dead were everywhere.

Forty miles outside of Missoula, Roger's cell phone received a flicker of reception, and immediately the phone rang. Roger dropped speed, from 90 to 80, and answered, "Martin."

It was not Martin, but Vivienne.

"Where are you?" she asked.

"About eight hours, Viv. Less."

"Oh eight hours I'm sick I don't know if I can hold on to my thoughts Roger eight hours that's a long time and Roger the thought of you your handsome eyes where is my memory?" something metal hit the floor; someone shouted, Vivienne screamed.

Roger didn't shout into his phone, didn't cry out his sister's name. He dumped his phone onto the passenger seat, reception gone.

Two years before, the day after he left San Francisco, he stopped in Missoula, early in the afternoon. He stopped because he still had a day or two before he had to be in Decker, where he'd gotten a job delivering frozen food. He stopped for no other reason than to sightsee, which he did, he wandered aimlessly, amazed by how good it could be in a city that was not cosmopolitan, that was not San Francisco or New York, the two poles his life had him caught between—had once had him caught between. Spokane had been nice, had shown Roger a little city, emptier on a workday than he'd thought possible and Missoula was like that, too, though less industrial, more kind. He ate a fish taco in a restaurant where people could still smoke, and he liked the way people were dressed, some for office work, surely, but many more for enjoying the place they were in and nothing else.

That Roger was romanticizing this place was evident even as he was doing so; a stop at a dingy bar cleared his head, kept the idea that maybe he'd settle in Missoula from fully forming. Afternoon light slanted into the dark bar decorated with license plates and empty bottles, some quite old, all beneath a film of dust. A few obvious alcoholics sat at the bar, a grad student who either thought the alcoholics were noble or who was a young alcoholic himself, and a skinny red head who turned out to be the bartender. She served Roger his beer, washed some glasses in a metal sink, then disappeared into a back room, the door marked with a sign that read: "hot dogs $1." A man in a once shiny baseball jacket turned to Roger and began to talk, without an invitation to do. He told Roger that he accepted his people's defeat, "Indians," he said, "didn't have weapons as good as yours and that's how it goes, I accept that, that's okay. But you should know, you might not have known this, but we have Custer's leg."

Roger, amused, asked, "What?"

"Custer's leg. The Blackfoot. We have it in a bag."

"The whole leg?"

"It's dust now."

The Blackfoot opened his mouth—presumably to smile—but without teeth, what his open mouth indicated was unclear.

"We pass it from tribe to tribe. Depending on the season."

"You mean, Custer, like, 'Custer's last stand' Custer? The general?"

"The government wants it back, so we pass it, tribe to tribe, keep it safe in a medicine bag."

Roger drove, he pushed 100. The feel of the car changed; eventually felt right. He checked for reception—as he passed through the Hellgate, reception returned, and Roger redialed.

Roger left San Francisco shortly before Vivienne married Martin. Martin's family thought it rude that Roger left town before the wedding, and one of Martin's aunt's was foolish enough to say so in Vivienne's presence. Vivienne didn't lose it, in the way she'd lost her mind from time to time while living with her brother, but she did explode, at first delivering a rich assemblage of Czech profanities, followed by an eerily calm explanation of Roger's importance in her life and of his right to do just exactly what he felt had to do, and concluded with an un-invite of Martin's aunt, which was not reversed, as everyone on Martin's side of the family—even Martin though he never admitted as much—assumed would happen. As Roger was never discussed by his own family, he was never discussed by Martin's.

The phone connected to Martin's phone, and Roger heard noise like people arguing. Roger shouted his brother-in-law's name, shouted, "Vivienne!" A voice, high and hysterical. Roger said, "Vivienne?" But it wasn't Vivienne. "Martin. Shut up. Stop carrying on." A clatter, as if in the phone, the phone must have been dropped. Martin's voice, Martin apologized. "Fine," Roger said. "What's going on with Vivienne?" Martin's explanation made little sense. He said something like:

"The doctors don't know. An epidemic. Hardly any staff here at all. Vivienne is sick, man, sometimes she seems okay and sometimes she loses her mind. And that's what the doctors say, too, that people are losing their minds, like, not crazy, like, their minds are dying. You gotta get us out of here. We can't get out. And Vivienne wants to go."

A scream, Vivienne's, for sure. An animal loped onto the highway. At 100 miles per hour, Roger could not stop for it, dropped his cell phone, gripped the steering wheel so as to keep the car steady, and drove into the animal. Its pliant body burst over the hood of the car, a dog, perhaps, or even a wolf. The car skidded a little, but Roger kept control. The wipers cleared the windshield adequately. When he found the phone, the connection was gone, and no reception.

Roger slowed to navigate the winding roads of Idaho, but was in Washington in less than an hour. Out this way, Route 90 was rarely heavily trafficked, but there was simply no traffic. A couple times Roger swerved to avoid an abandoned vehicle, but he no longer worried about oncoming traffic, and straddled both lanes, preferring to stay clear of the shoulder, where many cars were either abandoned or was the site of unwholesome activity, peripheral glimpses of writhing and bloodied men and women. He crossed into Washington state. Soon, Spokane was below him. Here, he passed cars and trucks, people driving slowly to survey the damage, people heading east. He passed one car headed west, a little Rabbit that quickly receded in his rearview mirror, a red speck on faded gray highway.

Past Spokane, he stopped again for gas. He didn't look for an attendant. He was grateful the pumps were on. He considered the very good possibility that gas stations would dry up, maybe not in the next few days, maybe not in a week, but soon enough. He thought maybe he'd find a gas can and fill it. Maybe grab some food, too, though for now what he'd bought in Billings was plenty. Roger's freezers, back in Decker, were still humming, drawing power from the generator shed. Peter, who'd volunteered to drive Roger's route, didn't make it out of the driveway, crashed Roger's truck into a tree; Peter's head smashed open against the steering wheel.

A man, "Hey, man."

Roger's shotgun lay across the roof of his car.

"Hey man, can you give me a lift?"

The man was not dead, he was a young guy in torn jeans and a waffle shirt, with a dusty pack and dusty boots. Roger weighed the pros and cons of a passenger.

"This pack is killing me." The man dropped his pack between his feet, which revealed a bleeding wound on his shoulder. "I feel terrible, too. Look at this bullshit." The man pointed to his shoulder. "There's some fucked up shit going on."

Roger remained cool, determined to wait until the pump clicked off, then to fill the neck. No gas can, though. Roger sighed. No time, now.

The man asked, "Where are you headed?"

"Seattle."

"Great!"

"To see my sister."

"Seattle's great."

"She's sick. In the hospital."

"Sorry to hear it, man. But that's good for me. I could get this shit looked at, maybe get something for this damn headache."

The pump clicked. Roger squeezed the pump trigger, once, twice, then locked the cap.

"No," Roger said.

"'No' what?"

"I won't give you a ride."

"Why not, man?"

"You're sick."

"You're going to a hospital!"

"You're sick and you're going to die."

"Why the fuck would you say that?"

"How does it feel?"

"I feel pretty bad, that's how I feel."

"No. How does *it* feel?"

Roger lifted the shotgun from the roof of his car.

"You gonna shoot me? You're fucked up, you know that? Stay the fuck away from me. I'll get a ride from a human being. So just stay the—"

And Roger saw it happen. A moment of confusion, a jerky step back, a tremor that traveled the spine to the eyes.

"—fuck—"

Discharging his shotgun at the gas station would be stupid, and the man was no threat. Roger put the shotgun on the passenger seat, and brought out the tire iron.

"—away—" The man shook his head, as if to clear it.

There was plenty time for Roger to get into his car and drive away. The man saw what Roger held and stepped back, appeared to struggle with himself, took another step back. "Just let me go, man."

With the iron raised, Roger closed the distance between himself and the man, brought the iron down, let its own weight do most of the work, splitting open the left side of the man's head. *Not rotten yet,* Roger thought. The man jumped, something electric lifted him from the ground, and Roger swung again, up from his leg, and knocked the man to the dirt with a blow to the man's shoulder. *He's still alive.* Another blow, to the chest, broke ribs. The man cried out. Roger leaned over the man, beating him with the iron, beating him to death.

Roger tossed the tire iron into the passenger-side foot well, and drove away, his interest in the man gone, his need to reach his sister all the more keen.

When Roger left San Francisco, he quit a lucrative job and sold most of what he owned shortly after he learned of Martin's competent handling of a suicide attempt by Vivienne. Martin had returned from work and found Vivienne on the floor of their bathroom. He called for help, removed what pills were still in her mouth, and kept her awake. Once Vivienne was out of the hospital, Roger fully expected Martin to break up with Vivienne, leaving her once more in Roger's care. Instead, Martin took her on a short vacation and proposed. Roger waited for a little while after, suffered quietly and admired Vivienne's ring when she came home, which wasn't all that often. The night before Roger left, he and Vivienne spent one last evening together. They fell asleep together, in Roger's room, warmed by a fire and with no fuss at all.

Roger drove the rest of Washington in a haze. Deep forests. The falls of Snoqualmie. A white barn painted with the word "Cherries." All the energy it took to make the drive came from Roger's body, a knot of anger and lust and confusion untied from Decker to the bridge to Seattle. Route 90 terminates as a long bridge that crosses Lake Washington into Seattle. He would not be able to drive into the city. The sun was up, the sky, clear. Not blue, exactly. More—white. The bridge was crowded with people, a great, sluggish crowd, biting and clawing at each other and at nothing, spitting blood, smeared with blood, coated and crusted with blood. Roger thought of his sister. *Maybe.* He needed to get across the bridge. He filled his pockets with shells. He would clear a stretch of the bridge, get back into his car and drive until he needed to clear another stretch. He would drive across a bridge of corpses. When the path became too narrow for the car, he would walk. *I am ready to destroy whatever monsters lie between me and my sister and I'm ready to keep her alive forever.* He unlocked the door, stepped onto the bridge, and took aim.

The Quarantine Act

by Mehitobel Wilson

Let me tell you what little I know about the great Mehitobel Wilson.

For starters, she doesn't publish much. She's her own harshest critic. If only more were like her. As such, *the only* Bel *book on the market to date is* Dangerous Red: *a collection of short stories that is, to my mind, perhaps the finest I've seen in the fresh twenty-first century.*

Like the best of Harlan Ellison, her fiction walks in enraged, full of fearsome intelligence and balls out to here. Unlike Harlan, she keeps a low profile.

So *it is my great pleasure to help spread the legend.*

"The Quarantine Act" *is one of those stories that's far more afraid of* us *than it is of them.* The *net effect is one of slow, gut-squeezing paranoia, with a restless intellect and rigorous attention to detail that only serves to accentuate the doom.*

Showing us humanity on the ropes.

And wondering if it's worth saving.

I REFUSED THE INJECTION. I said nothing, held my ground, stood firm. I raised my chin against them and set my jaw and did not say anything as void as, "I have rights." I just stared at them.

They looked at me, at their handheld computers, and at my wife. One looked at my car.

Everyone looks at my car. That's why I bought it. But no man in full Anti-Biohazmat cadmium yellow had appraised it through a polarized facemask before, and the fact that this one did, it made sense, and it fucked all thought of rights clean out of my head.

So I'm here with the orange carpet and the dead language, in quarantine. There is closed-circuit television in the school. All news, all the time. I watch one of the regular loops meant to illustrate the dangers. This one shows a teenager. The surface of his skin shines with fluid when the rare light strikes it. His ever-open eyes are dry and do not shine. He grinds his teeth. I call him Gnashing Jack.

My own eyes, too, are dry, but I believe that I am still healthy. My eyes are dry because I stare through the darkness, trying to see what has happened to us, what we have done. The darkness itself is better than the truth, I think.

It was a shock the first time I saw someone I knew on television. That made me wonder, all over again. Annie. "Slopface."

The confinement, even with the flickering likes of Gnashing Jack and Slopface Annie and the others, might be better than the truth.

I'm clean, still. Alive, though? That's a question if there ever was one. Depends on what you mean by *alive*.

Slopface Annie (yeah, I'd called her that well before the ratification of the Act, and before the needle squads hit the streets, and before the infection spread)—Slopface Annie knelt before me in her beige motel room, her chapped lips scouring my cock as she smeared fishy dimestore lipstick along its length and back again. She kept frowning and shifting her unshaven legs. I'd tracked bits of gravel in with me from the parking lot and her knees ground into the tiny rocks. It hurt her—the princess and the pea—and made her frown. I liked how the frown hardened her lips as she worked, liked it a lot.

I pulled back. "Open your mouth and smile like a donut," I said, and she did. That's why she was Slopface, then.

Not now.

"Aim for the chin," she said, exaggerating the words so that her blurred mouth was very wide as she tossed her head back and faked royal joy, as she probably did with every john.

Don't get the wrong idea, here. Yes, Annie was a whore. Yes, I treated her like a whore when I fucked her. But we went way back, and there was real affection between us. We'd gone to college together. I lasted, she didn't.

She wasn't technically a whore until the time I paid her, I guess, but once that hurdle had been passed, she hit the streets and went whole hog.

"You need money," I had said.

"Of course I do, we all do. You do too. With all you have, do you still want more?" She'd been laying beside me, but pushed herself up then, sweeping her corkscrewed bleach-dead curls over her shoulder so they scratched my face.

"Sure. That's why I go to the office every day. But it wouldn't kill me to give you five hundred bucks, and it wouldn't kill you to take it."

"Five hundred?" Annie's dark brown eyes counted every bill in thin air and compared each to her rent. "Hell, if you're giving, I'll take." And she winked and sent her palm down to pay howdy to my balls, and added, "And I'll give, too."

And she did.

Maybe it did kill her, that money, after all.

Then again, maybe it didn't kill her at all. A whore's a whore. If enough money talks, even the dead can walk.

My wife, she didn't get the vaccine. She's not in quarantine, either, not Julia. Her value to society is different than my own, and than Annie's.

I can't love her anymore. That, too, is my choice. It's my necessity. No sense loving what's gone.

She's a pragmatic girl, my Julia. There is no doubt that she feels the same way as I do.

The assignations with Annie, and with all the others, ended the moment I noticed that I loved Julia. Just to be clear, there.

Julia was a good excuse to avoid Annie, anyway. I'll admit that now—

why the hell not? Annie made me feel guilty for having turned her into a whore.

Scratch that. No matter how much I stare into the darkness here, trying to see the truth of monsters past it, I can't see past myself. So, fine. I was guilty about Annie only when I reminded myself that I ought to be guilty about Annie. I was guilty only when I thought, "You called her 'Slopface.' That was your pet name and you called her that aloud. You prick. You should feel awful."

But I had to *tell* myself to feel awful. Because the first thing I felt when I thought of Annie then was disgust.

Now, in Quarantine, I tell myself to feel guilty about my disgust for her, there on the television screen. I think, *ho ho ho, ol' Slopface is aptly named—I sure called that one!* And then I try to stop, but can't, because the disgust is real.

The sounds that came from the set, the sounds of her chewing off her own tongue and loving it, seem real, too.

Julia and I had arrived home from dinner, two months ago, on a Monday night. She had worn backseamed stockings with her skirt, and I only noticed this when she ascended the steps of our house, just before she pivoted a bit on her black patent heels and waited for me to unlock the door. She'd dashed in ahead of me, darling sharkskin-skirted ass all a-wiggle, and disabled the alarm system.

"Tapioca," she whispered, "and beer!" and off she went, stepping out of her heels mid-prance, to get them.

I met her in the living room, our good, dim place, fragrant with the vanilla of her perfume and lit only by her quiet aquarium. She pressed a dry, cold long-neck into my hand and gave me a flirty look through the little dark veil of her bangs, and said, "We should watch the news first."

First.

She nipped the lip of her own bottle and I heard a tiny clink of tooth enamel on glass, and "first" seemed like a death sentence, right then. *Now* was much better than waiting for "first" to end.

Pretty little fingers, gray in the dimness, picked up the remote and, good girl, handed it to me. News, on.

A clean-shaven government spokesman stood at a podium. He didn't look quite wealthy enough to be Federal; I assumed he was a member of state government. "... thirty-eight percent failure rate, Professor Schneider notes, is a lower failure rate than that of the Polio vaccine, or of the prescribed drug courses for AIDS and HIV control."

"That's not true," I said. I remember saying that.

"Shhh," Julia said, pressing her beer to her cheek.

The bland man at the podium squared his shoulders and looked straight ahead; this didn't work particularly well for our channel's cameraman, who was lensing from the side. The effect made the Spinmaster look distant, and wholly untrustworthy.

But maybe I was just impatient with him for being First, when Julia was wearing backseamed stockings over there on her side of the sofa.

The Spin guy said, "All of that is good news. In addition, as you're likely aware, the State Emergency Health Powers Act was passed in December so that our state and our Governor would be prepared to protect you, the citizens."

Julia tongued tapioca from her spoon, held upright like a lollipop, and shot me a quizzical look. I returned it: this Health Powers Act thing was a new one on both of us, it seemed.

"Tonight I must announce that the State Emergency Health Powers Act must bear fruit immediately. The SEHPA was born of extreme and prudent wariness on the part of your Governor, and all of us, and all of you, fervently hoped we might never have to move forward. Though we do, I expect you're all as grateful as I that we have measures already in place."

"What measures?" Julia asked the television, her voice sharp. The spoon was no longer upright; her fingers were slack and the spoon drooped across them. A pearl of tapioca dressed her knuckle.

"Tomorrow at noon we will present another conference which will include further details. In addition to this, all citizens with state-issued identification or state income tax information on file, and all others whose addresses were taken during the last Federal census, will receive packets in the mail which include information and your appointment cards. Rest assured that we have full immunization supplies for everyone, and that we'll all be back to life as usual within a week or two. Thank you, and good night."

Our pretty blonde news anchor appeared onscreen; behind her was a graphic bearing the letters SEHPA and a syringe superimposed over our state flag. "Similar announcements have been made in all states that passed SEHPA, or their version of it. California, which had refused the terms of the Act when it was initially recommended by the CDC and other contributing departments, is holding an emergency session tonight to reconsider their decision. On a lighter note, California's governor also spoke today about a new environmental toxicity report which concluded that 40 percent of the detrimental carbon dioxide emissions in the atmosphere are caused by the exhalations of the world's human population."

The co-anchor, also blonde and pretty, casually turned to the anchor. "Didn't they make laws last year to reduce the carbon dioxide emissions from cars?"

"Yes, they did, Sheila! You have to wonder what laws they'll make to reduce our own emissions!"

"Talk about bad breath!" laughed Sheila.

"That's right!" laughed the anchor.

"What was all that about?" I asked, and Julia downed the rest of her beer, then just gripped the empty bottle.

"In weather news, Tropical Storm Hando is still under watch for a potential upgrade. Scientists now suggest that the storm is not purely a meteorological occurrence, but may have been prompted by the release of gases from a fault in the ocean floor. More on this from News Four's meteorologist, Tom Danner."

Julia plucked the remote from my hand and thumbed the channel buttons, scanning for more information on this SEHPA thing. No luck. She flung the remote back at me; it hit my thigh. Her frustrations always managed to find some painless but annoying projectile, which in turn always found some part of my body. I was used to it and let it pass.

I turned off the television and she followed me through the dark house, to bed.

"First" was out of the way, and her stockings were still sexy, but even when I'd anchored my fingers under her black silky garters and started licking that taut tendon inside her thigh, I was too distracted over the news to really notice.

So was she.

We paid just enough attention to each other to get off (or just end it, at least) and then, still in our own heads, we each feigned sleep.

If you're wondering, yes, it was the last time we touched one another. It was absentminded and terrible and it was the last time, ever.

The next day, I kept the radio in my office tuned to the news station. Environmental extremists were all over the talk shows, braying about the toxic breath of humankind. Seems every sigh makes the earth die, and shit like that. The BBC reported that a group of loonies had done their part to clear the air by ceremoniously pulling plastic bags over their heads, then snapping rubber bands around their necks.

At lunchtime, I knocked on each door that I passed. "The SEHPA news conference is about to start, and I'm going to watch it in the conference room," I said, over and over. Everyone looked blank, everyone of them. "Just come watch, they're going to give us details," I said.

Apparently the salad bars and secret martinis were more appealing than any news conference, though, because I watched it alone.

And my skin crawled.

Crawling skin, they said, was a symptom.

Never before was I a conspiracy theorist, but once your mind trips a conspiracy switch, vistas of paranoia and open inside you, warrens of hatred, and all of it makes sense.

And then you blow up, knowing that every possibility is founded on an "if" of some kind, "If their goal is *this*, then they're going to do *that*," and you realize that all of your "ifs" are based on things They have told you, which can't be true in the first place, if you distrust Them that much.

So the vistas become voids, and you're crippled—and all of this can happen in the space of a single lunch hour.

Because surely, surely there isn't some pervasive infectious agent on the scene that zombifies all its victims. No one said "zombies," they said truly stupid doublespeak things instead—the one that made me laugh until I gasped for breath was an acronym for a chain of words that included the word "consumer" (because, you see, they consume the flesh of others)—but they meant zombies.

I've seen my share of zombie movies, and the IMCCs and OARKs and all the other shit they called our new national threat seemed worse. The pathogen (which they speculated came from the fault under the ocean, but who cares?) was transmitted through fluids such as saliva and perspiration; just an infected host brushing against you, and you were doomed to walk and rot and crave the taste of live flesh.

But they were full of shit. Zombies. It was a joke, such a joke that they had to figure we'd buy it. Who would, though?

It didn't matter if we bought it or not, however.

Enter SEHPA.

The breakdown: the State Emergency Health Powers Act gave the governor of each state the absolute power, in the event of a bioterrorist attack or other epidemic threat, to mandate inoculations for all citizens. Though, in a cute concession to our Constitutional rights, refusal of the vaccine for religious or any other reason was legal, all those who refused were to be quarantined in prepared housing facilities.

Appointment cards would be issued to us all; upon receiving the inoculation, each person would receive a card that included a digitized fingerprint. Air travel and interstate travel of any kind was "on hold until further notice." Checkpoints would, within hours, be erected on many roads, and all police officers and deputized CDC officials had been issued print scanners so they might stop anyone, at any time, to verify that they'd been immunized.

Zombies couldn't be real—but SEHPA shouldn't have been real, either.

Yet it was.

So the vistas opened, and then my cell phone rang.

"Hello?"

"Did you see?" Julia asked, her voice shrill. "On TV?"

"Yes, I just watched it here," I said. Her own words overran mine.

"—last night they said thirty-eight percent failure rate. If everyone gets the shot, *thirty eight percent will die*, right?"

"Dear God," I said, but still she talked over me.

"—and forty percent of carbon dioxide, air pollution they say, is caused by us breathing, right? Which we won't do when we're DEAD, right?"

"Do zombies breathe?"

Vistas in other minds had opened. "Fuck the zombies, look at the shots! Look at the shots!"

"And what will they do with the property of those quarantined? Burn it? Impound it?"

I hadn't thought about that. What *would* they do with it?

Julia's voice was loud. "Come home, right now. I'm leaving, meet me at home right now, Alan, please."

"I can't do that. No one else here watched, no one knows."

"Well, tell them, then!"

"They wouldn't believe me."

"So fuck them and come home. Your job is nothing compared to this. Thirty-eight percent of them will be dead soon anyway! Come home!"

Then I heard a cracking sound on the line, and I knew she'd thrown the phone across the room.

And I went home.

Julia was a hurricane, storming through the house and raving, then pausing from time to time to croon at her fish or heave little wistful sighs at me. Her fingers worried her hair, snapping off split ends, leaving a drift of half-inch brown strands on her shoulders. She picked up my cell phone and flung it at me—"Call one of your friends, you've got to know *someone*."

I did know someone. I knew the General.

He'd offered to sell me guns before, but I had been against personal gun ownership. I had been a jackass, hadn't I. But he'd forged a number of personal documents for certain folks I'd wanted to hire, and he'd done an excellent job. He even had my prints on file.

If I was lucky, he'd have some pharmaceuticals around, too. It might not hurt to have some anti-anxiety meds on hand in case Julia never calmed down.

"We have a Lexus," she whispered as I dialed the General's pager number and entered the ID code he'd assigned me. "They're going to want that. They're going to want everything."

I ignored her, and prayed that he would recognize the code.

Three hours later, he called back.

At five o'clock in the morning, Julia and I met him at a gas station. He fingerprinted us again, hiding our hands under his own massive paws as he rolled our fingers across the pad before giving us each pre-moistened wipes to clean the ink from our skin. He's a thoughtful man, the General is. He'd be cast as a big gray Maine lobsterman if someone made a movie; he'd then be fired for boiling his lines down to one or two words each. I've never met anyone as gruff as the General.

I'm not certain that he ever was a General, or even in the military at all; he might have been a professor at some point, or a hit man.

He called Julia "madam."

She was somber throughout the transaction.

"Two days, I'll call," he said, and closed up his chocolate crocodile case. We went back to the Lexus and he climbed into his black van, and the noise of his engine starting covered the shivery sound of the General's bottled pills in my coat pocket.

Julia didn't come to bed after we got home from our meeting with the General. It's just as well; I didn't fall asleep for a long while, myself, but didn't feel like listening to whatever came out of her mouth every time a new one of those magical, paranoid vistas cracked wide within her formerly screwed-on head.

But in the morning, when I woke after sleeping late, I smelled coffee.

She'd been right about the job; now was not the time to worry about corporate bullshit. Maybe I'd thought of myself as a philanthropist, helping ex-felons and a certain caliber of illegal alien get a leg up in my world by hiring them via paperwork conjured by the General, but bullshit smells a lot different when you walk up on it from downwind, instead of just sitting smack in the middle of the loads you generate day after day.

Those pills the General had given me were tempting. Julia might end up with one or two slipped into her coffee, but a couple wouldn't kill me, either.

Why be disgusted with the world, when you can be disgusted with yourself?

Oh, yes. Yes. Yes, that's what let all this happen, let SEHPA mosey on in and piss all over the sofa, that very tendency of Americans to sink into self-absorption and masturbatory loathing.

Pitiful personal melodramas always ground emotions to depths sicker than any that could be plumbed by documentaries, or by monster movies.

Monsters—I wasn't thinking about them, not yet. If any thought of them crossed my mind, it was with disgust that the government had so little respect for its herd of citizen cattle that it thought we'd actually buy zombies as a great excuse to get vaccinated.

I slipped into the tacky velour robe Julia'd given me, my favorite, the Sheik robe, and walked barefoot down the hall and into the kitchen.

It could have been any lovely Sunday morning, but it was a sunny Tuesday, and the world was a joke.

In a way, that made it lovelier. For once, instead of barely taking note of them, I felt an actual fondness for the moist-petaled pink peonies piled in a basket on the oak table, and the symmetry of the two comfortable chairs squared across from one another there. The waxed wood glowed in the morning light. I appreciated the coolness of the clean white tiles underfoot. I wanted to sit in one of those chairs, roll my heels on the cool tile, rest my elbows on the sun-warmed wood, and smile over the fragrant pink flowers at my wife, while we drank coffee together.

Why had we never done that before? Not once. And here, the stage was set for it every day, and—not once had we done it. It would have been nice. She would have thought so, too. I just don't think it ever occurred to either of us to do something so simple.

From the living room, I heard the television tube fire up and the speakers blare forth unfamiliar voices. Their cadences were standard newscaster fare, and I dashed coffee into the mug Julia had left out for me, and hurried into the living room to join her. To check on her.

Julia sat erect on her side of the couch. She wore chinos and a clean white tank top, and her mountain boots, the ones with serrated soles. Her heels were aligned and her hands were on her thighs. She looked solid, military. Her hair was twisted hard and pinned to the back of her head, and without turning, she cut her eyes at me when I walked into the room.

"Paranoia," she spat, "is a symptom, they say now."

"They said the same thing about anxiety and alarm last night. They said the sensation of crawling skin was a symptom." I sipped the good, hot coffee and watched her carefully.

Julia glanced back at the television, then turned fully toward me, took a breath. She was very serious. "They showed footage of zombies. They called them something else, but they count as zombies in my book. SEHPA shit aside, I've spent the morning thinking: what if this is real?"

I had no answer. My morning had just begun, and I hadn't yet reached the point where I could put the SEHPA shit aside.

But I hadn't watched the news.

"There's one," she said. She leaned forward, gripped her khaki knees, and stared hard at the screen. "I really can't tell. Either it's a great makeup job, or one motherfuck of a disease. They're saying it spreads exponentially. I don't expect to see a herd of these guys on TV for a couple of days yet, but that might also be because the effects labs need a few days to get that much makeup ready. I doubt there's a secret government makeup lab, they'd have to contract out." Her fingertips pinched the creases of her slacks, slipped along them from mid-thigh to knee to mid-calf, released, began again. Still she watched the television.

I realized something then, something that made me want to touch her, but that welled so large within me that touching her seemed disrespectful: Julia truly, completely loved me. Trusted me. She trusted our transaction with the General—my plan to save us from SEHPA—so implicitly that SEHPA was no longer a worry to her at all.

And I felt terrible about the little pistachio-colored pills, that I'd even considered medicating her just to shut her up. Because that's what it was, at the heart of it.

The afflicted man onscreen looked like any standard movie zombie, and since he was on TV, he may as well have been one. I was unmoved. Julia's clinical rationale had probably encouraged my own distance, but there it was.

He had an expensive, if mussed, haircut. His suit was a tailored charcoal number that buttoned high, which was cutting-edge. This suggested to me that he was young enough to care about such things, or newly-salaried at a brokerage firm, or maybe an entertainment agency. There was no way to determine his precise age, though. Above the wilted white collar stained with septic fluid sat a slick wreck of a face, mottled cheeks and temples too hollow, eyelids and lips too fat. He was slightly in profile. The one gray sclera the camera caught seemed to be peeling. There was a dark brown bulb of matter protruding from his nostril; it did not move, suggesting either that the brown was solid, or that the man did not breathe.

His greased lips were curled to reveal beautiful teeth, Hollywood teeth.

Julia said, "All of the ones they've shown have been like this, upscale guys. There was one black woman—well, gray, anyway—but she was in a business suit. And tennis shoes, like she was on her lunch break. They were soggy around the ankles."

"They're trying to show us that it's going to happen to the best of us, which means it's definitely going to happen to the worst of us." I knew that we counted among the bests, and the knowledge meant little.

"Well, the vaccination clinics are mobbed by the worst of us. Guys with pieces of lumber with nails sticking out. Teenagers jumping around behind the reporters, waving their validation cards and showing off the ink on their fingers. Pressing their thumbs on their foreheads before the ink dries to leave a mark there."

I laughed at that. "We ought to do that. Call the General."

Julia shook her head. "I'm not looking forward to leaving the house, even to meet him," she said. "I'm more afraid of the vaccine mobs than I am of any zombies."

We watched the news all day, and I had to agree with her about the mobs.

We made no plans. There was no way to plan in the face of this; it was all too big to consider, really. Now and then the vague notion of flight would swim up into my forebrain, then meet my recollection of closed highways and locked airports.

So we watched the news, each gripping opposite arms of the sofa, exchanging little comments now and then, nothing either of us heard. We were thinking too hard with no solid ideas to grasp.

Julia remembered that we should eat. She made tuna salad with pickles for lunch, and used too much Chinese mustard, but I may have liked it anyway. The crumbs from the toast stayed on my lap until dinner. We opened a bottle of wine, some decent Cab, maybe, but didn't drink it, or even remember that it was there for us to drink.

We ate at the table. Chicken breasts and steamed broccoli. I think it was good. Hard to say. Hard, really, to remember if it was broccoli. Something green, I know that.

I wish I'd paid more attention.

Something that I do recall about that day, though, was the total absence of commercials on TV.

But I don't recall if either of us remarked upon that. If even the events that were so overwhelming didn't matter, simply because they were too large for comment, the lack of commercials probably didn't either.

Which means one of us probably did mention it, because those little random things are the only ones about which we can muster a word, it seems. Like how I'm thinking about it now, when I can smell the gun oil on the guards posted outside my classroom.

I am in a high school. The building, from the '70s, is arranged in pods: each one is a circle within a circle. The inner circle is a central common office that housed each department. I am in the Foreign Language pod. I am in the Latin classroom. Six wedge-shaped classrooms radiate off from the center office. On the narrow end of the wedge, a windowless door leads to the office. On each corner of the wide end, a door leads to the halls. Each door has a window of plexiglass-encased metal grilles, but they look into the halls, not out to the world. It is often dark here.

Now a unit of sixteen heavily armed soldiers occupies each inner office, and at least one soldier in biohazard gear guards each outer door. So I was told upon my incarceration here.

There are twenty-six pods in the school.

I assume there are more people like me—maybe infected, maybe Gnashing Jack and Slopface Annie in the flesh—in the school.

I'm supposed to assume that.

The carpet here is hot orange, that hard-knotted industrial carpeting from which you can scrape chewing gum without so much as fraying a fiber. It is stain-resistant. It would not, I doubt, withstand the leakage from Annie, or from that teenaged boy.

There's a new loop of him on the news. He grunts a lot. He rolls his shaggy, peeling eyes.

I wonder if he'd gone to school here, or taken Latin in this classroom.

As the hours pass, I continue to watch the television. There's nothing much else to see. The bolted steel brace that holds me by the throat to the tangerine cinder-block wall won't let me look away.

Julia snatched the telephone from the coffee table at the first chirping hint of a ring. "Yes," she said into it, and "yes" again, and I stood up. She listened, intent, and then reached without looking into the pocket of the jacket I'd thrown over the back of the couch. She drew forth my keys and gripped them in her hard little hand and said, "Yes, sir."

She handed the keys to me with one hand as she stood, and dropped the phone onto the couch with the other. "Half an hour, the grocery store on White Bluff. We're supposed to meet him in the detergent aisle."

"No cameras there, I guess. Nobody wants to shoplift detergent."

"There's a class statement in there, somewhere, I'm sure of it." She picked up my jacket and slipped her arms into it, and thought I'd never known her as a college girl, that's what she looked like then: gamine gone serious, bitter over the politics of social consciousness, a little flannel girl in a big twill coat.

She smoothed the jacket and her face creased; just as I remembered the bottle of pills, she plunged her hand into the pocket and fished it out. Checked the label. Gave, then, her classic little chin-snap nod, the same one that she gave when she stalked, critical-eyed, up and down, ceaselessly, in front of the long low aquariums at the goldfish store, then stopped—her chin popped up once, down once—because the decision was made. The nod could mean approval, or resignation, or determination, but all those were nuances of finality: it was the indication that there was no turning back.

She set the bottle of pills on the coffee table, turned to me, and said, "Ready?"

It was dark when the guard burst in, and I might have been asleep. If a place is too dark, and the nightmares far worse when you're awake, it's tough to tell whether your eyes are open or closed, whether your thoughts are conscious or unconscious.

But the television was off and the room was dark, and then he stumbled through the door and slapped his gloved hand against the wall. The fluorescent strips overhead shuddered alight. The lights settled into their full burn and I checked my hands for the lymph shine, and saw nothing, still.

The guard slammed the door shut behind him, leaned on it, and turned the thumb-bolt.

He whipped the oilslick lens of his face toward me. I wanted to see his expression: Was he repulsed? Afraid of me and what I might carry? Was he sorry?

Surprised to see me still healthy, or not surprised at all?

The guard turned back to the door and I heard the ticking sounds of his faceplate against the glass window. He wanted very badly to see something out in the hallway.

He spoke. "I'm out," he said. "Secure in I-A. Did you see that? Did you see that fucking thing?"

Was I supposed to actually answer? How could I have seen anything, other than the "*amo, amas, amat*" poster and orange carpet and suppurating, dead flesh on the television?

"Yeah, I know it was fucking fast, but I saw it." I realized he had a radio of some kind inside his mask, under his screaming yellow headdress.

The man paused; his body language, even under the near-shapeless protective suit, suggested that he was listening hard.

"I will. Full report. Yes, I terminated him as per instructions." He paused, and his face mask shot light at me as he turned his head. "No, sir, I couldn't get that little fucker, he's still out there, as far as I know."

What had he killed, human or zombie?

I wondered if it there was a difference any more.

Or, for that matter, if there had ever been a difference at all.

"Ready," I said to Julia. I wanted to take her hand, but did not.

We opened the front door, just a little, and a mustard-colored arm was right there. Black glove fingers flattened against the door and pushed. Other fingers reached from other crinkled yellow arms and caught me around the bicep. A hand wrapped around Julia's wrist.

That yellow blazed in the sunlight; it was semi-reflective, and blinding. Polarized glass masks hid the upper half of the face behind violet-tinged blackness, and the lower halves bristled with filtration canisters—five each.

I expected the one that stood before us, shoulders squared and feet planted solidly in rubber-sheathed boots, to read to us from a clipboard. Instead, he held a PDA at face level, and read from it. "Alan Carter Martin. Julia Sayers Martin. Your cards, please."

Someone else held Julia, someone other than me.

"We were on our way to the clinic," Julia said.

"I see," the man said. "Then you will agree to submit to the vaccination here." He raised a glove and one of the men massed behind him approached with a kit that rattled.

The General had turned on us.

Do or die, I thought.

In retrospect, I chose the latter.

So I said no, and Julia said no through a throat thickened by emotion, and some of the men entered our house, and others added my Lexus to their digital inventory list, and I knew that everything we owned was to be seized by the government due to noncompliance and a probable health risk.

As were we.

And I watched them confer over the notes on their small handheld screens, and watched sunlight glint off their facemasks as they inventoried Julia. I watched her take stock of them, too.

She gave that little chin-snap of hers. I saw it right before they turned me around and loaded me into the steel quarantine transport.

The State Emergency Health Powers Act had just protected the country from one woman, one man, one four-bedroom house, and one burgundy Lexus.

I said nothing, held my ground, stood firm. I raised my chin against them and set my jaw and never even said anything such as, "I have rights."

I just stared.

THE GOOD PARTS

BY LES DANIELS

Color me crazy, but to my way of thinking, this is the most adorable story in the book.

Mind you, it's also mind-boggingly hideous, and wrong on so many levels that enumerating them would run longer than the story itself.

But what "The Good Parts" *lacks in any sense of appropriate moral boundaries whatsoever, it more than makes up for with a giddy, whimsical charm that leaves me cackling and grinning every time I think about it.*

I'm not sayin' it's Dr. Seuss *or anything, but I will say that* Les Daniels' *greatest trick is making lightheartedness the single most subversive element in the telling of this terrible, terrible story. Which I think is fantastic.*

And I hope you will, too.

IN LIFE, he had been huge but hardly menacing; his four hundred and eighty-three pounds had been all fat and no muscle. It had actually been hard for him to move.

But now it was hard for almost everyone to move. Their muscles, their tendons, their bones, all were soft as slime, soft as rot, soft as his.

But he was bigger.

Instead of hunting with the pack he hunted behind it, waiting till they brought a victim down and only then moving in to help with the kill. The others in the pack never seemed to notice what he did, never fought against him as he shouldered them aside with his bloated bulk. They only had eyes for the meat, and they fell where they were pushed when he leaned down into the crimson trough and went for the good parts.

If there was any thought at all left in his jellied brain, it would have been expressed in those three words: the good parts.

He had always liked the good parts, even when he was alive. He had liked them in his books and he had read them over and over again, marking the margins in red so they would be easier to find next time. And he had liked them in his movies. Actually he never went to the movies (the seats were too small), but that didn't matter since he had his VCR. He could sit in the dark and watch the good parts over and over again. Forward and back, forward and back. In and out. Up and down. And while he watched, he ate.

He had books like *High School Gym Orgy* and *Hitchhikking Harlots*, he had films like *Romancing the Bone* and *Debbie Does Dallas*, and he had magazines like *Eager Beavers* and *Hot to Trot*. In a way the magazines were the best: if he found one with the right kind of pictures, there was nothing in it but good parts.

But all that had been back in the days before civilization had collapsed, before the dead had risen to devour the living. Now he was even better off. Once he had only stared at the good parts and stuffed himself, but now he had achieved his destiny. He was eating the good parts.

He didn't realize how safe he was; he didn't understand that being big and slow kept him out of the firefights till they were over and the living ones were down. The good parts were hard to reach, but that was lucky too: the quickest hunters were still pulling at extremities, arms and legs and heads, when he lumbered up and bulldozed his way toward the good parts. Sometimes he had to settle for a breast or a buttock, but most of the time he got what he really wanted. His favorite food tasted like a fish and cheese casserole basted with piss: no one had time to take a bath.

His yellow teeth were matted with pubic hair and mucous membrane; he never brushed.

He might have been a sexist when he was alive, but all that was behind him now. Anybody's good parts were his meat.

He was a virgin.

There wasn't much to do but eat and look for more to eat. One day he lurched into the Naughty Nite Bookstore, and he almost remembered it. A few of the usual crowd were there, bumping into the walls and moaning with dismay because no food was in the place. They left, but he lingered. He picked up a magazine called *Ballin'*. He couldn't read the title, but he could see the pictures, and he was still looking at them when he walked out of the store and found himself in a small apartment in the back. The couch looked cozy. He sat down on it for a few minutes to look at his magazine, and then went out to look for food, but later he came back again. He had to go somewhere.

He had a home.

Once in a while some of his friends followed him home (they had to go somewhere, too), but after milling around for a few minutes they decided that nothing was happening there and went away. Nobody understood him.

A meat shortage developed. Sometimes it hardly seemed worth getting up. He had quite a collection of magazines after a few months, and he was losing his teeth. Some of his fingers fell off.

Still, a guy's gotta eat, so sometimes he would haul himself up and look for lunch. Everyone he saw on the street looked sad. The city echoed with their howls. Some tried munching on each other, but the meat was rotten and the trend never caught on.

One day a female followed him home. He might have looked like he knew something, and he certainly looked well fed. In fact, he was a mountain of maggots, and he let her eat some. It was better than nothing.

Her clothes had rotted clean away, and he noticed that he could see her good parts. She looked like a picture in a magazine. Well, close enough. Some instincts never die.

He had an inspiration, and then he had a wife.

She didn't seem to mind. When he pulled away from her, vaguely confused, he left his penis inside of her. He never really missed it. It was too far gone to eat in any case.

After that they hunted together. The pickings were slim. Once he got a few bites out of a leg, which wasn't what he felt like having that night, but it was better than nothing. He didn't notice that she was getting fatter even though they hardly ever ate.

One day she took him to the Stop 'n' Shop, a place she knew almost as well as he knew the Naughty Nite Bookstore. She showed him how a can opener worked. He wasn't really interested, and he didn't care much for the food, but she was wolfing it down as if it still was hot and fresh.

Of course he didn't know that he would be a father soon.

After all, who knew what a zombie could do?

The human scientists who studied them had other things to think about than the possibility of zombie sex. The zombies seemed to be too busy working on oral gratification for anyone to worry about their genitals. Nobody had their minds in the gutter anymore; they had their bodies there instead.

But the female was pregnant. She was expecting. She was what used to be called full of life. And you know it could have happened, because it did.

The female began making regular trips to the Stop 'n' Shop, coming back home with all the cans that she could carry. He didn't get the point, but he began to go along to help her. It was something to do.

Their friends thought they were crazy.

Actually, they didn't see that much of their friends anymore. A lot of them were falling apart, especially the skinny ones. Decay was in the air. Parts of bodies lay in the streets. Some were moving and some were not. Being fat became suddenly fashionable: it made it easier to stay in one piece. Bulk was beautiful.

When the day finally came, the birth was unorthodox. The baby simply crawled out through its mother's bloated belly, and after that the female had trouble getting around. In fact, she came apart at the waist, and she would have died if she had been alive. He propped her top half up in a closet and gave it food from time to time, but it lost interest and disintegrated.

The child was a girl, and it was human.

When he first realized that, he almost took a big bite out of her, but suddenly he noticed that something was wrong. Her good parts weren't really good enough to eat yet. She wasn't ripe.

It was tempting, no doubt of that, but for all he knew this was the last fresh food that he would ever see. He wanted to wait. He wanted to care for her. He wanted the perfect banquet for his last meal. Not only would she be riper, but she'd be bigger, too. He might even invite some people over for a party.

They didn't wait for invitations. Only a few days later, while he was stuffing some concentrated chicken noodle soup into his daughter's little pink mouth with some of his stumps, he heard the old gang shuffling through the bookstore, their voices rising in a ravenous chorale. It was just like them to spoil his surprise.

He was protective of his only child, and he was still the biggest man in town. He shut the door that led into their little home and leaned his massive bulk against it. Of course the zombies tried to break it down, but most of them broke up instead. Their arms and legs snapped like spaghetti strands. Some of them crawled away as best they could, and some of them didn't even bother, but none of them got in. They just rotted and liquified and merged with the floorboards of the Naughty Nite Bookstore.

The little girl was fine. She grew stronger as the days and weeks and months sped past, and it was just as well she did, because her father was growing steadily weaker. Pages fell from the calendar, and pieces fell from him. He was still waiting, but the truth was that he had waited for too long. Now she was the one who opened up the cans and gave the food to him. His teeth were gone, and in fact there wasn't much left of his mouth, but she cheerfully packed what she could into his dripping, reeking, gaping maw. He couldn't move. He was trapped on the couch, a festering mountain of pus, and after dinner she would climb into his lap and turn the pages of his favorite magazines so they could enjoy them together. She liked the funny pictures, and they were pink the way she was.

Daddy was gray and green.

We can't go on like this, he would have said, but he couldn't speak, and he couldn't think much either. Of course that was nothing new, but he sensed dimly that things were getting out of hand when she perched on his knee one night and sank into it up to her armpits. She laughed and clapped her hands at Daddy's little joke, and in response he gave a sort of sigh, but that was about it.

The next morning, when she woke up, Daddy had soaked through the couch and spilled onto the carpet. At first she thought he might be kidding, but a few days later she decided she would have to face the facts. She'd been wondering about him for some time, but now there could be no doubt in her mind.

Daddy was history.

She stuck around for a while just to make sure, noticed that her supply of food was running low, cried for a few minutes, and then toddled toward the door. Armed only with her can opener, she went forth naked into the world.

There were some bones and puddles lying around, but nothing moved. She would survive, and perhaps she would find others like her, new humans born of dead desire. They might be living near a porn store, where only the will was wanted. There might even be, in time, an outbreak of new life.

She had seen her father's books, and she knew what to do with the good parts.

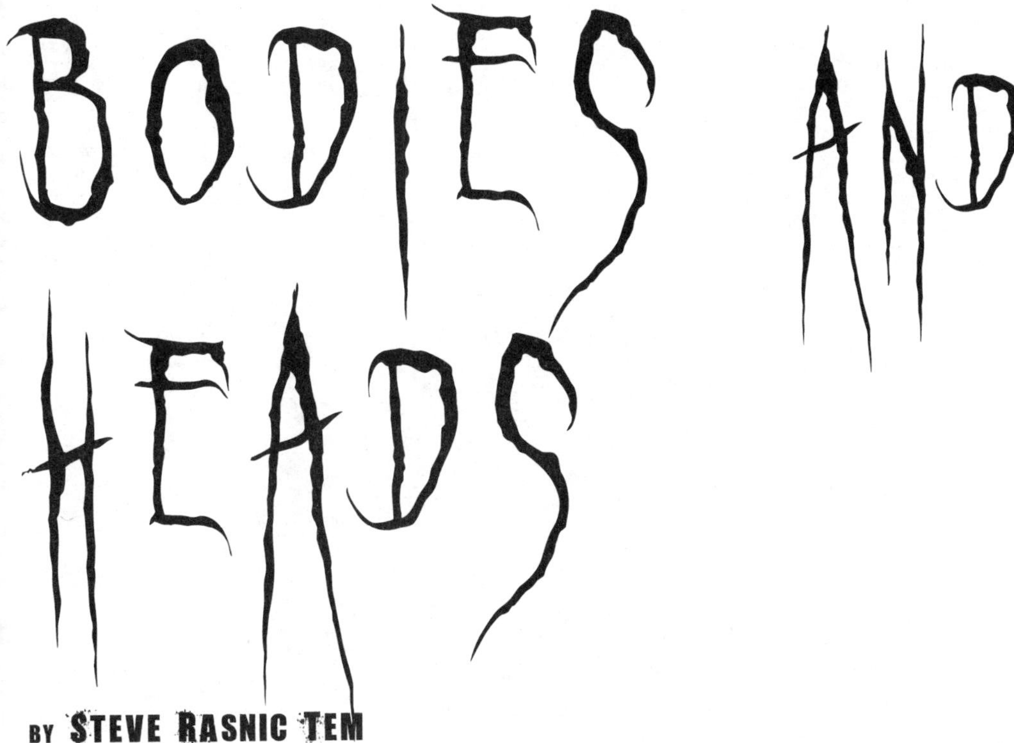

Bodies and Heads

BY **STEVE RASNIC TEM**

Steve Rasnic Tem is a horror writer's horror writer: not so much unsung as undersung, when one considers the sheer volume of visionary fiction he has published over the last several decades.

*When I first picked up "*Bodies and Heads*" twenty years ago, for* Book of the Dead*, I expected waves. But in the company of louder, more riotous stories, it seemed to have somehow faded into distance, like the essential humanity of the people it so richly invokes.*

But I gotta tell ya: this remains one of the most haunting and disturbing horror stories I've ever read, zombie or otherwise.

And it's an honor to return it to the world's attention.

IN THE HOSPITAL WINDOW the boy's head shook no no no. Elaine stopped on her way up the front steps, fascinated.

The boy's chest was rigid, his upper arms stiff. He seemed to be using something below the window to hold himself back, with all his strength, so that his upper body shook from the exertion.

She thought of television screens and their disembodied heads, ever so slightly out of focus, the individual dots of the transmitted heads moving apart with increasing randomness so that feature blended into feature and face into face until eventually the heads all looked the same: pinkish clouds of media flesh.

His head moved no no no. As if denying what was happening to him. He had been the first and was now the most advanced case of something they still had no name for. Given what had been going on in the rest of the country, the Denver Department of Health and Hospitals had naturally been quite concerned. An already Alert status had become a Crisis and doctors from all over—including a few with vague, unspecified governmental connections—had descended on the hospital.

Although it was officially discouraged, now and then in the hospital's corridors she had overheard the whispered word *zombie*.

"Jesus, will you look at him!"

Elaine turned. Mark planted a quick kiss on her lips. "Mark . . . somebody will see . . ." But she made no attempt to move away from him.

"I think they already know." He nibbled down her jawline. Elaine thought to pull away, but could not. His touch on her body, his attention, had always made her feel beautiful. It was, in fact, the only time she ever felt beautiful.

"You didn't want anyone to know just yet, remember?" She gasped involuntarily as he moved to the base of her throat. "Christ, Mark." She took a deep breath and pushed herself away from him. "Remember what you said about young doctors and hospital nurses? Especially young doctors with administrative aspirations?"

He looked at her. "Did I sound all that cold-blooded? I'm sorry."

She looked back up at the boy, Tom, in the window. Hopelessly out of control. No no no. "No—you weren't that bad. But I'm beginning to feel a little like somebody's mistress."

Some of the other nurses were now going into the building. Elaine thought they purposely avoided looking at the head-shaking boy in the window. "I'll make it up to you," Mark whispered. "I swear. Not much longer." But Elaine didn't answer; she just stared at the boy in the window.

There was now a steady stream of people walking up the steps, entering the hospital, very few permitting themselves to look at the boy. *Tom*, she thought. *His name is Tom.* She watched their quiet faces, wondering what they were thinking, if they were having stray thoughts about Tom but immediately suppressing them, or if they were having no thoughts about the boy at all. It bothered her not knowing. People led secret lives, secret even from those closest to them. It bothered her not knowing if they bore her ill will, or good will, or if for them she didn't exist at all. Her mother had always told her she cared far too much about what other people thought.

"I gather all the Fed doctors left yesterday afternoon," Mark said behind her.

"What? I thought they closed all the airports."

"They did. I heard this morning the governor even ordered gun emplacements on all the runways. Guess they left the city in a bus or something."

Elaine tried to rub the chill off her arms with shaking hands. The very idea of leaving the city in something other than an armored tank terrified her. It had been only a few months since the last flights. Then that plane had come in from Florida: all those dead people with suntans strolling off the plane as if they were on vacation. A short time later two small towns on Colorado's eastern plains—Kit Carson and Cheyenne Wells—were wiped out, or apparently wiped out, because only a few bodies were ever found. Then there was another plane, this one from Texas. Then another, from New York City. "It's hard to believe they could land a plane," had been Mark's comment at the time. But there were still more planes; the dead had an impeccable safety record.

"I'm just as glad to see them go," Mark said now. "Poking over that spastic kid like he was a two-headed calf. And still no signs of their mysterious 'zombie virus.'"

"No one knows how it starts," she said. "It could start anywhere. It could have dozens of different forms. Any vague gesture could be the first symptom."

"They haven't proven to me that it *is* a virus. No one really knows."

But Denver's quarantine seemed to be working. No one got in or out. All the roads closed, miles of perimeter patrolled. And no zombie sightings at all after those first few at the airport.

The boy's head drifted left and right as if in slow motion, as if weightless. "I missed the news this morning," she said.

"You looked so beat, I thought it best you sleep."

"I *need* to watch the news, Mark." Anger had such a grip on her jaw that she could hardly move it.

"You and most everybody else in Denver." She looked at him but said nothing. "Okay, I watched it for you. Just more of the same. A few distant shots of zombies in other states, looking like no more than derelicts prowling the cities, and the countryside, for food. Nothing much to tell you what they'd really be like. God knows what the world outside this city is really like anymore. I lost part of it—the reception just gets worse and worse."

Elaine knew that everything he was saying was true. But she kept watching the screens just the same, the faces seeming to get a little fuzzier every day as reception got worse, the distant cable stations disappearing one by one until soon only local programming was available, and then even the quality of that diminishing as equipment began to deteriorate and ghosts and static proliferated. But still she kept watching. Everybody she knew kept watching, desperate for any news outside of Denver.

And propped up in the window like a crazed TV announcer, young Tom's head moved no no no. At any moment she expected him to scream his denial: "No!" But no words ever passed the blurring lips. Just like all the other cases. No no no. Quiet heads that would suddenly explode into rhythmic, exaggerated denial. Their bodies fought it, held on to whatever was available so that muscles weren't twisted or bones torqued out of their sockets.

His head moved side to side: no no no. His long blond hair whipped and flew. His dark pebble eyes were lost in a nimbus of hair, now blond, now seeming to whiten more and more the faster his head flew. His expressionless face went steadily out of focus, and after a moment she realized she couldn't remember what he looked like, even though she had seen him several times a day every day since he had been admitted into the hospital.

What is he holding on to? she wondered, the boy's head now a cloud of mad insects, the movement having gone on impossibly long. His body vibrated within the broad window frame. At any moment she expected the rhythmic head to levitate him, out the window and over the empty, early-morning street. His features blurred in and out: he had four eyes, he had six. Three mouths that gasped for air attempting to scream. He had become a vision. He had become an angel.

"It's going to take more than a few skin grafts to fix that one," Betty said, nervously rubbing the back of her neck. "My God, doesn't he ever stop?" They were at the windows above surgery. He'd been holding on to a hot radiator; it had required three aides to pull him off. Even anesthetized, the boy's head shook so vigorously the surgeons had had to strap his neck into something like a large dog collar. The surgeries would be exploratory, mostly, until they found something specific. It bothered Elaine. Tom was a human being. He had secrets. "Look at his eyes," Elaine said. His eyes stared at her. As his face blurred in side-to-side movement, his eyes remained fixed on her. But that couldn't be.

"I can't see his eyes," Betty said with sudden vehemence. "Jeezus, will you look at him? They oughta do something with his brain while they're at it. They oughta go in there and snip out whatever's causin' it."

Elaine stared at the woman. *Snip it out. Where?* At one time they had been friends, or almost friends. Betty had wanted it, but Elaine just hadn't been able to respond. It had always been a long time between friends for her. The edge of anger in Betty's voice made her anxious. "They don't know what's causing it," Elaine said softly.

"My mama don't believe in 'em." Betty turned and looked at Elaine with heavily-shadowed eyes, anemic-looking skin. "Zombies. Mama thinks the zombies are something the networks came up with. She says real people would never do disgustin' things like they're sayin' the zombies do." Elaine found herself mesmerized by the lines in Betty's face. She tried to follow each one, where they became deeper, trapping dried rivers of hastily applied makeup, where pads and applicators had bruised, then covered up the skin. Betty's eyes blinked several times quickly in succession, the pupils bright and fixed like a doll's. "But then she always said we never landed on the moon, neither. Said they filmed all that out at Universal Studios." Milky spittle had adhered to the inside corners of Betty's mouth, which seemed unusually heavy with lipstick today. "Guess she could be right. Never read about zombies in the Bible, and you would think they'd be there if there was such a thing." Betty rubbed her arm across her forehead. "Goodness, my skin's so *dry*! I swear I'm flakin' down to the *nub*!" A slight ripple of body odor moved across Elaine's face. She could smell Betty's deodorant, and under that, something slightly sour and slightly sweet at the same time.

That's the way people's secrets smell, Elaine thought, and again wondered at herself for thinking such things. *People have more secrets than you could possibly imagine*. She wondered what secret things Betty was capable of, what Betty might do to a zombie if she had the opportunity, what Betty might do to Tom. "Tom's not a zombie," she said slowly, wanting to plant the idea firmly in Betty's head. "There's been no proof of a connection. No proof that he has a form of the virus, if there is a virus. No proof that he has a virus at all."

"My mama never believed much in *coincidences*," Betty said.

Elaine spent most of the night up in the ward with Tom and the other cases that had appeared: an elderly woman, a thirty-year-old retarded man, twin girls of thirteen who at times shook their heads in unison, a twenty-four-year-old hospital maintenance worker whose symptoms had started only a couple of days ago. As in every other place she'd worked, a TV set mounted high overhead murmured all evening. She couldn't get the vertical to hold. The announcer's head rolled rapidly by, disappearing at the top of the screen and reappearing at the bottom. But as she watched she began thinking it was different heads, the announcer switching them at the rate of perhaps one per second. She wondered how he'd managed the trick. Then she wondered if all newscasters did that, switching through a multitude of heads so quickly it couldn't be detected by the average viewer. She wanted to turn off the TV, but the doctors said it was best to leave it on for stimulation, even though their charges appeared completely unaware of it. Dozens of heads shaking no no no. Heads in the windows. Heads exploding with denial. Heads like bombs.

Two more nurses had quit that day. At least they had called; some had just stopped showing up. All the nurses were on double shifts now, with patient loads impossible to handle. Betty came in at six to help Elaine with feeding some of the head shakers.

"Now buckle the strap," Elaine said. She had the "horse collar," a padded brace, around the old woman's neck, her arms around the woman's head to hold it still. Betty fiddled with the straps.

"Damn!" Betty said. "I can't get it to buckle!"

"Hurry! I can't hold her head still much longer." Holding the head still put undue pressure on other parts of the system. Elaine could hear the woman's protesting stomach, and then both bladder and bowel were emptied.

"There!" Elaine let go and the old woman's head shook in her collar. Betty tried to spoon the food in. The woman's body spasmed like a lizard nailed to a board. Sometimes they broke their own bones that way. Elaine held her breath. Even strapped down, the old woman's face moved to an amazing degree. Like a latex mask attached loosely to the skull, her face slipped left and right, led by an agonized mouth apparently desperate to avoid the spoon. Elaine thought it disgusting, but it was better than any other method they'd tried. The head shakers choked on feeding tubes, pulled out IVs, and getting a spoon into those rapidly moving mouths had been almost impossible.

"I know it's your turn, but I'll go feed Tom," Elaine said.

Betty glanced up from the vibrating head, a dribble of soft brown food high on her right cheek. "Thanks, Elaine. I owe you." She turned back, aiming the spoon of dripping food at the twisting head. "I don't know. If I had to be like them . . . I don't know. I think I'd rather be dead."

Tom had always been the worst to feed. Elaine fixed a large plastic bib around his neck, then put one around her neck as well. He stared at her. Even as the spasms pulled his eyes rapidly past, she could see a little-boy softness in those adolescent eyes, an almost pleading vulnerability so at odds with the violent contortions his body made.

She moved the spoon in from the side, just out of his peripheral vision. But every time the metal touched the soft, pink flesh of the lips, the head jerked violently away. Again and again. And when some food finally did slip into the mouth cavity, he choked, his eyes became enormous, the whites swelling in panic, and his mouth showered it back at her. It was as if his mouth despised the food, reviled the food, and could not stand to be anywhere near it. As if she were asking him to eat his own feces.

She looked down at the bowl of mushy food. Tom reached his hand in, clutched a wet mess of it, then tried to stuff it into his own mouth. The mouth twisted away. His hand did this again and again, and still his mouth rejected it. Eventually his hands, denied the use of the mouth, began smearing the food on his face, his neck, his chest, his legs, all over his body, pushing it into the skin and eventually into every orifice available to receive it. He looked as if he had been swimming in garbage.

Tom's face, Tom's eyes, pleaded with her as his hands shoved great wet cakes of brown, green, and yellow food up under his blue hospital pajama top and down inside his underwear. Finally, as if in exasperation, Tom's body voided itself, drenching itself and Elaine in vomit, urine, and feces.

Elaine backed away, ripping off her plastic gloves and bib. "Stop it! Stop it! Stop it!" she screamed, as Tom's head moved no no no, and his body continued to pat itself, fondle itself, probe itself lovingly with food-smeared fingers. Elaine's vision blurred as she choked back the tears. Tom's body suddenly looked like some great bag of loose flesh, poked with wet, running holes, some ugly organic machine, inefficient in input and output. She continued to stare at it as it fed and drained, probed and made noises, all independent of the head and its steady no no no beat.

She ran into Betty out in the corridor. "I have to leave *now*," she said. "Betty, I'm *sorry*!"

Betty looked past her into the room where Tom was still playing with his food. "It's all right, kid. You just go get some sleep. I'll put old Master Tom to bed."

Elaine stared at her, sudden alarms of distrust going off in her head. "You'll be okay with him? I mean—he didn't *mean* it, Betty."

Betty looked offended. "Hey! Just what kind of nurse do you think I am? I'm going to hose him off and tuck him in, that's all. Unless you're insisting I read him a bedtime story, too? Maybe give him a kiss on the cheek? If I could *hit* his cheek, that is."

"I'm sorry. I didn't mean . . ."

"I know what you meant. Get some rest, Elaine. You're beat."

But Elaine couldn't bear to attempt the drive home, searching the dark corners at every intersection, waiting for the shambling strangers who lived in the streets to come close enough that she could get a good look at their faces. So that she could see if their faces were torn, their eyes distant. Or if their heads were beginning to shake.

Mark had been staying in the janitor's apartment down in the basement, near the morgue. The janitor had been replaced by a cleaning service some time back as a cost-cutting measure. Supposedly it was to be turned into a lab, but that had never happened. Mark always said he really didn't mind living by the morgue. He said it cut the number of drop-in visitors drastically.

Elaine went there.

"So don't go back," Mark said, nibbling at her ear. He was biting too hard, and his breath bore a trace of foulness. Elaine squirmed away and climbed out of bed.

"I have to go to the bathroom," she said. After closing the bathroom door, she ran water into the sink so that she would be unable to hear herself pee. People reacted to crisis in different ways, she supposed. Mark's way was to treat all problems as if they were of equal value, whether it was deciding what wattage light bulb to buy or the best way to feed a zombie.

Elaine looked down at her legs. They'd gotten a little spongier each year; her thighs seemed to spread a little wider each time she sat down. Here and there were little lumps and depressions which seemed to move from time to time. Her belly bulged enough now that she could see only the slightest halo of dark pubic hair when she looked down like this. And the pubic hair itself wasn't all that dark anymore. There were streaks of gray, and what had surprised and confused her, red. By her left knee a flowery pattern of broken blood vessels was darkening into a bruise. She tried to smell herself. She sometimes imagined she must smell terrible.

It seemed she had always watched herself grow older while sitting on the toilet. Sitting on the toilet, she found she couldn't avoid looking at her legs, her belly, her pubic hair. She couldn't avoid smelling herself.

She stood up and looked at herself in the mirror. She looked for scars, bruises, signs of corruption she might have missed before. She pretended her face was a patient's, and she washed it, brushed her hair. As a child she'd pretended her face was a doll's face, her hair a doll's hair. She'd never trusted mirrors. They didn't show the secrets inside.

"I have to go back," Elaine said coming out of the bathroom. "We're shorthanded. They count on me. And I can't let Betty work that ward alone."

But Mark was busy fiddling with the VCR. "Huh? Oh yeah . . . well, you do what you think is right, honey. Hey—I got us a tape from one of the security people. The cops confiscated it two weeks ago and it's been circulating ever since." Elaine walked slowly around the bed and stood by Mark as he adjusted the contrast. "Pretty crudely made, but you can still make out most of it."

The screen was dark, with occasional lighter shadows floating through that dark. Then twin pale spots resolved out of the distortion, moving rapidly left and right, up and down. Elaine thought of headlights gone crazy, maybe a moth's wings. Then the camera pulled back suddenly, as if startled, and she saw that it was a black man's immobile face, but with eyes that jumped around as if they were being given some sort of electrical shock. Frightened eyes. Eyes moving no no no.

But as the camera dwelled on this face, Elaine noticed that there was more wrong here than simple fright. The dark skin of the face looked torn all along the hairline, peeled back, and crusted a dark red. A cut bisected the left cheek; she thought she could see several tissue layers deep into the valley it made. And when the head moved, she saw a massive hole just under the chin where throat cartilage danced in open air.

"That's one of them," she said in a soft voice filled with awe. "A zombie."

"The tape was smuggled in from somewhere down South, I hear," Mark said distractedly, moving even closer to the screen. "Beats me how they can still get these videos into the city."

"But the quarantine . . ."

"Supply and demand, honey." As the camera moved back farther, Elaine was surprised to see live, human hands pressing down on the zombie's shoulders. "Get a load of this," Mark said, an anxious edge to his voice.

The camera jerked back suddenly to show the zombie pressed against gray wooden planks—the side of a barn or some other farm building. The zombie was naked: large wounds covered much of its body. Like a decoration, an angry red scar ran the length of the dangling, slightly paler penis. Six or seven large men in jeans and old shirts—work clothes—were pushing the zombie flat against the gray wood, moving their rough hands around to avoid its snapping teeth. The more they avoided its teeth, the more manic the zombie became, jerking its head like a striking snake, twisting its head side to side and snapping its mouth.

An eighth man—fat, florid, baggy tits hanging around each side of his bib overalls—carried a bucket full of hammers onto the scene and handed one to each of the men restraining the zombie. Then the fat man reached deeper into the bucket and came out with a handful of ten-penny nails, which he also distributed to the men.

Mark held his breath as the men proceeded to drive the nails through the body of the zombie—through shoulders, arms, hands, ankles—pinning it like a squirming lizard on the boards.

The zombie showed no pain, but struggled against the nails, tearing wider holes. Little or no blood dripped from these holes, but Elaine did think she could detect a clear, glistening fluid around each wound.

The men stared at the zombie for a moment. A couple of them giggled like adolescent girls, but for the most part they looked dissatisfied.

One of the men nailed the zombie's ears to the wall. Another used several nails to pin the penis and scrotum; several more nails severed it. The zombie pelvis did a little gyration above the spot where the genitals had become a trophy on the barn wall.

The zombie seemed not to notice the difference. The men laughed and pointed.

There were no screams on this sound track. Just laughter and animalistic zombie grunts.

"Jesus, Mark." Elaine turned away from the TV, ashamed of herself for having watched that long. "Jesus." She absentmindedly stroked his hair, running her hand down his face, vaguely wondering how she could get him away from the TV, or at least to turn it off.

"Damn. Look, they're bringing out the ax and the sickle," Mark said.

"I don't want to look," she said, on the verge of tears. "I don't want *you* to look either. It's crazy, it's . . . pornographic."

"Hey, I know this is pretty sick stuff, but I think it tells us something about the way things *are* out there. Christ, they won't show it to us on the news. Not the way it *really* is. We need to know things like this exist."

"I know goddamn well they exist! I don't need it rubbed in my face!"

Elaine climbed into bed and turned her back on him. She tried to ignore the static-filled moans and giggles coming from the TV. She pretended she was sick in a hospital bed, that she had no idea what was going on in the world and never could. A minute or two later Mark turned off the TV. She imagined the image of the zombie's head fading, finally just its startled eyes showing, then nothing.

She felt Mark's hands gently rubbing her back. Then he lay down on the bed, half on top of her, still rubbing her tight flesh.

"They're not in Denver," he said softly. "There's still been no sightings. No zombies here, ma'am." The rubbing moved to her thighs. She tried to ignore it.

"If there were, would people here act like those rednecks in your damn video? Jesus, Mark. Nobody should be allowed to behave that way."

He stopped rubbing. She could hear him breathing. "People do strange things sometimes," he finally said. "Especially in strange times. Especially groups of people. They get scared and they lose control." He resumed rubbing her shoulders, then moved to her neck. "There are no zombies in Denver, honey. No sightings. All the news types keep telling us that. You *know* that; you're always watching them."

"Maybe they won't look the same."

"What do you mean?"

"Maybe they won't look the same here as they do everywhere else. Maybe it'll take a different form, and we won't know what to look for. They think it's a virus—well, viruses mutate, they have different forms. Maybe the doctors and the Health Department and all those reporters aren't as smart as they think they are. Christ, it might even be some form of venereal disease."

"Hey. That's not funny."

"You think I intended it to be?" She could feel her anger bunching up the shoulder muscles beneath his hands. She could feel all this beginning to change her; no way would she be the same after it all stopped. If it ever stopped.

"I know. I know," he said. "This is hard on all of us." Then he started kissing her. Uncharitably, she wondered if it was because he'd run out of things to say to her. But she found her body responding, even though her head was sick with him and all his easy answers and explanations.

His kisses ran down her neck and over her breasts like a warm liquid. And her body welcomed it, had felt so cold before. "Turn out the light, please, Mark," she said, grudgingly giving into the body, hating the body for it. He left silently to turn out the light, then was back again, kissing her, touching her, warming her one ribbon of flesh at a time.

In the darkness she could not see her own body. She could imagine away the blemishes, the ugly, drifting spots, the dry patches of skin, the small corruptions patterning death. And she could imagine that his breath was always sweet smelling. She could imagine his hair dark and full. She could imagine the image of the zombie's destroyed penis out of her head when Mark made love to her. And in this darkness she could almost imagine that Mark would never die.

His body continued to fondle her after she knew his head had gone to sleep.

Mark's kiss woke her up the next morning. "Last night was wonderful," he whispered. "Glad you finally got over whatever was bothering you." That last comment made her angry, and she tried to tell him that, but she was too sleepy and he'd already left. And then she was sorry he was gone and wished he would come back so his touch would make her body feel beautiful again.

She stared at the dead gray eye of the TV, then glanced at the VCR. Apparently Mark had taken his video with him. She was relieved, and a little ashamed of herself. She turned the TV on. The eye filled with static, but she could hear the female newscaster's flat, almost apathetic voice.

"... the federal government has reported increased progress with the so-called 'zombie' epidemic ..." Then this grainy, washed-out bit of stock footage came on the screen: men in hunters' clothing and surplus fatigues shooting zombies in the head from a safe distance. Shootting them and then moving along calmly down a dirt road. The newscaster appeared on the screen again: silent, emotionless, makeup perfect, her head rolling up into the top of the cabinet.

It was after four in the morning. Betty had handled the ward by herself all night and would need some relief. Elaine dressed quickly and headed upstairs.

Betty wasn't at the nurse's station. Elaine started down the dim-lit corridor, peeking into each room. In the beds dark shadows shook and moved their heads no no no, even in their dreams. But no sign of Betty.

The last room was Tom's, and he wasn't there. She could hear a steady padding of feet up ahead, in the dark tunnel that led to the new wing. She tried the light switch, but apparently it wasn't connected. Out of her pocket she pulled the penlight that she used for making chart notations in patients' darkened rooms. It made a small, distorted circle of illumination. She started down the darkened tunnel, flashing her small light now and then on the uncompleted ceiling, the holes in the walls where they'd run electrical conduit, the tile floor streaked white with plaster dust, littered with wire, pipe, and lumber.

She came out into a giant open area that hadn't yet been divided into rooms. Cable snaked out of large holes in the ceiling, dangled by her face. Streetlight filtered through the tall, narrow windows, striping piles of ceiling tile, paint cans, and metal posts. They were supposed to be finished with all this by next month. She wondered if they would even bother, given how things were in the city. The wing looked more like a structure they were stripping, demolishing, than one they were constructing. Like a building under autopsy, she thought. She could no longer hear the other footsteps ahead of her. She heard her own steps, crunching the grit under foot, and her own ragged breath.

She flashed her light overhead, and something flashed back. A couple of cameras projected from a metal beam. Blind, their wires wrapped uselessly around the beam. She walked on, following the connections with her light. There were a series of blank television monitors, their enormous gray eyes staring down at her.

Someone cried softly in the darkness ahead. Elaine aimed her light there, but all she could see were crates, paneling leaned against the wall and stacked on the floor, metal supports and crosspieces. A tangle of sharp angles. But then there was that cry again. "Betty? Tom?"

A pale face loomed into the blurred, yellowed beam. A soft shake of the face, side to side. The eyes were too white, and had a distant stare.

"Betty?" The face shook and shook again. Betty stumbled out of a jumble of cardboard boxes, construction and stored medical supplies breaking beneath her stumbling feet.

"No . . ." Betty's mouth moved as if in slow-motion. Her lipstick looked too bright, her mascara too dark. "No," she said again, and something dark dripped out of her eyes as her head began to shake.

Elaine's light picked up a glint in Betty's right hand. "Betty?" Betty stumbled forward and fell, keeping that right hand out in front of her. Elaine stepped closer thinking to help Betty up, but then saw that Betty's right arm was swinging slowly side to side, a scalpel clutched tightly in her hand. "Betty! Let me help you!"

"No!" Betty screamed. Her head began to thrash back and forth on the litter-covered floor. Her cheeks rolled again and again over broken glass. Blood welled; smeared, and stained her face as her head moved no no no. She struggled to control the hand holding the scalpel. Then she suddenly plunged it into her throat. Her left hand came up jerkily and helped her pull the scalpel through muscle and skin.

Elaine fell to her knees, grabbed paper and cloth, anything at hand to dam the dark flow from Betty's throat. After a minute or two she stopped and turned away.

There were more noises off in the darkness. At the back of the room where she'd first seen Betty, Elaine found a doorless passage to another room. Her light now had a vague reddish tinge. She wondered hazily if there was blood on the flashlight lens, or blood in her eyes. But the light still showed the way. She followed it, hearing a harsh, wet sound. For just a moment she thought that maybe Betty might still be alive. She started to go back when she heard it again; it was definitely in the room ahead of her.

She tried not to think of Betty as she made her way through the darkness. *That wasn't Betty. That was just her body.* Elaine's mother used to babble things like that to her all the time. Spiritual things. Elaine didn't know what she herself felt. Someone dies, you don't know them anymore. You can't imagine what they might be thinking.

The room had the sharp smell of fresh paint. Drop cloths had been piled in the center of the floor. The windows were crisscrossed by long stretches of masking tape, and outside lights left odd patterns like angular spiderwebs on all the objects in the room.

A heavy cord dropped out of the ceiling to a small switch box on the floor, which was in turn connected to a large mercury lamp the construction crew must have been using. Elaine bent over and flipped the switch.

The light was like an explosion. It created strange, skeletal shadows in the drop cloths, as if she were suddenly seeing *through* them. She walked steadily toward the pile, keeping an eye on those shadows.

Elaine reached out her hand and several of the cloths flew away.

My god, Betty killed him! Betty killed him and cut off that awful, shaking head! The head was a small, sad mound by the boy's filthy, naked body. A soft whispering seemed to enter Elaine's ear, which brought her attention back to that head.

She stopped to feel the draft, but there was no draft, even though she could hear it rising in her head, whistling through her hair and making it grow longer, making it grow white, making her older.

Because of a trick of the light the boy's—Tom's—eyes looked open in his severed head. Because of a trick of the light the eyes blinked several times as if trying to adjust to that light.

He had a soft, confused stare, like a stuffed toy's. His mouth moved like a baby's. Then his naked, headless body sat up on the floor. Then the headless body struggled to its feet, weaving unsteadily. *No inner ear for balance*, Elaine thought, and almost laughed. She felt crazed, capable of anything.

The body stood motionless, staring at Elaine. Staring at her. The nipples looked darker than normal and seemed to track her as she moved sideways across the room. The hairless breasts gave the body's new eyes a slight bulge. The navel was flat and neutral, but Elaine wondered if the body could smell her with it. The penis—the tongue—curled in and out of the bearded mouth of the body's new face. The body moved stiffly, puppet-like, toward its former head.

The body picked up its head with one hand and threw it out into a darkened corner of the room. It made a sound like a wet mop slapping the linoleum floor. Elaine heard a soft whimpering that soon ceased. She could hear ugly, moist noises coming from the body's new bearded mouth. She could hear skin splitting, she could see blood dripping to the dusty floor as the body's new mouth widened and brought new lips up out of the meaty darkness inside.

The sound of a wheelchair rolling in behind her. She turned and watched as the old woman grabbed each side of her ancient-looking, spasming head. The head continued its insistent no no no even as the hands and arms increased their pressure, the old lady's body quaking from the strain. Then suddenly the no no no stopped, the arms lifted up on the now-motionless head, and pulled it away from the body, cracking open the spine and stretching the skin and muscle of the neck until they tore or snapped apart like rotted bands of elastic. The old woman's fluids gushed, then suddenly stopped, both head and body sealing the breaks with pale tissues stretched almost to transparency.

The new face on the old woman's body was withered, pale, almost hairless, and resembled the old face to a remarkable degree. The new eyes sagged lazily, and Elaine wondered if this body might be blind.

The old woman's head gasped, and was still. The young male body picked up the woman's dead head and stuffed it into its hairy mouth. Its new, pale pink lips stretched and rolled. Elaine could see the stomach acid bubbling on those lips, the steadily diminishing face of the old lady appearing now and then in the gaps between the male body's lips as the body continued its digestion. The old woman's denuded skull fell out on the linoleum and rattled its way across the floor.

Elaine closed her eyes and tried to remember everything her mother had ever told her. Someone dies and you don't know them anymore. It's just a dead body—it's not my friend. My friend lives in the head forever. Death is a mystery. Stay away from crowds. Crowds want to eat you.

She wanted Mark here with her. She wanted Mark to touch her body and make her feel beautiful. No. People can't be trusted. No. She wanted to love her own body. No. She wanted her body to love her. No. She tried to imagine Mark touching her, making love to her. No. With dead eyes, mouth splitting at the corners. No. Removing his head and shoving it deep inside her, his eyes and tongue finding and eating all her secrets.

No no no, her head said. Elaine's head moved no no no. And each time her vision swept across the room with the rhythmic swing of her shaking head, the bodies were closer.

Operated by seven men who sometimes work
round the clock putting calls through it averages
'Calling home is probably the greatest morale
It's great talking to home
said last month Alpha Zulu
calls than any other station both in
area of operation and in the
enjoy their work because it is a
be able to do something for other
rewarding work commented Spe
Beza, 19, of Toledo, Ohio
as a civilian operator in
to running patches, Beza and
It builds morale better than an
This magic is radio AB8AZ 'The
a serviceman's voice contact
with family and friends at home Called Alpha
it is one of many Military Affiliate Radio
System (MARS) stations in Vietnam and is locat
ed at this 9th Division base camp 41 miles south
of Saigon

On the Far Side of the Cadillac Desert with Dead Folks

by Joe R. Lansdale

If there's one man in all of writerdom that I'd want watching my back in a zombie apocalypse, it's Joe R. Lansdale. They don't come any tougher, more clear-eyed or brass-tacked. And like Texas toilet paper—to quote the old Gallegher joke—he don't take shit offa no one.

"On the Far Side of the Cadillac Desert with Dead Folks" is only one of many zombie yarns Joe has spun over the years. But for me, this one is the pure quintessence. All hardass zombie-fightin' survivalist fiction from that point on took its cues from this raucous motherfucker, as well they should have.

Cuz it don't get any better than this.

A note for the easily-offended: you'll know within a paragraph or three whether this story is for you. If not, feel free to mosey on down the table of contents for less unremitting fare.

But for those of you who came to see mayhem, you have come straight to the right damn place.

1

After a month's chase, Wayne caught up with Calhoun one night at a little honky-tonk called Rosalita's. It wasn't that Calhoun had finally gotten careless, it was just that he wasn't worried. He'd killed four bounty hunters so far, and Wayne knew a fifth didn't concern him.

The last bounty hunter had been the famous Pink Lady McGuire—one mean, mama—three hundred pounds of rolling, ugly meat that carried a twelve-gauge Remington pump and a bad attitude. Story was, Calhoun jumped her from behind, cut her throat, and as a joke, fucked her before she bled to death. This not only proved to Wayne that Calhoun was a dangerous sonofabitch, it also proved he had bad taste.

Wayne stepped out of his '57 Chevy reproduction, pushed his hat back on his forehead, opened the trunk, and got the sawed-off double barrel and some shells out of there. He already had a .38 revolver in the holster at his side and a bowie knife in each boot, but when you went into a place like Rosalita's it was best to have plenty of backup.

Wayne put a handful of shotgun shells in his shirt pocket, snapped the flap over them, looked up at the red-and-blue neon sign that flashed ROSALITA'S: COLD BEER AND DEAD DANCING, found his center, as they say in Zen, and went on in.

He held the shotgun against his leg, and as it was dark in there and folks were busy with talk or drinks or dancing, no one noticed him or his artillery right off.

He spotted Calhoun's stocky, black-hatted self immediately. He was inside the dance cage with a dead buck-naked Mexican girl of about twelve. He was holding her tight around the waist with one hand and massaging her rubbery ass with the other like it was a pillow he was trying to shape. The dead girl's handless arms flailed on either side of Calhoun, and her little tits pressed to his thick chest. Her wire-muzzled face knocked repeatedly at his shoulder and drool whipped out of her mouth in thick spermy ropes, stuck to his shirt, faded and left a patch of wetness.

For all Wayne knew, the girl was Calhoun's sister or daughter. It was that kind of place. The kind that had sprung up immediately after that stuff had gotten out of a lab upstate and filled the air with bacterium that brought dead humans back to life, made their basic motor functions work and made them hungry for human flesh; made it so if a man's wife, daughter, sister, or mother went belly up and he wanted to turn a few bucks, he might think: "Damn, that's tough about ole Betty Sue, but she's dead as hoot-owl shit and ain't gonna be needing nothing from here on out, and with them germs working around in her, she's just gonna pull herself out of the ground and cause me a problem. And the ground out back of the house is harder to dig than a calculus problem is to work, so I'll just toss her cold ass in the back of the pickup next to the chain saw and the barbed-wire roll, haul her across the border and sell her to the Meat Boys to sell to the tonks for dancing.

"It's a sad thing to sell one of your own, but shit, them's the breaks. I'll just stay out of the tonks until all the meat rots off her bones and they have to throw her away. That way I won't go in some place for a drink and see her up there shaking her dead tits and end up going sentimental and dewey-eyed in front of one of my buddies or some ole two-dollar gal."

This kind of thinking supplied the dancers. In other parts of the country, the dancers might be men or children, but here it was mostly women. Men were used for hunting and target practice.

The Meat Boys took the bodies, cut off the hands so they couldn't grab, ran screws threw their jaws to fasten on wire muzzles so they couldn't bite, sold them to the honky-tonks about the time the germ started stirring.

Tonk owners put them inside wire enclosures up front of their joints, started music, and men paid five dollars to get in there and grab them and make like they were dancing when all the women wanted to do was grab and bite, which muzzled and handless, they could not do.

If a man liked his partner enough, he could pay more money and have her tied to a cot in the back and he could get on her and do some business. Didn't have to hear no arguments or buy presents or make promises or make them come. Just fuck and hike.

As long as the establishment sprayed the dead for maggots and kept them perfumed and didn't keep them so long hunks of meat came off on a fella's dick, the customers were happy as flies on shit.

Wayne looked to see who might give him trouble, and figured everyone was a potential customer. The six foot two, two-hundred fifty pound bouncer being the most immediate concern.

But, there wasn't anything to do but to get on with things and handle problems when they came up. He went into the cage where Calhoun was dancing, shouldered through the other dancers and went for him.

Calhoun had his back to Wayne, and as the music was loud, Wayne didn't worry about going quietly. But Calhoun sensed him and turned with his hand full of a little .38.

Wayne clubbed Calhoun's arm with the barrel of the shotgun. The little gun flew out of Calhoun's hand and went skidding across the floor and clanked against the metal cage.

Calhoun wasn't outdone. He spun the dead girl in front of him and pulled a big pigsticker out of his boot and held it under the girl's armpit in a threatening manner, which with a knife that big was no feat.

Wayne shot the dead girl's left kneecap out from under her and she went down. Her armpit trapped Calhoun's knife. The other men deserted their partners and went over the wire netting like squirrels.

Before Calhoun could shake the girl loose, Wayne stepped in and hit him over the head with the barrel of the shotgun. Calhoun crumpled and the girl began to crawl about on the floor as if looking for lost contacts.

The bouncer came in behind Wayne, grabbed him under the arms and tried to slip a full nelson on him.

Wayne kicked back on the bouncer's shin and raked his boot down the man's instep and stomped his foot. The bouncer let go. Wayne turned and kicked him in the balls and hit him across the face with the shotgun.

The bouncer went down and didn't even look like he wanted up.

Wayne couldn't help but note he liked the music that was playing. When he turned he had someone to dance with.

Calhoun.

Calhoun charged him, hit Wayne in the belly with his head, knocked him over the bouncer. They tumbled to the floor and the shotgun went out of Wayne's hands and scraped across the floor and hit the crawling girl in the head. She didn't even notice, just kept snaking in circles, dragging her blasted leg behind her like a skin she was trying to shed.

The other women, partnerless, wandered about the cage. The music changed. Wayne didn't like this tune as well. Too slow. He bit Calhoun's earlobe off.

Calhoun screamed and they grappled around on the floor. Calhoun got his arm around Wayn's throat and tried to choke him to death.

Wayne coughed out the earlobe, lifted his leg and took the knife out of his boot. He brought it around and back and hit Calhoun in the temple with the hilt.

Calhoun let go of Wayne and rocked on his knees, then collapsed on top of him.

Wayne got out from under him and got up and kicked him in the head a few times. When he was finished, he put the bowie in its place, got Calhoun's .38 and the shotgun. To hell with pig sticker.

A dead woman tried to grab him, and he shoved her away with a thrust of his palm. He got Calhoun by the collar, started pulling him toward the gate.

Faces were pressed against the wire, watching. It had been quite a show. A friendly cowboy type opened the gate for Wayne and the crowd parted as he pulled Calhoun by. One man felt helpful and chased after them and said, "Here's his hat, Mister," and dropped it on Calhoun's face and it stayed there.

Outside, a professional drunk was standing between two cars taking a leak on the ground. As Wayne pulled Calhoun past, the drunk said, "Your buddy don't look so good."

"Look worse than that when I get him to Law Town," Wayne said.

Wayne stopped by the '57, emptied Calhoun's pistol and tossed it as far as he could, then took a few minutes to kick Calhoun in the ribs and ass. Calhoun grunted and farted, but didn't come to.

When Wayne's leg got tired, he put Calhoun in the passenger seat and handcuffed him to the door.

He went over to Calhoun's '62 Impala replica with the plastic bull horns mounted on the hood—which was how he had located him in the first place, by his well-known car—and kicked the glass out of the window on the driver's side and used the shotgun to shoot the bull horns off. He took out his pistol and shot all the tires flat, pissed on the driver's door, and kicked a dent in it.

By then he was too tired to shit in the backseat, so he took some deep breaths and went back to the '57 and climbed in behind the wheel.

Reaching across Calhoun, he opened the glove box and got out one of his thin, black cigars and put it in his mouth. He pushed the lighter in, and while he waited for it to heat up, he took the shotgun out of his lap and reloaded it.

A couple of men poked their heads outside of the tonk's door, and Wayne stuck the shotgun out the window and fired above their heads. They disappeared inside so fast they might have been an optical illusion.

Wayne put the lighter to his cigar, picked up the wanted poster he had on the seat, and set fire to it. He thought about putting it in Calhoun's lap as a joke, but didn't. He tossed the flaming poster out the window.

He drove over close to the tonk and used the remaining shotgun load to shoot at the neon Rosalita's sign. Glass tinkled onto the tonk's roof and onto the gravel drive.

Now if he only had a dog to kick.

He drove away from there, bound for the Cadillac Desert, and finally Law Town on the other side.

2

The Cadillacs stretched for miles, providing the only shade in the desert. They were buried nose down at a slant, almost to the windshields, and Wayne could see skeletons of some of the drivers in the car, either lodged behind the steering wheels or lying on the dashboards against the glass. The roof and hood guns had long since been removed and all the windows on the cars were rolled up, except for those that had been knocked out and vandalized by travelers, or dead folks looking for goodies.

The thought of being in one of those cars with the windows rolled up in all this heat made Wayne feel even more uncomfortable than he already was. Hot as it was, he was certain even the skeletons were sweating.

He finished pissing on the tire of the Chevy, saw the piss had almost dried. He shook the drops off, watched them fall and evaporate against the burning sand. Zipping up, he thought about Calhoun, and how when he'd pulled over earlier to let the sonofabitch take a leak, he'd seen there was a little metal ring through the head of his dick and a Texas emblem, being from there himself, but he couldn't for the life of him imagine why a fella would do that to his general. Any idiot who would put a ring through the head of his pecker deserved to die, innocent or not.

Wayne took off his cowboy hat and rubbed the back of his neck and ran his hand over the top of his head and back again. The sweat on his fingers was thick as lube oil, and the thinning part of his hairline was tender; the heat was cooking the hell out of his scalp, even through the brown felt of his hat.

Before he put his hat on, the sweat on his fingers was dry. He broke open the shotgun, put the shells in his pocket, opened the Chevy's back door and tossed the shotgun on the floorboard.

He got in the front behind the wheel and the seat was hot as a griddle on his back and ass. The sun shone through the slightly tinted windows like a polished chrome hubcap; it forced him to squint.

Glancing over at Calhoun, he studied him. The fucker was asleep with his head thrown back and his black wilted hat hung precarious on his head—it looked jaunty almost. Sweat oozed down Calhoun's red face, flowed over his eyelids and around his neck, running in riverlets down the white seat covers, drying quickly. He had his left hand between his legs, clutching his balls, and his right was on the arm rest, which was the only place it could be since he was handcuffed to the door.

Wayne thought he ought to blow the bastard's brains out and tell God he died. The shithead certainly needed shooting, but Wayne didn't want to lose a thousand dollars off his reward. He needed every penny if he was going to get that wrecking yard he wanted. The yard was the dream that went before him like a carrot before a donkey, and he didn't want anymore delays. If he never made another trip across this goddamn desert, that would suit him fine.

Pop would let him buy the place with the money he had now, and he could pay the rest out later. But that wasn't what he wanted to do. The bounty business had finally gone sour, and he wanted to do different. It wasn't any goddamn fun anymore. Just met the dick cheese of the earth. And when you ran the sonofabitches to ground and put the cuffs on them, you had to watch your ass till you got them turned in. Had to sleep with one eye open and a hand on your gun. It wasn't anyway to live.

And he wanted a chance to do right by Pop. Pop had been like a father to him. When he was a kid and his mama was screwing the Mexicans across the border for the rent money, Pop would let him hang out in the yard and climb on the rusted cars and watch him fix the better ones, tune those babies so fine they purred like dick-whipped women.

When he was older, Pop would haul him to Galveston for the whores and out to the beach to take potshots at all the ugly, fucked-up critters swimming around in the Gulf. Sometimes he'd take him to Oklahoma for the Dead Roundup. It sure seemed to do the old fart good to whack those dead fuckers with a tire iron, smash their diseased brains so they'd lay down for good. And it was a challenge. Cause if one of those dead buddies bit you, you could put your head between your legs and kiss your rosy ass goodbye.

Wayne pulled out of his thoughts of Pop and the wrecking yard and turned on the stereo system. One of his favorite country-and-western tunes whispered at him. It was Billy Conteegas singing, and Wayne hummed along with the music as he drove into the welcome, if mostly ineffectual, shadows provided by the Cadillacs.

My baby left me,
She left me for a cow,
But I don't give a flying fuck,
She's gone radioactive now,
Yeah, my baby left me,
Left me for a six-tittied cow.

Just when Conteegas was getting to the good part, doing the trilling sound in his throat he was famous for, Calhoun opened his eyes and spoke up.

"Ain't it bad enough I got to put up with the fucking heat and your fucking humming without having to listen to that shit? Ain't you got no Hank

Williams stuff, or maybe some of that nigger music they used to make? You know where the coons harmonize and one of them sings like his nuts are cut off."

"You just don't know good music when you hear it, Calhoun."

Calhoun moved his free hand to his hatband, found one of his few remaining cigarettes and a match there. H struck the match on his knee, lit the smoke and coughed a few rounds. Wayne couldn't imagine how Calhoun could smoke in all this heat.

"Well, I may not know good music when I hear it, capon, but I damn sure know bad music when I hear it. And that's some bad music."

"You ain't got any kind of culture, Calhoun. You been too busy raping kids."

"Reckon a man has to have a hobby," Calhoun said, blowing smoke at Wayne. "Young pussy is mine. Besides she wasn't in diapers. Couldn't find one that young. She was thirteen. You know what they say. If they're old enough to bleed, they're old enough to breed."

"How old they have to be for you to kill them?"

"She got loud."

"Change channels, Calhoun."

"Just passing the time of day, capon. Better watch yourself bounty hunter, when you least expect it, I'll bash your head."

"You're gonna run your mouth one time too many, Calhoun, and when you do, you're gonna finish this ride in the trunk with ants crawling on you. You ain't so priceless I won't blow you away."

"You lucked out at the tonk, boy. But there's always tomorrow, and every day can't be like at Rosalita's."

Wayne smiled. "Trouble is, Calhoun, you're running out of tomorrows."

3

As they drove between the Cadillacs, the sky fading like a bad bulb, Wayne looked at the cars and tried to imagine what the Chevy-Cadillac Wars had been like, and why they had been fought in this miserable desert. He had heard it was a hell of a fight, and close, but the outcome had been Chevy's and now they were the only cars Detroit made. And as far as he was concerned, that was the only thing about Detroit that was worth a damn. Cars.

He felt that way about all cities. He'd just as soon lie down and let a diseased dog shit in his face than drive through one, let alone live in one.

Law Town being an exception. He'd go there. Not to live, but to give Calhoun to the authorities and pick up his reward. People in Law Town were always glad to see a criminal brought in. The public executions were popular and varied and brought in a steady income.

Last time he'd been to Law Town he'd bought a front-row ticket to one of the executions and watched a chronic shoplifter, a red-headed rat of a man, get pulled apart by being chained between two souped-up tractors. The execution itself was pretty brief, but there had been plenty of buildup with clowns and balloons and a big-tittied stripper who could swing her tits in either direction to boom-boom music.

Wayne had been put off by the whole thing. It wasn't organized enough and the drinks and food were expensive and the front-row seats were too close to the tractors. He had gotten to see that the red-head's insides were brighter than his hair, but some of the insides got sprinkled on his new shirt, and cold water or not, the spots hadn't come out. He had suggested to one of the management that they put up a big plastic shield so the front row wouldn't get splattered, but he doubted anything had come of it.

They drove until it was solid dark. Wayne stopped and fed Calhoun a stick of jerky and some water from his canteen, then he handcuffed him to the front bumper of the Chevy.

"See any snakes, Gila monsters, scorpions, stuff like that," Wayne said, "yell out. Maybe I can get around here in time."

"I'd let the fuckers run up my asshole before I'd call you," Calhoun said.

Leaving Calhoun with his head resting on the bumper, Wayne climbed in the backseat of the Chevy and slept with one ear cocked and one eye open.

Before dawn Wayne got Calhoun loaded in the '57 and they started out. After a few minutes of sluicing through the early morning grayness, a wind started up. One of those weird desert winds that come out of nowhere. It carried grit through the air at the speed of bullets, hit the '57 with a sound like rabid cats scratching.

The sand tires crunched on through, and Wayne turned on the windshield blower, the sand wipers, and the headbeams, and kept on keeping on.

When it was time for the sun to come up, they couldn't see it. Too much sand. It was blowing harder than ever and the blowers and wipers couldn't handle it. It was piling up. Wayne couldn't even make out the Cadillacs anymore.

He was about to stop when a shadowy, whale-like shape crossed in front of him and he slammed on the brakes, giving the sand tires a workout. But it wasn't enough.

The '57 spun around and rammed the shape on Calhoun's side. Wayne heard Calhoun yell, then felt himself thrown against the door and his head smacked metal and the outside darkness was nothing compared to the darkness into which he descended.

4

Wayne rose out of it as quickly as he had gone down. Blood was trickling into his eyes from a slight forehead wound. He used his sleeve to wipe it away.

His first clear sight was of a face at the window on his side; a sallow, moon-terrain face with bulging eyes and an expression like an idiot contemplating Sanskrit. On the man's head was a strange, black hat with big round ears, and in the center of the hat, like a silver tumor, was the head of a large screw. Sand lashed at the face, embedded in it, struck the unblinking eyes and made the round-eared hat flap. The man paid no attention. Though still dazed, Wayne knew why. The man was one of the dead folks.

Wayne looked in Calhoun's direction. Calhoun's door had been mashed in and the bending metal had pinched the handcuff attached to the arm rest in two. The blow had knocked Calhoun to the center of the seat. He was holding his hand in front of him, looking at the dangling cuff and chain as if it were a silver bracelet and a line of pearls.

Leaning over the hood, cleaning the sand away from his windshield with his hands, was another of the dead folks. He too was wearing one of the round-eared hats. He pressed a wrecked face to the clean spot and looked in at Calhoun. A string of snot-green saliva ran out of his mouth and onto the glass.

More sand was wiped away by others. Soon all the car's glass showed the pallid and rotting faces of the dead folks. They stared at Wayne and Calhoun as if they were two rare fish in an aquarium.

Wayne cocked back the hammer of the .38.

"What about me," Calhoun said. "What am I supposed to use."

"Your charm," Wayne said, and at that moment, as if by signal, the dead folk faded away from the glass, leaving one man standing on the hood holding a baseball bat. He hit the glass and it went into a thousand little stars. The bat came again and the heavens fell and the stars rained down and the sand storm screamed in on Wayne and Calhoun.

The dead folks reappeared in full force. The one with the bat started through the hole in the windshield, unheeding of the jags of glass that ripped his ragged clothes and tore his flesh like damp cardboard.

Wayne shot the batter through the head, and the man, finished, fell through, pinning Wayne's arm with his body.

Before Wayne could pull his gun free, a woman's hand reached through the hole and got hold of Wayne's collar. Other dead folks took to the glass and hammered it out with their feet and fist. Hands were all over Wayne; they felt dry and cool like leather seat covers. They pulled him over the steering wheel and dash and outside. The sand worked at his flesh like a cheese grater. He could hear Calhoun yelling, "Eat me, motherfuckers, eat me and choke."

They tossed Wayne on the hood of the '57. Faces leaned over him. Yellow teeth and toothless gums were very near. A road kill odor washed through his nostrils. He thought: now the feeding frenzy begins. His only consolation was that there were so many dead folks there wouldn't be enough of him left to come back from the dead. They'd probably have his brain for dessert.

But no. They picked him up and carried him off. Next thing he knew was a clearer view of the whale-shape the '57 had hit. It was a yellow school bus.

The door to the bus hissed open. The dead folks dumped Wayne inside on his belly and tossed his hat after him. They stepped back and the door closed, just missing Wayne's foot.

Wayne looked up and saw a man in the driver's seat smiling at him. It wasn't a dead man. Just fat and ugly. He was probably five feet tall and bald except for a fringe of hair around his shiny bald head the color of a shit ring in a toilet bowl. He had a nose so long and dark and malignant looking it appeared as if it might fall off his face at any moment, like an overripe banana. He was wearing what Wayne first thought was a bathrobe, but proved to be a robe like that of a monk. It was old and tattered and moth-eaten and Wayne could see pale flesh through the holes. An odor wafted from the fat man that was somewhere between the smell of stale sweat, cheesy balls and an unwiped asshole.

"Good to see you," the fat man said.

"Charmed," Wayne said.

From the back of the bus came a strange, unidentifiable sound. Wayne poked his head around the seats for a look.

In the middle of the aisle, about halfway back, was a nun. Or sort of a nun. Her back was to him and she wore a black-and-white nun's habit. The part that covered her head was traditional, but from there down was quite a departure from the standard attire. The outfit was cut to the middle of her thighs and she wore black fishnet stockings and thick high heels. She was slim with good legs and a high little ass that, even under the circumstances, Wayne couldn't help but appreciate. She was moving one hand above her head as if sewing the air.

Sitting on the seats on either side of the aisle were dead folks. They all wore the round-eared hats, and they were responsible for the sound.

They were trying to sing.

He had never known dead folks to make any noise outside of grunts and groans, but here they were singing. A toneless sort of singing to be sure, some of the words garbled and some of the dead folks just opening and closing their mouths soundlessly, but, by golly, he recognized the tune. It was "Jesus Loves Me."

Wayne looked back at the fat man, let his hand ease down to the bowie in his right boot. The fat man produced a little .32 automatic from inside his robe and pointed at Wayne.

"It's small caliber," the fat man said, "but I'm a real fine shot, and it makes a nice, little hole."

Wayne quit reaching in his boot.

"Oh, that's all right," said the fat man. "Take the knife out and put it on the floor in front of you and slide it to me. And while you're at it, I think I see the hilt of one in your other boot."

Wayne looked back. The way he had been thrown inside the bus had caused his pants legs to hike up over his boots, and the hilts of both his bowie's were revealed. They might as well have had blinking lights on them.

It was shaping up to be a shitty day.

He slid the bowies to the fat man, who scooped them up nimbly and dumped them on the other side of his seat.

The bus door opened and Calhoun was tossed in on top of Wayne. Calhoun's hat followed after.

Wayne shrugged Calhoun off, recovered his hat, and put it on. Calhoun found his hat and did the same. They were still on their knees.

"Would you gentlemen mind moving to the center of the bus?"

Wayne led the way. Calhoun took note of the nun now, said, "Man, look at that ass."

The fat man called back to them. "Right there will do fine."

Wayne slid into the seat the fat man was indicating with a wave of the .32, and Calhoun slid in beside him. The dead folks entered now, filled the seats up front, leaving only a few stray seats in the middle empty.

Calhoun said, "What are those fuckers back there making that noise for?"

"They're singing," Wayne said. "Ain't you got no churchin'?"

"Say they are." Calhoun turned to the nun and the dead folks and yelled, "Ya'll know any Hank Williams?"

The nun did not turn and the dead folks did not quit their toneless singing.

"Guess not," Calhoun said. "Seems like all the good music's been forgotten."

The noise in the back of the bus ceased and the nun came over to look at Wayne and Calhoun. She was nice in front, too. The outfit was cut from throat to crotch, laced with a ribbon, and it showed a lot of tit and some tight, thin, black panties that couldn't quite hold in her escaping pubic hair, which grew as thick and wild as kudzu. When Wayne managed to work his eyes up from that and look at her face, he saw she was dark-complected with eyes the color of coffee and lips made to chew on.

Calhoun never made it to the face. He didn't care about faces. He sniffed, said into her crotch, "Nice snatch."

The nun's left hand came around and smacked Calhoun on the side of the head. He grabbed her wrist, said, "Nice arm, too."

The nun did a magic act with her right hand; it went behind her back and hiked up her outfit and came back with a double-barreled derringer. She pressed it against Calhoun's head.

Wayne bent forward, hoping she wouldn't shoot. At that range the bullet might go through Calhoun's head and hit him too.

"Can't miss," the nun said.

Calhoun smiled. "No you can't," he said, and let go of her arm.

She sat down across from them, smiled, and crossed her legs high. Wayne felt his Levis snake swell and crawl against the inside of his thigh.

"Honey," Calhoun said, "you're almost worth taking a bullet for."

The nun didn't quit smiling. The bus cranked up. The sand blowers and wipers went to work, and the windshield turned blue, and a white dot moved on it between a series of smaller white dots.

Radar. Wayne had seen that sort of thing on desert vehicles. If he lived through this and got his car back, maybe he'd rig up something like that. And maybe not, he was sick of the desert.

Whatever, at the moment, future plans seemed a little out of place.

Then something else occurred to him. Radar. That meant these bastards had known they were coming and had pulled out in front of them on purpose.

He leaned over the seat and checked where he figured the '57 hit the bus. He didn't see a single dent. Armored, most likely. Most school buses were these days, and that's what this had been. It probably had bullet-proof-glass and puncture-proof sand tires, too. School buses had gone that way on account of the race riots and the sending of mutated calves to school just like they were humans. And because of the Codgers—old farts who believed kids ought to be fair game to adults for sexual purposes, or for knocking around when they wanted to let off some tension.

"How about unlocking this cuff?" Calhoun said. "It ain't for shit now anyway."

Wayne looked at the nun. "I'm going for the cuff key in my pants. Don't shoot."

Wayne fished it out, unlocked the cuff, and Calhoun let it slide to the floor. Wayne saw the nun was curious and he said, "I'm a bounty hunter. Help me get this man to Law Town and I could see you earn a little something for your troubles."

The woman shook her head.

"That's the spirit," Calhoun said. "I like a nun that minds her own business . . . You a real nun?"

She nodded.

"Always talk so much?"

Another nod.

Wayne said, "I've never seen a nun like you. Not dressed like that and with a gun."

"We are a small and special order," she said.

"You some kind of Sunday school teacher for these dead folks?"

"Sort of."

"But with them dead, ain't it kind of pointless? They ain't got no souls now, do they?"

"No, but their work adds to the glory of God."

"Their work?" Wayne looked at the dead folks sitting stiffly in their seats. He noted that one of them was about to lose a rotten ear. He sniffed. "They may be adding to the glory of God, but they don't do much for the air."

The nun reached into a pocket on her habit and took out two round objects. She tossed one to Calhoun, and one to Wayne. "Menthol lozenges. They help you stand the smell."

Wayne unwrapped the lozenge and sucked on it. It did help overpower the smell, but the menthol wasn't all that great either. It reminded him of being sick.

"What order are you?" Wayne asked.

"Jesus Loved Mary," the nun said.

"His mama?" Wayne said.

"Mary Magdalene. We think he fucked her. They were lovers. There's evidence in the scriptures. She was a harlot and we have modeled ourselves on her. She gave up that life and became a harlot for Jesus."

"Hate to break it to you, sister," Calhoun said, "but that do-gooder Jesus is as dead as a post. If you're waiting for him to slap the meat to you, that sweet thing of yours is going to dry up and blow away."

"Thanks for the news," the nun said. "But we don't fuck him in person. We fuck him in spirit. We let the spirit enter into men so they may take us in the fashion Jesus took Mary."

"No shit?"

"No shit."

"You know, I think I feel the old boy moving around inside me now. Why don't you shuck them drawers, honey, throw back in that seat there and let ole Calhoun give you a big load of Jesus."

Calhoun shifted in the nun's direction.

She pointed the derringer at him, said, "Stay where you are. If it were so, if you were full of Jesus, I would let you have me in a moment. But you're full of the Devil, not Jesus."

"Shit, sister, give ole Devil a break. He's a fun kind of guy. Let's you and me mount up . . . Well, be like that. But if you change your mind, I can get religion at a moment's notice. I dearly love to fuck. I've fucked everything I could get my hands on but a parakeet, and I'd have fucked that little bitch if I could have found the hole."

"I've never known any dead folks to be trained," Wayne said, trying to get the nun talking in a direction that might help, a direction that would let him know what was going on and what sort of trouble he had fallen into.

"As I said, we are a very special order. Brother Lazarus," she waved a hand at the bus driver, and without looking he lifted a hand in acknowledgment, "is the founder. I don't think he'll mind if I tell his story, explain about us, what we do and why. It's important that we spread the word to the heathens."

"Don't call me no fucking heathen," Calhoun said. "This is heathen, riding around in a fucking bus with a bunch of stinking dead folks with funny hats on. Hell, they can't even carry a tune."

The nun ignored him. "Brother Lazarus was once known by another name, but that name no longer matters. He was a research scientist, and he was one of those who worked in the laboratory where the germs escaped into the air and made it so the dead could not truly die as long as they had an undamaged brain in their heads.

"Brother Lazarus was carrying a dish of the experiment, the germs, and as a joke, one of the lab assistants pretended to trip him, and he, not knowing it was a joke, dodged the assistant's leg and dropped the dish. In a moment, the air conditioning system had blown the germs throughout the research center. Someone opened a door, and the germs were loose on the world.

"Brother Lazarus was consumed by guilt. Not only because he dropped the dish, but because he helped create it in the first place. He quit his job at the laboratory, took to wandering the country. He came out here with nothing more than basic food, water, and books. Among these books was the Bible, and the lost books of the Bible: the Apocrypha and the many cast-out chapters of the New Testament. As he studied, it occurred to him that these cast out books actually belonged. He was able to interpret their higher meaning, and an angel came to him in a dream and told him of another book, and Brother Lazarus took up his pen and recorded the angel's words, direct from God, and in this book, all the mysteries were explained."

"Like screwing Jesus," Calhoun said.

"Like screwing Jesus, and not being afraid of words that mean sex. Not being afraid of seeing Jesus as both God and man. Seeing that sex, if meant for Christ and the opening of the mind, can be a thrilling and religious experience, not just the rutting of two savage animals.

"Brother Lazarus roamed the desert, the mountains, thinking of the things the Lord had revealed to him, and lo and behold, the Lord revealed yet another thing to him. Brother Lazarus found a great amusement park."

"Didn't know Jesus went in for rides and such," Calhoun said.

"It was long deserted. It had once been part of a place called Disneyland. Brother Lazarus knew of it. There had been several of these Disneylands built about the country, and this one had been in the midst of the Chevy-Cadillac Wars, and had been destroyed and sand had covered most of it."

The nun held out her arms. "And in this rubble, he saw a new beginning."

"Cool off, baby," Calhoun said, "before you have a stroke."

"He gathered to him men and women of a like mind and taught the gospel to them. The Old Testament. The New Testament. The Lost Books. And his own Book of Lazarus, for he had begun to call himself Lazarus. A symbolic name signifying a new beginning, a rising from the dead and coming to life and seeing things as they really are."

The nun moved her hands rapidly, expressively as she talked. Sweat beaded on her forehead and upper lip.

"So he returned to his skills as a scientist, but applied them to a higher purpose—God's purpose. And as Brother Lazarus, he realized the use of the dead. They could be taught to work and build a great monument to the glory of God. And this monument, this coed institution of monks and nuns, would be called Jesus Land."

At the word "Jesus," the nun gave her voice an extra trill, and the dead folks, cued, said together, "Ees num be prased."

"How the hell did you train them dead folks?" Calhoun said. "Dog treats?"

"Science put to the use of our Lord Jesus Christ, that's how. Brother Lazarus made a special device he could insert directly into the brains of dead folks, through the tops of their heads, and the device controls certain cravings. Makes them passive and responsive—at least to simple commands. With the regulator, as Brother Lazarus calls the device, we have been able to do much positive work with the dead."

"Where do you find these dead folks?" Wayne asked.

"We buy them from the Meat Boys. We save them from amoral purposes."

"They ought to be shot through the head and put in the goddamn ground," Wayne said.

"If our use of the regulator and the dead folks was merely to better ourselves, I would agree. But it is not. We do the Lord's work."

"So the monks fuck the sisters?" Calhoun asked.

"When possessed by the Spirit of Christ. Yes."

"And I bet they get possessed a lot. Not a bad setup. Dead folks to do the work on the amusement park—"

"It isn't an amusement park now."

"—and plenty of free pussy. Sounds cozy. I like it. Old shithead up there's smarter than he looks."

"There is nothing selfish about our motives or those of Brother Lazarus. In fact, as penance for loosing the germ on the world in the first place, Brother Lazarus injected a virus into his nose. It is rotting slowly."

"Thought that was quite a snorkel he had on him," Wayne said.

"I take it back," Calhoun said. "He *is* as dumb as he looks."

"Why do the dead folks wear those silly hats?" Wayne asked.

"Brother Lazarus found a storeroom of them at the site of the old amusement park. They are mouse ears. They represent some cartoon animal that was popular once and part of Disneyland. Mickey Mouse, he was called. This way we know which dead folks are ours, and which ones are not controlled by our regulators. From time to time, stray dead folks wander into our area. Murder victims. Children abandoned in the desert. People crossing the desert who died of heat or illness. We've had some of the sisters and brothers attacked. The hats are a precaution."

"And what's the deal with us?" Wayne asked.

The nun smiled sweetly. "You, my children, are to add to the glory of God."

"Children?" Calhoun said. "You call an alligator a lizard, bitch?"

The nun slid back in the seat and rested the derringer in her lap. She pulled her legs into a cocked position, causing her panties to crease in the valley of her vagina; it looked like a nice place to visit, that valley.

Wayne turned from the beauty of it and put his head back and closed his eyes, pulled his hat down over them. There was nothing he could do at the moment, and since the nun was watching Calhoun for him, he'd sleep, store up and figure what to do next. If anything.

He drifted off to sleep wondering what the nun meant by, "You, my children, are to add to the glory of God."

He had a feeling that when he found out, he wasn't going to like it.

5

He awoke off and on and saw that the sunlight filtering through the storm had given everything a greenish color. Calhoun seeing he was awake, said, "Ain't that a pretty color? I had a shirt that color once and liked it lots, but I got in a fight with this Mexican whore with a wooden leg over some money and she tore her. I punched that little bean bandit good."

"Thanks for sharing that," Wayne said, and went back to sleep.

Each time he awoke it was brighter, and finally he awoke to the sun going down and the storm having died out. But he didn't stay awake. He forced himself to close his eyes and store up more energy. To help him nod off he listened to the hum of the motor and thought about the wrecking yard and Pop and all the fun they could have, just drinking beer and playing cars and fucking the border women, and maybe some of those mutated cows they had over there for sell.

Nah. Nix the cows, or any of those genetically altered critters. A man had to draw the line somewhere, and he drew it at fucking critters, even if they had been bred so that they had human traits. You had to have some standards.

Course, those standards had a way of eroding. He remembered when he said he'd only fuck the pretty ones. His last whore had been downright scary looking. If he didn't watch himself he'd be as bad as Calhoun, trying to find the hole in a parakeet.

He awoke to Calhoun's elbow in his ribs and the nun was standing beside their seat with the derringer. Wayne knew she hadn't slept, but she looked bright-eyed and bushy-tailed. She nodded toward their window, said, "Jesus Land."

She had put that special touch in her voice again, and the dead folks responded with, "Eees num be prased."

It was good and dark now, a crisp night with a big moon the color of hammered brass. The bus sailed across the white sand like a mystical schooner with a full wind in its sails. It went up an impossible hill toward what looked like an aurora borealis, then dove into an atomic rainbow of colors that filled the bus with fairy lights.

When Wayne's eyes became accustomed to the lights, and the bus took a right turn along a precarious curve, he glanced down into the valley. An aerial view couldn't have been any better than the view from his window.

Down there was a universe of polished metal and twisted neon. In the center of the valley was a great statue of Jesus crucified that must have been twenty-five stories high. Most of the body was made of bright metals and multicolored neon, and much of the light was coming from that. There was a crown of barbed wire wound several times around a chromium plate of a forehead and some rust-colored strands of neon hair. The savior's eyes were huge, green strobes that swung left and right with the precision of an oscillating fan. There was an ear to ear smile on the savior's face and the teeth were slats of sparkling metal with wide cavity-black gaps between them. The statue was equipped with a massive dick of polished, interwoven cables and coils of neon; the dick was thicker and more solid looking than the arthritic steel-tube legs on either side of it; the head of it was made of an enormous spotlight that pulsed the color of irritation.

The bus went around and around the valley, descending like a dead roach going down a slow drain, and finally the road rolled out straight and took them into Jesus Land.

They passed through the legs of Jesus, under the throbbing head of his cock, toward what looked like a small castle of polished gold bricks with an upright drawbridge interlayed with jewels.

The castle was only one of several tall structures that appeared to be made of rare metals and precious stones; gold, silver, emeralds, rubies, and sapphires. But the closer they got to the buildings, the less fine they looked and the more they looked like what they were: stucco, cardboard, phosphorescent paint, colored spotlights, and bands of neon.

Off to the left Wayne could see a long, open shed full of vehicles, most of them old school buses. And there were unlighted hovels made of tin and tar paper; homes for the dead, perhaps. Behind the shacks and the bus barn rose skeletal shapes that stretched tall and bleak against the sky and the candy-gem lights; shapes that looked like the bony remains of beached whales.

On the right, Wayne glimpsed a building with an open front that served as a stage. In front of the stage were chairs filled with monks and nuns. On the stage, six monks—one behind a drum set, one with a saxophone, the others with guitars—were blasting out a loud, rocking rhythm that made the bus shake. A nun with the front of her habit thrown open, her headpiece discarded, sang into a microphone with a voice like a suffering angel. The voice screeched out of the amplifiers and came in through the windows of the bus, crushing the sound of the engine. The nun crowed "Jesus" so long and hard it sounded like a plea from hell. Then she leapt up and came down doing the splits, the impact driving her back to her feet as if her ass had been loaded with springs.

"Bet that bitch can pick up a quarter with that thing," Calhoun said.

Brother Lazarus touched a button, the pseudo-jeweled drawbridge lowered over a narrow moat, and he drove them inside.

It wasn't as well lighted in there. The walls were bleak and gray. Brother Lazarus stopped the bus and got off, and another monk came on board. He was tall and thin and had crooked buck teeth that dented his bottom lip. He also had a twelve-gauge pump shotgun.

"This is Brother Fred," the nun said. "He will be your tour guide."

Brother Fred forced Wayne and Calhoun off the bus, away from the dead folks in their mouse-ear hats and the nun in her tight, black panties, jabbed them along a dark corridor, up a swirl of stairs and down a longer corridor with open doors on either side and rooms filled with dark light and spoiled meat and guts on hooks and skulls and bones lying about like discarded walnut shells and broken sticks; rooms full of dead folks (truly dead) stacked neat as firewood, and rooms full of stone shelves stuffed with beakers of fiery-red and sewer green and sky blue and piss yellow liquids, as well as glass coils through which other colored fluids fled as if chased, smoked as if nervous, and ran into big flasks as if relieved; rooms with platforms and tables and boxes and stools and chairs covered with instruments or dead folks or dead-folk pieces or the asses of monks and nuns as they sat and held charts or tubes or body parts and frowned at them with concentration, lips pursed as if about to explode with some earth-shattering pronouncement; and finally they came to a little room with a tall, glassless window that looked out upon the bright, shiny mess that was Jesus Land.

The room was simple. Table, two chairs, two beds—one on either side of the room. The walls were stone and unadorned. To the right was a little bathroom without a door.

Wayne walked to the window and looked out at Jesus Land pulsing and thumping like a desperate heart. He listened to the music a moment, leaned over and stuck his head outside.

They were high up and there was nothing but a straight drop. If you jumped, you'd wind up with the heels of your boots under your tonsils.

Wayne let out a whistle in appreciation of the drop. Brother Fred thought it was a compliment for Jesus Land. He said, "It's a miracle, isn't it?"

"Miracle?" Calhoun said. "This goony light show? This ain't no miracle. This is for shit. Get that nun on the bus back there to bend over and shit a perfectly round turd through a hoop at twenty paces, and I'll call that a miracle, Mr. Fucked-up Teeth. But this Jesus Land crap is the dumbest fucking idea since dog sweaters.

"And look at this place. You could use some knickknacks or something in here. A picture of some ole naked gal doing a donkey, couple of pigs fucking. Anything. And a door on the shitter would be nice. I hate to be straining out a big one and know someone can look in on me. It ain't decent. A man ought to have his fucking grunts in private. This place reminds me of a motel I stayed at in Waco one night, and I made the goddamn manager give me my money back. The roaches in that shit hole were big enough to use the shower."

Brother Fred listened to all this without blinking an eye, as if seeing Calhoun talk was as amazing as seeing a frog sing. He said, "Sleep tight, don't let the bed bugs bite. Tomorrow you start to work."

"I don't want no fucking job," Calhoun said.

"Goodnight, children," Brother Fred said, and with that he closed the door and they heard it lock, loud and final as the clicking of the drop board on a gallows.

6

At dawn, Wayne got up and took a leak, went to the window to look out. The stage where the monks had played and the nun had jumped was empty. The skeletal shapes he had seen last night were tracks and frames from rides long abandoned. He had a sudden vision of Jesus and his disciples riding a roller coaster, their long hair and robes flapping in the wind.

The large crucified Jesus looked unimpressive without its lights and night's mystery, like a whore in harsh sunlight with makeup gone and wig askew.

"Got any ideas how we're gonna get out of here?"

Wayne looked at Calhoun. He was sitting on the bed, pulling on his boots.

Wayne shook his head.

"I could use a smoke. You know, I think we ought to work together. Then we can try to kill each other."

Unconsciously, Calhoun touched his ear where Wayne had bitten off the lobe.

"Wouldn't trust you as far as I could kick you."

"I hear that. But I give my word. And my word's something you can count on. I won't twist it."

Wayne studied Calhoun, thought: Well, there wasn't anything to lose. He'd just watch his ass.

"All right," Wayne said. "Give me your word you'll work with me on getting us out of this mess, and when we're good and free, and you say your word has gone far enough, we can settle up."

"Deal," Calhoun said, and offered his hand.

Wayne looked at it.

"This seals it," Calhoun said.

Wayne took Calhoun's hand and they shook.

7

Moments later the door unlocked and a smiling monk with hair the color and texture of mold fuzz came in with Brother Fred, who still had his pump shotgun. There were two dead folks with them. A man and a woman. They wore torn clothes and the mouse-ear hats. Neither looked long dead or smelled particularly bad. Actually, the monk smelled worse.

Using the barrel of the shotgun, Brother Fred poked them down the hall to a room with metal tables and medical instruments.

Brother Lazarus was on the far side of one of the tables. He was smiling. His nose looked especially cancerous this morning. A white pustle the size of a thumb tip had taken up residence on the left side of his snout, and it looked like a pearl onion in a turd.

Nearby stood a nun. She was short with good, if skinny legs, and she wore the same outfit as the nun on the bus. It looked more girlish on her, perhaps because she was thin and small-breasted. She had a nice face and eyes that were all pupil. Wisps of blond hair crawled out around the edges of her headgear. She looked pale and weak, as if wearied to the bone. There was a birthmark on her right cheek that looked like a distant view of a small bird in flight.

"Good morning," Brother Lazarus said. "I hope you gentlemen slept well."

"What's this about work?" Wayne said.

"Work?" Brother Lazarus said.

"I described it to them that way," Brother Fred said. "Perhaps an impulsive description."

"I'll say," Brother Lazarus said. "No work here, gentlemen. You have my word on that. We do all the work. Lie on these tables and we'll take a sampling of your blood."

"Why?" Wayne said.

"Science," Brother Lazarus said. "I intend to find a cure for this germ that makes the dead come back to life, and to do that, I need living human beings to study. Sounds kind of mad scientist, doesn't it? But I assure you, you've nothing to lose but a few drops of blood. Well, maybe more than a few drops, but nothing serious."

"Use your own goddamn blood," Calhoun said.

"We do. But we're always looking for fresh specimens. Little here, little there. And if you don't do it, we'll kill you."

Calhoun spun and hit Brother Fred on the nose. It was a solid punch and Brother Fred hit the floor on his butt, but he hung on to the shotgun and pointed it up at Calhoun. "Go on," he said, his nose streaming blood. "Try that again."

Wayne flexed to help, but hesitated. He could kick Brother Fred in the head from where he was, but that might not keep him from shooting Calhoun, and there would go the extra reward money. And besides, he'd given his word to the bastard that they'd try and help each other survive until they got out of this.

The other monk clasped his hands and swung them into the side of Calhoun's head, knocking him down. Brother Fred got up, and while Calhoun was trying to rise, he hit him with the stock of the shotgun in the back of the head, hit him so hard it drove Calhoun's forehead into the floor. Calhoun rolled over on his side and lay there, his eyes fluttering like moth wings.

"Brother Fred, you must learn to turn the other cheek," Brother Lazarus said. "Now put this sack of shit on the table."

Brother Fred checked Wayne to see if he looked like trouble. Wayne put his hands in his pockets and smiled.

Brother Fred called the two dead folks over and had them put Calhoun on the table. Brother Lazarus strapped him down.

The nun brought a tray of needles, syringes, cotton and bottles over, put it down on the table next to Calhoun's head. Brother Lazarus rolled up Calhoun's sleeve and fixed up a needle and stuck it in Calhoun's arm, drew it full of blood. He stuck the needle through the rubber top of one of the bottles and shot the blood into that.

He looked at Wayne and said, "I hope you'll be less trouble."

"Do I get some orange juice and a little cracker afterwards?" Wayne said.

"You get to walk out without a knot on your head," Brother Lazarus said.

"Guess that'll have to do."

Wayne got on the table next to Calhoun and Brother Lazarus strapped him down. The nun brought the tray over and Brother Lazarus did to him what he had done to Calhoun. The nun stood over Wayne and looked down at his face. Wayne tried to read something in her features but couldn't find a clue.

When Brother Lazarus was finished he took hold of Wayne's chin and shook it. "My, but you two boys look healthy. But you can never be sure. We'll have to run the blood through some tests. Meantime, Sister Worth will run a few additional tests on you, and," he nodded at the unconscious Calhoun, "I'll see to your friend here."

"He's no friend of mine," Wayne said.

They took Wayne off the table, and Sister Worth and Brother Fred and his shotgun directed him down the hall into another room.

The room was lined with shelves that were lined with instruments and bottles. The lighting was poor, most of it coming through a slatted window, though there was an anemic yellow bulb overhead. Dust motes swam in the air.

In the center of the room on its rim was a great, spoked wheel. It had two straps well spaced at the top, and two more at the bottom. Beneath the bottom straps were blocks of wood. The wheel was attached in back to an upright metal bar that had switches and buttons all over it.

Brother Fred made Wayne strip and get up on the wheel with his back to the hub and his feet on the blocks. Sister Worth strapped his ankles down tight, then he was made to put his hands up, and she strapped his wrists to the upper part of the wheel.

"I hope this hurts a lot," Brother Fred said.

"Wipe the blood off your face," Wayne said. "It makes you look silly."

Brother Fred made a gesture with his middle finger that wasn't religious and left the room.

[8]

Sister Worth touched a switch and the wheel began to spin, slowly at first, and the bad light came through the windows and poked through the rungs and the dust swam before his eyes and the wheel and its spokes threw twisting shadows on the wall.

As he went around, Wayne closed his eyes. It kept him from feeling so dizzy, especially on the down swings.

On a turn up, he opened his eyes and caught sight of Sister Worth standing in front of the wheel staring at him. He said, "Why?" and closed his eyes as the wheel dipped.

"Because Brother Lazarus says so," came the answer after such a long time Wayne had almost forgotten the question. Actually, he hadn't expected a response. He was surprised that such a thing had come out of his mouth, and he felt a little diminished for having asked.

He opened his eyes on another swing up, and she was moving behind the wheel, out of his line of vision. He heard a snick like a switch being flipped and lightning jumped through him and he screamed in spite of himself. A little fork of electricity licked out of his mouth like a reptile tongue tasting air.

Faster spun the wheel and the jolts came more often and he screamed less loud, and finally not at all. He was too numb. He was adrift in space wearing only his cowboy hat and boots, moving away from earth very fast. Floating all around him were wrecked cars. He looked and saw that one of them was his '57, and behind the steering wheel was Pop. Sitting beside the old man was a Mexican whore. Two more were in the backseat. They looked a little drunk.

One of the whores in back pulled up her dress and pressed her naked ass against the window, cocked it high up so he could see her pussy. It looked like a taco that needed a shave.

He smiled and tried to go for it, but the '57 was moving away, swinging wide and turning its tail to him. He could see a face at the back window. Pop's face. He had crawled back there and was waving slowly and sadly. A whore pulled Pop from view.

The wrecked cars moved away too, as if caught in the vacuum of the '57's retreat. Wayne swam with his arms, kicked with his legs, trying to pursue the '57 and the wrecks. But he dangled where he was, like a moth pinned to a board. The cars moved out of sight and left him there with his arms and legs stretched out, spinning amidst an infinity of cold, uncaring stars.

". . . how the tests are run . . . marks everything about you . . . charts it . . . EKG, brain waves, liver . . . everything . . . it hurts because Brother Lazarus wants it to . . . thinks I don't know these things . . . that I'm slow . . . I'm slow, not stupid . . . smart really . . . used to be a scientist . . . before the accident . . . Brother Lazarus is not holy . . . he's mad . . . made the wheel because of the Holy Inquisition . . . knows a lot about the Inquisition . . . thinks we need it again . . . for the likes of men like you . . . the unholy, he says . . . But he just likes to hurt . . . I know."

Wayne opened his eyes. The wheel had stopped. Sister Worth was talking in her monotone, explaining the wheel. He remembered asking her "Why" about three thousand years ago.

Sister Worth was staring at him again. She went away and he expected the wheel to start up, but when she returned, she had a long, narrow mirror under her arm. She put it against the wall across from him. She got on the wheel with him, her little feet on the wooden platforms beside his. She hiked up the bottom of her habit and pulled down her black panties. She put her face close to his, as if searching for something.

"He plans to take your body . . . piece by piece . . . blood, cells, brain, your cock . . . all of it . . . He wants to live forever."

She had her panties in her hand, and she tossed them. Wayne watched them fly up and flutter to the floor like a dying bat.

She took hold of his dick and pulled on it. Her palm was cold and he didn't feel his best, but he began to get hard. She put him between her legs and rubbed his dick between her thighs. They were as cold as her hands, and dry.

"I know him now . . . know what he's doing . . . the dead germ virus . . . he was trying to make something that would make him live forever . . . it made the dead come back . . . didn't keep the living alive, free of old age . . . ."

His dick was throbbing now, in spite of the coolness of her body.

"He cuts up dead folks to learn . . . experiments on them . . . but the secret of eternal life is with the living . . . that's why he wants you . . . you're an outsider . . . those who live here he can test . . . but he must keep them alive to do his bidding . . . not let them know how he really is . . . needs your insides and the other man's . . . he wants to be a God . . . flies high above us in a little plane and looks down . . . Likes to think he is the creator, I bet . . ."

"Plane?"

"Ultra-light."

She pushed his cock inside her, and it was cold and dry in there, like liver left overnight on a drainboard. Still, he found himself ready. At this point, he would have gouged a hole in a turnip.

She kissed him on the ear and alongside the neck; cold little kisses, dry as toast.

". . . thinks I don't know . . . But I know he doesn't love Jesus . . . . He loves himself, and power . . . . He's sad about his nose . . ."

"I bet."

"Did it in a moment of religious fever . . . before he lost the belief . . . Now he wants to be what he was . . . . A scientist. He wants to grow a new nose . . . knows how . . . saw him grow a finger in a dish once . . . grew it from the skin off a knuckle of one of the brothers . . . He can do all kinds of things."

She was moving her hips now. He could see over her shoulder into the mirror against the wall. Could see her white ass rolling, the black habit hiked up above it, threatening to drop like a curtain. He began to thrust back, slowly, firmly.

She looked over her shoulder into the mirror, watching herself fuck him. There was a look more of study than rapture on her face.

"Want to feel alive," she said. "Feel a good, hard dick . . . . Been too long."

"I'm doing the best I can," Wayne said. "This ain't the most romantic of spots."

"Push so I can feel it."

"Nice," Wayne said. He gave it everything he had. He was beginning to lose his erection. He felt as if he were auditioning for a job and not making the best of impressions. He felt like a knothole would be dissatisfied with him.

She got off of him and climbed down.

"Don't blame you," he said.

She went behind the wheel and touched some things on the upright. She mounted him again, hooked her ankles behind his. The wheel began to turn. Short electrical shocks leaped through him. They weren't as powerful as before. They were invigorating. When he kissed her it was like touching his tongue to a battery. It felt as if electricity was racing through his veins and flying out the head of his dick; he felt as if he might fill her with lightning instead of come.

The wheel creaked to a stop; it must have had a timer on it. They were upside down and Wayne could see their reflection in the mirror; they looked like two lizards fucking on a window pane.

He couldn't tell if she had finished or not, so he went ahead and got it over with. Without the electricity he was losing his desire. It hadn't been an A-one piece of ass, but hell, as Pop always said, "Worse pussy I ever had was good."

"They'll be coming back," she said. "Soon . . . Don't want them to find us like this . . . . Other test to do yet."

"Why did you do this?"

"I want out of the order . . . . Want out of this desert . . . . I want to live . . . . And I want you to help me."

"I'm game, but the blood is rushing to my head and I'm getting dizzy. Maybe you ought to get off me."

After an eon she said, "I have a plan."

She untwined from him and went behind the wheel and hit a switch that turned Wayne upright. She touched another switch and he began to spin slowly, and while he spun and while lightning played inside him, she told him her plan.

9

"I think ole Brother Fred wants to fuck me," Calhoun said. "He keeps trying to get his finger up my asshole."

They were back in their room. Brother Fred had brought them back, making them carry their clothes, and now they were alone again, dressing.

"We're getting out of here," Wayne said. "The nun, Sister Worth, she's going to help."

"What's her angle?"

"She hates this place and wants my dick. Mostly, she hates this place."

"What's the plan?"

Wayne told him first what Brother Lazarus had planned, On the morrow he would have them brought to the room with the steel tables, and they would go on the tables, and if the tests had turned out good, they would be pronounced fit as fiddles and Brother Lazarus would strip the skin from their bodies, slowly, because according to Sister Worth he liked to do it that way, and he would drain their blood and percolate it into his formulas like coffee, cut their brains out and put them in vats and store their veins and organs in freezers.

All of this would be done in the name of God and Jesus Christ (Eees num be prased) under the guise of finding a cure for the dead folks germ. But it would all instead be for Brother Lazarus who wanted to have a new nose, fly his ultra-light above Jesus Land and live forever.

Sister Worth's plan was this:

She would be in the dissecting room. She would have guns hidden. She would make the first move, a distraction, then it was up to them.

"This time," Wayne said, "one of us has to get on top of that shotgun."

"You had your finger up your ass in there today, or we'd have had them."

"We're going to have surprise on our side this time. Real surprise. They won't be expecting Sister Worth. We can get up there on the roof and take off in that ultra-light. When it runs out of gas we can walk, maybe get back to the '57 and hope it runs."

"We'll settle our score then. Who ever wins keeps the car and the split tail. As for tomorrow, I've got a little ace."

Calhoun pulled on his boots. He twisted the heel of one of them. It swung out and a little knife dropped into his hand. "It's sharp," Calhoun said. "I cut a Chinaman from gut to gill with it. It was easy as sliding a stick through fresh shit."

"Been nice if you'd had that ready today."

"I wanted to scout things out first. And to tell the truth, I thought one pop to Brother Fred's mouth and he'd be out of the picture."

"You hit him in the nose."

"Yeah, goddammit, but I was aiming for his mouth."

10

Dawn and the room with the metal tables looked the same. No one had brought in a vase of flowers to brighten the place.

Brother Lazarus's nose had changed however; there were two pearl onions nestled in it now.

Sister Worth, looking only a little more animated than yesterday, stood nearby. She was holding the tray with the instruments. This time the tray was full of scalpels. The light caught their edges and made them wink.

Brother Fred was standing behind Calhoun, and Brother Mold Fuzz was behind Wayne. They must have felt pretty confident today. They had dispensed with the dead folks.

Wayne looked at Sister Worth and thought maybe things were not good. Maybe she had lied to him in her slow talking way. Only wanted a little dick and wanted to keep it quiet. To do that, she might have promised anything. She might not care what Brother Lazarus did to them.

If it looked like a double cross, Wayne was going to go for it. If he had to jump right into the mouth of Brother Fred's shotgun. That was a better way to go than having the hide peeled from your body. The idea of Brother Lazarus and his ugly nose leaning over him did not appeal at all.

"It's so nice to see you," Brother Lazarus said. "I hope we'll have none of the unpleasantness of yesterday. Now, on the tables."

Wayne looked at Sister Worth. Her expression showed nothing. The only thing about her that looked alive was the bent wings of the bird birthmark on her cheek.

All right, Wayne thought, I'll go as far as the table, then I'm going to do something. Even if it's wrong.

He took a step forward, and Sister Worth flipped the contents of the tray into Brother Lazarus's face. A scalpel went into his nose and hung there. The tray and the rest of its contents hit the floor.

Before Brother Lazarus could yelp, Calhoun dropped and wheeled. He was under Brother Fred's shotgun and he used his forearm to drive the barrel upwards. The gun went off and peppered the ceiling. Plaster sprinkled down.

Calhoun had concealed the little knife in the palm of his hand and he brought it up and into Brother Fred's groin. The blade went through the robe and buried to the hilt.

The instant Calhoun made his move, Wayne brought his forearm back and around into Brother Mold Fuzz's throat, then turned and caught his head and jerked that down and kneed him a couple of times. He floored him by driving an elbow into the back of his neck.

Calhoun had the shotgun now, and Brother Fred was on the floor trying to pull the knife out of his balls. Calhoun blew Brother Fred's head off, then did the same for Brother Mold Fuzz.

Brother Lazarus, the scalpel still hanging from his nose, tried to run for it, but he stepped on the tray and that sent him flying. He landed on his stomach. Calhoun took two deep steps and kicked him in the throat. Brother Lazarus made a sound like he was gargling and tried to get up.

Wayne helped him. He grabbed Brother Lazarus by the back of his robe and pulled him up, slammed him back against a table. The scalpel still dangled from the monk's nose. Wayne grabbed it and jerked, taking away a chunk of nose as he did. Brother Lazarus screamed.

Calhoun put the shotgun in Brother Lazarus's mouth and that made him stop screaming. Calhoun pumped the shotgun. He said, "Eat it," and pulled the trigger. Brother Lazarus's brains went out the back of his head riding on a chunk of skull. The brains and skull hit the table and sailed onto the floor like a plate of scrambled eggs pushed the length of a cafe counter.

Sister Worth had not moved. Wayne figured she had used all of her concentration to hit Brother Lazarus with the tray.

"You said you'd have guns," Wayne said to her.

She turned her back to him and lifted her habit. In a belt above her panties were two .38 revolvers. Wayne pulled them out and held one in each hand. "Two-Gun Wayne," he said.

"What about the ultra-light?" Calhoun said. "We've made enough noise for a prison riot. We need to move."

Sister Worth turned to the door at the back of the room, and before she could say anything or lead, Wayne and Calhoun snapped to it and grabbed her and pushed her toward it.

There were stairs on the other side of the door and they took them two at a time. They went through a trap door and onto the roof and there, tied down with bungie straps to metal hoops, was the ultra-light. It was blue-and-white canvas and metal rods, and strapped to either side of it was a twelve-gauge pump and a bag of food and a canteen of water.

They unsnapped the roof straps and got in the two seater and used the straps to fasten Sister Worth between them. It wasn't comfortable, but it was a ride.

They sat there. After a moment, Calhoun said, "Well?"

"Shit," Wayne said. "I can't fly this thing."

They looked at Sister Worth. She was staring at the controls.

"Say something, dammit," Wayne said.

"That's the switch," she said. "That stick . . . forward is up, back brings the nose down . . . side to side . . ."

"Got it."

"Well shoot this bastard over the side," Calhoun said.

Wayne cranked it, gave it the throttle. The machine rolled forward, wobbled.

"Too much weight," Wayne said.

"Throw the cunt over the side," Calhoun said.

"It's all or nothing," Wayne said.

The ultra-light continued to swing its tail left and right, but leveled off as they went over the edge.

They sailed for a hundred yards, made a mean curve Wayne couldn't fight, and fell straight away into the statue of Jesus, striking it in the head, right in the midst of the barbed wire crown. Spot lights shattered, metal groaned; the wire tangled in the nylon wings of the craft and held it. The head of Jesus nodded forward, popped off and shot out on the electric cables inside like a Jack-in-the-Box. The cables popped tight a hundred feet from the ground and worked the head and the craft like a yo-yo. Then the barbed wire crown unraveled and dropped the craft the rest of the way. It hit the ground with a crunch and a rip and a cloud of dust.

The head of Jesus bobbed above the shattered craft like a bird preparing to peck a worm.

11

Wayne crawled out of the wreckage and tried his legs. They worked.

Calhoun was on his feet cussing, unstrapping the guns and supplies.

Sister Worth lay in the midst of the wreck, the nylon and aluminum supports folded around her like butterfly wings.

Wayne started pulling the mess off of her. He saw that her leg was broken. A bone punched out of her thigh like a sharpened stick. There was no blood.

"Here comes the church social," Calhoun said.

The word was out about Brother Lazarus and the others. A horde of monks, nuns and dead folks, were rushing over the drawbridge. Some of the nuns and monks had guns. All of the dead folks had clubs. The clergy was yelling.

Wayne nodded toward the bus barn. "Let's get a bus."

Wayne picked up Sister Worth, cradled her in his arms, and made a run for it. Calhoun, carrying only the guns and the supplies, passed them. He jumped through the open doorway of a bus and dropped out of sight. Wayne knew he was jerking wires loose and trying to hotwire them a ride. Wayne hoped he was good at it, and fast.

When Wayne got to the bus, he laid Sister Worth down beside it and pulled the .38 and stood in front of her. If he was going down he wanted to go like Wild Bill Hickok. A blazing gun in either fist and a woman to protect.

Actually, he'd prefer the bus to start.

It did.

Calhoun jerked it in gear, backed it out and around in front of Wayne and Sister Worth. The monks and nuns had started firing and their rounds bounced off the side of the armored bus.

From inside Calhoun yelled, "Get the hell on."

Wayne stuck the guns in his belt, grabbed up Sister Worth and leapt inside. Calhoun jerked the bus forward and Wayne and Sister Worth went flying over a seat and into another.

"I thought you were leaving," Wayne said.

"I wanted to. But I gave my word."

Wayne stretched Sister Worth out on the seat and looked at her leg. After that tossing Calhoun had given them, the break was sticking out even more.

Calhoun closed the bus door and checked his wing mirror. Nuns and monks and dead folks had piled into a couple of buses, and now the buses were pursuing them. One of them moved very fast, as if souped up.

"I probably got the granny of the bunch," Calhoun said.

They climbed over a ridge of sand, then they were on the narrow road that wound itself upwards. Behind them, one of the buses had fallen back, maybe some kind of mechanical trouble. The other was gaining.

The road widened and Calhoun yelled, "I think this is what the fucker's been waiting for."

Even as Calhoun spoke, their pursuer put on a burst of speed and swung left and came up beside them, tried to swerve over and push them off the road, down into the deepening valley. But Calhoun fought the curves and didn't budge.

The other bus swung its door open and a nun, the very one who had been on the bus that brought them to Jesus Land, stood there with her legs spread wide, showing the black-pantied mound of her crotch. She had one arm bent around a seat post and was holding in both hands the ever-popular clergy tool, the twelve-gauge pump.

As they made a curve, the nun fired a round into the window next to Calhoun. The window made a cracking noise and thin crooked lines spread in all directions, but the glass held.

She pumped a round into the chamber and fired again. Bullet proof or not, this time the front sheet of glass fell away. Another well-placed round and the rest of the glass would go and Calhoun could wave his head good-bye.

Wayne put his knees in a seat and got the window down. The nun saw him, whirled and fired. The shot was low and hit the bottom part of the window and starred it and pelleted the chassis.

Wayne stuck the .38 out the window and fired as the nun was jacking another load into position. His shot hit her in the head and her right eye went big and wet, and she swung around on the pole and lost the shotgun. It went out the door. She clung there by the bend of her elbow for a moment, then her arm straightened and she fell outside. The bus ran over her and she popped red and juicy at both ends like a stomped jelly roll.

"Waste of good pussy," Calhoun said. He edged into the other bus, and it pushed back. But Calhoun pushed harder and made it hit the wall with a screech like a panther.

The bus came back and shoved Calhoun to the side of the cliff and honked twice for Jesus.

Calhoun down-shifted, let off the gas, allowed the other bus to soar past by half a length. Then he jerked the wheel so that he caught the rear of it and knocked it across the road. He speared it in the side with the nose of his bus and the other started to spin. It clipped the front of Calhoun's bus and peeled the bumper back. Calhoun braked and the other bus kept spinning. It spun off the road and down into the valley amidst a chorus of cries.

Thirty minutes later they reached the top of the canyon and were in the desert. The bus began to throw up smoke from the front and make a noise like a dog strangling on a chicken bone. Calhoun pulled over.

12

"Goddamn bumper got twisted under there and it's shredded the tire some," Calhoun said. "I think if we can peel the bumper off, there's enough of that tire to run on."

Wayne and Calhoun got hold of the bumper and pulled but it wouldn't come off. Not completely. Part of it had been creased, and that part finally gave way and broke off from the rest of it.

"That ought to be enough to keep from rubbing the tire," Calhoun said.

Sister Worth called from inside the bus. Wayne went to check on her. "Take me off the bus," she said in her slow way. ". . . I want to feel free air and sun."

"There doesn't feel like there's any air out there," Wayne said. "And the sun feels just like it always does. Hot."

"Please."

He picked her up and carried her outside and found a ridge of sand and laid her down so her head was propped against it.

"I . . . I need batteries," she said.

"Say what?" Wayne said.

She lay looking straight into the sun. "Brother Lazarus's greatest work . . . a dead folk that can think . . . has memory of the past . . . . Was a scientist too . . ." Her hand came up in stages, finally got hold of her head gear and pushed it off.

Gleaming from the center of her tangled blond hair was a silver knob.

"He . . . was not a good man . . . I am a good woman . . . I want to feel alive . . . like before . . . batteries going . . . brought others."

Her hand fumbled at a snap pocket on her habit. Wayne opened it for her and got out what was inside. Four batteries.

"Uses two . . . simple."

Calhoun was standing over them now. "That explains some things," he said.

"Don't look at me like that . . ." Sister Worth said, and Wayne realized he had never told her his name and she had never asked. "Unscrew . . . put the batteries in . . . Without them I'll be an eater . . . . Can't wait too long."

"All right," Wayne said. He went behind her and propped her up on the sand drift and unscrewed the metal shaft from her skull. He thought about when she had fucked him on the wheel and how desperate she had been to feel something, and how she had been cold as flint and lustless. He remembered how she had looked in the mirror hoping to see something that wasn't there.

He dropped the batteries in the sand and took out one of the revolvers and put it close to the back of her head and pulled the trigger. Her body jerked slightly and fell over, her face turning toward him.

The bullet had come out where the bird had been on her cheek and had taken it completely away, leaving a bloodless hole.

"Best thing," Calhoun said. "There's enough live pussy in the world without you pulling this broken-legged dead thing around after you on a board."

"Shut up," Wayne said.

"When a man gets sentimental over women and kids, he can count himself out."

Wayne stood up.

"Well, boy," Calhoun said. "I reckon it's time."

"Reckon so," Wayne said.

"How about we do this with some class? Give me one of your pistols and we'll get back-to-back and I'll count to ten, and when I get there, we'll turn and shoot."

Wayne gave Calhoun one of the pistols. Calhoun checked the chambers, said, "I've got four loads."

Wayne took two out of his pistol and tossed them on the ground. "Even Steven," he said.

They got back-to-back and held the guns by their legs.

"Guess if you kill me you'll take me in," Calhoun said. "So that means you'll put a bullet through my head if I need it. I don't want to come back as one of the dead folks. Got your word on that?"

"Yep."

"I'll do the same for you. Give my word. You know that's worth something."

"We gonna shoot or talk?"

"You know, boy, under different circumstances, I could have liked you. We might have been friends."

"Not likely."

Calhoun started counting, and they started stepping. When he got to ten, they turned.

Calhoun's pistol barked first, and Wayne felt the bullet punch him low in the right side of his chest, spinning him slightly. He lifted his revolver and took his time and shot just as Calhoun fired again.

Calhoun's second bullet whizzed by Wayne's head. Wayne's shot hit Calhoun in the stomach.

Calhoun went to his knees and had trouble drawing a breath. He tried to lift his revolver but couldn't; it was as if it had turned into an anvil.

Wayne shot him again. Hitting him in the middle of the chest this time and knocking him back so that his legs were curled beneath him.

Wayne walked over to Calhoun, dropped to one knee and took the revolver from him.

"Shit," Calhoun said. "I wouldn't have thought that for nothing. You hit?"

"Scratched."

"Shit. "

Wayne put the revolver to Calhoun's forehead and Calhoun closed his eyes and Wayne pulled the trigger.

13

The wound wasn't a scratch. Wayne knew he should leave Sister Worth where she was and load Calhoun on the bus and haul him in for bounty. But he didn't care about the bounty anymore.

He used the ragged piece of bumper to dig them a shallow low side-by-side grave. When he finished, he stuck the fender fragment up between them and used the sight of one of the revolvers to scratch into it: HERE LIES SISTER WORTH AND CALHOUN WHO KEPT HIS WORD.

You couldn't really read it good and he knew the first real wind would keel it over, but it made him feel better about something, even if he couldn't put his finger on it.

His wound had opened up and the sun was very hot now, and since he had lost his hat he could feel his brain cooking in his skull like meat boiling in a pot.

He got on the bus, started it and drove through the day and the night and it was near morning when he came to the Cadillacs and turned down between them and drove until he came to the '57.

When he stopped and tried to get off the bus, he found he could hardly move. The revolvers in his belt were stuck to his shirt and stomach because of the blood from his wound.

He pulled himself up with the steering wheel, got one of the shotguns and used it for a crutch. He got the food and water and went out to inspect the '57.

It was for shit. It had not only lost its windshield, the front end was mashed way back and one of the big sand tires was twisted at such an angle he knew the axle was shot.

He leaned against the Chevy and tried to think. The bus was okay and there was still some gas in it, and he could get the hose out of the trunk of the '57 and siphon gas out of its tanks and put it in the bus. That would give him a few miles.

Miles.

He didn't feel as if he could walk twenty feet, let alone concentrate on driving.

He let go of the shotgun, the food and water. He scooted onto the hood of the Chevy and managed himself to the roof. He lay there on his back and looked at the sky.

It was a clear night and the stars were sharp with no fuzz around them. He felt cold. In a couple of hours the stars would fade and the sun would come up and the cool would give way to heat.

He turned his head and looked at one of the Cadillacs and a skeleton face pressed to its windshield, forever looking down at the sand.

That was no way to end, looking down.

He crossed his legs and stretched out his arms and studied the sky. It didn't feel so cold now, and the pain had almost stopped. He was more numb than anything else.

He pulled one of the revolvers and cocked it and put it to his temple and continued to look at the stars. Then he closed his eyes and found that he could still see them. He was once again hanging in the void between the stars wearing only his hat and cowboy boots, and floating about him were the junk cars and the '57, undamaged.

The cars were moving toward him this time, not away. The '57 was in the lead, and as it grew closer he saw Pop behind the wheel and beside him was a Mexican puta, and in the back, two more. They were all smiling and honked the horn and waved.

The '57 came alongside him and the back door opened. Sitting between the whores was Sister Worth. She had not been there a moment ago, but now she was. And he had never noticed how big the backseat of the '57 was.

Sister Worth smiled at him and the bird on her cheek lifted higher. Her hair was combed out long and straight and she looked pink-skinned and happy. On the floorboard at her feet was a chest of iced beer. Lone Star, by God.

Pop was leaning over the front seat, holding out his hand, and Sister Worth and the whores were beckoning him inside.

Wayne worked his hands and feet, found this time that he could move. He swam through the open door, touched Pop's hand, and Pop said, "It's good to see you, son," and at the moment Wayne pulled the trigger, Pop pulled him inside.

Like Pavlov's Dogs

by Steven R. Boyett

Time has been extremely kind to Steven R. Boyett's Like Pavlov's Dogs. *Like the best speculative fiction, its concerns have only gotten more germane, as the world spirals closer to whatever the hell we all know is coming (though we still don't know what that is).*

As with Lazarus, *this story tackles the big themes on a massive scale, this time with every stratum of society mirrored by their relative position either in or out of the ecosphere.*

Unlike Lazarus, *this is also a rip-roaring action/adventure, layered with sharp gags, genuine laughs, and eye-popping set pieces galore. Which is to say, it's both dark and fun.*

If I had to pick one story from this book to make into the next $60 million zombie extravaganza, it would be Like Pavlov's Dogs. *Hollywood, please take note.*

In the meantime, kick back and watch the walls come down in the hands of the brilliant Steve Boyett.

1

"*Good* morning, happy campers!" blares the loudspeaker on the wall above the head of Marly Tsung's narrow bed. "It's another beautiful day in paradise!" A bell rings. "Rise and shine!"

Marly the sleepy camper slides out from her pocket of warmth. "Rise your own fucking shine," she mutters as she rises from her pallet and staggers to the computer screen that glows a dull gray above her desk. The word UPDATE pulses in the middle of the monitor; she flicks it with a finger and turns away to find the clothes she shed the night before.

"Today is Wednesday, the twenty-ninth," says her recorded voice. "Today marks the three hundred seventy-second day of the station's operation." Marly sniffs and makes a sour face at how pleasant her earlier self sounds. How *enthused*. "Gung ho," she says.

"The structural integrity of the Ecosphere is ninety-nine point five percent," the recording continues brightly, "with indications of water-vapor leakage in panels above the northern quadrant of the Rain Forest environment."

"Christ," says Marly, hating the daily cheerfulness of her own voice. She slides into faded, baggy jeans, then scoops on peasant sandals.

"Unseasonal warm weather in this region of Arizona has increased the convection winds from the Desert environment, and as a result the humidity has increased in the Rain Forest environment. Rainfall may be expected in the late afternoon. Soil nitrogenating systems are—"

Marly puts on a T-shirt, sees the neck tag pass in front of her, pulls the shirt partway off, and turns it around.

Leaving, she pauses at the door and looks back. Computer console on oak desk, dirty laundry, precariously stacked pop-music cassettes, rumpled bed. If someone were to come in here, someone who knew Marly but wasn't on Staff, would they be able to figure out who lived here?

She looks away. The question is moot. The only people in the entire world who know Marly are the Ecostation personnel.

She slides shut the door on her own voice and heads down the narrow hall to one of the station's two bathrooms.

FLUSH TWICE—IT'S A LONG WAY TO THE KITCHEN is scrawled in black felt-tip on the wall facing her. It's been there a year now. More recently—say, ten months ago—someone wrote, below that, EAT SHIT. And below that—with a kind of prophetic irony—WE'RE ALL IN THIS TOGETHER.

Marly never did think these were very funny.

She flushes—once—and heads for the rec room and the inevitable. Her waste heads for reclamation and the (nearly) inedible.

Four of the other seven station personnel are in the rec room ahead of her. Billtheasshole stands on the blue wrestling mat. He's wearing his gray UCLA sweat suit again. If clothes could get leprosy, they'd look like that sweat suit. On a leather thong around his neck is a silver whistle. Marly thinks her usual idle morning thought about what it would feel like to choke Billtheasshole by that lanyard. She imagines his stern face purpling, his reptilian eyes dimming. Watching his tinfoil-colored eyes staring at the door, Marly invents Tsung's law: The biggest shithead and the person in command can usually be shot with the same bullet.

Pale Grace sits glumly at an unplugged gaming table, drumming her nails against the dark glass tabletop. Marly shakes her head. A year now, and Grace still looks like someone desperate for a cigarette. She catches Marly watching her and ducks her head and twitches a smile. Marly thinks of just staring at her to drive her even more crazy, but what's the point?

Slumped against the heavy bag in the corner like a determined marathon dancer is Dieter. He smiles sleepily at her and scratches his full, brown beard. "Grow me coffee," he says in his pleasant Rotweiler growl, "and I will unblock your pipes for the next year."

She smiles and shakes her head. "No beans," she replies. This has become their daily morning ritual. Dieter knows what that headshake is really for: He's unblocked her pipes enough already, thank you.

Sitting barefoot in lotus on the folding card table is little carrot-topped Bonnie. She smiles warmly at Marly, attempting to get her to acknowledge the spiritual kinship that supposedly exists between them because Bonnie is into metaphysics and Marly is Chinese.

Marly makes herself look inscrutable.

In walk Deke and Haiffa, a mismatched set: him burly, her slight; him hairy, her smooth; him Texas beefeating good-ole-boy-don't-shoot-till-you-see-the-black-of-their-skin, her Israeli vegetarian educated at Oxford. Naturally they are in love. Marly pays them little mind beyond a glance as they walk in holding hands like children and sit on the unraveling couch; Deke and Haiffa return the favor. They have become Yin and Yang, a unit unto themselves, outside of which exists the entire rest of the world. Proof again that there is such a thing as circumstantial love, love in a context, love-in-a-box.

Last in is Leonard Willard. Marly still spells his name LYNYRD WYLLYRD on the duty roster, long after the last drop of humor has been squeezed from the joke, which Leonard never got anyway. Leonard is the youngest staff member, always compensating for his inexperience with puppyish eagerness to please. But despite the fact that Leonard could have been one of the original Mouseketeers, Marly takes his constant good cheer as an indication of his bottomless well of self deception. The Ecosphere station is his world; everything outside it is . . . some movie he saw once. In black and white. Late at night. When he was a kid. He really doesn't remember it very well.

Predictably, Billtheasshole blows his whistle the moment the last person walks in. "Okay, troops," he says. "Fall in." He likes to call the staff members "troops." He would still be wearing his mirrored aviator sunglasses if Marly hadn't thrown them into the Ocean.

She falls in behind the others as they line up on the wrestling mat to begin their calisthenics. Or, as Billtheasshole calls them, their "cardiovascular aerobic regimen."

2

Sweetpea spits gum onto low-pile, gray carpet. "Flavor's gone," she explains.

Doughboy laughs. Shirtless, his hairy belly quivers. "Where you gonna get some more, girl?"

("Sailor?" someone calls from the stacks upstairs. "Goddamn motherfucker—*Sailor!*")

Sweetpea just shrugs and turns her back on Doughboy. She goes to join a group gathered behind one of the tall bookshelves. 0900: American History. One of the group pulls a book from a shelf and heaves it, then gives the finger to someone Doughboy can't see. The hand is snatched back as a return salvo is launched from Engineering. The book tumbles across the floor and stops facedown like a tired bat near Doughboy's left boot. *Alloy Tensile Strength Comparisons*. He doesn't attempt to interpret the title, but bends down, picks up the book, and pulls Sweetpea's gum from where it has stuck against a page that shows a graph. He brings fingers to chapped lips and blows. Fingers in mouth, then out, and wiped against blue jeans that have all the beltloops ripped loose. "Dumb bitch," he says, and chews.

A loud slap from above. Doughboy looks up to see gangly Tex being thrown against a tall shelf. The shelf tips, but does not fall. Books do.

"What the fuck you *yelling* for, man?" Sailor stands above Tex, who has set a hand to his reddening cheek. Sailor remains there a moment, looking down at Tex with hands on hips, then bends and pulls Tex to his feet. He dusts him off and pats his shoulder. "Look, I'm sorry I hit you, man," he says. "Only, don't run around *yelling* all the time, okay?"

"Sure," says Tex. His hand leaves his inflamed cheek, and he glances at his palm (for blood? wonders Doughboy). "Sure. But, I mean, I was just wonderin', y'know? I mean—" He looks around the library. "What're we gonna find here?"

Sailor frowns. He looks around. One hand tugs at the face of Mickey Mouse hanging from his right ear. When he looks back at Tex, he's smiling wryly.

"Books," he says.

Doughboy nearly chokes on his gum, he thinks this is so goddamn funny.

"What are *you* laughing at?" from above. Doughboy only shakes his head.

Sailor shakes his head, too, but for completely different reasons. "Fuck," he says. "I used to *go* to this school." He comes down the stairs with two hardcover books tucked under one arm. "Yoo of A."

Doughboy angles his head to see the titles; Sailor hands him the books. Doughboy holds one in each hand before him. His lips move. Furrows appear in his forehead.

Sailor taps the book in Doughboy's left hand. "*Principles of Behavior Modification*," he supplies. He taps the thicker in Doughboy's right. "*Radiation and Tissue Damage*." He clasps his hands behind him and rocks back and forth, beaming.

"You taking a test?"

Sailor shakes his head. "Nope. Deadheads are. I think I can teach them to find food for us. *Real* food."

Doughboy makes a farting noise. "Shit. *We* can't find real food; how you expect them to?"

"The name 'Pavlov' ring a bell?"

"No."

Sailor sighs. "Why I stay with you limpdicks I will never know," he says.

Doughboy stacks the books. "But how you gonna get—"

"*God damn you, nigger!*"

They turn at the shout from Engineering.

"That *hurt*, motherfucker!"

"Why you didn't move, then, home?" replies American History. "What you been throwing at *me* the last—"

Shouts, something heavy thrown against a wall, a bookshelf falling against a bookshelf, scuffling, and cheers as American History and Engineering begin beating the living shit out of each other.

Sailor walks over to break it up. He takes his time, wondering why the hell he's bothering in the first place. He oughta just let evolution sort 'em out. Well, he's there he might as well do something to split 'em up.

It's Cheesecake and Jimmy. Figures. Cheesecake's got the upper hand, which is no surprise, and with no more than two or three blows he's already made a mess of Jimmy's face. White boys never could fight.

He leans forward to grab Cheesecake's teak arm as the knotted fist at the end of it rises, but something stops him. Around them

(*"You gonna let that nigger put a hurt on you, boy?"*)

are scattered newspapers. One lies spilled like a dropped deck of cards

(*"Fuck 'im up! Yeah! Yeah!"*),

fanned out to expose the Local section.

Dull slap of bone-backed meat on softer meat.

Sailor bends to pick up the paper.

(*"Cheese, man, ease up. C'mon, man."*)

'Space
Breaks

(*"Motherfucker hit me on my head with a book. A big book, motherfucker!"*)

Sailor turns the paper over.

Station'
New Ground

He unfolds the paper.

(*"Ah! Fucking nigger! I'll kill you, fuckin'—"*)

'Space Station'
Breaks New Ground

Sailor frowns. An artist's conception accompanies the article.

"Let him up," Sailor says mildly, and they stop.

(Tucson)—Official groundbreaking ceremonies were held Monday morning in a tent 60 miles northwest of Tucson, to mark the beginning of construction on Ecosphere—a self-contained "mini-Earth" environment that may prove a vital step in mankind's eventual colonization of other planets.

Budgeted at a "modest" $30 million, according to project director Dr. William Newhall of the University of Arizona Ecological Sciences division, Ecosphere will be a completely self-sufficient, 5-milllion-cubic-feet ecological station. The station will contain five separate environments, including a tropical rain forest, a savanna, a marshland, a desert, and a 50,000-gallon salt-water "ocean," complete with fish. There will also be living quarters for the Ecosphere staff, scientific laboratories, livestock, and an agriculture wing—all on two acres covered by computer-controlled "windowpanes" that regulate the amount of sunlight received. Even Ecosphere's electrical energy will come from the sun, in the form of arrays of solar-power cells.

"Ecosphere will be a sort of model of our planet," says chief botanist Marly Tsung. "We'll have a little of everything"—including several thousand types of trees, plants, animals, fish, birds, insects, and even different kinds of soil.

If all goes well after Ecosphere is constructed and stocked, eight "Ecosphereans" will bid goodbye to the outside world and enter the station's airlock, and they will remain as working residents of this model Earth for two years.

Designed to reproduce and maintain the delicate balance of the Earth's ecosystem in the midst of a hostile environment—presently the Arizona desert, but conceivably Mars by the end of the century—Ecosphere will also serve as an experiment in how future interplanetary colonists might get along working in close quarters for long periods. However, Grace Havland, team psychologist, does not foresee any problems. "We're all self-motivated, resourceful, problem-solving people," she says. "But we're also very different from one another, with widely varied interests. I think that will help. That, and the fact that the station itself provides a lot of stimuli."

What could go wrong? In the first place, Ecosphere's delicate environment could suffer a

(turn to page 16D)

"I remember this," says Sailor as the others gather around to see what's got him so interested. Jimmy mops his face with his torn, white T-shirt. "They started building it when I was in school." He turns to 16D. "They interviewed a bunch of these assholes before they went to live in it. There was this Chinese girl with blue eyes." He whistles appreciative recollection and lowers the paper. Suddenly he frowns and hands the paper to Florida, who scans the article and studies the cutaway drawing of the Ecosphere (which is not a sphere at all). Florida's dark eyebrows flex toward his hairline. One big-fingered, skull-ringed hand strays to his scarred leather hunting vest. He passes the paper around for the others to read and scratches the back of his neck under the red elastic band that holds his long pony tail.

Ed the Head squints at the article as if it is out of focus. His lips move as he reads, then he turns bleary eyes to Sailor. "So they, like, built some kinda space station in the middle of the goddamn desert. So fuckin' what?"

"So now you know why no one lets you do the grocery shopping," says Sailor. "You wouldn't recognize an opportunity if it gave you a whip-cream enema."

Ed fingers his matted beard. "Chill out, dude. Ain't nobody fuckin' with *you*."

Sailor shakes his head. "It's all just one big mystery to you, isn't it?" He looks around at the group. "Jesus," he and takes back the paper before leaving them.

"What he mad about?" Cheesecake rubs cut knuckles with two ragged-nailed fingers.

Florida folds his Popeye arms, making himself look twice as big as he already is. "That space station's set up to go for years without any help from outside," he says in surprising melodic baritone. He pulls off his silver ear cuff and massages the outside curve of his ear. "They control their environment. They grow their own food. They raise their own livestock. Get it now?" His arms unfold. "Apples. Oranges. Chicken. Eggs. Bacon."

"Oh, man . . ." from someone behind Jimmy.

"Aw, those dudes're wasted by now," says Ed the Head.

"Reefer," adds Florida.

Ed the Head straightens. "No shit? Hey, Florida, man, you wouldn't fuck with me, now. . . ."

"How we know they still there?" demands Cheesecake. "They be walkin' around dead and shit, by now."

Florida smiles and replaces his earcuff. "We don't know," he says. He glances at Sailor and raises an eyebrow. "Yet."

"Doughboy. Hey, Doughboy!"

Doughboy turns with a finger still up his nose. "Yo, Sailor," he says mildly. He twists, pulls out—

"We still got that baby?"

—and puts the finger in his mouth. He withdraws it with a wet smack and shrugs. "I dunno. Maybe. You wanna go to the zoo an' see?"

Outside the hurricane fence at the juncture of Optical Sciences and Physics: Sailor and Doughboy peer about the corral.

"I don't see it," says Sailor. "Maybe they ate it?"

"Nah. They don't do that, much. Somehow they know the difference." He bangs the fence with both palms.

Shambling figures turn.

"Hey," shouts Doughboy. "*Hey, you deadhead fuckheads!*" He bangs harder. " 'Course," he says, more conversationally, watching their stiff approach, "they coulda tore it up. They're kinda dumb that way."

Watching them shuffle toward him and Doughboy, Sailor suddenly begins to giggle. He bends forward and his mouth opens, as if he has been kicked in the stomach. The giggle expands and becomes full-throated. He can't control it. Eventually he drags a bare, anchor-tattooed forearm across one eye, saying "Oh, shit . . ." in a pained way, and wipes the other eye with the other arm. "Oh, Jesus. Whose idea was *this*?"

Doughboy grins and rubs a palm across sparse blond billy-goat beard. "You like it?" The hand lowers to hook a thumb in a front pocket of his Levi's. "Florida ran across a T-shirt shop in the Westside Mall. He brought back a shitload of 'em. And a bunch of us got the deadheads outta of the zoo one at a time and put 'em on 'em."

Sailor shakes his head in amazement.

A little old lady deadhead reaches the fence ahead of the others. Part of her nose is missing, and the rest flaps against one wrinkled, bluegray cheek in time with her sleepwalker's gait. She runs face-first into the fence, then steps back with a vaguely surprised look that quickly fades. Hanging shapelessly about her upper body is a ridiculously large, blue T-shirt. I'M WITH STUPID, it reads, with an arrow pointing to her left.

Sailor begins to laugh again.

Doughboy is laughing now, too.

The dead old lady is joined by an enormous Hispanic deadhead with the figure of a bodybuilder. His skin is the color of moss. A strip of bone shows above his ear where a furrow of scalp has been ripped away. His arms and chest look overinflated. He wears a tight, red maternity blouse. Centered over his bulging pectorals is:

BABY ON BOARD

The deadheads make plaintive little noises as they reach like sad puppies for Sailor and Doughboy, only to regard the fence that blocks their hands as some kind of miraculous object that has inexplicably appeared in front of them.

There are twenty of them clustered around the fence now, purpled fingers poking nervelessly through the wide mesh.

"No baby," says Doughboy. "But it wouldn't be here anyway. Can't walk yet."

"Walk?" Sailor frowns. "It probably never will." He regards the hungry drowned faces as he speaks. "I wonder if they age?"

Doughboy's eyes narrow. "Baby doesn't have to have been like that from the start. Coulda been born after everything turned to shit, then died an' gone deadhead."

"Yeah, but still—how would we know? Do they get older as time goes by?" He nods toward the fence. "Can a deadhead die of old age?"

Doughboy shrugs. "We'll find out someday," he says. Sailor looks away from the fence. "Are you an optimist or what?"

Doughboy only snorts.

"Who's the one by himself back there?" Sailor points. "He doesn't move like a deadhead."

"Whozzat? Oh, Jo-Jo? Yeah, he's pretty fuckin' amazing, ain't he? He's a regular Albert fuckin' Einstein—for a deadhead, I mean. Quick, huh?"

The figure standing alone turns to face them. He wears a brown T-shirt with white letters that spell out HE'S DEAD, JIM.

Sailor's frown deepens. "He's *watching* us."

"They all do that, man. We look like those big ol' steaks in the cartoons."

"No, I mean . . ." He squints. "There's something going on in that face. His *tabula* ain't quite *rasa*."

"Yeah, what you said. Here—" Doughboy leaves the fence and goes to a plastic milk crate. He pulls out a disk that glints rainbow colors. "Cee Dee," he says, grinning, and holds it up. "Michael Jackson. *Thriller*."

In his other hand is a rock.

He steps to the left of the knot of deadheads who still claw vaguely toward them. He glances at Sailor and angles the compact disk to catch the sunlight.

"Jo-Jo," he calls. "Hey—Io-Jo!" He jumps (*light on his feet, for a jelly-belly,* thinks Sailor) and lobs the rock.

"Jo-Jo!"

hunger me jojo they call jojo and throw at me without hurt only eat and i with move them to jojo from their meat mouths i reach to hunger with light of hot above with bright the fence the hunger-others grab and pull but shining outside they hold the shining thing and forward i into the fence grab against press into my face and raise my hands in hunger not to the shining thing but to the hand that holds it in hunger jojo they say and i will eat

"He," declares Sailor, watching the deadhead toss the rock it has caught from hand to hand, "is smarter than the average deadhead."

Doughboy nods. "Fuckin' A, Boo-Boo."

3

Bill hangs around after the others leave, sweating from their cardiovascular aerobic regimen. They will disperse to attend to the many jobs that await them each day; maintaining the Ecosphere is a full-time job for eight people. And keeping those eight people in shape and responsive to the needs of the ecological station, maintaining their *esprit de corps*, making them understand their responsibilities to the station's investors, to science—indeed, to the human race—is quite a burden. That's why Bill is glad that he is the one in charge—

because, of the eight, only he has the discipline and organizational abilities, the qualities of *command*, to keep them functioning as a unit. And—*as a unit*—they will persevere. He imagines he is a lifeboat captain, forcing the others to share their labor and rations, sometimes extreme in his severity and discipline. But when rescue comes, they will all thank Bill for running his tight little ship. Yes they will.

He goes to a locker and removes a French fencing foil. He tests the grip, slides into stance, and holds his left hand loosely above and behind his head. *En garde*. Blade to *quarte*. Block, parry, riposte. Lunge, *hah!* He is D'Artagnan; the wine of his opponent's life spills upon the wrestling mat. *Touché*.

The pigs in their small pen near the corner formed by the human habitat and the agricultural wing are slopped by Grace. Of all the dirty work in the station she must perform (even though it is not her job to), the team psychologist finds working with the pigs almost pleasurable, and certainly less troublesome than working with Staff. Grace is a behaviorist, and a behaviorist will always work better with pigs than with people. The pigs in their uncomplicated Skinner box of a muddy pen are easier to direct and adjust than those upright pigs in their bigger, labyrinthian pen.

The ground darkens around her and she looks up at a cloud passing in front of the sun, distorted by the triangular glass panes above. She idly wonders how long it's been since she went outside the station. She shrugs. What difference does it make?

She bends to pat Bacon's globular head. She has named the pigs so that she will remember their prime function, to prevent her from becoming too sentimentally attached to them: Bacon, Fatback, Pork Chop, Hot Dog, Sausage, and Hambone. The pigs are wonderful: not only do they clear the quarter acre of land devoted to raising vegetable crops, and fertilize it as well, but they are astonishingly gregarious, affectionate, and intelligent animals. Which any farm girl knows—but Grace has devoted her life to the exacting science of manipulating human beings, and has only recently become devoted to the emotionally admirable pig.

If only the staff were as easy to manage. Humbly she tries to tell herself that she's only doing her job, but, truth to tell, if they hadn't had someone to keep them psychologically stable all this time, she doubts they'd have lasted even this long. She thinks of the other staff members one at a time as Pork Chop and Sausage nuzzle her calves. She maintains a file on each one of them and updates it every day with her observations and impressions of their sessions together. Luckily the sessions have diminished in importance, which is as it should be, since everybody is so mentally healthy. So goddamned healthy. So *enormously* adjusted.

Pork Chop squeals, and Grace realizes she has been squeezing his poor ear as hard as she can. She lets go and pats his thick head. "There, there," she says. "There, there."

She thinks again of the book she will write when all this is over. It will sell well. She will be on Phil Donahue. Holding an imaginary pen, she practices signing her name.

Bonnie is not far from Grace; she works, shirtless in the early-morning sun, on her knees in the three tall rows of cornstalks. The agricultural wing is like the playing board of a child's game, with squares devoted to corn, potatoes, beans, peas, squash, carrots, and tomatoes. She wishes they had watermelon, but it would require far too much water to be ecologically justifiable. But at least there's the fruit grove by the wall, there—right beside the vegetables—with apples, oranges, and lemons. The soils are as rich as possible, having originally been procured from all parts of the United States.

Is it *still* the United States? Bonnie wonders. Surely somewhere it *must* be.

She returns to her work, examining stalks and peeling back husks to check for insects. There are screen doors in the narrow access corridors between the agricultural wings and the Environments, but still, insects manage to get through. Despite their productive yield the Ecosphere is actually never very far away from starvation, and the loss of a single crop to insects could be—well, it just didn't bear thinking about.

Bonnie likes to work with plants. Not in the same way that Marly does—that appraising, sterile, *scientific* way—but in a sort of . . . *holistic* way. An *organic* way. Yes, that's right: organic. She smiles at the word. Bonnie feels a kinship to the plants, with the interrelatedness of all living things. She likes to feel the sunlight on her bare, freckled skin because it reminds her of the ironic combination of her specialness and insignificance. The sun is an indifferent ball of burning gases ninety-three million miles away, yet without it there could be no life. "We are all made of the same star-stuff," Carl Sagan used to say. Well, Bonnie feels that stuff in her very cells. It sings along the twined strands of her DNA.

She certainly doesn't miss sex. She doesn't need sex. She hardly ever even *thinks* about sex.

She sits up and shuts her eyes. She breathes deeply. *Om mani padme om*. Who needs sex when there is such passion in as simple an act of life as breathing?

She finds a bug in a cornhusk and crushes it between thumb and forefinger.

Leonard Willard takes everybody's shit every day. He puts it in phials and labels it and catalogs it; he analyzes it and files the results. He operates and maintains the waste-reclamation systems and biological and mechanical filtering systems. It's a dirty job, but someone has to do it. If no one did it, the Ecosphere wouldn't work. Leonard likes to think of himself as the vital link in the Ecosphere's food chain. Filtration is his life. Ecosphere gives him an abundance of opportunity to feel fulfilled: there are filtration systems in the sewage facilities, in the garbage-disposal units, in the water-reclamation systems; there are desalinization units between the Ocean and the freshwater marsh; there are air filtration units, and air is also cleaned by pumping it beneath the Ecosphere and allowing it to percolate through the soil from several areas.

Leonard loves to purify things. To take a thing that is unusable in its present form, and by passing it through buffers and barriers and filters, distill a usable, needed thing—that makes him feel useful. Needed. Staff couldn't breathe without him. Staff couldn't drink without him. Without Leonard, staff couldn't take so much as a healthy shit. Without Leonard, the shit would never hit the fans.

Leonard has Hodgkin's disease, a cancer of the lymph system. Years ago radiation therapy made all his hair fall out and stabilized his condition enough that he could be put on chemotherapy, which only made him stupid and violently ill for two days out of every month. He began putting on weight again, and his hair grew back in, even thicker than before, and the doctors felt encouraged that his condition had stabilized. Somehow his body learned to live with the disease.

Or, from a different perspective, he thinks (reaching a gloved hand into a water conduit to withdraw what looks like a dirty wet air-conditioning filter), the disease has allowed his body to live. So that it can continue to feed. This is why Leonard rarely worries about the things that roam the Outside, the things Bill has dubbed carnitropes. He doesn't worry about them because his body is being eaten from the *in*side. Or, to distill it in a very Leonard-like way, there is shit in his blood, and he can't filter it out.

He shakes the wet filter over a plastic sheet. Ropy black strands drip down. Leonard cleans the filter with a compressed-air hose, returns it to the conduit, then bundles and twist-ties the plastic sheet.

Walking with it dripping to the lab, Leonard realizes that there is nowhere else on Earth, anymore, where he could perform his job. Leonard feels he is the most realistic of all the Staff—and he knows what it's like outside their brittle little environment. Though he helps maintain the station, and therefore the illusion the station represents, he understands intuitively that his reasons for doing so are quite different from theirs. They maintain Ecosphere as a denial of what has changed Outside. He maintains it as a triumphant affirmation of the same. As above, so below. None of the others, being physically fit, can appreciate this. Therefore none of the others can adequately appreciate Leonard.

But he keeps up a cheery façade. It's important to him that he do this.

In the lab he unbundles the plastic and breathes deeply. T*hat* is the stuff of life, and don't let anyone tell you otherwise.

Deke and Haiffa are fucking on the thirty-foot beach. Deke and Haiffa are always fucking somewhere. "Oh, look," Haiffa says. She points, and their rhythm halts. Deke rolls his head to look out on the water, not minding sand that grinds into his brush-cut hair.

"Don't see nothin'," he says.

"A fish," she says. She sets her hands on his chest and resumes.

"Fish on Friday," he says. "Maybe I'll hook 'im. What's today?"

"I don't know." Her accent, which used to charm him, is invisible to him now. "Wednesday."

"Anything-Can-Happen Day," he says, and arches his back as he begins to come.

Above them on the roof, Dieter the marine biologist watches through the glass. Sometimes the Ecosphere to him is a big aquarium. He watches Deke and Haiffa not from a need to accommodate voyeurism so much as from a desire to alleviate boredom. The first couple of months, everybody went at everybody else in various combinations, then settled into a few pairings that dissolved, either from attrition or from entropy, and now everybody is more or less an environment unto his or her self. In this they are like the scientific wonder in which they all live, but which none calls home.

Dieter is supposed to be cleaning solar panels. Dust from the Arizona desert accumulates on the Ecosphere's glass-and-aluminum roof, and when it is thick upon the solar cells, the station's power supply is diminished. But there are a lot of solar-power cells, and it is a hot July day in the Arizona desert. Dieter takes frequent water breaks.

Below him Haiffa and Deke seem to be finished, and he looks away. He stands and puts his hands on his hips, turning to take in the gleaming, sloping geometry of glass and aluminum that is the station. Ecosphere is built into the side of a gently sloping hill; the rain forest uphill is forty feet higher than the desert downhill, which is also nearly six hundred feet distant. Hot air rises from the desert and flows uphill; condensers in the rain forest cool the air and separate the moisture. It actually rains in the indoor rain forest.

Dieter looks at the terraced Aztec pyramid of glass and aluminum that caps the rain forest. What would it feel like, he wonders, to jump from the top?

A sense of freedom, the exhilaration of weightlessness, and then the ground, stopping all thought. All worry. All pain. All fear.

But an eighty-foot fall might not kill him. And even if it did, he'd just get back up and start walking around again. No, a bullet in the brain is about the only way to go, he thinks laconically, bending to pick up his rags and economy-size bottle of Windex. Shame Bill had to have the foresight to lock up the guns they obtained on that one expedition to Tucson, a year ago.

He looks left, over the edge and down at the parking lot behind the human habitat. The Jeep Cherokee and the Land Rover are still there. It would be so goddamned easy. Just get in, crank up one of those babies—might need to juice up the battery, but there was plenty of that to go around—put her in gear, and fucking *go*.

He'd do it in a minute, too, if there was someplace to fucking go *to*.

And Marly. She climbs down from a tree, drops her pruning shears, unties her harness, and lets it fall at her feet. She mops her brow. It is amazingly humid in here. "Tropical" is such a misleading word, she thinks, conjuring mai tais and virgin beaches. In the higher branches of the tree she has been pruning it is not so bad; the eternal trade wind from the downhill desert is cooling. On the surface, though, the breeze is broken up by the thick foliage, and the climate is dank and wet.

She watches a squirrel dart along branches. They've been having trouble with the squirrels. They're dying out, and no one is sure why. Marly was against their presence from the start; they're filthy little rodents that carry disease and live by stealing whatever they can get their grubby little paws on. Everybody likes them because they have neotenic characteristics: big heads in relation to the body, big eyes in relation to the head. They look, in other words, like babies, and *everybody* likes babies. Well, small-scale evolution is taking care of the little shits, so Marly guesses she showed them. Nobody would listen to her because she's a botanist, which everybody knows is just a fancy word for gardener. Have you met Miss Tsung, our Chinese gardener—oh, I *do* beg your pardon: Ms. Tsung, our *Asian botanist.*

She wipes palms on denim and walks from the rain forest to the sparse growth near the beach. She pulls open a screen door and walks down an access corridor, then out the screen door at the far end. Bare-breasted Bonnie waves to her as she cuts across a corner of the Agricultural wing. Marly ignores her and enters the Supply section of the human habitat.

"Supplies, supplies!" she says.

From a closet whose door is marked EXT STORES she takes the two-man tent and a sleeping bag.

Walking toward the front door she meets Billtheasshole walking in. He stops in front of her, eyebrows rising, and does not get out of her way. "Again?" he says, looking at the blue nylon tent bag and rolled sleeping bag. "I don't know that I altogether approve of this antisocial behavior, Marly. Everybody needs his privacy—or *her* privacy—but you are *actively segregating* yourself from us."

She holds the camping supplies before her like a shield. Her mouth forms an O as she mimics sudden recollection. "Oh, I *am* sorry," she says. "We were having the Tupperware party tonight, weren't we? Or were Haiffa and Deke going to sell us Amway? I forget."

"Grace tells me you didn't show up for your last two scheduled sessions." He rubs his jaw (tending toward jowls) with the span of thumb and forefinger. Of the four men on Staff, only Bill continues to shave—his badge of civilization endeavoring to persevere. Striking a blow for *homo gillette*.

She laughs. "Who has? I don't have time for her bullshit. She's more fucked-up than the rest of us. Just tell her it was my bad toilet training, okay?"

"I am merely attempting to express my concern over your lack of cooperation," he says with the mildness of psychotic conviction. "Everyone has to contribute if we're going to pull through—"

"Pull through? Pull *through*, Bill? What is this, some *phase* the world's going through? Going to grow out of it, is that it?"

"I think I understand your resentment toward authority, Marly, but you must see that some sort of hierarchy is necessary in light of—"

"Authority?" She looks around, as if expecting a director to yell "Cut!" "Why don't you do me a favor, Bill, and fuck off?" She shoulders past him.

"This will have to go into my report," he warns.

She opens the door. "More demerits!" she wails to the vegetable crops. "Golly. I'm—I'm so *ashamed*." She turns back to smile meanly, then tries to slam the door behind her. The hydraulic lever at the top hisses that she'd better not.

A last swipe with a dirty rag, and Dieter grins at his reflection. "I can *see* myself!" he says.

He collects the dirty rags scattered around him on the glass. Waste not, want not: the Golden Rule of the Ecosphere. He stands and surveys the surrounding Arizona desert. As an experiment in maintaining an artificial environment in the midst of an alien one, Ecosphere is immensely successful: They are an island of glass on the rusted surface of Mars.

He stretches cramped muscles and breathes in the dry Martian air. Dieter Schmoelling, naked to the alien plain, the only human being able to withstand—

He frowns. Wipes sweat from his brow. Shades his eyes, squints, bends forward.

A tunnel of dust, a furrow in the desert. A giant Martian mole burrowing toward the invading glass island. A Martian antibody come to attack the invading foreign cell.

A car.

4

Marly is pitching her tent in the downhill desert when the P.A. sounds an electronic bell: *Bong!* "All personnel to the fruit grove," commands Billtheasshole. *Bong!* "All personnel report to the fruit grove immediately." And clicks off.

What confidence, what assurance! The son of a bitch just *knows* that everybody will show up there, *bong!* Marly thinks of not showing up, just to remind him that his authority lies entirely in their acquiescence, but curiosity gets the better of her. Despite her dislike of him, she knows that Bill wouldn't call them together in the middle of their working day for no good reason.

But what Bill thinks of as a good reason is not necessarily dreamt of in her philosophy.

Marly sighs, pulls up stakes, and walks around the bluff, past scrub, into savanna, beside the ocean, into the southern access corridor, across croplands, and into the fruit grove.

The others are already there, except for Bill. Their backs are to her as they look out the windows. "I suppose we're all wondering why he called us here," says Marly.

Dieter turns and beckons her over. She pulls an apple from a tree and heads toward them. She bites into the apple and Dieter frowns. She grins and offers it to him, Chinese Eve. His frown deepens, and she laughs at his seriousness.

He makes room for her and points to the ruler-straight desert road, but he really doesn't need to. Marly can see the car heading for them. It's only three or four miles away.

"Should've baked a cake," she says, but inside she feels a pang, something tightening.

Bill joins them, holding a double-barreled shotgun. Her heart slams, and for a moment she is certain Bill is going to kill them all. This is it; she knew it would happen someday—

Deke steps forward and takes the shotgun from Bill's hands. Bill is so surprised by this . . . this *usurpation*, that he allows him to.

Deke breaks the shotgun and removes the corrugated red plastic shells. He returns shells and broken shotgun to Bill, shakes his head in contempt, and steps back.

"They'll probably pull into the parking lot," says Bill. "I'm going out on the roof, in case they try anything." From a back pocket he pulls out a slim walkie-talkie. He hands it to Dieter. "I'll call you if I need you," he says. He turns to Leonard. "Talk to them over the P.A. in the monitor room," he orders. "Find out what they want and get them out of here. Ladies—"

"We'll make coffee," suggests Marly.

"I want you to keep out of sight."

"I want a gun."

Bill shakes his head. He turns away and heads for the human habitat, where the airlock is. They follow him, since the monitor room is at the north end of the human habitat anyway. Marly catches up to Bill. "Then give me the key to the armory," she persists. "You're not taking it out of here so you can get your ass shot off on the roof."

He frowns, but cannot fault her logic. He draws a many-keyed holder from a retractable line attached to his belt and selects a key. He gives it not to Marly but to Deke, then turns and trots ahead of them.

Marly glances back toward the apple trees. The car is perhaps two miles away.

Inside the habitat Bill veers right at a T intersection; the others veer left and climb a flight of stairs. They enter the monitor room—all but Deke, who grins at Haiffa, tosses the armory key, catches it, and hurries down the hall.

Camera One already stares unblinkingly at the asphalt parking lot. Leonard activates Camera Two and sends it panning. The others cluster at his chair.

"Check, check," says the walkie-talkie in Dieter's hand. "Do you read me? Over."

"Loud 'n' clear, man," replies Dieter. He rolls his eyes.

"I'm on the roof, making my way toward the agricultural wing where the cover's better. Over."

"Right. I mean, yeah . . . over?"

Leonard turns from the control panel. "I'm guh-guh-*going* to test the puh-puh-P.A. Ask him if he c-c-can *hear* it. "

Dieter relays the message, and Leonard says "T-testing wuh-wuh-one t-two three," into the microphone.

"Loud and clear," says Bill. "Listen, if there's any—here they are. Over and out."

The car is a dusty black El Camino. They watch on Monitor One as it pulls into the asphalt lot, slows, and parks beside the Land Rover. The driver waits for the dust to clear. Over the speakers they can hear the engine idle, can hear it knocking after it is switched off.

The driver opens the door and steps out holding a pump shotgun. He turns, says something to a passenger (there isn't room for more than two in the El Camino), and straightens. He shuts the door and approaches the Ecosphere.

He is the first live human being they have seen in over a year.

"Hello?" he calls. Squeak of feedback, and Marly winces. Leonard adjusts the gain. "Hello, is anybody there?"

Leonard pushes a button and Camera Two zooms in.

He is young—early twenties. His hair is dark, straight, shiny, tied in a pony tail, to his waist. Faded gray jeans with white-threaded holes in the knees below a long, unbuttoned, black-and-white-checked shirt with rolled sleeves. Earring dangling from right earlobe.

"Hello?" he calls again.

Leonard thumbs the mike switch. He clears his throat self-consciously and the man steps back. The shotgun comes up.

"Wuh-wuh-we *hear* you," Leonard says.

The man looks around for the source of the voice.

Leonard glances at the others. "Wuh-wuh-*what* do you want?" he says into the mike.

The shotgun dips, lowers. "Food. Just—food. Me and my wife are . . . we haven't eaten in a while—"

Deke arrives carrying an armload of rifles and ammunition. Silently he gives one to each of the other six, continually glancing at the monitor.

"—and our baby is pretty sick. We just want some food; we'll leave you alone, after."

Bonnie refuses a rifle. Deke shrugs. "Your funeral," he says.

"If we give them food now they'll only come back for more later," says Grace.

"Prob'ly with friends," adds Deke, handing Marly a rifle.

Leonard fiddles with the monitor controls. Camera Two pans left, centers on the El Camino, and zooms. Leonard adjusts the focus. There is a young woman in the holding a bundle that might be a baby.

Leonard looks at Dieter, who shrugs.

On Camera One the man waits.

Leonard frowns and thumbs the mike again. "How you nuh-nuh-*know* we w-were here?"

A breeze billows the tail of the young man's shirt. "There was an article in the paper," he says. "In the Tucson library. I thought maybe you were still here." He looks around and wipes his brow. "Hot out here," he says.

"Suffer, bud," says Deke. Marly glares at him.

Dieter goes to stand beside Leonard. "Maybe we should, like, tell him to get his wife out of the car," he says.

Leonard glances up. "W-w-what if he won't?"

"What if *she* won't?" adds Bonnie.

"Hey, beggars can't be choosers," Dieter replies. "They'll do it."

Leonard turns back to the mike. "Tell your w-w-*wife* to step out of the cuh, car," he says.

"You didn't say please," murmurs Marly.

"She—our baby's pretty sick," says the man. "I don't . . ." He seems indecisive, then turns toward the car and walks from Monitor One to Monitor Two. He opens the passenger door and leans in. He glances back once or twice as he speaks.

Leonard fiddles with the gain knobs.

"—ust do it. No one's going to hurt you. . . . I don't care what the little fucker feels like, just do it. And keep your cakehole shut."

The passenger door opens and a girl gets out. She wears khaki pants, sandals, and a dirty white T-shirt. She is perhaps seventeen years old. She wears a lot of make-up and bright red lipstick. The breeze tugs her tangled hair.

She holds a bundle before her. A little hand protrudes from it, grabs air, finds her breast, clasps.

"All right," says the man. "Now, please—can you spare us some food?" Leonard pulls back Camera One until he's in view again. They watch him gesture expansively. "You have a lot; we just want enough for a few days. Just enough for us to drive across the desert. We're trying to get to California."

Again Leonard glances at the others. "Cuh, Cuh, California? What's there?"

"My brother."

"I'll just bet he is," mutters Grace.

"Hold on a m-m-minute," says Leonard, and kills the mike. He swivels in his chair with a questioning look.

"I don't like it, man," says Dieter.

"Not one bit," says Deke.

"Maybe just some apples, or something . . ." says Bonnie.

Marly pulls back the bolt of her carbine and begins feeding little missile shapes to the breech.

"Sure," says Deke. "You wanna take it out to 'em?"

"Belling the cat," muses Grace.

"Dieter? Dieter, do you read me?" Bill's voice, a loud whisper.

Dieter lifts the walkie-talkie. "Roger . . . Bill."

At the console, Leonard suppresses a giggle. Behind him on the monitors, the man, the girl, and the baby await their reply.

"Keep it down; I don't want them to hear me up here. Don't tell them we'll give them any food. Over."

"We were just voting on it," says Dieter.

"It's not a voting issue. They don't get any."

Marly finishes loading her rifle and slaps the bolt in place.

"Just a couple of apples?" asks Bonnie.

Marly glares at her, hating her every milquetoast fiber.

"We have to remember the Ecosphere," continues Bill's tinny voice. "We can't upset the balance. We can't introduce anything new or take anything away. We breach the integrity of the station."

Marly shoulders her rifle and leaves the room.

"Hey, listen, Bill—" begins Dieter, but Bill is still transmitting.

"—ink of what this station represents: we're a *self-contained* unit. We grew that food ourselves. We live on a day-to-day basis."

"They're not asking for very much," mutters Bonnie. She sits in a chair and stares sullenly at the television monitor.

Dieter thumbs the "send" button. "We think it's a bad idea for other reasons," he says. "Grace feels that if feed them, they'll just, like, come back for more. Probably they'll tell others, y'know? Uh . . . over."

"Exactly! And *they'll* tell others, and we'll be barraged. We'll be like a . . . a free McDonald's out here."

"Golden arches," says Haiffa solemnly, and steeples her hands. Deke pinches her butt.

"We've got a consensus, then?" asks Dieter.

"Tell them no," says the walkie-talkie.

"They don't look too hungry to me," says Deke. "Get 'em outta here."

"Still," mutters Bonnie, "it seems such a shame . . . ." She watches the monitor and does nothing.

"Hello? Hey, hello?"

Leonard activates the mike. "Wuh-wuh-we're still here," he says. He seems much more confident now that a decision has been made for him. "Listen, we . . . we've taken stock of our, um, *situation* here, and we've talked it over, and examined the, uh, *parameters* of our food-intake quotients. You have to understand: we're rationed out ourselves. A meal for you means a meal less for someone here." His tone has become warm, congenial. "I'm sure you understand."

"You're saying no?" The beggar seems incredulous.

"I'm saying I'm sorry, but we've analyzed your situation with regard to ours, and we simply can't . . . *accommodate* you at this time."

"I don't fucking believe—you won't give us three days' food?" He keeps glancing around, as if persuasive arguments lie around the asphalt parking lot. "What about my wife?" he asks. "What about our *baby*?"

"I'm very sorry," says Leonard. He does not sound very sorry. He sounds, in fact, glad to be in a position to refuse something to someone, for a change. Like a hotel manager effusively sympathetic because there's no room at his inn. "But you come here asking a favor," he continues stutterlessly, "and you don't have any right to blame us for declining to grant it."

"Favor?" The man raises the gun. "You want a *favor*, you god—"

"Hold it *right there*, son." Bill's voice, over the speakers.

The young man hesitates.

"Don't do it. I don't want to shoot, but I will." Bill doesn't sound reluctant to shoot. He sounds very excited. "Now, you've asked for help and we can't give it. We would if we could. My advice to you is for you and your wife to get back in your car and head out of here. Don't head for California; head for Phoenix. There's bound to be food there, and it's only a few hours' drive."

"But we just *came* from—"

"Then head south. But you can't stay here. You got that? We don't have anything for you."

"We'll *work* for it!"

"There's no work for you here. This is a highly sophisticated station, and it takes a highly trained staff to operate it. There are a lot of us, and we're all armed. We need everything we have, and there isn't enough to go around. I'm sorry, son, but that's life in the big city. I—"

Bill breaks off. The young man and his wife look at something off camera.

"Get back inside!" yells Bill. "Back inside, now! That's an *order*!"

Leonard pans Camera One as close as it can come to the airlock entrance, which is below it and to the right. He shakes his head and gives a low whistle.

"Well," says Dieter. "Fuck me."

[5]

The rifle is braced on its strap on her shoulder. Her finger is on the trigger. In the other hand she holds a wicker basket. She's not nervous as she heads toward them—in fact, she's surprised how calm she is. Behind and above her, Billtheasshole yells for her to get back inside. She ignores him, but she feels a curious itching between her shoulder blades—probably because Bill is more likely to shoot her than they are.

They don't look as good off camera. A scar splits his eyebrow; another runs the length of his upper arm, bisecting a blue-gray anchor tattooed on his muscular biceps. He's not thin, but he looks undernourished. Vitamin deficiencies.

And the girl looks . . . well, *worn* is the only word Marly can think of. Used up. Her eyes are dull and unresponsive.

The hand gropes again from the bundle the girl carries. She presses it protectively to her, and Marly glimpses mottled flesh when the baby tries to suck the girl's nipple through the cotton of her T-shirt.

Marly stops ten feet from the man and sets down the basket. The girl glances down and holds the baby farther from her body.

The man and Marly stare at each other for a moment.

"What's it like?" asks Marly. She inclines her head to indicate the Arizona desert. "Out there."

"Pretty rough," he says.

She nods a few times. "Well . . ." She indicates the basket and steps back from it. "I'm sorry I can't do more. There's fruit, some vegetables, a little meat. A can of milk for the baby—what's wrong with it?"

"I don't know."

"Well, none of us is a medical doctor," she says. "But you might want to try a pharmacy whatever town you go through next. Or a doctor's office. If it's an infection, try ampicillin. If it's some kind of disease . . . well, antibiotics shouldn't hurt anyway. But keep her—him?" They don't say; Marly raises an eyebrow and continues. ". . . on liquids, and get her out of this heat."

Since setting down the basket she's been backing toward the airlock. The man comes forward. Instead of picking up the basket, he glances at the roof of the habitat.

"No one's going to shoot you," says Marly. "Just take it and go. And don't come back."

He lifts the basket and backs toward the El Camino. The girl is already behind the open passenger door, and now she eases into the cab. He sets the basket next to her, gets in, and shuts the door.

The man studies Marly. He nods, slowly. He starts the car and backs out. He backs up until he is out of the parking lot, then turns around and drives away.

For several minutes Marly watches the settling of the receding rooster tail raised by the car, and then she goes inside.

"Just who the hell do you think you are?"

"I'm one-eighth of this station, same as you, and I grew that food as much as anybody else did."

"You defied a direct order—"

"From someone with no authority over me. You know as well as I do that the hierarchy depends on the nature of the crisis."

"We put it to a *vote*, damn you—"

"Nobody asked for mine. How about you, Grace? Haiffa? Leonard? Bonnie?"

"Did you give any thought whatsoever to the repercussions this might have on us? You've just sent ripples through a very small pond."

"For Christ's sake, Bill, I gave them enough food to last them three *days*—if they're careful."

"We're not much more than three days from food depletion ourselves. *Every* change affects *all* of us. You of all people should know that, Marly. The experiment can't continue if outside—"

"The experiment ended over a *year* ago, Bill! Along with the rest of civilization! Why don't you fucking wake up!"

"All the more reason for us to hold out. Maintaining this station *is* maintaining civilization."

"But not humanity."

"Hey, Marly—the guy's just tryin' to say that, y'know—sometimes hard decisions have to be made. I'm sure he didn't like turning them down. Did you, man?"

"Of course not."

"Oh, Christ! Look, I'll *skip* a meal a day for three days, to make everything nice and even, all right? Will that make you happy?"

"*I* thought we should give them some food."

"Yeah, Bonnie. But you didn't do shit."

6

"*Motherfuckers.*" Sailor has the pedal to the metal. "Those mother*fuckers*, man. I thought we'd just grab some food from them, you know? As an excuse to case the place. See how many of them are left, see how good their security is, all that shit. But, god damn, I never thought they wouldn't give us any food. Fuck, *we'd* have given us food, I know we would've. We've *done* it before! Sons of fucking bitches." He bangs the steering wheel. "They wouldn't feed a goddamn *baby*, man!" He glances at Sweetpea. "You *believe* that?"

Sweetpea is holding the baby at arm's length, staring at it with loathing. "It was chewing," she says dully.

"Of course it was chewing; it's a goddamn—"

She drops the baby and begins batting her hands about her as if fighting off wasps. "It was *chewing*, it was *chewing*, it was *trying to eat me through my shirt*, its *mouth* was on me, oh, God, and it was moving, and I thought, that poor baby, and then I *realized*—"

Sailor grabs her arm and yanks. The El Camino swerves. "Calm down. Calm fucking *down*."

She stares at him wide-eyed. On the floorboard the baby paddles air like a roach on its back. Half out of its swaddling, the skin around its neck blues where the make-up leaves off, its left arm missing, ripped from the socket some unknown time ago. Its right arm reaches; its toothless mouth opens and closes. Its eyes are like flat plastic.

Sweetpea pulls her legs up to the seat.

"We have to drive straight out of here," says Sailor. "We can't give them any reason to think something's not right. Just stay calm until we get over the rise, there, all right? All right?"

"I want it out of here."

"In a minute." He seems amused at her revulsion. He snorts. "Just close your eyes and think of England."

Huddled on the seat, she turns to look at him. A mile later she says, "You wanna know why I fuck all the others and not you?"

Sailor gives her a you-can't-be-serious look. "Because I don't *want* to fuck all the others?" he asks innocently.

She ignores him. "Sometimes the others are nice to me, you know? They give me things, they show me things. They take me where good things are. You give me the fucking creeps. You're like a fucking deadhead; you live inside your brain all the time and hardly ever come out, and when you do, it's fucking creepy. You got maggots in your brain, or something. I wouldn't fuck you if you were the last man on earth."

"Well, gosh," Sailor says meanly. "There can't be many more to go." He sighs. "Maybe someday . . ."

She slits her eyes and he laughs.

They top the rise. On the other side Sailor pulls off the road and fishes out his .45 semiautomatic from under the seat. He works the action and turns off the engine. He takes the keys, not about to leave them with her. He goes to her side and opens the door. He picks up the baby and turns to face the desert.

Its head lolls. Its mouth works. Its single hand grabs gently at the hair on his forearm. Its mouth opens and closes, opens and closes.

He holds the baby at arm's length, puts the barrel of the pistol against one unblinking flat-plastic eye, and fires.

7

hands: remember other hands of other food that touch and make the hunger go without the need of food from her *a* her *i remember but the hunger and without her now the hunger still but her* hands

8

Marly takes soil samples from the savanna. She must determine whether the recirculated air is percolating properly throughout all the environments; she suspects blockage in places.

Dieter leans against a mangrove tree, arms folded, left leg crossed over right.

"Hey, I'm not saying that you did the wrong thing," he is saying. "I'm just playing devil's advocate here. I mean, from Bill's standpoint, you've violated the integrity of the Ecosphere. You risked possible contagion; you depleted a carefully regulated—"

She stands with a metal scoop and a dripping, mud-filled plastic baggie in hand. She turns away from him and squishes toward another section of mangrove. She squats and gropes in the stagnant water.

Other than their brief sexual liaison in the first months of the station's operation, Dieter and Marly have something in common: They both helped design environments for the EPCOT Center at Walt Disney World in Florida. Under contract from Kraft, Marly worked on a pavilion called The Land, which raised its own crops in various experimental ways, including hydroponics and alternate-gravity centrifuge environments. Dieter helped stock a million-gallon, walk-through ocean called The Living Seas, complete with sharks and dolphins.

Marly wonders how ol' Walt Disney World is faring these days. The personnel and guests probably look and act pretty much the same. Down & Out in Tomorrowland, same as her.

Now, a week after reality so rudely impinged upon their own little world, Marly is trying to sever all connections with Staff as best she can, under the confined circumstances. She has slept in a tent in the desert every night. She has eaten only food she picks and prepares herself from the Agriculture wing. She does not report for morning exercises with Bill, psychiatric consultation with Grace, the weekly Staff gripe sessions, or the twice-weekly operations reports. She receives all environmental updates from the computer. She stands night watch on the monitor screens when scheduled to—a duty increased since what she has come to think of as the Food Incident.

So now Dieter stands around, dragging the Incident out into ridiculous academic discourse, and the jissum of his mental masturbation falls all over her. She wants to spill his alleged brains with her garden trowel, but what she does is continue working and ignore him. It's not very difficult. Thinking about it, Marly realizes that she's already spent over a year in solitary with these seven people.

For the others it's life as normal—as normal as they can make it, which is very normal indeed, if you apply a now-anachronistic standard. The Food Incident was simply an unplanned-for contingency; they tap its pertinent minutiae into their data banks and schedules and allotments; they compensate, and adjust, and otherwise act as though it were no different than any of the other minor inconveniences that must be dealt with to keep the Ecosphere going.

Marly knows better. She knows their heads are in the sand. She knows that, one day, the real world will show up and kick them in the ass.

But Marly also knows that it's a lot easier to get by in here than Outside. She is torn: she certainly does not want to leave the station, but she is not sure how much longer she can tolerate these whitebread martinets. Self ostracism is her temporary compromise. She's on hold. She is a weather vane, shaping herself around the direction of the wind.

9

"Again."

Florida turns on the flashlight. Sailor watches as Jo-Jo's hands, knotted in the T-shirt (HE'S DEAD, JIM), extend before him. Jo-Jo trudges toward the source of the light like Frankenstein's monster.

Florida clicks off the light and Jo-Jo stops. He looks confused. Through the fence Sailor extends a broom handle from which dangles a fresh piece of cat. Jo-Jo grabs it and begins gnawing, string and all.

"How are the others coming along?"

Florida shrugs. "Not as good. Jo-Jo's still smartest. We can get 'em to go for the light, though, as long as we give 'em munchies after. They'll follow a piece of meat anywhere, particularly if it's alive. It's got so that every time they see a light, they expect food. But Jo-Jo's the only one you can get to carry things. Got him to open a door, a couple times."

One deadhead (SHIT HAPPENS) trips over a lounging deadhead whose shirt proclaims that she is BORN AGAIN.

Sailor shakes his head. "Pretty fucking stupid."

Florida nods. "Don't see what good all this is gonna do us."

"They taught pigeons to run machines by pecking buttons. Deadheads are as smart as pigeons."

"Not by much."

"No," Sailor agrees. "They're like plants that turn to follow the sun. Only they follow live meat. But we can redirect that impulse to get them to go after something else if we give them meat as a reward. Clustered stimuli and delayed gratification. They used to do the same thing to get people to quit smoking."

Florida laughs and scratches a muscular arm. "Dead? Call Schick! But Sailor, what do we need 'em for? We do all right by ourselves."

Sailor shrugs. “I want to use them,” he says simply.

“You’re still pissed at those techno-weenies out in the desert? Fuck ’em, bud. Let ’em rot. Ain’t nothing those peckerwoods got that we can’t get ourselves.”

“There’s more to it than that,” Sailor mutters.

“You’re taking this pretty personally,” says Florida.

Sailor turns on him. “They wouldn’t feed a fucking *baby*.”

“Sailor, it was a deadhead.”

“They didn’t know that.”

“So what? What possible difference can it make?”

“Aw, man, fuck you, all right?”

At the fence, finished with his bit of cat, cyanotic-tinged face against the broad steel mesh, Jo-Jo watches. Beside him now are the others, carnitropically attracted. They jostle and vie mindlessly, like teenagers before the gate at a rock concert. The upraised elbow of a deadhead (PARTY ANIMAL) strikes the temple of a skinny woman wearing a blank T-shirt that has a bumper sticker slapped onto it: I EAT ROAD KILL.

Sailor and Florida turn at the sound of approaching music. Cheesecake has a ghetto blaster the size of a suitcase on his muscular shoulder. Run D.M.C. are demanding that sucker emcees call them sire. How Cheesecake can walk and dance at the same time is a mystery to Sailor, whose musical taste always ran to Tangerine Dream and King Crimson anyhow. Well-ordered, high-tech music. White-boy stuff.

Cheesecake’s eyes glint in the light from the building the others are burning down across the quad. His irises are bright, mirrored rings.

“Fuck,” whispers Florida, and reaches for his holster.

Sailor stops him with a hand on his elbow. Florida glances at him, and Sailor shakes his head.

Cheesecake stops before them and sets the ghetto blaster down, dancing jointlessly.

“I thought you’d gone deadhead,” Florida says mildly.

Cheesecake dances. “Say what?” The music is pretty goddamn loud.

“I nearly shot your nigger brains out!” yells Florida.

"Wha' for?"

Florida and Sailor glance at each other and laugh.

"Oh, man . . ." says Florida, shaking his head.

"Hey, you like these?" Cheesecake points to his eyes. "They bad, or what?"

"Where'd you get 'em?" yells Sailor.

"I dunno. Some building." He waves across the quad, where the building burns.

"Optical sciences," says Sailor.

"Yeah."

The song changes; the beat doesn't.

"You're gonna get your ass shot off with those on," yells Florida.

"Say what?"

Florida shakes his head and turns to Sailor. "I don't think the others are gonna be too enthused on coming down on that place, Sailor," he says. "No percentage in it. "

Sailor nods. "Figured."

"I have to tell you, too." He watches Cheesecake dancing. "Sweetpea thinks . . . well, she wants some of the guys to split up, you know, and come with, her. You aren't exactly Number One on her hit parade."

"She wants to leave, let her."

"Yeah, but . . . a lot of the guys'd go with her. You know how it is."

"There's girls at that station in the desert."

"Yeah?" Hearing this last, Cheesecake brightens. "Hey, yeah?"

Sailor nods, and begins to elaborate, but stops when he sees Florida staring at the zoo pen. He turns to look.

"Hey, Jo-Jo!" Cheesecake points and grins. "Check you out, bro!"

sounds they make i remember from boxes it made me move not toward *like food but* with *and sometimes with sounds and moving with* her

"Jesus Christ," Sailor breathes, watching Jo-Jo stiffly dancing. "He *remembers*."

Later that night Jimmy sees Cheesecake coming down steps of the Student

Union and blows his nigger brains all over the concrete. Engineering defeats American History.

"He was walkin' funny an' his eyes was all fucked an' shit," he tells Sailor. "What the hell was I *supposed* to think?"

"Fuck if I know," replies Sailor, certain now that it's time he moved on.

10

Leonard in the monitor room is drawing circles on a yellow legal pad. He draws them two lines tall and one after the other, circle beside circle. He is trying to teach himself to draw a perfect circle every time. He will not stop until he draws two consecutive rows of perfect circles.

At the end of each row he surveys the monitor screens. Cameras are placed around the station, along with an alarm system on the bottom row of glass panes around the perimeter.

Leonard does not see the Ryder truck with its lights out glide to the base of the slope and stop several hundred yards from the south end of the Ecosphere. He does not see the driver's-side door open and close (without the cab light coming on), nor the black-clad driver hurrying to the back to raise the door. He does not see the masked Pied Piper with a flashlight beam lead a group of shambling figures toward the Ecosphere.

Leonard draws a row of nearly perfect circles and surveys the monitors. He looks directly at the Ryder truck at the bottom left of Monitor Five, but motionless in the dark it looks like the rest of the angular landscape and he returns to drawing circles.

He completes a perfect row, and is halfway through a second when the alarm goes off.

11

Marly awakens to the sound of a distant bell. It is dark inside her two-man tent. She slips out of her sleeping bag and pushes past the entrance flaps.

Stars shine in the Arizona sky above glass above desert built in desert.

She zips her coverall and tries to get her bearings. It's the general alarm; somebody on monitor watch must have hit it.

Monitor watch?

A chill clenches her stomach. She retrieves her carbine from the tent and heads down the bluff, then around the miniature oasis and toward the marshlands. Marshwater has begun to soak through her Reeboks when she hears the screams. She stops, and chill water saturates.

From the animal pens. She splashes toward the savanna and the nearest access corridor.

The sound of the pigs squealing in terror awakens Grace. Her room is right next to the animal pens, and she hurriedly throws on a robe and looks out the window. There is motion, but it is too dark to make out anything.

She leaves her room and hurries down the corridor, out the front door, and past the bean poles toward the animal pens. Only then does she notice that an alarm bell is ringing. Her feet are getting dirty and there is a cold draft blowing from the apple orchard. She should have thought to put on her slippers, at least, but no, if something's happened to Bacon, or Pork Chop, she'd want to get—

She stops. The cool breeze is coming from the end of the apple orchard. In the dim light she can see two triangular glass panes are missing from the wall past the trees. What could have caused that? It could have just . . . *blown* in—the difference in external air pressure, maybe, or even just a strong gust. Maybe *that's* what had upset the poor little piggies: the sound of breaking glass.

The squealing comes again, startling her. She rushes toward the pens, unmindful of cold air or dirty feet. "There, there," she calls as she opens the waist-high gate. "Mommie's here. It's all right." She finds the switch for the bare bulb above the pigpen and flips it up. "Mommie's—"

Bacon is standing on top of a man. The man has arms and legs wrapped around Bacon. Bacon is gnawing on his shoulder. His round head tosses, tearing flesh and pulling tendon.

Beside them is the gutted body of Hambone. Grace is horrified to see that Hambone is still alive.

The man's head comes up. Bacon's ferocious gnawing does not seem to bother him. He opens his mouth and bites her neck. Pork flesh tears and blood gouts. Bacon squeals.

"*What are you doing?*" Grace is heading toward him before she knows what *she* is doing. "*You get away from her!*"

Bacon slips loose. Blood squirts rhythmically from her neck. The man stands amid snuffling pigs. He turns toward her. Pig blood streaks his Grateful Dead T-shirt. Bloodless flaps of flesh fold from torn fabric at his shoulder.

Grace is only beginning to register what it is that turns toward her. That heads toward her with vacant eyes and outstretched arms. That needs her as no one has. She backs up a step. "No," she says. "No, wait." Snuffling pigs nuzzle her calves. "You can't—you don't *belong*—"

She falls backward over Fatback. The frenetic pig tramples her stomach. The breath is knocked from her. Something tugs her foot. She looks up. Hot Dog's mouth is around her instep. She jerks back her leg. The pig makes a guttural noise like the growling of a dog. Its eyes are wide and dull in the light from the bare bulb.

She sits up. The intruder bends to her. He places a hand on either shoulder. He opens his mouth. Pork gobbets hang from green-coated teeth. She cannot get breath enough to scream. She pushes him away and tries to stand. Hot Dog tears into her calf. The intruder bends again. Her leg is burning. She kicks away. Hot Dog squeals and bites again. The intruder lowers his face to her breast. Ringing bells and squealing pigs. His teeth come together. It burns. He turns his head. It tears. She pushes him away. Wetness warms her hands. Tatters of herself in his mouth. Her fingers smear dark wet across his face. Into his mouth. He bites. Bone crunches. She pulls back her hand. Two fingers gone. Leg numb. Why so cold? Vague pressures. Distant sound of chewing.

Burning white flashes as he feeds the pigs feed on rip of meat stripped from bone pull tendons bitten tugged snapped like hot strands of cheese that pulse the pulse that beats that ebbs that slows and fades away.

12

Marly hurries along the access corridor, wet shoes squishing. The Ecosphere is very dark; they do not like to keep "exterior" lights on at night because they would be visible for miles.

At the screen door leading to the agriculture wing she pauses.

Pop. Pop-pop!—and breaking glass.

She unslings her carbine and opens the door.

Dieter jumps awake at the sound of the bell. He sits up in bed and glances at the flashing computer screen on his desk. INTEGRITY BREACH. He rubs his eyes, gets out of bed, and puts on his clothes. He fastens his belt and opens his closet to retrieve a .45 automatic in a shoulder holster and the pump 30.06 Deke gave him the day of the Food Incident.

He is halfway up the stairs to the monitor room when he hears the screams from outside. He pumps the rifle, *chuk-chik!* and hurries into the corridor, where he meets Bonnie in her white kimono. They run for the front door.

The screams have stopped by the time they are outside. Neither has a flashlight, and they stand in the darkness for a moment, letting their eyes adjust. Bonnie gestures nervously toward the animal pens, and they head that way, Dieter in the lead and Bonnie clinging close behind, both trying to be silent but making a lot of noise.

At the low barrier to the pigpen they stop. The pigs are gathered and snuffling, hind ends wiggling. Dieter vaults the barrier and claps his hand against the rifle stock. The pigs scatter, and Dieter stops in his tracks. Spread before him is emptied Grace, and before her in the flesh kneels a real live dead carnitrope. The carnitrope raises its head and opens its mouth. A quivering strip of flesh hangs on its upper lip, then slides off.

Behind him Bonnie vomits.

Dieter levels his rifle and pulls the trigger. It will not depress. The carnitrope is getting to its feet. For some reason Dieter does not think to check the safety, but drops the rifle and pulls the .45 from its holster. The carnitrope shambles toward him, dragging a worn wing-tip shoe through Grace. Dieter thumbs the safety and pulls the trigger. The bullet makes a small hole going in and a large hole going out of the carnitrope's chest. The corpse staggers back under the impact, heel squirting something rubbery from beneath, then comes forward again. Dieter aims higher and fires twice. The back of the carnitrope's head sprays away, and behind it a pane shatters. The corpse slams backward to land in the remains of Grace.

Bill pops awake the second he hears the alarm bell. He's anticipated something like this, and he's ready. They'll never catch old Bill with his pants down. He pulls a Smith & Wesson .44 magnum from under his bed, snatches his brown coverall from across the back of the chair at his desk, where he has left it so that he can find it in the dark, and pulls it on without letting go of the enormous pistol. He goes to his door and raises the pistol alongside his head. Purple light flickers from his desk as the computer monitor screen comes to life. INTEGRITY BREACH, it reads, and begins blinking. Bill narrows his eyes and turns back to the door. He snatches it open and peers into the corridor.

Nothing.

The bell continues to ring.

He jumps into the corridor and lands in a policeman's firing stance, legs straddled, left hand around right hand holding the gun, back straight, arms a little bent. He didn't read *Soldier of Fortune* for nothing.

He turns quickly. The corridor is clear. He straightens and moves for the stairwell and the monitor room.

Leonard is puh-puh-panning cameras like mad, searching for any sign of motion, when Bill bursts into the room. He starts, then bolts out of his chair when he sees that Bill clutches the buh-buh-biggest pistol he has ever seen, aimed square at his chest. He glances at the monitors and Bill lowers the gun.

"You sounded the alarm?"

Leonard shakes his head. "Window buh-buh-broke. In the orchard."

Bill frowns, still looking at the monitors. "False alarm?" He sounds disappointed.

Leonard shrugs.

Bill peers forward. "Hold Camera Five," he says.

Leonard hits a button on the console. Bill leans until his face is five inches from the screen. "Bring it up."

"Do you mean zoom, or p-p-*pan* up?"

Bill glares. "Zoom," he says.

Leonard works the controls until Bill is staring at a Ryder truck not three hundred yards downhill from the desert environment. He turns to look at Leonard. He raises the gun. Leonard raises his hands as if to ward off bullets.

From outside they hear gunshots. *Pop. Pop-pop.*

13

Haiffa swims naked in cool tropical water. She cannot bear to open her eyes in salt water and so swims blindly, coming up for a breath and flipping back down again. Her long hair streams behind her; she is a mermaid. Or a Siren, perhaps, to torture the naked ears of Ulysses.

She likes to swim after making love. She likes to think of Deke lying spent on the shore, waiting for his Venus to emerge.

She swims out past the sandbar and surfaces. She waves toward the narrow shore, but Deke does not see her because he is facing the Staff Quarters to the west and scratching his head. She draws a deep breath and dives.

The bottom is less than twenty feet down, here; she grabs it with her hands. Grit collapses in her palms. Sometimes she has accidentally grabbed crabs here, or scraped herself against rock, or been startled when—

—something slides across her leg. She jerks, but of course it is only a fish, though for a moment it felt—

Her ankle is grabbed. The grip is cold and firm. She whirls and opens her eyes. Salt water stings. Dark water. She reaches. Her fingers brush the cloud of her hair. She kicks out, but encounters nothing. Her leg is tugged. She jackknifes to free herself from whatever holds her. Something with ridges. It feels like a *hand*, but that's ridic—

Agony as something rips along the blade of her foot. Air bubbles contain her scream, float to the surface, and pop without a sound. Haiffa curls up and grabs at her foot. Her hands encounter something round, with hair. A head. But it can't be a head, not down here. Her hands slide across it as her foot pulses into the cold water. Her fingers trace cold flesh and opened eyes.

Following her next scream is a short gasp. It contains water. She forces herself to check it. Salt water in her throat. She coughs. The little air that remained to her bubbles up. Her lungs feel scoured. Her foot throbs. Her leg is pulled in again. Two hard crescents press into her thigh, and press harder. In the sudden pain of tearing flesh she rips away a clot of hair in one hand. Thrashing now. She tries to scream, but there is nothing. Her mouth works to call, but the world lies above a veil of water she cannot part. The only sound is the beating of her heart.

The flailing arm that holds the hair is grabbed, is pulled. Her mouth stretches horribly as arm muscle is pulped and torn away. Mottled red tinges the darkness in her eyes. A tone builds in her ears, the sustained ringing of a distant underwater bell. Some threshold is crossed in her brain, a line of resistance past which the instinct to breathe defeats the knowledge that there is no breath to draw. She inhales. Her lungs fill with water. Relief floods into the midst of her pain. Coolness quenches the burning in her chest.

Something tears loose inside her. The ringing grows, her heartbeat slows. Red lace webs her vision. Pain spreads up her arm as she is drawn into a cold embrace, is held like a lover, is kissed with great passion, is consumed, while around her the water grows warm.

Deke rises from the beach at the sound of gunfire. *Pop. Pop-pop!* Pistol, sounds like. He brushes sand from his butt and turns toward the agricultural wing. He opens his mouth to improve his hearing, but there is nothing further to hear. He does not see the hand rise from the water behind him, wave a frantic goodbye, and sink again.

He picks up his jeans, shakes them out, and begins pulling them on. "Haiffa," he calls. "Haiffa!"

He peers forward, straining to see in the darkness. The Olympic-sized ocean is placid.

Been under an awful long time now. Prob'ly swam out past the sandbar, but she oughta be able to hear him call. Should check out that gunfire. Better make sure Haiffa's okay first.

He walks to the end of the beach and skirts the ocean to the west, where the savanna begins.

"Haiffa?"

Probably somebody finally had enough of ol' Billy-boy and did it to him. More than likely idjit did it to himself, way he handles a gun. Damn fool could screw up a two-car funeral on a one-way street. Three shots, though.

"Haiffa!"

Well, it'd probably take him three shots to find a brain in that head to blow out anyway, the stupid son of—

Something in the water there? Not big enough to be Haiffa, though. But what the hell *could* it be? Gator? Sheeeit. Something else appearing beside it, something smaller. *Oh, forgot to tell you, man.* Dieter's voice in his head. *Put a little tiger shark in the ocean. Full stock, right? Scavengers of the deep, y'know?*

Splashing as something rises from the water. Dripping as it emerges.

"Haiffa . . ."

Reaches the smaller object in the water, grabs it, picks up. Brings it toward itself. Heading toward him. Taking shape from the darkness. Wet figure. Woman. Not Haiffa. Pulls the object away from its head, dangles it by its side. In silhouette he sees the object is a leg from ragged-ended knee to foot. Pulled in again. Piece ripped away.

Deke sprints toward the beach. Fucking pistol on the towel. He splashes through the muddy ground, hits soft, wet sand, heads to the dark square of towel. Yep, pistol's there. Smith and Wesson beats four aces, his daddy used to say. Take that to the bank. Bill had wanted the guns back. "Sure you can have it back," he'd replied, and repeats it now. "You take it from me, it's yours."

He wipes palms on jeans and grips the pistol firmly. On the sand he waits as the figure stumbles onto the beach, recovers, and gropes toward him. *Carnitrope.* What the fuck was *that* supposed to mean? Plant's *photo*tropic, Bill explained. Turn toward sunlight. Biochemical reaction. Stimulus/response. *Ding!*—slobber. *Carni* = meat.

Fuck.

He raises the pistol and thumbs back the trigger—

Carnitrope his goddamn ass. They can call it that if it makes 'em feel better, but his momma didn't raise no fools.

—sights down the long barrel—

"*The only thing working is their hindbrains—the reptilian complex,*" Marly had lectured. "*They're like snakes that wait in one place all day for something to come along. The* R*-complex lets the carnitropes move, and the only reason they move is to get live meat.*" Chink bitch. He may be just a glorified fucking janitor, but where did she come off—

—fires.

The figure staggers back and drops the leg onto the sand. It comes forward again.

"*Cut off the* R*-complex—decapitation, massive neural destruction,*" Marly had continued, "*and the tropism is removed.*" In memory Bill smiles. "*In other words,*" he elaborated, "*if you blow their brains out they have a motivation problem.*"

"Blow your fuckin' brains out," breathes Deke. He cocks the hammer and fires again.

A sudden furrow glistens above the creature's left eye. The creature takes two more steps. Stops. Reaches up an inquiring hand. Fingers sink to knuckles. Hand lowers. Another step. Front knee buckles, and it pirouettes to the sand.

Deke holds the gun on it for a few more seconds, then straightens and nears it cautiously. Yep. Dead for good.

Writing on its wet T-shirt. LIFE'S A BITCH, THEN YOU DIE. Different lettering beneath: THEN YOU COME BACK. Nipples beneath the wet fabric. Peekaboo.

Deke looks out over the little ocean. A little log, propelled by the eternal north wind, drifts toward the sandbar.

Crack! More gunfire. Rifle, this time. He better—

—searingblindwhiteness. Jesus *fucking*—

He sinks to his knees. His belly is turning warm. Somebody pushed a hot soldering iron through his chest. He looks down at his knees. Grit-ringed wet spots in the denim. I *hate that. Fuckin' cold spots when I walk—*

You never hear the one that gets you. Goddamn lie. Heard that one just fine. Oh, *shit.* He tries to rise, something shudders to a halt inside.

14

Sailor lowers his nine-millimeter Ingram submachine gun. The man he has just shot arches his back and spasm once. God, he hates that. Like all the nerves are screaming at once. Gives him the fuckin' willies.

He turns away from the beach. Invisible in his black jeans and sweatshirt, he works rapidly but quietly from tree to tree, heading uphill from the palms on the beach to the dense foliage of the rain forest. At the north end vegetation meets slanting glass panes. He pulls a box from his nylon backpack, wedges it between two aluminum struts, and turns a Radio Shack wireless intercom to "receive." He hurries toward the west wall, where he places another box and attaches another intercom.

He pauses at the screen door to the access corridor that leads back to the agriculture wing, where he broke in ten minutes ago. Floodlights are on outside the staff quarters, illuminating neat rectangles of crops. Getting in there isn't going to be easy.

Bill looks from the carnitrope lying in tattered Grace to the missing panes at the end of the orchard. "All right, now, let's not jump to any conclusions," he says. "It could be that one just got in here and went for the pigs, and Grace found it."

"Right," says Leonard. "It ruh-ruh-*rented* a Ryder truck and d-d-*drove* on up here to see if it could buh, buy a bacon, lettuce, and tomato sandwich." He wipes a shaking hand across his mouth.

Bill narrows his eyes.

"It was eating her," Bonnie says flatly. She looks strangely calm, as if Grace's death at the teeth of a reanimated corpse is yet another factor to account for in the many trivial events that accrue during the normal operation of the

Ecosphere. Yes, Grace is dead; now work schedules will have to be adjusted, and the sudden one-eighth surplus of food and water will have to be noted, and of course a new person will have to be appointed to moderate the weekly gripe sessions, not to mention someone else having to slop the remaining pigs.

Bill, Dieter, and Leonard regard her stonily. It is as if her casualness toward Grace's death is more repulsive than the fact and manner of Grace's death. There is something alien about it. If only she would go into hysterics, they would understand. That's what a woman is *supposed* to do when this sort of thing happens; they're *conditioned* by society. They can't help it. So why doesn't Bonnie just have a screaming fit and get it over with?

"I guess we shouldn't assume there aren't any more of them," Dieter says.

Bill nods. "Someone let them in here deliberately. An infiltration."

"Huh-who?" asks Leonard.

Dieter cradles his arms and rocks them, humming "Rock-a-bye Baby."

Bill frowns. He inclines his head, slowly. "We have to stay together," he says. "I don't want—"

Pop.

Their heads jerk.

Pop.

"Beach," says Leonard.

"Deke and Haiffa," says Diefer.

Bill brandishes his pistol. "Leonard, you come with me. Dieter, stay with Bonnie."

Bill trots away without waiting for Leonard, pistol in the lead.

Crack! Different sound from the beach. Bill stops. He glances back. "Leonard?"

Leonard swallows and cuh-cuh-catches up to Bill, his rifle held before him like a shield he doesn't trust.

15

Marly in the southern access corridor, trying to decide what to do. First three shots from near the agriculture wing to the northwest, and now three more from the vicinity of the beach. Which way should she go?

Well . . . assuming it's the same people shooting, she ought to head in the direction of the most recent shots.

She firms her grip on the carbine and turns back.

"I don't want to wait here."

Dieter looks at Bonnie as if suddenly remembering she is there. "We have to wait till they find out what's going on."

"I *don't* want to wait here." She glances toward the pen at the bodies of the two pigs, the carnitrope, and Grace. The other pigs snuffle and make nervous sounds, run into one another, trample the bodies, sometimes stop to nuzzle the freshly dead, and raise their piggy heads with piggy noses freshly red.

Dieter goes to the pen and bangs the low wall to calm the pigs, but they only bleat louder. "I'm gonna let 'em out," he decides. Bonnie says nothing, and Dieter opens the little wooden gate. The pigs do not bolt, so Dieter enters the pen and drives them out.

"I'm going inside," says Bonnie. "I'm going to my room. Until this is over."

"Hey, you can't do that. You heard what the man said."

"He's got no authority over me. There's no rank here. I wouldn't have volunteered if there was. Fuck that supremist bullshit."

"I mean about the zom—the carnitropes." He walks from the pen, and they head toward the front of the staff quarters. "There are probably others in here," he continues. "And *someone* let them in. You don't even have a gun."

"I despise the things. They're *male* weapons. Extensions of the male sexuality. If you can't rape something, you exterminate it."

Dieter gives a moment's thought to exterminating Bonnie, but none to raping her.

"I'm going to my room," Bonnie continues, "and locking the door. No one will bother me there. I'm not going to be a party to you people acting out your primal hunting instincts. I am civilized, and I refuse to collaborate."

"You are one fucked-up asshole," says Dieter. "You know that? I use the word asshole because it is nonchauvinistic. Everyone has one, y'know?"

Bonnie opens the front door to the staff quarters and goes inside. Dieter shakes his head. He levels the 30.06 extension of his male sexuality and surveys the flood-lighted area. He wishes he had a cigarette, the first such craving he has felt in a while. Or a joint. They had to give up cigarettes when they entered the Ecosphere, and bringing in marijuana seeds was out of the question, even though Marly claimed they'd grow fine in the tropics.

He stands stiffly and swiveling, trying to make his face hard. Dieter the Martian colonist standing sentry duty within the lone glass island, the only thing between safety and the living-dead invaders who threaten their very—

Something pokes his back. "Don't move." The voice is tight, as if the throat that produced it is constricted.

He begins to move anyway, then stops.

"Drop the gun. Now."

He lowers the rifle. Holds it at arm's length. Lets go.

Loud thud of a large-caliber handgun from somewhere near the ocean.

Someone shoves his shoulder. "That way. Inside."

Dieter attempts to walk normally. If he passes an opened door, a corner to scuttle around—

"Keep your hands up. I have a submachine gun, and you wouldn't get five feet without looking like an outtake from *Bonnie and Clyde*. Got it?"

He glances back despite himself. "*Bonnie and Clyde?*"

Poke in the kidneys. "Move, asshole."

"Where are we going?"

"Power room. Battery room. Whatever the fuck you people call it."

"I don't know how—"

"I don't care what you don't know. You take me to it. Fuck with me and I'll kill you. And I'll put the bullet in your heart so you come back, like my friends out there."

Dieter imagines himself an automaton: stumbling, agape, hands outstretched, eyes needy, drawn to living flesh. Turning left toward the power room, he finds himself wondering just how different it would really be.

16

"It's Deke."

"It got him? The, the carnitrope, it got him?"

Bill toes Deke's face-down body, which yields jointlessly. There is a small, nearly bloodless hole between the shoulder blades. Bill bends and turns the body over. The torso rolls, but the legs stay knee-down, body twisted at the waist.

That's how you know someone's dead, Leonard thinks. Because they don't care what position they're in.

Bill rolls the lower half of Deke's body as well. Out of some sense of decorum? Whatever; he squats before the big man's chest. A larger, more ragged exit hole exactly at the solar plexus. "Someone shot him in the back," Bill says.

Leonard glances around the beach. They're pretty exposed here. Something floats against the sandbar in the water. A sniper there, prone in the water? Too far, too dark, to tell. "Shouldn't we take cuh, cuh, *cover*?" he asks.

"Whoever shot him wouldn't remain in one position." Bill stands and goes to the corpse of the carnitrope, "They'd sweep the terrain, continue mobile. Tactical maneuvering. Offensive advantage. Search and destroy. Divide and conquer."

Leonard comes up beside him. "Took one with him," Bill observes.

They do not see Deke's body stir behind them.

"Lot of guh-good it did him," Leonard replies.

They do not hear it regain its feet and begin to slouch toward them.

Leonard maintains a respectful distance from the morbid X of the carnitrope. "So . . . w-what should we duh-do now?"

Bill never answers, because Leonard's shoulder is grabbed. He turns and finds himself face to face with Deke. At first he is relieved: They made a mistake and Deke is not duh-duh-dead after all. But realization floods in: Deke is wall-eyed and slack-faced. Thickened blood stains his chin. Sand clings to the right side of his face, to his eyelashes—Leonard can even see grains in his eye. But Deke does not blink. He does not breathe. He does not have any light of life in his eyes. His cold fingers curl on Leonard's shoulder, and pull. What do you want to say, Deke? What are you trying to tell me? Nuh-nuh-nothing. His mouth opens. Bill is shouting something, but Leonard is so fascinated by the sight of Deke back from the dead like some redneck Jesus that he doesn't really hear Bill. Deke the Resurrected pulls him nearer, and Leonard knows he ought to do something, but all he can do is stare. The rifle is a piece of wood in his hand. *Flesh of my flesh, good buddy.* That's what Deke would say if the front part of his brain was still working. *You gonna be baptised now! You gonna get the faith! The Holy Spirit gonna enter you! Whosogoddamnever believeth in me shall not perish, but shall dwell in the House of the Bored forever.*

But Deke the Saviour stops. He stares at Leonard in a kind of open-mouthed sorrow, a wistfulness like a child denied a sugary cereal on a trip to the grocery store with Mom. The hand still holds his shoulder, but no longer clutches with need, no longer pulls imploringly. A dog-like, questioning look enters the dull eyes. Leonard feels a kind of stupid disappointment. He feels a sudden compulsion to reason with Deke, dead or no, to ask him just what the heck is going on here, good buddy, you gonna eat me or what? But the enormously long, black barrel of a pistol enters the scene and taps Deke on the temple. Leonard sees the hand curled around the handle, bite-nailed index finger curved over the trigger, hammer cocked. Bill to the rescue. Bill who nightly yearns for rabid dogs, broken legged horses, mortally wounded soldiers in a platoon pursued by enemy soldiers. It is the proof of your grit to shoot your own dog; it is the token of your humanity to put a thing out of its misery. Bill has wanted to put something out of its misery for as long as he can remember. An unnatural and unsanctified reanimation stands between Deke and his heavenly reward; Bill as God's agent shall liberate his spirit.

The finger squeezes, the hammer descends, the bullet flies, the locker of Deke's being sprays onto the sand. Father forgive them.

Marly ducks back behind the tree. Jesus Christ, they *killed* him; they shot Deke—

No. No. Think. Piece it together. Deke was dead already.

All right. Then maybe Bill and Leonard knew what was happening here, what this madness was all about.

Sweating in the artificial subtropic night, she steps out from behind the tree. She lowers her rifle and waves. "Hey," she calls.

Bill whirls and fires. The .44 magnum goes off like a cannon. Behind her she hears the bullet slam into the tree. A splinter strikes her arm.

She drops, rolls sideways, and ends up prone with the butt of her carbine against her right shoulder, left eye sighting. "It's Marly," she calls. "Drop your gun."

"Marly—" Bill heads toward her.

"Drop your gun, or Deke's gonna hold the door for you on his way in."

He hesitates, possibly thinking about the independent clause of Marly's sentence, but drops the gun. His left hand goes to his wrist.

"You, too, Leonard."

"Listen, Marly, there's muh, muh, *more* of those things around here. I don't think it's such a g-g-good—"

She pulls the trigger. The rifle doesn't buck nearly as much as she thought it would. A plume of sand kicks up behind Leonard's right leg, and he drops his rifle. Marly stands and heads toward them. "Now what the hell's going on?" she demands as she approaches.

"Someone's b-b-broken into the station," Leonard says from the beach.

"Infiltration," adds Bill. "Carnitropes for distraction. Behind enemy lines. Liberating the soles in limbo. Tactical incursion, hit and run, select firepower for multienvironment guerrilla warfare. Strategic placement, Staff on alert." He is breathing heavily. His right wrist is swelling.

Marly looks at Leonard, who shrugs and looks momentarily worried. Bill, he seems to be indicating, is playing poker with a pinochle deck.

"Grace is dead," says Leonard, and Marly feels someething with blades unfold in her chest. Not because she cares especially for Grace, to be quite honest, but because their hermetic group is irretrievably reduced. Change has been introduced into the system; ripples will spread from this splash. About fucking time.

She indicates the corpses on the sand behind Leonard. "One of them?"

He nods. "Huh-Haiffa, too, we think."

"I saw what happened with Deke. Why did he stop? He had you, but he just stopped."

"Because I liberated him," replies Bill. "I freed him, I cast him from limbo. Because I blew his god damn brains out."

"Why did he stop attacking you before Bill shot him?" Marly firmly directs her question to Leonard, who shrugs.

"I don't know. One m-minute he was all over me, and the nuh, next it was like he'd smelled bad muh-muh-*meat*, or someth . . ." He stops.

Marly frowns.

"B-b-bad meat," says Leonard. "Oh, my God. That's it. Culls from the herd. Cellular awareness." He looks at Marly. "Jesus Christ, that's it." His stutter is much slighter.

"It's an extremely good pistol, actually," says Bill.

Marly ignores him. She is uncertain what to do. Now Leonard seems to be popping his excelsior, too.

"Hodgkin's disease," says Leonard, and thumps his chest. For a moment Marly thinks it's another *non sequitur*, but then she realizes.

"You son of a bitch," she says. "You never said—"

And the lights go out all over the Ecosphere.

17

Bonnie sits in lotus on her bed. *Om mani padme om. Om mani padme om.* She uses the litany as a kind of squeegee to wipe away the karmic scum she feels she has accumulated tonight.

She is just beginning to feel relaxed when the lights go out. She sits in darkness for a moment, waiting for her eyes to adjust.

She hears a faint noise like popcorn popping in the distance.

She debates whether she should stay in her room. What decides her is the realization that the air vents probably aren't working if the power is out. She'll want to be outside.

But . . . outside? The men are stalking each other, and probably Marly playing their adolescent army games along with them. Outside? No; let them get it out of their systems. Of course there are carnitropes out there, the reanimated corpses, but Bonnie feels no superstitious dread whatsoever toward them. They didn't *ask* to be what they are, and what they are is really not very different from plants. Hungry plants, mobile plants, but plants all the same. And Bonnie feels a kinship with plants. She certainly does not feel *threatened* by them, just as she does not feel threatened by the carnitropes. You could outrun them, outsmart them, out-anything them.

She gropes around her modular dresser until she finds miniature Tekna flashlight. She twists the ridged section ringing the lens; and the light comes on. She slides the circle of light around her room and is reminded of a germ under a microscope. Light is the only weapon she needs. She fixes the circle of light on her door and makes her way toward it.

"This is it." Dieter opens the power-room door and begins to enter.

"Stay right there. Turn on the light."

"I can't stay where I am and turn on the light."

"Turn on the light, asshole."

Dieter leans in and turns on the light. He takes short steps as he is prodded in. The door is shut behind him. He turns to look at his captor for the first time and is unsurprised to recognize the long-haired young man who came begging last week. Was it last week? He's not sure how long ago it was. Time flies.

"Yeah, it's me," says the young man. "You just stay right there. Lace your fingers and put your hands on top of your head. We're playing charades and you're a sequoia, got it?"

Dieter doesn't get it, but he nods anyway and does as he's told.

The man keeps the submachine gun trained on him as he shrugs out of a nylon daypack. He bends and unzips it, keeping the gun on him, then pulls out a box about the size of a cardboard pencil case. The box is olive-drab and curved like a hip flask. In upraised letters one side reads FRONT TOWARD ENEMY. He carries box and backpack toward power-convertor controls, circuit breakers, generator controls, voltmeters, regulators, and stacked banks of power-storage batteries. He sets the box face-down on a bank of controls, pulls out a little white box with square buttons that looks like a portable radio, connects it to the curved box, and trips a toggle switch. He sets another curved box against the battery bank. "Nice little ratbox you people have here," he says conversationally as he goes about his work. "All the comforts of home. Air conditioning. Barcaloungers. MTV."

"What do you want from us?" Dieter asks.

"Nothing." He glances at him. "Really." He shrugs. "Used to want a hamburger or two, but hey, that's life in the big city, now, isn't it?"

"Look, man, *I* wanted to give you some food. I *told* them we should, that it was only the right thing to do. But they wouldn't—"

The man waves him to silence. "Water under the bridge," he says. "Let the dead past bury its dead, I say." He indicates the row of circuit breakers. "Main power switch?" he asks.

Dieter shrugs. "I'm a marine biologist," he says.

"Mmph. Chust followink orders, huh?"

Dieter says nothing. The man rises and goes to the row of circuit breakers. He throws a knife switch. Nothing happens. He pulls another one. Nothing. Another.

" 'S awright," he says. "They're doing something somewhere." He continues throwing switches.

The lights go out, and Dieter makes his move.

Sailor waits until he hears the door latch jerked down and the door snatched open. He fires a burst on full auto, sweeping the barrel in a tight crescent. The clip is empty in seconds. He thumbs the release, pulls out the empty drops it, pulls a fresh one from his back pocket, and slaps it in. He bends and gropes until he encounters the backpack. He pulls out a penlight and switches it on, then attaches it beneath the squarish gun barrel with electrical tape and plays it around the room.

The body props open the door. Bulletholes in a slight diagonal to either side of the door frame. Sailor shoulders his pack and steps over the body. "One duuumb fucker," he says. He trains the penlight beam down. All back shots, a whole bunch of them. They don't count for shit in the long run, but that's all right. It's Sailor's party. The more, the merrier.

Flashlight beam guarded with one hand, he steps past the body and makes his way down the hall.

Bill doesn't waste a second: He knows where his gun is and when the lights go out, he bends, scoops it up, and runs. He doesn't need light to find his way. Hyperacute kinesthesia. Night sense. Geared to register motion. Under siege. Trojan horse. Marly and Leonard calling, but he keeps running. Charlie's out there. In the bush. In the desert. In the marsh. In the fields. In their own back yard. Gotta deploy. Gotta recon. Stay low. Hit and roll. Hit and run.

He reaches the screen door easily and negotiates the access corridor in a westerly direction. He emerges in fresher air and croplands. Out there. Waiting.

Footsteps. Running toward him. Breathing, low, from the ground. *Crawling*, sneaky sons of bitches. Pale figure coming toward him on hands and knees. He raises the magnum and fires. Pain stitches his sprained wrist. Tough shit. Gotta be tough, son. No pain, no gain.

Squealing, labored breathing. Stubby, flailing legs in front of him. A goddamn *pig*, for Christ's sake!

Wrist throbbing, he stalks the cornfields. There, *there*, two of the fucks. Zip, zip, good as dead. *Good as dead*—hah! Better soon.

He stalks. Three shots left? Let's see: one that liberated Deke, one that missed Marly, one for makin' bacon. Yep: three left.

They're turning for him now. Stupid bastards, not even brains enough to hide. Couldn't sneak up on a goddamn slug. He walks right up to the nearest. Gun against the nose. It grabs the barrel. "Say goodnight, Gracie," he says, and pulls the trigger—but the sonofabitch has grabbed around the *back* of the gun, and the hammer won't cock back. Bill tugs the gun and the creature merely follows. The other one is pretty close now. Bill puts a foot on its stomach and shoves. The gun slides free. Bill steps back. Too close to take time to aim. Head a hard target. Policeman crouch, good form, squeeze . . .

Boom! and the fucker slams backward like it's been sledgehammered by God himself. In the muzzle flash the T-shirt reads SAVE THE WHALES.

Bill ignores the pain in his wrist as he takes aim and fires at the second staggering figure. *Boom!* EAT ME, reads the shirt.

Bill laughs. "Eat *this*, shit-for-brains!" He waves the magnum. His wrist is on fire. He is alive.

He runs for the staff HQ. Ten feet in front of it, the door is flung open. He fires automatically: last bullet, quick on the draw, and right in the goddamn *forehead*, yeah! What's her T-shirt say? He bends, pulls a flashlight from the twitching fingers, shines it down.

No T-shirt. Kimono, parted to expose one breast. Doesn't say a thing. Germ circle of light slides up to dead eyes, drilled forehead, red hair.

Bonnie.

18

Leonard walks the forest of the dead. He is one of them and they leave him alone. He is tainted. He is taboo. He is *bad meat.*

Leonard laughs.

In the distance, gunfire.

Sweating he wanders smiling through lush tropics. He'll make it. They'll leave him alone. Leonard alone may run the gauntlet of the dead. The rejected cull triumphant. Darwin in reverse: Those who have not survived will allow the genetic undesirable to continue.

Another shot.

Leonard pauses. There is more to fear from the living he realizes.

Then I shall climb a tree. I will sit in a branch and await the dawn. And then? I will be free. To do whatever I want. For as long as . . . as I have left.

He finds a tree and hoists himself up from the leaf-carpeted ground.

Marly thinks it's about time to abandon ship. At the first sound of gunfire she was acting out of concern for the Ecosphere and the safety of the others, but now she realizes that the Ecosphere has been a ghost ship for quite some time, Flying Dutchman in the Arizona desert, and the truth about her crew is that it's *always* been every man for himself. The current situation merely brings the point home.

Nope: too late to repair the leaks, to Band Together As A Unit; no returning to Those Golden Days of Yesteryear. Time to jump in a lifeboat and row for shore.

Marly exits the access corridor and crouches low near the glass. In her pocket is the key to the armory, taken from Deke's body on the beach. In the armory are the keys to the Land Rover, along with more guns and ammunition.

She runs forward, bent low, carbine ready. She nearly trips over the body of a pig. Half its head has been blown away.

Billtheasshole.

She hurries on toward the habitat. In the darkness every shape is a threat. Why didn't she think to grab a flashlight? Well, this wasn't exactly the sort of emergency they'd planned on.

But wasn't it exactly the sort of emergency they should have considered? Didn't crop blights sort of pale in comparison?

She heads toward the three tall rows of corn; from there she can survey her surroundings before proceeding.

Body among the stalks. Face up, face gone. SAVE THE WHALES beneath. She steps around it and puts some distance between it and herself, then kneels in the rich soil. Tang of nitrogenated fertilizers.

She looks toward the staff quarters. The door is partway open, propped by a body. She can see it only from the waist down; from the waist up it is inside the building. Too dark to tell who it is.

Cornstalks rustle.

Marly grows still. She strains to hear, but it is difficult because of the sound of her breathing, of her heartbeat in her ears. She turns her head slowly. The sound is approaching from her right.

She turns that way and steadies in a marksman's stance, right leg back and weight over the knee, left leg forward, left elbow on left knee, rifle steady.

There.

It lurches toward her almost drunkenly. It's moving pretty slowly; she has plenty of time. She steadies, sights, and fires. The rifle bucks slightly. The drunken figure staggers back, trips over the body behind it, and lands on its butt. It gets to its feet again.

Go for the head, Marly remembers. *The chest is the easier target, but the head is the only thing that powers it. Medulla oblongata.*

She slaps the bolt of the carbine with the heel of her hand and pulls it back.

The cartridge spits out. She pushes the bolt forward, and it sticks. She pulls back, push again. No good. She glances again. Scarecrow approaching through the corn. *If I only had a brain.* She stands and turns—

—into the arms of another. It hugs her. Stink of rotten meat. Opens its mouth. Gold filling glints. Half-moon crescent in one earlobe where an earring has been ripped away. Its head bends toward her.

Marly gets an arm up and grabs it by the throat, forcing its head back. The flesh against her palm is loose and leathery cool, like touching the neck of a turtle. She bats her rifle against its side, but can get no room for a powerful swing. The creature bleats softly. Smell of stale air from dead lungs. Quiet, so quiet; absurdly, she thinks there ought to be more noise.

Her hair is tugged from behind.

She turns and the hungry thing turns with her, wedged now between her and the first one. She pushes against the unbreathing throat while the other tries to reach around the one holding her. She can't get loose.

Pop! like a champagne cork. The carnitrope not holding her cants to one side, balances on one leg like a street mime doing an obscure impression, and falls. The one holding her works its head from side to side and snaps its teeth to bite the hand it wants to feed it. *Clack-clack! Clack!*

"Turn it!" someone yells. "Turn it toward me! Goddammit—"

Marly strains. For a panicked moment she feels overbalanced, about to fall over with the creature on top of her, but she jerks a leg back, brings it up into the creature's groin, and pivots.

A loud riveting sound from her right. The creature's head peels away like a rotten plum. It holds her a moment longer, and she feels its dead fingers spasming against her. Then it drops, and she pushes it away and jumps back, turning toward the sound of the gunfire.

A flashlight, but who's behind it? Bill? Dieter? Leonard?

He walks closer. The light shines beneath the squarish barrel of his submachine gun.

"You . . . ?"

He nods. The light does not waver. He cups it with his left hand. "Get out of here," he says.

"But—I don't—"

"Go on. Party's winding down."

Marly considers him for a moment, then nods. "I was just leaving," she says.

"Good idea."

She starts to thank him, but stops. Thanks are not called for here. He hadn't thanked her for the basket, had he? She nods again. "I have to get ammunition and supplies."

"You have about ten minutes."

"The others," she begins. "I have to—"

"Fuck the others. Get your shit and get out of here."

Still she hesitates. "I—I'm a botanist. I can keep this place going. I know how. It can keep you and your wife—and your baby—"

"Wasn't a real baby." The light dips, then raises again. "Deadhead."

"Dead . . . ? Ohmigod."

"There's a lot of 'em out there, deadheads. But you wouldn't know. You've been in here."

She feels a clammy turning inside. World of dead babies, relentless crawling, toothless chewing. "You want the station," she says. "I understand that. But look, I know how to maintain it. It won't last without—"

"I don't want it to last. I want to bring it down."

"To . . ." She searches out his face above the light. Again she nods. "Yes," she says. "Yes, I guess so."

"Eight minutes." The light clicks off, and he's gone.

19

Bill with his Tekna light in the apple orchard. Gun in hand, swollen wrist. Incursion. Evasion. Stealth. Sentry removal.

There's one up ahead. HE'S DEAD, JIM. No shit, Sherlock.

things on trees food once but no more smell i remember made water in my mouth but nothing now is light toward light for food with light she *with light her hands would hold the treefood would feed would let into my mouth and i would eat the food of the tree but not the food that is her hand that holds the light and behind the light is food and if i reach the light i will eat and i will be and i will know*

Bill holds the flashlight in sprained right wrist and raises the gun in his left hand. Marly unlocks the dark storage closet-become-armory, takes a flashlight from a shelf, plays it around the room, and begins cramming boxes of ammunition into an orange crate. Dieter pushes his bullet-riddled body from the floor and staggers down the dark hall; behind him the power-room door thuds shut. Bonnie grows cold half-in, half-out the front door of the habitat. Leonard awaits the dawn on the limb of a South American tree. Haiffa bobs gently on the ocean, nuzzling the little sandbar. Sailor sets a final charge. Pigs run blindly through dark geometry of cropland. Bill aims and fires at the thing that gropes toward his light, bracing for the recoil. Marly shoves packets of dried food into a plastic garbage bag. *Click:* Bill stares in wonder at the gun. *the light i reach for behind the light is always food* Heading for the front door with supplies and a slung carbine, Marly sees Dieter shambling away from her down the dark corridor. Sailor pauses at the air-lock door when he hears Bill's scream. He smiles, he claps softly, he bows. He leaves; wait for the encore, folks. "Dieter?" Marly ventures. Leonard stands in the tree and peers into the lightening east. Dieter turns toward Marly. Sailor trots down the hill and opens the driver's door of the Ryder truck. Marly drops orange crate and garbage bag, saying, "Shit." Dieter's eyes fill with something not recognition. Leonard drinks in the faint coral tinge bleeding into the horizon. Jo-Jo drinks in tincture a Bill beneath apple blossoms. Marly raises the carbine. Dieter's face is a rictus she remembers from orgasm. Sailor turns the key, depresses the clutch, puts the truck in gear, and eases onto the road. Bill stares unblinking at the infinity of departing night above the glass roof of his little pocket of civilization. Marly lowers the rifle. Dieter reaches for her needfully. Leonard sits again on his leafy throne, feet dangling, to watch the sunrise. Marly picks up garbage bag and orange crate, turns, and steps over Bonnie holding the front door for her. *light then food i move from sound not from the box but sounds i hear anyway and she holds out her hand* Sailor drives a mile away and pulls off the road beside a low hill, turning the truck to face the Ecosphere. Sparkle of glass and aluminum by dawn's early light. Marly runs from the air lock, throws bag and crate into the back of the Land-Rover, sets carbine on passenger seat, slides key into ignition. Sailor glances into the long side-view mirror. He will wait until the sun clears the horizon. Faint buzz from under the hood: battery dead. *Shit.* *and the sound louder and others move with and she looks at me with her hand out to me and her mouth opens and sound from it* Leonard on high looks down on Marly opening the hood of the Land-Rover outside. Let her go; let them all go. Leonard knows who he is now; the death inside him has found the pure unfilterable fundament of death without. Sailor opens the door and gets out. The sun is a dome on the horizon, a frozen nuclear explosion, the Eye of God. Marly removes the battery and tosses it onto the asphalt. Spare in the back of the Rover; Bill is—was?—nothing if not redundant. Motion turns her head: A figure inside the Ecosphere presses against the glass, flattened dead features of its face above a T-shirt that reads RUGBY PLAYERS EAT THEIR DEAD. Sailor breathes in the cool morning air that blows across the desert floor. He pulls the elastic band from his hair for the breeze to have its way. He feels very alive. In the distance the ecosphere gleams like a discarded toy. Marly slams down the hood, gets in the Land-Rover, and turns the key. Once, twice, and it starts. She squeals out of the lot, and Leonard waves good-bye.

20

The sun clears the crooked line of mountain-limned horizon. Sailor goes to the back of the truck and raises the door. He removes a box from the wood-slatted bed, and from it removes another box. He raises the telescoping antenna in back of this, and presses a button. A red light glows: CHARGE OKAY. He carries the box to the front of the truck and sets it on the high hood. He hoists himself up beside it, then sets it in his lap and throws another switch. Another red light winks on above the white-painted word ARMED. Sailor cracks his knuckles and looks to the framework of aluminum struts supporting triangular glass panels in the distance.

"It is a far, far better thing I do," he says, and flourishes a finger.

"Oh, no, you don't."

The finger pauses. He glances right. The wind blows his hair over his eyes.

He shakes his head to move it out of the way. The Chinese woman stands on top of the hill, carbine trained on him. They stare at each other across the orange-lit slope. The rifle barrel traces a curt line to the right; Sailor sets the transmitter aside. She juts her jaw; Sailor eases down from the warm hood of the truck. She heads down the hill toward him; Sailor spreads his fingers and holds his hands away from his body.

"Have a seat," she says.

Sailor sits.

"Hands on top of your head."

Sailor puts his hands on top of his head. "You never let me have any fun," he says.

"What were you going to do," she asks. "After this?"

Sailor shrugs. "Don't know. Got a bunch of shit in back of the truck. Oregon, maybe. Find some asshole survivalist's nuclear bomb shelter, set up camp. I try not to think that far ahead anymore. How 'bout you?"

Her turn to shrug. "Yosemite, maybe."

He grins. "Bears and 'possums. Raccoon stew."

"This what I think it is?" She nods toward the transmitter on the hood.

"Ain't about to play no rock and roll, if that's what you mean."

"That's what I mean." She keeps the carbine aimed toward him and grabs the transmitter. The two red lights shine steadily: CHARGE OKAY. ARMED. And a button with no light: DETONATE.

She looks back to see him wincing under the vacant, one-eyed stare of the rifle. "Nervous?"

"We've got to stop meeting like this."

"I can't let you do it," she says. "I'm sorry."

"Why not?" Sailor lowers his hands. "You like the rest of those assholes? Are you *endeavoring to persevere*?"

"No." She lowers the rifle to the road and holds out the transmitter. She takes a deep breath. "Because *I* want to."

She extends her hand—

21

—Dieter exploring the aquarium of the dead, intrepid Martian explorer alone and yet accepted, finally where he belongs, cartographer of the damned—

—Bill reborn, rising with the dawn, finally at peace with the world, content at last with a single purpose and mission: to feed—

—Leonard arboreal, monument to Darwin descending; Leonard *Rex Mortura*, King of the Dead; Leonard with power at last, returning to earth enlightened to survey these his new people, this the new necropolis—

others but nothing for them i walk there is light past the treefoods i go near i press my face against the clear toward the light i shut my eyes and she *is there with the soft of her hands and there is music and roger she says* Roger *come dance with me, and* I *take her hand, and* I *open my eyes, and there is music, and light, and* I remember—

22

—and brings her finger down.

JERRY'S KIDS MEET WORMBOY

BY DAVID J. SCHOW

You know, sometimes ya just gotta fuck shit up. Lay waste to all that you survey, and dance in the smoldering ashes. It's a mad nihilist impulse that each of us harbors, though most of us manage to bury it well. And while, in real life, it's an incredibly bad idea, apocalyptic zombie stories have proven a magnificent place to vent it. As witness this case in point.

David J. Schow's "Jerry's Kids Meet Wormboy" *isn't just a gross-out classic. It's a* legendary virtuoso gross-out classic: *the literary equivalent of* Peter Jackson's Dead Alive, *or the* Zombie Mystery Paintings *of outsider art guru* Robert Williams.

In this case, the allure is not so much in the "plot" but in the setup and characters, which are fucking insane; and in the sheer ungodly dynamo that is the power of Schow's prose.

In the word-by-word, image-by-image, perfectly calibrated sentence by you-get-the-idea, "Jerry's Kids" is a master's course in making things blow up, squirt, shred, or otherwise disgorge their contents. Its gleeful and shameless savagery, its overheated machine-gun barrages of language, its sheer unbridled cartoon chaos matched by flawless photorealistic technique, together combine to make "Jerry's Kids" the gold standard of hyperviolent literary gore. Plus, I think it's funny, too!

I trust you will enjoy.

EATING 'EM WAS MORE FUN than blowing their gnarly green heads off. But why dicker when you could do both?

The fresher ones were blue. That was important if you wanted to avoid cramps, salmonella. Eat one of them green ones and you'd be yodeling down the big porcelain megaphone in no time.

Wormy used wirecutters to snip the nose off the last bullet in the foam block. He snugged the truncated cartridge into the cylinder of his short-barreled .44. Full deck. When fired, the flattened slug would pancake on impact and disintegrate any geek's head to hash. Them green ones weren't really "zombis," because no voudou had played a part. They were all just geeks, slow as syrup and stupid as hell, and Wormboy loved it that way. It meant he would not starve in this cowardly new world. He was eating; millions weren't.

Wormboy's burden was great. It hung from his Butthole Surfers T-shirt. He had scavenged dozens of such shirts from a burned-out rockshop, all Extra-Extra Large-Large, all screaming about dead 'n gone bands of which he had never heard—Dayglo Abortions, Rudimentary Penii, Shower of Smegma, Fat & Fucked Up. Wormboy's big personal in-joke was one that championed a long-ago album titled *Giving Head to the Living Dead*. That one didn't get washed much.

The gravid flab of his teats distorted the logo, and his surplus flesh quivered and swam, shoving around his clothing as though some subcutaneous revolution was aboil. Pasty and pocked, his belly depended earthward, a vast sandbag held in check by a wide weightlifter's belt, notched crotch-low. The faintest motion caused his hectares of skin to bobble like mercury.

Wormboy was more than fat. He was a crowd of fat people. A single mirror was insufficient to the task of containing his grandeur.

He was preening when the explosion buzzed the floor beneath his hi-tops. Vibrations slithered from one thick stratum of dermis to the next, and gradually brought him the news.

The sound of a Bouncing Betty's boom-boom always worked like a Pavlovian dinner gong. It could smear a smile across Wormy's jowls and start his tummy to percolating. He snatched up binoculars and stampeded out into the graveyard.

Valley View Memorial Park was a classic cemetery of venerable lineage, far preceding the ordinances that required flat monument stones to benchmark the dear departed. The granite and marble jutting from its acreage was the most ostentatious and artfully-hewn stonework this side of a Universal monster movie boneyard, despite the fact that the tract had been brought low in its dying years by the lawn-efficiency dorks and their weed-whackers, grooming character-less vanity plates in a suburbia for the lifeless. In the older sections, stone cold angels still reached toward heaven. Stilted verse, deathlessly chiseled, eulogized the more venerable departees.

Most of the graves were unoccupied now. They had prevailed without the fertilization of human decay and were now choked with loam and healthy green grass. Those newer tenants had clawed out and waltzed off several seasons back.

Wormboy's current address was at the crest of Valley View's oldest hilltop, reached by a modest road which formed a spiral ascent path and terminated in a cul-de-sac—parking, way back when. Midway up it was interrupted by a trench ten feet across and twelve deep. Wormboy had excavated this "moat" using the cemetery's scoop-loader, and seeded it with lengths of two-inch pipe sawn at an angle to form funnel-knife-style pungi sticks. Tripwires knotted gate struts to tombstones to booby traps, and three hundred antipersonnel mines lived in the earth, waiting. (Well, two hundred and ninety-nine, just now. Wormy was big on inventory. It kept him alive.)

Every longitude and latitude of Valley View had been lovingly nurtured into a Gordian Knot of killpower which Wormboy had christened his "spiderweb." The Bouncing Bettys had been a godsend. Anything that wandered in unbidden would get its legs blown off, or become immovably gaffed in the moat.

Not long after the day the geeks woke up, shucked dirt, and ambled away with their yaps drooping open, Wormboy had claimed Valley View for his very own, fulfilling that aspect of the American Dream. He knew that the dead tended to "home" toward places important to them back when they weren't green—pre-green—and therefore, they would never come trotting back to a graveyard.

Wormboy's previous squat had been a defrocked National Guard armory. Too much traffic in walking dead weekend warriors, there; blowing them into unwalking lasagna just took too much damned time and powder, plain and simple. After seven Land Rover-loads of military rock-and-roll, Wormy's redecoration of Valley View began to reflect his personality, as good homes should. The whole graveyard was one big mechanized ambush. The reception building and non-denominational chapel were ideally suited to his needs . . . and breadth. Outfitting the prep room was more stainless steel than in a French kitchen in Beverly Hills; where stiffs were once dressed for interment, Wormboy now dressed them for din-din. There was even a sub-zero morgue locker seating thirty, the world's biggest refrigerator. Independent generators chugged out wattage (since power had stopped coming from the cities several years ago). Wormy's only real lament is that there would never be enough Julia Child videotapes to keep him jolly. Her final season show wasn't even a wrapup; that had been disappointing, too. She never saw what was coming.

His binocs were overpriced Army jobs that had cost taxpayers, on paper, $7500 per pair. Wormboy thumbed up his bottle-bottom specs, focused, and swept the base of the hill, using the illuminated reticule. Smoke was still rising from the breach point. Fewer geeks actually blundered in, these days, but now and again one could still be snagged.

That in itself was peculiar. As far as Wormboy could reckon, geeks functioned on the level of pure motor response with a single directive—seek food—and legs that made their appetites mobile. Past Year One, the locals shunned Valley View altogether, almost as though the geek grapevine had warned them this place was poison to their kind. Could be that Valley View's primo kill ratio had made it the crucible of the first bona fide zombi superstition.

Wormboy was tickled by the thought of being an innovator.

God only knew what geeks were munching in the cities, by now. As the legions of ambulatory expirees had swelled, their preferred food—live citizens—had gone underground, so to speak. Predator and prey had swapped positions without noting the mordant irony of it all. Survivors of what Wormboy had named Zombi Apocalypse had gotten canny, or gotten eaten. Geek society itself was akin to a gator pit; he'd seen them get cheesed off and chomp hunks out of one another. Though their irradiated brains kept their limbs supple and greased with oxygenated blood, they were still dead . . . and dead people still rotted. Their structural integrity (not to mention their freshness) was less than a safe bet past the second or third Hallowe'en. Most Wormy spotted these days were minus at least one limb. They digested—sort of—but did not eliminate. Sometimes the older ones simply exploded. They clogged up with gas and decaying food until they hit critical mass, then *kerblooey*—steaming gobbets of brown mulchy crap all over the perimeter. It was enough to put you off your dinner.

Life was so weird. Sometimes Wormboy felt like the only normal person left.

This movable feast, this walking smorgasbord, could last another year or two, max, and Wormboy knew it. His fortifications insured he would be ready for whatever trundled down the pike when the world changed again. It wasn't nice to fool Mama Nature, but for now, it was a matchless chow-down, and grand sport besides.

The six-wheeled ATV groaned and squeaked its usual protests when Wormboy settled into the wide saddle. A rack welded to the chassis secured his geek tools—pinch bar, fire axe, scattergun sheath, and a Louisville Slugger sporting a lot of chips, nicks, and dried blood. Papaw had given him that bat; it was virtually Wormboy's sole childhood souvenir. He kick-started and the all-terrain balloon tires did not burst under his weight; he was good to putter down and meet his catch of the day.

Geeks were capable of sniffing live human meat from a fair distance. Some had actually gotten around to elementary tool use. But their maze sense was zero-zero; they always tried to proceed in straight lines. Even a non-geek would need a load of deductive logic just to pick a *normal* path toward Valley View's chapel without getting divorced from his or her vitals—much more time than generally elapsed between Wormboy's feedings.

Up on this hilltop, his security was assured. He piloted his ATV down his specially-configured escape path, twisting, turning, pausing at several hot junctures to gingerly reconnect tripwires and det cord between him. He dropped his folding-metal Army fording bridge over the moat and tootled across.

Some of the meat hung up in the heat flash of the explosion was still sizzling on the ground in charred clumps. Dragging itself doggedly up-slope was half a geek, still aimed at the chapel and the repast that was Wormboy. Straight lines. Everything from its navel down had been blown off.

Wormboy dismounted and unracked his pinch bar, one end of which had been modified to accept a ten-pound screw-on harpoon head of machined aluminum. A swath of newly-muddied earth quickly matured into a trail of strewn organs resembling smashed fruit. The geek's brand-new prone carriage had permitted it to evade several of the Bouncing Betty trips. Wormboy frowned. His announcement was pointed—and piqued—enough to arrest the geek's uphill crawl.

"Welcome to Hell, dork breath."

It humped around on its palms with all the grace of a beached haddock. Broken rib struts had punched through at jigsaw angles to present mangled innards, swinging from the empty chest cavity like pendent jewels. One ear had been sheared away; the side of its head was caked in thick, stale blood, dirt, and pulverized tissue that reminded Wormboy of a scoop of dogfood. The geek returned Wormboy's gaze with bleary drunkard's eyes, virulently jaundiced and discharging gluey fluid like those of a sick animal.

It was wearing a besmirched Red Cross armband.

A long, gray-green rope of intestine had paid out behind the geek. It gawped with dull hunger, too long unwhetted, and did an absurd little push-up in order to bite it. Teeth crunched through geek-gut and gelid black paste evacuated with a blatting fart noise. *Sploot!*

Disinclined toward autocannibalism, it tacked again on Wormboy. A rotten kidney peeled loose from a last shred of muscle and rolled away to burst apart in the weeds. The stench was unique.

Impatient, Wormy shook his head. Stupid geeks. "C'mon, fuckface, come and get it." He waggled his mighty belly, then extended the rib-roast of his forearm. "You want Cheez-Whiz on it or what? C'mon, chow time."

It seemed to catch his drift. Mouth champing and slavering, eyes straying in two directions, it resumed its quest, leaving hanks and clots of itself behind all the way down. It was too goddamned slow . . . and wasting too many choice bits.

Hefting the pinch bar, Wormboy hustled up the slope, one mountain conquering another. He slammed one of his size eighteens thunderously down within biting range and let the geek fantasize for an instant about what a crawfull of Wormboy Platter might taste like. Greedy; they were always too obvious and greedy. Wormboy threw his magnificent tonnage behind a downward thrust, spiking his prey between the shoulderblades and staking it to the ground with a moist crunch.

It thrashed and chewed air. Wormboy imitated it, crunching up his pillow face into a mimic of zombi maceration. He strained, red-faced, and liberated a basso fart as punctuation, then waved bye-bye, boo-hoo, letting the geek watch him pick his way back down to the ATV. He wanted it to see him returning with the axe. His work sweat had broken freely; the exertion already had him huffing and aromatic, but he loved this part almost as much as swallowing mouthful after mouthful of that ole style, down-home, Country Kitchen cookin'.

The axe hissed down, overhand. A bilious rainbow of decomposing suet hocked from the neck stump while the blue-green head pinballed downhill from one tombstone to the next. It thonked to rest against the left rear wheel of the ATV. Wormboy lent the half-torso a disappointed inspection. Pickings were lean; this geek had been on the hoof too long. Burger night . . . again.

He looked down and sure enough, the lone head was fighting like hell to redirect itself. Hair hung in its eyes, the face was caved in around the flattened nose, the whole of it now oozing and studded with cockleburs, but by God it tipped over, embedded broken teeth into packed graveyard dirt, and tried to pull itself toward Wormboy—it was *that* hungry.

Wormboy ambled down to meet it, humming. He secured the axe in its metal clip and drew the ballbat. Busting a coconut was tougher. The geek's eyes stayed open. They never flinched when you hit them. On the second bash, curds of blood-dappled brain jumped out to meet the air. It ceased moving then, except to crackle and collapse. The cheesy brain stuff looked tainted, the color of fish-bellies. Wormboy pulled free a mucilaginous fistful and brandished it before the open, unseeing eyes. He squeezed hard. Glistening spirals unfurled between his fingers with a greasy macaroni noise.

"I win again."

He licked the gelid residue from his trigger finger and smacked his lips. By the time he got back to the torso with a garbage bag, the Red Cross armband had begun to smolder. He batted it away. It looped in midair and flared, newborn fire gobbling up the swatch of cloth and the symbol emblazoned thereon, leaving Wormboy alone to scratch his eczematous scalp over what it might have meant.

Little Luke shot twin streamers of turbid venom into the urine specimen cup against which his fangs were chocked, Providing like a good Christian. He did not mind being milked (not that he'd been asked); it was necessary as a preamble to the ritual. He played his part and was provided for—a sterling exemplar of God's Big Blueprint. His hypodermic teeth were translucent and fragile-looking. Cloudy poison pooled in the cup.

Maintaining his grip just behind the hinge of Little Luke's jaws, the Right Reverend Jerry thanked his Lord for this bounty, that the faithful might all partake of communion and know His peace. He kissed Little Luke on the noggin and carefully deposited all four feet of him into the pet caddy. Little Luke's Love Gift had been generous today. Perhaps even serpents knew charity.

Jerry pondered charity, and so charitably ignored the fact that his eldest Deacon was leaking. Weaving back and forth in the vestibule was Deacon Moe, his pants soaked and dripping, on standby. He was not breathing, and his cataracted eyes saw only the specimen cup. The odor that surrounded him in the cramped space was that of maggoty sausage. Without a doubt, he was a creature of wretchedness, but he was also proof to the Right Reverend Jerry that the myth had delivered at last, all skeptics be damn'd.

The dead has risen from their graves to be judged. If that was not proof, a real miracle, what was? Back in the days before, the regular viewers of Jerry's tri-county local access video ministry had long drawn succor from miracles infinitely more pallid—eased sprains, exposed Jezebels, restored control of the lower tract, that sort of thing. Since this new ukase had flown down from Heaven, it would be foolish for Jerry to shun its opportunities.

Jerry savored the moment the dead had walked. He relished this revelation which had vindicated his own lagging faith, dispelling in one masterstroke the doubts that had haunted his soul for a lifetime. There *was* a One True God, and there *was* a Judgement Day, and there *was* an Armageddon, and there was *bound* to be a Second Coming, sooner or later, and as long as these events came to pass correctly, who cared if their order had been juggled a bit? The Lord had been known to work in mysterious ways before.

Once his suit had been blazing white, and pure. With faith, it would shine spotlessly again. Right now he did not mind the skunky miasma exuding from the pits of what had once been a $1500 jacket. It helped blanket the riper and more provocative stench of Deacon Moe's presence. The congregation was on the move, and there was little time for dapper grooming in mid-hegira.

Jerry beckoned Deacon Moe forward to receive communion. From the way poor Moe shambled, this might be his last chance to drink of the Blood, since none of the faithful had meshed teeth lately on the Body, or any facsimile thereof.

In an abandoned library, books had told Jerry what rattlesnake venom could do.

In human beings, it acted as a neurotoxin and nerve impulse blocker, jamming the signals of the brain by preventing acetylcholine from jumping across nerve endings. The brain's instructions were never delivered. First came facial paralysis, then loss of motor control; the heart and lungs shut down as the victim began to drown in backed-up fluids. Hemolytic (blood-destroying) factors caused intense local pain. Jerry had tasted the venom he routinely fed his quartet of Deacons, and it was nothing to fret about—so long as your stomach lining had no tiny holes, ulcers, or perforations to convey the stuff into your bloodstream. The bright yellow liquid was odorless, with a taste at first astringent, then sweetish. It numbed the lips. There was so much books could not know.

In *walking dead, former* human beings, however, Jerry discovered that the venom, administered orally, easily penetrated the cheesecloth of their internal pipework and headed straight for the motor centers of the brain, unblocking them, allowing a certain Right Reverend to reach inside the reanimated dead mind to tinker with light hypnosis. He could program his Deacons not to hunger for him in *that* way. More importantly, this imperative was then passed among the faithful in some unspoken and mystical way reserved to only these very special children of God.

The talent for mesmerization came effortlessly to a man who had devoted years to charming the camera's unblinking and all-seeing eye. Jerry preferred to consider his ability innate, a divine, God-granted sanction pre-approved for the new use he now made of it: *Don't eat the Reverend.*

Deacon Moe moistened his cracked and greenish lips with a mildew-furred tongue, not in anticipation so much as a wholly preconditioned response to Jerry's act of holding the cup into the light. The demarcations of the urine container showed a level two ounces. Little Luke could be fully milked slightly more often than once per month, if Jerry's touch was gentle and coaxing. He tilted the cup to Deacon Moe's lips and the poison was glugged down *in nomine Patris, et Filii . . .*

"AND GOD WAVED HIS HAND!" Jerry belted out.

"And when God did wave His hand, He cleansed the hearts of the wicked of evil. He scoured out the souls of the wolves, and set His Born-Agains to the task of reclaiming the Earth in His name. The Scriptures were right all along, brethren—the Meek did inherit! Now the world is grown green and fecund again. Now must the faithful seek strength from their most holy Maker. The damned Sodom and Gomorrah of New York and Los Angeles have fallen to ruin, their false temples pulled down to form the dust which makes the clay from which God molds the God-fearing Christian! Our God is a loving God, yet a wrathful God, so he smote down those beyond redemption. He closed the book on secular humanism. His mighty Heel did trample out radical feminism. His good right Fist did mete out rough justice to the homosexuals; His good left Fist likewise did silence the pagans of devilspawn rock and roll. And He did spread his Arms wide to gather up the sins of this evil world, from sexual perversion to drug addiction to worship of all the false gods. And you might say a Memo did come down from the Desk of the Lord, and major infidel butt got kicked doubleplusgood!"

Now he was cranking, impassioned, his pate agleam with righteous perspiration. His hands clamped down on Deacon Moe's bony shoulders. His breath misted the zombi's dead-ahead eyes. His conviction was utter. Moe salivated.

"And today, right here right now, the faithful walk the land, Brother! God's legions grow by the day, by the hour, by the very minute, as we stand here and reaffirm our faith in His name! We are all Children of God, and God is a loving

Father, a Big Daddy who *pro-vides* for his pro-geny! Yes, we must make sacrifices and forsake transient comforts. But though our bellies be empty today, our hearts are full up with God's greatness—*aren't they*?!" His voice was cracking now; it was always good to make it appear as though an overload of passion was venting accidentally, spilling out despite decorum. "From that goodness, Brother, you and I must draw the strength to persevere until tomorrow, when the Millennium shall come and no child of the Lord shall want! Peace is coming! *Food* is coming! Go forth unto the congregation, Deacon Moe, and spread this good news! Amen! Amen! *Can I hear an Amen*?!"

Jerry reaped what he had asked for. Deacon Moe wheezed, his arid throat rasping out acknowledgment that sounded like an asthmatic trying to say *rruuaah* through a jugfull of snot. Jerry spun him about-face and impelled him through the curtain to disseminate the Word. He heard Moe's stomach-load of accumulated detritus slosh. Corrosion was amok in there. Any second now, God's gravity might fill Deacon Moe's pants with his own zombi-fied tripe.

Tonight they were billeted inside an actual church—long looted, windows smashed, pews askew amid dust and vermin. Most of the faithful loitered in the deconsecrated sanctuary. The four Deacons led the faithful through Jerry's motions; the response quotient of the entire group, twoscore and ten, was about as dependable as a trained but retarded lab rat. Less control, and Jerry would have starred at his own Last Supper months ago. Right now he saw his congregation as vessels itching to be filled to the brim with the prose of God. He tried to keep them fed as best he could manage.

He permitted himself modest pride in remembrance of the glorious day he had commenced his latest cross-country revival. It had come to pass at a Baton Rouge honkytonk called the Corner Pocket, a rural watering hole festooned with strings of Christmas lights—*Christmas* tree lights!—whose trailer-hitch rollaway marquee announced the presence of some musical entity known as Slim Slick and his Slick Dicks. Jerry strode boldly into the murky bar and drank in the hellacious noise of the band (damn'd souls, tormented by pitchforks), inhaled the brimstone of cigarette and marijuana smoke, and Witnessed, with his own eyes, the drinking of alcohol, the pawing of loose women, the degradation of the entire human race right there in microcosm.

He had raised his Bible high and begun Testifying. Even the band stopped playing to pelt him with garbage.

Jerry had marched deeper into this bottomless pit of vice, unafraid . . . and right behind him were twenty hungry Born-Agains. What began as a holy purge quickly waxed into his new congregation's first big feed. Slim Slick, et al, had been *forced* to see the light. Some of them had even joined the marching ministry, those not too chewed up to locomote.

Like Jesus to the temple, the Right Reverend Jerry had come not to destroy, but to fulfill. To fill full.

He poked his snakestick into the hatch of the pet caddy. Nobody buzzed. Nobody could. Rattling tended to upset the faithful, so Jerry had soaked the rattle of each of his four favored wine-makers until they rotted into silence. Little Matthew was disengaged from the tangle of his brothers. Eastern diamondbacks were legendary for their size and high venom delivery; full contact bites were almost always fatal. Little Matt was five feet long, with large glands that could effortlessly yield a Love Gift capable of converting six hundred and sixty-six adults to the cause, and wasn't *that* a significant coincidence of mathematics? Jerry had shoved the figures around a smidgen, converting milligrams to grains to ounces; how a lethal dosage was administered was also a big variable. But the final number summoned by his calculator was 666, repeating to infinity. That was how many sinners could swing low on three ounces of Little Matt's finest kind. To Jerry, that number had been a perfect sign, and wasn't that what really counted in the Big Book? Perfection just tickled God green.

Deacon Curly had not come forth to receive communion. Perhaps he had wandered astray?

Back in the days before comedy had become synonymous with smut, Jerry had enjoyed a good laugh. Upon his nameless Deacons he had bestown the names of famous funnymen, the classics, the unspoiled ones from the days of black-and-white nitrate film. As his ramrods wore out or were retired with honors, Jerry's list of available names dwindled. Just now, the Deacons in charge were Moe, Curly, W. C., and Fatty. Curly was running late. Tardiness and disobedience were a compound sin.

The Right Reverend Jerry felt secure his flock would follow him even without the able assistance of his Deacons. He represented the Big Guy. His tent-revival roots ran deep and wide and his TV version of the same had pealed out the Word into the ozone. Mental messages, invisible vibrations, sheer goodness proved Jerry had always trodden the upward path, so it was no surprise to him that his congregation followed him, because they would burgeon beneath his loving ministrations. When he sermonized, the Born-Agains seemed to forget their earthly hungers. He could not pinpoint why, exactly, past his own Rock-solid certainty that the Word held the power to still the restless, and quiet gnawing bellies. There were other kinds of nourishment; these lost ones were spiritually starved, as well. Jerry, hyper-aware as always, held a deep reverence for sheer unsupported faith, which he fancied he saw in the eyes of his flock when he vociferated. It was during a sermon he realized it had been a miracle—he looked out upon the milling throng and just *knew*. These Born-Agains depended on him as much for the Word as his Deacons counted on him to deliver the holy imbibitions. Venom governed the Deacons, but had been a new kind of faith that had thrown an umbrella over the entire marching ministry. Had to be.

They needed saving. Jerry needed to save. Symbiosis—plain, ungarnished, and God-sanctioned as all get-out. In a most everlasting way, they fed each other. Maybe it was not such a big whodunit, after all.

Still no sign of Deacon Curly in the vestibule. Jerry motioned Deacon Fatty inside. Fatty's lazy eye had popped out to hang from its stalk again. Jerry tucked it in and brushed the bugs from this Deacon's shoulders, then re-knotted the armband which had drooped to the zombi's elbow. Each member of the congregation had been outfitted with a Red Cross, which seemed appropriate as a symbol for this New Dawn, and gave Jerry a handy way to take quick head counts while on the march, or track his disciples from afar.

The sudden, flat boom of an explosion not far away made Jerry's heart slam on the brakes. Deacon Fatty stood unimpressed, awaiting his communion, insects swimming in his free-floating drool.

It was in the prep room that Wormboy first encountered the brand-new living dead lifeform.

Valley View's mortuary was a stainless steel holy-of-holies in Wormy's personal religious lexicon, and the cleanest thing in his entire life. There were three canted dressout tables with flushable drain troughs, and an overhead conveyance resembling an upside-down model racing track, used so a single mortician could transfer clients from freezer to slab without a lot of wrestling, like an assortment of treats in an automat. He routinely sluiced the trays with a ten-percent bleach solution to wipe out stray viruses.

By the time he delivered the bisected cemetery intruder onto the center table, there was not much left, and he could hoist the unmoving jumble of body parts one-handed. Soon he was going to have to venture beyond the safety of Valley View merely to procure fresher kills.

He cut a fair imitation of a mad doktor in his double-wide rubber apron and goggles (you never wanted to get zombi spew in your eyes if you could help it). His PVC gauntlets strapped at the bicep and had to be adapted to his manly dimensions using modified trouser belts. While he was filleting the reeking remains of the zombi, the backbone *squirmed* in his grasp as though it had other ideas.

The zombi was less one head, therefore minus a dead-alive brain, ergo nothing should still be wiggling around. Wormboy actually startled and dropped the slippery spine on the floor, where it splatted on the tiles . . .

. . . and then righted itself, coiled, and—apparently—looked right at him.

The backbone from tip to tail looked less like a spine and more like one of those wooden snake marionettes made in Mexico. Two pellets, igneously faceted like kidneystones, had sprouted from the top knob of cervical vertebrae, completing the illusion of eyes. The tip of the coccyx vibrated. It was not unlike a finned sea-snake, with blind, atavistic eyes akin to those found on the scolex of a tapeworm.

Wormboy was blinking very fast and breathing shallowly. Before he could think *what the FUCK?* the damned thing tried to bite him on one massive calf. It struck bluntly, without a mouth, teeth, or equipment to sting. Without musculature, it nonetheless mustered a formidable hit that would raise a bruise. Wormboy's expression darkened, fat and adipose slithering beneath his face to convey annoyance, anger, mild fear. He kicked the knotwork of bones across the room. It curled up defensively in the corner near the meat lockers.

Eventually he used tongs to deposit the alien, with much thrashing drama, into a vacuum-locked specimen container, a confined cylindrical space in which it whipped around until it calmed down. Only then did Wormboy's blood drain as though a tub drain had been freed. He felt the vertigo-lurch of impending shock and sat down heavily on the bare floor, his sandbag butt vibrating the steel tables with impact. He had to get some sugar, and pronto, to avert nausea.

He poured down, virtually without swallowing, two liters of a fondly remembered brown fizzy soft drink, feeling regret that the gross supply of this beverage would eventually deplete. He wondered how much of it he could drink before the end of the world. Thoughts of food always calmed him. Then he glanced again at the animated backbone with eyes-that-weren't, its skeletal structure clinking against the tempered glass of the jar. It did not seem to need air.

Great, now your food tries to murder you even after it's dead—twice. He imagined eating a whole baked trout, keeping weapons ready so the spine did not jump up and try to gouge out his eye. Hysterical.

He preferred heavy caliber projectile peace of mind. Cordite calm. He had named his M60 "Zombo" and it was swell, a devastating auto-weapon sized to his own bounty. One round (the size of his sausage finger) made raspberry slush out of anything organic it hit. Vaporize the head and the leftovers could not eat you or infect you with the geek germ. And spraying on Pam kept them from sticking to the cookery.

Wormboy hated it when the rules decided to change on him with no warning and no lubrication, just *wham*! and you're stuck up the hiney-hole with an express missile of bad news. The snaky bone-thing clattered about, offering no clues.

On the other hand, maybe he had just discovered something new. Maybe he had the scientific right to name it. Which made him better than Dukey Mallett, the first person Wormboy had ever eaten, a giver-of-names without portfolio.

"Yo, Wormy, whatcha got in your locker, more WORMS, *huh?"*

Quoth Dukey Mallett, who bestows the epithet upon Wormboy (15th Street Junior High's resident wimp, blimp, pussywhip, and pariah), who, per Dukey, sucks up three squares chock full 'o nightcrawlers every day, with squiggly snacks between. Just because. This is always good for a chorus of guffaws from Dukey's intimates, 15th Street's other future convicts.

Dukey smokes Camels. His squeeze, Stacey, has awesome boobs and a lot of pimples around her mouth. She uses bubblegum-flavored lipsmacker. Two weeks prior to becoming a high school freshman, Dukey wraps a boosted Gran Torino around a utility pole at ninety. He, Stacey, and a pair of their joyriding accomplices are barbecued by sputtering wires and burning Hi-Test. Paramedics pile what parts they could retrieve onto a single stretcher, holding their noses.

Tompkins Mortuary provides local ambulance service. Wormboy races there as fast as his sweaty, obese teen corpus could move him, once he catches wind of the news. Old Man Tompkins admires his spunk and gristle when he requests to view the remains of his beloved classmates. "I HAVE TO BE SURE!" Wormy blurts, having rehearsed his grief. Tompkins is one of those guys of a mind that youngsters can never be exposed to death too soon, and so buys Wormboy's melodrama, and consents to give the kid a peek at the carbonized component mess filling Drawer Number Eight.

Wormboy thinks Tompkins smells like the biology lab at shark-dissecting time. While the old man averts his gaze with a sharp draw of untainted air, Wormboy sucks wind, fascinated. This flash-fried garbage staining the slab and blocking up the drains is Dukey. Harmless now. The sheer joy of this moment threatens to effervesce, create pressure, explode, so Wormboy quickly swipes a small sample. When Tompkins turns back, Wormy has to remember to look mortified. He sheepishly claims to have seen enough. He is lying.

Later, alone, he wallows.

Papaw had always said that orthodoxies had spent too long screwing up the world. That whole religion thing? Yeah, come to America, and enjoy religious freedom . . . as long as you pick one of these. Damned hypocrites, Papaw had said; enough was enough and too much. Idiots in the real world blundered blindly about, expending their existence by accident, begging unseen gods for unavailable mercies, trusting in supernatural beings and nebulous powers of "good" or "evil" that predetermined what breakfast cereal they ate. Papaw's doctrine was Get Some, and if there was any "evil," now, its name was either Starvation or Stupidity—two big helpings of which could make you instantly gone. True Believers spent their time preparing to die. Wormboy preferred fighting to live.

His honed survival ethics could conceivably become the first writ of a new doctrine— Get Some, Now. Better that than any other system that would rise, given time. Nobody in the real world ever learned a goddamned thing.

Wormboy dumped his dishes in the surgical sink and relaxed on another of his prizes, a sort of lazy-boy loveseat that held his mammoth buttocks tight as a lover. His alarm system primed, he dozed.

The piece of Dukey Mallet he has purloined from Tompkins turns out to be one of Dukey's fricasseed eyeballs. It has heat-shrunken and wrinkled into a raisin pattern, deflated on one side, mildly petrified, but without a doubt one of Dukey's baby blues. The eye that has directed so much scorn at Wormboy is now in the grasp of Wormboy himself, subtracted of blaze and swagger and no more threatening than a squashed seed grape. It gives under the pressure of Wormy's fingers, like stale cheese. It is sour-smelling, like an eggshell in the trash, with no insides.

Wormboy pops the eye into his mouth and bites down before his brain can say no. He gets a crisp bacon crunch. His mental RPMs redline as flavor billows across his tongue and floods his meaty squirrel cheeks.

Mamaw would not approve. This sort of thing was . . . well, it just wasn't DONE. Good thing Wormy is locked in the bathroom.

"Nobody on God's green Earth takes half an hour to comb their hair," Papaw's voice comes through the door, simultaneous with a disdainful THUD. "Finish up in there, boy—I gotta potty."

They think he's in here beating off, and in a way, they are right.

Mamaw is cooking dinner for eight, which means only she, Papaw, and Wormy will be dining tonight. The short corridor leading to the bathroom of the mobile home is only wide enough to accommodate one of them at a time, in any direction. And all of a sudden, those chicken wings, those potatoes, all that gravy and butter, doesn't raise that familiar, pleasant tectonic plate shift in Wormboy's gut.

Biting Dukey's eye brings a rush of . . . liberation, yeah, that's what it is. The ultimate expression of revenge, of power wielded over Dukey the dick-nosed shitheel. It is the nearest thing to sex that Wormboy will ever experience, damned close to religious.

Once Wormboy gets older, he scores a part-time, after-school job at Tompkins' place. By then, his future is cast in bronze, and his extra weight gain attracts no notice at all.

When history delivers him to the National Guard Armory, nostalgia compels him to tuck into a few boxed, Type-A government-issue combat meals. The gel-packed pucks of mystery meat he pries from inside the olive drab tins is more disgusting than anything he ever sliced off down at the morgue.

Wormboy's wet dream was just sneaking up on the gooshy part when another explosion, outside, jerked him back to reality and put Zombo's trusty rubber-banded grip in his hand faster than a samurai's katana. The vast flow of his stomach rippled in waves. *Brriiittt!* Lunch was still in there, fighting. But what his binoculars revealed flushed the need for a bromo right out of his mind.

Two dozen geeks, maybe more, were lurching toward the front gate of Valley View. Wormboy's jaw unhinged. That did not stop his mouth from watering at the sight. It was getting to be a busy Monday.

The Right Reverend Jerry unshielded his eyes and stared toward the corpulent sinner on the hilltop as smoking wads of Deacon W. C. rained down on the faithful. Something fist-sized and mulchy smacked Jerry's shoulder and blessed it with a smear of yellow. He shook steaming glop off his shoe and thought of Ezekiel 18:4: *The soul that sinneth—it shall die!*

Boy, he was getting a mad on now.

Deacon Curly and Deacon W. C. had both bitten the big one and bounced up to meet Jesus. The closer the congregation staggered to the graveyard, the better they could smell this sinner, and his fatted calves. The hour of deliverance—and dinner—so long promised by Jerry seemed nigh.

Jerry felt something else skin past his ear faster than sound. Behind him, another of the Born-Agains came unglued, skull and eyes and brains all cartwheeling off on different trajectories. Jerry recoiled, stepping blind, his heel skidding through yet something *else*, moist and slick. His feet took to the air and his rump introduced itself to the pavement and much, much more of Deacon W. C., who had always been the biggest. New colors soaked into his coat of many.

The Right Reverend Jerry involuntarily took his Lord's name in vain.

Another of the faithful to burst into a pirouette of flying parts, followed by the flat crack of the gunshot. Chunks and stringers spattered the others, who had the Christian grace not to take offense and continued marching forward.

Jerry scrambled in the puddle of muck, his trousers slimed and adherent, his undies coldly bunched. Just as wetly, another Born-Again ate a bullet and changed tense from present to past. Jerry caught most of the jetwash in the bazoo.

It was high time for him to bull in and start doing God's work.

Wormboy cut loose a throat-rawing war whoop of pure joy at what was heading his way. Home delivery! One guy in the rear did not twitch and lumber the way most geeks did, so Wormy reslung his Remington hunting rifle and checked through the scope. He saw a dude in a stained suit smearing macerated slush out of his eyes and hopping around in place with Donald Duck fury. It was apparently a live guy, among the dead guys.

Like all the others, he wore a Red Cross armband.

While Wormboy had the rifle up, he zeroed a fresh geek in the crosshairs, squeezed off, and watched another head screw inside-out in a pizza-colored burst of flavor. With a balletic economy of motion for a human his size, he ejected the spent brass and left the rifle open-bolted, because Zombo was still hot for mayhem. Zombo was itching to pop off and hose stragglers. A stretch belt of high velocity armor-piercers was draped over one sloping hillock of Wormboy's shoulder; the sleek column of shell casings obscured the Dirty Rotten Imbeciles logo on his T-shirt. Casserole time. Zombo lived. Zombo ruled.

The next skirmish line of Bouncing Bettys erupted, ooh, ahhh, fireworks. They were halfway to the moat. The stuff pattering down from the sky sure looked like manna.

Jerry let the faithful have it in his stump-thumper's bray, full-bore: "Onward! Onward! *Look unto me, and ye be saved, all the ends of the earth!*" Isaiah 45:22 was always a corker for rousing the rabble. They surged as one. By now even the hindmost had scented the plump demon on the hilltop in his false palace. He was bulk and girth and mass and calories and salvation. Valley View's iron portals were smashed down. Within seconds, a holy wave of living dead arms, legs and innards were airborne and graying out the sunlight.

"Onward!" Jerry frothed his passion to scalding and dealt his nearest disciple a fatherly shove in the direction of the enemy, the sinner, the monster. "*Onward!*" The flat of his hand met all the resistance of cold oatmeal. A cow patty had more tensile strength and left less mess. Jerry ripped his hand free with a yelp. Gooey webs followed it backward. The Born-Again gawped hollowly at the tunnel where its left tit had been a second before, then stumped *onward*, sniffing fresh Wormboy meat.

The sequential explosions had become deafening, slamming one into the next, thunderclaps that mocked God. Jerry thought he could hear a low, vicious chuddering in the interstices, not a heavenly sound, but an evil noise unto the Lord that was making the faithful go to pieces faster than frogs with cherry bombs inside. He tried to snap away the maggot-ridden brown jelly caking his hand and accidentally boffed Deacon Moe in the face. The zombi's nose tore halfway off and dangled. Moe felt no pain. He had obediently brought the pet caddy, whose occupants writhed and waxed wroth.

Zombo hammered out another gunpowder benediction and Jerry flung himself down to kiss God's good earth. Hot tracers ate pavement and jump-stitched through Deacon Moe in a jagged crotch-to-chin zig-zag. The pet carryall took two big hits and fell apart. Moe did likewise. His ventilated carcass executed a juice dump and the Right Reverend Jerry found himself awash in gallons of zombi puree garnished with four extremely aggravated rattlesnakes.

Jerry never identified the first to betray him. The first bite pegged him right on the balls, and the rest of his time was spent howling.

Deacon Moe, his work on this world finished, keeled over with a *ker-splat*. It was like watching a hot cherry pie hit a concrete sidewalk.

Wormboy rubbed his salt-stung eyes. He had not been aiming for the caddy. Zombo had *missed*. It was not just the sweat that had spoiled his aim. His vision was bollixed. The oily drops oozing from his vast pate were ice cold.

Probably somebody's something he ate.

Zombo's beak was dipping, pissing away good ammo to spang off the metal spikes crowding the moat. The huge gun was growing too heavy, too frying-pan hot to control. Wormboy gritted his teeth (always flossed), clamped his trigger finger down hard, and seesawed the muzzle upward with a bowel-clenching grunt. He felt himself herniate below the broad weightlifter's belt. Zombo continued his speech as geeks blocked tracers, caught fire and sprang apart at the seams. Those in front were buffaloed into the moat by those behind. They seated permanently onto the pungi pipes with spongy noises of penetration, to wriggle and gush bloodpus while reaching impotently toward Wormboy.

Zombo demanded a virgin belt of fresh slugs. Wormboy's appetites had churned into a platinum-class acid bath of indigestion. This night would belong to Maalox.

The air blackened with the tang of geek beef in no time. One whiff was all it took to make Wormboy vomit long and strenuously into the moat. Steaming puke pasted a geek who lay skewered through the back, facing the sky, mouth agape. It spasmed on the barbs, trying futilely to lap up as much fresh hot barf as it could collect.

Wormboy dropped the tagged-out Zombo and unholstered his beloved .44 to send a pancaking round into Barf Eater's brain pan. Its limbs stiffened straight as hydrostatic pressure blew its head apart into watermelon glop. Then it came undone altogether, collapsing into a mound of diarrheic putrescence that bubbled and flowed around the pipework.

Now *everything* was beginning to look like vomit. Wormboy's ravaged stomach said heave-ho to that, and contracted to expel what was no longer vomitable. This time he brought up blood, fizzing like soda pop from both nostrils. He spat and gagged, crashing to one catcher's mitt knee. His free hand vanished into the cushion of his stomach, totally inadequate to the task of clutching it.

The Right Reverend Jerry saw the sinner genuflect. God was still in Jerry's corner, punching away, world without end, hallelujah, amen.

Jerry's left eye was smeared down one cheek like a lanced condom. Little John's fang had put it out (it must have offended him). Jerry seized Little John and dashed his snaky brains out against the nearest headstone. Then he rose and began his trek uphill, through the valley of death, toting the limp, dead snake as a scourge. Consort with serpents had won him several dozen bites, but Jerry knew the value of immunization. He stung all over and wobbled on his feet, but so far he was still chugging, and his wherewithal had to have a Divine source.

This must be Hell, he thought, dazed, as he Witnessed most of his congregation get sliced and diced to droop all over Valley View's real estate like wet Christmas tinsel. Tendrils of smoke curled heavenward from the craters rudely gouged in the soil. Dismembered limbs hung, spasming their last. A few Born-Agains had stampeded over the fallen and made it halfway across the moat.

Jerry could feel his heart thudding, impelling God knew how much snakebite nectar through his veins. He could feel the Power working inside him. Blood began to leach freely from his gums, slathering his lips. His left hand snapped shut into a spastic claw and stayed that way. His good eye tried to blink and could not; it was frozen open. The horizon tilted wildly. Down below, his muscles surrendered, sending down shit and piss express delivery.

He wanted to raise his voice to his children, and tell them in the name of the Lord that the famine was ended, to hoot and holler about the feast at last. He lost all sensation in his legs instead. He tumbled into the violence-rent earth of the graveyard and began to drag himself further with his functioning hand, the one still vised around the remains of Little John.

He wanted to declaim, to shout, but his body had gone too stupid too fast. What came out, in glurts of blood-flecked foam, sounded like *nam He hess ed begud!*

Just the sound of that fucker's voice made Wormboy want to blow his ballast all over again.

Jerry clawed his way to the lip of the pit. The remaining Born-Agains congregated around him, including his only still-standing Deacon, Fatty. Ironic. His eye globbed onto his face, his body jittering as the megadose of poison took firmer hold, Jerry nevertheless raised his snake and prepared to Spake.

Wormboy had just enough gumption left to drag his .44 into the firing line and blow the evangelist's mushmouthed head clean off, before that mouth could pollute the air with any further religious noise. Papaw would have beamed with pride.

"That's . . . better," Wormboy ulped, his gorge pistoning. Then he ralphed again anyway and blacked out.

Weirder things had happened, and none of it had been a dream. Wormboy's brain insisted these were true things. It added that one eye was shut against the dark of dirt and his nose was squashed sideways. When he opened his other eye, the incoming light and information was going to hurt, but it would permit him to survey the situation, feigning sleep or death while peering over the topography of regurgitated lunch in front of his face.

Keystone Kops, he thought. Chowing down on a headless corpse. Wormboy watched strips of meat get ripped and gulped without the benefit of mastication, each glistening shred sliding down a gullet like a snake crawling into a wet red hole. One geek was busily gnawing a russet ditch into a Jerry drumstick with the foot still attached. Others played tug-o-war with slick spaghetti tubes of evangelist intestine, or wolfed double facefuls of thinner, linguini strands of tendon or ligament, all marinated in that special, extra-chunky maroon secret sauce.

Wormboy's tummy recommenced grumbling jealously. It was way past dinnertime. The surviving geeks would not just enjoy dessert and leave, no, not with Wormboy uneaten. Sick or not, subpar or handicapped, he'd have to crop 'em right now, unless he wanted to try a mop-up in total darkness with half his tools missing in action, and maybe waiting all the way to sunup to snack. He got cranky when he missed any feeding.

He saw one of the geeks in the moat wrench free of the pungi. Its flesh no longer meshed strongly enough for the barbs to hold it. It spent two seconds wobbling on its feet, then did a clumsy header onto three more pipes. Ripe plugs of rotten tissue spat upward and acid bile burbled forth.

Wormboy rolled toward Zombo, rising like a wrecked semi-righting itself. His brain rollercoastered; his vision strained to focus; what the *fuck* had been wrong with lunch? He was no more graceful than a geek himself, now. His heavy-bag muscles grated as he put one pillow-sized hand against a headstone to steady himself. The marker memorialized someone named Eugene Roach, *Loving Father*. The late Mr. Roach had lurched off to consume other folks' children a long time ago.

What happened next, happened fast.

Wormboy had to pitch his full weight against the tombstone just to keep from keeling over. When he leaned, grass and sod levered free with a sound like hair tearing out by the roots. His bloodshot eyes bugged and before he could arrest his own momentum, the headstone hinged back, a loose tooth freed from the tissue of Valley View's overnourished turf. Arms windmilling, Wormboy fell on top of it. His mind registered a flashbulb image of the tripwire, twanging taut to do its job. The mine detonated with an eardrum-compressing clap of bogus thunder beneath him, and two hundred pounds of headstone took to the air, with four hundred-plus pounds of Wormboy on top of it like a floundering surfer. The stone protected him from the blast, but the blast catapulted him over the moat to land right in the middle of the feeding frenzy on the other side.

Wormboy did a complete somersault, another first for his life.

With movie slo-mo surreality, he saw his pal, the hunky .44 Magnum, drop away like a bomb from a zeppelin. It landed with its trigger guard snugged around one of the moat's deadly metal speartips. The firmly impaled Deacon W. C. was leering down the bore when it went *bang*. Everything above the Adam's apple rained down to the west as goulash and flip chips.

Wormboy heard the shot but did not witness it. Just now, his overriding concern was gravity, and impact.

A geek turned as Wormboy flew in, raising its arms as if in supplication, or a pathetic attempt to catch the UFO that isolated it in the center of a house-sized, ever-growing shadow. Eugene Roach's overpriced monument stone veered into the moat. The geek struggling off the spears, the mushy one, watched it right up until the instant it hit. The fallout was so thick you could eat it with a fondue fork.

Wormboy clamped shut his eyes and screamed as he bellied in, headfirst. Bones snapped when he touched down. Only the yellows of the skywatching geek's eyes were visible in the end. It liquefied with a *poosh* and became a wet stain at the bottom of the furrow excavated by Wormboy's crash-landing.

All heads turned.

I've got it. Little snaky backbone serpent things, brand new. I discovered them so I get to name them. Yeah, that would be an accomplishment. I captured the first one. I saw others born of the smashed carcasses of geeks during the battle, wriggling free of living dead afterbirth, holding blind snouts up to the moonlight. I shall call them Z.A.V.S., *for*

Zombi Armored Venomous Serpent. Papaw and Mamaw could say that their son discovered something; might even get him into the World Book, if Papaw or Mamaw or the encyclopedia existed anymore. That was the tragedy of real accomplishment: sometimes there were no other humans around to take note of it, or fuss over it, or affirm it had even happened at all.

His brain was a boardroom riot of yelling stockbrokers. The first report informed him that aerial acrobatics did not agree with his physique. The second, enumerated fractures, shutdown, concussion, and one eardrum that had popped with the explosive decompression of a pimento vacuumed from an olive. The third, confirmed the equitable distribution of slag-hot agony to every outback and tributary of his body . . . and the dead taste of moist dirt, back again.

Then came the surprise, bonus news flash: He had not been gourmandized down to nerve peels and half a dozen red corpuscles. Yet.

He filed a formal request to roll back his eyelids. It took about an hour to trickle down through channels. And all the while, he could hear the geeks, eating. If they were eating *him*, he sure could not feel it.

He finally recognized starlight, in the post-midnight sky above him. He was on his back, legs straight, arms out in a plane shape. What a funny.

Eight pairs of reanimated dead eyes appraised his worth.

Dead bang, no argument, they've got me, Wormboy thought. *For more than a year they've whiffed me, and gotten smithereened, and now I've jolly well been served up as payback, air freight, gun-less, laid out flat on my own flab. Maybe they waited just so I could savor the sensual cornucopia of being devoured alive, firsthand. Dr. Moreau time, kids. Here's the part where Uncle Wormy checks out for keeps.*

He tried to wiggle his numbed fingers at them. "Yo, dudes." It was all he could think of to say. These guys didn't want a story and were uninterested in hearing about Z.A.V.S.

The zombis surrounding him in a funereal wake configuration—three up, three down, one at his feet and one at his head—rustled as though stirred by a soft breeze. They communed, in their odd way.

Now Wormboy could discern that the skull of the Right Reverend Jerry had been perched upon his chest. He could barely see it up there. The blood-dyed and tooth-scored fragments had been leaned together into a fragile sort of card ossuary. Now Wormboy could see that one of his bullets had gone in through Jerry's left eyebrow; good shot.

An uppercut of pain convulsed his insides and Wormy coughed weakly. The skull clattered apart like an inadequately-glued clay pot.

This caused more introspective commotion, among the zombis.

The Right Reverend Jerry had been sharked down to a jackstraw clutter of bones; the bones had been cracked, their marrow greedily drained. All through this feast, Wormboy had lain unconscious and available, mere feet distant, representing bigger portions for everybody, but he had gone unmolested for hours. Instead of tucking in, the zombis had gathered 'round and waited for him to wake up. They had, in fact, flipped him over and touched him without biting. They had pieced together Jerry's headbone and now seen it blown apart by a cough from the immense fat man. They had Witnessed.

The eyes that sought Wormboy did not judge him. They did not see a grotesquely obese pig who snarfed up worms and eyeballs and rarely bathed. The watchers did not snicker in a Dukey Mallett drawl, or lower their heads in disappointment that way Mamaw and Papaw often had. They did not reject Wormy, or find him lacking in any social particular. They had waited for him to revive. Patiently, on purpose, they had waited . . . for him.

They had never sought to eat of his lard or drink of his cholesterol. The Right Reverend Jerry had taught them that there were hungers other than physical.

He considered the litter of soda cracker skull frags confined by his own teats, and felt the same rush of revelation he had experienced by examining Dukey's eyeball, back in the pre-world. So fitting now, to relish that crunchy stone-ground goodness. He tipped a flake into his mouth and chewed with bloody teeth. Not bad, kind of like a wafer. As he ate, he abruptly realized he was not breathing—just like the geeks above, who rustled and communicated in their insect, tactile way, watching him.

One of his legs felt busted, but did not pain him any more. With effort, he found he could roll, his weight reforming like a Silly Putty lava flow until he could hike himself up onto both elbows. The zombis shuffled dutifully back to make room for him to rise, and when he could not, they helped him, wrestling him erect yet crooked, copying the dogfaces who had hoisted the Stars and Stripes over Iwo Jima. Wormboy realized that right now, he could order them to march into one of Valley View's crematory ovens according to height, and they would probably comply.

It seemed that at long last, he had gained the devoted approval of a peer group.

His back was broken. He indicated a ropy Z.A.V.S. coiled near his hassock feet. It was delivered unto him and with little effort he found he could guide it beneath his flesh, where it aligned according to instinct and quickly firmed up his carriage. It was miraculous.

Soon enough, some asshole would come along and try to whore up this resurrection for posterity in a big, bad black notebook . . . and get it all wrong. Wormboy decided on the spot that anybody who tried would have a quick but meaningful one-way interview with Zombo.

I *win again*. This, he had thought and said countless times before, in reference to those he had once dubbed geeks. Bacterial warmth flooded through him. He was dead, and not a geek, therefore *they* were not, either.

When he at last Spake unto them, he said something like, "Awww . . . shit, you guys, I guess we oughta go hustle up some potluck, huh?"

He began by passing out the puzzle pieces of the Right Reverend Jerry's skull. As one, they all took and ate without breathing.

And they saw that it was Good.

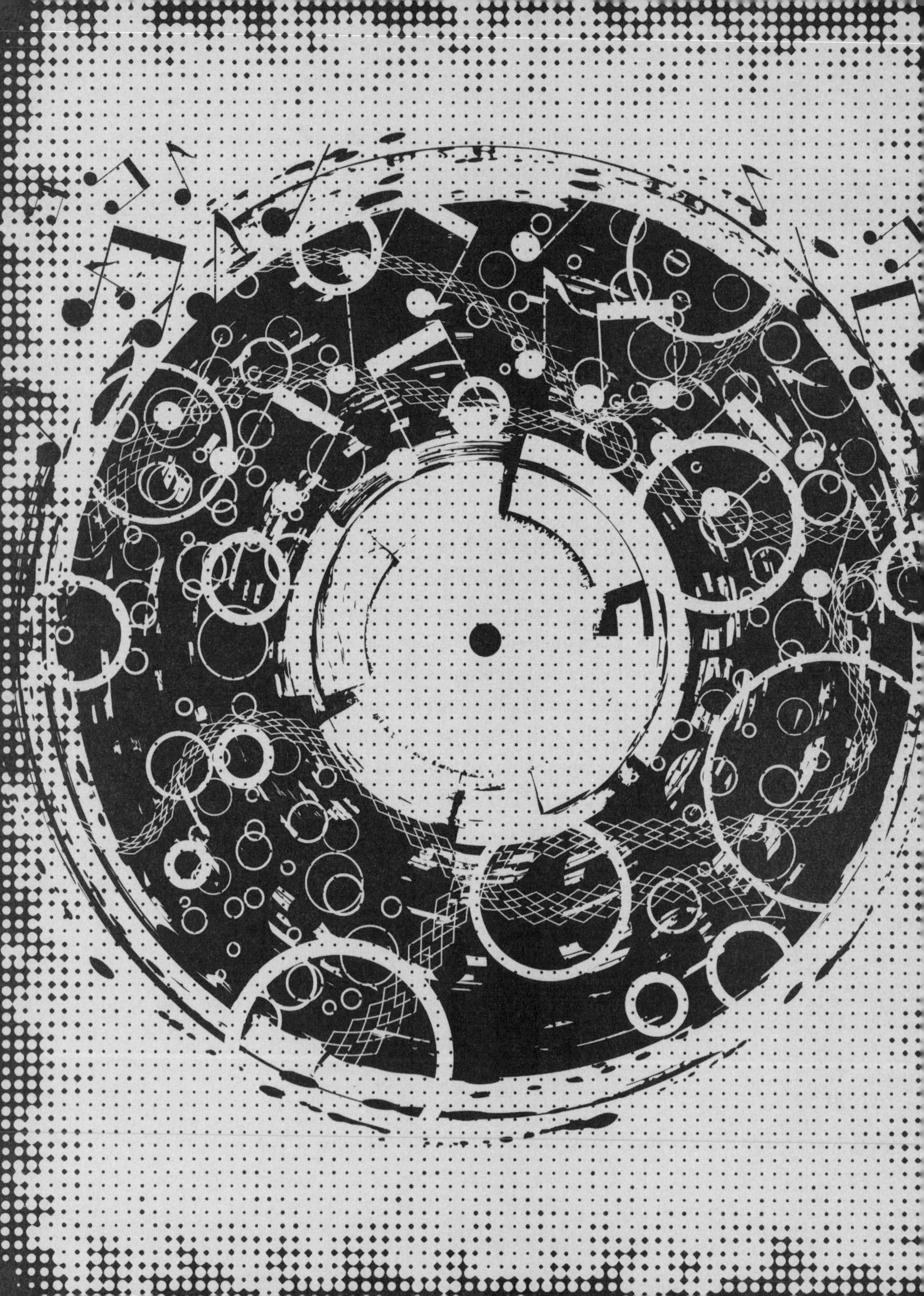

Red-hot romance is not something one expects to find amongst the cold and green. And though I hear there've been some recent attempts to market zombie erotica (good luck with that!), the truth is that most folks hope to live their whole lives without ever having to watch dead people fuck.

In fact—though you may know from previous anthologies that I'm not personally recalcitrant about such matters—zombies with big ol' raging hard-ons were the ones least apt to make it through the publishing gates this time. By and large, this is just not that kind of a book.

And yet . . . and yet . . .

With "Eat Me," Robert R. McCammon *manages the highly unlikely with enormous skill. Which is to say, he takes something deeply appalling and makes it almost entirely beautiful.*

It's a rare gift, as is this story, which closed the original Book of the Dead *and came less than a half an inch from doing so here.*

A QUESTION GNAWED, DAY AND NIGHT, at Jim Crisp. He pondered it as he walked the streets, while a dark rain fell and rats chattered at his feet; he mulled over it as he sat in his apartment, staring at the static on the television screen hour after hour. The question haunted him as he sat in the cemetery on Fourteenth Street, surrounded by empty graves. And this burning question was: when did love die?

Thinking took effort. It made his brain hurt, but it seemed to Jim that thinking was his last link with life. He used to be an accountant, a long time ago. He'd worked with a firm downtown for over twenty years, had never been married, hadn't dated much either. Numbers, logic, the rituals of mathematics had been the center of his life; now logic itself had gone insane, and no one kept records anymore. He had a terrible sensation of not belonging in this world, of being suspended in a nightmare that would stretch to the boundaries of eternity. He had no need for sleep any longer; something inside him had burst a while back, and he'd lost the ten or twelve pounds of fat that had gathered around his middle over the years. His body was lean now, so light sometimes a strong wind knocked him off his feet. The smell came and went, but Jim had a caseload of English Leather in his apartment and he took baths in the stuff.

The open maw of time frightened him. Days without number lay ahead. What was there to do, when there was nothing to be done? No one called the roll, no one punched the time-clock, no one set the deadlines. This warped freedom gave a sense of power to others; to Jim it was the most confining of prisons, because all the symbols of order—stoplights, calendars, clocks—were still there, still working, yet they had no purpose or sense, and they reminded him too much of what had been before.

As he walked, aimlessly, through the city's streets he saw others moving past, some as peaceful as sleepwalkers, some raging in the grip of private tortures. Jim came to a corner and stopped, instinctively obeying the DON'T WALK sign; a high squealing noise caught his attention, and he looked to his left.

Rats were scurrying wildly over one of the lowest forms of humanity, a half-decayed corpse that had recently awakened and pulled itself from the grave. The thing crawled on the wet pavement, struggling on one thin arm and two sticklike legs. The rats were chewing it to pieces, and as the thing reached Jim, its skeletal face lifted and the single dim coal of an eye found him. From its mouth came a rattling noise, stifled when several rats squeezed themselves between the gray lips in search of softer flesh. Jim hurried on, not waiting for the light to change. He thought the thing had said "*Whhhyyy?*" and for that question he had no answer.

He felt shame in the coil of his entrails. When did love die? Had it perished at the same time as this living death of human flesh had begun, or had it already died and decayed long before? He went on, through the somber streets where the buildings brooded like tombstones, and he felt crushed beneath the weight of loneliness.

Jim remembered beauty: a yellow flower, the scent of a woman's perfume, the warm sheen of a woman's hair. Remembering was another bar in the prison of bones; the power of memory taunted him unmercifully. He remembered walking on his lunch hour, sighting a pretty girl and following her for a block or two, enraptured by fantasies. He had always been searching for love, for someone to be joined with, and had never realized it so vitally before now, when the gray city was full of rats and the restless dead.

Someone with a cavity where its face had been stumbled past, arms waving blindly. What once had been a child ran by him, and left the scent of rot in its wake. Jim lowered his head, and when a gust of hot wind hit him he lost his balance and would have slammed into a concrete wall if he hadn't grabbed hold of a bolted-down mailbox. He kept going, deeper into the city, on pavement he'd never walked when he was alive.

At the intersection of two unfamiliar streets he thought he heard music: the crackle of a guitar, the low grunting of a drumbeat. He turned against the wind, fighting the gusts that threatened to hurl him into the air, and followed the sound. Two blocks ahead a strobe light flashed in a cavernous entrance. A sign that read THE COURTYARD had been broken out, and across the front of the building was scrawled BONEYARD in black spray paint. Figures moved within the entrance: dancers, gyrating in the flash of the strobes.

The thunder of the music repulsed him—the soft grace of Brahms remained his lullaby, not the raucous crudity of Grave Rock—but the activity, the movement, the heat of energy drew him closer. He scratched a maddening itch on the dry flesh at the back of his neck and stood on the threshold while the music and the glare blew around him. The Courtyard, he thought, glancing at the old sign. It was the name of a place that might once have served white wine and polite jazz music—a singles bar, maybe, where the lonely went to meet the lonely. The Boneyard it was now, all right: a realm of dancing skeletons. This was not his kind of place, but still . . . the noise, lights, and gyrations spoke of another kind of loneliness. It was a singles bar for the living dead, and it beckoned him in.

Jim crossed the threshold, and with one desiccated hand he smoothed down his remaining bits of black hair.

And now he knew what hell must be like: a smoky, rot-smelling pandemonium. Some of the things writhing on the dance floor were missing arms and legs, and one thin figure in the midst of a whirl lost its hand; the withered flesh skidded across the linoleum, was crushed underfoot as its owner scrabbled after it, and then its owner was likewise pummeled down into a twitching mass. On the bandstand were two guitar players, a drummer, and a legless thing hammering at an electric organ. Jim avoided the dance floor, moving through the crowd toward the blue-neon bar. The drum's pounding offended him, in an obscene way; it reminded him too much of how his heartbeat used to feel before it clenched and ceased.

This was a place his mother—God rest her soul—would have warned him to avoid. He had never been one for nightlife, and looking into the decayed faces of some of these people was a preview of torments that lay ahead—but he didn't want to leave. The drumbeat was so loud it destroyed all thinking, and for a while he could pretend it was indeed his own heart returned to scarlet life; and that, he realized, was why the Boneyard was full from wall to wall. This was a mockery of life, yes, but it was the best to be had.

The bar's neon lit up the rotting faces like blue-shadowed Halloween masks. One of them, down to shreds of flesh clinging to yellow bone, shouted something unintelligible and drank from a bottle of beer; the liquid streamed through the fissure in his throat and down over his violet shirt and gold chains. Flies swarmed around the bar, drawn to the reek, and Jim watched as the customers pressed forward. They reached into their pockets and changepurses and offered freshly-killed rats, roaches, spiders, and centipedes to the bartender, who placed the objects in a large glass jar that had replaced the cash register. Such was the currency of the Dead World, and a particular juicy rat bought two bottles of Miller Lite. Other people were laughing and hollering—gasping, brittle sounds that held no semblance of humanity. A fight broke out near the dance floor, and a twisted arm thunked to the linoleum to the delighted roar of the onlookers.

"I know you!" A woman's face thrust forward into Jim's. She had tatters of gray hair, and she wore heavy makeup over sunken cheeks, her forehead swollen and cracked by some horrible inner pressure. Her glittery dress danced with light, but smelled of gravedirt. "Buy me a drink!" she said, grasping his arm. A flap of flesh at her throat fluttered, and Jim realized her throat had been slashed. "Buy me a drink!" she insisted.

"No," Jim said, trying to break free. "No, I'm sorry."

"You're the one who killed me!" she screamed. Her grip tightened, about to snap Jim's forearm. "Yes you are! You killed me, didn't you?" And she picked up an empty beer bottle off the bar, her face contorted with rage, and started to smash it against his skull.

But before the blow could fall a man lifted her off her feet and pulled her away from Jim; her fingernails flayed to the bones of Jim's arm. She was still screaming, fighting to pull away, and the man, who wore a T-shirt with *Boneyard* painted across it, said, "She's a fresh one. Sorry, mac," before he hauled her toward the entrance. The woman's scream got shriller, and Jim saw her forehead burst open and ooze like a stomped snail. He shuddered, backing into a dark corner—and there he bumped into another body.

"Excuse me," he said. Started to move away. Glanced at whom he'd collided with.

And saw her.

She was trembling, her skinny arms wrapped around her chest. She still had most of her long brown hair, but in places it had diminished to the texture of spiderwebs and her scalp showed. Still, it was lovely hair. It looked almost healthy. Her pale blue eyes were liquid and terrified, and her face might have been pretty once. She had lost most of her nose, and gray-rimmed craters pitted her right cheek. She was wearing sensible clothes: a skirt and blouse and a sweater buttoned to the throat. Her clothes were dirty, but they matched. She looked like a librarian, he decided. She didn't belong in the Boneyard—but, then, where did anyone belong anymore?

He was about to move away when he noticed something else that caught a glint of frenzied light.

Around her neck, just peeking over the collar of her sweater, was a silver chain, and on that chain hung a tiny cloisonné heart.

It was a fragile thing, like a bit of bone china, but it held the power to freeze Jim before he took another step.

"That's . . . that's very pretty," he said. He nodded at the heart.

Instantly her hand covered it. Parts of her fingers had rotted off, like his own.

He looked into her eyes; she stared—or at least pretended to—right past him. She shook like a frightened deer. Jim paused, waiting for a break in the thunder, nervously casting his gaze to the floor. He caught a whiff of decay, and whether it was from himself or her he didn't know; what did it matter? He shivered too, not knowing what else to say but wanting to say something, anything, to make a connection. He sensed that at any moment the girl—whose age might be anywhere from twenty to forty, since Death both tightened and wrinkled at the same time—might bolt past him and be lost in the crowd. He thrust his hands into his pockets, not wanting her to see the exposed fingerbones. "This is the first time I've been here," he said. "I don't go out much."

She didn't answer. Maybe her tongue is gone, he thought. Or her throat. Maybe she was insane, which could be a real possibility. She pressed back against the wall, and Jim saw how very thin she was, skin stretched over frail bones. Dried up on the inside, he thought. Just like me.

"My name is Jim," he told her. "What's yours?"

Again, no reply. I'm no good at this! he agonized. Singles bars had never been his "scene," as the saying went. No, his world had always been his books, his job, his classical records, his cramped little apartment that now seemed like a four-walled crypt. There was no use in standing here, trying to make conversation with a dead girl. He had dared to eat the peach, as Eliot's Prufroc lamented, and found it rotten.

"Brenda," she said, so suddenly it almost startled him. She kept her hand over the heart, her other arm across her sagging breasts. Her head was lowered, her hair hanging over the cratered cheek.

"Brenda," Jim repeated; he heard his voice tremble. "That's a nice name."

She shrugged, still pressed into the corner as if trying to squeeze through a chink in the bricks.

Another moment of decision presented itself. It was moment in which Jim could turn and walk three paces away, into the howling mass at the bar, and release Brenda from her corner; or a moment in which Brenda could tell him to go away, or curse him to his face, or scream with haunted dementia and that would be the end of it. The moment passed, and none of those things happened. There was just the drumbeat, pounding across the club, pounding like a counterfeit heart, and the roaches ran their race on the bar and the dancers continued to fling bits of flesh off their bodies like autumn leaves.

He felt he had to say something. "I was just walking. I didn't mean to come here." Maybe she nodded. Maybe; he couldn't tell for sure, and the light played tricks. "I didn't have anywhere else to go," he added.

She spoke, in a whispery voice that he had to strain to hear: "Me neither."

Jim shifted his weight—what weight he had left. "Would you . . . like to dance?" he asked, for want of anything better.

"Oh, no!" She looked up quickly. "No, I can't dance! I mean . . . I used to dance, sometimes, but . . . I can't dance anymore."

Jim understood what she meant; her bones were brittle, just as his own were. They were both as fragile as husks, and to get out on that dance floor would tear them both to pieces. "Good," he said. "I can't dance either."

She nodded, with an expression of relief. There was an instant in which Jim saw how pretty she must have been before all this happened—not pretty in a flashy way, but pretty as homespun lace—and it made his brain ache. "This is a loud place," he said. "Too loud."

"I've . . . never been here before." Brenda removed her hand from the necklace, and again both arms protected her chest. "I knew this place was here, but . . ." She shrugged her thin shoulders. "I don't know."

"You're . . ." *lonely*, he almost said. As *lonely as* I *am*. ". . . alone?" he asked.

"I have friends," she answered, too fast.

"I don't," he said, and her gaze lingered on his face for a few seconds before she looked away. "I mean, not in this place," he amended. "I don't know anybody here, except you." He paused, and then he had to ask the question: "Why did you come here tonight?"

She almost spoke, but she closed her mouth before the words got out. I know why, Jim thought. Because you're searching, just like I am. You went out walking, and maybe you came in here because you couldn't stand to be alone another second. I can look at you, and hear you screaming. "Would you like to go out?" he asked. "Walking, I mean. Right now, so we can talk?"

"I don't know you," she said, uneasily.

"I don't know you, either. But I'd like to."

"I'm . . ." Her hand fluttered up to the cavity where her nose had been. "Ugly," she finished.

"You're not ugly. Anyway, I'm no handsome prince," He smiled, which stretched the flesh on his face. Brenda might have smiled, a little bit; again, it was hard to tell. "I'm not a crazy," Jim reassured her. "I'm not on drugs, and I'm not looking for somebody to hurt. I just thought . . . you might like to have some company."

Brenda didn't answer for a moment. Her fingers played with the cloisonné heart. "All right," she said finally. "But not too far. Just around the block."

"Just around the block," he agreed, trying to keep his excitement from showing too much. He took her arm—she didn't seem to mind his fleshless fingers—and carefully guided her through the crowd. She felt light, like a dry-rotted stick, and he thought that even he, with his shrunken muscles, might be able to lift her over his head.

Outside, they walked away from the blast of the Boneyard yard. The wind was getting stronger, and they soon were holding to each other to keep from being swept away. "A storm's coming," Brenda said, and Jim nodded. The storms were fast and ferocious, and their winds made the buildings shake. But Jim and Brenda kept walking, first around the block and then, at Brenda's direction, southward. Their bodies were bent like question marks; overhead, clouds masked the moon and blue streaks of electricity began to lance across the sky.

Brenda was not a talker, but she was a good listener. Jim told her about himself, about the job he used to have, about how he'd always dreamed that someday he'd have his own firm. He told her about a trip he once took, as a young man, to Lake Michigan, and how cold he recalled the water to be. He told her about a park he visited once, and how he remembered the sound of happy laughter and the smell of flowers. "I miss how it used to be," he said, before he could stop himself, because in the Dead World voicing such regrets was a punishable crime. "I miss beauty," he went on. "I miss . . . love."

She took his hand, bone against bone, and said, "This is where I live."

It was a plain brownstone building, many of the windows broken out by the windstorms. Jim didn't ask to go to Brenda's apartment; he expected to be turned away on the front steps. But Brenda still had hold of his hand, and now she was leading him up those steps and through the glassless door.

Her apartment, on the fourth floor, was even smaller than Jim's. The walls were a somber gray, but the lights revealed a treasure—pots of flowers set around the room and out on the fire escape. "They're silk," Brenda explained, before he could ask. "But they look real, don't they?"

"They look . . . wonderful." He saw a stereo and speakers on a table, and near the equipment was a collection of records. He bent down, his knees creaking, and began to examine her taste in music. Another shock greeted him: Beethoven . . . Chopin . . . Mozart . . . Vivaldi . . . Strauss. And, yes, even Brahms. "Oh!" he said, and that was all he could say.

"I found most of those," she said. "Would you like to listen to them?"

"Yes. Please."

She put on the Chopin, and as the piano chords swelled, so did the wind, whistling in the hall and making the windows tremble.

And then she began to talk about herself: She had been a secretary, in a refrigeration plant across the river. Had never married, though she'd been engaged once. Her hobby was making silk flowers, when she could find the material. She missed ice cream most of all, she said. And summer—what had happened to summer, like it used to be? All the days and nights seemed to bleed together now, and nothing made any of them different. Except the storms, of course, and those could be dangerous.

By the end of the third record, they were sitting side by side on her sofa. The wind had gotten very strong outside; the rain came and went, but the wind and lightning remained.

"I like talking to you," she told him. "I feel like . . . I've known you for a long, long time."

"I do, too. I'm glad I came into that place tonight." He watched the storm and heard the wind shriek. "I don't know how I'm going to get home."

"You . . . don't have to go," Brenda said, very quietly; "I'd like for you to stay."

He stared at her, unbelieving. The back of his neck itched fiercely, and the itch was spreading to his shoulders and arms, but he couldn't move.

"I don't want to be alone," she continued. "I'm always alone. It's just that . . . I miss touching. Is that wrong, to miss touching?"

"No. I don't think so."

She leaned forward, her lips almost brushing his, her eyes almost pleading. "Eat me," she whispered.

Jim sat very still. Eat me: the only way left to feel pleasure in the Dead World. He wanted it, too; he needed it, so badly. "Eat me," he whispered back to her, and he began to unbutton her sweater.

Her nude body was riddled with craters, her breasts sunken into her chest. His own was sallow and emaciated, and between his thighs his penis was a gray, useless piece of flesh. She reached for him, he knelt beside her body, and as she urged "Eat me, eat me," his tongue played circles on her cold skin; then his teeth went to work, and he bit away the first chunk. She moaned and shivered, lifted her head and tongued his arm. Her teeth took a piece of flesh from him, and the ecstasy arrowed along his spinal cord like an electric shock.

They clung to each other, shuddering, their teeth working on arms and legs, throat, chest, face. Faster and faster still, as the wind crashed and Beethoven thundered; gobbets of flesh fell to the carpet, and those gobbets were quickly snatched up and consumed. Jim felt himself shrinking, being transformed from one into two; the incandescent moment had enfolded him, and if there had been tears to cry, he might have wept with joy. Here was love, and here was a lover who both claimed him and gave her all.

Brenda's teeth closed on the back of Jim's neck, crunching through the dry flesh. Her eyes closed in rapture as Jim ate the rest of the fingers on her left hand—and suddenly there was a new sensation, a scurrying around her lips. The love wound on Jim's neck was erupting small yellow roaches, like gold coins spilling from a bag, and Jim's itching subsided. He cried out, his face burrowing into Brenda's abdominal cavity.

Their bodies entwined, the flesh being gnawed away, their shrunken stomachs bulging. Brenda bit off his ear, chewed, and swallowed it; fresh passion coursed through Jim, and he nibbled away her lips—they *did* taste like slightly overripe peaches—and ran his tongue across, her teeth. They kissed deeply, biting pieces of their tongues off. Jim drew back and lowered his face to her thighs. He began to eat her, while she gripped his shoulders and screamed.

Brenda arched her body. Jim's sexual organs were there, the testicles like dark, dried fruit. She opened her mouth wide, extended her chewed tongue and bared her teeth; her cheekless, chinless face strained upward—and Jim cried out over even the wail of the wind, his body convulsing.

They continued to feast on each other, like knowing lovers. Jim's body was hollowed out, most of the flesh gone from his face and chest. Brenda's lungs and heart were gone, consumed, and the bones of her arms and legs were fully revealed. Their stomachs swelled. And when they were near explosion, Jim and Brenda lay on the carpet, cradling each other with skeletal arms, lying on bits of flesh like the petals of strange flowers. They were one now, each into the other—and what more could love be than this?

"I love you," Jim said, with his mangled tongue. Brenda made a noise of assent, unable to speak, and took a last love bite from beneath his arm before she snuggled close.

The Beethoven record ended; the next one dropped onto the turntable, and a lilting Strauss waltz began.

Jim felt the building shake. He lifted his head, one eye remaining and that one sated with pleasure, and saw the fire escape trembling. One of the potted plants was suddenly picked up by the wind. "Brenda," he said—and then the plant crashed through the glass and the stormwind came in, whipping around the walls. Another window blew in, and as the next hot wave of wind came, it got into the hollows of the two dried bodies and raised them off the floor like reed-ribbed kites. Brenda made a gasping noise, her arms locked around Jim's spinal cord and his handless arms thrust into her ribcage. The wind hurled them against the wall, snapping bones like matchsticks as the waltz continued to play on for a few seconds before the stereo and table went over. There was no pain, though, and no reason to fear. They were together, in this Dead World where love was a curseword, and together they would face the storm.

The wind churned, threw them one way and then the other—and as it withdrew from Brenda's apartment it took the two bodies with it, into the charged air over the city's roofs.

They flew, buffeted higher and higher, bone locked to bone. The city disappeared beneath them, and they went up into the clouds where the blue lightning danced.

They knew great joy, and at the upper limits of the clouds where the lightning was hottest, they thought they could see the stars.

When the storm passed, a boy on the north side of the city found a strange object on the roof of his apartment building, near the pigeon roost. It looked like a charred-black construction of bones, melded together so you couldn't tell where one bone ended and the other began. And in that mass of bones was a silver chain, with a small ornament. A heart, he saw it was. A white heart, hanging there in the tangle of someone's bones.

He was old enough to realize that someone—two people, maybe—had escaped the Dead World last night. Lucky stiffs, he thought.

He reached in for the dangling heart, and it fell to ashes at his touch.

BY **JACK KETCHUM**

Jack Ketchum is known best for hyperviolent and emotionally grueling novels such as Off Season, Offspring, *and* The Girl Next Door: *bare-knuckled, punishing works that leave you on your belly in the dirt, knowing you've just been worked over by a particularly savage pro.*

Maybe that's why I fell so deeply in love with "The Visitor"*: a story of such raw sympathy and rare understanding that I almost couldn't believe it was written by the same guy.*

Of course, all the rhythms of the language are there, and the rich grasp of human complexity. He's a student of human moves, and he nails them unerringly here.

But this time, instead of punching us repeatedly in the face and neck, Ketchum quietly holds our hand while we wait for the end. Which, if anything, takes even more serious balls.

How sweet and strange and wonderful, then, that Ketchum would join Bradbury here at the tenderest end of the undead spectrum.

I love this story, and hope you do, too.

THE OLD WOMAN IN BED NUMBER 418B of Dexter Memorial was not his wife. There was a strong resemblance though.

Bea had died early on.

He had not been breathing well that night, the night the dead started walking, so they had gone to bed early without watching the news though they hated the news and probably would have chosen to miss it anyway. Nor had they awakened to anything alarming during the night. He still wasn't breathing well or feeling much better the following morning when John Blount climbed the stairs to the front door of the mobile home unit to visit over a cup of coffee as was his custom three or four days a week and bit Beatrice on the collarbone, which was not his custom at all.

Breathing well or not, Will pried him off of her and pushed him back down the stairs through the open door. John was no spring chicken either and the fall spread his brains out all across their driveway.

Will bundled Beatrice into the car and headed for the hospital half a mile away. And that was where he learned that all across Florida—all over the country and perhaps the world—the dead were rising. He learned by asking questions of the harried hospital personnel, the doctors and nurses who admitted her. Bea was hysterical having been bitten by a friend and fellow golfer so they sedated her and consequently it was doubtful that she ever learned the dead were doing anything at all. Which was probably just as well. Her brother and sister were buried over at Stoneyview Cemetery just six blocks away and the thought of them walking the streets of Punta Gorda again biting people would have upset her.

He saw some terrible things that first day.

He saw a man with his nose bitten off—the nosebleed to end all nosebleeds—and a woman wheeled in on a gurney whose breasts had been gnawed away. He saw a black girl not more than six who had lost an arm. Saw the dead and mutilated body of an infant child sit up and scream.

The sedation wore off. But Bea continued sleeping.

It was a troubled, painful sleep. They gave her painkillers through the IV and tied her arms and legs to the bed. The doctors said there was a kind of poison in her. They did not know how long it would take to kill her. It varied.

Each day he would arrive at the hospital to the sounds of sirens and gunfire outside and each night he would leave to the same. Inside it was relatively quiet unless one of them awoke and that only lasted a little while until they administered the lethal injection. Then it was quiet again and he could talk to her.

He would tell her stories she had heard many times but which he knew she would not mind his telling again. About his mother sending him out with a nickel to buy blocks of ice from the iceman on Stuyvesant Avenue. About playing pool with Jackie Gleason in a down-neck Newark pool hall just before the war and almost beating him. About the time he was out with his first-wife-to-be and his father-in-law-to-be sitting in a bar together and somebody insulted her and he took a swing at the guy but the guy had ducked and he pasted his future father-in-law instead.

He would urge her not to die. To try to come back to him.

He would ask her to remember their wedding day and how their friends were there and how the sun was shining.

He brought flowers until he could no longer stand the scent of them. He bought mylar balloons from the gift shop that said *get well get well soon* and tied them to the same bed she was tied to.

Days passed with a numbing regularity. He saw many more horrible things. He knew that she was lingering far longer than most did. The hospital guards all knew him at the door by now and did not even bother to ask him for a pass anymore.

"Four eighteen B," he would say but probably even that wasn't necessary.

Nights he'd go home to a boarded-up mobile home in an increasingly deserted village, put a frozen dinner into the microwave and watch the evening news—it was all news now, ever since the dead started rising—and when it was over he'd go to bed. No friend came by. Many of his friends were themselves dead. He didn't encourage the living.

Then one morning she was gone.

Every trace of her.

The flowers were gone, the balloons, her clothing—everything. The doctors told him that she had died during the night but that as of course he must have noticed by now, they had this down pretty much to a science and a humane one at that, that once she'd come back again it had been very quick and she hadn't suffered.

If he wanted he could sit there for a while, the doctor said. Or there was a grief counselor who could certainly be made available to him.

He sat.

In an hour they wheeled in a pasty-faced redhead perhaps ten years younger than Will with what was obviously a nasty bite out of her left cheek just above the lip. A kiss, perhaps, gone awry. The nurses did not seem to notice him there. Or if they did they ignored him. He sat and watched the redhead sleep in his dead wife's bed.

In the morning he came by to visit.

He told the guard four eighteen B.

He sat in the chair and told her the story about playing pool with Gleason, how he'd sunk his goddamn cue ball going after the eight, and about buying rotten hamburger during the Great Depression and his first wife crying well into the night over a pound of spoiled meat. He told her the old joke about the rooster in the henyard. He spoke softly about friends and relations, long dead. He went down to the gift shop and bought her a card and a small potted plant for the window next to the bed.

Two days later she was gone. The card and potted plant were gone too and her drawer and closet were empty.

The man who lay there in her bed was about Will's age and roughly the same height and build and he had lost an eye and an ear along with his thumb, index and middle fingers of his hand, all on the right side of this body. He had a habit of lying slightly to his leftas though to turn away from what the dead had done to him.

Something about the man made Will think he was a sailor, some rough weathered texture to this face or perhaps the fierce bushy eyebrows and the grizzled white stubble of beard. Will had never sailed himself but he had always wanted to. He told the man about his summers as a boy at Asbury Park and Point Pleasant down at the Jersey shore, nights on the boardwalk and days with his family by the sea. It was the closest thing he could think of that the man might possibly relate to.

The man lasted just a single night.

Two more came and went—a middle-aged woman and a pretty teenage girl.

He did not know what to say to the girl. It had been years since he'd even spoken to a person who was still in her teens—unless you could count the cashiers at the market. So he sat and hummed to himself and read to her out of a four-month-old copy of *People* magazine.

He bought her daisies and a small stuffed teddy bear and placed the bear next to her on the bed.

The girl was the first to die and then come back in his presence.

He was surprised that it startled him so little. One moment the girl was sleeping and the next she was struggling against the straps which bound her to the bed, the thick grey-yellow mucus flowing from her mouth and nose spraying the sheets they had wrapped around her tight. There was a sound in her throat like the burning of dry leaves.

Will pushed his chair back toward the wall and watched her. He had the feeling there was nothing he could say to her.

On the wall above a small red monitor light was blinking on and off. Presumably a similar light was blinking at the nurse's station because within seconds a nurse, a doctor and a male attendant were all in the room and the attenddant was holding her head while the doctor administered the injection through her nostril far up into the brain. The girl shuddered once and then seemed to wilt and slide deep down into the bed. The stuffed bear tumbled to the floor.

The doctor turned to Will.

"I'm sorry," he said. "That you had to see this."

Will nodded. The doctor took him for a relative.

Will didn't mind.

They pulled the sheet up over her and glanced at him a moment longer and then walked out through the doorway.

He got up and followed. He took the elevator down to the ground floor and walked past the guard to the parking lot. He could hear automatic weapons-fire from the Wal-Mart down the block. He got into his car and drove home.

After dinner he had trouble breathing so he took a little oxygen and went to bed early. He felt a lot better in the morning.

Two more died. Both of them at night. Passed like ghosts from his life.

The second to die in front of him was a hospital attendant. Will had seen him many times. A young fellow, slightly balding. Evidently he'd been bitten while a doctor administered the usual injection because the webbing of his hand was bandaged and suppurating slightly.

The attendant did not go easily. He was a young man with a thick muscular neck and he thrashed and shook the bed.

The third to die in front of him was the woman who looked so much like Bea. Who had her hair and eyes and general build and coloring.

He watched them put her down and thought, this was what it was like. Her face would have looked this way. Her body would have done that.

On the morning after she died and rose and died again he was walking past the first-floor guard, a soft little heavyset man who had known him by sight for what must have been a while now. "Four eighteen B," he said.

The guard looked at him oddly.

Perhaps it was because he was crying. The crying had gone on all night or most of it and here it was morning and he was crying once again. He felt tired and a little foolish. His breathing was bad.

He pretended that all was well as usual and smiled at the guard and sniffed the bouquet of flowers he'd picked from his garden.

The guard did not return the smile. He noticed that the man's eyes were red-rimmed too and felt a moment of alarm because he seemed to sense that the eyes were not red as his were simply from too much crying. But you had to walk past the man to get inside so that was what he did.

The guard clutched his arm with his little white sausage fingers and bit at the stringy bicep just below the sleeve of Will's short-sleeved shirt. There was no one in the hall ahead of him by the elevators, no one to help him.

He kicked the man in the shin and felt dead skin rip beneath his shoe and wrenched his arm away. Inside his chest he felt a kind of snapping as though someone had snapped a twig inside him.

Heartbreak?

He pushed the guard straight-arm just as he had pushed John Blount so long and far ago and although there were no stairs this time there was a fire extinguisher on the wall and the guard's head hit it with a large clanging sound and he slid stunned down the face of the wall.

Will walked to the elevator and punched four. He concentrated on his breathing and wondered if they would be willing to give him oxygen if he asked them for it.

He walked into the room and stared. The bed was empty.

It had never been empty. Not once in all the times he'd visited.

It was a busy hospital.

That the bed was empty this morning was almost confusing to him. As though he had fallen down a rabbit-hole.

Still he knew it wasn't wise to argue when after all this time he finally had a stroke of luck.

He put the slightly battered flowers from his garden in a water glass. He drew water in the bathroom sink. He undressed quickly and found an open-backed hospital gown hanging in the closet, slipped it on over his mottled shoulders and climbed into bed between clean fresh-smelling sheets. The bite did not hurt now and there was just a little blood.

He waited for the nurse to arrive on her morning rounds.

He thought how everything was the same, really. How nothing much had changed whether the dead were walking or not. There were those who lived inside of life and those who for whatever reason did not or could not. Dead or not dead.

He waited for them to come and sedate him and strap him down and wished only that he had somebody to talk to—to tell the Gleason story, maybe, one last time. Gleason was a funny man in person just as he was on TV but with a foul nasty mouth on him, always cussing, and he had almost beat him.

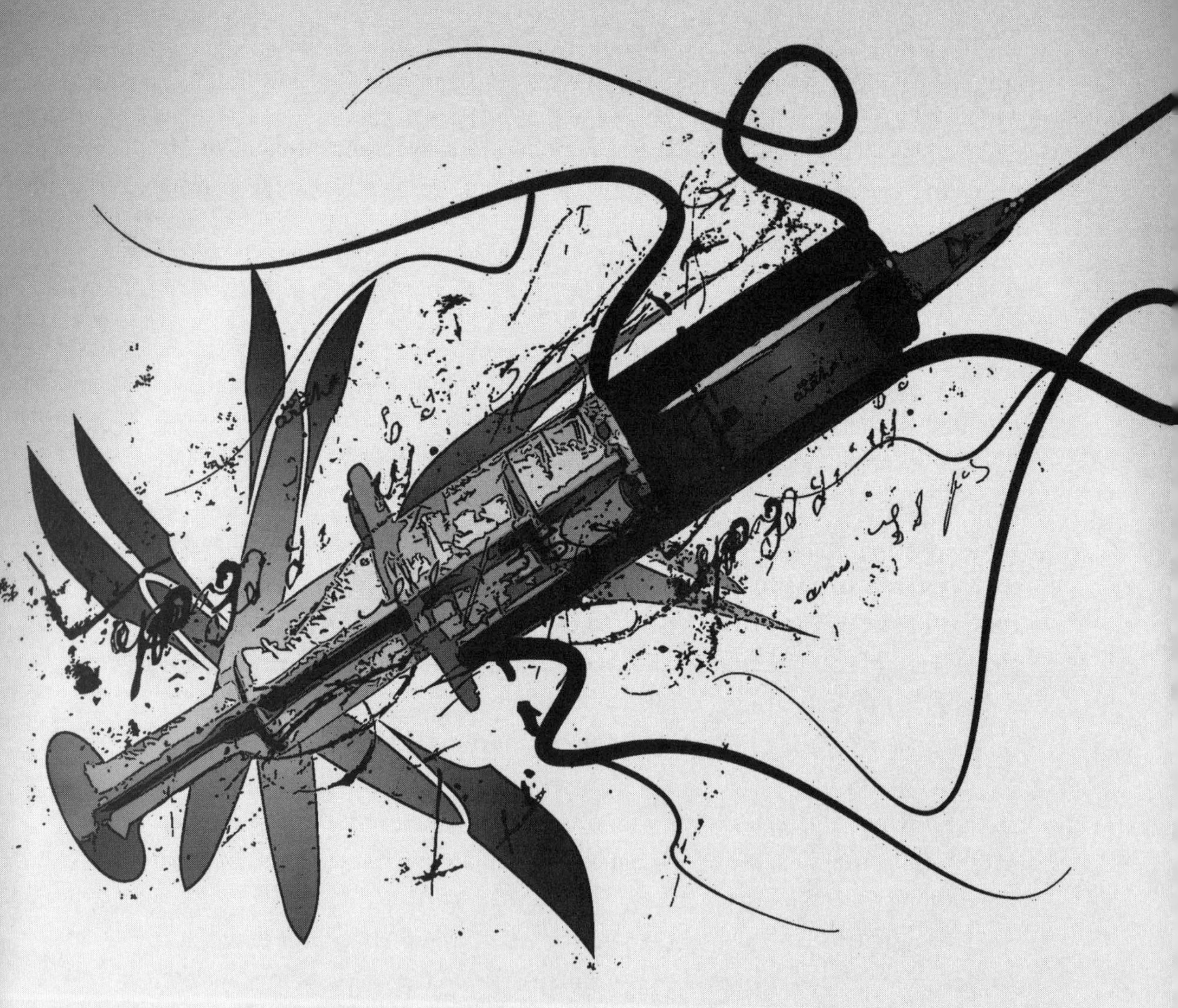

The Prince of Nox

BY **KATHE KOJA**

I once said to Kathe Koja, "The best shit I've ever written was like a gateway drug to you." Which is one of the biggest compliments I've ever paid a human being.

What I meant by it was this:

When I write, what I hope to do is open doors—of thought, and emotion, and revelatory connection—with the understanding that there will always be doors beyond those doors, revealing even deeper insight and information.

When I read Kathe, I sense doors opening that I haven't even scratched at. As Dali loved to proclaim vis-a-vis himself, she is the drug, using language skills and points of view so startlingly unique that anyone writing remotely like her is probably just copping her licks.

And so with "The Prince of Nox": as odd and haunting a tickle to the zombie hindbrain as you are ever liable to read. May it open some doors for you.

THE PRINCE OF NOX UPON A TABLE, pinned by plastic, praying for death.

The lights were recessed blue above him; his sky. Punishing medicinal smell, reek of plasma and clean gore. Directly beneath him, the smooth gurney landscape; they would not waste a real bed on him. His restraints, ignored because ubiquitous, specially made to bind the strong and mobile dead: hurried fruit of a terrible specialization but not a growth industry, no, or at least not anymore; what had the drivers of the plague wagons done with their vehicles when the crisis was over? Slimly constructed gauntlets of some heavy material, not precisely cloth nor precisely plastic, the dull metal fasteners like nickel scabs on the pale false flesh pinning forehead, chest, arms, legs, abdomen. They were smart enough, here, to be very careful.

He stretched, a little, the hemisphere of his restraints. To his left was the unwindowed wall, to his right the door bristling its redundancy of locks. He had a call button—perhaps the ultimate grotesquerie—and a long-empty saline drip. From a small metal tree hung his chart, a monstrous thing with a definite life of its own. His name was written in fading blue capitals, alongside it and underlined (twice), his date of death.

He remembered everything.

His name was Death; the yang to birth's yin and he had gone through it heedless as a tramp, stunned by plain sensation when he should have been most aware. Still, how was he to guess that that first metamorphosis was itself the gate to a grander change, how could he have foretold? The nervous parking lot of a Piggly Wiggly, one of the few stores still open at night, the assault a surprise more dreadful than death would be: grabbed from behind by hands missing fingers, teeth on his body like porcelain chips and his own blood spraying stupid across the windshield of his Chevette, brown-bagged milk, cigarettes, lunchmeat smashing to a pulpy goulash on the blacktop. Lunchmeat. That's what it all came down to, the gift of life. Kiss of life. Lust for life. Crouched and dying against the hood of his car, his assailant's brute heedless attention now bestowed on the man trying for the car next to his, a big gray late model Ford like an elaborate moving sarcophagus, the man struggling with those stubborn jaws on his throat as if they were the hinges on the gates of hell. Good luck.

The hood of his own car still warm, his temples and bowels one swimming migraine; disorientation; the plunging loss of control, horrible, *horrible.* And then: resuscitating agony, tissues lurching not back to life but back to service. All the smells. His own shit. His own blood. Meat, somewhere, very ripe. Hiding behind the store, its back door open—the clerks were all dead, all two of them, he had watched them die—he hunched sideways in the pour of fluorescence, staring at his hands, unable to believe they could now reduce a human body to chunks and shreds.

Until he did it. Murder; but he was starving, the meat smell was *everywhere*: so absolute it reduced to the status of whim the greedy threshold quest for orgasm, until then the strongest physical emotion he could imagine. To this hospital moment he still did not consciously remember whom he had killed, how, recalled only the sense of vomitfullness before he lay where he was to sleep, less than half a mile from the parking lot where he had achieved zombiehood, Piggly Wiggly everlasting,

His sleep was not as it had been, less dreams than random firings of misdirected neurons, cessation but no rest. He woke like an appliance turning on, itchy with dried blood, the yellowish gravel of broken patio blocks stubbling his cheek, the backs of his hands. He lay in the driveway of a house, fake brick, fake farmhouse mailbox and lurching gutters, the whole carelessly abandoned like a bad idea: there were still toys in the overgrown yard, a garden hose half-coiled, gritty chunks of charcoal in a rusting grill. When he stood up he was very dizzy; it was almost impossible to keep an even gait. So, he thought, remembered thinking (remembering now in the slow radiation of blue above him, the heinous scent of meat he could smell but not touch), that's why they walk so funny.

Inside the house through the open back door, cereal box still on the kitchen counter, more toys underfoot. Newspapers in the living room, he could not read them, he could not properly focus his eyes, In the bathroom, a small dog recently dead behind the toilet. More toys' in the tub, a duckie, a pair of red flat-bottomed boats that fit, moored, in the palms of his cold hands. He did not realize he was crying until he smelled his own tears.

He put everything back the way it had been and left the house, doors locked this time; it seemed important that the house stay undefiled. It was easier to keep to the sidewalk, less chance of stumbling. He walked back to the main road, careful to keep away from the infrequent cars until he realized there was no longer a reason to care.

The Piggly Wiggly had been looted, but was empty now, broken windows shivered lightly by the building wind. There was a car in the parking lot, a blue Toyota slewed defensively diagonal before the phone stand. It was empty as well.

How much time had passed, for him, for the world? Had everyone died? And if they had, where were they now?

Inside the store there was a radio, cheap and forgotten under the counter. He turned it on, sat atop the counter to listen while sorting through the contents of his wallet; he could not read any of the various identification, but he recognized himself on the driver's license.

Apparently the plague, the infestation, had finally reached downstate; they had all said it could not happen, that the Army, the National Guard had the outbreaks contained to the heavily populated metro areas, that if you stayed away from the big cities you would be okay. The usual smug rural paranoia, glaringly reinforced by daily newscast scares, closer and closer until there were sightings, here and there, more and more but no actual deaths. Stay out of the cities, they said. Lock your doors. Of course now they had been proved completely wrong, but then again they probably no longer cared. The only question left half-worth wonder was Who; who finally brought the death, who rode the pale horse; and did it matter?

No. Of course not.

He killed and ate a pregnant teenager that afternoon; her bones snapped in his hands like fragile clasps of cheap jewelry. Soon afterward he walked in front of a truck, a quarter-ton pickup driven by two women whose vast and rolling eyes were almost blinded by outrage and terror, and found what it was like to fly.

It was possible to walk a long way without feeding. He tried to go as long as he could, and as far. He was moderately successful.

He had forgotten that his name was Peter, that he was a cost accountant, that he had no close friends and a wife who did not particularly like him.

He thought he might live forever.

Did you use alcohol? Did you use prescription drugs? Stimulants or anti-depressants of any kind? How about nonprescription drugs? Cocaine? Amphetamines?

No.

Were you ever diagnosed as having hypertension? Diabetes? AIDS? MS? CP? Huntington's? Hodgkin's? All the brain diseases, finally, which at least made some sense if not enough: no, he told them. I was perfectly healthy. I didn't even smoke cigarettes regularly.

Senses: enhanced olfactory, to a level of sophistication comparable only to the most advanced carnivores. Enhanced night vision. Auditory unchanged. Tactile senses deteriorated to a large degree. They never asked about his sense of taste.

Angry eyes. Notations. Without adequate medical records, without a formal autopsy they were reduced to that old fallback standby, asking questions. They asked the same questions a lot. He wondered if they knew that.

They smelled so good.

Irony: having died once, stupid and fast and too dumbfounded for real awareness as he crossed the line from life to hyperlife, now all he wanted was to die again, passing this time into the fullness of erasure; to unbecome. Irony once more, but one infinitely warmer: in his first life he was not much, in fact he was nothing and no one, *no one*, his problems, the sorrows of his emptiness less than cliché and his heart too dull to even notice the rolling time sucked from him by cold attrition; but now in death, the answer.

The vessel must be emptied before it can be filled.

He had not been transformed, as if from frog to royalty, all in a moment, in fact it took him the better part of a season, warm to cold, to realize that he had changed. Again. In his dark vagabond travels, street to street to highway and death after death after death, he assumed of the others he saw, the ones he watched without joining, an aimlessness informed by innocence and more than equal to his own. At last, shy and stealthy, he followed and then joined a trio met outside what had been a parochial school, standing blanched and faintly steaming in blind yellow streetlight circles.

He told them, haltingly in their silence, of his theories—he had a lot of theories then, many of them to prove subsequently untrue, one or two in the next few minutes—and spoke of his ideas, his belief that there must be a different way to live, that this course of wandering, of empty killing, was wrong. Death is *good*, he told them earnestly; it should not be randomly bestowed, there should be a *purpose*, a reason behind it. Kill and eat, yes, it had to be done and was in its way perhaps not so bad, perhaps not even as bad as the old way which was the same thing, really, wasn't it? Hadn't it been? Just disguised. It had still been eater and eaten, but without blood, and maybe this new way was better. Cleaner, because everyone *gained*, wasn't it so?

Wasn't it?

It was like talking to the light poles. No answering. No talking.

No thinking.

No nothing.

He remembered trying again, simpler words, louder in his frustration, louder until he was screaming at them, right there in the parking lot, they were *nothing*, less than animals, stupid eating machines; in the bland reflection of their eyes was his first serious consideration of suicide. The last immortal man on earth. What a joke. He left them there and promised himself he would live—and die if he had to—alone, he would never come near any of them again, he was *different*.

He stayed different.

He became lonely.

Eventually, after nights in the snow, curled like a sad surly insect in a bitter cocoon, he realized what was happening, had been, what he had truly become.

Was it a coincidence that he alone retained the gift of awareness, of a consciousness more severely tempered and refined than even those who had never died? Was it a coincidence that he alone understood what a *gift* it all was?

No. It was not. There is more in heaven and earth, more than the dead and the living: there was a place inside him that death did not hamper nor life release, that had blossomed now in this terrible half-life to make of it, and him, something new.

And there was work to do.

He cried then, he was so happy.

We transcend death, we *are* death, we are the afterlife. His message, preached to a herd begun as worse than cows, grisly cud and slack stares. Quite the congregation, clustered together like flies around a sore, wandering away, then back to stand as stupid as before. But they had listened, he knew they had. Because even those eyes could widen, even there was the echo of the place inside him: Emptiness fined calling to the guttering void of others: Here is what you need. Be filled. And eventually, through reservoirs of patience and demand, they learned. Not much, even after all his efforts, but enough to rise at least a step or two above the level of simple slaughtering machines, dumb animals feeding at the living trough of the ever-lessening pool of victims—because of course the others, the ones left alive, were learning too, after a shockingly long period of numb terror that decimated them through its fostering of stupid theories, ruinously reckless modes of action; that vaccine, for example, what a disaster that had turned out to be.

Not for him, though, or his people. For them it was not apocalypse but transformation, a changed order of being. Fruit of his relentless teachings, as slow as they, finally he had guided them in choice of their victims—who in deepest fact were truly victims no longer: choose not the healthy but the ill, the old, the sleepers on benches, the hiders in crevices too small for living eyes to find: take from them the sorrows life has forced upon them; empower them all. They are empty: fill them. And painlessly, it must be done painlessly: no ugliness, no slobbering feast, just a seamless entrance to the infinite. And his people, relieved now of the burden of total senselessness, restored in some distant way to the habit of order, had responded with tenacity collective, a dark unconscious charity that absolved, rather than bestowed, pain. They had given all that was left for them to give, they had given of *themselves*, not taking but making, no longer the heedless gobble it had been—although unfortunately that continued, there were still some he could not reach, usually the ones gone so far for so long that nothing but a well-placed bullet could get their attention—now the process had become more than a process, it had evolved into nothing less than the sacramental.

But in the end what difference had it made? They all died again at last, painfully, in clumps and lowing droves; he had never taught them a way to save themselves; it had not seemed necessary. Why fear death when death is what you are? His own survival had been almost a comic fluke, found as he was pinned beneath an unused refrigerator in the basement of an abandoned community center, their summer's hive, lair, church; he had tried to block the door, found his strength distracted until it was too late, and lay there stunned as an idiot bug, unable to escape the grim combat faces in their hypersterile suits, saved only—irony again—by his sudden terrified cries of Please. Over and over: Please, please. Ask nice, his mother used to say. The inability to do so had killed his people, sent them en masse to crematoria, their bewildered cries of hunger and unease unmarked by him, incarcerated as he was in this monolithic facility, unable to hear or help.

Still he had loved them, in away, and needed them certainly, and certainly they needed him. God help us if they ever get smart—if he had heard it once in the days before his own sloppy exit, he had heard it a million times, and twice that afterward. Well, he was smart, and more than mere intelligence: he was aware. By his being he brought epiphany; from emptiness, the first intelligence of what it meant to be full. He had enough brains for all of them.

And now he *was* all of them, all by himself.

How long had it been, they wanted to know, since he had eaten real food? As opposed, he supposed, to the synthetic humanity they fed him, the hideous fake flesh. God. Real food. Don't make me laugh, he said. That *was* the real food. Realer than dead animals and dead fish. You drink blood too, you just call it gravy.

They hadn't liked those answers, liked others even less, liked least of all his answers incomplete, his silences that fed their frustration, boiling to a shout, We have to *know*! We have to find out.

Why do you ask me? Yelling now himself. Why me.

Because you're the only one whose brain didn't turn to neuron puree, you're the only one who still has an IQ. Because there isn't another one like you.

Slowly, there in his prison, he came to new theories, black knowledge seeping as cruel and inevitable as infection through the blood. The zombie epidemic, the reign of the rapturous dead, was effectively over. What few shambling wanderers remained—none of them *his*, he was sure—were walking a very short line thanks to the Army's new improved assembly line techniques, practice evidently having finally made perfect.

So. Why then were the doctors, the NIH bullies, so greedy to find out what differed in his post-death physiology, what possible difference could it make at this late date? And why do it with such idiotic Twenty Questions sloth, for God's sake? Why not just perform a lengthy slice and dice, study each cell individually if that was what it took to get where they wanted to go?

Where did they want to go?

He had a theory for that, too, and the more he pondered it the more correct he knew himself to be. They wanted to make themselves like him. Immortal. But without struggle, or pain. Or work, real work, his work, the plumb and scorch of the heart, the soul. No. They were doctors, they didn't believe in souls. Just find out what he has so we can get it too, synthesize it, something. We have the greatest concentration of experts in the history of medicine, for fuck' s sake, we ought to be able to do *something*. He's just a zombie. He's just a zombie.

Stropping his wrists against the restraints, a slow and antique care, trying to slough to the bone. No, he told them. I won't cooperate with you anymore. There is nothing more for me to do here, and I want to die.

They did not answer. If he wished to eat, he could not help but cooperate, and they all knew it, he most of all in the warm depths of his degraded capitulation. He had tried to starve himself once; they had not permitted it. They had their own lengths, how far they would go.

But they would never let *him* go.

His people, such as they were, had been—and even if they had been nothing, they had still been his—were all dead forever, passed beyond that second life into the only place he wanted now to be, the last fulfillment, the final step taken. So easy, with access to the right weapons, weapons nothing, the right *mindset*. Goad the wrong orderly, presto. But that was for dreary daydreams, he never in fact saw any orderlies, any nurses, anyone other than the increasingly sullen doctors and he had goaded them plenty already, they were unimpressed with his reasonings, his message and pity writ large; they wanted bodily fluids, they wanted to measure his eyeballs, they wanted him to flex his right arm twenty times and twenty times again, they wanted to see if he remained capable of a bowel movement, of a rise in temperature, of an erection. How human are you, they asked with their tests. How are you still like us?

Too much, he thought, and told them so.

"Why don't you just kill me?"

The doctor, young, thin; swift gloved brown hands, faintly cool pink palms. Large eyes that said nothing at all.

"You know why."

Tears. He could still cry. "I want to die. Please just let me die."

Swabbing at his restraints, swiping lubricant beneath to keep the friable flesh intact. "It's not up to me." Making notes on the file, it was already *War and Peace*, what else was there to say? How long was this going to go on?

"Please," he said. "Let me go. Tell them to let me go."

Cold eyes, now. "Did you give your victims—pardon me, your *converts*—did you give them any choice? Did you *ask* them if they—"

"Yes! Yes, I did." Earnestly. "I asked them all, I never forced anybody. Once I explained to them how it was, that death is inevitable, they understood and they—"

"Let me explain something to *you*. You didn't bring anybody to a better life, you just killed them, all those people, you and that Salvation Army you organized, as if they weren't bad enough on their own."

And in his eyes, the question. The how.

Still, forever the unspoken how: when it was only why that mattered: how did you do it, how did you train them, how are you different? Weakness, calling to weakness, *made* for it, weak himself unto a loathing so pure it had gone for so long unrecognized that it became part of his body, his inner skin, did no one understand what it was to be *nothing*? "I did it for them," he said, and felt the truth of it, elemental as the taste itself; but how explain the helpless beauty of smell to the noseless and the blind?

Leaning down, now, and close, right in his face like they never did. "Who the hell do you think you are, anyway? Jesus? The Second Coming? If Jesus saw you he would puke. You killed people, and you ate them, and you knew what you were doing! All the time!"

And did he realize, that young doctor, did he begin to understand how the sudden fresh gust of his scent was in and of itself so incredible, so overwhelming, that those angry words were lost in it, contempt drowned delicious in the river of that smell, he was so *close*—

"God, *look* at you!" in new horror and disgust, actually leaping back, away, far away so his scent dwindled to a faint sweet ribbon, gone entirely when he left the room.

And left behind, abashed, his mouth weeping helpless drool, to turn his trembling head away.

To sink into nervous proto-dreams, thrashing against the restraints to rejoin his people, whom he had tried to save, empower by emptiness: his happy twice-dead people in the painless landscape of Nox, a heaven of endless night unfolding now before him in the space behind his eyes as in the cubicles and offices beyond his room that day's conclusions, findings, results unto minutiae were entered into list after list, as the lights above his twisting body glowed continuous blue, a pitiless illumination for his helplessness and grief, extinguished by immortality to the status of the everlasting dead.

Call Me Doctor

BY **ERIC SHAPIRO**

Eric Shapiro is a new guy on the scene, writing psychological horror of unusual probity. He first came to my attention with immaculately observed end-of-the-world small-press novellas like It's Only Temporary *and* The Strawberry Man *(for which I was proud to write the intro).*

Since then, I've seen his ultra-low-budget directorial debut, The Rule of Three, *which only served to confirm my suspicions that Eric Shapiro is a new guy worth watching.*

With "Call Me Doctor," *he brings his meticulous verbal acuity to a short-short that's akin to a series of snapshots, laid out across your desk, giving you the worst of it with no chaser whatsoever. Just a lingering feeling that the worst has only begun.*

BY NATURE, YOU ARE NOT A MAN OF ACTION.

You were the one, in the classroom, who sat and watched quietly.

You were the one whom the teachers suspected were judging them. Their perceptions were accurate. You knew you were brighter.

And yet, although the world contains men of mind, it remains a thing of action, and so—

—you're going to drive to the house on the red rock street.

You're going to come to a modest, stout home. You'll be wearing a suit, this in spite of the sun. You'll be dressed like New York, even though it's New Mexico. You will knock at the door; your heart will knock at your chest. Mrs. Gomez will greet you. She will hold out her arms.

Your eyes will bear the iced tea. They will bear the wall clock. They will bear all of the things of the Gomez abode, provided that you don't have to look at one thing. It is chafing and moist. It's what brought you here.

Not for you were the jobs where you woke with the sun. Not for you was the life where the cuff links just clinked. For your cuff links *chime*. For you is red wine. For you are the evenings when your wallet squares off with the city.

And the wife, yes. All yours. Without her, you might have misplaced your heart. For she's the one who nods and says, "You can do this, Max. You can go on."

And says, "I love you."

And, "I believe in your mission."

Your trainers, too, they believed in the mission. On a practical level, it makes excellent sense. The ones who bear the virus are to be your central targets. For to let them beat the virus is to let them spread it 'round.

And to let it be spread is to let us fall dead.

For you, then, came the gun, came the holster, came the badge. Came the dark glasses. The headaches. The hundred-hour nights.

But you will still chat with Mrs. Gomez. You will chat with Mrs. Gomez, and you will look her (*anywhere*) in the eye (*but there*).

You will chat with Mrs. Gomez because you know that there are cabinets in your kitchen. And you know that those cabinets are meaningless without the fluff of bread upon their shelves.

And to get the bread, you must perform the task.

"Finish your drink!"

This is Mrs. Gomez. Her mouth's deformed. It's a nice deformity; they call it a "smile." But it doesn't belong there. It was born out of lies. Like the ones which emanate from your bedside-manner mouth:

"You'll be fine in several days . . ."

This you say, despite your gut.

"Fortunately, our new medicinal supplements can cut this off at the pass . . ."

This you recite, courtesy of the manual.

Despite the gun at your breastbone.

And the false label screaming from your badge.

"Doctor?" you asked him.

"Doctor," he said.

You looked at your badge. Then back at your trainer. You said to him, "But how can . . . ?"

"We have the authority."

A grin 'round his lips. A pat at your shoulder. As he walked off, whistling.

No medical school, not for one single day. And yet they called you doctor, these people. *All* people. The ones at the firm. At the town hall gatherings. All around your lime-grass neighborhood.

And needless to say, in the dim swell of those living rooms where you chattered, week after week after week . . .

The room now, again. The tea and the woman. Your keys shining like fallen moon shards.

"Those men," Mrs. Gomez says, "they came into my yard."

But those men were not men; they were viruses walking. For them was true gray, of an everlasting shade. Stuffed in their non-minds like aging hot cotton.

She explains, "They bit me *here.*"

And shows you her leg. She could've risked stockings, but that's have been risking pain. Your eyes, they seek the wall, the curtains. But you're a doctor, so you have to look.

"Mrs. Gomez," you say, because you have to say something.

But that wound, it speaks louder, saying nothing at all. It is, one could say, like a chain-hole with meat. The chain: her bone. The meat: her flesh. The color: off-blackness. The spots: conjunctivitis pink.

You stand. Make more eye contact. It's safe up here. You're going to have to inhale before you can speak.

"It's nothing" *(it's)* "we haven't" *(getting worse)* "seen before."

She hasn't a sense of your lies.

Two days till the grayness would descend down upon her. Soon an upright corpse where the widow once walked.

Yet you wept on the night of your first assignment. His name won't escape you: it was Mr. Lyons. The name of a restaurant where you order the eggs. A widower, parallel to Gomez.

Would she be your last, just as he was your first?

You seek out such symmetries because you know the world is mad.

You can stick a fork in a bowl of water. You can thrust religion toward the mystery of dying. You can launch hard science at the face of unreason.

But the face will stay there, smiling. And wink.

The moment, now, finally.

Your mind leaves the living room, goes to fields of the night. Fields of flat-button eyeballs and reaching, cracked hands.

Mrs. Gomez speaks of flowers. The garden out back, it will summon her soon. When she's back from her treatments—

Reach for your gun, one upward slash of your hand. Mrs. Gomez: not scared, nor shocked, nor confused, for there is simply not enough time. That's how good you've gotten.

Clean snap, through the frontal lobe.

Where the bone is less thick.

It's what they taught you.

Doctor . . .

It's always quiet, the nighttime ride. No other cars care to dare the roads. Sometimes you rebel, though the light isn't green. Oftentimes, though, you stop, as expected.

And bear the crickets, the creaking, the wind.

Please now reach for yourself, though—for the strength which you bear. The might which bore the still of the womb.

Cruise now with confidence, beside leafy roads, and past fields upon which lone lights shudder, squat middle schools seated in the empty dark. Ponder the little towns on the way back to your own, and wonder at the lives and near-lives beneath those roofs.

Your wife: think of her, also. She awaits you in bed. Although she is sleeping, in her heart is a wait. Go to her, briskly, for she will save you.

Pray to arrive with the sun.

And to someday stop being the monster you've become.

Great Wall: A Story from the Zombie War

by **Max Brooks**

I gotta say, the greatest literary revelation I've experienced while perusing the latest in zombie fiction is World War Z *by Max Brooks, hands down. It's the biggest, broadest, best sustained and gamut-spanning single-author zombie work in the history of the written word. I shit you not. If ever a book deserved to be a huge best seller, this is it. I was utterly floored by that thing.*

And the element that stunned me most was its fluent internationalism: its ability to not just recognize the danger as a global pandemic, but then meticulously play it out across a staggering range of multinational lines.

I plowed through that thing like a geek through gray matter, jaw agape and giddy heart soaring, trying to find the "interview" I'd most want to include in Zombies. *But the simple fact is, there's not a single part I wouldn't want to include in* Zombies.

So I'm particularly thrilled to present a rare "deleted scene" from World War Z: *a chapter Max loved, but which hit the proverbial cutting-room floor in the final edit, as so many great scenes do.*

THE FOLLOWING INTERVIEW was conducted by the author as part of his official duties with the United Nations Commission for postwar data collection. Although excerpts have appeared in official UN reports, the interview in its entirety was omitted from Brook's personal publication, now entitled *World War Z* due to bureaucratic mismanagement by UN archivists. The following is a first-hand account of a survivor of the great crisis many now refer to simply as "The Zombie War."

THE GREAT WALL: SECTION 3947-B, SHAANXI, CHINA

Liu Huafeng began her career as a sales girl at the Takashimaya department store in Taiyuan and now owns a small general store near the sight of its former location. This weekend, as with the first weekend of every month, is her reserve duty. Armed with a radio, a flare gun, binoculars, and a DaDao, a modernized version of the ancient Chinese broadsword, she patrols her five-kilometer stretch of the Great Wall with nothing but the "the wind and my memories" for company.

This section of the Wall, the section I worked on, stretches from Yulin to Shemnu. It had originally been built by the Xia Dynasty, constructed of compacted sand and reed-lined earth encased on both sides by a thick outer shell of fired mud brick. It never appeared on any tourist postcards. It could never have hoped to rival sections of the Ming-Era, iconic stone "dragon spine." It was dull and functional, and by the time we began the reconstruction, it had almost completely vanished.

Thousands years of erosion; storms and desertification, had taken a drastic toll. The effects of human "progress" had been equally destructive. Over the centuries, locals had used—looted—its bricks for building materials. Modern road construction had done its part, too, removing entire sections that interfered with "vital" overland traffic. And, of course, what nature and peacetime development had begun, the crisis, the infestation and the subsequent civil war finished within the course of several months. In some places, all that was left were crumbling hummocks of compact filler. In many places, there was nothing at all.

I didn't know about the new government's plan to restore the Great Wall for our national defense. At first, I didn't even know I was part of the effort. In those early days, there were so many different people, languages, local dialects that they could have been birdsong for all the sense it made to me. The night I arrived, all you could see were torches and headlights of a few broken-down cars. I had been walking for nine days by this point. I was tired, frightened. I didn't know what I had found at first, only that the scurrying shapes in front of me were human. I don't know how long I stood there, but someone on a work gang spotted me. He ran over and started to chatter excitedly. I tried to show him that I didn't understand. He became frustrated, pointing at what looked like a construction sight behind him, a mass of activity that stretched left and right out into the darkness. Again, I shook my head, gesturing to my ears and shrugging like a fool. He sighed angrily, then raised his hand toward me. I saw he was holding a brick. I thought he was going to hit me with it so I started to back away. He then shoved the brick in my hands, motioned to the construction sight, and shoved me toward it.

I got within arm's length of the nearest worker before he snatched the brick away. This man was from Taiyuan. I understood him clearly. "Well, what the fuck are you waiting for?" He snarled at me, "We need more! Go! Go!" And that is how I was "recruited" to work on the new Great Wall of China.

(She gestures to the uniform concrete edifice.)

It didn't look at all like this that first frantic spring. What you are seeing are the subsequent renovations and reinforcements that adhere to late and postwar standards. We didn't have anything close to these materials back then. Most of our surviving infrastructure was trapped on the wrong side of the wall.

On the south side?

Yes, on the side that used to be safe, on the side that the Wall . . . that every Wall, from the Xia to the Ming was originally built to protect. The walls used to be a border between the haves and have-nots, between southern prosperity and northern barbarism. Even in modern times, certainly in this part of the country, most of our arable land, as well as our factories, our roads, rail lines and airstrips, almost everything we needed to undertake such a monumental task, was on the wrong side.

I've heard that some industrial machinery was transported north during the evacuation.

Only what could be carried on foot, and only what was in immediate proximity to the construction sight. Nothing farther than, say, twenty kilometers, nothing beyond the immediate battle lines or the isolated zones deep in infested territory.

The most valuable resource we could take from the nearby towns were the materials used to construct the towns themselves: wood, metal, cinder blocks, bricks—some of the very same bricks that had originally been pilfered from the wall. All of it went into the mad patchwork, mixed in with what could be manufactured quickly on sight. We used timber from the Great Green Wall* reforestation project, pieces of furniture and abandoned vehicles. Even the desert sand beneath our feet was mixed with rubble to form part of the core or else refined and heated for blocks of glass.

Glass?

Large, like so . . . [*she draws an imaginary shape in the air, roughly twenty centimeters in length, width and depth*]. An engineer from Shijiazhuang had the idea. Before the war, he had owned a glass factory, and he realized that since this province's most abundant resources are coal and sand, why not use them both? A massive industry sprung up almost overnight, to manufacture thousands of these large, cloudy bricks. They were thick and heavy, impervious to a zombie's soft, naked fist. "Stronger than flesh" we used say, and, unfortunately for us, much sharper—sometimes the glazier's assistants would forget to sand down the edges before laying them out for transport.

(*She pries her hand from the hilt of her sword. The fingers remain curled like a claw. A deep, white scar runs down the width of one palm.*)

I didn't know to wrap my hands. It cut right through to the bone, severed the nerves. I don't know how I didn't die of infection; so many others did.

It was a brutal, frenzied existence. We knew that every day brought the southern hordes closer, and that any second we delayed might doom the entire effort. We slept, if we did sleep, where we worked. We ate where we worked, pissed and shit right where we worked. Children—the Night Soil Cubs—

*The Great Green Wall: a prewar environmental restoration project intended to halt desertification.

would hurry by with a bucket, wait while we did our business or else collect our previously discarded filth. We worked like animals, lived like animals. In my dreams I see a thousand faces, the people I worked with but never knew. There wasn't time for social interaction. We spoke mainly in hand gestures and grunts. In my dreams I try to find the time to speak to those alongside me, ask their names, their stories. I have heard that dreams are only in black and white. Perhaps that is true, perhaps I only remember the colors later, the light fringes of a girl whose hair had once been dyed green, or the soiled pink woman's bathrobe wrapped around a frail old man in tattered silken pajamas. I see their faces almost every night, only the faces of the fallen.

So many died. Someone working at your side would sit down for a moment, just a second to catch their breath, and never rise again. We had what could be described as a medical detail, orderlies with stretchers. There was nothing they could really do except try to get them to the aid station. Most of the time they didn't make it. I carry their suffering, and my shame with me each and every day.

Your shame?

As they sat, or lay at your feet . . . you knew you couldn't stop what you were doing, not even for a little compassion, a few kind words, at least make them comfortable enough to wait for the medics. You knew the one thing they wanted, what we all wanted, was water. Water was precious in this part of the province, and almost all we had was used for mixing ingredients into mortar. We were given less than half a cup a day. I carried mine around my neck in a recycled plastic soda bottle. We were under strict orders not to share our ration with the sick and injured. We needed it to keep ourselves working. I understand the logic, but to see someone's broken body curled up amongst the tools and rubble, knowing that the only mercy under heaven was just a little sip of water . . .

I feel guilty every time I think about it, every time I quench my thirst, especially because when it came my time to die, I happened, by sheer chance, to be near the aid station. I was on glass detail, part of the long, human conveyor to and from the kilns. I had been on the project for just under two months; I was starving, feverish, I weighed less than the bricks hanging from either side of my pole. As I turned to pass the bricks, I stumbled, landing on my face, I felt my two front teeth crack and tasted the blood. I closed my eyes and thought, *This is my time.* I was ready. I wanted it to end. If the orderlies hadn't been passing by, my wish would have been granted.

For three days, I lived in shame; resting, washing, drinking as much water as I wanted while others were suffering every second on the wall. The doctors told me that I should stay a few extra days, the bare minimum to allow my body to recuperate. I would have listened if I didn't hear the shouts from an orderly at the mouth of the cave,

"Red Flare!" he was calling. "Red Flare!"

Green flares meant an active assault, red meant overwhelming numbers. Reds had been uncommon, up until that point. I had only seen one, and that was far in the distance near the northern edge of Shemnu. Now they were coming at least once a week. I raced out of the cave, ran all the way back to my section, just in time to see rotting hands and heads begin to poke their way above the unfinished ramparts.

[*We halt. She looks down at the stones beneath out feet.*]

Here, right here. They were forming a ramp, using their trodden comrades for elevation. The workers were fending them off with whatever they could, tools and bricks, even bare fists and feet. I grabbed a rammer, an implement used for compacting earth. The rammer is an immense, unruly device, a meter-long metal shaft with horizontal handlebars on one end and a large, cylindrical, supremely heavy stone on the other. The rammer was reserved only for largest and strongest men in our work gang. I don't know how I managed to lift, aim, and bring it crashing down, over and over, on the heads and faces of the zombies below me . . .

The military was supposed to be protecting us from overrun attacks like these, but there just weren't enough soldiers left by that time.

[*She takes me to the edge of the battlements and points to something roughly a kilometer south of us.*]

There.

[*In the distance, I can just make out a stone obelisk rising from an earthen mound.*]

Underneath that mound is one of our garrison's last main battle tanks. The crew had run out of fuel and was using it as a pillbox. When they ran out of ammunition, they sealed the hatches and prepared to trap themselves as bait. They held on long after their food ran out and their canteens ran dry. "Fight on!" they would cry over their hand-cranked radio, "Finish the wall! Protect our people! Finish the wall!" The last of them, the seventeen-year-old driver held out for thirty-one days. You couldn't even see the tank by then, buried under a small mountain of zombies that suddenly moved away as they sensed that boy's last breath.

By that time, we had almost finished our section of the Great Wall, but the isolated attacks were ending, and the massive, ceaseless, million-strong assault swarms began. If we had had to contend with those numbers in the beginning, if the heroes of the southern cities hadn't shed their blood to buy us time . . .

The new government knew it had to distance itself from the one it had just overthrown. It had to establish some kind of legitimacy with our people, and the only way to do that was to speak the truth. The isolated zones weren't "tricked" into becoming decoys like in so many other countries. They were asked, openly and honestly, to remain behind while others fled. It would be a personal choice, one that every citizen would have to make for themselves. My mother, she made it for me.

We had been hiding on the second floor of what used to be our five-bedroom house in what used to be one of Taiyuan's most exclusive suburban enclaves. My little brother was dying, bitten when my father had sent him out to look for food. He was lying in my parent's bed, shaking, unconscious. My father was sitting by his side, rocking slowly back and forth. Every few minutes he would call out to us. "He's getting better! See, feel his forehead. He's getting better!" The refugee train was passing right by our house. Civil Defense Deputies were checking each door to find out who was going and who was staying. My mother already had a small bag of my things packed; clothes, food, a good pair of walking shoes, my father's pistol with the last three bullets. She was combing my hair in the mirror, the way she used to do when I was a little girl. She told me to stop crying and that some day soon they would rejoin me up north. She had that smile, that frozen, lifeless smile she only showed for father and his friends. She had it for me now, as I lowered myself down our broken staircase.

[*Liu pauses, takes a breath, and lets her claw rest on the hard stone.*]

Three months, that is how long it took us to complete the entire Great Wall. From Jingtai in the western mountains to the Great Dragon head on the Shanhaiguan Sea. It was never breached, never overrun. It gave us the breathing space we needed to finally consolidate our population and construct a wartime economy. We were the last country to adopt the Redeker Plan, so long after the rest of the world, and just in time for the Honolulu Conference. So much time; so many lives, all wasted. If the Three Gorges Dam hadn't collapsed, if that other wall hadn't fallen, would we have resurrected this one? Who knows. Both are monuments to our shortsightedness, our arrogance, our disgrace.

They say that so many workers died building the original walls that a human life was lost for every mile. I don't know if that it was true of that time . . .

(*Her claw pats the stone.*)

But it is now.

Calcutta, Lord of Nerves

by Poppy Z. Brite

If I were to have to pick one reason why "Calcutta, Lord of Nerves" *is one of the most oft-reprinted zombie stories of all time—and deservedly so—it would probably be this:*

What Max Brooks accomplished broadly with the whole of World War Z, *Poppy Z. Brite compressed into one shimmering, pulsating, multifaceted gem of South Asian exotica: less a story than a stunning travelogue, dripping with sensual detail so ripe you can taste it, ripping the average Western reader far away from familiar zombie stomping grounds and into a landscape so alien-yet-utterly-grounded that the sense of transcendence—in the moment-to-moment—comes almost as naturally as breathing.*

(Of course, some guy from Calcutta would probably just shrug and mutter, "About fucking time!")

Would that there were a thousand stories that accomplished the magnitude of what Poppy does here, from a thousand nations. But as of this writing, that's just not the case.

Which is to say, there's just nothing else like it.

And this is how legends are born.

I WAS BORN IN A NORTH CALCUTTA HOSPITAL in the heart of an Indian midnight just before the beginning of the monsoon season. The air hung heavy as wet velvet over the Hooghly River, offshoot of the holy Ganga, and the stumps of banyan trees on the Upper Chitpur Road were flecked with dots of phosphorus like the ghosts of flames. I was as dark as the new moon in the sky, and I cried very little. I feel as if I remember this, because this is the way it must have been.

My mother died in labor, and later that night the hospital burned to the ground. (I have no reason to connect the two incidents; then again, I have no reason not to. Perhaps a desire to live burned on in my mother's heart. Perhaps the flames were fanned by her hatred for me, the insignificant mewling infant that had killed her.) A nurse carried me out of the roaring husk of the building and laid me in my father's arms. He cradled me, numb with grief.

My father was American. He had come to Calcutta five years earlier, on business. There he had fallen in love with my mother and, like a man who will not pluck a flower from its garden, he could not bear to see her removed from the hot, lush, squalid city that had spawned her. It was part of her exotica. So my father stayed in Calcutta. Now his flower was gone. He pressed his thin chapped lips to the satin of my hair. I remember opening my eyes—they felt tight and shiny, parched by the flames—and looking up at the column of smoke that roiled into the sky, a night sky blasted cloudy pink like a sky full of blood and milk.

There would be no milk for me, only chemical-tasting drops of formula from a plastic nipple. The morgue was in the basement of the hospital and did not burn. My mother lay on a metal table, a hospital gown stiff with her dying sweat pulled up over her red-smeared crotch and thighs. Her eyes stared up through the blackened skeleton of the hospital, up to the milky bloody sky, and ash filtered down to mask her pupils.

My father and I left for America before the monsoon came. Without my mother Calcutta was a pestilential hellhole, a vast cremation grounds, or so my father thought. In America he could send me to school and movies, ball games and Boy Scouts, secure in the knowledge that someone else would take care of me or I would take care of myself. There were no *thuggees* to rob me and cut my throat, no *goondas* who would snatch me and sell my bones for fertilizer. There were no cows to infect the streets with their steaming sacred piss. My father could give me over to the comparative wholesomeness of American life, leaving himself free to sit in his darkened bedroom and drink whiskey until his long sensitive nose floated hazily in front of his face and the sabre edge of his grief began to dull. He was the sort of man who has only one love in his lifetime, and knows with the sick fervor of a fatalist that this love will be taken from him someday, and is hardly surprised when it happens.

When he was drunk he would talk about Calcutta. My little American mind rejected the place—I was in love with air-conditioning, hamburgers and pizza, the free and undiscriminating love that was lavished upon me every time I twisted the TV dial—but somewhere in my Indian heart I longed for it. When I turned eighteen and my father finally failed to wake up from one of his drunken stupors, I returned to the city of my bloody birth as soon as I had the plane fare in my hand.

Calcutta, you will say. What a place to have been when the dead began to walk.

And I reply, what better place to be? What better place than a city where five million people look as if they are already dead—might as well be dead—and another five million wish they were?

I have a friend named Devi, a prostitute who began her work at the age of fifteen from a tarpaper shack on Sudder Street. Sudder is the Bourbon Street of Calcutta, but there is far less of the carnival there, and no one wears a mask on Sudder Street because disguises are useless when shame is irrelevant. Devi works the big hotels now, selling American tourists or British expatriates or German businessmen a taste of exotic Bengal spice. She is gaunt and beautiful and hard as nails. Devi says the world is a whore, too, and Calcutta is the pussy of the world. The world squats and spreads its legs, and Calcutta is the dank sex you see revealed there, wet and fragrant with a thousand odors both delicious and foul. A source of lushest pleasure, a breeding ground for every conceivable disease.

The pussy of the world. It is all right with me. I like pussy, and I love my squalid city.

The dead like pussy, too. If they are able to catch a woman and disable her enough so that she cannot resist, you will see the lucky ones burrowing in between her legs as happily as the most avid lover. They do not have to come up for air. I have seen them eat all the way up into the body cavity. The internal female organs seem to be a great delicacy, and why not? They are the caviar of the human body. It is a sobering thing to come across a woman sprawled in the gutter with her intestines sliding from the shredded ruin of her womb, but you do not react. You do not distract the dead from their repast. They are slow and stupid, but that is all the more reason for you to be smart and quick and quiet. They will do the same thing to a man—chew off the soft penis and scrotal sac like choice morsels of squid, leaving only a red raw hole. But you can sidle by while they are feeding and they will not notice you. I do not try to hide from them. I walk the streets and look; that is all I do anymore. I am fascinated. This is not horror, this is simply more of Calcutta.

First I would sleep late, through the sultry morning into the heat of the afternoon. I had a room in one of the decrepit marble palaces of the old city. Devi visited me here often, but on a typical morning I woke alone, clad only in twisted bedsheets and a luxurious patina of sweat. Sun came through the window and fell in bright bars across the floor. I felt safe in my second-story room as long as I kept the door locked. The dead were seldom able to navigate stairs, and they could not manage the sustained cooperative effort to break down a locked door. They were no threat to me. They fed upon those who had given up, those too traumatized to keep running: the senile, abandoned old, the catatonic young women who sat in gutters cradling babies that had died during the night. These were easy prey.

The walls of my room were painted a bright coral and the sills and door were aqua. The colors caught the sun and made the day seem cheerful despite the heat that shimmered outside. I went downstairs, crossed the empty courtyard with its dry marble fountain, and went out into the street. This area was barren in· the heat, painfully bright, with parched weeds lining the road and an occasional smear of cow dung decorating the gutter. By nightfall both weeds and dung might be gone. Children collected cow shit and patted it into cakes held together with straw, which could be sold as fuel for cooking fires.

I headed toward Chowringhee Road, the broad main thoroughfare of the city. Halfway up my street, hunched under the awning of a mattress factory, I saw one of the catatonic young mothers. The dead had found her, too. They had already taken the baby from her arms and eaten through the soft part at the top of the skull. Vacuous bloody faces rose and dipped. Curds of tender brain fell from slack mouths. The mother sat on the curb nearby, her arms cradling nothing. She wore a filthy green sari that was ripped across the chest. The woman's breasts protruded heavily, swollen with milk. When the dead finished with her baby they would start on her, and she would make no resistance. I had seen it before. I knew how the milk would spurt and then gush as they tore into her breasts. I knew how hungrily they would lap up the twin rivers of blood and milk.

Above their bobbing heads, the tin awning dripped long ropy strands of cotton. Cotton hung from the roof in dirty clumps, caught in the corners of the doorway like spiderweb. Someone's radio blared faintly in another part of the building, tuned to an English-language Christian broadcast. A gospel hymn assured Calcutta that its dead in Christ would rise. I moved on toward Chowringhee.

Most of the streets in the city are positively cluttered with buildings. Buildings are packed in cheek-by-jowl, helter-skelter, like books of different sizes jammed into a rickety bookcase. Buildings even sag over the street so that all you see overhead is a narrow strip of sky crisscrossed by miles of clotheslines. The flapping silks and cottons are very bright against the sodden, dirty sky. But there are certain vantage points where the city opens up and all at once you have a panoramic view of Calcutta. You see a long muddy hillside that has become home to a *bustee*, thousands and thousands of slum dwellings where tiny fires are tended through the night. The dead come often to these slums of tin and cardboard, but the people do not leave the *bustee*—where would they go? Or you see a wasteland of disused factories, empty warehouses, blackened smokestacks jutting into a rust-colored sky. Or a flash of the Hooghly River, steel-gray in its shroud of mist, spanned by the intricate girder-and-wirescape of the Howrah Bridge.

Just now I was walking opposite the river. The waterfront was not considered a safe place because of the danger from drowning victims. Thousands each year took the long plunge off the bridge, and thousands more simply waded into the water. It is easy to commit suicide at a riverfront because despair collects in the water vapor. This is part of the reason for the tangible cloud of despair that hangs over Calcutta along with its veil of humidity.

Now the suicides and the drowned street children were coming out of the river. At any moment the water might regurgitate one, and you would hear him scrabbling up the bank. If he had been in the water long enough he might tear himself to spongy gobbets on the stones and broken bricks that littered the waterfront; all that remained would be a trace of foul brown odor, like the smell of mud from the deep part of the river.

Police—especially the Sikhs, who are said to be more violent than Hindus—had been taking the dead up on the bridge to shoot them. Even from far away I could see spray-patterns of red on the drab girders. Alternately they set the dead alight with gasoline and threw them over the railing into the river. At night it was not uncommon to see several writhing shapes caught in the downstream current, the fiery symmetry of their heads and arms and legs making them into five-pointed human stars.

I stopped at a spice vendor's stand to buy a bunch of red chrysanthemums and a handful of saffron. The saffron I had him wrap in a twist of scarlet silk. "It is a beautiful day," I said to him in Bengali. He stared at me, half amused, half appalled. "A beautiful day for what?"

True Hindu faith calls upon the believer to view all things as equally sacred. There is nothing profane—no dirty dog picking through the ash bin at a cremation ground, no stinking gangrenous stump thrust into your face by a beggar who seems to hold you personally responsible for all his woes. These things are as sacred as feasting day at the holiest temple. But even for the most devout Hindus it has been difficult to see these walking dead as sacred. They are empty humans. That is the truly horrifying thing about them, more than their vacuous hunger for living flesh, more than the blood caked under their nails or the shreds of flesh caught between their teeth. They are soulless; there is nothing in their eyes; the sounds they make—their farts, their grunts and mewls of hunger—are purely reflexive. The Hindu, who has been taught to believe in the soul of everything, has a particular horror of these drained human vessels. But in Calcutta life goes on. The shops are still open. The confusion of traffic still inches its way up Chowringhee. No one sees any alternatives.

Soon I arrived at what was almost invariably my day's first stop. I would often walk twenty or thirty miles in a day—I had strong shoes and nothing to occupy my time except walking and looking. But I always began at the Kaalighat, temple of the Goddess.

There are a million names for her, a million vivid descriptions: Kali the Terrible, Kali the Ferocious, skull-necklace, destroyer of men, eater of souls. But to me she was Mother Kali, the only one of the vast and colorful pantheon of Hindu gods that stirred my imagination and lifted my heart. She was the Destroyer, but all final refuge was found in her. She was the goddess of the age. She could bleed and burn and still rise again, very awake, beautifully terrible.

I ducked under the garlands of marigolds and strands of temple bells strung across the door, and I entered the temple of Kali. After the constant clamor of the street, the silence inside the temple was deafening. I fancied I could hear the small noises of my body echoing back to me from the ceiling far above. The sweet opium glaze of incense curled around my head. I approached the idol of Kali, the *jagrata*. Her gimlet eyes watched me as I came closer.

She was tall, gaunter and more brazenly naked than my friend Devi even at her best moments. Her breasts were tipped with blood—at least I always imagined them so—and her two sharp fangs and the long streamer of a tongue that uncurled from her open mouth were the color of blood, too. Her hair whipped about her head and her eyes were wild, but the third crescent eye in the center of her forehead was merciful; it saw and accepted all. The necklace of skulls circled the graceful stem of her neck, adorned the sculpted hollow of her throat. Her four arms were so sinuous that if you looked away even for an instant, they seemed to sway. In her four hands she held a noose of rope, a skull-staff, a shining sword, and a gaping, very dead-looking severed head. A silver bowl sat at the foot of the statue just beneath the head, where the blood from the neck would drip. Sometimes this was filled with goat's or sheep's blood as an offering. The bowl was full today. In these times the blood might well be human, though there was no putrid smell to indicate it had come from one of the dead.

I laid my chrysanthemums and saffron at Kali' s feet. Among the other offerings, mostly sweets and bundles of spice, I saw a few strange objects. A fingerbone. A shrivelled mushroom of flesh that turned out upon closer inspection to be an ear. These were offerings for special protection, mostly wrested from the dead. But who was to say that a few devotees had not lopped off their own ears or finger joints to coax a boon from Kali? Sometimes when I had forgotten to bring an offering, I cut my wrist with a razor blade and let a few drops of my blood fall at the idol's feet.

I heard a shout from outside and turned my head for a moment. When I looked back, the four arms seemed to have woven themselves into a new pattern, the long tongue seemed to loll farther from the scarlet mouth. And—this was a frequent fantasy of mine—the wide hips now seemed to tilt forward, affording me a glimpse of the sweet and terrible petalled cleft between the thighs of the goddess.

I smiled up at the lovely sly face. "If only I had a tongue as long as yours, Mother," I murmured, "I would kneel before you and lick the folds of your holy pussy until you screamed with joy." The toothy grin seemed to grow wider, more lascivious. I imagined much in the presence of Kali.

Outside in the temple yard I saw the source of the shout I had heard. There is a stone block upon which the animals brought to Kali, mostly baby goats, are beheaded by the priests. A gang of roughly dressed men had captured a dead girl and were bashing her head in on the sacrificial block. Their arms rose and fell, ropy muscles flexing. They clutched sharp stones and bits of brick in their scrawny hands. The girl's half-pulped head still lashed back and forth. The lower jaw still snapped, though the teeth and bone were splintered. Foul thin blood coursed down and mingled with the rich animal blood in the earth beneath the block. The girl was nude, filthy with her own gore and waste. The flaccid breasts hung as if sucked dry of meat. The belly was burst open with gases. One of the men thrust a stick into the ruined gouge between the girl's legs and leaned on it with all his weight.

Only in extensive stages of decay can the dead be told from the lepers.

The dead are greater in number now, and even the lepers look human when compared to the dead. But that is only if you get close enough to look into the eyes. The faces in various stages of wet and dry rot, the raw ends of bones rubbing through skin like moldy cheesecloth, the cancerous domes of the skulls are the same. After a certain point lepers could no longer stay alive begging in the streets, for most people would now flee in terror at the sight of a rotting face. As a result the lepers were dying, then coming back, and the two races mingled like some obscene parody of incest. Perhaps they actually could breed. The dead could obviously eat and digest, and seemed to excrete at random like everyone else in Calcutta, but I supposed no one knew whether they could ejaculate or conceive.

A stupid idea, really. A dead womb would rot to pieces around a fetus before it could come halfway to term; a dead scrotal sac would be far too cold a cradle for living seed. But no one seemed to know anything about the biology of the dead. The newspapers were hysterical, printing picture upon picture of random slaughter by dead and living alike. Radio stations had either gone off the air or were broadcasting endless religious exhortations that ran together in one long keening whine, the edges of Muslim, Hindu, Christian doctrine beginning to fray and blur.

No one in India could say for sure what made the dead walk. The latest theory I had heard was something about a genetically engineered microbe that had been designed to feed on plastic: a microbe that would save the world from its own waste. But the microbe had mutated and was now eating and "replicating" human cells, causing basic bodily functions to reactivate. It did not much matter whether this was true. Calcutta was a city relatively unsurprised to see its dead rise and walk and feed upon it. It had seen them doing so for a hundred years.

All the rest of the lengthening day I walked through the city. I saw no more dead except a cluster far away at the end of a blocked street, in the last rags of bloody light, fighting each other over the bloated carcass of a sacred cow.

My favorite place at sunset is by the river where I can see the Howrah Bridge. The Hooghly is painfully beautiful in the light of the setting sun. The last rays melt onto the water like hot *ghee*, turning the river from steel to khaki to nearly golden, a blazing ribbon of light. The bridge rises black and skeletal into the fading orange sky. Tonight an occasional skid of bright flowers and still-glowing greasy embers floated by, the last earthly traces of bodies cremated farther up the river. Above the bridge were the burning *ghats* where families lined up to incinerate their dead and cast the ashes into the holy river. Cremation is done more efficiently these days, or at least more hurriedly. People can reconcile in their hearts their fear of strangers' dead, but they do not want to see their own dead rise.

I walked along the river for a while. The wind off the water carried the scent of burning meat. When I was well away from the bridge, I wandered back into the maze of narrow streets and alleyways that lead toward the docks in the far southern end of the city. People were already beginning to settle in for the night, though here a bedroom might mean your own packing crate or your own square of sidewalk. Fires glowed in nooks and corners. A warm breeze still blew off the river and sighed its way through the winding streets. It seemed very late now. As I made my way from corner to corner, through intermittent pools of light and much longer patches of darkness, I heard small bells jingling to the rhythm of my footsteps. The brass bells of rickshaw men, ringing to tell me they were there in case I wished for a ride. But I could see none of the men. The effect was eerie, as if I were walking alone down an empty nighttime street being serenaded by ghostly bells. The feeling soon passed. You are never truly alone in Calcutta.

A thin hand slid out of the darkness as I passed. Looking into the doorway it came from, I could barely make out five gaunt faces, five forms huddled against the night. I dropped several coins into the hand and it slid out of sight again. I am seldom begged from. I look neither rich nor poor, but I have a talent for making myself all but invisible. People look past me, sometimes right through me. I don't mind; I see more things that way. But when I am begged from I always give. With my handful of coins, all five of them might have a bowl of rice and lentils tomorrow.

A bowl of rice and lentils in the morning, a drink of water from a broken standpipe at night.

It seemed to me that the dead were among the best-fed citizens of Calcutta.

Now I crossed a series of narrow streets and was surprised to find myself coming up behind the Kalighat. The side streets are so haphazardly arranged that you are constantly finding yourself in places you had no idea you were even near. I had been to the Kalighat hundreds of times, but I had never approached it from this direction. The temple was dark and still. I had not been here at this hour before, did not even know whether the priests were still here or if one could enter so late. But as I walked closer I saw a little door standing open at the back. The entrance used by the priests, perhaps. Something flickered from within: a candle, a tiny mirror sewn on a robe, the smoldering end of a stick of incense.

I slipped around the side of the temple and stood at the door for a moment. A flight of stone steps led up into the darkness of the temple. The Kalighat at night, deserted, might have been an unpleasant prospect to some. The thought of facing the fierce idol alone in the gloom might have made some turn away from those steps. I began to climb them.

The smell reached me before I ascended halfway. To spend a day walking through Calcutta is to be assailed by thousands of odors both pleasant and foul: the savor of spices frying in *ghee*, the stink of shit and urine and garbage, the sick-sweet scent of the little white flowers called *mogra* that are sold in garlands and that make me think of the gardenia perfume American undertakers use to mask the smell of their corpses.

Almost everyone in Calcutta is scrupulously clean in person, even the very poor. They will leave their trash and their spit everywhere, but many of them wash their bodies twice a day. Still, everyone sweats under the sodden veil of heat, and at midday any public place will be redolent with the smell of human perspiration, a delicate tang like the mingled juices of lemons and onions. But lingering in the stairwell was an odor stronger and more foul than any I had encountered today. It was deep and brown and moist; it curled at the edges like a mushroom beginning to dry. It was the perfume of mortal corruption. It was the smell of rotting flesh.

Then I came up into the temple, and I saw them.

The large central room was lit only with candles that flickered in a restless draft, first this way, then that. In the dimness the worshippers looked no different from any other supplicants at the feet of Kali. But as my eyes grew accustomed to the candlelight, details resolved themselves. The withered hands, the ruined faces. The burst body cavities where ropy organs could be seen trailing down behind the cagework of ribs.

The offerings they had brought.

By day Kali grinned down upon an array of blossoms and sweetmeats lovingly arranged at the foot of her pedestal. The array spread there now seemed more suited to the goddess. I saw human heads balanced on raw stumps of necks, eyes turned up to crescents of silver-white. I saw gobbets of meat that might have been torn from a belly or a thigh. I saw severed hands like pale lotus flowers, the fingers like petals opening silently in the night.

Most of all, piled on every side of the altar, I saw bones. Bones picked so clean that they gleamed in the candlelight. Bones with smears of meat and long snotty runners of fat still attached. Skinny arm-bones, clubby leg-bones, the pretzel of a pelvis, the beadwork of a spine. The delicate bones of children. The crumbling ivory bones of the old. The bones of those who could not run.

These things the dead brought to their goddess. She had been their goddess all along, and they her acolytes.

Kali's smile was hungrier than ever. The tongue lolled like a wet red streamer from the open mouth. The eyes were blazing black holes in the gaunt and terrible face. If she had stepped down from her pedestal and approached me now, if she had reached for me with those sinuous arms, I might not have been able to fall to my knees before her. I might have run. There are beauties too terrible to be borne.

Slowly the dead began to turn toward me. Their faces lifted and the rotting cavities of their nostrils caught my scent. Their eyes shone iridescent. Faint starry light shimmered in the empty spaces of their bodies. They were like cutouts in the fabric of reality, like conduits to a blank universe. The void where Kali ruled and the only comfort was in death.

They did not approach me. They stood holding their precious offerings and they looked at me—those of them that still had eyes—or they looked through me. At that moment I felt more than invisible. I felt empty enough to belong among these human shells.

A ripple seemed to pass through them. Then—in the uncertain candlelight, in the light that shimmered from the bodies of the dead—Kali did move.

The twitch of a finger, the deft turn of a wrist—at first it was so slight as to be nearly imperceptible. But then her lips split into an impossibly wide, toothy grin and the tip of her long tongue curled. She rotated her hips and swung her left leg high into the air. The foot that had trod on millions of corpses made a pointe as delicate as a prima ballerina's. The movement spread her sex wide open.

But it was not the petalled mandala-like cleft I had imagined kissing earlier. The pussy of the goddess was an enormous deep red hole that seemed to lead down to the center of the world. It was a gash in the universe, it was rimmed in blood and ash. Two of her four hands beckoned toward it, inviting me in. I could have thrust my head into it, then my shoulders. I could have crawled all the way into that wet crimson eternity, and kept crawling forever.

Then I did run. Before I had even decided to flee I found myself falling down the stone staircase, cracking my head and my knee on the risers. At the bottom I was up and running before I could register the pain. I told myself that I thought the dead would come after me. I do not know what I truly feared was at my back. At times I thought I was running not away from something, but toward it.

I ran all night. When my legs grew too tired to carry me I would board a bus. Once I crossed the bridge and found myself in Howrah, the even poorer suburb on the other side of the Hooghly. I stumbled through desolate streets for an hour or more before doubling back and crossing over into Calcutta again. Once I stopped to ask for a drink of water from a man who carried two cans of it slung on a long stick across his shoulders. He would not let me drink from his tin cup, but poured a little water into my cupped hands. In his face I saw the mingled pity and disgust with which one might look upon a drunk or a beggar. I was a well-dressed beggar, to be sure, but he saw the fear in my eyes.

In the last hour of the night I found myself wandering through a wasteland of factories and warehouses, of smokestacks and rusty corrugated tin gates, of broken windows. There seemed to be thousands of broken windows.

After a while I realized I was on the Upper Chitpur Road. I walked for a while in the watery light that fills the sky before dawn. Eventually I left the road and staggered through the wasteland. Not until I saw its girders rising around me like the charred bones of a prehistoric animal did I realize I was in the ruins of the hospital where I had been born.

The hole of the basement had filled up with broken glass and crumbling metal, twenty years' worth of cinders and weeds, all washed innocent in the light of the breaking dawn. Where the building had stood there was only a vast depression in the ground, five or six feet deep. I slid down the shallow embankment, rolled, and came to rest in the ashes. They were infinitely soft; they cradled me. I felt as safe as an embryo. I let the sunrise bathe me. Perhaps I had climbed into the gory chasm between Kali's legs after all, and found my way out again.

Calcutta is cleansed each morning by the dawn. If only the sun rose a thousand times a day, the city would always be clean.

Ashes drifted over me, smudged my hands gray, flecked my lips. I lay safe in the womb of my city, called by its poets Lord of Nerves, city of joy, the pussy of the world. I felt as if I lay among the dead. I was that safe from them: I knew their goddess, I shared their many homes. As the sun came up over the mud and glory of Calcutta, the sky was so full of smoky clouds and pale pink light that it seemed, to my eyes, to burn.

GOD SAVE THE QUEEN

BY JOHN SKIPP AND MARC LEVINTHAL

Now this is an interesting story: and by that, I primarily refer to the story behind the story.

Over the many years it took me to assemble Book of the Dead, Still Dead, *and what became* Mondo Zombie, *I always had it in my head that* Clive Barker *had to get in on this. Though he had written some phenomenal stories in* The Books of Blood*—notably* "Sex, Death and Starshine" *and* "Scapegoats"*—I really wanted to see his brilliant take on the* Romero *mythos, which I knew he loved every bit as much as I.*

But to call Clive *a busy man is to call the* Grand Canyon *an acne scar; and as much as he admitted to delight at the possibility, there was never nearly enough time to see it through. His wild imagination had too many other places to go, and which demanded to be borne witness to as only he could.*

Then in 1993, much to my immense delight, came Night of the Living Dead London: *a graphic novella co-written by* Clive *and his longtime co-*

conspirator, Steve Niles. Alarmingly illustrated by Carlos Kastro, it took the zombie outbreak to Buckingham Palace, in a truly grand display of collapse and corruption that was precisely what I'd been craving all those years.

Except that it was a comic book.

"You guys?" I asked. "Would you mind if I adapted your astonishing story myself?"

The color of the light, to my great delight, was green.

So, alone, I set about the rigorous task of nailing Night of the Living Dead London *in prose. I wasn't working from the script but from the visualized narrative: trying to paint the pictures with words, get behind the images to the unspoken.*

I banged on that shit off and on for a year and a half, to no avail. Certain sequences were playing really well. But I couldn't quite get to the heart.

Enter Marc Levinthal.

Marc is a phenomenal musician and voracious reader turned writer, with whom I had just completed an insanely fun novel called The Emerald Burrito of Oz.

Marc instantly pegged the problem I was having, and simultaneously nailed the one key element Clive and Steve had hoped to illuminate with their version, but hadn't quite gotten to, either.

What it's like for a zombie to dream.

Once Marc wrote that opening sequence—grounding the perspective from the point of view of the nameless boy on the street—"God Save the Queen" fell together with staggering speed. And I devoted myself to invoking the verbal vivacity and audacity so ragingly apparent in Clive's original Books of Blood.

It is my hope that the experiment was a success.

PART ONE
THE BOY

1

He drifted through black waters of sleep, across an oceanic silence; and when the dark waters parted, the nameless boy found himself once again walking. Walking through the haunted slumber land remains of London, in what seemed to be the East End, alone.

The air was freezing—cold damp off the river. Funny that, now wasn't it, how he could feel the cold in a dream?

He was looking for his house, but he just couldn't find it. No roof, no door, no window registered. There were rows upon rows of lifeless homes, stretching out endlessly before him; and though with his gaze he groped hard for his bearings, not one single recognizable detail appeared.

And yes, he felt lost. And yes, he felt frightened

And no; as in his waking life, there was no one left to ask.

The dead were all around him, of course: lumbering, stupid, eternally hungry. Reeking of old meat: their victims', their own. Husks of selfhood, on unstinting auto drive. They were looking for something, too. But evidently, it was no longer him. He could at least thank God for that.

It wasn't, it seemed, that the dead couldn't see him. They could. They just didn't seem to care. They were all honed in on some inscrutable postmortem live-meat vibe, and evidently he no longer aired on that station.

Like an apparition so dense as to simulate mass, he watched them walk around him, then pass right by.

The boy touched himself: gaunt girlish features, sparrow chest to genitals, across the ass and back. He ran long bony fingers through dark matted hair still streaked with red, blue, violet, green. He felt himself alive. Felt righteously so. Felt more alive than anyone he knew.

And yet, at times—when he looked in their eyes—he could almost hear and smell and feel the necro-frequency's whispered breath: a subcutaneous static tickling, at the furthest marrow-depths.

Whatever its message, it would not come clear.

As if, for him, it were not yet time.

And he couldn't find the house. Couldn't remember what it looked like. Couldn't remember much at all. He felt empty, hopeless desperation, as though he'd been searching forever; and so far as he knew, he quite possibly had. For all he knew, he'd already passed the place a million fucking times.

It made him so lonely, this disconnection: this pointed loss of time, place, self. Most of the time, in waking life, he didn't let it bother him. But in the dream, it was soul-crushing lonely.

Strange indeed, how emotional sensation was so much more vivid in the context of the dream.

And then, all at once, Vince blundered up, out of the crowd of milling dead. The shock of recognition—of any at all—blew the boy back in his tracks, put a shudder through the membrane of sleep.

He looked at Vince—yes, he of the pocked chin and Husky-blue eyes; ol' ten-inch Vince—and found himself yelling, "Hey!' Actually shouting and waving for the attention of the living dead.

Vince was snuffling at a garbage container. Like the others, he looked up, then away. The boy stepped forward, felt a clean surge of rage, slammed into the bin and sent his dead ex-lover sprawling.

Vince hit the moist dream-cobblestones hard, staring up in blank zomboid confusion. No stir through the shuffling community "It's me!" the boy screamed. "It's me!"

Vince stared up as the others shambled past, and his look would have said *what do you want from me?* if his look had said anything at all. But it didn't. It was vacant as an enema's rectum. It was barren as a fresh-aborted womb.

And it was there, in that blank-met stare, that the boy abruptly snapped out of the dream.

✠

He woke up, shivering in the record shop on King's Road sleeping behind a barricade of album crates in the stockroom. The sun had freshly fallen, but he could see his breath in the dim candlelight, and wrapped his overcoat more tightly around his delicate frame.

It was a chill evening, which was a good thing. The cold slowed the bastards down. Not enough to stop them, but any edge is a good edge, especially when the odds are a million to one against you.

The stockroom was a favorite hiding place, one of more than twenty at the top of his rotation. The boy found it wise to break things up: never stay in one place too long, or return too often. The dead had no strategic mental capabilities, but their short-term memory could surprise you.

In the well over a year he'd been surviving all alone—the rest of the last of his fellow street rats having been duly shredded, or converted by default to the opposite camp—this was perhaps the thirtieth time he'd stayed here overnight. And it was a testament to just how alone he truly was that, in all that time, nobody had raided his stash. The last tins of meat, the last packs of smokes were right where he'd left them. And thank God for that. Pickings had gotten mighty slim in the days turned to months turned to years since the End.

The boy stretched, took a stale John Player from his pocket, lit it off the candle's stub. The nicotine went straight to his head, amping the peculiar Buzz that always seemed to be with him these days. It was good to get that initial disorienting blast out of the way, first thing, in a place that was relatively safe from harm; and once he'd realized that the dead couldn't really smell past their own rotting brains, it had become his waking ritual.

It gave him roughly ten minutes, at the start of each night, to put his daily ducks into a row. Figure out where he was off to next. Muse a little.

Maybe even remember who he was.

When that didn't happen, he snubbed out the butt, loaded his pockets and put out the candle. Then he carefully took a small section of the crates down, slid out of his hidey-hole, put his ear against the stockroom door and listened. He couldn't hear anything knocking around out in the store, but there was no way to be sure. Sometimes they just stood still, for hours on end: not sleeping, but not exactly conscious either. Just waiting for some little sound or motion to activate them.

Slowly, he cracked open the door and peered out. In the dim evening light, the aisles between the rows of ransacked album bins appeared to be empty. He thought, and not for the first time, what an astonishing waste it all was: all that excellent music, and no way to play it. Figures that when vinyl died, it had to take all of western civilization with it. The boy had always felt that digital was a bad idea.

It took a minute for the sound from the street to register.

It began, for starters, from so far away that it bled rather than erupted into his consciousness. And said consciousness, still rocking from the confluence of nicotine and his new perma-Buzz had gone off on a little idle speculation of its own, (something about how, if the sounds of real life were best reflected by the wholeness of full-bodied analog waves, then maybe living death was like a bad digital simulation: trillions of little squared-off wave-bits, attempting to replicate the sweep of true sound. Fake life, not real life. Catching bits, but missing out on the whole.)

(Which led him to think about migrating factors like distortion and static: vibrational corrosives that snuck in sideways to coarsen or devour the original signal. Whatever that might be. And whatever it might mean.)

(Which begged the question: how and why had God or whatever changed the format of human experience?)

This type of thought was relatively new to him. In the past, insofar as he could recall, he'd been a fairly shallow young man: a survivor, to be sure, but one far more concerned with *what, who,* and *when* than the esoterics of *how* or *why.*

But as time had gone on, and the Buzz had slowly grown, he'd found himself increasingly prone to Deep Thoughts. They came to him frequently, surprisingly, cogently.

And as he was thinking these things, the sounds were getting closer.

It wasn't till the first distant gunshots cut through that he noticed the rowling under growl. A truck or something. No more than six blocks away.

"Fuck," he said, hands clenching, trying to get a bead on the situation. Unless the dead had finally learned how to drive, and fire off guns, these were people that he might want to meet.

Over the years, he'd heard such sounds before. But always too distant. Or the timing was wrong. There had been times, along the way, when the last thing he wanted was to run into still-extant human beings. Especially ones with guns.

He did not miss the threat of rape, much less the actuality. He did not miss having his shirt stolen. And he did not, as a rule, miss people much at all.

But it had been a long time since bands of predators roamed. Most of them were dead, and there was not much left to steal. He figured that anyone left with bullets was doing way better than he was.

More shots went off, and tires squealed. He looked out the shattered front windows, and thought he saw headlights glimmer, dim, off the bricks of the chemist shop on the corner.

"Fuck," he said again, and then went quickly back into the hidey-hole for his axe. If they were shooting, that meant that there were dead out on the street. And the more they shot, the more dead would come. Which would doubtless be bad news for him.

Because he was going out.

Did this make sense? He wasn't sure. If he went out there, he was exposing himself. If they didn't pick him up, he would probably get eaten. If they did, then . . . what? God only knew. Slavery. Friendship. A few extra meals. Hopefully sex, and lots of it.

Or maybe just a bullet in the head.

He thought all this as the truck and the gunshots drew nearer, as he grabbed the fire axe and made his way to the front door, on impulse pulling another cigarette out and lighting it, as if to say *the dead don't smoke!* Already committed, without quite knowing why, to what he was about to do.

Then he was out the door. Out on the street.

Surrounded by the dead.

And it was not like the dream. They saw him right off, and they were moved. Their body language, as they tilted toward him, more than said it all.

Terror flared, and the boy began to run: fire axe in one hand, cigarette in the other. He ran in the direction of the sound, the light that was even now blasting toward him. When he looked down the King's Road, he was half-blinded by the high beams that nailed him, could almost see the shape of the vehicle that bore them.

But mostly what he saw was the dead, in silhouette: a dozen shapes caught in the headlight glare, suddenly undecided as to which way to turn.

He held up the axe, saw the light reflect off it.

At that, he heard yelling, excited: a living sound, so different from the low moan of the dead. The firing stopped, and the engine-sound amped.

They had spotted him.

Good.

Behind him, the three advancing dead made sounds of desire. He paused, turned round, assessed the distance. The middle-aged woman was closest by far. The businessmen lagged by several feet. A narcotized panic, a galvanizing calm swept through him, bought him a moment of strange equilibrium. The boy slipped the cigarette twixt his teeth, chomped it, brought both hands to the axe handle. Feeling *muy macho* in the moment of the swing.

The woman could have been his mum, but it wasn't. Fair enough. The sound her head made as it detached was twig-like, dry and over fast.

It felt good, but then he turned, and saw that not everyone had veered toward the light.

The boy was not a fighter. He had not survived by strength. He did not win. He got away. There was a world of difference. By rooftop, by shortcut, by hidey-hole, yes. By cunning. By stealth.

There were twenty of them now.

It had been a long time since he'd been face-to-face with the living dead in waking life. A survival imperative. *Keep out of their way.* You forgot just how awful it fucking was, until you found yourself back there again. The up-close stench of it. The nightmare of their faces. The absurdity of the socially-prescribed uniforms that still pointlessly draped their frames. The singular abhorrence of rotting flesh. The total indignity of it all. The gag reflex which was perfectly natural, but also your absolute worst enemy. Unless you counted empathy, which was even worse.

Because this was the joke God had played. They used to be you. *And you might still become them.* They were mirrors that threw yourself right back at you: swaddling your hope in maggots, your dreams in a shambling infinitude of blankness.

They were everything that you never wanted to be.

And now there were easily thirty.

The truck was still roughly a block away, but closing fast. He ran toward it, feet clomping on pavement, axe raised, eyes calculating distance and proximity of the dead. They were mostly spread out, and he tried to remind himself that they went down pretty easily.

But now the first one was upon him, and he knocked it aside, but it clawed at him; and the moment its nails raked across his jacket, he remembered how easily he could die. The next one wore a butcher's apron, but the meat from its torn-open face could easily account for all the bloodstains across it. He sidestepped the grasping hands, veered dangerously near to a hospital midwife who once had been comely, but whose bulging gray breast implants now protruded like balloons from the rot of her bosom. He used the head of the axe to knock her over, and she fell, just as another pair of desiccated dandies stepped forward, buttressed by five behind.

The guns resumed firing, on semi-automatic.

Projectile brain gobbets struck the boy in the face as the row of five jittered and fell. He screamed, and a bullet wisked right past his ear as he veered sharply to the left. His axe came up, down, imbedded in a green-black face and stuck, crushed skull gripping at the blade like forceps. The fucker on the right made a move for him. He let go of the handle and screamed again, suddenly grappling with the dead.

His hands came down on corduroyed shoulders and squished there, old meat sickly giving way. Then all he could see was the zombie's face: green scum-slick teeth, yellow eyes rolled back.

That head exploded, inches from the boy's own; faintly, from a distance, he heard the high yip of the marksman's boisterous delight.

The body fell, and the Buzz took over, rendering everything in slo-mo. The multiple muzzle-flashes. The spastic collapses of the smithereening dead. The truck, as it screeched to a shuddering halt. The door, flying open.

The fat man, moving into the light.

There was one zombie left: its legs blown off, dragging itself forward with its spindly arms, toward him. The boy just stared at it, numb into weightless. The fat man approached on the zombie's absent heels. The expression on the dead thing's face was exactly the same as it would have been if it were still walking around.

Nothing could distract it from its hunger for him.

The boy stared into the dead thing's eyes; and all at once, the static roared. He felt it at the core of him, a subsonic resonant crackle and boom. For the first time, he felt he heard something within it.

For the first time, he almost understood.

The fat man had a very large revolver. He took a long time brandishing it, waiting until he was directly upon the crawling dead before aiming and firing. The crawling stopped. The silence was huge.

"Bloody papist," said the fat man, and spat on the corpse.

The boy just stared, enveloped by the silence.

Then the world went blacker than the night, and he fell.

卌

What followed was a blur punctuated by moments: the interior of the truck, which was leather and softness; the words *poor boy* and *he's doubtless in shock*; the occasional *tac* of weapons fire; the howl of the dead outside as majestic gates parted before him.

And then he was up, being ushered down corridors stately and chill: a labyrinthine sequence over which the fat man presided, as if he'd done it many times before. Another man, whose name was Lewis, helped the boy along, essentially walking him toward wherever they were going.

And then there was a room too right to articulate, as if all the world's treasures had been secreted here: glimmers of gold and gem, sumptuous fabric, exquisite sculpture, high art, and sacred iconography amassed in unbelievable scale and scope.

It was hard, at this point, to disbelieve that this was just some heavenly dream. Or perhaps, in fact, that he had died, and this was the literal Heaven.

But then he was ushered into the bath. A cathedral for bathing. An altar for the act. And as Lewis undressed him, there was no missing the look in the fat man's eyes.

If this was Heaven, then God sucked cock.

Alright, then, the boy thought. He was back in the world he knew, and the politics of flesh.

The boy watched the bathtub fill, felt a bit of himself creep back. He looked first at Lewis, who fell back, impassive. Then he met the fat man's gaze. Giving nothing up himself. As if the shock had never left.

The fat man gave it all away. His nakedness thrummed at the impact of that gaze. He checked himself out. He was nothing if not trim. There were bruises and zits, but that was to be expected.

This was going to work out just fine.

After the exquisite bath came bed: solo at first, and then with the fat man. All told, it went quite well. There was no getting around the simple solace of human contact, and the flavor of man bore no small satisfaction. He had long waxed nostalgic on the virtues of come; and when it came, he swallowed large. He felt it was the least he could do.

Of course, then it was his turn; and discharging was no problem at all. The fat man was both ardent and tender. In pig heaven, he was.

After that came dreamless sleep.

And when he awoke, still deeply buzzed, the fat man was dressing. Not in last night's streetwear, either. These were lavish, luxuriant flowing vestments: outrageously pompous, to be sure, but totally in keeping with the lush, archaic splendour of it all.

Watching—feigning sleep, with mute and slowly-mounting awe—he realized that he had spent the night with no less than Bishop Hallam, the head of the Church of England.

Which placed him squarely behind the gates of Fuckingham Palace itself.

It was a given, if you'd spent any time on the street at all, that you resented the tits off the Royal Family. Never more so than now. No matter what horror was being foisted upon you, day after day, in this New Hell on Earth, you could rest assured that the Queen and her kin were doing just as fine as could be.

If, say, for example, you awoke on a given Sunday to find that your lover had died; and that, because you knew he was dying, you had strapped him to the cleanest mattress you could find, in some shithole flat in the middle of hell, then slept beside him, offering him all the scant comfort you had.

And say that you awoke to a growl and sudden motion, the bed shuddering beneath and especially beside you; and you knew he was dead because now he was back; and you, careless with love and compassion, had fallen asleep with your head on his shoulder.

Say, then, that you looked in his eyes, backing up just in time, backing up because you had to; and say that your heart broke in that moment. Say that your beautiful friend and lover—who had moved you to tears, orgasms, laughter—was gone, but that all of his flesh and his bone remained. And say that said flesh and bone tried to devour you now: not with love, but with hunger alone . . .

Well, you could assume that the Queen was just dandy: sipping tea and nibbling bisquits.

And say that you had made a deal with your wounded love, in your final days together. Say that you had promised to take care of it. To make sure that he wandered the earth no longer.

And say that you began to cry, when you found that the moment was finally upon you; and you found that your tears meant nothing to him now, no, and never again and say that the sound alerted the dead, who broke down the door and set upon you . . .

Well, at least you knew that the Queen was safe, and snuggly-warm, within Buckingham Palace.

And, just to bring an end to this, say that you managed to crush your loved one's skull, watching his fine body's final twitching as you rose, faced the dead, then took off up the stairs. Not knowing if they were waiting up there, too. Not knowing if it mattered. Not caring if you knew . . .

Well, guaranteed, filet mignon was waiting for the Queen. (Boiled, no doubt. She was, after all, British.)

This was all, of course, just hypothetical. It had only happened to him once. And he had no idea if the Queen's chronology had been in step with his own travails.

But he knew, as he rose—his host at last gone—that some issues were arising within him. Little matters of class, of justice and vengeance.

Or maybe just making the best of it. He was, after all, no longer outside.

And much remained to be seen.

There was a note at the foot of the bed. It read:

> *Dear boy,*
>
> *I thank God that I found you last night. Lord only knows how much you must have suffered. I trust you will unburden to me, in the day's to come.*
>
> *I have important business, in the service of the Queen. I hope that you will excuse me. When the day is done, I will return.*
>
> *Until then, feel free to explore my quarters. There is much beauty here. Food is on the table by the windows. Please help yourself.*
>
> *Unfortunately, as for now, I must restrict you to my quarters. Strict protocols govern our comings and goings. When the time comes, if it is your desire, you will be issued a uniform and duties that allow you greater access to the larger realm. All this I will explain in full.*
>
> *Until then, please enjoy.*

This was followed by a scribble far less legible than the text.

The boy got up blearily, looked around. It was indeed a fabulous place. It looked like they'd looted every church of note in Europe, so that even the least of the artifacts were splendid by any ordinary standard.

It was all God, God, and God some more, but there were a number of interesting spins. Aside from the hundred thousand Jesii, there were Jehovan constructs aplenty. Jehovah the Creator. Jehovah the destroyer Jehovah the Omniscient. Jehovah the Just Barely There. Not to mention innumerable pagan doodads, more than sufficient to fill in all of the metaphysical blanks.

When that got boring, there was beef and cheese and bread so fresh it was free of mold.

And then there was the view.

From the windows, all of London spread out before him; and for the first time, he got a handle on the regal perspective. Looking down, of course.

There were the sculpted grounds below. Then the guards. Then the fences. And only then came the walking dead: hundreds and hundreds of them, pressed together, as if waiting for Elton John to do a benefit concert. *Dead Aid*, they would doubtless call it. And it would be sold out.

The boy was horrified, looking down. There were so many of them. Were they always there? Was this like a mecca?

Of course it was. There were living here, right out in the open and everything. Flaunting what they had. Virtually daring the dead to take it.

"Filthy peasants," he heard himself mutter, and felt the black oil of history move through his veins.

Suddenly, the Buzz welled up, and he could no longer eat, no longer look out the window. Vertigo smacked him a dizzying whack, strange voices hissing gibberish in the back of his skull. The sandwich he had made dropped from his hand, squished into the carpet beneath his feet as he staggered back and away, groping for balance, his palms at last landing heavily on the sturdy oak of the bishop's writing desk.

He steadied himself there, eyes snapped shut, and let the world stop spinning.

When he looked back clown, the jewel-encrusted cover of a leather-bound book glimmered up at him, fired by the morning sun. Oh my, he thought, and flipped it open, revealing page after page of the bishop's tidy handwriting.

A journal? Most likely. Left out? Indeed!

And oh, what secrets it might reveal!

The boy flipped to the first page and proceeded to read.

Understand this, my dears: beauty has always been my downfall, a long slow shipwreck on the siren's rock. Would that I could resist the call, but I have always felt too long at sea. Adrift in this bloated, ridiculous body. Riding the black tide, alone.

At least the bishop had no illusions about himself. The boy skimmed a little, then flipped toward the back.

And so it began, my sweets: the search for the new Princess. Prince Randolph would have his bride, and the bloodline would continue. No detail was to be overlooked, no option ignored. Of the two hundred plus servants alive and working in the Palace, all were informed of the quest, and all were put on active duty. An army of cars were sent out blazing in every direction. The shortwave radios were scanned and searched twenty-four hours a day. Randolph even launched his beloved pigeons.

If there was a surviving female member of any of the Royal Families, Queen Florence would make sure she was found.

The madness here has steepened precipitously, as evidenced by this morning's episode, which I will attempt to describe in all of its lunatic detail.

I was walking in the garden with the Queen and Queen Mother as they busily planned the wedding. I had been brought in to consult. Florence read aloud from a crabbed list of worthies who simply must attend; and in all cases, the intended quest was dead.

From the Queen Mother? "Oh, bother," was the general response.

It was then that we came across the body . . . or, rather, the remnants thereof.

The base of the rib cage was wedged tight against the bars: the legs long since snapped off and dragged to zombie gourmand heaven, the pelvis shattered and likewise gone, along with the base of the spine. The one-limbed torso had fallen back to describe one-quarter of the Crucifixion. But there was no flesh on the face, nor organ to speak of within the fractured ribs.

Even the scalp was gone, eliminating the possibility of identification through hairstyle. But gauging from the shredded garb, it was clearly a male member of our servant staff; and based on the positioning of the body, I could envision all too clearly what must have transpired.

"Suicide," I muttered, tasting bile on the word.

The Queen cast a shocked gaze in my direction, as though such a thought were inconceivable. But I, alas, understood all too well why a soul would want out of this place.

I imagined the poor man, lurking unseen by the vast liquor cache, drinking himself wretched in the wee hours of the morning. Imagined the moans of the walking dead as they echoed and droned inside his head. Trapped like a rat was how he felt, hopeless and lonely and sick to death of life. So, at long last, he half-snuck and half-staggered out into the moonlit garden, most likely with bottle in hand.

And there were the dead, with their arms outstretched; wanting him, needing him, calling him home.

How long did he stand there, thinking it over, weighing the moment in his mind? Did he race straight into their starving embrace, hellbent kamikaze without a cause? Or did he linger for hours there, weaving, cursing, taunting the dead with the last of his spark? Did he, indeed, launch himself willfully into the fence? Or did he stumble, perhaps, coming a little too close to those grasping hands in a final burst of ersatz courage and drunken devil-may-care?

In the end, it doesn't matter, and I have no way of knowing. But I was sickened then, as I am sickened now, by contemplation of his end. Because, indeed, the hands did seize him, pull him flush against the bars, bring him face to rotting face with the hordes that would not let him fall until every last edible speck had been devoured.

I imagined these things without wishing to—far more than I wished to, that much is certain—prey to the terrible empathy I ascribe to a still-functioning human soul.

But the Queen Mother had no such problems. Clearly, she had other things on her mind.

"Do get that cleaned up," she said, looking down at the body like it was so much dog feces.

"Fucking bitch," the boy heard himself mutter, letting the bishop's words play vividly in his mind. The sordid and soulless atrocity of it confirmed every negative assumption he had.

It was tempting, at that moment, to break out and throttle the wicked old cunt, maybe snuff the whole lot of them. It was also, of course, impossible; so he look a deep breath and poured himself back into the journal.

There followed several pages of self-indulgent childhood musings, which the boy quickly skimmed right past. Looking for the next informative section. Which followed, quickly enough.

She is here!

The princess Sara Marie Hargrove of Norway arrived today, quite exceeding all of our possible expectations. She arrived via helicopter, which she piloted herself, in a stunning display of initiative and valor.

Evidently, she and her father, King Agar, had been living alone in the Palace these last few years. They had survived on their wits and cunning, with only a handful of servants in attendance; and they were thrilled when they received word that other Royalty still lived.

The most important thing, as Florence has repeatedly stated, is that the bloodline remain unsullied. It appears that she will get her wish. If anything, the Princess is far too impressive to imagine mating with Randolph under any other circumstances.

She is, in a word, stunning: red-blond hair cascading to either side of a face that, in a saner world, might adorn the cover of Vogue. *When she emerged from the copter in her leather flight jacket, white blouse, and black slacks, I found myself smitten with not lust, but envy for the lust she instantly inspired in every other male attending.*

It is the central absurdity of my sinful condition that I wished, not to have her, but to be her.

"Ah, ha" the boy said. No big surprises there. The Buzz swelled once again, huge in his head; still, he could not help but continue on.

And so, it seems, that the wedding will take place exactly as I hoped for. On Christmas Day. And I will preside, as is my duty: dispensing God's sanction on the union of souls.

But before I do, I must venture out once again into poor dead London. Searching, as ever, for my own counterpart—the one who will be mine, as she will be his. I will say that I'm merely charting the way to the Abbey; and, in a sense, I am.

If I die, they will have to pursue their Godless course without me. If I fail, I will function as their guide.

But what if I find my beautiful boy? What if my prayers are somehow answered? What if I find that I am wrong, and that God is listening after all?

As ever, I trust myself into Your hands. Though all my faith is vanquished. Though I curse You night and day.

I remain your faithful servant, in deed if nothing else.

There was only one more entry, dated November 24th. The boy was numb as he turned to it.

God save me. And God save the Queen.

I have found my beautiful boy.

PART TWO
THE ROYAL FAMILY

V.

Christmas day, and the wedding at last. After weeks of frenzied prep, the Royal Knot was finally fit to be tied. The boy had observed the preparations, numbed by the Buzz but still three parts attentive: those parts divided neatly between awe, contempt, and glee.

From his multiple vantage points, at room within the Palace, he was forced to conclude that he was not the only one losing his mind.

When the bishop had come back that night, with all of his terms and conditions, the boy had been most monosyllabic in expressing his consent. Part of it was his version of the dumb blonde act. Most of it was the fact that he felt thoroughly stunted when it came to actual speech. He could think a fucking mile a minute, and frequently did, through the psychic fog; but when it came to putting it out there verbally, he was just one and a half steps up from Karloff's Frankenstein.

"Yes." "Thank you." "Sorry." "No." That was the bulk of the lexicon. "Yes, I liked it." "That was good." Phrases pretty much reserved for the bishop and bed.

The dumb-show had become less of an act as time passed. He found himself staring at nothing for hours, gazing absently out the wide balcony window, and the sea of walking corpses would disappear into the background as his mind slowly erased itself.

He'd hear the echo of that thing from his dream; whatever called to those dream-zombies, he was sure it called to him now. It was faint, but each day he heard it more: a static with a voice, with an agenda that made no literal sense, but spoke with a surety that calmed him. As if his unraveling mind was puzzled, but the very cells of his body understood.

He shared the bishop's bed since that first night, and was surprised to find the arrangement not altogether unpleasant. True, the old cleric was somewhat grotesque: all wattles and flab and limp, watery eyes. On the other hand, he was very clean, and impeccably scented, by and large; and as most of their fucking was done in the dark, or with the boy blindfolded . . . well, one did what one could.

And then again, the bishop had some charming qualities. He was generous, gentle, respectful, compassionate. He was also full of stories he seemed desperate to tell: many of them scandalous, quite a few of them hilarious. He seemed always most gratified when he got the boy to laugh; and even just a smile was a delight to the old bastard, as the boy gave up so little of himself in that regard.

Hallam was, in all, a very complex man; and the boy respected that, even as his own complexity unraveled.

The servant's uniform served the boy well: he had become proficient, during his several weeks in the palace, at hiding in plain sight; at looking as though he belonged, yet remaining all but invisible.

And as the wedding drew nearer, the boy's non-sexual duties gradually grew. He found himself increasingly used as a courier, shuttling hastily-hand-scribbled messages from the bishop to the various departments of the Palace apparatus. In that capacity, where questions demanding more than a "yes" or "no" answer were rarely asked, he found himself becoming somewhat familiar, while remaining essentially unknown.

He was, in that sense, almost beginning to belong.

Even so, he could not believe the bishop's audacity when he insisted that the boy ride in the carriage with him, as part of the wedding entourage. It was one thing to have him serve as an informal valet. But to have him at his side, accompanying him to the Abbey, seemed completely dangerous, given the caution the bishop had used up until then. If they were found out, what would the mad royals do about it? Have him shot? Hanged? Exiled? Or worse?

Maybe, in their madness, they'd choose to ignore the bishop's indiscretions. Maybe. But probably not.

At any rate, how could you second-guess the motivations of people like that: people so insane, so removed from reality, that they would leave the safety of Buckingham Palace, en masse, to stage their wedding amongst the dead?

Down in the courtyard, the air was thick with panic. Over a hundred brave soldiers were falling into formation, on either side of the processional vehicles lined up before the gate. To a man, they looked ready to shit their pants.

The boy could not have empathized more.

This was the closest he'd come to the dead since the night he'd left the streets. And though he'd logged more survival time out there than the rest of these people put together, he still didn't relish going back.

There were literally thousands of them out there now. More than he'd ever seen in one place. Even at the height of it—pin the early days, during the riots that ultimately tore the throat out of the city—there was still enough doomed civilization extant to put some spread and balance into the equation. (50,000 looters and berserkers + 500,000 walking dead + 5,000 armed defenders of the Empire + 1,000,000 civilians caught in the crossfire = the flash-point, London watching its life pass before its eyes in the final moments before The End.)

Hallam hustled the boy toward the last of the three open-air carriages in formation. It was—to the boy's stupefaction—horse-driven, as were the one's designed to transport the royal family. The horses were, of course, terrified; and the boy watched faithful Lewis comfort the poor three under his bridle's command.

There was an armored tank at the front of the procession, and another at the back. In between, flanking the carriages, were six jeeps, all bearing machine guns and flame throwers. This was, of course, all somewhat comforting; but despite the little macho displays of comraderie that flickered between them, there was not a man present who was not, at heart, crawling with dread.

"Come on," the bishop said. "Get in." And as the door was already held open, the boy obeyed, taking his seat by the right-hand window. Staring out at the soldiers who stood by now, so very still. Preparing to march to their deaths.

The bishop did not follow, but rather turned back toward the music that was even now beginning to blare (pre-recorded, as few musicians had managed to survive). The words *Pomp and Circumstance* leapt to mind, though the boy wasn't at all sure he was right; he had never been much up on the classics.

And then, sure enough, came the Royal Family: slowly, slowly, as if someone had slipped God some 'ludes; as if they were thoroughly convinced that their terrified subjects, gathered here for this command performance, just couldn't get enough of looking at them.

There was the Queen Mother herself: Old Florence, that gnarled little gnome, her face a mazed city of wrinkles beneath a tidal wave of makeup, with hair twice the size of her head. There was Queen Margaret, only three-quarters as old and hideous; and with her was the doddering King, who looked nearly as shriveled and somnambulant as the dead.

Then came Prince Randolph, a tall, gangly man whose nose and ears were so large that his mouth and eyes seemed stolen from a substantially smaller person.

And beside him was the Princess Sara Marie Hargrove.

Two words sprang to mind as the boy looked at her. They were *holy* and *shit*. In precisely that order.

She was gorgeous, and that was just the half of it. She was alive to a nearly alarming extent. The British Royals were already museum pieces; but next to her, they more resembled animate wax figures in some lurid Chamber of Horrors.

The boy could not stop staring as they advanced. Could not stop staring at her. Nor could the rest of the men there assembled. It was as if a common thought were passing between them all: a thought so horrid that it screamed to be expressed, and so forbidden that it forcibly stifled the scream.

And the thought was: "Wait a minute! We're going out there, and facing death, so that she can marry him?"

And all the while, the dead were amassing: drawn by life, by the music, by the palace itself. Upping the voltage with every moment that the Royals dragged it out.

Until, at last, they were loaded into their carriages. At which point the bishop returned, taking his seat beside the boy. A servant handed the bishop a pair of semi-automatic weapons, then closed the door. The bishop carefully set the weapons on the floor: one for himself, and one for the boy.

"You're a survivor," said the bishop, still staring at the floor. "I thank God for that. And I thank you for being . . ." He swallowed hard. ". . . here."

He looked hard at the boy, who returned the gaze, empty.

VII

The gate guards were ready, machine guns in hand. At their commander's signal, they opened fire upon the crowd.

Vaporized cranium plumed from the front ranks, showering the dead behind with shrapnel. Faces imploded and pasted their scraps on the next wave to shatter, then onto the next. Aiming always at head level, with minor deviations for size, they gunned down a hundred in a minute or less.

It was time to open the gates.

The lead tank leapt forward, aiming straight into the breach. Its razored cow-catcher sliced meat as it plowed its way though the waiting herd. The gunners on top laid waste to the dead that stumbled in from either side. Clearing the way.

The horses whinnied—a frantic, heartbreaking sound—but did as they were told. To either side, the foot soldiers did likewise. And then the bishop's carriage, like the rest, was off as well. The boy watched the gate loom, crown, then recede.

As they passed over into undead London.

And the rotting proletariat laid siege.

Almost as soon as the gates were closed behind them, soldiers began to die. There were too many bodies, in too close an area, with the entire procession moving far too slowly. Even under the deafening battery of fire, the dead would not stop coming.

The boy watched limbs cascade through the air, torsos empty, bones burst into flames. And still the dead would not stop coming. They tripped over each other, their fallen comrades. Got up. And would not stop coming.

There were five soldiers clustered to the right of the boy, keeping pace with the carriage as they fired and fired. A few of them had shouldered their rifles, drawing handguns for accuracy. But one of the men stood slightly out from the pack, moving sideways, assault rifle blasting away.

A nun on fire came at him from an angle, grabbing his barrel on the way to his face. He moved to shake her off, and a dead rugby player came in from the front. The soldier let go of the gun too late, hands raking his face as he fell over backwards. The nun and the rugby player met him on the pavement, tearing him apart as all three burst into flames.

"Keep it moving!" yelled the squad leader, firing his pistol into the crowd. "Keep it moving, slow and steady!"

Slow and steady? The boy stared at Hallam, thinking it so hard that the bishop flinched. *Slow and steady?*

To the left of the bishop's carriage, two zombies wrestled a fine young soldier back into the door. His jacket caught on the handle and stuck, dragging him along as they assailed him with their teeth. The soldier screamed and jammed his revolver into the left eye socket of the housewife at his throat. She fell as he fired, taking his larynx with her. Blood sprayed. The other zombie hung on, tearing off his cheek, working its way toward his lips.

The soldier's death-noises were unbearable. Bishop Hallam slid to the left door and stood: firing first at the zombie, whose skull turned to vapor; then at the soldier, whose did much the same.

"Give me a hand, here!" the bishop howled. Unsteadily, the boy obliged:

taking the now-headless soldier by the shoulders and hefting the carcass free. Letting it drop, soon to be devoured.

And still the dead kept coming.

The boy could only imagine the Queen Mother up ahead, waving and shouting "Happy Christmas! Happy Christmas!" at the undead throngs that swelled toward them. As if they still remained her subjects. As if her subjects really cared. From what little he had seen of her, she was so far gone as to be without fear.

"Everything's fine," the bishop said, patting the boy's bloody hand with sweaty palm. "Everything's fine."

As another soldier screamed, feeding the bottomless hunger.

What saved the cavalcade was no more planned than wanted or imagined. As more and more soldiers fell, the zombies stopped and fed: as many as twenty or thirty converging upon one fallen man, and devouring what they could.

So as people died, and distance mounted, the attacking army thinned; and soon the caravan was under control, leaving behind a hideous trail of carnage and mutilation.

By now the bishop was fighting back tears, though he still convulsively patted the boy's hand. The boy tried not to hear the lingering screams of the young men being eaten alive.

There would be a wedding, but at no small expense. He pictured the Queen Mother, and felt his blood boil. This was her madness. She alone brought it on.

You miserable bitch, he thought to himself.

I hope to God you pay.

It took over an hour to arrive at and secure Westminster Abbey.

The army grouped outside, preparing for the return. It had started to snow, a surreal blanket of peace falling over the streets as the soldiers built fires and reloaded weapons.

Inside, the wedding had begun.

VIII

That night, the bishop wrote in his journal:

> *Today, I performed what I suspect will be the last royal wedding in human history; and I hope that this does not sound cruel.*
>
> *But I pray that I am right.*
>
> *We have crossed the line, and we are damned. I know of no other way to say it. We have crossed the line, and there will be no forgiveness. Not from God. And not from me.*
>
> *As I spoke the holy words of wedlock, I felt my soul constrict, recede: recoiling from the utter wrong, then sinking to a place so deep I fear I may never see it again.*
>
> *I felt a humm rise up in me, then: some sound I'd never heard before. It was emptiness, profound and hollow. It was nothingness.*
>
> *Inside me now, and forever.*
>
> *And I sensed that God at last was gone. That He'd had enough, and could bear no more. From this point on, I suspect that we are thoroughly on our own. As well we deserve.*
>
> *We deserve just what we get.*

But it would be hours before the boy read that particular journal passage.

That night, he had a few adventures of his own.

IX

In the aftermath of the wedding, there was much jubilation. At least amongst the Royals, who had lost none of their own, unless you counted the thirty-seven men who had given up their lives in the interests of pageantry, and so that the dead might feed again.

Only a few had died on the return trip. Three, to be precise, although a fourth had alas been bitten. Florence had seen this as some sort of benediction; and though the bishop didn't corroborate her view, precisely, he didn't seize the opportunity to debate it with her, either.

The bishop was depressed—that much was clear—and he took his leave at the earliest diplomatic juncture. Leaving the boy seated at the farthest corner of the largest of the sittings rooms, observing the madness at play.

From there, in the warmth of the hearth-fires burning, the boy watched as they celebrated the union, feting the newest member of the British Royal family.

And, for hours on end, he listened.

In their delirium, they assumed they could rebuild their empire by continuing the bloodline. To them, it was as simple as that. They discussed the reentrenchment of sovereignty, the reemergence of a viable working class. They spoke as if they sincerely believed that this whole living-dead business was just an inconvenience, some annoying historical glitch. That some day all would be as it once was.

The idea made him sick.

Because things would never be the same. He knew this in his blood and bones. The dead would rot to nothing eventually, but what they'd done would take hundreds of years to redo. If ever. A gargantuan *if*.

And without precautions—as yet nonexistent—the new dead would continue to rise. Keeping the living ever vigilant.

And that was the least of it.

The boy looked at the Princess Sara; and every so often, she looked back at him. Eye contact had been established. Discreetly. But there it was. She was gorgeous, and so was he. At least they alone had something in common.

He imagined that she knew that this all was bullshit. From the twinkle in her eyes, he surmised that he was right.

He looked at her, and then he looked at the Prince.

And thought to himself, no fucking way.

Later, as night descended in full, the boy began to wander the halls. This had become his routine, a way to ease the growing boredom. He'd found rooms he was sure no one had visited for years, rooms filled with antique furniture and long-forgotten gifts from foreign dignitaries.

But more to the point, he now knew where everyone and everything was quartered, knew who stayed up and what time they went down. The night was his time; and as the corridors cleared, the Palace became his own.

And so it was, late into that night, that he found himself moving toward the grand new quarters that the Prince and his wife had drawn.

The boy knew that Randolph had retained his old rooms, and no wonder; he had only spent his entire life there. It was a boy's room, albeit effete; and remodeling it into a royal love nest would not only obliterate its personal value, but leave him with nowhere to retreat.

And so the room where he and Sara were destined to commingle was in another wing entirely. It was, in essence, Sara's room: designed for sharing, but hers in the clinch.

And, lo and behold, the clinch had already come.

"What do you mean, you can't?" This from the Princess, loud behind the closed doors.

The boy paused, listening in the hall.

From the unmistakable voice of the Prince came some vague, halted stammering. Something about ". . . me old fella."

The boy stifled a laugh.

"But we were so close!"

More muted stammering then, slowly groping towards regal command.

Then the volume went down on both of them, as if they were suddenly concerned about being overheard. Which would have been absurd, under ordinary circumstances. They literally had the wing to themselves.

But tonight, the boy was listening hard.

Not more than a couple of minutes passed before the door to the bedroom opened; and from it stepped Prince Randolph, draped in a fabulous robe, some lovely slipper, and a long-faced expression of furious shame. The boy ducked back into the bountiful shadows and waited. The Prince turned away from him, then off down the hall.

"Randolph!" the Princess shouted after him. "You could at least shut the door, if that's all you can do!"

The Prince walked faster. There was a bend at the end of the hall. The Prince took it, his footsteps receding.

The boy waited till the footsteps were more than gone.

From inside the bridal chamber, he heard crying. It barely penetrated through the Buzz that swelled up in him now. The Buzz had nothing to do with hearing; his hearing, he'd found, was painfully acute; the Buzz existed wholly apart from the senses. It had something to do with the soul.

And if he had a soul left, after today, the boy couldn't find it with a map. Instead, he followed the Buzz, which spoke to him with words no more coherent than before, but suffused now with a meaning that was coming increasingly clear, moment to moment and step by step.

The crying was quiet, an internal affair with only a few strategic leaks; and it slowly approached the door from within as he quickly approached from without. He found himself carefully calculating distance, and slowed just at the brink of arrival, so that he got there just as she reached the door.

And she saw him, stepping into the doorway just as she moved to close it off. And they saw each other. Stopped. And stared.

Caught in a moment inexplicably huge.

She was draped in a blanket she'd torn from the bed, and absolutely nothing else. She looked wounded and doomed and profoundly aware and more exquisitely sexually ripe for the taking than any human being in the history of man.

And the boy had no problem with his old fella. Not then. Not in the hours that ensued. The Princess, as it turned out, was a wallow in the finest that earthly woman-flesh could offer; and he found himself coming there again and again, acutely aware of the womb that was doused by his unrestrained issue. Over and over.

The bloodline, indeed.

PART THREE
THE DEAD

X

The months passed, and the spring thaw made the stench from the streets nearly unbearable. By the summer, burning incense was common all along the labryinthian hallways, and perfumes were sprayed on furniture and clothing, to limited result.

The stench could be masked, but not eliminated.

The boy hardly seemed to notice. He could smell it, but it had ceased to matter. He had become more and more like a ghost: transparent, haunting the hallways, and the bedrooms of the bishop and the princess. He marveled at how nothing seemed to get through to him now. It was all just fucking. And pretending.

He'd become even more pale and thin, hardly venturing into the sunlight. Waiting until dusk to begin his activities: an innocuous ghoul, rendered unscary by the ambient backdrop of horror.

The boy had taken to borrowing the princess' make-up to heighten the effect, darkening his eye sockets, and whitening his already-anemic skin. Imitating them outside. Mocking them. Mocking them all. He wondered what his old goth friends would have made of all this, and suspected delight. He wished he could shoot some video, and send it back in time.

The bishop, for his part, had seemed incensed by his new appearance at first, then gradually excited.

The Princess—as it turned out, an old Cure fan—was nothing less than thrilled.

Lately he'd even stopped wearing the servant's uniform, dressing instead in expensive cast-offs he found about the Palace. No one seemed to care; people seemed to be folding into themselves as time went on.

Bishop Hallam had recently told him about stopping the King from opening the front gates. The poor old shriveled bastard had been poised, with a confused guard barring his way, to walk right up to the reaching arms of the undead.

He had wanted to "let his people in."

The bishop had managed to talk him down, convincing him that the zombies were Nazis instead. This notion had sent the King into a comical dance of outrage. His demand that the guards open fire at once was obeyed, with a nod from the bishop. The outside ranks were thinned once again, at the cost of several hundred rounds from their dwindling stockpile of ammunition.

But later, the King had confided to the bishop, "I go in and out, but I see." Then, with a gentle smile, he'd added, "We're not going to make it, are we, Hallam?"

To which the bishop could only sigh, then give the King a heartfelt embrace.

And then there'd been the night—which the boy observed firsthand—when the bishop and the Queen Mother nearly collided in the hall. The bishop had nearly hopped out of his skin, but Florence herself seemed merely flustered.

"Oh, bother," she'd said. "I'm lost again. Would you be so kind as to guide me to my room? My lady in waiting is dead, you know."

The bishop had bowed and said he was honored, then taken her by the arm and led her back down the hall. The boy, unseen, had followed discreetly, listening to every word exchanged. Much of it was mere chit-chat—the baby this and the kingdom that—but at a certain point, her gait had changed, and her tone went deeper, more profound.

"I'm worried, you know," she'd said, and sighed. "Things are very different now, and I want it stopped at once." The bishop said nothing, and silence hung thick in the still, rank Palace air.

"May I ask you a question," she'd continued at last, "as you are of the cloth?"

"Of course," he replied. "Again, you honor me."

At that, she'd stopped and turned to him. Concern swam in her pitted eyes.

"Has God . . ." drawing it out ". . . abandoned us?"

"No, no. Not at all!" the bishop replied at once. "He is merely challenging us."

Florence smiled. "And ridding us of those mad Catholics."

"Yes, that as well."

"Well, then, bully!" she'd said, resuming her forward momentum, self-important assurance returning with every step. "Then we must meet His challenge, and continue what is ours by right."

"That's the spirit!" he'd assured her, with a bland smile on his lips.

And so she had toddled on back to her quarters, flush with her own delirium; in the end, less on top of the facts than the poor pathetic King.

Afterwards, the bishop had cried for hours. He was no fool. Or, at least, he wasn't stupid.

Later that night, he wrote:

The buy is bored with me. And, more surprisingly, I am bored with him. There is no future in our static hold upon the present tense.

I suspect that he's found some other place to ply his talents. Or perhaps he's merely as lost as Florence. As lost as all of us now.

Ah, well.

Very soon, I will venture out again with faithful Lewis, the last and only friend I have. Trolling for loveliness, once again. Or, more likely, trolling for death.

I find myself thinking about the King, and his impulse to open the gates: absurd, of course, but how much more absurd than mine, in the final analysis?

The urge to destroy it all is—at heart, I suspect—the core desire. The urge to give in to the dying tide, to merge with the only remaining reality. To see the last preposterous boundaries fall would be, at the least, some sort of closure.

Be it heaven, or hell, or nothing at all, I suspect that it would have to be better than this.

Which seemed almost sane, until the boy caught the bishop masturbating square into the face of Jesus: not once, not twice, but again and again. Thrusting into paintings one thousand years old. Squeezing the wet spurting tip of his cock into mouths sculpted wide with the pain of crucifixion. Dousing the Savior in desperate jizzum.

Perversely praying for the One Love he would never have.

XI

So it was madness, and sex, and wandering the halls, and the boy's new fascination with the dead things outside: an advancing obsession, as autumn led into the empire's final days. There he found himself, as in the dream, searching for something he recognized. Even stupid Vince would do.

Often, this led the boy down to the fence, where he stood just inches from their skeletal reach. Staring into the sea of faces. Listening to the siren song imbedded in the Buzz.

Sometimes he looked into their eyes, and thought he caught them dreaming: not dead, not asleep, not awake, not alive, but merely adrift in dream.

And it was there that he found some sense of what might lie beyond.

✶

The eyes of the dead were emptiness incarnate. The only light that played there was reflected from without. The boy tuned into that, letting go, abandoning himself to the beckoning Buzz. He slowly absorbed the incoherence, the nothing that echoed with rattle and clambor.

And, as he settled in, the sorting-out began.

Behind the Buzz was infinite flow, information careening through infinite space. What it said was perhaps less important than the simple fact that it spoke at all.

Because what it said was everything, spoken with every conceivable voice. What it described was the hollow, the husk, and the animating spark, in all of their particulars. Emptiness, when viewed as such, was no less a thing than the coalesced matter that marked it off, the flying impulse-data that defined its boundaries.

This was no less true of the dead than of the living.

All of it was here, and now.

The universe was huge and hungry, boundless in its phylum form. Species, spectrums, realms, dimensions rose in flickers, collapsed into voids. God was a dancer in infinite drag, and a voyuer esconsed on a pivoting throne. Watching. Watched. Devouring. Fasting. On-and-offing, in a binary code.

He would see all this, and then pull back: a boy in a body surrounded by corpses.

Then the Buzz would resume its song.

And, sated, he would return to the royal halls.

Occasionally, he ventured downstairs to the kitchen, in order to scavenge a personal treat. Increasingly, it was raw meat he craved: taken from the walk-in freezers, then thawed in the ovens until the blood flowed warm.

The kitchen staff had considerably thinned, mostly due to suicide. In the absence of judgment or opposition, this arrangement worked out just fine.

The Princess Sara's advanced pregnancy did nothing to slow their love-making; she'd announced the zygote with some fanfare in mid-February, and was now almost due. But still she craved sex with him, taking him sometimes three times in one day. Which was, again, perfectly fine with him. She'd descended into her own strange fantasy world—again, totally par for the course—and the bigger she got, the deeper she wanted him. Eventually, he wound up strapping on toys. (Some borrowed from the bishop, and some of her own.)

And just when that was no longer enough, Prince Randolph came back into their lives.

For the longest time, Randolph had stayed away from her bedchambers altogether. A few more fitful attempts, in the early days, had left him so thoroughly humiliated that he retreated to his own quarters entirely.

Though they were polite together at daily meals and other social functions, they'd not spent a private moment together since February.

With regards to her extracurricular coupling, both she and the boy assumed that Prince Randolph was either clueless or apathetic. He certainly seemed to revel in her pregnancy, and seemed quite excited about "his" child, apparently disregarding the fact that he'd never been inside her.

But then, one night, after an hour of frenzied fucking that had left her unable to climax, she bemoaned out loud her horny state.

And at that moment, Prince Randolph stepped in through the balcony curtains. He had, evidently, been there all night, observing every thrust.

Sara screamed, and the boy had to admit that he was a wee bit stunned as well. He rolled off the Princess and stared at Randolph, shuddering despite himself.

The Prince held up a silencing hand as he stepped deeper into the room. He was wearing his robe and slippers. "Did you think that I didn't know?" he said. "Honestly. I have known for some time. You're a very talented couple, and I've enjoyed watching you very much; but really, darling, you should always check the balcony before taking such risks."

His calm was unnerving, as was his relative good cheer. "Actually," he said, "I've given this much thought, over all these many months. It would seem that I have two choices." Holding up that many fingers. "One: to have the boy shot . . ."

Sara jumped, clutched the boy to her. "No!"

Randolph waved her off. "But . . . the second is better. Much better." A wide smile played across his face. Casually, he began to untie the robe's sash. "You see, it would seem that watching the two of you rutting has . . . solved my little problem."

His robe fell open, revealing an erection that was actually quite impressive.

Sara looked at the boy, then back at her husband. The range of expressions on her face was marvelous to behold. She was shocked and scared and embarrassed and angered and more than a little bit turned on.

The boy, in that moment, almost loved her.

But the Buzz welled large.

Then the Prince, unexpectedly, turned away from the bed and headed for the chamber door. Confusion trailed him, Sara and the boy exchanging a glance that was rife with the stuff. Randolph reached the door and threw it open, then turned around and grinned.

"I don't know if danger works for you," he said, "but it certainly does for me."

That night, the Bishop Hallam penned his final entry; hours later, in the aftermath, the boy would find it. The penmanship was shaky, and the ink was blotched where a trio of tears had slipped free of their defenses, exploded upon the page.

Nonetheless, his last words were duly noted, for all those generations to come . . .

My dears.

The end, at last. After what I have seen, there can be no doubt.

And God, you malevolent prick: grant me if you dare the wherewithal to describe it, before I go.

Spent hours today in council with the raving Florence, who, in my eyes, cannot die badly enough. Nothing new said. Such a huge surprise, there. Just more spinning of lunatic dreams that will never come to pass.

Then, just now, as I paced the corridors—emulating, I suppose, my sweet cuckolding boy—I found myself drawn to the corridor where the Princess Sara's bedchambers lay. Anticipating, as ever, the sounds of fuck.

Not expecting the door to be open.

It was not within my power to withstand the temptation. As many hours as I'd spent shamelessly masturbating there, I could not resist the urge to see for myself what I'd always imagined.

But when I saw the three of them together, as if spotlighted by the hallway's glare, it was as if some final threshold snapped within me. My cock went hard, and I loathed it more than I ever had before.

Because I could have waddled in, and inserted myself into Randolph's ass; and no doubt, I would have come. A jolly time had by all.

But the stink of decay, more profound than the dead, overcame my DNA, It was the crotch-rot of civilization, the ultimate betrayal of God by the flesh.

And then the boy, rectum stuffed, turned back to look at me, his eyes empty and black as the eyes of the dead.

And so help me God, he blew me a kiss.

Thanking me.

And saying goodbye,

I made it almost all the way to my rooms before vomiting. Three cheers for me, I have endured more betrayal than anyone should; and if I passed it back on, then more's the pity.

In a couple of minutes, I will go to see Lewis. Engage in idle banter. Just enjoy him, one more time.

The bullet that I place in his brain will be clean and instantaneous.

It is the last act of kindness of which I am capable.

There are only two guards at the gate tonight. If I am swift and capable, they should expire just as discreetly.

As for me, I anticipate agony.

But there it is. If there's an epitath, I would suggest that it be this:

"The Bishop John Hallam was a walrus in a frock, albeit one anointed by the mighty hand of God. He lusted after boys. Was that why he was punished?

"Who fucking knows?"

"Who fucking cares?"

If anyone survives in this Hell, I leave you now, just as I began.

Beauty has always been my downfall.

For God's sake, don't let it be yours.

XIII.

The boy was deep in the Prince's ass when the gunfire in the courtyard erupted. A total of three shots in all, but it was enough to disrupt the uber-coitus. The Prince and Princess, face to missionary face, caught themselves abruptly staring at each other in panic.

The boy continued thrusting.

And the Buzz went crystal-clear.

"Oh my God!" screamed the Prince, and it was plain from his quiver that he was just about to come. First time in a woman's cunt; and last, as it all turned out.

She grabbed his hips and felt him flood her, propelled in midspasm by the still-humping boy. And all at once, a moisture huge blew out of her, washing the Prince's spunk away.

Water sloshed the length of the bed, soaking the mattress from her ass to her feet. There was a moment of complete abstraction.

And then the first contraction hit.

The Prince pulled out, as if fired from a cannon. The boy slid out of him, as well. The men fell back as the woman howled and writhed on the bed in anguish.

A yell from the courtyard was met with a clipped staccato burst of gunfire.

Then the moan of the dead, heading back to the balcony. The curtains closed behind him. The boy looked at the bed.

Blood and water were staining the sheets.

Outside, the bishop began to scream.

And then the boy was off the bed, parting the curtains and staring down at the open gates in the courtyard flooding with the shambling dead. The bishop was pieces of wriggling red, detatching in stringers of shredding flesh. His mouth was a black hole that filled with fingers. Then he vanished altogether, and that was that.

The Prince stood at the balcony, gripping the railing with white-knuckled hands. His naked shoulders and neck and back were exposed to the boy who advanced now, transforming.

The Buzz blew into a sonic flare that flensed him of identity. In that moment, the boy was reborn, and instinctively knew what to do.

Veins popped as teeth scraped bone, and the Prince shrieked as his neck tore open, but the boy had pinned his arms back, and so there was no way to fight. The boy spat meat, with quite a bit left to swallow, and the world stung red as blood sprayed in his eyes.

There was struggle galore. Then the boy bit again, coming up with a mouthful of soft shoulder flesh. It came away hard, its structural integrity fighting, resisting the damage, to no avail. The Prince's knees buckled. He hit his head on the rail. Perhaps he blacked out, or just gave up entirely.

The boy flipped him over and took out his throat. Then his tongue. Then his eyes. Then his big flappy. Let him wander around like that for a while.

Let him wander around till the end of time.

There was gunfire resounding, but it sounded half-hearted. The last soldiers were dead, and they knew it. The boy listened to the shouting of names, of men entreating each other to survive. But all of them ended in screams; and fairly soon, the guns stopped firing altogether.

There were noises, then, inside the Palace: some of them living, but not nearly all. Sacred icons were breaking; the walls shuddered with violence; and the last of the staff was being turned into chum.

But there was one scream that went on and on.

The boy turned from the balcony, reentered her bedroom.

There was very much blood there now. It called to him, but there was much still left to do.

She called to him, as well; but it was no longer him that she was calling to. He had ceased to be that person: not dead, but no longer a man.

Into the hall he went. It was, as yet, vacant. But soon. Very soon. There was a bend at the end of the hall, and he took it, took it further, until he reached the wing where the last of the Royals were quartered. He imagined tea and bisquits, and, surprisingly, laughed.

The King and the Queen were still together. Or, rather, the King was all together. The Queen was mostly parts. Evidently, he had passed on in the course of the night, then reconnoitered with both his flesh and her own.

So much for that. The King eyed him blankly as he moved resolutely toward Florence's chambers.

At this point, a small mob joined him; but he felt no dread as he advanced toward the door. They saw him; they noted him; it was very much like the dream, except that they deferred to him in the strangest way. As if he were Royalty itself.

The boy was the first to reach the door; and as such, the first to reach the cowering Queen Mother. She was so tiny, in those final moments—such a creeching, piteous thing—that it was more than anti-climactic.

He simply tore her open.

And then let her people in.

"Happy Christmas," he muttered as he headed for the door. At least it felt like he had said that. Who fucking knew anymore.

All the way down the corridors, a huge contingent mounted. They were following him; that much was clear. And the Buzz was a fanfare of static distortion: real life, hideously sampled and then blared back at reality in ruins.

Maybe God had reformatted badly. Or maybe there was just a scratch in the record. Maybe Hallam was right, and Elvis had simply left the building:

leaving the needle to scratch away at the smooth grooves at the end of Earth's record, forever and ever.

Whatever. He followed the Princess's screams, which grew louder and louder with every step. Hearing a new voice that keened as hers faltered: high-pitched and wailing, ringing out through the night.

The room was full when he arrived, but nobody was feeding. Indeed, it was flush with reverence: a rare thing, in this place of barren symbol.

The Princess was barely alive. With its teeth, the newborn had delivered itself. There was blood everywhere, but the dead still held back, instinct reined in by a dictate that was wholly religious.

The crowd parted as the once-boy stepped forward, and the Princess's eyes flared up. The last impulse of light, in a world that had fallen. She was truly a beautiful woman. It was a shame, he guessed.

Ah, well.

She died, and he lifted the baby, turning toward the dead. It let out a keening sound, and as one, the dead stiffened, as if in prayer.

"It's a girl." They were his very last words.

God save the Queen.

We Will Rebuild

BY **CODY GOODFELLOW**

Cody Goodfellow is smarter than I am, a fact I Zenfully and gleefully acknowledge ever second of every day we collaborate together, on books or scripts or stories or whatever-the-hell else we might be up to at the time. Fact is, he was a badass writer before we met, and will doubtless still be one long after I'm gone.

That did not automatically qualify him to be in this book, all groans of ersatz nepotism to the contrary.

What qualified him was "We Will Rebuild": the small-town zombie apocalypse cop story to end all small-town zombie apocalypse cop stories.

Redneck zombie horror is so ubiquitous—from B movies and the small press all the way to the top—that calling 'em a dime a dozen is overrating the currency by more than half.

But what Cody does goes way the hell deeper than dime-store racism and traditional heartland slurs. It takes the time to get both provincialism and police procedure right, drawing the line between us and them in terms that illustrate the true nature of civic pride and cultural identity. Cutting through cliché to far more harrowing truth.

And when the punch line comes, that pretty much says it all.

That's the difference that quality makes.

ON THE FIRST MONTHLY ANNIVERSARY of V-D Day, some residents of Ocotillo still came out to wave or put Old Glory up on their porches as Deputies Snopes and Bascomb rolled up the nameless main drag in their armored cruiser, siren blaring to lift the curfew.

"Happy Death Day, suckers," Bascomb hollered.

"Leave 'em alone," Snopes said. "Everybody loves a parade."

Bascomb made V-D Day medals out of X-mas ribbon and teeth for the occasion, but only Bascomb wore his, along with his Army purple heart and the special citation for the Battle of the Calexico Wal-Mart, two weeks ago. A Wal-Mart greeter's nametag hung from the ribbon; *Hi! My Name is Sole Survivor.*

Verna Schepsi swept the sidewalk in front of the feed store, but it was a fool's errand. The particles of ash that still rained down out of the sulfurous yellow sunrise were like downy snowflakes, merging into gray dust devils battling in the empty street.

Chubby Beckwith lumbered out of the Circle K and waved at them when he got to the end of his chain. Chubby was a good kid, always kept a fresh pot of coffee on until they ran out of it, but he got grabby when they stopped to top off the cruiser once, so they had to chop off his hands. It was all legal, the papers on file with the judge.

"Wanna go out to the canal and look for deadbeats?" Bascomb was crocked early and itchy today, because his wife got into it with Taffy, their doberman pinscher. Reluctant to put either of them down, he was damned if he wasn't going to shoot something today.

"Waste of ammo," Snopes replied. "Besides, we got to go out and change the sign."

The sign marking the Interstate 8 off-ramp used to read *Ocotillo; Elev. 47; Ft. Pop. 220; Gas Food Lodging.* As soon as the dust settled after V-D Day, they revised the list of amenities with big stenciled red No's, and shortwave and CB frequencies to call those inside.

Snopes had the idea to borrow the scoreboard numbers from the little league field. He displayed the number of the alive with the black numbers for the home team, and the number of the dead in the red for the visitors. The score was not encouraging: 32 to 67. Gabe Gonzalez got bit by his daughter last night, and after they woke the judge up to sign the order, she was put down. Everyone pretty much knew what he was trying to do when he got bit, so no one was overly exercised about it.

Still and all, a pretty normal day . . .

Bascomb wanted to tack a 1 in front of the black number. "If any more gangs come looking for shit, we got to look tough."

"When the Army comes, we got to look meek, so they don't just bomb us. You heard on the radio what the Marines did to them rich dicks in Palm Springs."

Snopes went up the road with his binoculars to check the perimeter. Ocotillo straddled the I-8/S.R.46 junction, snug between the Anza-Borrego mountains, studded with fractured granite boulders and the dusty, drained lakebed of the Imperial Valley.

Nothing alive or dead had come up the 8 or down from the hills in over a week. Gangs and deadbeat stragglers from the conflagration that destroyed El Centro and Calexico still dribbled in from the east, but deadbeats couldn't cross the canal; burnt up with hunger and half-mummified by the desert sun, most of them dissolved like soda crackers in the swift current. Everything on wheels stopped where the deputies had blown the I-8 overpass at the canal, and either turned north on the 46 or abandoned their vehicles.

After that doctor from La Jolla, nobody had successfully pled for asylum in Ocotillo. When they let him in with his wife and three daughters, they thought they'd turned a corner; but three days later, the shitbird gassed himself and his whole family with their propane tank. The house blew up and burned down both its neighbors.

People from the cities couldn't handle desert life, before or after Day Zero. Nothing out here had changed. There had always been laws on the books for dealing with aliens. If they were from outside the town's jurisdiction and had nothing to offer, they had to be treated accordingly.

A couple deadbeats had wandered into the minefield along the highway a while back, and parts of them still tried to crawl through the tumbleweed snarls of razor wire that flanked the interstate and encircled the town. The fields were clearly marked for living and dead alike, cardboard signs and rotting, chattering heads on pikes, but nobody took time to read anymore.

Vultures and crows feuded over the last scraps on the skeletons of the latest live invaders—a small herd of runaway horses that had blundered into the claymores set up between the outbuildings of the abandoned Pernicano ranch. The yard sale scatter of long, elegant bones and stringy flesh looked like the ruins of something built to fly. Sometime ago, he might have seen something sad or beautiful in it, but now the waste of meat just made his mouth water.

In the crisp heat haze of the quickening day, everything seemed to squirm with a tortured thirst for blood and sweat. Snopes went back to the cruiser. With sheet metal and chainlink fence for windows, it was already a sweat lodge inside. Bascomb was in the driver's seat, hooting at the radio like football was back. "Hell yeah!"

Snopes pushed him over and got in, turned back down the off-ramp. Bascomb loaded shells into the shotgun and stuffed the rest of them in his pockets. "Dead wetbacks!"

They passed Chubby again, who waved a stump at them as he chewed on the other, and a couple of boarded-up houses. Mrs. Chesebro wandered her dusty yard in her housecoat, looking for her cats. Next door, Chet Bamberger strained at the end of his leash to get his month-old morning paper. He wore only a wifebeater tanktop—second-skinned to him by yellow seepage, and drizzling maggots out the armpits. His muzzle was splashed with bright red blood, which, since his own was black and clotted in his feet and ass, clearly solved the mystery of the missing cats.

Bamberger was unemployed, and lost his license for a third DUI coming back from the Golden Acorn casino, so he and the deputies knew each other pretty well. He liked to tune up his wife, but she never pressed charges. He beat up Connie in Pal Joey's Bar on V-D Day, and got locked up with some deadbeat tweaker from San Diego who'd crashed a stolen car on the off-ramp. The tweaker bit Chet, who died but got up and ate two of his cellmates.

Chet was one of the first locals to stir, and Snopes put four bullets into his torso that night. He sorely regretted that he didn't know, back then, that you have to shoot them in the head. Order was restored, Connie took him home, and he hadn't attacked anyone since. How they stayed together under one roof with no AC was a mystery to Snopes, but their problems were none of his business, until someone complained.

At the stoplight, Ocotillo showed that somebody really believed it would be a proper town, once. A shabby little bandstand and a pocket park once sat in the middle of the road, but now, the town square was a field of black, greasy ash. A sun-bleached and smoke-blackened banner hung over the street, reminding him to catch the Ocotillo Settlers' Days festival that should have started last weekend.

The town hall was a sturdy whitewashed brick monument to itself, with a sheriff's station, courtroom, mayor's office, basement holding cells, and a broom closet that doubled as a library and civil defense shelter.

V-D Day was mostly peaceful in Ocotillo, until the panicked mass exodus from San Diego swept through, with the dead in its wake. Half the town bugged out for the hills, while the rest hunkered down in attics and cellars, or the town hall building.

Ocotillo was overrun and picked clean. Sheriff Lorber and the deputies holed up on the town hall roof when the remaining civilians fled or went down in the shelter. The dead converged on the town hall, wading into the ankle-deep gasoline pool Sheriff Lorber had drained into the square, and gawking up at them as they tossed road flares.

When the fire died down, the wave had crested and fallen, and the remaining deadbeats were easy to put down or contain.

Judge Dooling came down from his ranch that morning, and since the Mayor was dead, he took over and restored order. Painting the town hall white again had been the first order of business.

The people in the shelter weren't so lucky. When the power failed and the water pressure dropped, rats boiled out of the toilets and bit them in the dark. All the rats had feasted on the bodies in the streets, and were rife with the bug that made them walk and eat.

Whatever still knocked around inside was too dumb to work the hatch, but the Judge ordered them to open it. Three deputies had family in the shelter, and at first, they were just happy to have them back. Benedetto got careless, and was bit by his son. He looked happy, when he and his family lurched out of their trailer for the chow wagon. Espinoza ate his gun that night, after executing his deadbeat wife and his mother. Bascomb and his hogbitch wife fought almost every night, so for them, nothing much had changed at all.

In all, they identified seventy-nine walking dead residents, and sixty-three living. Getting the deadbeat locals to go home was easy; once chained down in their houses or at their jobs, most just did more or less what they always had, knocking around aimlessly until chow time, or until live meat got too close. Putting the muzzles on, though, was a king-hell bitch.

Deputy Mark Snopes had no family in town. He came over from the San Diego Police Department two years before, and was damned lucky to have a job. The cop mentality—us versus them, with any civilian more or less one of them—ground on his nerves. He tasered an enormous lady shoplifter when she got aggressive with him. She turned out to be five months pregnant, and miscarried.

In a burg like Ocotillo, it was the same problems, but smaller and simpler. Half the town out of its head on drink or drugs or God, and beating on the other half; shitheads and deadbeats passing through, littering, and shooting up the signs; and wetbacks, creeping over the border and eating all the livestock. But it was better than the city. The desert took care of those who couldn't take care of themselves. You knew who the good people were, and the right and the wrong of a situation was writ plain. Now, more than ever . . .

Snopes swung the cruiser into the town hall lot and jumped out. Bascomb called after him, "Fuck you, then, I'm driving!"

Betty Olson saw him coming, and unlocked the door, then locked and bolted it when he barged through the saloon doors that led to the courtroom. "I wouldn't" she whispered, "The generator's out, so he's in a mood."

Snopes didn't knock. The courtroom was darker than the other rooms, with no slits cut into the boards over the windows, and no lamplight. The dark was all violet fireworks until his eyes adjusted to the pinprick spiderwebs of daylight seeping into the courtroom.

In the stifling heat and silence, Snopes believed he could feel something scratching, like claws, on the concrete underneath his feet. Somewhere in the room, the dispatch radio crackled.

"Your Honor, even if there was something out there, we got bigger shit—beg pardon, sir—issues, to contend with, and I'm worried about Bascomb—"

"He's worried about you, Deputy."

"I can't see you, Your Honor."

A match flashed and kissed the mantle of a Coleman lamp on the judge's desk. "The dark makes it feel cooler." Only the gavel, drinking glass, revolver, and pale, liver-spotted hands came into view. "If we had gas to spare for the generators . . . but never mind. You wanted to resign, then?"

"You know I don't. I take this job seriously, and since Sheriff Lorber got bit, me and Doug are pretty much the only law left. But this patrol duty isn't going to solve anything. We're just wasting gas."

"Deputy, the migrant illegal traffic through this area is more of a scourge now than ever. You saw, yourself, what they did in Seeley and Calexico. You'd like to see them gather at the wire, I suppose, and overrun us again?"

Snopes couldn't lose his temper with the judge, but the way he tied you up with his questions made his head hurt. "I'd like to clean up the mess *inside* the wire."

"What mess is there? What haven't you been reporting to me?"

Snopes came closer to the light. The outline of Dooling's head floated in the dark above the perfect black of his robe. Hairless, blank as the moon. "Your Honor hasn't been outside in a while, so far as I know, but I have, and I file reports on everything. Five of our people got killed this month in, uh, domestic disputes—"

"*Nine* died this month, don't you mean, Deputy Snopes?"

"No sir, the other four were already—"

"They were citizens of this town, each and everyone, never forget that. We take care of our own."

"Sir, we have a responsibility to the living to protect them from the dead . . . don't we?"

Judge Dooling looked Snopes up and down, his bifocals and his dentures winking in the yellow light. "Deputy, do you know why the dead got up last month?"

Snopes felt as if the courtroom at his back was packed with laughing ghosts, laughing at him. "No sir, I don't."

The judge clucked his tongue, a dry baby rattler sound. "Then how can you say you know what will happen tomorrow?"

Snopes headed for the door. "I don't get it, Your Honor."

Dooling's chair creaked. "You are the arm of the law, young man, not its brain. The police have ever had the thankless duty of standing between the citizenry and their own worst impulses."

"*Your Honor might take a different view of the law if he ever got off his fossilized ass and tried enforcing it.*" That was what Snopes wished he'd said. Instead, he said, "Yes, Your Honor."

Dooling's voice got higher and louder as Snopes walked away. When Snopes stopped at the door, it went down low, but the superb acoustics of the courtroom delivered it to his ear. "This could be divine retribution, and it could be a disease, Deputy. But tomorrow, if it is a disease, there may be a cure; and if it is the judgment of God, then we will go to our greater reward with our sins against the innocent and ill weighing heaviest in our hearts."

Snopes tried hard not to shout. "Your Honor, Bascomb and I are more than ready to take care of business with a clean conscience—"

"Have him start with his wife, then, would you, Deputy? You haven't lost anyone, so you can't relate. The state can't presume to write the law, but should act to preserve order and normality, until the rest of the world does likewise."

"Right, everything's normal."

"Yes, if we say so, and we do. We have restored order, and we will rebuild our town. Now there's a mob of dead illegal aliens massed somewhere around the fence. See to it."

Snopes left, stopped in the library to get a tripod-mounted M-60 and two extra belts. Judge Dooling was also a retired Brigadier General in the National Guard, and had the keys to the armory in Seeley. All the heavy stuff went out to blockade the 8 to the east, to stop the deadbeat armies marching out of Mexico. Nothing came back.

Snopes got blindsided by the daylight when he went outside. He slipped on his shades. Bascomb hung out the window with his arms thrown wide for the machinegun. "OK, you can drive."

They drove south, down the perimeter to where it swerved east to parallel the interstate. "All clear, shit!" Bascomb growled, and cracked open a blood-hot beer.

Most of the ash came from El Centro, Calexico, and Mexicali, which the Marines torched with fuel-air bombs a week after V-D Day. They boiled over like anthills doused in gas, never-ending waves of deadbeats, scorched black and ravenous. The Marines got eaten or bugged out, and that was the last they saw of any order outside their own fence.

Snopes went up the canal to where the fence picked up at the trailer park at the north end of town. He cut across the back end of Bascomb's yard on the cul-de-sac. Bascomb waved to his wife, who drooled and banged on the bars of their bedroom window.

They followed the fence along the canal and turned north, and were almost back to the main drag when Bascomb called, "Wetbacks!"

Snopes braked on the shingled dirt road beside the abandoned Milbank ranch, which stood half in and half out of the perimeter. Donnie Milbank was a small-time TV minister, and when the Rapture found him still on earth, he packed up the family in the Winnebago and hauled ass for some born-again survivalist enclave in Texas.

Where the fence circled behind Milbank's stables, he saw twenty or thirty ragged scarecrows loping across the dead brown lawn. They shambled jerkily through a gap in the razor wire, where it was trampled flat.

Snopes jerked to a stop. The nearest wetback was inside the fence, not ten feet away, flannel and denim rags caked with mud and dust and blood, greedy claws outstretched, slack jaws snapping in dumb, bottomless hunger. Bascomb jumped out, laid the M-60 across the hood and opened up.

Bascomb hosed them down like leaves off a driveway, walking the spray of lead across their midsections to slash them in half and pile them up against the wire.

Snopes stayed behind the wheel, but opened fire with the shotgun. He saw big scoops of meat lifted out of heads and chests and knew he was connecting; at this range, how could he miss?

It was hard to hear with the atomic-typewriter clatter of the machinegun, but when Bascomb finally stopped to reload, Snopes could see how a few survivors tried to run for the open desert. He could hear how they screamed and cried and prayed.

His stomach filled with nightcrawlers and battery acid. "Stop! Bascomb, Doug, Jesus Christ, stop! *They're not dead!*" He hit the siren and jumped out, ran around the cruiser to knock Bascomb down, because his partner just laughed and kept shooting.

Snopes tore down the gun and shut off the siren. If any got away, he didn't see them moving.

Bascomb got up and dusted off, punched Snopes in the shoulder. "Fuck you thinking, fucker? You wanna die?"

"Didn't you hear that? They were fucking screaming!"

"They were screaming in Spanish! They're fucking wetbacks, dude, and they look pretty fucking dead now. Come on, let's clean up."

Bascomb covered while Snopes checked for survivors. There were none, and nothing got up. The bodies lay in mounds like wet laundry in the gap, which they'd made by throwing plywood from Millbank's stables over the wire. There were nineteen of them, as near as he could tell, what with their being blown open and running into each other like a casserole.

He saw two women with babies in slings, and another who might've been pregnant.

"Give me a hand, asshole," Snopes said. He turned and vomited into the dust, wrapped a bandana over his face. They rolled out some tarp and got them ready for the chow wagon.

The bodies were pitifully light, skeletal, blistered skin flaking away, but they had walked out of Mexico alive. "We gotta get this shit in the chipper before lunchtime," Bascomb said. "Stiffs'll think it's Thanksgiving."

"Your wife'll be so happy," Snopes said, "she might even let you get some."

"Fuck you, Mark. Least I got something to come home to . . ."

They lifted one by the hands and feet, and were trying to sling it over on the tarp without spilling its innards, when Chet Bamberger came limping across the yard, with his chain and a chunk of drywall dragging behind him.

"Oh fuck," Snopes cried, and let go of the corpse's feet.

Bascomb let go a hair too late, and blundered into the piles of razor wire. He shrieked, "Eeeeyagh!" and jerked up, but the curling steel teeth snagged his uniform and flabby back and dragged him back into the thickest of it.

Like all Ocotillo's registered dead citizens, Chet wore a chain and a leather muzzle with a bike lock on the back, and only a tiny hole for eating. They were fed slurry and carrion from the chow wagon, but said supply had petered out as even the dead stopped coming down the road.

Chet wasn't wearing his muzzle.

Snopes's left hand went out to pull Bascomb free, while his right tried to draw his gun. Neither effort met with much success.

Chet ignored them. He ambled over to the pile of bodies and squatted over one, lifted a neatly bisected hemisphere of a woman's skull and slurped at it like a slice of cantaloupe. Snopes smashed Bamberger's grill in when he put on the muzzle, so the slobbering hole he chewed his food with had no teeth in it.

Somehow, this only made him more repulsive, more threatening. His crumbling gray hide was pocked with burns and brands, and carved words. A Camel Filter butt jutted out of his left ear, and his right ear was melted off. With no TV and no Indian casinos down the road, Connie had been forced to take up a new hobby, but nobody had filed a complaint, so who was he to judge?

The jingling music of the approaching chow wagon echoed through the streets. "Music Box Dancer" today, thank God. Snopes didn't know why, but if he heard "Do You Know The Way To San Jose" one more time, *he* was going to eat somebody's brains.

Chet's eyes were pointed at Snopes, but they were as vital as soft-boiled eggs, and was there any remorse in them, any horror, at what he'd become? Was there any spark of anything worth saving, in the rancid mayonnaise behind those dead eyes? Had there ever been?

Snopes drew his gun and shot Chet Bamberger through the left eye, and then, because it wouldn't close, through the right.

The chow wagon pulled up in a cloud of dust. Something about the old ice cream truck always creeped Snopes out, even when it still sold ice cream. Now, with racks of chainsaws, baling hooks and flamethrowers and a wood-chipper in tow, and all the Rocket Pop and Dove Bar stickers slathered in sun-baked blood and clouds of ecstatic flies, the chow wagon only brought relief; somebody else to clean up this mess.

"Murderer! Fucking murderer!" Fists drummed on Snopes's back, ineffectual against his bulletproof vest, but knocking him off-balance when he tried to help Bascomb get free.

Connie Bamberger kicked Snopes in the crotch. He tripped and fell on the body pile. His hand snagged in a body cavity and half a baby spilled down the back of his neck.

"Murderer! Arrest him, Doug! I *want justice!*"

They grabbed him when he came into the courtroom. It was dark, but he recognized the deep-fried roadkill smell of Torres, who ran the Indian Skillet across the street, and Sturtevant's livestock stink, McBride by the whiskey on his breath. Bascomb unsnapped his holster and took his gun.

Connie Bamberger sobbed uncontrollably on the witness stand. Judge Dooling sat at the edge of the lampglow with his hand on the revolver. "Now, Mrs. Bamberger has given her testimony, and her complaint has been reviewed."

"What is this shit?" Snopes shouted. "Get off me, it was self defense."

"Witnesses say otherwise. Mr. Bamberger was not aggressive, and the illegal aliens' refuse was going to be processed for feed, in any event. You took a citizen's life in cold blood, Deputy. You broke the law, and it is very clear."

"That's not the real goddamned law! It's not murder! Chet was already dead!" Snopes struggled in the arms of the other men, but Bascomb jabbed him in the back with his own gun. As his eyes adjusted to the light, he saw the gloomy courtroom was packed with people, half the surviving town gathered to watch.

"All of us are equal before the law, Mark. I can't sentence you to death, but you've shown that you cannot be trusted to wield force in our defense. We'll have to ask for your badge."

Someone ripped it off his uniform. "Fine, take it and fuck you all."

"Excellent. And now, Doctor, tie off his arms."

Snopes bucked backwards, throwing Sturtevant into Torres, and driving Bascomb back into the door. His gun went off into the ceiling. Snopes jumped for the door, but Bascomb was quicker, and smashed him across the back of the head. The lamplight turned into a golden lava lamp glow, and he collapsed on a plastic tarp.

Dr. McBride was a veterinarian and a drunk, but he was Ocotillo's only medical authority, so he tied Snopes off at the elbows, and pumped him with a syringe that made the trippy light into a pointillist cloudscape.

"Son, I'm sorry as hell," McBride whispered in his ear. "We all know why you did it, but there's gotta be law, and the law's gotta be blind. My son, he's dead, but he's walking, so who's to say he won't get better? If we let you go on like you done—"

Judge Dooling banged his gavel. "Don't badger the prisoner, Walter. Deputy Bascomb, proceed."

Bascomb still bled from divots the razorwire gouged out of his neck, scalp and arms, but he did not hesitate to drag his partner's right arm out across the floor and step on the wrist, heft the axe and slam it into the inside of Snopes's elbow.

From head to toe, he was bathed in lightning. Screaming blood and vomit and streaming tears, Snopes tried to fight, but he couldn't even get the breath to scream for mercy when they tugged the other one away from his chest and chopped it off, as well.

A little blood oozed out of the tourniquets, but Dr. McBride cauterized the stumps with a blowtorch and pronounced him sound.

The gavel banged again. "Court is adjourned. Deputy, leave the defendant where he is. I'd like a word. No, touch nothing—"

Snopes lay there, watching the silhouettes of the people he'd sworn to protect and serve file past the tarp. The sight of his severed arms, splayed out in front of him like spare parts from a model kit, was very unsettling; but he couldn't remember why until he reached out to touch them.

He still couldn't scream, but he found it very easy to cry.

When the courtroom was empty, Judge Dooling rose from the bench, shuffled over to Snopes, and knelt beside him.

"I know you think this is very cruel and unusual, Mark, but we all have to learn to submit to something bigger than ourselves."

Snopes's response was garbled, even to himself.

The judge sighed, touched his shoulder. "You think this is insane, but you are fortunate not to be able to understand. You probably won't remember this, but I wish you would, so you could see how wrong you were, as time goes by, about the risen population of Ocotillo.

"The dead are not wholly incapable of recovery, Mr. Snopes."

Dooling brought his face down closer to the deputy and picked up his severed left forearm. He stroked Snopes's face with his own fingers, then took a bite out of the meaty belly of the exposed muscle, just above the clean cut at the elbow.

"We *are* getting better," His Honor said around a mouthful of flesh. "Order has been restored. We will rebuild our town, and it will be better than it ever was, with equal liberty and justice for *all* its citizens."

Snopes had all but blacked out. His last clear memory was of the Judge: wiping his blood-slick lips, taking the scorched stumps of his arms in his hands, and licking them with his gray, ulcerated tongue, just like a stamp.

But he heard him get up and call for Bascomb. "You're free to go."

SPARKS FLY UPWARDS

BY LISA MORTON

I've always felt that social commentary is one of the things that horror fiction excels at. The conditions that promote heartbreak, loss, pain, and terror are its natural stomping grounds.

This little beauty by Lisa Morton explores the deep divide between pro-life and pro-choice in a way that stunningly spans the chasm. You may not agree with its ultimate conclusions—statistically, the odds are roughly fifty-fifty that either you will or you most definitely won't—but you can't argue with the heart and thoughtfulness evinced in this harrowing domestic drama writ large.

Those who look to survivalist horror for answers to the hard questions need to keep this one in their active checklist. It is, as they say, a keeper.

My breath is corrupt, my days are extinct, the graves are ready for me.

Job 17:1

Blessed and holy is he that hath part in the first resurrection . . .

Revelation 20:6

JUNE 16

Tomorrow marks one year ago that the Colony was begun here, and I think just about everyone is busy preparing for a big celebration. We just had our first real harvest two weeks ago, so there'll be plenty of good things to eat, and as for drink—well, the product of George's still is a little extreme for most tastes, so Tom and a few of the boys made a foray outside yesterday for some real liquor.

Of course I was worried when Tom told me he was going (and not even for something really vital, just booze), but he said it wasn't so bad. The road was almost totally clear for the first five miles after they left the safety of the Colony, and even most of Philipsville, the pint-sized town where they raided a liquor store, was deserted. Tom said he shot one in the liquor store cellar when he went down there to check on the good wines; it was an old woman, probably the one-time shopkeeper's wife locked away. Unfortunately, she'd clawed most of the good bottles off to smash on the floor. Tom took what was left, and an unopened case of good burgundy he found untouched in a corner. There are 131 adults in the Colony, and he figured he'd have a bottle for every two on Anniversary Day.

It's been two weeks since any of the deadheads have been spotted near the Colony walls, and Pedro Quintero, our top marksman, picked that one off with one shot straight through the head from the east tower. It would be easy to fool ourselves into thinking the situation is finally mending . . . easy and dangerous, because it's not. The lack of deadheads seen around here lately proves only one thing: That Doc Freeman was right in picking this location, away from the cities and highways.

Of course Doc Freeman was right—he's right about everything. He said we should go this far north because the south would only keep getting hotter, and sure enough it's been in the 80's here for over a week now. I don't want to think what it is down in L.A. now—probably 120, and that's in the shade.

Tomorrow will be a tribute to Doc Freeman as much as an anniversary celebration. If it hadn't been for him . . . well, I suppose Tom and little Jessie and I would be wandering around out there with the rest of them right now, dead for a year but still hungry. Always hungry.

It's funny, but before all the shit came down, Doc Freeman was just an eccentric old college professor teaching agricultural sciences and preaching survival. Tom always believed Freeman had been thinking about cutting out anyway, even before the whole zombie thing, because of the rising temperatures. He told his students that agriculture in most parts of the U.S. was already a thing of the past, and it would all be moving up to Canada soon.

When the deadheads came (Doc Freeman argued, as did a lot of other environmentalists, that they were caused by the holes in the ozone layer, too), it was the most natural thing in the world, I guess, for him to assemble a band of followers and head north. He'd chosen the site for the Colony, set up policy and government, designed the layout of fields, houses and fences, and even assigned each of us a job, according to what we were best at. It had all been scary at first, of course—especially with three-year old Jessie—but we all kind of fell into place. I even discovered I was a talented horticulturist—Doc says the best after him—and in some ways this new life is better than the old one.

Of course there are a lot of things we all miss—ice cream, uncalloused hands, TV—Del still scans the shortwave radio, hoping he'll pick something up on it. In a year, he has only once, and that transmission ended with the sound of gunshots.

So we accept our place in the world—and the fact that it may be the last place. Tomorrow we do more than accept it, we celebrate it.

I wish I knew exactly how to feel.

JUNE 17

Well, the big day has come and gone.

Tom is beside me, snoring in a blissful alcoholic oblivion. Tomorrow he'll be in the fields again, so he's earned this.

Jessie is in her room next door, exhausted from all the games she played and sweets she ate. Tom actually let me use a precious hour of videotape to record her today.

And yet I wasn't the only one crying when Doc Freeman got up and made his speech about how his projections show that if we continue at our present excellent rate, we'll be able to expand the colony in three years. Expand it carefully, he added. Meaning that in three years there'll be probably forty or fifty couples—like Tom and me—begging for the precious right to increase our family.

I know Doc is right, that we must remember the lessons of the old world and not outgrow our capacity to produce, to sustain that new growth . . . but somehow it seems wrong to deny new life when we're surrounded by so much death.

Especially when the new life is in me.

JUNE 24

I've missed two now, and so I felt certain enough to go see Dale Oldfield. He examined me as best he could (he's an excellent G.P., but his equipment is still limited), and he concluded I'd guessed right.

I am pregnant.

Between the two of us we figured it at about six weeks along. Dale thanked me for not trying to hide it, then told me he would have to report it to Doc Freeman. I asked only that Tom and I be allowed to be there when he did. He agreed, and we decided on tomorrow afternoon.

I went home and told Tom. At first he was thrilled—and then he remembered where we were.

I told Tom we'd be seeing Doc Freeman tomorrow about it, and he became obsessed with the idea that he'd somehow convince Doc to let us have the baby.

I couldn't stand to hear him torture himself that way, so I read stories to Jessie and held her until we both fell asleep in her narrow child-sized bed.

JUNE 25

We saw Doc Freeman today. Dale Oldfield confirmed the situation, then gracefully excused himself, saying he'd be in his little shack-cum-office when we needed him.

Doc Freeman poured all three of us a shot of his private stock of Jim Beam, then he began the apologies. Tom tried to argue him out of it, saying a birth would be good for morale, and we could certainly handle just one more in the Colony . . . but Doc told him quietly that, unlike many of the young couples, we already had a child and couldn't expect special treatment. Tom finally gave in, admitting Doc was right—and I'd never loved him more than I did then, seeing his pain and regret.

He went with me to tell Dale we'd be needing his services next week, and Dale just nodded, his head hung low, not meeting our eyes.

Afterwards, in our own bungalow, Tom and I argued for hours. We both got crazy, talking about leaving the Colony, building our own little fortress somewhere, even overthrowing Doc Freeman . . . but I think we both knew it was all fantasy. Doc Freeman had been right again—we did have Jessie, and maybe in a few more years the time would be right for another child.

But not now.

JULY 2

Tomorrow is the day set for us to do it.

God, I wish there was another way. Unfortunately, even after performing a D&C three times in the last year, Dale still has never had the clinic's equipment moved to the Colony. It's ironic that we can send out an expedition for booze, but not one for medical equipment. Doc Freeman says that's because the equipment is a lot bigger than the booze, and the Colony's only truck has been down basically since we got here.

So tomorrow Tom, Dale, and I will make the eighteen-mile drive to Silver Creek, the nearest town big enough to have had a family planning clinic. Dale, who has keys to the clinic, assures me the only dangerous part will be getting from the car to the doors of the clinic. They can't get inside, he tells me, so we'll be safe—until we have to leave again, that is.

Funny . . . when he's telling me about danger, he only talks about deadheads.

He never mentions the abortion.

JULY 3

I didn't sleep much last night. Tom held me but even he dozed off for a while. It's morning as I write this, and I hear Jessie starting to awaken. After I get her up, I'll try to tell her mommy and daddy have to leave for a while, and nice Mrs. Oldfield will watch her. She'll cry, but hopefully not because she understands what's really going on.

It's later now—Jessie's taken care of, and Dale's got the jeep ready to go. Tom and I check our supplies again: an automatic .38 with full magazine, an Uzi with extra clips, a hunting rifle with scope and plenty of ammo, three machetes, and the little wooden box. Dale's also got his shotgun and a Walther PPK that he says makes him feel like James Bond. Everyone teases him about it, telling him things like the difference is that Bond's villains were all alive to begin with. Dale always glowers and shuts up.

It's time to go.

We climbed into the Jeep. Tom asked why I was bringing you (diary) along, and I told him it was my security blanket and rabbit's foot. He shut up and Dale gunned the engine. We had to stop three times on the way out to exchange hugs and good luck wishes with people who ran up from the fields when we went by.

We're about 15 miles out now, and it's been the way Tom said—quiet. After the gates swung open and we pulled onto the dusty road, it must've been ten minutes before we saw the first deadhead. It was lumbering slowly across a sere field, still fifty yards from the road as we whipped by.

A few miles later there was a small pack of three in the road, but they were spaced wide apart. Dale drove around two of them; they clawed in vain at the Jeep, but we were doing 60 and they just scraped their fingers. The third one was harder to drive around—there were car wrecks on either side of the road—so Dale just whomped into him. He flew over the welded cage at the front of the Jeep and landed somewhere off to the side of the road. We barely felt it.

We'd just reached the outskirts of Silver Creek when Dale slowed down and cleared his throat. Then he said, Listen, Sarah, there's something you ought to know about the clinic. He asked me if I'd talked to any of the others he'd already escorted out here.

Of course I had, but they had only assured me of Dale's skilled, painless technique, and that they'd be there if I needed to talk. None of them had said much about the clinic itself.

I said this to Dale, and he asked me something strange.

He asked if I was religious.

Tom and I looked at each other, then Tom asked Dale what he was getting at.

Dale stammered through something about how the deadheads tend to go back to places that were important to them, like their homes or shopping malls or schools.

We nodded—everyone knew that—and Dale asked if we'd ever heard of Operation SoulSave.

I swear I literally tasted something bad in my mouth. How could I forget? The fundamentalists who used to stand around outside abortion clinics and shout insults and threats at people who went in. I was with a friend once—a very young friend—when it happened to her.

Then I realized what he was saying. I couldn't believe it. I tried to ask him, but my words just tripped all over each other. He nodded and told us.

They're still here.

Most of Silver Creek was empty. We saw some of them inside dusty old storefronts, gazing at us stupidly as we drove by, but they probably hadn't fed in well over a year and were pretty sluggish. Either that, or they'd just been that way in life—staring slack-jawed as it passed them by.

That wasn't the case, however, with the group before the clinic.

There must have been twenty of them, massed solidly before the locked doors. As we drove towards them, I saw their clothes, once prim and starched, now stained with all those fluids they'd long ago feared or detested. One still held up a sign (I realized a few seconds later he had taped it to his wrist as he died) which read **Operation SoulSave—Save a Soul for Christ!** Several sported the obligatory **Abortion Is Murder** t-shirts, now tattered and discolored.

Their leader was the Priest. I remembered him from before, when he'd been on all the news programs, spouting his vicious rhetoric while his flock chanted behind him. Of course, he looked different now—somebody had snacked on his trapezius, so his Roman Collar was covered in dried gore and hung askew, and his head (he was also missing a considerable patch of scalp on that same side) canted strangely at an odd angle.

I saw Dale eyeing them and muttering something under his breath. I asked him what it was so I could write it down: *Yet man is born unto trouble, as the sparks fly upward.* He said it was from the Bible. I was surprised; I didn't know Dale read the Bible.

Tom responded with a quote from one of the more contemporary prophets: I *used to be disgusted, now* I *try to be amused.* Then he asked Dale what we were going to do. Dale, who was practiced in this, said he'd drive around the building once, which would draw most of them away from the front long enough for us to get in. They wouldn't bother the Jeep when we weren't in it.

Dale headed for the next corner. Tom pulled the .38 and held it, and I remembered.

I was thinking about the time I had to go to a different clinic with my friend Julie. It was before I started you, diary; in fact, I started you about the time Julie disappeared with most of the rest of the world. So I've never written any of this down before.

Julie had gotten pregnant from her boyfriend Sean, who split when she told him. Abortions were legal then (this was a long time ago), but could be costly, and Julie, who was still going to college (as I was), had no money. She went to her parents, but they threw her out of the house. She thought about having the baby and putting it up for adoption, but she had no health insurance, wouldn't be able to afford the actual birth, and regarded overpopulation as the end of the world. This, obviously, was before the deadheads arrived and clarified *that* issue.

So I'd lent her the money, and agreed to go with her to the clinic. She made the appointment, worried about it so much she didn't sleep the night before, almost backed out twice on the drive there—and all so she could be confronted by the fine Christian citizens of Operation SoulSave.

They had seated themselves on either side of the walkway leading into the clinic. Even though it was in another state and time, they wore the same T-shirts and held the same signs. They were mainly male, or women in clothes so tight they seemed life-threatening. They all had vacuous smiles on their faces, that gave way to cruel snarls of contempt whenever anyone went into or out of the clinic doors.

Julie took one look at them and didn't want to leave the car. I told her we'd be late, and she said it didn't matter.

We'd talked about the morality of abortion already, and had agreed that it was obvious that the unformed, early fetus was only an extension of the mother's body, and as such each woman had the right to make her own decision. I reminded Julie of this as she sat shivering in the car, and she'd said that wasn't why she didn't want to go past them.

She was afraid of *them*. She said they seemed like a mindless horde, capable of any violence they were directed to commit.

She'd had no idea how right she was.

We drove slowly around one corner. Sure enough, they stumbled after us. Then Dale threw it into fourth, and we screeched the rest of the way around the block.

When we got back to the main entrance, there were only five or six still there, not including one that dragged itself around on two partially-eaten legs. Tom handed me the Uzi, while he took the .38 and cradled the box. Dale opted for a machete (I didn't want to have to see him use it minutes before he operated on *me*).

We sprinted from car to door. Tom shot two right between the eyes. I raised the Uzi, forgetting its rapid-fire design, and ripped one of them completely apart. I felt my stomach turn over as I saw some stale gray stuff splatter the doors. Dale just kept running, shouldering the last two aside. One rebounded and grabbed his left arm. He whirled and brought the machete down, severing the thing's hand, then kicked the deadhead away. He pried the dead hand from his arm, threw it aside, and told us to cover him while he unlocked the door.

As Dale fiddled with the keys, Tom shot the two Dale had barreled through. Then the .38 jammed. He began to fieldstrip it, and I looked nervously down the street, where the ones we'd tricked were shambling back, led by the gruesome

Priest. Suddenly I felt something on my ankle. I looked down to see the legless one had dragged itself up the steps, and was bringing its gaping maw to bear on my lower calf. I freaked out and grabbed the Walther from Dale's holster; I think I was screaming as I fired into the zombie's peeling head. It died and let go, thick brown liquid draining onto its **Save a Soul—Close a Clinic** T-shirt.

Then Dale had the doors open and we were in.

Later, Tom told me he had to pry the pistol from my fingers while Dale started up the generator and got things ready.

Then before I knew it Dale was there, in gloves and mask, saying he was ready.

I don't remember much of the actual operation, except that I asked Tom to wait outside—and the sound. The horrible sound the whole time we were in there:

Them, pounding on the doors, slow heavy thuds, relentless, unmerciful.

Dale was, as I've said before, an excellent doctor, and it was over soon. He made sure I didn't see what he put into the tiny wooden box Tom had carried in, and I didn't ask. The box, which had been beautifully crafted by Rudy V., would be taken back to the Colony and buried there.

There was one thing I had to ask, though, as morbid a though as it was. I had to know if—I had to be sure Dale had—God, I can't even write it.

But he knew what I was asking, and as he stripped off the gloves he told me I didn't have to worry. None of the ones aborted had ever come back. The rest of us had to be cremated or have the brain destroyed upon death, or we'd resurrect.

How ironic, I thought, that this was how we would finally lay to rest the Great Debate. They weren't human enough to come back. Abortion isn't murder.

Getting out would be harder than getting in, but Dale had it all down. Tom would crawl out a side window, drawing them away from Dale and me. Dale would lock the front door while Tom and I covered him, then we'd all head for the Jeep. I was, of course, still weak, and Tom didn't want to leave my side, but Dale told him it was the safest way, and he'd be sure I was okay. Tom reluctantly agreed.

It went down without mishap. They were slow and easily confused, and by the time they saw two of us on the stoop and one by the Jeep, they didn't know which way to turn. Tom shot a couple who were in our way. Once Dale had the doors locked, he pocketed the keys, took the Uzi from me, and I carried the little coffin as we ran for the Jeep.

Once we were inside, Dale started it up and pulled away. They were already hammering on the sides, clawing the welded cage, drooling a yellowish bile. One wouldn't let go as we drove off, and it got dragged fifty feet before its fingers tore off. Tom actually shouted something at it.

Dale was ready to speed out of town when I asked him to stop the Jeep and go back. He stopped, then both he and Tom turned to stare at me, as open-mouthed as any deadhead. They asked why, and I just handed Tom our box, took the rifle, got out and started walking back.

They ran up on either side of me, Tom saying I was still delirious from the operation, Dale arguing I could start hemorrhaging seriously. I ignored them both as I saw the deadheads at the end of the street staggering forward now.

I had to wipe tears out of my eyes—I didn't even know I was crying—as I raised the rifle and sighted on the first one. I fired, and saw it flung backwards to lie unmoving in the street, truly finally dead. Tom and Dale both tried to take the rifle from me, but I shrugged them off and fired again. Tom argued we were done here, and there was no point in wasting ammo on these fuckers, but I told him I had to. Then I told him—told them both—why.

After that they left me alone until all the deadheads were gone but one—the Priest. My arms were shaking so bad I almost couldn't hold the gun steady, but he was close—thirty feet away now—and hard to miss. My first shot blew away part of his neck—and whatever was left of the collar—away, but the last one brought him down.

I dropped the gun, and Tom and Dale had to carry me back to the Jeep.

But now I'm at home in bed, and Dale says I'm physically okay. I miss the child I'll never know, a pain which far outweighs the physical discomfort, but Jessie is here, and she hugs me a long time before Tom sends her to bed.

Now I'm smiling as I think of that street, and write this. Because I know that none of the women who come after me will have to endure more than the horror of giving up part of themselves.

LEMON KNIVES 'N' COCKROACHES

BY **CARLTON MELLICK III**

This is one of the few stories in this collection to come with a warning label, which I am proud to provide:

Caution! May result in loss of appetite, sensory dislocation, palpable queasiness, the urge to laugh even though you're not sure if it's okay to.

There. I have done my civic duty.

Carlton Mellick III is a founding father of the growing Bizarro movement in twenty-first century literature. It's been alternatively described as absurdist horror and the literary equivalent of the "Cult" section in a really cool video store.

The best practitioners of Bizarro—and Mellick is definitely one of the best—bring an amazing playful sweetness to the atrocities on hand: somewhere between David Lynch, John Waters, William Burroughs, Kurt Vonnegut Jr., S. Clay Wilson, and Alejando Jodorowsky on the off-the-charts weirdness scale.

"Lemon Knives 'n' Cockroaches" is another story. Like his latest book, Apeshit, *it found itself following a path so dark that the whimsy couldn't quite survive intact. It's still there, but drowning in what I can only describe as genuine nightmare: an all-swallowing delirium so self-contained that you can only pray you might someday wake up from this horrible dream.*

Good luck with that! And again, be forewarned: if you let it into your brain, this is a hard one to shake.

WE ARE SPIDER-CRAWLING THROUGH the dark places between the walls, like maggots under dead skin. Boney limbs and hooks on our fingertips to help us slither through the tight pathways.

Alyxa and all of her dirty smells ahead of me, her cricket legs creeping the crawlspace, greases scraping off of her and coating the walls as she moves, leaving a path for me to follow.

Every time she spreads her legs to move a rotten stench attacks me in the face, makes my eyes water, almost collapsing me from my position.

One of the boys is following behind, Paul I think his name is, not sure. All of the school boys look alike now with their black-painted bodies, bald heads, goggles over their eyes. They don't really speak anymore, driven mindless, inhuman. The boy crawls like a cockroach behind me, overlapping my limbs if my pace slows, cutting into my leg flesh when he misses the wall.

Alyxa stops, freezes in a position with her legs apart to brace herself. Her smell sweeps over me and I try not to breathe, even when breathing through my mouth I can taste the thick scent of her filth. She turns to us and opens her lips to release two lemon knives, sharp handmade knives greased with sour acids yellow in color, dropping them into each of her hands. Dirt-crusted teeth and a cat-dry tongue, looks at me deep through my eyes.

"I love you," she whispers, petting my arm with her bare toes.

I continue to hold my breath, my eyes seal themselves shut from the sting of her fumes, she can't see my expressions in the shadows. The cockroach boy tugs on my legs behind me.

"Let's go," she says, and continues on.

I open my eyes and follow, rubber kneecaps helping me through the crawlspace. More cautious now. We're in the dangerous region, where they are most likely to find us. So many have been killed here, so many that were stronger than me, smarter. Alyxa's the only one left worth saving.

We move vertically through the crawlspace now, into a hole in an air vent, shifting to the space over the ceiling of the first story of the facility, beneath the floor of the second story. And pause, balancing ourselves on the framework so that we do not fall through.

My leg slips and clanks into the frame. That was sloppy. Alyxa puts a metal hooknail to my lips, *hussshhh*, and points down to the vent at our knees.

I nod and slowly pull the vent away, a rush of musty pungent odor surges into the crawlspace, even more rancid than Alyxa's dirty smells. I hand the vent to the cockroach boy who in turn hands me a wire-rope tied in a noose. The opening leads to a deep blackness. I can't see all the way to the ground. A cloth over my nose as I focus on them.

"There they are," Alyxa whispers, but she doesn't have to say anything. They are right below us, like they were waiting for us. They peel open their decayed leathery lips and release deep hungry moans.

I can only see parts of them in the shadows, their cold faces glowing in the dim moonlight from a half-boarded window somewhere down the hallway. No clue how many there are. Their moans are echoing in such a way that it sounds like hundreds. But those are just echoes. Have to be . . .

"Lower the rope," Alyxa says, and I slide it into the pool of dark as the cockroach boy ties the other end to the metal framework.

"It's just like fishing," she says.

She knows I've never done this before, that I was lying when I said that I was the fisher on the runs that I used to go on with her brother. Back when there were enough people to spread out the runs evenly, so that everyone only had to go on one run every eight days. As of yesterday, we go every other day.

I wiggle the rope slowly at their heads, waving it at them. Alyxa sighs hard at me, sniff-shaking her head. I'm used to having the cockroach boy's job, hiding in the back, in the safe place.

One of them snatches onto my noose, tugs violently at it, tries to pull me down to him. The noose slips tight around its fingers. "Pull," Alyxa screams and I tug the wire-rope, the creature tumbles from its feet and the wire goes limp.

"Did it break?" my words slurred. My nerves feel like ants crawling up my neck.

"No, it slid from his hand." Alyxa fingers my waist like it's a pat on the back.

We reclaim the rope and retie the noose, lowering it back into the pit of living death. The moaning grows louder as more of them enter the hallway, this kind of commotion brings them all out of hiding.

"Hurry up," Alyxa says. "We can't afford to attract any more of them."

"You think I don't know that?"

Before she can respond a groan pops out of my lungs, my breath is knocked out of me as one of the creatures snatches the wire-rope and rips it from my grip.

"Watch it," Alyxa cries as the rope slashes around at us, the monster below convulsing against the chord, throwing my balance.

I seize the wire-rope and pull, the noose hooking tight around the creature's arm.

"Come on," Alyxa shrieks into my ear. "Pull, pull!"

All three of us reel in the wire, the cockroach boy uses the framework as leverage.

"It's a big one!" I say, as if it really is a fish, "Will it fit through the walls?"

Alyxa doesn't answer, concentrating, the lemon knives propped in her mouth.

The creature comes into focus: a very large corpse, white and naked, its skin wrinkled with rot. It growls as we pull it in, swinging at us with its free arm.

Just a few inches away from us, we stop pulling. The boy wraps the excess wire-rope to the frame and Alyxa releases her portion, slipping the lemon knives from her lips.

"Okay," Alyxa sighs, leering down at the living corpse at her feet, a hazy film over its eyes. "Are we ready?"

But before we can respond, the dead man grabs hold of the edge of the opening with its free hand and pulls himself up into the crawlspace.

I scream, jerking back away from the zombie, kicking to move, hitting Alyxa in the ankle and she drops one of the knives. I shove myself into the cockroach boy who slips from the framework, falls back and drops through the ceiling.

He quietly disappears into the darkness below.

Alyxa retrieves her lemon knife and stabs both of them through the sides of the zombie's head, their tips touching each other in the middle of the dead man's mind.

She pulls his corpse away from me as I lie here, staring at the quiet hole where the cockroach boy was situated. He went without a scream or complaint, just dropped into the mass of living dead underneath.

"Are you going to drain him?" I ask.

"No time," she says. "We're taking him as he is. Just don't get any blood on you."

Through crawlspaces back to our home, the only room hidden from the undead, deep inside of the walls of the facility, brightened by fire light. We shove the large fleshy corpse through the tight spaces as quick as we can. This one is hardly able to fit, but we grease him up with the oils built up in our scalps and privates to ease him through.

"Don't look at me," I tell Alyxa as she pets my cheek. "Don't touch me."

Upon arrival, several cockroach boys rip the body from our arms and immediately string it upside-down from the ceiling, poke holes into its neck and wrists with bones carved into knives, bleeding it into a large saucer.

"Ahh, dinner is here," says a scratchy voice behind me. "And a very good piece of meat I see."

The voice forms into the shape of a man as he steps out of the shadows and into the fire light.

"Everything went perfect then, I see."

"Not exactly," we tell him.

"What do you mean, *not exactly*?"

"I'm sorry, Thomas . . ." I say. "We lost the boy."

The man's eyes droop from their lids, and his mouth shivers. He lets out a shriek and fails to his chubby knees, covering his face to cry. "No, not Charlie, anyone but Charlie," he says in his tears. He sounds almost sarcastic.

"He didn't scream," I tell him. "It couldn't have been a painful death."

"Of course he didn't scream," Thomas shrieks at me. "I taught him not to scream, not to give in to pain or fear."

"I'm sorry, Thomas," I say, but the man curls into a fat ball and rocks back and forth.

"Come warm me," the man says to the cockroach boys draining the corpse, and they stop their work to huddle around him, pressing their sickly forms against his fleshy breasts, gurgling.

I step away from time, into the cold shadows to Alyxa who drinks from the drippy pipes. The corners of the room are littered with sick dying children and an old woman.

Alyxa kneels to the old woman.

"Take the blanket off," the woman begs with a leechy voice, her head swaying from side to side. And Alyxa removes the blankets, rubs the places where her arms and legs used to be, the stumps still scabbed and infected.

"Thank you," says the woman. Alyxa smiles.

The woman's name is Mrs. Boontide. I don't know if she has a first name. Her husband was killed by Thomas several months ago, for breaking his rules. Thomas was always looking for an excuse to kill and eat the elderly. Mrs. Boontide is the last.

For having an unruly husband, Thomas has been taking her limbs from her one at a time. Cutting them off and feeding them to his children.

The cockroach boys will do anything he tells them to do. They aren't human anymore. Just empty shells. Insects. He commands them like an army. Faceless, soulless soldiers.

I can hear Thomas whispering to the boys: "Oh, Charlie and I were so close, so friendly. I can't believe he's gone. He was the only man here, you know? Now I have to wait for one of you to become a man. Who is the oldest? Paul? You will be a man in almost a year, won't you? That's not very long at all. You can be the new captain of the swim team. Oh, thank God I have you, Paul. Thank you God."

*

"Why don't you sleep with me anymore?" Alyxa asks me.

We are sitting on a ledge in the elevator shaft, a candle between us, far away from Thomas and his cockroach boys, our feet dangling into the darkness.

"I mean you never even sleep next to me, let alone fuck me," she continues. "Why can't you be affectionate? You say you love me but won't lay a finger on me."

"I don't feel like it anymore," I tell her.

"You don't feel like making love with me?" she says. "You're the one who said the only thing left worth living for is sex, you told me that living in the walls is passionate, our flesh trapped closely together."

"I do love you, Alyxa," I tell her. "And the only reason I don't kill myself right now is because I want to be with you. I'm just bored with it, it's all we've been doing for the past three years. All day, every day. And I can't handle all those abortions. You say it provides food for us, but I just can't deal with it anymore."

"It's safer than eating the dead," Alyxa says. "I can't help but wonder if I'm going to catch the disease every time I take a bite of their flesh. With the abortions, I can actually eat in without worries. The idea that I'm eating my babies doesn't even bother me anymore. It seems almost natural."

"*Our* babies," I tell her.

"I don't know why you refuse to eat them."

She doesn't see my head shaking at her in the dark.

I let her screw me in the elevator shaft, digging her nails deep into my chest. Her dirty smells encase my body, cut into me like razors. I try not to breathe through my nose or mouth, trying to inhale through my eyes, ears, pores on the skin . . .

"Do you remember what the light looks like, what the sun looks like?" I ask Alyxa, her greasy head lying in my armpit.

"I don't remember these things."

"Sometimes I want to take a chance and go to the roof. Just to see the sun again."

"There's no sun anymore," Alyxa tells me, her eyes shifting to mine, glistening in the dark. "It disappeared when the dead came out of their graves."

"We don't know that for sure."

"It might as well be true," she says, kissing my gritty hand and licking some sweat away.

The dead man hanging from the ceiling has lost most of his meat. All the cockroach boys scrabbling his flesh into their throats, their only form of communication being growls and snorts. Thomas says there isn't enough food to go around, so Alyxa and I have to go searching for beetles and rats. It's an exhausting job with little reward, but we like the idea of leaving the company of our twisted leader, escape into the walls.

"Is it time to kill ourselves yet?" Alyxa asks me.

"Not yet," I say. "I won't die until I see the daylight again."

"It's a sweet dream, but we both know it will never happen."

"It will happen," I tell her. "Some day."

She wraps her sweaty palm around my mouth and licks my ear.

"Let's kill ourselves now," she says. "Let's feed the zombies."

"Not yet," I say.

"Let's become zombies together," she says, a chuckling whisper. "Let's be undead flesh-eating corpses." Then a slitting sound close to my eardrum.

I scream in pain, blood gushes from the side of my head. I jerk to look at her, she's holding a lemon knife in one hand and my ear in the other.

"I'm a zombie," she says, folding the ear into her mouth and chewing.

I can hardly breathe from shock. She swallows my ear, licking her lips at me. And she's just playing a game . . .

"I'm going to eat you," she screams out. "Let me taste more of you."

I stagger, holding the blood inside of my head.

"Get away," I scream.

She cuts me across the shoulder. I shriek, scrambling back, trying to get away. No room for agility when between the walls, especially for a man.

"Let me eat you," she screams. "I'll fuck you and eat you at the same time."

I lunge at her, grab her knife and bite her ear. My molars grind against it and tear it off, nearly choke on it. Blood rivers down her shoulder and her eyes widen. She howls at me, breaks free from my hold. I feel the blade enter my muscle and loose skin, cutting my arms and legs. Alyxa drops the knife, licking the blood, drinking pieces of my flesh into her mouth and chewing it free.

She sucks her severed ear from my lips and gulps, licking my forehead and laughing at herself.

"I'm never going to die," she tells me. "Help me die."

Thomas becoming more insane every day. He has started painting murals on the walls with a young boy's shit. We have to go onto our elevator ledge to escape the smell. Our heads and my limbs all bandaged with a dead cockroach boy's clothes. Alyxa becomes more and more ready to commit suicide, excited for it, depressed when she realizes she is not yet dead.

"Want to try getting to the parking lot?" I ask Alyxa and she smiles. "I don't want to die until I see daylight. I was thinking . . . maybe we should try to make it outside. Steal a car. You know, see how far we can get."

"There's no chance we can make it out of the building. We've tried before, remember?"

"That was years ago. There aren't as many of them as there used to be."

"It sounds good to me . . ." she says. "But I hope you realize we most likely won't get twenty feet outside these walls. I don't want you to be disappointed if you die before making it outside."

I throw bits of rock down the shaft. "I've thought about it all day long."

Alyxa is jealous when Mrs. Boontide passes away.

She presses her fingers against the woman's dead face and curls the skin into odd expressions, making her look happy or sad or just warped. Flaying with her face like silly putty.

"It's weird," she tells me. "It feels fake."

She pulls my hand towards the skin but I resist.

"What's wrong with you?" she asks.

"I just don't want to touch her," I say.

"You'll eat her but you won't touch her skin?"

"I don't see what's so fun about playing with a dead woman's face," I say.

"You're becoming such a bore," she says.

"You're becoming another person," I say.

"When are we going to try the escape?" she asks.

She menstruates onto a plate for the cockroach boys' dinner.

"Later," I say.

"You've been saying that for the past two days," she says.

"I'm not ready yet," I say.

"I'm going to go without you," she says.

"We'll go for it soon," I say. "I promise."

Alyxa flicks at Mrs. Boontide's cheeks and nose.

"I just want us to be dead . . ." she says.

I pick the maggots out of the old woman's wounds and swallow them without chewing.

✶

"Come here," Thomas screams at Alyxa. "Take your clothes off and come to me."

We are lying in bed, half of the cockroach boys are gone on a run, and Thomas has his wild twisty voice testing our obedience to him.

"Alyxa, my patience is a weak little thread. Come here quickly."

"I'm not going to fuck you," she tells him, calm and stern.

"Get over here!" his voice grinding into the back of his throat.

She stands and drops her clothes, her naked smells forcing me to look in the other direction. By the way she walks to him, I can tell she has her lemon knives hidden between her legs.

"After all this time, you now want to fuck me."

Thomas laughs. "I'm not going to fuck you," raises an eyebrow. "But Timmy here wants you to fuck him. He's been begging me to make you take his virginity for so long . . . I just can't refuse him anymore."

Alyxa chuckles. "You're joking."

This is no joke. I stand up.

The other two cockroach boys lunge for me and tackle me to the ground, hard knees in the back of my neck, vision getting dizzy. The hole where my ear used to be opens up and spills blood onto the cement.

"I never joke, Alyxa," Thomas says. "You are a birthday present, from me to him. Please be a nice present and give yourself with a smile."

Thomas grabs hold of her shoulders and pushes her to the skinny boy in the corner. "Are you ready, Timmy? Beautiful little Timmy . . ."

The boy nods furiously and Alyxa struggles against Thomas.

Trying to hold her still, he says, "If you don't behave yourself, I will have to give presents to all the boys."

"You're sick," she says. "He's just a boy."

"Yes, that's why he wants you. He's going through that phase in his life. Only boys want women."

Alyxa slips to the ground and jerks her eyes at me. She is starting to tear. Thomas has overpowered her arms and she cannot reach the lemon knives she has hidden. I struggle to get off the ground, but the cockroach boys bend my legs and arms back until they hear high-pitched squeals coming from me.

"Your man over there is not really a man," says Thomas. "I thought he was a man a long time ago, when I loved him. I wanted him so badly, but he rejected me. Because of you. That's when I realized he wasn't a man at all. Just a boy. No more than any of these teenagers we share the walls with. A little worthless boy. How can a man love a boy? Only *women* love boys."

He pulls my lover's arms, dragging her. "But some boys, like my Timmy and my Paul, have the ability to someday become men. Like caterpillars becoming butterflies."

Thomas stops tugging on Alyxa, pausing to gaze into Timmy's eyes. The boy's goggles shine the fire light back into his leader's smile. They are frozen long enough for Alyxa to pull the lemon knives out of her secret places and stab Thomas in the inside of his leg.

A deep scream and Thomas is thrown to the ground, blood leaking down his legs.

The cockroach boys leap from me and charge Alyxa, I catch one of their ankles, but his foot slips through. They move in silence, drawing sharp blades longer than Alyxa's, rise them high above her and then they pause. They are frozen in mid-strike.

"Don't move," Alyxa says, calmly.

I get up. Move to a better view. A lemon knife is at each of their throats, one of them is partially inside a boy's neck, just a twitch away from the jugular.

Thomas grabs a pipe from Timmy's feet and lifts it like a baseball bat.

"Drop it, Thomas," Alyxa tells him. "Or they'll both die right here in front of you."

"You wouldn't," Thomas puts the pipe down slowly. "They're only children."

"We're all children," Alyxa tells him, inching the blades deeper into their necks.

"Don't, please," Thomas cries.

His body folds into a ball. He screams, "Let them go now!"

"If I let them go they will kill me."

"If you kill them you will die, I promise you."

"It sounds like it's worth the risk." Alyxa smiles at the young men, their eyes jiggling in their goggles.

"Alyxa . . ." I say, taking the blades away from the boys. "Don't do it. We can try to escape now. We'll see the sunlight."

I smile at her, but she will not look at me.

As if shrugging, Alyxa turns away from them to look at Timmy.

"Happy birthday," she tells him, smiling.

Then a slicing sound and blood sprays into musty air, the two cockroach boys holding their wide-open necks as they fall to the ground. Redness pools under our bare feet.

And she just stares at Thomas coldly. Her eyeballs are black pools without any white in them.

The shock has taken the breath out of Thomas. "You . . . bitch," he chokes, too weak to cry. "I can't believe . . . you . . . killed them. You fuck . . . ing bitch."

"What did you do?" I yell at her, and her face twitches back at me. "Kill Thomas. He's the only one who deserves to die."

"I'd rather see Thomas suffer."

I gather our things, dressing myself in the correct attire for fighting the living dead, collecting the sharpest homemade weapons.

"Hurry up," I tell Alyxa, throwing the rubber outfit at her. "We need to go before the others get back."

"What about Thomas?" she asks.

I look down on the pathetic retch, his face wrinkled downwards. "Kill him, quickly."

"No, I want him to come with us." She laughs, cutting her own shoulder with a lemon knife.

"No time for games," I tell her. "He's just going to slow us down."

"I won't rest until I make this perverted asshole suffer," she tells me, bringing her knife to his chin. "Either I stay here and do it or I feed him to the dead."

"Fine, take him," I tell her.

And she runs up to me and licks all the blood off the side of my head.

*

Last week, Alyxa was lying next to me in the darkness. She was cradling her stomach as if pregnant again. It was too dark to see, but I swear I could hear her smiling, her eyes closed just smiling at the thoughts that were spinning around in her head.

"Do you remember when mom used to make pies in the summer?" she asked me.

"My mom never made pies," I told her.

"She made them on Saturday afternoons when the sun was directly above us," her voice like a little girl's. "The sun was so big, warming up the garden in the backyard, hugging flavor into mom's pies through the window."

"I thought you hated the sun?"

"No, not before mom died," she told me. "It was big and warm and comforting, just like my mom. And I'd play in the sunshine all day long, squishing frogs into jelly and rubbing it on the sidewalk to cook."

"Yes, of course," I say.

But she's never known her mom . . .

We leave the sick people behind. Most of them only have a few days left anyway. The very young cockroach boys hide behind the skeleton piles, waiting for us to leave so they can eat the two freshly dead teenagers.

Thomas doesn't put up a fight as we push him through the crawlspace, but he's so fat that he can hardly get through. Fat from eating people.

"Let's not go down through the ceiling," I say. "They'll be expecting us there."

"Where then?" Alyxa asks.

"One of the office vents," I say.

"But those are farther from the exit," she says.

"But they won't be waiting for us there," I say.

She nods.

I was right. Peering through a vent into one of the stale offices, there aren't any corpses in sight. Unfortunately, the vent is screwed shut. We'll have to break through and the noise will probably attract them into the room.

The door to the office is shut. It might even be locked. That helps a little, but we don't want them to swarm in the hallway outside the door. We'd never be able to get through them that way.

Alyxa kicks the vent in. The bang echoes through the room but we don't hear any noises in response.

"Come on," she says, sliding through the opening.

She pulls Thomas's plump legs and I push on his shoulders with my feet until he can get through the vent hole. He cries out as his flesh compacts. His breaths heavy, like he's suffocating. He hasn't gone through enough of the crawlspaces to get over the claustrophobia.

This attracts the dead. I can hear them in the next office, pounding on the walls to get through.

"Hurry up," Alyxa cries.

I shove all my weight into Thomas, not worried if I hurt him or break his neck in the process. Let out all my anger to get him through.

He plops out on the other side, lands on his legs weird.

"Get up," Alyxa tells him, but he won't get to his feet.

I crawl out of the shaft and hurry to the door. No sounds when I put my ear to it, but the scratching against the other wall might be interfering.

"Leave him," I say.

"But I want to watch him die . . ."

"Come on," I say.

She pulls Thomas up by the hair. His ankle must have been twisted because he can't stand on it anymore.

"You don't want to do this," Thomas cries. "We'll die horribly."

"As long as I get to see you die first," she says.

Out in the hallway, the corpses are animated mannequins. Naked, mechanical, featureless. Spread out but not close enough to be a problem yet.

Alyxa and I drag the fat man across the tile floor, over rubble and mummified body parts scattered around like old laundry.

"We've got to run," I say. "Drop him."

"Not yet," she says. "I want to feed him to them."

The fat man oozes a yellow substance from his mouth.

"You . . ." he chokes on the goop in his throat. "I'll kill . . ."

He falls to his knees and pukes up a blanket of yellow muck. Alyxa pulls on him to get up, but he's glued to the floor. The regurgitation becomes violent. Yellow squirts from his nostrils, through the corners of his eyes.

"What's wrong with him?" I ask.

Snails crawl through the soup. They stick to Thomas' hands, to the sides of his face. A slug stretches out of his nostril and dribbles grease onto his upper lip.

"Help me," Alyxa says.

I grab Thomas by the other shoulder and we lift him off of his knees, but he jerks out of our grasp and stabs me in the chest.

We let him go and he backs away, pointing a knife at us. I look down at my chest: a little round hole. Black blood squirts out of it with a swirl of mucous.

It's not a knife, it's a pen. But he holds it like a knife, threatens us to back off.

"Murderers!" he cries, snails and slime still pouring out of his mouth. A thick yellow waterfall pooling onto his belly.

Alyxa curls her eyebrows at the undead.

"Eat him!" she cries. "You're too slow!"

The closer the corpses get, the slower they seem to move.

She runs up to the zombies and smacks them in the face, gets behind them and shoves them at Thomas. They don't attack her. They just groan at her through holes in their skulls.

"Come on! Eat him!" she cries.

Thomas just points his pen at me, holding his mouth shut with his other hand, snot dripping through his fingers.

"I'll eat him then!" she cries.

Thomas turns to point his pen at her as she leaps onto him, grabs him around the shoulders and wraps her legs around his waist. He stabs at her with the pen but it does not break the skin.

Alyxa bites into his neck and chews through his flesh until she opens a major blood vessel. But instead of blood gushing out of him, it is the same yellow snot that he has been regurgitating. It leaks down Alyxa's lips and chest. She growls at him, a flesh-hungry ghoul.

He falls to the floor and seizures. Alyxa squeezed around him like a spider, trying to hold down his flapping limbs as she eats him.

The living dead pass me and pile on top of Thomas. They tear him apart, taking pieces of him into their black mouths. But they don't attack Alyxa. They eat with her, like she is one of them.

"Come on," she says to me with yellow slop all over her face. "Join us."

I back away from them, holding the blood in my chest by plugging the hole with my little finger, and she returns to feasting on the fat man.

The living dead do not attack me either for some reason. They bump me out of their way to get to Thomas. I stagger down the hallway, looking for a room to duck into.

A hand grabs me.

"Come back," she says. "We're safe."

She digs her fingers into her crotch and rubs it on my face.

I cough at her.

"It smells like death," she says. "That's why they aren't attacking us. The menstrual blood stains on our bodies have turned rancid. They think we're dead like them."

She rubs more rotten smells onto my neck and stomach. I hold my nose and mouth but still feel like puking.

"Let's go," she says, smiling, kissing me on the forehead.

But instead of taking me towards the exit, she goes back to Thomas's body to eat more of him.

"What are you doing?" I whisper.

"I want to feed," she says.

"We've got to get out of here," I say.

"No," she says, "we don't have to leave anymore. We can fit in with the living dead now. We can live with them."

"We must leave," I say.

"We'll never leave," she says.

And she goes back to Thomas.

She drops her weight next to the gurgling zombies, but her knees don't hit the ground. A wire has hooked her by the neck. She opens her eyes wide at me as the noose tightens around her throat.

"Alyxa . . ."

She doesn't have the air to cry out as the wire pulls her off of her feet, staring at me with baby eyes and kicking her legs. I see the cockroach boys up in the ceiling, their minds as dead as the zombies behind those black goggles. They don't realize Alyxa is not one of the zombies as they reel her in, lift her up into the ceiling and stab her in the head with a lemon knife.

They bleed her like a cow, then fold her limp body under their arms and pull them with her deep into the crawlspace.

I lay down in the puddle of Alyxa's blood and press my face against the floor to feel the last of her warmth, rubbing my arms in it like I'm making a snow angel.

Staggering through the halls like I'm one of the corpses, blood no longer gushing from the hole in my chest, looking for a way out. Hours pass. I can't find an exit anywhere. The hallways seem to go for miles in every direction. After a day, I camp out in an office, eat a spider and the contents of its web, then continue to search for a way into the street. to see the sun one more time before I die.

Days go by. Still nothing but corridors and empty rooms crowded with the living dead.

They look at me as if I'm one of their own. Just another walking corpse that refuses to die. And I'm beginning to look at myself in the same way.

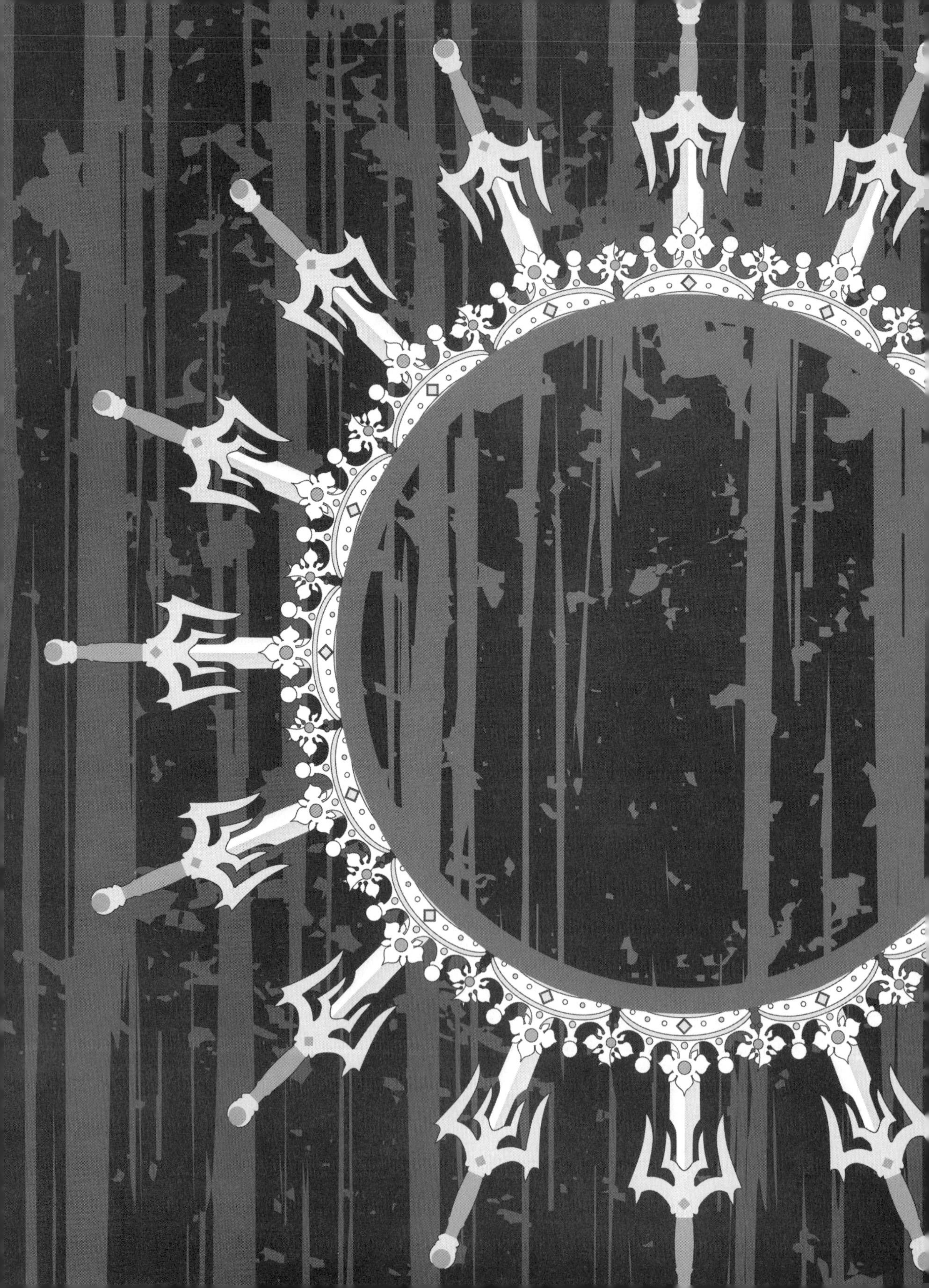

ZAAMBI

BY **TERRY MORGAN & CHRISTOPHER MORGAN**

Christopher Morgan and Terry Morgan are brothers, so I couldn't begin to tell you who did what. But together, they have conjured a samurai mini-epic with a ticking clock that operates somehow outside of time, to marvelous effect.

Rumor has it that the comic-book version of "Zaambi" is about to land in my mailbox. It is something that I very much long to see.

But in the meantime, satisfy yourself with the vivid pictures and stunning ramifications implicit in the awesome prose before you, rife with martial arts action and a whole lot more. Deeper than fun, funner than art, this is deep art fun, and sheer pleasure from start to finish.

I. In Which I Become A Man. Year of Our Sorrows 103

I killed three zaambi today before my father returned from Honchu Village. My younger brother Kisai watched as I dispatched the vermin, his eyes very wide. After it was through and the bonfire was burning Kisai told me in an overloud voice that he had been standing as a second for me, should the battle get too pitched. I thanked my six-year-old brother for his assistance and had him clean my father's blade of the zaambi foulness. Upon returning home Kisai waited no more than five seconds to regale Mother and Hiroko with my adventure, the telling of which upset them no little amount. Mother cried and told me I was a foolish boy, but her tears, truly, were those of relief. Hiroko questioned Kisai about the details, trying not to seem too curious. I didn't mind all the fuss. Today I had proved myself a man. My father upon his return would have to recognize me as such when I handed him my kill bag with the three heads in it. It had been a very good day.

I had dreamed, as had all boys my age, of joining the Shinsei-Na-Senzo-Sentai (Holy Ancestor patrol) for Honchu Village. It was rare enough to see zaambi within the perimeter of Honchu; I had only seen eight in my fourteen years. It was not a sight you could forget. My first sighting of the Sonkei Shisha (Revered Dead) happened midday in a crowded marketplace. Hiroko and I were helping Mother to carry her shopping. The vendor was mistakenly trying to convince my mother that the meat he sold was of ancient Kobe stock and was receiving the whip-end of her tongue when we heard horrified screams from behind us in the crowd. I dropped my basket when I saw the three zaambi. Two of them were entirely black with the rot of long earthly internment, their bones shiny with mud. The third was more freshly possessed of demonic life and still wore the work clothes he had died in. A gash ran across his entire face where an axe perhaps had opened the flesh, his staring eyes separated by a gory chasm. I would have screamed but I was struck dumb at the awful sight. A boy I knew, Kimitake, had fallen before the hideous pair of zaambi. As my mother pulled Hiroko and me behind the vendor's stall I saw the boy torn in three pieces.

For years afterward I could not force that sound from my head, the popping and ripping and rending of sinew, not unlike the sound made when Father is enjoying his chicken. The fresher of the beasts was approaching our hiding place, and grown men were running rather than take their chances against it. In desperation my mother raised the vendor's meat cleaver before her, but it proved unnecessary as a detachment of the Holy Ancestor patrol arrived in the marketplace. The zaambi threatening us was knocked to the ground by a running man, who proceeded to quarter it with his long blade. Peeking around the corner of the stand I could see an arm feebly grabbing at the air, detached from its owner. I gaped at this sight until I was startled into a loud yell by a man's head peering over the edge of the stand. It was my father. The two other zaambi had been dealt with by other members of the patrol, and Honda, my father's second-in-command, was piling firewood for an immediate bonfire. The boy, Kimitake, was going into the fire as well. All was screams and smoke and chaos. I have never been prouder of my father.

Today as Mother and Hiroko are making a fuss over me, buying sweet rice cakes and pouring liberal amounts of sake for myself and the neighbors, my father is pulling me aside for the talk I knew would come. Outside, it is a spectacular sight as the sun dips into a violet sky and the air is cool and crisp. This is what it is like to be a man, I think. This clarity.

My father is not a man given to foolish overpraise. He wastes no time.

"You committed their souls to the air," he asks, brusquely, his mind elsewhere.

"I have the ash on my hands," I say, displaying my gray palms for his perusal. He doesn't look. He doesn't need to. From the time I could understand stories I had heard again and again of the proper treatment of the Revered Dead, of the respect that must be paid to the souls of our ancestors.

"The ceremonial bonfire on which we cremate the fallen zaambi serves both a practical and spiritual purpose," my father had begun countless times, on walks through Honchu Village, by the river, in front of the fire. "Practically, the excresence that is the corrupt body of a zaambi must be burned to prevent contagion. Spiritually, the demon that possessed the physical body of the Revered Dead upon the opening of the Gate of Hell must be exorcised in its own element. The evil spirit recognizes that its place is that of flame and not of flesh, and departs. The soul of the Revered Dead, no longer under siege, may rise into the afterlife untroubled and exalted, as it should do."

I know this advice better than I know my own name.

"Perhaps when we are back inside with the rest of the family you and I shall drink a toast together to your adventure," my father begins.

"It was nothing much," I interrupt.

I don't wish to make my father praise me more than he wishes. In all truth I did a clumsy and terrified job on the three zaambi, who came upon Kisai and myself unawares. What was humiliating was that, secretly, I was looking for zaambi to kill. I felt I was ready for the Holy Ancestor patrol, whether my father thought so or not. I was only looking for a lone zaambi, however, and being surprised by three of them was not in my plan. Only sheer bravado and the excellent sharpness of my father's blade allowed my victory over the pathetic creatures, but from small seeds grow great trees. This almost-accident would serve to allow me to tryout for the Holy Ancestor patrol.

"It was sacred and vital," my father returned, a note of reproof for my disrespect in his voice. "I would hope that one soon to seek entry to be a ronin in the Holy Ancestor patrol would have appropriate respect for the gravity of his duties."

"Yes, father," I said, chastened. He turned to look closely at me, his serious face scrutinizing my frivolous one.

"The test will be tomorrow morning at dawn. Are you ready?"

"Yes, father."

He clapped me on the back. "Then we drink to you. You'll need whatever spirits you can get to help you."

I followed him inside, my stomach in turmoil. The test. In less than twelve hours.

I saw Father twice before my testing in a period following the many toasts of my novitiate companions that carried our benevolent and merry prayers to the spirits on rivers of sake and sweet plum wine. The first meeting occurred when he brought me the kimono of the Holy Ancestor Guild in which I was to test, a silken affair the colors of tea rose and ochre with the ice blue insignia of the Patrol stitched neatly onto its back. The second time he shook me heartily to bring me from the most sound sleep I had ever known. As I walked beside my father to the Yamato Temple I shook the fog of the bibulous from my head and took in the rich and heavy odor of hours-old vomit that stuck dried to the raiments of my compatriots, who were also to be tested.

I was the third of the boys to breach the temple. We entered into a large darkened anteroom that was almost entirely empty of furnishings, yet filled to overflowing with the imperious mingling of scents from the ginger root, vanilla bean, and anise incense sticks smoldering within. From here our group, who numbered ten, was ushered down a flight of dangerously narrow stairs and into a cavernous chamber so complete in its lack of light that, for a moment, I began to reconsider my desire to become ronin. Samurai. We ten sat in the pitch, some praying nervously, some joking obscenely, all wondering if this was part of the test.

Fire sprung to life in a hanging pot eight feet off the ground, and a stern voice guided us to the small circle of light in the middle of the room. The voice, one I was sure that I had heard before, ordered the initiates to kneel and recite the *Obeisance for the Revered Dead*. As I knelt, I felt a not so timid tap upon my left shoulder. When I turned to look, I was greeted by the face of Honda's son, my best friend, Kenji-Tango. Presently, he was aping the bloated face of Madame Mutsu, the fat and hateful matriarch of the Mutsu family. It was his best impression; I had to think of Kimitake being torn into thirds to keep from laughing.

We ten started the *Obeisance* at the same time.

"I am the arm of my brother who has none,
I am his blood that has long been dust,
I am his flesh that has gone to rot,
I am his guide toward the Holy Separation."

The oath continued in this fashion for some time. Afterwards, we sat in silence in a circle of light bounded by darkness deeper than the raven's hue. We waited apprehensively, hoping for someone to come. When we heard the shuffling-shambling foot-slides nearing our circle of light, even Kenji-Tango, who is the bravest of my friends, looked at me mouth agape and eyebrows raised very high, mocking no longer. We two were at the edge where light met dark, right where the awkward thing, which a moment ago was far off to the right, was now heading. The walk was distinctive.

When the rotting, grinning corpse materialized into the light four feet in front of me, I held my steps. Most of the other boys, excepting Kenji-Tango and another I couldn't make out, were pulled by fear to the other side of the lit circle, afraid to commit themselves to the dark. The zaambi slavered and drooled. Its one good eye turned to look at us, oxblood-colored pustulence oozing from the socket. The beast lumbered toward us, the organic fetor rising off its putrifying body, making the low gutteral chokings of a wild dog retching from the too-rich garbage he had earlier scavenged.

The boy I could not recognize ran dry of his courage when the decaying creature dropped its black and sore-covered tongue onto the ground with as much notice as a horse gives to its newly fallen dung. He ran to join the fraternity of the other boys. With painful and spasmatic movements, the zaambi turned toward me. I too was readying my legs for flight, but I refused to move even the distance of an inchworm unless Kenji-Tango ran first. We had tarried longer than all others, but if I were to bolt first, it would be as if Nature were to say that Honda's son and Honda himself, as the flower arises from the seed, were more brave and more honor-worthy than myself and Father. No one is braver than Father, nor more noble. I stood.

The zaambi bellowed in my ear its satisfaction at finding a slow-moving meal. The creature craned its head around until our noses touched. The monster grunted, and just as my traitorous feet were about to betray my vow, I smelled shaved ice mixed with liana syrup. The fiend drew back and looked on at me curiously as I sniffed the air about its face. Kenji-Tango, he later told me, thought I had gone mad, smelling a zaambi in such a way. Shaved ice and liana syrup put in a new silver bowl was favorite of Abbot and Abbess Yamato, and as far as I knew, they were the only two who ate the wretched, bitter substance. So, I knew that Abbot and Abbess Yamato had either just been eaten by this monstrosity, or . . .

I reached forward and pulled the zaambi mask from the startled face of Abbot Yamato. Kenji-Tango laughed quite unrestrainedly, and soon the other boys followed.

"Enough!" This from the lips of the presently enraged Abbot Yamato. "You in the corner dare not laugh! Laughter is the privilege of the courageous only! Fear is not a quality with which ronin regard zaambi. Ronin feel only anger and sorrow. Anger for the violation by the possessing demon, and sorrow for our brethren whose souls are being ravaged."

The Abbot paused, regarding us in turn. He then knelt and opened a panel in the floor. Inside this small storage area was a pile of ten escrima sticks, slender wooden swords to be used for fighting practice.

"You are now to undergo the examination for entrance into the Holy Ancestor Guild. The test is as follows: You are each allotted one escrima stick. Defend yourselves from the Guild members who will attack you by dealing them blows to areas that would be fatal to true zaambi. Do not hold back; they are well protected. They will attempt to drag you from the room. If they do, you are disqualified and you may test again next year. Use any means you must to stay in the room. You will be judged on technique as well as courage. That is all. Good luck."

With this, Abbot Yamato walked out of our circle of light and disappeared into the blackness.

We each picked up our allotted escrima, and began practice fighting with the other boys. Well before we were prepared, a bodiless voice from the shadows intoned: "Begin."

The first attacker came from the opposite side of the circle from where I was standing. Like the Abbot, it was another member of the Patrol dressed convincingly as a zaambi. The mask he wore was that of a man who had died from having his face flayed. It was all wet, red muscle with white rolling eyes. One of the boys, trying to regain his honor after running from the Abbot, stepped up to the beast and gave it a swift cut to the temple. The zaambi fell, defeated, and returned to the darkness. Two more appeared from the depths of the room. One zaambi wore the mask of a woman with nests of maggots for eyes, and the other was a lipless old man who shrieked loudly, without ceasing. Kenji-Tango dispatched the lipless fiend, while another boy named Shotoku thrust at the padded mask of the she-demon. They both fell and slid back into the shadows. Shotoku turned back toward us and cried, "This is easy!"

Fifty zaambi stepped into the light, completely surrounding the circle. By the time that Shotoku could turn and raise his sword, he had already been grabbed by four of the zaambi and was being carried, screaming, into the darkness. An icicle of fear slid securely into the meat of my heart. Even though we knew that the zaambi were just disguised members of our village, the trickery of the light and the horrific craftsmanship of the masks were enough to convince us otherwise. Some had rotted holes for noses. Others seeped black blood from the corners of their mouths. All looked hungry. The zaambi stumbled closer. We began to fight.

I sent three zaambi sprawling to the ground, though I swung at perhaps twice that number. All at once I was surrounded by a chaos of swords flying and bodies falling. When I had slain the last of the zaambi near me, I looked to my right and saw a boy named Little No pulled into the air by his head and carried off, praying to Amida for mercy. Hands clutched at my garments, and I batted them away with the flat of my escrima. Fifteen more zaambi stepped into the light. The fighting would not let up. As soon as so many were dispatched, more stepped in to take their place. Kenji-Tango and I stood together, defending a portion of the light-circle six zaambi in width.

Quickly, our circle of defense began to get smaller and smaller, due to novitiates being carried away and the mass of gore-covered zaambi bodies that pressed increasingly harder to reach us. The six of us who remained stood in a small circle, fighting for our lives. I was using such energy that twice I almost lost my sword from the sweat that coated both palms.

Kenji-Tango and I fought hard, side by side, neither of us willing to be outdone by the other. I had just decapitated a zaambi to my left, and was preparing to do the same to another who was feasting on its own bowels, when I was bumped from behind. I had assumed that our defensive circle had just gotten smaller, until I turned and found my face less than a hair's breadth from the snapping teeth of the skinless zaambi who had been vanquished earlier.

"This is impossible! We kill them and they return to fight! Find an exit or we'll be slaughtered!"

The words came from the mouth of Dogen, perhaps the strongest boy of our group, who had cleared away a path through the zaambi big enough to escape the circle of light. Four boys, including Dogen, stood at the edge of the lit area and were preparing to make a dash into the darkness.

"Come you two," Dogen shouted. "There is safety in numbers!"

"Not in the darkness," I yelled back. "There could be a hundred just beyond the light, waiting to grab you after yelling so loud! Stay where we can see the enemy approach!"

"I'll not come back to save your foolish souls," said Dogen as he ran from the light. Two other boys followed him, but the third, Gen, looked back at us undecidedly and then turned to follow the others. It was too late. The pathway that Dogen had cleaved had been closed by new ranks of zaambi. Gen tried to run back toward us, but was grabbed by his leg. Gen dropped his escrima as he clawed at the ground, bloodying his fingers in a desperate attempt to keep from being dragged away. I picked up his sword as he was consumed by the dark.

Kenji-Tango and I positioned ourselves back to back, I double-sworded. The weapons grew heavy in my arms, as I swung at this zaambi and stabbed at that one. Every blow connected with leg, hand, or head of the groaning mass of bodies. The zaambi pressed closer against us until Kenji-Tango and myself were crushing into each other. As I brought my escrima down upon the head of a zaambi that was eating a lock of human hair, I heard the screams of Dogen and his two as they were carried away by zaambi like so many sacks of ground beef.

Startled by the screams, I had forgotten to continue striking with my blade. Two hands grabbed me firmly from behind, embracing me so that I could not escape. I tried to pull the hands away, and as I did, I noticed that the palms were entirely smoothed with puffy scar tissue.

My father's samurai blade is unique. He wraps the hilt in roughened shark skin, and circles the guard with snake fangs pointing downward toward his hands. He says he does this to keep the proper focus during fights. Often after a battle Father's hands will be bloody and raw. He then offers his hands to the East and says, "I have been cleansed."

The hands that dragged me from the circle of light were Father's. I did not resist, for it would not be right for a son to stand against the wishes of his father. I saw Kenji-Tango in the now far away circle of light become swarmed by zaambi. I watched as he was lifted into the air by many hands, and turned to yell at me.

"Fight! You are only being held by one! I am held by many! Fight! Fight!!"

I could not disobey the will of my father.

"May the gods damn your soul if you do not fight that zaambi!! Save us! Fight you coward!!!"

I knew what Kenji-Tango had meant. If he called me a coward, then he in turn called my father a coward. I would rather take the punishment for disobedience than have Father suffer the extent of such an insult!

I stood and tried to break free of Father's firm grasp. He would not yield. So I had to fight dirty. The Abbot did instruct us to use any means possible for escape, so . . .

I reached up under Father's zaambi mask and performed the martial defense known as Monkey Paw Crushing Lotus Blossom upon his ear. Father yowled in pain, and I rushed to the aid of Kenji-Tango. Picking up a fallen escrima, I struck at the mass of zaambi carrying him, until he was freed.

"I knew that would get you," he said, picking up a sword.

All the zaambi in the room turned and rushed toward us, slow no longer. Kenji-Tango looked around desperately for some means of escape. As they closed in on us, I decided that we had only one option. When the zaambi got close, I struck the hanging brazier with my escrima and all my might. The pot that provided the room's only source of illumination fell to the ground, overturned, crushing out all light. I jumped up as high as I could and managed to grasp the chain that held the brazier. I climbed up until I was perhaps eight feet from the ground, and held on as the zaambi wandered below. I could hear them circling just below my feet, silent sharks looking for blood in a dark sea.

As I clung to the chain, I must admit that I began to get frightened. I was hanging in pitch blackness inches above a room full of men dressed as corpses whose only purpose was to search the darkness and grab me. I wondered where Kenji-Tango was. How could he stand this? I knew at any moment a decayed hand was going to grab my foot and pull me to the ground to be devoured. What if they weren't masks? What if they were real zaambi?

As I was pondering this last terrible thought, my hands, now slick with perspiration, slipped slowly down the length of the chain. I tried desperately to hold onto the last link, but the effort was in vain. My hands slipped from around the chain, and I fell to the ground.

Almost instantly, groping hands found my form and attempted to drag me away. I reached under the overturned brazier, grabbed a still red-hot coal, and forced it against the hands and feet of my attackers. I was released almost instantly amidst howls of pain. I did not mind the burning of my own flesh. It kept me focused.

I fended off the demons until the coal grew cold in my hand, and I was so weary from exhaustion that I could no longer resist. Many hands bore me upwards as I was carried from the room, heavy with the knowledge of failure.

When we entered the antechamber, a great roar filled my ears. I wrenched my body violently to escape my captors, but then I saw. The room was lit with many ceremonial candles, and I noticed Kenji-Tango smiling at me, his head shaved and with upright ponytail in the tradition of samurai. Father, now without mask, was one of the men who bore me. His ear was very red. He smiled.

"A single man cannot defeat the world," Father said. "The purpose of the test is to measure your endurance and fighting skills."

"Did I pass?" said I.

"We've been searching around for you in the dark for over an hour now," said Abbot Yamato. A red, blistering patch the exact size of a briquette of coal was burned neatly onto the backside of his hand.

Dogen and the others watched with jealous eyes as I was fed the congratulatory meal of spiny oysters and spicy fried noodles. Dogen's gaze told me that he might do more than just consider the nobility of the act of seppuku this evening.

Father laid before me a fine sword sheathed in a white ashwood scabbard. I grinned quite wide, forsaking the Virtue of Humbleness, as my head was shaved in the manner of the ronin, Banisher of Demons.

2. In Which I Become A
Year of Our Sorrows 108

Mother was dead. Father cremated her himself. A large part of him died that day, I am certain. I was blessed in the presence of my wife, Ayako, during this tragedy; but for her I might have been tempted to kill myself. Some time after Honchu was overrun by zaambi my attitude concerning my own life had changed for the worse. If there was nothing to fight for, why resist? I hadn't succumbed to this depression, nor had I given it voice, but Ayako felt it there in my heart and did her best to replace this black misery with the light of love. Still, I was glad she was not with child.

One of the first things I learned after inclusion in the Holy Ancestor Guild was that my home was not my home, not as I knew it. As Kasuri, Kenji-Tango and I sat in the Guild's anteroom our world disappeared before Abbot Yamato's words. Nippon had long ago been infested with zaambi, he told us. Due to its small size it was indefensible and the few groups to survive the opening of the Gate of Hell centuries ago had escaped across the sea to the Chinese mainland. Our group was led by a man named Daimatsu Honchu, who started the village as well as the Holy Ancestor Guild, fortifying and drilling his men until the area for miles around was reasonably secure. Yamato had personally known Honchu's grandson, he told us, going into an anecdote, but I could not follow the story.

All of my life I believed that I lived in Nippon, that the land was my heritage and in my blood, that Nippon lived in me. I knew nothing of China other than vague stories and historical rumors of the inferiority of the Chinese people compared to pure Japanese stock. Now to find that I had been born and raised in the bosom of China . . . I felt profoundly betrayed. By my father, mother, the Abbot, everyone. Of course, now I know that only those in the Guild knew this fact, but at the time I first learned the truth I was blind with anger. I did nothing about this feeling, but the beginning of my present malaise, I believe, stems from this event.

There were 106 of us left from Honchu, and we were a mobile band as much as possible. The zaambi had grown exponentially in number during the past five years. This was a mystery to us all as we had grown used to infrequent sightings of the beasts. The Holy Ancestor patrol would dispatch ten to twenty stragglers a day without much effort and everything was manageable; when I began my perimeter watch for Honchu the number had risen to a pretty regular thirty a day. Six months later it was worse, and three months past that there was much distress in the Village. It was not uncommon to see the Revered Dead walking our streets. I got no sleep, and when I did, I dreamed of decay taking root in my own flesh, of my face sloughing off like the chrysalis of a butterfly to reveal the blackened skull grinning underneath. The boy who had dreamed of honor and adventure had withered away into ash; in his place slumped an ancient nineteen-year-old warrior tired beyond his saddest imaginings.

It was determined that the growing population or the zaambi was due to the almost endless presence of the dead in the ground. It had taken them years to claw their way up through the soil, and they looked it. Most often I would be fending off mere skeletons from attacking our compounds. They didn't care about what they ate; their demon was that or prepossessing and fathomless hunger. At night I could not sleep without wondering what lay scrabbling beneath me in the unquiet earth. I cursed the wretchedness of the world in the night, and at the coming of dawn I became death so that I and mine might live another miserable frightened day longer.

Mother died because she was too brave. We were traveling inland on what long ago had been a paved road but now was little but stone blocks grown over with vegetation. The group of zaambi appeared before us suddenly as we crested a hill; they had been enjoying themselves on the burning remains of a small town. Many of the recently dead had joined their ancient brothers in the feasting; neighbor ate neighbor and parent ate child. When they saw, or more likely, smelled us, as one mass they groaned forward. We had no time to set up a line of defense.

The fighting was person to person and the zaambi had broken through into the very center of our group. Women screamed as they were bitten or as their children were ravaged; there were over 100 zaambi surrounding us. As fast as we could, the members of the Holy Ancestor Squad, forty-three of us, circled the women and children and fended off the vermin. At one point I impaled three zaambi with one thrust of my sword, and a fourth crawled over the bodies of the other three while my sword remained within its compatriots. We moved the group into the center of the burning village, hoping that the flame would scare off the beasts. It didn't.

I was crushing the skull of a zaambi with the hilt of my sword when I heard my sister Hiroko scream. I turned and saw instantly that she was unharmed. Before I could look away a severed head fell to Hiroko's feet, its teeth still chomping. Beside the head slumped the body of my Mother. Her face was a mass of blood, and a bone stuck out of her chest. The roar I heard then ripped through the fabric of my soul and I joined it, stepping forward into the mass of the dead, berserk with rage. I kept up my father's cry as I mowed down beast after beast, inhuman and unstoppable. Anything that got in my way was soon quartered at my feet, squashed under my boots. I tore the skin off of arms, faces, chests. I ripped a head straight off a zaambi's shoulders and flung it into the rampaging fire. I didn't stop until I couldn't find another victim. Ayako later told me I was covered head to toe in gore. There was rotting flesh in my teeth. As I stepped forward from the fallen village I saw my Mother's body begin to burn. I wept.

Mother had moved to assist a member of the patrol, Raichi, when his weapon was torn from his hands, Hiroko told me. She had been handing him a long knife when an arm shot out from the zaambi crowd and pulled her forward. Raichi chopped at the zaambi's arm but another beast had its teeth in his neck as soon as he'd looked away. Father was there in an instant, but it was too late. Mother died because she was brave and now Father too is dead, inside.

We have traveled many days through country wild and unknown, our group feeling less strong by the day. This was discouraging, for we had been followed by zaambi ever since we left the place of my mother's death. At first there were perhaps only twenty of the vermin that gave chase. Too weak to fight then, we walked on in hopes of evading them. We did not. Now others have joined their diseased confederacy, filing in from the forests, the small villages, and the cemeteries, raising their number from twenty to ten times that. They have tracked us as wolves to their prey. Even now, they are little more than a mile behind us, marching steadily, incessantly, without need for sleep, or food, or concern for health. We fast outdistance them by day, but at night, when we are stationary with sleep, the dead continue to shamble forward, hunger gnawing at their bellies. Old Man Yayoi says that the zaambi track us by our smell. He spends all of the day rubbing himself with the acrid leaves of the mulberry tree, hoping that the dead will find him unpleasant to the palate. We living find him unpleasant to the nose. He walks alone.

Today we breasted a high hill and in the distance saw a thin plume of smoke rising toward the heavens. A tell-tale sign of a battle waged against the dead. Kenji-Tango, myself, and another named Tamakura ran toward the sight at full gait. The other ronin, my father included, kept formation behind us.

Kenji-Tango and I reached the seven-foot brick barricade that circled a village encampment. Kenji-Tango lifted me upon his shoulders so that I might have a look. I was shocked by what I beheld.

Men on horseback rode around the village. These riders were backed up in triplicate by footsoldiers. All were armed. Some carried quarterstaff and sword, while others rode with lasso and pike. Every member of this group wore slick leather armor and a metal helm crested with the aubergine feathers of the starling. What was most startling about this batallion of skilled warriors was what they were doing to the living men and women of this simple village.

In the matter of a few seconds, I saw a brigand on horseback ride in pursuit of a man and woman fleeing through the rice paddies. The man was lassoed around the neck and dragged over the furrows in the ground until he moved no longer. I glanced at a woman, no older than fifteen, being raped by a gang of three men in full body armor. I saw man and woman alike joined by manacles, cuffed to their necks, pushed into a line of slaves who were being marched from the village. As I heard the straining voice of Kenji-Tango ask, "What do you see?" my blood boiled over. I could watch no longer.

I jumped over the wall, unsheathed my bitter-edged sword, and ran toward the maurauding band. Hearing my cry of battle a footsoldier turned, only to find himself cleaved into two sloppy parts, the upper half of his body staring from the ground at his still standing lower half. I ran with quick strides, my blade bloodied and singing in the rush of wind. The soldiers who were forcing themselves upon the young girl had a sudden urge to reach for their heads, only to find them missing. A second later, their ears heard the rhythmic drumbeat of three heads hitting the ground—the last sound they ever heard.

I ran straight into the heart of the brigand pack, cold fury coursing through my veins. How could men do this to one another when they had a common enemy to fight? The only answer I was given to my question was a fount of brigand's red blood hotly spraying my body. I had been cleansed.

Suddenly, a lasso fell around my neck. I tried to force it back over my head, but the knot had drawn tight. I saw a horse start to ride away, and the rope had lost all its slackness. Just as I was about to be dragged off into the paddies to have my bones and spirit broken, a sword severed the rope. I turned and saw my savior. Kenji-Tango stood there, aping the ugly face of the brigand who just about took my life.

The brigand on horseback turned around to face us, not pleased with his unflattering portrayal. He hefted a large pike that had been strapped to the horse's saddle and began riding toward my friend. Kenji-Tango and I both scattered in opposite directions, making hard targets, but when I looked back, I saw that he had lost his footing in the wet earth, and was face-down in the mud.

I ran as fast as I could across the slippery ground, and when I saw that I would not reach the charging steed with my sludge encumbered footsteps, I lunged through the air and hurled my sword javelin-style. Despite the balance and sharpness of my blade, it flew low and missed the brigand. Not forsaking me entirely, though, my sword embedded itself deep within the horseflesh, causing the rider to be thrown. The man landed inches from Kenji-Tango's now upright body. He slew the wretch easily.

By now, the other ronin had arrived. A true battle was underway, samurai against trained killers. In the distance I heard a shrill yell, the sound of a sparrow chick crying when threatened by a tree snake. I looked about and discovered the source of the commotion. Off to the right, deep in the rice paddies, a girl child was hiding behind a well, pursued by a man astride a sorrel mare. Again, I asked myself, what kind of man, in armor and on horseback, would pursue a frightened child?

I ran, splashing across the rain-flooded paddies, trying to reach the child. Her pursuer turned and charged at me, his lance pointed forward to impale. I faked going to the left and then threw my body to the right, narrowly avoiding the six-foot lance aimed between my eyes. By the time that the horseman turned his steed, I had reached the child. I had expected her to hide, thinking me another brigand, but she ran forth from behind the stone well and jumped into the cradle of my left arm. I held her. The horseman charged. When the brigand neared within twenty feet, I faked a dodge to the left and again threw myself to the right.

White hot pain shot from just below my right shoulder into every part of my body, and then the wind was forced from me as if I had fallen from the farthest star all the way down onto the hard rocks of China. When the chaos stopped, I opened my eyes. The horseman, a huge and muscled Chinese bastard, was laughing at me. From just below my right shoulder, the brigand's lance protruded. It was speckled with blood and bits of tattered flesh. Sickened, and on the verge of passing out, I looked over my right shoulder. This produced a gale of laughter from the massive Chinaman. I had been impaled straight through by the brigand's lance, and then jammed into the stony side of the well. Things did not look good.

I tried to move, to stab the man with my sword, but the giant pushed on the lance with his strong arms, forcing me back against the well. I grimaced, and I think I passed out for a moment.

"This will wake you," roared the Chinaman, as he lifted me with the lance and positioned me above the mouth of the well. My brain itched furiously with rage. I threw the little girl clear of the mouth of the well, and saw her running off as I swung my sword against the lance. The lance shattered, and I began to fall, grabbing onto the portion of the lance that the Chinaman was holding. The lanyard that tied the lance to his hands during battle now was dragging him with me down the long and narrow throat of the well. My laughter echoed toward the belly of the stone well while my companion was struck dumb with surprise.

We landed amidst a mighty splashing of fetid water at the bottom of the well. By the overpowering stench of feces and urine, I knew instantly that the well was not constructed for drinking water. It was where the chamber pots were emptied.

The great brigand brought himself to his feet, the awful muck being only thigh deep, before I could even begin to get my footing. He pounded my face with a meaty fist and then held me underneath the surface to drown. I tried to overpower him with strength, only to find all of mine gone. I tried to find my sword, but it had vanished into the depths of the cesspool. I tried to play dead, only to find out that he knew better. He was a man experienced in killing. I didn't know how many tens of seconds had gone by, but my lungs were nearly filled to drowning with black, putrid water. I could feel the giant shake with laughter every time he saw me convulsively swallow the foamy liquid. As I was beginning to lose consciousness, I used this successfully to my advantage.

I opened my mouth wide, until I thought it might unhinge, and pretended to swallow the filthy brew. Then I did my best imitation of Kenji-Tango mimicking Madame Mutsu eating something foul. That did it. The brigand doubled-over in laughter, and my hand shot out of the water, two extended fingers finding his eyes. This sufferance, taught by Abbot Yamato, is known as Spider's Fangs. The Chinaman fell back clutching his blood-slicked face, as I stood, taking in air thick with flies. After I coughed heartily, I went over and broke his neck. His heavy body sunk quickly to the bottom of the well.

I tried to scale the wall to reach the land above, but every time I thought I had a good hold, I slipped back down on lichen that beslimed my route. When I was not quite ten feet up, there was a great stirring in the water. I glanced back to see the giant brigand, now zaambi, sniff the air and walk toward me. I saw that his eyes were pulpy and the biting flies at the bottom of the well were massed around the gore, burrowing for the rich meat. I turned and began to climb faster. When I had neared within two feet of the top, my left hand gave way, and I held on by fingertips. Not strong enough to continue climbing, not willing to fall back into the well, I cried for help.

After a moment, someone heard my call. There was a great amount of noise at the top of the well. When I thought I could hold on no longer, a seeking arm clothed in ronin kimono reached down to assist me. I grasped the arm and tried to climb to the surface. When I pulled, the face of the owner hove into view. It was Tamakura. He had been cleaved straight down the center with what looked like a large halberd. He hissed the hungry cry of the zaambi, but the torn bits of muscle that affixed his arm to his body ripped loudly. I fell toward the giant zaambi roaring at the bottom of the well, the arm of Tamakura still jerking in my hands.

I landed again in the scrofulous mess, but this time I landed on my feet. Flies were upon me in an instant, probing my wound. Two, I think, went up my nose quicker than I could smash them. The zaambi approached me, hand outstretched. I grabbed his arm with my right hand and shattered the elbow joint with a blow from my left. Tamakura bellowed at the top, and I could feel reverberations at the bottom. The giant zaambi still moved forward. I sidestepped his lunge, and holding him up against the stone wall, broke his spine in as many as six different places with a maneuver known as Picking Apples.

This did not seem to affect the zaambi. He rolled over and, with much of the strength he had had while amongst the living, pressed me up against the stone wall. I was immobilized by his bulk. His fingers dug into my wound, scraping out muscle and yellowy tissues. He brought a handful from the hole in my chest and smeared the soggy pulp into his mouth. He chewed, and I swear to Amida that he smiled. His hand thrust back into my wound, quick with longing. I struggled, but was absolutely trapped. He ate another handful of my body, and deciding that grabbing it was too slow, leaned his head toward my chest, jaws snapping their need.

Just as the beast was to devour me, a sharp tugging clamped around my outstretched hand. It was a lasso.

"Pull!" I shouted in a shamefully high voice, and was lifted with the speed of a falcon toward the top. When I reached the edge, I crawled from the well to be greeted by father on horseback. This explained the speed of my ascent. Before I could find voice for my thanks, Father was riding back toward the village with the body of Tamakura. Taking him to the fire.

After the brigands had been either killed or captured, the zaambi that were following us slain, and the villagers released from their enslavement, the members of the Holy Ancestor Patrol were invited to feast with the warrior leaders of the village encampment. Old Man Yayoi refused to sit near me, complaining that I smelled. The Chinese village generals, two men known as Yang Hsien and Tsing Chan, told how it was no longer possible for the living to survive among the dead. The victory of the zaambi was assured in the coming year, as their numbers measured in the hundreds attacking the village every single day. A silence fell over us all.

Outside the generals' quarters, a brigand prisoner known as Whining Wu spoke up.

"I know how you might defeat the dead," he said in the direction of the room. "We were heading there when we saw your village. Our leader, who is now at the bottom of your well, said that we must take your people as slaves for farming and breeding. I would be happy to trade this information for my life."

"Do not listen to him," advised Tsing Chan. "He is just trying to save his filthy hide."

"I am sure your opinion of his hide is correct," flattered Abbot Yamato, "but what can it hurt to hear him out? We should turn away no options in such desperate straits."

"Very well, master," said Whining Wu to Abbot Yamato.

3. In Which I Become
Year of Our Sorrows 110

Outside of the burial chamber I can hear the moans and scratchings of the dead. There must be over a thousand of them milling about both overhead and at the stone entrance to the chamber; soon, although the zaambi are not bright, they will overpower the strength of stone with sheer quantity and our present location will become an inescapable trap. No one knows when this will happen, we only know that it will. This is truly our last chance. If we fall, all of the survivors of Honchu and the two hundred or so Chinese who have joined us will fall as well. By now Ayako has probably delivered our child into the world.

Is it a boy? We were going to name it Akira if it was, my father's name. How many days will Akira live if I fail now?

Seven of us, Honda, Kenji-Tango, Abbot Yamato, my father, our Chinese compatriots Yang Hsien and Tsing Chan, and myself, made it across the Yellow River Valley into Lin-t'ung county. We started as a party of twenty well-armed men leaving our loved ones in Tsing Chan's protected compound, and ended up in this chamber barely alive, three of us badly wounded and surrounded by a sea of zaambi. We were not even able to burn or behead our fallen brothers and they are probably zaambi now, their souls in torment. This has weighed heavily on us all. Father looks very old now, but he continues as he always does, gripping his blade and blood dripping from his hands. We were lucky to get here, however, no matter the cost, if Whining Wu's information was correct.

They stood at all sides of us, the warriors. Some with sword and others bearing spears, men on horseback and men bearing packs, six thousand terracotta statues in a series of chambers over a mile long, standing at attention as they had done for probably 2,500 years. It is the quietest army on earth, the eternal retinue of Chinese Emperor Ch'in Shih Huang Ti, and we walked among its precise rows by torchlight in underground chamber after chamber. I had never before witnessed an eerier sight, I who had spent my life staring grim death down. We were all affected by the unholy silence, the smiles of these clay men as tall as ourselves holding actual weapons. I had the horrible feeling that we were walking into a trap. No man had yet entered the emperor's actual burial chamber, Yang Hsien told us back at the compound, and none knew what wonders or terrors lay within. There was a legend that Ch'in Shih Huang Ti, builder of the Great Wall of China, knew all of the secrets of the supernatural, and it is this slim hope we were traveling on. This was the secret Wu had for us. We had nothing else.

Abbot Yamato had lost three fingers from his right hand but he marched on regardless. Kenji-Tango had probably broken one of his arms and yet he propped up his father, Honda, as we made our way to the emperor's chamber; Honda was only semi-conscious and babbled in a mystic delirium talking alternately to his dead wife Soo and to Amida-Buddha. As Kenji-Tango answered the old man, playing all of the roles his father's fevered brain could summon, I was prouder of my friend than I can say. Kisai is my true brother but Kenji-Tango and I were more than that—we were one and the same. If he was wounded I would bleed. It was good that he was there. even if this was to be the end.

At the end of the final chamber of warriors we came to the place no man was said to have entered, but immediately found this to be untrue. Before us were a pair of doors large enough for a mammoth of old to have passed through, and inset in the larger door, a smaller, open one. Within the stone portal there was an iron gate blocking the path, and underneath it, the skeletal remains of a man who had attempted to enter the tomb, his skull on the floor of the next chamber. The back of his shirt was inscribed in a strange language I and the rest of the party were unfamiliar with. It read: K. Koepfli. National Geographic.

Yang Hsien groaned in defeat, but I saw telltale orange marks in the gate and proceeded to give it a hard shove, toppling the rusty edifice to the chamber floor, raising a cloud of powdery dust about our heads. I was thus the first man in 2,500 years to enter the emperor's tomb alive. All I could tell at first was that it was vast, and that the floor was of green marble, the like of which I had never seen. I stepped ahead into the unknown darkness, expecting to fall at any moment into a pit filled with spikes or to have a large stone descend from above and crush me, but nothing of this sort happened. My footsteps, and those of the group behind me, echoed loudly and gave rise to the thought that maybe the zaambi had broken through the outer door. I shook these thoughts from my head, my grip on my sword iron-tight. There it was before me. The burial monument of the emperor.

The coffer was surprisingly small for such a large room. I believed, at a single look, that it was composed entirely of gold with a jade lid. Standing directly before the tomb was the largest statue we had seen yet, at least seven feet tall and in full battle armor, a gigantic scimitar hanging from his hand to the chamber floor. His face was terrifying, a snarl of fanged teeth and a blaze of ruby eyes, a muscled body that seemed primed to explode from sheer animal tension. Next to this titan was a teakwood box on a silver stand, an inscription in Chinese etched onto the box's surface.

Yang Hsien cried out and opened it before any of us could think. I ducked as I heard the sound, and a moment later I saw Yang Hsien fall to the ground, a crossbow bolt buried between his blood-spattered eyes. Tsing Chan, after a moment's hesitation, beheaded his friend to be sure he wouldn't rise as zaambi.

"What did the inscription read?" asked Abbot Yamato, out of breath.

"It read: For those who seek enlightenment. Death is supposed to be very enlightening, I'd warrant," said Tsing Chan. "I wouldn't open the emperor's coffin unless you wish the same fate as poor Yang," he added, bitterly.

I heard a rustling and turned to see my father wrench the breastplate off the great statue before the tomb. A sealed cylinder fell to the floor, and rolled to my feet. Chan snatched it up, and broke the iron seal by smashing the cylinder hard against the floor. A brown roll of parchment slid out, and he feverishly began to read. He laughed loudly to himself, but would not share his findings with us until he had finished reading. He was not laughing anymore.

"This is the finest tea you have ever served me, Soo," said Honda from further back in the darkness. "Amida-Buddha will be pleased with its high quality. Why do you frown so?"

"I am afraid that my tea will not be up to the standards of the gods," said Kenji-Tango softly. I looked away.

"Speak to us," said my father to Tsing Chan. Chan stood, his face gone quite pale.

"It is too horrible," Tsing faltered. I placed the edge of my blade at his sweaty throat.

"Speak," I said. My father did not move to stop me.

"Ch'in Shih Huang Ti did not intend to lay in his coffin this long, I believe," started Chan. "The great warrior that stands before him was supposed to house his spirit and lead his immortal troops into world conquest, but some brave soul must have made sure the transfer never took place. What this scroll explains is the process of that supernatural transfer."

"This is exactly what we seek," cried the Abbot, excitement giving his old frame energy. "If we may raise these statues to do our bidding we will have an army like the world has never seen! The zaambi shall trouble us no more!"

"What is required for the transfer," asked my father, practical as always. Chan took a long breath.

"One of us must take his own beating heart from his chest and place it in the chest of the great warrior. As you see, there is a spot set aside for that."

We all looked at the hollow chest of the ferocious statue. There, in the center, was an obsidian stone, hollowed to fit the placement of a human heart.

"I vote the honor to Akira," said the Abbot, in all respect. "He is the most noble man I have ever known, and the finest warrior. If there is anyone who can close the Gate of Hell, it is he."

"I second," I cried, followed by Kenji-Tango. My father smiled wearily in recognition of our great respect for him, and then shook his head no.

"To my great shame, I cannot do this," said my father. "This life is hateful to me; I cannot bear the thought of immortality, even at the cost of the entire world. Honda is as fine a man as I, and he is near death. Perhaps in this manner he may be saved."

"The person who wishes the transfer must do this to himself," said Tsing Chan sadly. "Honda would be unable to do this in his present state. For myself, I do not possess the courage. I am wretched in your brave company."

We all started as a great vibration ran through the chamber. Fresh air followed the sound shortly.

"The beasts have burst open the doors," I said, tearing my kimono from my shoulders and baring my chest. "I must do what I can. There is no time left." Kenji-Tango cried out his despair.

"I shall do it," he said, but I cut him off.

"Your father and the rest need you. I will be back to fight by your side shortly," I said, trying to be comforting. My heart was racing and I felt sick, but I couldn't falter. Not now. He clasped my hands tightly.

"You will always be my greatest friend, Kenji-Tango. Protect my father and Ayako and my child." Kenji-Tango stepped aside, tears in his eyes, for my father to hand me his long bladed knife. His hands shook as they handed me the weapon. His dark eyes burned into mine, sending me his courage by sheer force of will.

"I will await you, my son. There is work to do." He turned away. I could hear the many footsteps of the zaambi as they poured into the first chamber of warriors, and the crash of terra-cotta as it shattered on the floor. The moans of the dead magnified around us in the echoing emperor's chamber, a miasma of hunger and death. I could hear the Abbot praying to Amida-Buddha for my soul.

I placed the tip of my father's knife directly underneath my ribcage. Taking a shuddering breath I cut deeply, pulling the blade sharply to the left. The pain was indescribable. I looked up as if to beseech the gods to cease my agony and beheld the ruby eyes of the statue beginning to glow with a bloody fire. My gaze was drawn in inexorably, as though by control of another force. I felt my hand reach inside the wound I had made and thrust up amongst my body's heat to grip upon the pumping heart and wrench it forcibly from its mooring. I watched with dimming vision as I staggered upwards to place my convulsing offering into its obsidian home. A surge of black electricity rippled through my body, tearing it asunder in its force. My soul screamed . . .

And I opened my eyes. The darkness was as nothing to me. I could see very clearly the pathetic zaambi stumbling towards the source of their hunger; I could see through the fallen door well into the landscape outside a mile away. I stepped forward with a roar of triumph, crushing the bones of my previous body into red powder. I felt my new teeth drawing blood from my shredded lips, and laughed as the gore dripped from my monstrous mouth. I was so very strong. Memory flooded into my consciousness and I barked out a single word that bellowed through the chambers like a fire through parchment. Through sheer force of my will I demanded the warriors to rise before their new lord.

The tomb shook as the warriors, as one body, took up their defensive positions. Dust and pieces of masonry fell about us, but I was singularly unconcerned. I strode forward at ten times my normal speed and reached the forefront of the vermin in no time at all. I grabbed two zaambi without breaking stride and propelled them into each other with such violence that they simply exploded. I gave my second command, that of battle, and my warriors moved behind me in a wave of cutting blades and stabbing spears, decimating the zaambi force within the chamber in moments. I bent over the nearest beast and wrenched its head from its rotting shoulders using my teeth, flinging it aside with a laugh. Revered Dead, indeed. Insects.

Much later, after I loosed my army in the surrounding countryside, I returned to the emperor's chamber to find my father dead by his own hand.

"The knife was not dry from your blood before he committed seppuku," Kenji-Tango informed me, staring at the floor where his own father lay babbling. Was it out of respect for the dead he wouldn't look at me or was it out of fear and disgust at my new body? I thought about this for a moment but I felt entirely too fine to mourn. A noble thought had occurred to me, and I addressed the men before me knowing that my army heard my every thought and would obey.

"After we have cleared this place of filth and provided for the safety of our families I shall take my army back across the sea to Nippon to free her from her dishonorable masters. Nippon shall once again be our home. After this, is there anything that dare stand in our way? We shall be as gods on this earth, and after we have conquered all things on the face of the earth we shall follow the very demons through the Gate of Hell itself and I personally shall eat the heart of the Prince of Demons! As my father said to me, there is much work to do. Go to it, my men! Banzai!"

4. IN WHICH I:
YEAR OF OUR SORROWS 364

Many times now have I attempted to pull my loathsome heart from my chest, but whatever supernatural power imbued me with this life does not see fit to take it away from me. I have found the most consolation to my soul here in the Forbidden City, my troops massed before me in the Great Courtyard, but that consolation is little. I have seen all parts of the world, the great empty towers of America and the silent Egyptian pyramids, and I have led my warriors all places with me. We have killed all dead things, but not before all living things perished in the battle. I cannot be everywhere at once, and in our absence the dead have had the last laugh on me. They are centuries gone now, my family and countrymen, all humanity.

In time I will have read every book ever written in every language; I will have seen every film and examined closely all artwork. I will know every single grain of this benighted earth. I am master of all that I survey, and what I survey is desolation itself. I have eaten the heart of the Prince of Demons and have found it to be my own. There is a thought that repeats itself in my mind derived from the Old Testament creation myth.

It rolls around the interior of my skull like a pebble spiraling down an endless well.

If I am God, where is my Seventh Day? When do I, Toshiro Hiraoka, get my rest?

THE ZOMBIES OF MADISON COUNTY

BY **DOUGLAS E. WINTER**

Douglas E. Winter is the poet laureate of zombie fiction. And also the most "meta," in the literary sense, in that the stories that compose his collection American Zombie *("Less Than Zombie," "Bright Lights, Big Zombie," "The Zombies of Madison County") are all staggeringly-realized riffs on popular fictions of the time. Try to guess which ones.*

I feel honored to have commissioned each of those astonishing stories—one apiece—for each of my previous zombie anthologies. I feel responsible only in that I somehow created the opportunity for him to do it not once, not twice, but thrice.

And now, being forced to choose, I have no choice but to go with this one: the only zombie story in all my years that made me weep uncontrollably copious tears, over the phone, at the author who dredged such wracking emotion out of me.

Also the most meta, and most personal, of them all.

Jesus raised the dead . . .
but who will raise the living?
—Pearls Before Swine

THE END

There are songs that come weighted with debt from the stormclouds of a hundred smokestacks, from the grey ashes of a thousand lives, a million deaths. This is the last of them. On another long morning after the dead began to walk, I'm at my desk, staring into the wide blank screen of my computer, waiting for the words that never come, the telephone that never rings.

Nothing but the manuscript is left. The world outside is gone, at least the world as I knew it, and in its place the New Age. Inside there is nothing more to say. Only the manuscript remains, a shuffled stack of pages, for the most part typed, but by its midpoint nicked and scratched with ink and at last given over entirely to handwriting. A story; perhaps a fable. Whether a book of lies, or of revelations, it is the final missive from Madison County.

Its writer has extracted a solemn promise: If I decide not to publish his manuscript, I must agree to tell in my own words what happened in Madison County, Illinois, in the late summer of this year—what, for all I know, is happening there still. As usual, his ambition and conceit are intense, his compulsion to tell a story so demanding as to try to make that story mine.

Still, with the manuscript complete, the puzzle parts in place, I read his story through to the end. At times I stop, put the pages aside and wish them away. But I cannot help myself; I read, and read again. As I read, I begin to see the images, black type on white paper blurring, finally swallowed up in a wash of gray. To see the images is to know the truth of words. And I begin to hear those words, rising like smoke off these brittle pages. The story whispers to me. At times it shouts; at other times it cries. Sometime just after midnight, I know that there is no alternative but to try to publish the story—if anyone is left alive, or cares, to read it—though its telling may seal my fate as surely as it sealed that of Douglas Winter.

In a world where death is life, and life, in all its forms, seems nothing more than a rehearsal for death, I could feel the hunger created by this story, the need to know its truth or deception. I believed then that, in a world where movies have become reality, where the dead walk and eat the living, there was still a place for fiction. I believe even more strongly now that I was wrong. But I had read his story, and I needed to know if it was truly a story, or something more. And the knowing could bring me to one place, and one place only.

Journeying to Madison County through these pages—and now, as I must, by wing or wheel or foot—I felt that, in many ways, I had become Douglas Winter. Finding the way into his essence is something of a challenge. His story provides few certainties, and a handful of vague clues from which only the most cautious of deductions may follow. He is an enigmatic person. At times he seems mysterious yet mundane, for in the days before the dead, he was one of those Washington lawyers, walking and talking through corridors and courthouses, aloof in Armani suits, fast cars, fast tracks. At other times he seems ethereal, perhaps even imaginary. He was not simply a lawyer but a writer, lost so deeply in himself that he would fall into the well of the subconscious and emerge with a story, a book—not about the law, but about horror. In his legal work he sought, no doubt, to be a consummate professional; probably he worked too hard at it, worsening his own wounds in seeking cures for others. Since he saw the world through different eyes, in time he inevitably would count himself one of the hunted, not the hunters. Given the law's implacable need for order, consider the agony of his vision, which saw that very likely there was none. Consider his plight, in the darkest hours of the night, awake, watching, waiting for the answer to come.

Too many questions remain without answer, and they, too, draw me onward, a wary moth to the flame of Madison County. I have been unable to determine what became of anything else Winter wrote there, which, as his story suggests, may have included other stories, perhaps in the hundreds of pages. The best guess—and this would be consistent with what I know of him—is that he destroyed it all before vanishing into the midnight existence that tells us nothing and everything. For, having reached this story's end, I know nothing more of Douglas Winter than is written here, nothing at all about his life, if indeed there is one, after the zombies of Madison County.

His story has revised the very way that I read, I write, I think—and, most of all, reminded me of how we lived for so very long in a fragile kind of light, that light known as faith. For some people, there was faith in God or some other spiritual source of goodness, but for most of us, there was simple faith in a neighbor, a friend, a lover, a parent, the proverbial fellow man. We slept our peaceful nights in a darkness that was incomplete, pierced and illuminated by the shining stars of our faith: holes in the floor of Heaven. Coming to know Stacie Allen and Douglas Winter as I have in reading, and now writing, this story, I think that we were lucky, far more lucky than we knew. When the dead finally rose to teach us, it was too late for us to learn.

A story is always something more than its writer; it is also its reader. If you approach what follows, as I did, with the willingness to believe, you may find yourself on a journey that leads inexorably to his unspoken words: The End. You may wonder if you were meant to be entertained. In the increasingly indifferent furnace of your heart, you may even find, as Stacie Allen did, room to die again.

DOUGLAS E. WINTER

At dawn in late August, in the year of the dead, Douglas E. Winter locked the door of his suburban split-level house in Alexandria, Virginia. He carried a black leather dufflebag filled with handguns and ammunition and pharmaceuticals, the currency of the day, down a short curve of cement steps to the driveway. There, his 1971 Ford Mustang, taken from a used car dealer for a song and six clips of Black Talons, was waiting to take him home. The Mustang's once-bright racing blue was tainted red with rust, but its tires were new, and he would ask it only to make one last ride. A knapsack containing notebooks, pens, and a laptop computer snuggled in the tiny back seat among canned goods and bottled water, the box of novels, the sleeping bag, the Coleman lantern, the Mossberg .410 pump shotgun.

He sat in behind the wheel, fed an old Beatles cassette to the tape deck, and began the long and winding road that would lead, in two or three days, to the heart of the Midwest. Driving through the tranquil streets of Alexandria, he took in the familiar landscape for the final time before heading north on the Shirley Highway and then cutting onto the George Washington Parkway, which snakes west to the Beltway. Across the Potomac, invulnerable Washington, its ghettoes burned and streets patrolled by Marines, shone back its white wisdom: Order has been restored.

Above Langley, the Cabin John Bridge still stood, and took him through an armed checkpoint and out of Virginia. There was no looking back, not now, not after the knowledge, that thief in the night, had come to him and whispered its summons. Something was calling him, some uncomfortable urge that grew with each sleepless night; something he knew, in that place kept for secret knowledge and that now needed to be confirmed. He had grown tired of the movie, the endless replay of images from horror films that flooded the television screen, which with each passing day became more unreal, more fictional than the words he would type onto the page. He realized then that he was expendable, that in a world made up of horror, there might be nothing left to tell, no one left who wished to read his words.

He had written books, he had written articles, he had written stories; for nearly twenty years he had scrawled his message on the wall. Often he had written about the human need for horror, the passion with which the films, the fiction, had been embraced as his nation slouched toward the Millennium. By then he had quit the law and begun to argue his case alone, facing a computer screen instead of short-tempered judges, recalcitrant witnesses, blank-faced jurors. It was a good life, one in which his pain could be managed, in which he could retreat to the interior world, where everything mattered, and be done with the outside, the surface that the years had lacquered with layer after layer of lies to keep him safe. But then, when the dead rose, nothing could keep him safe. The law had also quit him, its façade of lofty ideals fallen into grim rituals of revenge, at first overseen by lynch mobs and shooting parties, but in time made formal by military tribunals, death squads, detention camps.

The highways were restricted but clear, said the talking heads on the nightly news, for Interstate 70 was the throat for the food and fuel supplies that kept the Northeast, what was left of it, alive. The convoy was formed near Frederick, Maryland, where he pressed the eject on his tapedeck and inserted the soundtrack to *Dawn of the Dead*. A bored M.P. glanced at his papers and waved him into line. The Mustang clung close to the heels of a pack of vans and eighteen-wheelers. In his rearview he watched an ever-lengthening tail of land rovers and tractor trailers, ridden herd by full-throttled Humvees as helicopter gunships fluttered overhead. There were detours, delays, diversions, wide and weary loops around the free-fire zone south of Pittsburgh, the ravaged remains of Columbus, but as evening brought down its veil, he made his bed within the gates of Fort Benjamin Harrison, and slept there encircled by the victorious army of the righteous, the living.

He had secured the rarest of commodities, a travel pass, which, like everyone and everything, had its price. But money, lies, and favors, the fair trade of the nation's capital, meant nothing to him now; their spending loosed him of what had become shackles, imprisoning him first in the law, and then at his writer's desk. Now he had the freedom to know. By mid-morning of the second day, the convoy split at Indianapolis, and he was caught up in a new column that followed the great scythe of I-70 southwest toward St. Louis, the Gateway to the West and now a mighty fortress for the cause of humanity, spared from the curse of the living dead by a trick of geography and a quick-tempered general who had seized power and levelled, in rapid order, its cemeteries, bridges, and crowded ghettoes.

His destination was there, just a few miles east of St. Louis, on the near shore of the Mississippi. Interstate 70 wove through the last of the Illinois countryside, through Vandalia and Highland, until reaching, just before Edwardsville, a cusp of low hills whose green had faded, the outpost of urban decay, erratic corridors of condominiums and convenience stores, acres of earth torn open, laid bare, mere symptoms of the suffering that lay beyond: the inner-city despair of East St. Louis, the blue-collar barrios of Madison and Venice, and at their crest, his hometown, the great gray ghost of Granite City.

But first he sought the strength that only could be found in pain: the pain of remembering. It brought him from the protection of the armored escort to the two-lane twist of blacktop that carried up into the hills and to the marker, the place of departure and forgetting, the place where he had stopped nearly twenty years before, on the day he left Madison County. His mother was buried there, on a sleepy knoll named Sunset Hills; she had lived long enough to see him as a lawyer, but not to see him happy. When God in His cruelty took her, he had started to write again.

The cemetery, once secluded, as peaceful and precious as an autumn sunset, was blanketed in black, its innocent fields now cratered char where even the earth was dead, sacrificed on the altar of fuel-air explosives or napalm. He closed his eyes and saw the silver-winged fighter-bombers of Scott Air Force Base, their howling dive and breath of flame, and he prayed that she was there when the airplanes struck, that she suffered only one death—for that, indeed, was enough. He vowed not to think about it again, and then faltered, sitting in the ashes as he began to cry.

He wished for the thousandth time in his life that he had married, and unmade the wish, as he often did, with the thought that it would have meant another betrayal, another loss. Then he asked his mother for forgiveness, and asked his God, what was left of Him, for the mercy He had not shown to her.

As he returned to the Mustang, he looked to the west, where the sun retreated through a sky he had never forgotten, the sky that shadowed his dreams, his nightmares, his stories: the sky of burnt steel, smokestack lightning, roiling above the mighty forge of Granite City, whose mills, long dead, were alive like the zombies, burning again, burning brightly, churning thunderclouds that never rained. A grey hope once, in the '40s, '50s, and '60s; a gray hope that, like so many American dreams, had turned to dust and despair instead. Foreign imports, labor unions, environmentalists, Arabs and Israelis, Democrats and Republicans, the energy crisis, the recession—he had heard all the stories and in the end believed none of them. For growing up in this burning world, he had seen neither hope nor despair, only gray.

That the shadow lingered still, snuffed out the sun, was no surprise. This place was waiting for him, waiting for his return. If asked, he could not have told anyone why. There was only the knowledge that had come to him that long and lonely night the week before, as he watched the government's video footage from St. Louis, the city of the miracle, the city that had escaped the dead, the city that stood at the banks of a mighty river, the promise of the New America. It was then that he saw this sky, the clouds that were not clouds but the dark breath of smokestacks, lingering in the distance. Just as he saw them now, saw them and felt their call.

At the First Baptist Church of Granite City, a little boy named Doug Winter had stood every Sunday morning, every Sunday night, as the evangelist closed each service with an invitation, arms upraised as if to embrace some invisible giant, *Just as* I *am, without one plea*, summoning those in the congregation who had heard the call of blessed Jesus, who had been touched by the hand of God, *But that thy blood was shed for me*, to join him before the altar, to join him in salvation, and when that little boy, seven or eight years old, had stumbled forward, down the long and lonely aisle and into that empty embrace, *And that thou bids't me come to thee*, he did not know why, he did not know what he heard, what had called him, just as he did not know now, or care to know, save that for once he had heeded the call: O *Lamb of God*, I *come . . .* I *come.*

STACIE

Darkness measured time for Stacie Allen, and darkness settled swiftly in this world of shadows. She watched the darkness, looked through it to the tall hurricane fence and its weave of barbed wire, thinking, if indeed there were thoughts, of the man who stood at the other side. Soon he would gesture to her, approach the wire, and soon she would stagger toward him from the crowded interior of the holding pen. Sometimes it was hard for her to walk, and impossible for her to talk; the words she tried to speak coughed from her lips in immutable moans, and however she sought to form them, they meant only hunger. It was hard to remember her name, how she looked, hard to remember the man who waited on the outside, harder still to remember how she had looked to him then, twenty years before. A girl in a red turtleneck sweater, plaid skirt, reel tights, black patent leather shoes, her hair long and dark and alive with the wind as she turned away, eyes wet—with tears or rain, he never knew. She kissed him goodbye, ran to the waiting car and ducked down out of the sudden spring shower, out of his life. Douglas Winter did not know then that she was pregnant with the child of another man, or that two months later she would be married and a housewife in a farm town somewhere in central Illinois. Certainly he did not know that some twenty years after that, he would be facing her again, their eyes still locked in that stare: his eyes filled with hope, hers blank and dead.

That he should find her here, at this time, this place, was the stuff of fiction. It was something that did not happen save in stories, including one that he had written. But it happened in movies, too, and the world, for all its dreaming, had at last become a motion picture.

If she could still read, she would know that she was fiction. His words had found her, or what remained of her, in sullen moments of introspection that he called stories. In their pages, her hair was black, her body lithe, her legs taut and athletic, curving into what her mother had called racehorse ankles; but her face was missing, without description, always in shadow, unseen, unknown—the cipher with raven hair. With three words, she had left him; with thousands upon thousands of words, he had brought her back.

It did not take long to find her. When he left his mother's grave, he followed the state highway down from the low hills and through the decades, past the ghost of the Bel Air Drive-In, whose screen still shone somewhere inside his head, past Pontoon Beach and its polluted pools and streams, past Tri-City Speedway and Bowland and the first of the housing projects, and then stopped at the railroad tracks, where he waited, counting the endless train of passing freight cars until, near one hundred, he noticed their cargo. Soon he crossed the web of tracks and was there, on Nameoki Road, driving into his hometown.

Thomas Wolfe was right: You can't go home again. The reason is that you have never left. Douglas Winter may have lived his adult life in places far from Granite City, but Granite City lived on in him. When he saw St. Elizabeth's Church, made the left turn onto Johnson Road, he was not only driving the Mustang, but its immaculate twin, and then a 1968 Ford Galaxie 500, riding in the back of a 1956 Ford Woodie, the front of a Volkswagen Beetle, pedaling a bicycle, running, walking, carried along in his father's arms; it was a journey he had probably taken more often in dreams than in life. Twice he met police cars, first at the sharp turn of Johnson, where he offered his ID, and then at Fehling Road, where he had to offer a fifth of whiskey as well. In the few minutes it took to circle the east of town, going as far as Bellemore Village, he felt the old pains, the ones that cut through him as certain as his mother's cancer: the Ben Franklin five-and-dime where he had bought his first toys, the pharmacy where he had bought his comic books and paperbacks, the confectionary that had become a funeral home, all of them gone, replaced by mocking strip malls and merchandise marts whose windows were smashed, their goods as stolen as his youth.

He drove past Frohardt School, where his mother had taught and he had written his first stories, past all the houses where he had lived, down Lindell Boulevard, over to Franklin Avenue and then the short distance back to Riviera Drive and Miami Court, the town's middle-class neighborhood, home to the Catholic merchants, the Jewish dentists and doctors, and the few others, his father among them, who had stepped from the shadow of the steel mills into a life outside. Douglas Winter drove through that shadow, knowing, not knowing, simply trusting in that instinct that had called him home as inevitably as a sparrow in late autumn.

The town had closed in on itself, the homes and shops abandoned, what was left of life waiting in the armed camp that surrounded the smokestacks of Granite City Steel. He found Nameoki Road again, took it south past the high school, where troops in the hundreds were now billeted, then farther along to the sullen projects of Kirkpatrick Homes, where plainfaced men and women in workclothes stared past him with tired and uncaring eyes. And at last he reached the unholy hive in which they labored: the mills, the chemical plants, the furnaces, the pipelines, insectile monstrosities of metal and flame that stalked Route 203 like some vast alien war machines from the science fiction films of his childhood.

He parked the car at the Nash Street entrance of Granite City Steel and sat on the hood, waiting for something to come to him—inspiration, antagonism, admonition—through the smoke and fog of his youth. He bought off the civilian security guards and watched the trains pull through like clockwork. The night brought nothing, so he drank his way into the next day, sleeping when he could, curled in the tiny back seat of the Mustang, the laptop computer hugged to his chest like a firstborn child. When he woke, the faded, dying searchlight of the sun was almost gone. Darkness prowled down, but a brighter light, borne of the blast furnaces, kept his vigil. He could feel its warmth, breathe its fumes, a pungence that burned his lungs more than his brief foray with cigarettes, the smoke that cancelled vision, silenced life, and it moved him as it never had before. Home was a city dressed in gray, forever shrouded, eternally in mourning. A place where even the dead came to die.

In the distance he heard the shuffle of another train, the latest in the ceaseless caravan that hauled restless cargo into the mills. Its whistle mourned a new night of grief, a cry that had echoed down the miles of rail from decimated Minneapolis and St. Paul, Milwaukee and Chicago and all points south, where parentless children, sundered spouses, the childless, the friendless, wept over a world gone so wrong that nothing could put it right but order. If only he had known—known and not seen what waited for him in Madison County—then perhaps he could have lived still in Virginia, watched his television with a bottle in hand like so many others, rested in the embrace of that greater sorrow. But the roaring furnaces burned through him now, heat melting the weariness of years spent in hiding; and he had touched the smoke, which gave back nothing to the world but a stain, a taint, that would never be washed away.

In the shriek of braking metal, the night's wailing engine found its resting place beneath the great burrow of corrugated steel that enclosed the railhead. He wiped the sleep and ash from his face as, in the deepening gloom, soldiers dropped from the cars, exchanged salutes and salutations with their kin at the yard, and then formed up into lazy ranks. The scene had been replayed with minor variations throughout this day, and the day before: the troops dispersing, reforming with weapons ready at the first of the boxcars as the process of unloading began. A huddle of zombies would be herded out of the car and into a jagged run of wooden chutes and fences that funneled and divided them like cattle until, one by one, they emerged into a final chute. There, soldiers with air hammers would hobble them at ankle or knee before letting them stagger into the wide fields of slag that bordered the mills, a makeshift prison secured with wire and cinderblock and steel.

He was too tired to count the zombies, or to count the mass of undead bodies that already crowded each wide rectangle of fence-work with emigrants from the grave. But he remembered each one of them, fascinated by the faces of the American dead; for here, at last, was a democracy where all men were created equal, mindless husks of grey with little to distinguish them but hair, clothing, shoes—and hunger. The tired, the poor, the huddled masses, yearning, yearning . . . to feed.

In time he watched the last of the passengers, what once had been a woman, stumble down the plank of the boxcar. Stop. Head lolling off to the side as if she were sleepwalking. Turn. Eyes raising to him. As if he had been waiting there for her.

And, of course, he was waiting. For her.

It was Stacie Allen.

The Book of Saturday

She could see him, vaguely, in the ever-slowing trickle of memory. Each moment she saw him, saw through him, a patchwork quilt, pieces of time sewn into what once was. He was tall, over six feet, weighted with the beginnings of middle age, and he moved like the smoke itself, tentative, ominous, hovering over her. His eyes were ice blue, now faded to gray, halfmoons of weariness etched beneath them, and there was only the trace of a smile, a mask to tame the world outside.

He was tired, that would have been the word she had tried to form while watching him. Tired for lack of sleep, and for lack of something else. He told her he had been a lawyer, though she knew that, and that his work had been long and hard, trials in distant places, trials about the dead and dying—dreadful accidents, air disasters—but Stacie could no longer imagine what this meant, could only see men in staid suits huddled among the victimized, the guilty, in courtrooms of winedark wood, shifting paper that meant money or life and sometimes both.

Douglas Winter was not meant to be a lawyer; he was a dreamer of sorts, who lived within himself in strange, almost threatening ways. Stacie had sensed as much on that distant Monday, the first day of school in that long-lost enigma of the 1960s, after a president had died but before his brother was killed, when Douglas Winter stopped by her desk in the ninth grade English class at Granite City Junior High School and asked if she were Clark Allen's sister.

She had been waiting for him, waiting for this question, for if it went unasked, she would have come to him and told him. She knew that from the moment she saw him. But she would wait, and wish, and across the room at the ringing of the bell he came, looking like a lost boy stepping painfully into that actor called a man.

He smiled, pushed at his glasses. "Are you Stacie?" A fat stack of books nearly wormed out from his hands. He set them carefully on her desk, and atop the shopping-bag-covered textbooks she could see a paperback novel: *The Puppet Masters* by Robert Heinlein. When her eyes returned to his, she felt something shift inside. The eyes, the voice, the face, the stance, the silence, an uncomfortable moment as something new, something disturbing, touches and then breaches the abyss that separates two hearts, makes them beat as one. Stacie knew this moment, though she had never known it before, might never know it again. And there began the thing that would change them both forever.

They spoke about that moment only once, late at night in a house emptied of her roommates, the beginning of a long holiday weekend together at the farthest point she had traveled from home: one hundred miles to college in Charleston, Illinois. She curled against him, naked yet chaste, and asked him if even then he knew that it would come, six years later, to this place where children no longer played at love but began to make love.

He leaned back into the pillow and looked at the poster scotch-taped above her bed, a sunny seascape whose caption told them *Virginia Is For Lovers*. "I don't know if I want to go back." That he was looking at the poster confused her, but only for a moment. "Back home. To Granite City . . . to Madison County."

"Yes." Stacie pulled in closer to him, placed her head upon his chest. "I know what you mean." But even then she didn't know. His knapsack, a tattered mangle of surplus-store canvas and rope, huddled on the floor beside the bed. The flap was folded back to expose the sheaf of papers, unkempt manila envelopes and file folders from which typescript pages fanned out. The nearest of the envelopes, thick to overflowing, contained a novel, she knew—a novel that would never end, he said. Even though it was fiction, the novel was called *Autobiography*, and it was about violence and Vietnam, madness and the Mississippi; most of all, it was about Madison County.

This package of paper that wanted one day to become a book was good. At least the parts she understood. He had read it to her, parts of it, and it had given her an excuse to glance inside him, to those places he had not opened, even to her.

He was going places, she knew that. Law school, lawyer. And what then? Washington, he sometimes told her, and that was near Virginia, the place for lovers. People. Power. Wealth. Those words didn't seem to apply to him. He was still lost, and there was little she could do about it except hold him in the night and wait and wait until the day came, and in time it would, when another man would cross another room to ask if she were Stacie Allen.

"Write another poem for me." Douglas Winter had smiled then. "A poem about Virginia."

He had written through the night, sitting on a broken angle of sidewalk, balancing the computer between his knees as his fingers tap-tapped at its keyboard, the arcane code of the storyteller.

He wrote, saved files, wrote again, shifted his body, and talked quietly to her as he worked, forever telling her about her beauty and how much he loved her. "Stacie, I . . ." Admissions of love. Sometimes he stopped and simply stared at her, a moment of inexpressible rapture.

Her throat was torn open from just beneath the left jawline, a gash that widened as it zigzagged down to a gaping hollow where flesh and marrow had been scooped from above her breasts. Most of her left arm had been chewed away, the forearm dangling on threads of muscle. She was not concerned about the wounds, or the blood that had dried into mudbrown patterns on her ashen skin and foul, torn J.C. Penney clothes.

Douglas Winter asked questions of her, and the words upset her, confused her, until he had whispered, "No, no, please, stay there." Then he held his silence, but after a time he could not help himself. There was so much to say, so little time left in which to say it. He would start to tell her something, then stop and type instead. Sometimes he slipped into moments of self-conversation. But then he would look at her, and his face would fall from its anguish into a kind of peace.

Near dawn, his confused emotions and the battery of his laptop computer were drained. On the spiral of his homecoming tour, he had taken the time to hide his backup battery, along with most of his belongings, in a closet of the house on Lindell Boulevard, sold by his parents late in the '50s, now abandoned, its roof partially collapsed—beneath the weight of time or explosives, it did not matter. He had taken back the house, the neighborhood, and it was home again.

He stood, shaking the aches from his back and hands, and stepped up to the fence, its heavy links, steel posts, and coiled parapet of barbed wire no barrier to what he first said to her. Then, remembering perhaps, or drawn only by the sound of his footsteps, the smell of his flesh, she came toward him as far as the barrier would allow. Reaching carefully through the small hole that he had cut in the fence, he could almost touch her wounded face. But it was time to leave.

Just short of his car, Douglas Winter stopped, looking back at her as another train sighed out its blast of steam, its aching weight finding rest in the Nash Street terminal. Through the jigsaw puzzle of chain he could see the mountains of slag that still marked the city's southern boundary, the coke plant and its blast furnaces belching their dirty mist into the dead sky beyond. Stacie was framed in a perfect circle of light, the raging furnaces brighter than the rising sun.

She was about five feet four, and from what he could tell her face had not seemed to age, though her body, like his, had thickened. Two children could do that to a woman. Her physical attraction had been immense, at first, to his teen-aged rage of hormones and happiness. But there was something in Stacie Allen that interested him still. There was no intelligence, he could see that. And there was no passion, though he never quite knew if there had been passion there for something other than stability, for a house and two cars and two children and a cat or a dog, in a town like Granite City, in a place like Madison County.

Later, he would tell her that in ways undefinable, finding her at the rail-yard that day was the most important moment of his life. Why was not spoken. That was the way he approached his life. He would write, not speak, about what was important, and even then, what he wrote was veiled, hidden, encoded, protected.

"Why is it that you write, exactly—I mean, this stuff."

He looked across another barrier, one no less daunting, to her. She stirred at her Coca-Cola with a straw, wrinkled her nose at the pile of pages on the dining room table between them. In the kitchen, only paces away, her mother made quiet noises, shuffling plates, rinsing silverware, letting them know she was still there.

"If I knew, do you think I would be writing it?" His smile went unreturned. "Sometimes I look down into my typewriter and there's this space there, white space, just emptiness. And it has to be filled. Like it's my job, that if these words don't get written down then they will never matter. I will never matter. And sometimes, when somebody, usually you, or my mother, sometimes a teacher, reads them and then looks at me a certain way, sometimes I think I've managed to matter. The rest of the time I'm just having fun. Trying to have fun. So why is it that you read what I give you?"

Stacie hadn't expected him to ask that question. He wondered if she thought before she spoke. She did stir again at her Coke; soon, he thought, the straw might become a cigarette.

"Well, because you gave it to me. So I thought that meant you wanted me to read it. That I was supposed to read it. Or that maybe you had written it for me." Her face brightened, a smile that held, waiting for him to respond.

"What if I didn't care?"

There was truth in there, somewhere. She knew it, and knew, for the first time, that she had looked into the soul of Douglas Winter.

"I'm supposed to say, 'Then I don't care, either.' Which is true, mostly. But I think you care. I think that you think you love me. And that you want me to love you. But you don't want me to love you, not really. You want me to love your poems, your stories. And"—she hesitated, glancing back over her shoulder toward the kitchen and the ghost of her mother—"it's not what I dreamed about as a girl."

Back in the house on Lindell he found the shower still working, though its water was cold and colored with corrosion. He could not remember ever bathing inside these walls. Perhaps the later dwellers had repainted, remodeled, rearranged the rooms. The tile was recent, only a decade or so old. The mirror above the sink was cracked, a jag of lightning that cut his face into a kind of Jekyll and Hyde. Like most people thought of him: Lawyer and writer and never the twain shall meet.

During the last good days, before the dead returned, he had thought, more and more often, of giving in to despair, of writing the John Grisham novel that everyone seemed to expect or demand of him. He had neglected this kind of thinking since the last months of their first love affair, in the Spring of 1971, when he had talked of a novel about the law, about the chaos they witnessed around them, the war in the streets, the war in the jungle. She watched in wonder as he slipped a joint from his pocket, raised it then in half-salute: "To steel mills and coke plants, Dow Chemical and napalm. Or better yet, to cold, coughed-up mornings in good old Granite City, Illinois."

Stacie said nothing, but looked off to the side of him and hugged herself against something, a chill in bright April, the University of' Illinois campus alive with parties and protest. There were four dead in Ohio, and many, many more in Vietnam, and in another month or so he would be receiving his draft notice. He was the love of her past six years and yet a stranger, talking now about peace and justice and freedom, but writing through the night as if alive on the chaos spinning around him, watching the endless stream of helicopters and bodybags on TV, watching nags burn, stomach burning with an ulcer, living hard, drinking harder, now slipsliding to dope. It was the child finally grown, punching his way into manhood, and it was more than she could deal with. She had an answer, but as usual, he was not listening, and gave her his own instead.

"Jesus raised the dead," he told her, summoning up one of the strange songs that sobbed from his stereo. "But who will raise the living?"

He passed the joint over to her; she pushed his hand away. And at last she said it: "I've got something to tell you." Words that he could have written, should have written, then. He wished that he could find them now, always thought that he would remember—that, for as long as he lived, he would never forget them.

Words that slipped from her like a confession. "I *don't think* . . ." Words that seemed rehearsed. ". . . *that* I *should* . . ." And they were rehearsed, of course they were rehearsed. ". . . *see you* . . ." Words that gave way to tears, expected tears, scripted tears, soap opera tears. ". . . *anymore*."

NEW MORNINGS, DISTANT MUSIC

When, in the hour after dawn, he had returned to the house on Lindell Boulevard, its yard of dead grass was blackened with the curious wash of fading night and oncoming shade. He moved through the uncertainty of that evolving darkness, beer in one hand, pistol in the other, listening for its sound.

Nothing spoke to him, not even bird or insect. He could hear only the distant drumming of the morning trains, arriving from the east with the sun.

Once inside the house, he checked the doors and boarded windows, then took his shower. He replaced the computer battery, printed out what he had written, and placed the pages inside his knapsack, loose and unsettled as ever. Everything obviously had its place, but in a pattern known only to him. He finished the beer and took another with him as he curled on the floor, his knapsack a pillow, and tried for a time to sleep. The sounds of the trains, implacable, mechanical, forever forceful, turning their great wheels around and around and around, lured him toward a calm, a peace, he had not felt in years. In a place where he had not slept for almost four decades, he tried but still could not feel safe.

"You're afraid," Stacie had told him. "You write because you're afraid. Not of the monsters, not of the dark, not of any of this stuff you make up . . . That isn't real to you, is it? You try to make it real to other people because it gets in their way. So they can't know you. Because that's what you're afraid of. Other people."

It was Christmas. Their last Christmas together. He had given her a sweater, perfume, a poem. She had given him a framed picture of her. It did not do her justice; the angle invoked her brother's face, and her smile was fixed and false. Later he wondered if even then she knew, even then the clock of their love was winding down.

"That's not fear," he said at last. "That's living. I write because each day is like the twist of the handle on a jack-in-the-box. But they tell you that that's God in the box. You turn the handle, slowly, swiftly, however you live, but you know—or you think you know—that God is somewhere inside, and that sooner or later He's going to pop out and take you. Or maybe you don't believe in Him, so you keep winding and winding that crank. Maybe the box never opens. Maybe the crank breaks off, or you get tired of turning it. Maybe it just winds on forever."

She pulled the soft wool of her new sweater between her fingers and felt her brow wrinkle, felt a kind of desperate headache push its way up from somewhere deep inside, a guilty place where the hands and lips and cock of a phantom had touched her. Stacie supposed that, for Douglas Winter, this was everyday talk. For her, it was the stuff of danger, darkness, plague years. People in Madison County didn't talk this way, about these things. The talk was about weather and the steel mills and the labor problems, the high school wrestling team and the new environmental regulations and the dangerous Negro boys from East St. Louis. Not about art or nightmares. Not about Gods who might or might not exist.

He put the framed photo aside, reached for her and brought her into his arms. She started to cry, for reasons he did not then know, and told him how much she loved him, wanted him, wanted to be with him.

As they kissed, slowly slipping to the floor, to lay entwined as the evening fell into night, he thought about what life would be like in twenty years. About the place on her poster, Virginia, with its sunny seascape, a beach on which a mother, unchanged by time, walked with a leopard's grace, her mane of black hair tied up in a knot, two children scurrying after her, dancing in the wash of salt water and sand, as her husband, their father, a happy man with a law degree and a fistful of novels, stood off-camera, watching.

He kissed her and told her something, something he had never said before. Outside the snow cut through the cloud cover and brought a blanket of white over the grey streets of Granite City. The lights of the Christmas tree twinkled like fallen stars. An angel watched over them. Stacie Allen was nineteen years old, and the Moody Blues sang of nights in white satin. Never reaching an end.

The Use of Ashes

Now what? thought Stacie Allen. But there could be only one thought: Food, always food.

He sat on the same bent angle of sidewalk he had used before and watched her and the city become one. The old ways, the old times, coming back to him again. He wondered at how much had returned; how far he had traveled, only to find himself back here. He wondered how her hair would feel to his touch, how the curve of her back would meet his hand, how she would fit beside him.

The old ways came to him so easily, despite all that was learned, dispensing so quickly with the lessons of the years, the hard rules of growing up and old. He tried to think of something else, writing or even the law. Anything but how she looked, now and then. But he failed and wondered again how it would feel to touch her, to put his face and hands and heart against hers.

He could feel her eyes on him constantly, hear her ceaseless back and forth, here and there, on her side of the barrier made of steel and time. He wanted to know, just as he wanted her to know, how much he cared.

Like the best of lovers, he fulfilled her desires. A newspaper, print blurred with greasy stains, brought from the folds of his knapsack and passed through the ragged portal in the wire. There he unfolded the paper for her and let the contents loose. They fell in a scramble at her feet. The air seemed wet, awash with seared metal. Her nostrils flared, head suddenly erect, like a dog capturing a scent.

She knelt, penitent, hands digging into the offering, not so much clutching at the wet meat than fondling it, the slick fat and strips of skin and sinew wound in her fingers as she brought it to her lips. He fell against the fence, the barbed wire cutting into one hand, the other seeking anxious purchase, a steady place, as he watched her eagerly press the meat to her mouth. Strings of fat leaked from her teeth and along her chin like ragged vomit; the sound of her chewing pained his own stomach. At last he turned away, unable to watch the guileless greed of her swallowing.

His uncertain steps trailed after the false beacon of the moon, cloaked in a sky of smoke whose lower reaches shined with the bloom of blast furnaces, replaying the nights of his childhood, when the mills, ferociously alight, marked the boundaries of his world. He stumbled on, deepbreathing the stench, the flurry of ashes, oblivious to the great gray hills that rose all around him. He had seen it all before: the heaps of coal and limestone, rusted metal and slag, all of it fodder or waste, and that the mounds had multiplied, grown taller with the years, meant nothing to him—nothing but the inevitable.

It had been too long since he had taken this kind of a walk, and soon he was short of breath, and his thigh ached, a quiet but lingering lament. He dry-swallowed a Percocet and kept on going. In the distance the civilian guards and soldiers lit cigarettes and spoke of something, nothing. He had taken care of them and their clones on each shift: cigarettes, ration slips, dollars, drugs—everyone of them had his price, and it was cheap. Enough to buy him the time he needed, though now it was almost gone, as shift replaced shift and day followed night, and soon there would be nothing left for him to trade. They would need her for their labors, and with the sound of a morning whistle, an angry foreman or NCO, the scuffle of the swing shift, a rattle of M-16s, he would awaken from this dream. Now that he had found her, she would be lost again.

Awakening always generated a summons. So did the zombies when they first appeared on the CBS News Bulletin. He had looked with surprise at the television screen, searching through the channels but finding only the same story, the old story, watching these shambling undead creatures rise from the grave as he had so many times before in horror movies—walking out of fields, forests, ruined cities, walking out of film after film and into reality.

For a short time, that first night, he wondered how many people knew that there was a difference, how many had died while watching their television sets, never thinking to look outside. But he lived in the sanctified shadow of the nation's capital: the body counts were for the most part distant, and as the days turned into weeks, and the weeks into months, the dead were simply statistics that tickertaped like stock market quotations beneath CNN broadcasts. He didn't need to be told to stay inside at night, to clean and load his shotgun, to walk calmly into the Drug Emporium and trade a fistful of Krugerrands for a shopping list of prescription drugs—painkillers, antibiotics, antidepressants. By then elements of the Rapid Deployment Force had moved into position, and soon the fifty-mile perimeter was drawn around the capital, while Marine Force Recon units prowled the streets within, shooting first, not even asking later.

Then came the night when the sky over the District of Columbia was lit, a patriotic celebration of superior firepower, a cleansing flame whipped by the wind of hovering helicopters. Just north of the Pentagon, a ruby rain showered down, the first of the gunship assaults on Arlington National Cemetery, where an army of the dead made their encampment. Later there would be airstrikes, napalm; and later, silence. More ashes.

After she walked out of his life, and the Army took him into its embrace, his father bought a car for him, a 1971 Mustang Mach I in racing blue, the sleek stuff of Team McLaren. He liked to drive the Mustang at night, to push the pedal down and down until he hit 100 miles per hour, letting the Interstate lead him into the dark, uncharted territory beyond Madison County. There he would find a dirt road, park on some quiet corner of farmland and wander into the embrace of fields of tall corn, convincing himself that he was lost, that if he went far enough, he could never be found; that no one could ever touch him again. In a year he was driving the car across the country to law school, and within three years more, to Washington, D.C.

Without any conscious plan, he reached the end of 21st Street, and looked west down a range of wall and wire as far as he cared to see. Inside were zombies by the thousands, tens of thousands, an inhuman ocean of gray whose restless tide washed up on shores of waste. Past them, across Route 203, the sickly cumulus brewed out from a hundred smokestacks. There, he knew, on the far side of the coke plant, lurked more avenues of rail, routes spiderwebbing north from Arkansas and Tennessee, Louisiana, perhaps even Texas. He looked up at the long stretch of fencing, the angry furnaces, the eternal ghost dance of fire and smoke, and shook his head at the industry of men. And then he looked back, just before his view would be lost to plateaus and peaks of slag, and he saw her sitting cross legged in the dust, her head in her hands.

By the time he returned to the cut in the wire, his leg taut and forcing him to limp, another dawn wept over them, the sun pulling itself reluctantly into the sky. Stacie said nothing, her eyes simply following a man to whom the idea of darkness seemed important. Empty eyes; accusing eyes. The question, unasked, unanswered, consumed him. The wire that separated her from him was nothing; it was the darkness, most of all, that kept them apart. The darkness defied him; and yet it defined him, made him into someone—someone who played at being a lawyer, who couldn't earn his living with words, so sold his soul to write them. Who once was lost. And who now, in the shadow of the smokestacks, had been found.

Soon she was only inches away. The wire blurred, almost disappeared from sight. Her face was slack, almost saddened; the meal seemed to calm her. Perhaps she was remembering. The image of glowing candles, the mills alight in storm clouds of smoke, had stalked her childhood, too, and now that darkness was returning again. There were so many memories: frail, uncertain flowers of flesh and blood that might blossom in the desert of her consciousness.

He embraced the darkness, wishing that it were her. "A gray hope," he told her, calmly reciting the words, another song out of another time. And slowly he raised his hand, brought it to the gap in the fence.

She looked up at him, past him. Her face, what was left of it, was without passion, without memory, eyes locked in a television game-show stare: all-seeing, never knowing. She remembered nothing, no one, then moonlight, a window, a flight of birds, the cry of a child, the pain of birthing, a gray hope . . . and then she remembered no more.

"Hope," he said again. Whether this night, alight with its furnaces, or another, it did not matter. There were few words left that mattered, and in the darkness there was only one:

"Love."

As if conjured by this word, the halo of a furnace flared over them, loosed by the opening of a distant gate. A team of workers, orange and yellow helmets, plaid flannel shirts, blue jeans and boots, faces and hands dark with grime and nightmare, emerged from the backdrop of flame, then melted into their counterparts, arriving for the morning shift.

"Love," he told her again, and his fingers touched her, softly, gently, on the curve of her wet cheek. From somewhere over all unseen rainbow rose the sigh of another train, bringing the zombies home.

THE WAFER AND THE WINE

On that evening of another unnamed, unnumbered day after the Second Coming, Douglas Winter looked steadily at Stacie Allen. She looked back in kind. From ten feet apart, through a web wad of rusted metal, they were locked in to one another, solidly, intimately, and eternally.

A train whistle blew. Still looking at him, she did not move on the first whistle, or the second. In the long silence after the second whistle, and before the third, he took a deep breath and looked down at his pants, the left leg streaked and shiny with new blood. In that instant of inattention, she urged herself forward, fingers twining in the chain links, face pressed against the barbed wire so tightly that her brow was etched and split.

He came closer, hesitated, and then moved closer still. She reached out with her hand, beckoning, bidding him to her. The fingers opened, clawed, pulled into a fist, then opened again. In only forty-eight hours she had come to remember Douglas Winter, to want him again, need him again. To love him again.

Her hand waved inches in front of him. The tear at his thigh was nothing, a tender scratch of the knife, the first of the wounds made fresh. He could feel the second cut, the awkward slice he had made from his neck along his shoulder, which took a layer of muscle from just back of the collarbone. Its urgent pain overwhelmed the latest, more cautious carving at his waist, where he had begun to run to fat. She was looking down at this wound, the freshest, where blood clotted in a wet slew against his shirt.

He was conscious of the warmth, the smell of his blood. The warmth came into her hand, moved up her arm, and from there spread to her mouth, her stomach, wherever it wanted to go, with no effort on his part. He kept his silence, watching this quiet power, this queer control.

Her hand spread like a talon, reaching, reaching, and when daunted, snaked back through the wire, fingers thrust into her mouth as if the taste of the air, warm with his blood, were enough.

He noticed all of this, just as he noticed all of her. He could have walked out on this earlier, could still walk. Rationality shrieked at him, but rationality had died long ago. In its place, the old slow song had begun. Somewhere it played, he could hear it, a 45 rpm single spinning inside a plastic-cased GE stereo, voices calling down an empty corridor that he had walked and walked until there was nowhere left to go, except toward Stacie Allen.

"We knew something once," he told her. Hands fumbling with the buttons of his shirt. Another sound in the distance, a voice calling, the bark of a guard dog; then the rattle of chain, the shuffle of restless feet, marching, marching.

By then he had reached out, placed his hand against the fence, felt her hand come up, slowly, slowly, to grasp it. Her head followed, the long now of raven hair, now a crop, half curls, half shorn, slivered with the gray of age, the brown of dried blood. Then her lips, peeling back to offer a row of stained and broken teeth and a tongue that darted forward to kiss his hand.

"No." His hand pulled away. "No." Left her hand as she bit at air, chewed at nothing, turning to face him with a hiss of sour spittle. "No." That softened to a purr as she saw him ease open the left side of his shirt, his shoulder and chest bared to her, a swamp of cotton and tape and blood. As he peeled the pressure dressing back, slipped the knife from his belt, cut at the strands of tape.

Three shots came in rapid fire from the distance behind him, whether warnings or kills he did not know, or care to know. Here, on this small island in a sea of gray, the music had started again. A needle scratched at vinyl skin, and the music, spun from its black circle, played. And played. Strange how these songs aged, lost meaning, became the background noise of elevators and doctors' offices, then somehow, in the night, returned.

She felt cold. So did he. But he took her right hand, brought it through the opening in the wire, her fingers moving into the wound at his side, and the pain vanished. Somehow it vanished as her nails clawed at the puddle of blood and muscle. He moved her hand in tighter.

She could smell him, his breath on her face, his meat on her busy fingers. The inescapable smell of a man from whom the veneer of civilization had been stripped forever and who seemed, in every eager part of himself, ready to acknowledge his kinship with the animal.

They danced, slowly, each on their side of the fence. He could feel her hand digging relentlessly into his side, coming away with a piece of him, and then returning, now squirming into his pectoral muscle, somehow searching for his heart, their bodies touching again and again through the wire.

The song ended, but he held on to her, humming that distant melody into her unhearing ear, and they stayed as they were until at last she tore the strand of muscle from his chest. He stifled a cry, of pain, of loss, and leaned into her, face pushed against the wire, his flesh to her lips, and the dance went on and on.

Her hand found his shoulder next, tore at the thin shirt and then tore at him. She was real, this was real, more real than anything he'd ever known. He bent slightly as the nails of her hand tightened, tore, then brought his bounty to her lips.

During the last night they had spent together, in his half-sleep, he thought she had slipped the covers from his chest and kissed at him, gently, tenderly, lips moving over his abdomen and down between his legs. He never knew if it was a dream, or real. Now as he watched her tasting him, he knew that it was a dream. That only this could be real.

There was no denying the feeling. She felt so good to him, her breasts and stomach and legs rubbing against him. He wanted this to run forever. More old songs, more of his body taken into hers. She had become a woman again, his woman. In a slow, unremitting way, she was turning for home, toward a place they had been and now might never leave.

He was falling into her now. And she into him. The barrier between them was giving way, the wire parting as her hand thrust at him and he pressed back against her. She bit at him, teeth grazing his throat, tongue licking at the vein beneath the skin. She looked up at him with dark, uncaring eyes, and he kissed her, kissed her gray and riven and moldering and pustulent cheek, and she snapped back, biting, biting, razor cuts at his face and at last blood, a silent stream of it that she licked and lapped and drank in thirsty mouthfuls.

The images of their long night together were blurred, obscured by passion and pain. He remembered the vague storm of sleep, her body curled against the fence, against him, her face placid, her appetite at last fulfilled, and then her smile, eyes opening slowly to look into him, to drink up this picture, one memory that would last for her brief eternity. When she kissed at him again, he was helpless, could only fall back into the wire as her lips worked on him. And in the midst of it, this fatal act of love, she had whispered the totality of her knowledge to him, spoken that single sentence: "I love you."

With her face buried in his neck, his torn skin open to her, he could smell the old smells, the smells of smoke, could hear steaming trains in that gray gulley, could see soldiers in autumnal camouflage moving steadily along the railhead, the sounds of the night unloading, unloading, urging the sleepwalkers onward, ever onward. Granite City swept over him, again and again and yet again, like a dirty rain that would never end. As he bled into her mouth, he murmured into her unhearing ears, "Oh, Stacie, Stacie . . . You love me."

She who had ceased consciousness days before paused at the sound of his voice, swallowing. "That was what you told me, wasn't it?" Teeth chewing at air. "Wasn't it?" Then he heard the words she had once whispered to him, now spoken in a voice other than her own. "I love you," he said, to her, for her.

And in that moment, he knew, after so many years, the meaning of love.

That was when he began to write this story.

ROOM TO DIE AGAIN

Douglas Winter wrote without stopping for the next several days. He spent most of his time with her, letting the old wounds, and the new ones, heal. Alcohol helped, poured onto his torn skin and then down his throat. Antibiotics and painkillers were his only other sustenance. Nothing but his story really mattered. The battery of the laptop computer soon expired, then its replacement, and he turned to paper instead, writing with an old pen whose bent nib seemed to weep with words.

Sometimes, when the need struck him, he would take the car on a long drive, finding this place or that, excavating memories, restoring the town to the museum of his mind. He pressed hard on the accelerator, trying to remember and trying to forget, weaving through silent streets on which ash danced like fallen snow, past the abandoned City Hall, the firegutted Public Library, the First Baptist Church and its blood-drenched sanctuary, where he had once walked a long and lonely aisle; where, he often thought, he had first found fear.

She rode with him, side-by-side, restored, like the town, to her youth. She was not a ghost, though only he could see this part of her. He kept wiping at his eyes, the sunlight and the smoke blurred into tears. If the songs could return, why not Granite City, and with it, Stacie Allen? All it took was love.

On the night that he finished writing, they made their new love again, touching at the fence until it was nearly sunrise, her fingers working endlessly at his flesh, her mouth tearing at the gift of his body and blood. Hers was a hunger that would not end. Soon, he knew, there would be nothing left to give.

When this sorrow, this pain that transcended any other pain, swept past the Percocet, past the fever, and into that place of secrets that was his heart, he cried out against the darkness. She did not move, just buried her face in the wire, teeth snapping at the remaining shreds of metal that kept them apart; he stumbled backward, fell prostrate into the dust, spent. Searching for the solace of sleep.

On that other endless night, after she told him that it was over, he wondered how she could sleep, and whether he would ever sleep again. She lay in his bed, wrapped in the covers of some hidden knowledge, while he lay awake, part of him forever torn away. In time he would sleep; in time, he knew, anyone would sleep. But time would heal no wounds. Time would only pass, and the wounds, once and forever open, would remain for her to touch and savor again.

"Tell them I love you," he had said the following morning, his last, helpless words as she pulled from a long and, until then, silent embrace and ran to the waiting car. He had no idea what those words meant: resignation, protestation, a dismal plea. Or to whom they should be spoken, save perhaps himself; that, whoever she was meant to speak them to, they were probably dead by now.

He imagined that he slept, and that as he slept, his fevered dreams gathered a circle of uniforms around him, dour and dreary faces peering out from beneath their helmets and gas masks with expectancy. He wanted to tell these men and women something, but the words could not be spoken; he had to write them down. When he tried to take the pen from his pocket, he felt what must have been a kick, a combat boot that caught his elbow, then his stomach; but there was no pain. He knew pain, and this was nothing like it. "It's over." Were those his words? His tongue tasted dirt and rock, and he spat out the chalky grit, saw the blood that sprayed from his lips instead. He wanted to waken, at least to roll over and let his body lay more comfortably in the concrete and ash on which he made his bed. More movement; another kick, and he opened his eyes again, watched a rifle butt slam down twice into the plastic case of the computer, watched shattered pieces spin away in all directions. He joined in the laughter; at least this time he could hear his voice. Then something hit his head, and the dream faded, far and away, and he found his black sleep.

Toward morning, he raised himself from the sidewalk, saw with muddled vision the stains where his blood had leaked into the earth. He turned anxiously to the holding pen, but she stood there, watching, waiting. He tried to meet her unseeing eyes, asked himself if she indeed could hear his words, understand them as something more than the grunt of an animal. He knew what had to happen, but he had been delaying the moment, wishing it away. The voice that echoed his knowledge was his own. "It's over." The great yards to the left and right were vacant, emptied; even the ranks of her holding pen had thinned. But she was still there, watching, waiting, watching, waiting.

Standing by the picture window on her twentieth birthday, sipping but not tasting a Diet Rite Cola, feeling the weight of the child growing inside her, Stacie Allen watched the bright August sunlight and decided that she would no longer imagine. She had looked into the sudden cloud that swelled high above the birch tree, and found a place where the two of them would stand, divided by a barrier more profound than that of marriage or years. The feelings inside her would change, of that she was sure. Sure enough that she would return to that place only once or so a year, and perhaps, if she were lucky, never again.

Her abstinence from imagining had been the first of the concessions. In the early years of her marriage, there had been many more: the new house, the children, the bills, the lack of money, the constant call of the real. She had needed nothing to stop him from coming into her. Until the night, one Halloween, that she saw the movie. The images were warped, fractured, as if seen from a distance through a veil of smoke, a maze of wire and steel. Twenty years forward, and quickly, so very quickly, twenty years back. With a flick of the dial, these frightening dreams, these fantasies, were banished, and she gave herself over to the here and now, marriage and motherhood, Taco Bell and TV, the only reality in which she cared to live.

She knew she was twenty and accepted it, but she could not imagine Douglas Winter being forty. Could not think of it, would not think of it. He was here with her, somewhere inside of her, as palpable as her unborn child. He was here with his long hair and wire-rimmed glasses and wrinkled fatigue jacket and that knapsack with its frantic sheaf of papers. No other version of him could exist, would exist; certainly not one older or wiser. Or that could be desired.

He hobbled across the uncertain path from the broken concrete to the fence, each few steps bringing the drill bit of pain to play at his chest, his shoulder, his leg, his side. But he wandered through the pain, jazzed by his morning cocktail of pharmaceuticals and the vision of her. There was little he could say, but it took some time for him to try to find the words.

"What are we going to do?" he said.

She was silent, walking-dead silent. Then: "I don't know," he answered, softly, for her. But he knew, in that part of him that believed she was inside of him, that knew he was inside of her, that wanted so desperately to believe in another being the two of them had created called "us." They had lost themselves and tried to create something else, something that existed only as an intermingling of the two of them. They were in love.

He pulled the pages of his manuscript from his back pocket, opened them and brought them to her, a final offering, a piece of him more intimate than flesh or blood.

"You can't come with me, Stacie. To that place, faraway, to that beach, the one in the poster. Virginia. Or anywhere."

Something brought her closer. He willed himself to believe it was the pages, everything that he had written; not the blood, not the sick smell of his life.

"But I can go with you."

He folded the pages into a tight square and slipped them through the break in the wire and into the pocket of her blouse.

There was only one thing left to do. He turned, wincing with the shift of his weight, and made his way back to the car. He opened the door, reached down into his knapsack, pulled free the pistol that had called to him with each new dawn. Knowledge in his eyes. Tears stealing down his cheeks. Gauze webbed around his breast, his side, his left arm; the wrappings of her love.

His hands trembled as he limped toward her, stopped ten feet short of the fence. Finally he flicked the slide of the Glock 17, chambering the first round. Just keep firing until it's empty, his friend Michael had told him once, on a day of blue skies and sunshine that must have been a dream. Until it's empty.

Only this was real: a man, a woman, and the gray hope that clouded over them. But when he readied himself, raising the pistol to stare over its unblinking eye into the face of Stacie Allen, he found that there was one more thing he wanted to do: he wanted to pray. Trying to find the old words, the words that had brought him down the aisle of the Interstate, to the altar of this city, to the faith that at last was his only faith: the faith in the artist, the writer, to tell the truth. And thus to know the truth before it is finally told. He had no faith in those distant, ever-dwindling stars above-the light, they had told him, that flickered through holes in the floor of Heaven.

He knew that he could not pray to that God above, but only to this idiot Goddess who reigned eternal in the shadows of the mills, the shadows of his heart. Her love would live forever; but his love? His love had to die.

He looked down the barrel, his unsteady hands lining the sight between the empty eyes that stared back at him, and he swallowed a long breath. His finger closed down on the trigger. And in that moment, he saw the same eyes, staring back at him across the gulf of years as he stood beside her desk and asked her name.

"Are you Stacie?" he had said then; and now, again, aloud: "Are you Stacie?"

And at last, swathed in the smoke of this burning world, he found the answer to his riddle, the conclusion of his story. He tossed the pistol aside.

He could not kill that which was already dead.

Postscript: The Furnace of the Heart

As I read the story of Douglas Winter and Stacie Allen, I understood how little any of us knew, or cared to know, about the zombies of Madison County. When I found its final words, there was little choice: I needed to know the truth—or the lie. I talked my way aboard one of the newly resumed commercial flights to St. Louis, and paid whatever it took for an enterprising cabbie to cross one of the precarious bridges laid by the Corps of Engineers to span the wide and swollen Mississippi.

On the Illinois side, a potholed four-lane road veered away from the flatland of crushed concrete and glass that once had been East St. Louis and north into ghostly villages named Venice and Madison. There the smoke descended, and with each minute dimmed the red brick houses, the pillaged storefronts, into a long forgotten past. It was like driving into a black-and-white photograph from the 1950s, worn and faded, a mist-shrouded landscape watched over by an anemic sun.

After the gypsy taxi made a confusing series of turns, and then found the wide lanes of Madison Avenue, we faced a phalanx of tanks and armored personnel carriers: the end of my ride, and the beginning of the long walk into Hell. That the soldiers let me pass was no surprise; their weapons were pointed away, in the other direction, guarding the world from whatever waited inside.

I needed no guide but the smoke and the flame. I walked in a snow of gray ash, following the curve of Madison Avenue until the great demon of Granite City Steel roared into view. The heat pulsed over me in waves, bringing sweat in December and, in time, tears. In row after row the smokestacks cut into the sky, venting the angry furnaces where once iron and carbon had melted, mated, formed the backbone of a nation, where once the locomotives had hauled in coal, hauled out shining steel. Now no kind word could describe this place; it was no city, no town, but an inferno whose fires had raged throughout eternity. It was where the dream that was America had come to die.

When I reached Nash Street and, at its midpoint, the entrance to the terminal where he had waited with sanguine expectancy, there were no longer civilian guards: I was questioned at length, turned away by a squad of blackbereted Army Rangers. Something was happening; I heard talk of shutting down, a laugh, and then stony silence. The railhead inside was barely visible, a rusted locomotive fallen from the nearest siding like an ancient, toppled monument. There was nothing else to be seen, they told me. Hands gripped at gunbelts; eyes offered a mortal desire. So I turned away, taking the same path he had taken, across 14th Street, following the high fences that stretched down and along Route 203, finally confronting the raging furnaces, the mountains of slag.

At first I believed them: nothing could be seen, nothing but gray. Yet I walked his path, and the smoke walked with me. I searched the miles of wire strung along steel girders that had been driven into the ground at fifty-meter intervals. In time I found the car, the rusted memory of a Ford Mustang, its tires stolen, interior picked over by scavengers. I found a broken angle of sidewalk and scattered pieces of a laptop computer. I even found a pen. And as approached the fence nearby, I found something else: something that was nothing, a space torn in the wire and painted with dried blood, the space where, for a time, a kind of love had been made. On the other side of the fence, in what he had called a holding pen there was only dust, slag in endless heaps and mounds, the waste dumped from the furnaces, the grey that had risen from the smokestacks to bleach every inch of the earth with its sadness.

It was the absence, I realized then, that was the presence at Madison County. The absence of life, and the presence, all around me, of every element of death. And at last I saw, I truly saw, where I stood, not just at this place, this moment in time, but in all places, at all times, lost in this burning world.

Standing there before me, he had seen Stacie Allen, or what he thought or wished or dreamed was Stacie Allen; but what he had written there made me see something else: the terrible something that is nothing. The hills, the mounds—there were so many grey rises that to the eye they seemed like so much litter, the refuse of the mills, and though of course they were, the act of seeing was one that for some time defied belief. But the smell could not be ignored. The smell is what made me believe.

The hills nearest to me were made up of shoes, piles and piles of shoes—leather and rubber and Corfam, women's pumps, children's Keds and Nikes, sandals, work boots, high heels and low, all shapes and all sizes, all kinds and all colors, and all of them empty. Whether it was the smell of them or the sight inside, that first instant of understanding, that bent me, I do not know. I simply wanted, so very desperately, to be sick, to vomit out their teaching.

But still I walked on, forced entry through that breach in the wire and into those forlorn hills, where clothing was heaped to the height of houses, sweaters mingled with suits, pyjamas with parkas, anything with everything: dirty, clean, wet, dry, bloody, white, synthetic, woolen. At uneven intervals I found troves of cheap jewelry, watches, eyeglasses, belts that curled like sleeping snakes; I stumbled over a prosthetic arm, pink with the tint of blood, and found a torn and empty baby blanket. Still I walked on and on, until I was to the farthest reaches of this place, and of my comprehension: to the dark, unsettled hills that dared me to approach, to know them, to caution me never to forget them. I could not deny their mystery, their gentle weave of brown and black, laced with auburn and gold, gray and white; and when I touched them, felt their silky yet brittle threads—felt my fingers flecked with hair—I did not need to look back to the smokestacks, the furnaces, the ovens, to know what burned inside.

First it was the dead, the things we called zombies, who had passed out of what we knew as life and into an existence of their own. But the fires are eager, they are hungry, they burn and they burn and, while we still live to stoke them, they will never stop. It was not long until the living dead would have given way to the legally dead—the prisoners, from the penitentiaries at Marion and Springfield, Leavenworth and Little Rock—and in time to the mental patients from Columbia and Alton, and then the near-dead, the dying, the defective, the disabled, and sooner or later the dissidents, the white-hot ovens forging a new world for a new age of harmony and love. For it was love that brought the zombies, like it brought Douglas Winter, to Madison County—a love made of fragile lies, the love of storybooks and sociopaths who believe in such conceits as love at first sight, a love that lasts forever, a love without consequences; a love without the effort that itself is love. A love that makes for bestsellers and bad movies. A love that denies the certain truth: that love, like any miracle, does not happen; it must be made.

I know these things, of course, because I know that I invented Douglas Winter, that he is just a character in what is, after all, just a story. I created him and the ground on which he walked. It did not take seven days. But now, having found my way to this place that he once called home, this trap of smoke and steel, I wonder how much I understand. The dead and the living, the living and the dead . . . what difference does it make? In the end they are the same; they are us. Now that I have seen his world, seen through the veil of gray that most of us mistake for clouds or mist or fog, I wonder if perhaps he created me, crafted me from the clay of this place of shadow and sorrow, in order to bring you here with me.

There is no end to his story, only the end of mine. In my dreams I want to believe that he somehow made his way to a world where words may still be spoken freely, if such a place exists—to Toronto or Quebec or some other unlikely Valhalla where he would find an audience that could still know horror, understand its meaning, its lessons. Who would read and perhaps be moved, swayed, cajoled into caring. Into waking, and living.

In my dreams he has found the right weapons. For it is possible that mere words are no longer enough; their powder, wet with so much blood, so many tears, may never again ignite the imagination. It is the time of the gun; perhaps it always has been, and those of us who thought otherwise were indeed poets, dreamers, fools.

In my dreams he lives, and he has finally found the nerve to fire back.

But in my nightmares I know better; I know that he walked with her, hand in hand, into the steaming shadow of the mills, shorn of shoes and clothes and at last of his hair, and then cast, like Daniel, into the flames.

Yet my dreams and my nightmares, like my story, have come to an end, because I know one other thing: I have the courage that Douglas Winter lacked.

I grip the slide of the pistol and chamber the only round I need. The barrel is black and tastes of blood and magazine oil as I press it into my mouth. My hand is steady; my will, not his, be done.

I stand in the smoke of his childhood and I watch the signal fires, a burning world whose only gift is grey. In the ever-darkening sky above, nothing shines down. The stars have gone out; the holes in the floor of Heaven are sealed.

The only light now is the light of man, burning brightly in the furnace of the heart.

for Lynne
without whom

BY ADAM-TROY CASTRO

And so we come to the kicker, with my personal number one choice for the coveted "Why Zombies Scare the Living Shit Out of Me" Award.

Because with "Dead Like Me," *Adam-Troy Castro has nailed to the ground everything I fear most about the Great Zombie Emancipation. The thing I first recognized in* Night of the Living Dead, *and which has haunted me ever since.*

The ultimate conformity is utter loss of self. And in a way, even Orwell's 1984 *is preferable, because at least we got to pretend we were still human.*

To say more would be stupid. Just read it, and weep.

And let us never, ever let it come to this.

SO. LET'S SUMMARIZE. You held out for longer than anybody would have ever dreamed possible. You fought with strength you never knew you had. But in the end it did you no damned good. There were just too many of the bastards. The civilization you believed in crumbled; the help you waited for never arrived; the hiding places you cowered in were all discovered; the fortresses you built were all overrun; the weapons you scrounged were all useless; the people you counted on were all either killed or corrupted; and what remained of your faith was torn raw and bleeding from the shell of the soft complacent man you once were. You lost. Period. End of story. No use whining about it. Now there's absolutely nothing left between you and the ravenous, hollow-eyed forms of the Living Dead.

Here's your Essay Question: How low are you willing to sink to survive?

Answer:

First, wake up in a dark, cramped space that smells of rotten meat. Don't wonder what time it is. It doesn't matter what time it is. There's no such thing as time anymore. It's enough that you've slept, and once again managed to avoid dreaming.

That's important. Dreaming is a form of thinking. And thinking is dangerous. Thinking is something the Living do, something the Dead can't abide. The Dead can sense where it's coming from, which is why they were always able to find you, back when you used to dream. Now that you've trained yourself to shuffle through the days and nights of your existence as dully and mindlessly as they do, there's no reason to hide from them anymore. Oh, they may curl up against you as you sleep (two in particular, a man and woman handcuffed together for some reason you'll never know, have crawled into this little alcove with you), but that's different: that's just heat tropism. As long as you don't actually think, they won't eat you.

Leave the alcove, which is an abandoned storage space in some kind of large office complex. Papers litter the floor of the larger room outside; furniture is piled up against some of the doors, meaning that sometime in the distant past Living must have made their last stands here. There are no bones. There are three other zombies, all men in the ragged remains of three-piece suits, lurching randomly from one wall to the other, changing direction only when they hit those walls, as if they're blind and deaf and this is the only way they know how to look for an exit.

If you reach the door quickly they won't be able to react in time to follow you.

Don't Remember.

Don't Remember your name. Only the Living have names.

Don't Remember you had a wife named Nina, and two children named Mark and Kathy, who didn't survive your flight from the slaughterhouse Manhattan had become. Don't Remember them; any of them. Only the Living have families.

Don't Remember that as events herded you south you wasted precious weeks combing the increasing chaos of rural Pennsylvania for your big brother Ben, who lived in Pittsburgh and had always been so much stronger and braver than you. Don't Remember your childish, shellshocked hope that Ben would be able to make everything all right, the way he had when you were both growing up with nothing. Don't Remember gradually losing even that hope, as the enclaves of Living grew harder and harder to find.

The memories are part of you, and as long as you're still breathing, they'll always be there if you ever decide you need them. It will always be easy to call, them up in all their gory detail. But you shouldn't want to. As long as you remember enough to eat when you're hungry, sleep when you're tired, and find warm places when you're cold, you know all you need to know, or ever will need to know. It's much simpler that way.

Anything else is just an open invitation to the Dead.

Walk the way they walk: dragging your right foot, to simulate tendons that have rotted away; hanging your head, to give the impression of a neck no longer strong enough to hold it erect; recognizing obstructions only when you're in imminent danger of colliding with them. And though the sights before you comprise an entire catalogue of horrors, don't ever react.

Only the Living react.

This was the hardest rule for you to get down pat, because part of you, buried deep in the places that still belong to you and you alone, has been screaming continuously since the night you first saw a walking corpse rip the entrails from the flesh of the Living. That part wants to make itself heard. But that's the part which will get you killed. Don't let it have its voice.

Don't be surprised if you turn a corner, and almost trip over a limbless zombie inching its way up the street on its belly. Don't be horrified if you see a Living person trapped by a mob of them, about to be torn to pieces by them. Don't gag if one of the Dead brushes up against you, pressing its maggot-infested face up close against your own.

Remember: Zombies don't react to things like that. Zombies are things like that.

Now find a supermarket that still has stuff on the shelves. You can if you look hard enough; the Dead arrived too quickly for the Living to loot everything there was. Pick three or four cans off the shelves, cut them open, and eat whatever you find inside. Don't care whether they're soup, meat, vegetables, or dog food. Eat robotically, tasting nothing, registering nothing but the moment when you're full. Someday, picking a can at random, you may drink some drain cleaner or eat some rat poison. Chance alone will decide when that happens. But it won't matter when it does. Your existence won't change a bit. You'll just convulse, fall over, lie still a while, and then get up, magically transformed into one of the zombies you've pretended to be for so long. No fuss, no muss. You won't even have any reason to notice it when it happens. Maybe it's already happened.

After lunch, spot one of the town's few other Living people shuffling listlessly down the center of the street.

You know this one well. When you were still thinking in words you called her Suzie. She's dressed in clothes so old they're rotting off her back. Her hair is the color of dirty straw, and hideously matted from weeks, maybe months of neglect. Her most striking features are her sunken cheekbones and the dark circles under her gray unseeing eyes. Even so, you've always been able to tell that she must have been remarkably pretty, once.

Back when you were still trying to fight The Bastards—they were never "zombies" to you, back then; to you they were always The Bastards—you came very close to shooting Suzie's brains out before you realized that she was warm, and breathing, and alive. You saw that though she was just barely aware enough to scrounge the food and shelter that *kept* her warm and breathing, she was otherwise almost completely catatonic.

She taught you it was possible to pass for Dead.

She's never spoken a word to you, never smiled at you, never once greeted you with anything that even remotely resembled human feeling. But in the new world she's the closest thing you have to a lover. And as you instinctively cross the street to catch her, you should take some dim, distant form of comfort in the way she's also changed direction to meet you.

Remember, though: she's not really a lover. Not in the proper emotional sense of the word. The Dead hate love even more than they hate Thought. Only the Living love. But it's quite safe to fuck, and as long as you're here the two of you can fuck quite openly. Just like the Dead themselves do.

Of course, it's different with them. The necessary equipment is the first thing that rots away. But instinct keeps prodding them to try. Whenever some random cue rekindles the urge, they pick partners, and rub against each other in a clumsy, listless parody of sex that sometimes continues until both partners have been scraped into piles of carrion powder. The ultimate dry hump.

So feel no fear. It doesn't attract their attention when you and Suzie grab each other and go for a quickie in the middle of the street: to knead your hands against the novelty of warm skin, to smell stale sweat instead of the open grave, to take a rest from the horror that the world has become. Especially since, though you both do what you have to do, following all the mechanics, of the act, neither one of you feels a damn thing. No affection, no pleasure, and certainly no joy.

That would be too dangerous.

Do what you have to do. Do it quickly. And then take your leave of each other. Exchange no kisses, no goodbyes, no cute terms of endearment, no acknowledgment that your tryst was anything but a collision between two strangers walking in opposite directions. Just stagger away without looking back. Maybe you'll see each other again. Maybe not. It really doesn't matter either way. .

Spend the next few hours wandering from place to place, seeing nothing, hearing nothing, accomplishing nothing. But still drawing breath. Never forget that. Let the part of you still capable of caring about such things count that as a major victory.

At mid-afternoon pass the place where a school bus lies burned and blackened on one side. A small group of Living had trusted it to carry them to safety somewhere outside the city; but it didn't even get five blocks through the obstacle course of other crashed vehicles before hundreds of Dead had imprisoned them in a cage of groping flesh. You were a block and a half away, watching the siege, and when the people in the bus eventually blew themselves up, to avoid a more horrific end, the heat of the fireball singed the eyebrows from your face. At the time, you'd felt it served you right for not helping. These days, if you were capable of forming an opinion on anything, you'd feel that the Living were silly bastards.

It's stupid to resist. Only the Living resist. Resistance implies will, and if there's one thing the Dead don't have it's will. Exist the way they do, dully accepting everything that happens to you, and you stand a chance.

That's the one major reason your brother Ben is dead. Oh, you can't know what happened to him. You know what happened to your wife and kids—you know because you were watching, trapped behind a chain-link fence, as a lurching mob of what had once been elementary school children reduced them to shredded beef—but you'll never ever find out what happened to Ben. Still, if you ever did find out what happened to him, you would not be surprised. Because he'd always been a leader. A fighter. He'd always taken charge of every crisis that confronted him, and inspired others with his ability to carry them through. He was always special, that way. And when the Dead rose, he brought a whole bunch of naive trusting people down into his grave with him.

You, on the other hand, were never anything special. You were always a follower, a yes-man, an Oreo. You were always quick to kiss ass, and agree with anybody who raised his voice loudly enough. You never wanted to be anything but just another face in the crowd. And though this profited you well, in a society that was merely going to hell, it's been your single most important asset in the post-plague world that's already arrived there. It's the reason you're still breathing when all the brave, heroic, defiant, mythic-ones like your brother Ben and the people in the school bus are just gnawed bones and Rorschach stains on the pavement.

Take pride in that. Don't pass too close to the sooty remains of the school bus, because you might remember how you stood downwind of their funeral pyre, letting it bathe your skin and fill your lungs with the ashes of their empty defiance. You might remember the cooked-meat, burnt rubber stench . . . the way the clouds billowed over you, and through you, as if you were far more insubstantial than they.

Don't let that happen. You'll attract Dead from blocks away. Force it back. Expunge it. Pretend it's not there. Turn your mind blank, your heart empty, and your soul, for lack of a better word, Dead.

There. That's better.

Still later that afternoon, while rummaging through the wreckage of a clothing store for something that will keep you warm during the rapidly approaching winter, you find yourself cornered and brutally beaten by the Living.

This is nothing to concern yourself with.

It's just the price you have to pay, for living in safety the way you do. They're just half-mad from spending their lives fleeing one feeding frenzy or another, and they have to let off some steam. It's not like they'll actually kill you, or hurt you so bad you'll sicken and die. At least not deliberately. They may go too far and kill you accidentally, but they won't kill you deliberately. There are already more than enough Dead people running around, giving them trouble. But they hate you. They consider people like you and Suzie traitors. And they wouldn't be able to respect themselves if they didn't let you know it.

There are four of them, this time: all pale, all in their late teens, all wearing the snottily evil grins of bullies whose chosen victim has detected their approach too late. The closest one is letting out slack from a coil of chain at his side. The chain ends in a padlock about the size of a fist. And though you try to summon your long-forgotten powers of speech, as their blows rain against your ribs, it really doesn't matter. They already know what you would say.

Don't beg.

Don't fight back.

Don't see yourself through their eyes.

Just remember: the Living might be dangerous, but the Dead are the real bastards.

It's later. You're in too much pain to move. That's all right. It'll go away, eventually. One way or the other. Alive or dead, you'll be up on your feet in no time.

Meanwhile, just lie there, in your own stink, in the wreckage of what used to be a clothing store, and for Christ's sake be quiet. Because only the Living scream.

Remember that time, not long after the Dead rose, when there were always screams? No matter how far you ran, how high you climbed or how deep you dug, there were always the screams, somewhere nearby, reminding you that though you might have temporarily found a safe haven for the night, there were always others who had found their backs against brick walls. Remember how you grew inured to those screams, after a while, and even found yourself able to sleep through them. And as the weeks turned to months, you found your tolerance rewarded—because the closer the number of survivors approached zero, the more that constant backdrop of screaming faded away to a long oppressive silence broken only by the low moans and random shuffling noises of the Dead.

It's a quiet world, now. And if you're to remain part of it, you're going to have to be quiet, too. Even if your throat catches fire and your breath turns as ragged as sandpaper and your sweat pools in a puddle beneath you and your ribs scrape together every time you draw a breath and the naked mannequins sharing this refuge with you take on the look of Nina and Mark and Kathy and Ben and everybody else who ever mattered to you and the look on their faces becomes one of utter disgust and you start to hear their voices saying that you're nothing and that you were always nothing but that they'd never known you were as much as a nothing as you've turned out to be. Shut up. Even if you want to tell them, these people who once meant everything to you that you held on as long as any normal man could be expected to hold on, but there are limits, and you exceeded those limits, you really did, but there was just another set of limits beyond them, and another beyond those, and the new world kept making all these impossible demands on you and there were only so many impossible things you could bear. Be silent. Even if you hear Nina shrieking your name and Mark telling you he's afraid and Kathy screaming for you to save her. Even if you hear Ben demanding that you stand up like a man, for once.

Endure the pain. Ignore the fever. Don't listen to what your family is trying to tell you.

Why should you listen to *their* advice? It didn't help them.

No, this is what you should keep in mind, while you're waiting to see if you'll live or die:

On the off-chance you are still alive when you stumble to your feet tomorrow, don't look at the fitting mirror on the wall behind you. It's the first intact mirror you've encountered in months. Nothing unusual about that, of course: there just isn't much unshattered glass left in the world these days. But the looters and the rioters and the armies and the Living Dead have left this particular mirror untouched, and though it's horrendously discolored by dust, it still works well enough to destroy you.

If you don't look at it you'll be okay.

If you do look at it you'll see the matted blood in your tangled shoulder-length hair and the flies crawling in your long scraggly beard and the prominent ribs and the clothes so worn they exist only as strips of rags and the dirt and the sores and the broken nose and the swollen mouth and the closed slit that was until recently your left eye and you'll realize that this is as close to being Dead as you can get without actually being there, and that it sucks, and you'll be just in the right frame of mind, after your long night of delirium, to want to do something about it.

And you'll stagger out into the street, where the Dead will be milling about doing nothing the way they always do and you'll be in the center of them and you'll be overcome with a sudden uncontrollable anger and you'll open your mouth as wide as you can and you'll scream: "*Hey!*"

And the Dead will freeze in something very much resembling a double-take and slowly swivel in your direction and if you really wanted to you could bury everything burning you up inside down where it was only a minute ago and you won't want to and you'll scream "*Hey!*" again, in a voice that carries surprisingly far for something that hasn't been used in so long, and the Dead will start coming for you, and you won't care because you'll be screaming "*You hear me, you stinking bastards? I'm alive! I think and I feel and I care and I'm better than you because you'll never have that again!*"

And you'll die in agony screaming the names of everybody you used to love.

This may be what you want.

And granted, you will go out convinced you've just won a moral victory.

But remember, only the Living bother with such things; the Dead won't even be impressed. They'll just be hungry.

And if you let yourself die, then within minutes what's left of you will wake up hungry too, with only one fact still burning in its poor rotting skull: that Suzie's faking.

APPENDIX A

ZOMBIE ROOTS: A HISTORICAL PERSPECTIVE

BY CHRISTOPHER KAMPE AND ANTHONY GAMBOL

THE ZOMBI ORIGINATED in the Caribbean at some point in history, and wasn't brought to English-speaking peoples until the late 1800s. In an essay titled "The Un-History of the Undead" published in *Verbatim*, Tim Kane argues that the contemporary image of the zombie and the vampire have been drastically altered by cinema and modern fiction, such that they are not now what they once were. He outlines the origins of the term and its passing into English vocabulary and attempts to explain what the "real" zombie is:

> A central precept of Voodoo, a hybrid of African animism and Catholicism, is the possession of a body by the *loa* [or spirit]. A person was believed to have two souls, the *gros-bon-ange* (the big good angel), and the *ti-bon-ange* (the little good angel). Each soul served a purpose. The gros-bon-ange served to give the body life, while the ti-bon-ange gave the person their personality. During a Voodoo ceremony, the loa would displace the ti-bon-ange, and thus control the person's body.
>
> A Voodoo sorcerer, called a *bokor*, had the ability to transform any person into a zombie. The bokor would sprinkle a powder on the doorstep, and when the intended victim stepped on it, the magic entered through the soles of the feet. The person died soon after. Within three days the bokor snuck into the graveyard, recited a magical chant, and called the victim's name several times. The zombie had no choice but to answer and come out of the ground. [To prevent the zombie from answering this call, precautions were taken. The mouth might be sewn up or tied shut using a strip of cloth fastened over the head and under the chin.] The bokor then beat the body with a whip to keep the ti-bon-ange from returning. [Often the *bokor* kept the *ti-bon-ange* in a jar. This was called a zombie astral, while the body that walked around, soulless, was called a zombie cadaver.]

Although this perspective is immensely helpful in understanding the Haitian *zombi*, it might be too specific. Myth is often inspired by reality, but myth is more than reality; when dealing with a term so grounded in religion, superstition, and folktale, it's overly simplistic to look at human slave zombies, while disregarding the myths surrounding them. Lafcadio Hearn, an adventurous correspondent working in the Caribbean for *Harper's* magazine, makes the first published mention of the word in English in *Two Years in the French West Indies*, and it's likened to a goblin or a ghost:

—"Adou," I ask, "what is a zombi?"

The smile that showed Adou's beautiful white teeth has instantly disappeared; and she answers, very seriously, that she has never seen a zombi, and does not want to see one.

[. . .]

Adou hesitates a little, and answers: "*Zombi? Mais ça fai désòde lanuitt, zombi!*"

Ah! It is Something which "makes disorder at night." Still, that is not a satisfactory explanation.

"Is it the spectre of a dead person, Adou? Is it *one who comes back*?"

—"*Non, Missié,—non; çé pa ça.*"

—"Not that? . . . Then what was it you said the other night when you were afraid to pass the cemetery on an errand,—*ça ou té ka di, Adou?*"

—["I do not want to go by that cemetery because of the dead folk,—the dead folk will bar the way, and I cannot get back again."]

—"And you believe that, Adou ?"

—"Yes, that is what they say . . . And if you go into the cemetery at night you cannot come out again: the dead folk will stop you—*moun-mò ké barré ou.*"

—"But are the dead folk zombis, Adou?"

—"No; the moun-mò are not zombis. The zombis go everywhere: the dead folk remain in the graveyard . . . .Except on the Night of All Souls: then they go to the houses of their people everywhere."

—"Adou, if after the doors and windows were locked and barred you were to see entering your room in the middle of the night, a Woman fourteen feet high?"

—"*Ah! pa pàlé ça!!*"

—"No! tell me, Adou?"

—"Why, yes: that would be a zombi. It is the zombis who make all those noises at night one cannot understand . . . Or, again, if I were to see a dog that high [she holds her hand about five feet above the floor] coming into our house at night, I would scream: "*Mi Zombi!*"

. . . Then it suddenly occurs to Adou that her mother knows something about zombis.

—"*Ou Manman!*"

—"*Eti!*" answers old Théréza's voice from the little out-building where the evening meal is being prepared over a charcoal furnace, in an earthen canari.

—"*Missié-là ka mandé save ça ça yé yonne zombi; —vini ti bouin!*" . . . The mother laughs, abandons her canari, and comes in to tell me all she knows about the weird word.

"I *ni pè zombi*"—I find from old Thereza's explanations—is a phrase indefinite as our own vague expressions, "afraid of ghosts," "afraid of the dark." But the word "Zombi" also has special strange meanings . . . . ["You pass along the high-road at night, and you see a great fire, and the more you walk to get to it the more it moves away: it is the zombi makes that . . . .Or a horse *with only three legs* passes you: that is a zombi."]

[. . .]

And then she tells me this:

—"Baidaux was a mad man of color who used to live at St. Pierre, in the Street of the Precipice. He was not dangerous,—never did any harm;—his sister used to take care of him. And what I am going to relate is true,— *çe zhistouè veritabe!*

"One day Baidaux said to his sister: ["I have a child, ah!—you never saw it!"]

His sister paid no attention to what he said that day; but the next day he said it again, and the next, and the next, and every day after,—so that his sister at last became much annoyed by it, and used to cry out: '*Ah! mais pé guiole ou, Baidaux! ou fou pou embeté moin conm ça!—ou bien fou!*' . . . But he tormented her that way for months and for years.

"One evening he went out, and only came home at midnight leading a child by the hand,—a black child he had found in the street; and he said to his sister:

— ["Look at the child I have brought you! Every day I have been telling you I had a child: you would not believe me,—very well, LOOK AT HIM!"]

The sister gave one look, and cried out: '*Baidaux, oti ou pouend yche-là?*' . . . For the child was growing taller and taller every moment . . . . And Baidaux,—because he was mad,—kept saying: '*Çé yche-moin! çé yche moin!*' [It is my child!]

"And the sister threw open the shutters and screamed to all the neighbors,—["Help! help! Come see what Baidaux has brought in here!"]

And the child said to Baidaux: '*Ou ni bonhè ou fou!*' [You are lucky that you are mad!] . . . Then all the neighbors came running in; but they could not see anything: the Zombi was gone."

The zombie is not so clearly defined here as we later see in the writings of William Seabrook, who describe the near-dead figures working the fields. This zombie is not articulated in the same terms Wade Davis uses to describe those men overcome by pufferfish poison and datura, buried, then pulled from the ground and commanded by a bokor. These zombies are not the cannibalistic undead later portrayed in the movies of Romero—they are beings that we don't quite understand, beings that exist as neither clearly living nor clearly dead that prey upon us. As Adou says, "It is the zombis who make all those noises at night one cannot understand . . . ." We must remember that outside of any tangible existence, the zombie was a creature of myth that frightened and disconcerted us. There isn't any easy way to explain where *our* zombies came from, but there is something so compelling and startling about the dead rising and the violation of human flesh that the myth transcends the boundaries of region, religion, and culture. Stories with these elements are found throughout history all over the world; the written and oral accounts abound.

At the most basic level, what we consider to be the hallmarks of the modern zombie, those characteristics that allow us to call it by that name, are: the rending or consumption of human flesh; a return to life or a facsimile of life after death or a facsimile of death; and a controlling or compelling force acting upon the subject, be it instinctual, spiritual, biological, or external. There is frequently but not exclusively a ritual element found in one or more of these parts. A zombie, to be identified as such, will contain one or more of these elements, if not all of them. These ideas are not new.

The Great Power, it is Unas; the powerful one of the powerful ones.
Whom he finds in his way, he eats him piecemeal.

The above is a portion of the "Cannibal Hymn," one of a series of inscriptions in the tomb of Unas, the ninth and last ruler of the Fifth Dynasty of the Old Kingdom of Egypt. The spells and hymns of this collection are the oldest known religious texts in the world, dating to around 2350 B.C. Unas, in the Pharaohic tradition, is a god-king on earth, and the text details how, at death, he consumes the flesh of men and gods alike to gain greater godly powers. Through this consumption, he secures his apotheosis and eternal life in death. This transition was a central tenet of Egyptian religious belief at the time. Although there is little evidence to suggest that cannibalism was ever habitually practiced in Egypt, many years later Diodorus Siculus writes in his history that cannibalism was ended in Egypt by the god Osiris, the Egyptian judge of the dead. It's coincidental that the earliest mentions of Osiris predate the Pyramid Texts by only a few years; perhaps it is too much to speculate that the end of Egyptian cannibalism and the emergence of the Pyramid Texts including Cannibal Hymn are related and that, among the other religious changes, it became only acceptable to consume human flesh after death.

The Greek ethnographer Herodotus recounts around 440 B.C. how certain tribes of Indian and Caucasian people consumed human flesh as a part of their death rituals. Although the Greeks may not have had such practices, their myths are full of other zombie elements. Kronos, the father of many of the classical Greek gods, upon hearing it prophesized that he would be usurped by a son, began to eat his children when they were born until he was tricked and deposed. The Greek god of wine, Dionysus, referred to as the "twice born," has an origin myth in which he is a human king whom the gods kill with a thunderbolt and who is then devoured by his priestesses, only to be reborn of the earth. After his rebirth the goddess Hera ordered that he be ripped apart, boiled in a cauldron, and devoured. After these ordeals he (like the grape vine) is eternally destined to be born, ripped apart, devoured, and born again. Robert Graves in *The Greek Myths* wrote that the process drove Dionysus quite mad, and he passes that madness on to his followers. The action of Euripides' tragedy *The Bacchae* has its protagonist, Pentheus, offending the god Dionysus. Pentheus refuses to honor Dionysus's deity and later spies on his sacred mysteries. In retribution, Dionysus removes the minds from his throng of followers and compels them to fall upon Pentheus, tear him to bits, and then play with the pieces.

Another interesting myth is that of Asclepius, who was so talented a healer that he roused the gods' ire by using his skills to raise people from the dead. The gods killed him for this; he had perpetrated what was considered an unnatural act and one of hubris, having stepped into the realm of godly power. The return to life from death was a feat reserved for the most powerful of heroes. Orpheus succeeded in traveling to Hades and making a safe return, but he failed in his quest to return with his wife. Theseus tried and failed to make the journey, only being freed by Heracles, who succeeded. Odysseus managed to travel to and from the land of the dead with Circe's help. There he convoked the shades by slitting the throat of a black ram and offered its blood to them as sacrifice. The dead comrades he encountered were unable to change in death: forever a shadow of what they were in life; it was not until they drunk the animal's blood that they were able to regain some semblance of their former function and communicate with him.

Perhaps the most famous person to have died and risen from the dead is Jesus, the Son of God in Christianity. He was killed by crucifixion and some doctrine holds that He descended into hell. Christians are, by reciting the Apostles' Creed, pledging their faith in the deity of Jesus Christ, displayed by His resurrection. This fact becomes even more relevant to our purposes when we consider Jesus' words at the last supper, paraphrased in the Catholic Liturgy of the Eucharist:

Take this, all of you, and eat it:
this is my body which will be given up for you.
Take this, all of you, and drink from it:
this is the cup of my blood,
the blood of the new and everlasting covenant.

Catholics are, by eating the flesh and blood of Jesus, entering into a covenant with God through which they will earn for themselves eternal life. From this we can see quite readily that even modern cultures utilize a large number of elements associated with zombie lore.

It's important to note that cultures that developed in the Mediterranean region are not unique in this respect. Aside from the Haitian *zombi* with its African and Mesoamerican heritage, most cultures throughout the world have myths and creatures with characteristic zombie elements. Throughout Buddhist mythology, there are tales of "hungry ghosts," physical spirits that must consume corpses (and very often excrement), without ever being able to satisfy their gnawing appetite. In *The Religious System of China*, Chinese folklore speaks of the *jiang shi*, reanimated corpses that must kill living creatures to absorb the essence of life. In Indonesia, the *pontianak* is a corporeal undead that kills its victims and consumes their entrails in order to sustain its own "life." There is the *ghoul* in Arabic folklore, the *draugr* in northern European, and even the *wendigo* of Algonquian myth: a supernatural being that possesses humans after they commit acts of cannibalism, transforming them into monsters and instilling in them a hunger for human flesh.

Going back to our earlier group of zombie hallmarks, the one that has been touched upon least thoroughly here is that force compelling the zombies' actions. Historically religion, be it Bacchic frenzy or faith in the Eucharist, has been the most prevalent compelling forces in zombie lore. It serves as the impetus that drives actions through piety or simple fear; fear of the *bokor* is just as powerful as his enchantments. Another is the insatiable desire for power, which might serve to explain Unas's feast. More recent depictions of zombies expand this list. The programming of the Borg in TV's *Star Trek* is a strong compelling force; the individuals affected by it have lost a component or the entirety of their personal agency. The films *28 Days Later* and *Quarantine*, as well as the Resident Evil video game franchise, have a form of undeath wherein the victims haven't actually died; rather, they ravaged by the effects of a particularly vicious virus. The biological function of the virus determines the actions of the host, who attacks uninfected individuals as the means of spreading the contagion. The zombies of Romero's *Land of the Dead* begin to display aspects of their former lives through the simple but powerful human urge to self-identify—what they were in life they will be a form of in death, no longer able to change. A viewer is reminded of Odysseus's shades.

This isn't an encompassing list of all things that display zombielike characteristics—that would be far too long. But even truncated it serves to illustrate why the zombie might be so attractive to our modern imaginations and why its character has developed so far from its strictly voodoo roots. The modern zombie is a compendium of the diaspora. The fears that it represents: of death, of consumption, of the loss of identity, of the loss of agency, are common, *human* fears. The Haitian *zombi* may have just been the catalyst. When one such idea gained traction, our sundry cultural identities were able to describe themselves using the same vocabulary. The zombie of today has been shaped by countless sources, both fictional and not. The zombie is infinitely adaptable because it's everywhere, or it's everywhere because it's infinitely adaptable. Regardless of the form it takes, we are able to identify its elements.

Zombies have lasted because they have been able reflect the fears of the moment. Whereas the fear of literal slavery dominated the late-nineteenth-century Caribbean cultural landscape, technological or viral or retributive biblical fears may now have replaced it in modern cultures and we can thoroughly expect to see further variations in the future. Fear is a mirror of desire and as such, our desires—eternal life, great power, perfect security in our social constructs, among others—are tempered by fear. Zombie stories reflect the undesirable results of these goals. Terrible things must sometimes be done to maintain them, and you can still be nothing more than a rotting husk of your former self.

We know that when you die you should stay dead. A person can do a great number of things to try to extend the natural human life, but it seems that we also know that there's something inherently unnatural about this process. We lose something in the transition, that something which makes us human. We lose all social conditioning and all emotion; nothing is left but base instinct and animal cruelty. Our self-control is loosened or lost, and we no longer function as the masters of our own destiny. We are slaves; we are decayed; we are terrible.

APPENDIX B

THEY'RE US AND WE'RE THEM: ZOMBIES IN POPULAR CULTURE

BY JOHN SKIPP AND CODY GOODFELLOW

ALTHOUGH THEY HAVE ALWAYS WALKED in the shadow of vampires, werewolves, and their snotty Eurotrash cousin Frankenstein's monster, zombies have shambled a long way: from a stiff, mute protestor of colonialism and consumerism to a rock icon, a dependable videogame unit-shifter and tireless TV pitchman.

The monster of choice for directors with bad dreams and no budget, zombies have become a cultural shorthand with a host of hooks in the mass-media mind.

MOVIES

First and last and always, zombies have thrived in the hothouse environment of darkened theaters. The zombie archetype born of F. W. Murnau's *The Cabinet of Dr. Caligari* and exotic tall tales of Haitian *vodun* rites spread slowly at first, but has evolved into an ecosystem unto itself in more than three hundred films.

Even after Bela Lugosi's dream of cheap labor blew up in his face in 1932's *White Zombie*, the exotic island undead (sort of) came back in the stylish *I Walked with a Zombie* (1943), and a host of cheapies such as *King of the Zombies* (1941), *Zombies of Mora Tau* and *Voodoo Island* (both 1957) and *Zombies*, a.k.a. *I Eat Your Skin* (1964). The island zombie got shortchanged until Wes Craven's liberal adaptation of Wade Davis's gonzo anthropology text *The Serpent and the Rainbow* (1988).

But island shoots are expensive; slave zombies are no fun until they rebel, and visions of dead-eyed workers turning on their masters gave the capitalist system the wrong kind of nightmares. With rare domestic exceptions such as the undead munchkins of *Phantasm* (1979), the whole damned town of Potter's Bluff in *Dead & Buried* (1981), and the adorable killer kid 'n' cat of *Pet Sematary* (1992), zombie slaves fell out of favor, but the dead are always hungry for dirty work, and soon went off to war.

In *Revenge of the Zombies* (1943), John Carradine played a Nazi raising a zombie army in the Louisiana swamps, whose undoing comes when his resurrected wife leads the inevitable revolt. The zombie Third Reich marched on to mediocrity in *The Frozen Dead* (1966), but returned to an island setting (and

Carradine) with striking results in *Shock Waves* (1977), trashed the African desert in the unforgivable *Oasis of the Zombies* (1981), and goosestepped into the future in *Dead Snow* (2009).

Nazis had the patent on reanimated cannon-fodder, but not the last word. On Showtime's *Masters of Horror* episode "Homecoming," a jingoistic pundit's rash invocation of dead soldiers to support a failed war incites a mass awakening, but the zombie soldiers come back only to vote the bums out of office.

Science-fiction action flicks project these ill-fated trends into the future; from *Universal Soldier* (1992), with its dubious decision to revive Dolph Lundgren and Jean-Claude Van Damme as enhanced combat-zombies, to cyborg juggernauts with human organ donors' wetware in *Terminator: Salvation* (2009), warmongers will always enlist the dead to fight their wars, and they'll always get fucked for it.

Of course, the dead often return with more on their mind than making a living. Almost every zombie with any memory of its past life soon turns to revenge. And no actor embodied that archetype better than Boris Karloff, the man who was Frankenstein's monster.

Karloff also played the titular lich in *The Mummy* (1932); and in *The Ghoul* (1933), he's a sinister, grabby Egyptologist who arises from his fake pharaoh's tomb to reclaim a stolen gem. In *The Walking Dead* (1936), he plays a gangster revived by medical science after he is framed and executed for murder. His hollow-eyed, pasty features here are the model for future zombies, but he was reborn for revenge, and not an empty eating machine.

Nearly all the popular walking dead before the Romero era were revenants; their short, unhappy tales played best in short, sharp shocks of pulp stories and comics. The creeping outlaw appeal of the banned EC horror comics inspired a rash of anthology flicks. The UK's Hammer and Amicus Pictures made the best of these, with *Tales from the Crypt* and *Asylum* (both 1972) and *The Vault of Horror* (1973) reviving the vengeful dead in all their gruesome glory alongside a host of other tools of poetic justice. The postmortem morality play reached its stylistic climax with *Creepshow* (1982), George Romero and Stephen King's loving tribute to the EC era.

Sometimes all it takes to piss off revenant zombies is to disturb their rest. Alan Ormsby's *Children Shouldn't Play with Dead Things* (1972) sets an angry zombie horde on hippies who dabble in satanic rituals, whereas the Spanish-Portuguese *Tombs of the Blind Dead* (1974) and its myriad sequels unleashes bloodthirsty Knights Templar on Eurotrash coeds.

The modern, plague, or Romero zombie—a product of science gone awry or nature's revenge on runaway human growth—came much later than its cousins but soon pushed the others to the brink of extinction, because its very blankness has made it an infinitely malleable monster. The unknowable and irrelevant origin of the plague makes them endlessly easy to reinvent, while their durability ensures that they're not invincible except in numbers, just that insanely violent means will have to be employed to dispatch them.

In *Things to Come* (1936), a utopian H. G. Wells future was beset by a plague that reduced its victims to aimless wandering and cadaverous appearance. U.S.-Italian potboiler *The Last Man on Earth* (1964) tried to adapt Richard Matheson's apocalyptic *I Am Legend*, but Romero's *Night of the Living Dead* (1968) gave the zombie a new lease on life, with a new diet plan and an infectious personality.

For the next decade, the zombie plague festered in the grind house underground, spawning the forgettable likes of the formaldehyde-huffing zombie chain gang of *Garden of the Dead* (1974). Two extraordinary exceptions were *Messiah of Evil* (1973), one of the most eye-popping hippie horror films ever made, and *Let Sleeping Corpses Lie* (1974), which has more alternative titles than there are zombies in the film. Both of these rarities come highly recommended.

Then Romero returned in 1979 with *Dawn of the Dead* [*Zombi*] to spell out the laws of the plague in bold, easy-to-mimic terms.

Always a hotbed of inspired imitation, Italy almost totally abandoned giallo/slashers to churn out *Dawn* knockoffs. Shot at the same time as *Dawn* and sold as a sequel in Italy and elsewhere, the crudely effective *Zombie* [*Zombi 2*] (1980) spearheaded an invasion as omnivorous as its subject. In 1980 alone, *Zombi Holocaust* [*Dr. Butcher, MD*], *Virus* [*a.k.a. Hell of the Living Dead, Zombie Creeping Flesh*], *Island of the Zombies*, *Le Notti del terrore* [*Zombi 3*], and

Nightmare City gnawed the hapless plague zombie to the bone. There were no survivors.

In America, the plague zombie enjoyed a slow explosion more inventive, if not always more entertaining, than in Europe, and helped to further blur the living and the dead. The toxic waste in C.H.U.D. (1984) finally made mutant homeless too hideous and hungry to ignore. *Night of the Comet* (1984) embraced the post-human apocalypse as a solipsistic paradise. Tobe Hooper's *Lifeforce* (1985) wrecked London with a runaway plague of energy-vampirism and gratuitous nudity. Stuart Gordon's *Re-Animator* (1985) and Brian Yuzna's *Bride of Re-Animator* (1990) inject gleeful perversity into H. P. Lovecraft's prim pulp tale of a mad med student's dead-defying elixir.

Dan O'Bannon's *The Return of the Living Dead* (1985) edges into sly parody while turning the shuffling zombies into crafty, party-hungry brain eaters who ran long before Zack Snyder's *Dawn* remake spiked the fast-zombie debate. Return's dioxin-dosed zombies also won some battles in the popular arena, with their fixation on "braaaiiins."

But Hollywood still wasn't hip to the untapped potential in zombies, and for want of decent financing, Romero scrapped his ambitious trilogy concluding script to make *Day of the Dead* (1985), a bleak, cramped closer that all but forces you to root for the zombies.

In the 1990s, studios finally discovered zombie cash cows, but have mostly taken their cues from video games as the sole innovation among diminishing crops of remakes, reboots, and reimaginings of old ideas. Amid global rehashes of the plague, such as Japan's *Shiryô-Gari* [*Junk*] (2000), a bright spot was *28 Days Later* (2002), where a rabies-Ebola hybrid plague renders its victims into hyperactive killing tools. Although its plague victims weren't true zombies at all, Danny Boyle's grim, stripped digital video put realistic human emotions back into the picture as only Romero had before. Zombies or no, his "Infected" changed the whole undead dialogue, and erased the line between the quick and the dead.

Zombie fans were sharply divided between purists and posers over the speedy zombies Zack Snyder put in his *Dawn of the Dead* remake (2004). But the film was a career-making hit for Snyder, whereas Romero's *Land of the Dead*

(2005) was sadly overshadowed, and *Diary of the Dead* [a.k.a. *Land of the Dead 2*] (2008) alienated many purists by adopting the "Blair Witch" reality format to his own remarkable, still-subversive ends.

Helpless to fend for themselves, zombies will keep getting pushed around like this until something moves into their empty skull that can push back. Zombies are, by definition, empty vessels. And if Nature hates a vacuum, Hell really, really loves them.

Inarguably a bastard brainchild of *The Exorcist*, Sam Raimi's *Evil Dead* (1983) created the demon zombie subgenre, which made its own ripple of imitators in Mario Bava's *Demons* (1985) and *Night of the Demons* (1988) before trashing its own legacy with two slapstick semiparody sequels. Ryhûhei Kitamura's *Versus* (2000) dares to reimagine *Evil Dead* with swordfights and gun-wankery.

Meanwhile, aliens have found human bodies a warm enough temporary home since they perfectly captured the mood of cold war fever. Imitating the infiltration schemes of *Invaders from Mars* and *It Came from Outer Space* (both 1953) and *Invasion of the Body Snatchers* (1956), outsider auteur Ed Wood upped the ante by putting his alien invaders into the corpses of the recently deceased in *Plan 9 from Outer Space* (1959). The sinister tableau of Vampira and Tor Johnson emerging from the cardboard graveyard to serve their saucer-borne masters outlived the awful material, and took the hoary idea of demonic possession to brave new worlds.

Fred Dekker's cult classic *Night of the Creeps* (1986) lingers in undeserved obscurity, but body-snatching alien invaders emerge again in James Gunn's homage/parody *Slither* (2006). Aliens hiding in human corpses are just one of the confusing convolutions of Alex Proyas's *Dark City* (1998), but alien-possessed zombies are somehow safer, less unsettling than their vacant cannibal cousins. By 1997, they're okay to leave the kids with, as in *Men in Black*.

People are funny, and dead people even more so. *Dawn of the Dead* indulges in plenty of whimsical gags at the zombies' expense, and anyone with a YouTube account can, and probably has, made a zombie parody. Bob Hope made creepy island locales and lurking voodoo zombies a backdrop for droll one-liners and screwball silliness in *The Ghost Breakers* (1941), which rendered the undead acceptable if audiences laughed, and kicked off endless unfunny, fright-free imitators. *Return of the Living Dead, Part 2* (1988), *My Boyfriend's Back* (1993) and *Fido* (2006) played the zombie holocaust purely as shtick, but the funniest zombie parodies were also kickass horror films in their own right, with wrenching tragedy and eye-popping violence shuffled into the deck. *An American Werewolf in London* (1980), *Dead Heat* (1986), *Dead Alive* [*Braindead*] (1993), *Dellamorte Dellamore* [*Cemetery Man*] (1994), *Undead* (2003), *Shaun of the Dead* (2004), *Tokyo Zombie* (2005), and *Slither* are all funny, yet they also pay more respect to the genre than they take out.

But in an age when almost nothing is funny on purpose, a banquet of botched delights awaits the most jaded hipster. Some misguided efforts were so cheap, vulgar, and/or inept that they witlessly blow away satires: try Ray Dennis Steckler's *The Incredibly Strange Creatures Who Stopped Living and Became Mixed-Up Zombies!!?* (1964) or *Oltre la morte* [*Zombie Flesh Eaters*] (1988) for their absurd incoherence, or *Street Trash* (1988) and *Wild Zero* (1999) for their sheer batshit insanity.

TV

If television is truly a vast wasteland, then zombies are the creatures best suited to inhabit it. But the living dead have gotten short shrift from TV until quite recently, due to the vast and vocal squeamish whiner demographic that rules the airwaves.

Among its futuristic and fantastic scenarios, Rod Serling's *Twilight Zone* (1961–65) probably first brought the living dead to TV, albeit with healthy respect for the kids and the oldsters. Vengeful ghosts abounded, but the bodily resurrected played the angles to keep viewers doubting in such episodes as "The Last Rites of Jeff Myrtlebank" and "Mr. Garrity and the Graves," or they worked their lonely, wrathful magic off-camera, as in "The Grave" and "Night Call." Serling's return to the genre anthology, *Night Gallery* (1970–73), offered some more explicit glimpses of revenant and pathetic zombies in "Cool Air, "The Return of the Sorcerer," and the astonishing "Green Fingers."

Many short-lived inheritors of the TZ formula have upped the ante in rounds. *Tales from the Darkside* (1984) adapted Robert Bloch's whimsical gross-out "A Case of the Stubborns" to awesome effect, whereas *Monsters* (1988) revived Romeo and Juliet tropes with "My Zombie Love." HBO broke the Serling curse with seven seasons of mostly masterful EC Comics adaptations in *Tales from the Crypt*, but zombies took a backseat to psychos and assholes meeting ironic earthly fates. "The Thing from the Grave" (season 2, episode 6), "Creep Course" (s.4, e.9), and "Half-Way Horrible" (s.5, e.12) are standouts. Showtime's ambitious *Masters of Horror* series offered the aforementioned "Homecoming" and the half-great, half-problematic Clive Barker adaptation "Haeckel's Tale" (s.1, e.12).

More often, zombies on TV played for laughs, as in the "Voodoo" (s.3, e.5) episode of *Gilligan's Island* (1964–67), when a witch doctor turns the Professor into a zombie, hilarity ensues, with Thurston Howell's confusing the hysterical zombie talk with an invitation to cocktails.

Even in jest, zombies could cut too close to the bone for TV audiences. When the late-night sketch comedy show *Fridays* aired its amazing Romero spoof "Diner of the Living Dead" on April 25, 1980, a third of affiliates cancelled the show, and repeats left out the offending sketch.

In their eponymous series, Canadian sketch troupe The Kids in the Hall were luckier, cleverly bashing lame zombie flicks in their "Zombie Nightmare" episode (s.1, e.11) without a whiff of reprisal.

Zombies only got serious air time with the advent of horror shows based on the police drama format, beginning with *Kolchak: The Night Stalker* (1974). The seedy reporter tangled with a resurrected assassin in "The Zombie" (s.1, e.2), and his *X-Files* and *Buffy the Vampire Slayer* heirs foiled several sort-of undead plots, but cathode zombies in the audience far outnumbered those on screen until quite lately.

One outstanding entry is *Dead Set*, a five-hour miniseries which aired on Great Britain's channel E4 in 2008. A faux-reality show set in the Big Brother House amid a zombie invasion, the ruthless celebration of selfishness inherent in these programs comes into harsh relief as contestants get "voted out" to be devoured.

ART

The living dead may own the streets, but the art galleries have held out on wine and cheese while all other survivors have surrendered. Whereas medieval devils and the dead literally munched the flesh of the sinful living on cathedral ceilings, genre themes brand modern artists as commercial or pulp. Still, immortal fine works such as Edvard Munch's *The Scream* or Salvador Dali's *The Face of War* are touchstones that resonate in the awful gaze of Romero's zombies.

Perhaps the strongest visual representations of living death come from European surrealists such as Zdzisław Beksinski and Hans Ruedi Giger, whose epic *Necronomicon* collection laces its biomechanical nightmares with vat-grown zombies, techno-witches with the face of his dead wife, and copulating undead body parts as components in an awesome panorama of death in life.

Defiant pop surrealists such as Robert Williams, with his *Zombie Mystery Paintings*, or Big Daddy Ed Roth, with his zombie-driven Rat Fink hot rods, made shrunken heads look like candy, and the dead guy into the coolest cat at the party. Taking cues from horror comics, grind house flicks, Mexican and Asian death-fetish art and urban graffiti, the new pop-surrealist school led by such artists as Chris "Coop" Cooper, Jeff Soto, and the zombie-obsessed Alex Pardee are gnawing away the barricades between blue-collar zombies and blue-blooded art patrons.

And no discussion of zombie art would be complete without a nod to the unsung heroes who ply their inks on human skin. Any horror convention is also a gallery on legs, and any die-hard zombie fan most likely carries a masterpiece under his black T-shirt, or her corset.

MUSIC

Zombies love to rock. Rock loves zombies.

A whole book would not suffice just to name-check all the metal, punk, Goth, industrial, and techno acts that have sung about zombie rampages and unquiet graves. Ever since Fats Waller's swinging "Abercrombie Had a Zombie," the dead have always got their props, though mostly in novelty tunes such as Bobby "Boris" Pickett's "Monster Mash." Cheesy teenage tragedy ballads and grave-robber torch songs such as "I Want My Baby Back" enabled such voodoo-crooning maniacs as Screamin' Jay Hawkins to raise the dead for love, and spawned the psychobilly subgenre epitomized by the Cramps.

The Zombies represented the undead in name, if not in any of their material or stage presence, but soon, musicians themselves began to resemble the living dead, and seemed to beckon fans from beyond the grave. Alice Cooper's Grand Guignol stage persona paved the way for death-trippers White Zombie, Joy Division, Christian Death, .45 Grave, the Misfits, Gwar, Marilyn Manson, and the Canadian goth-industrialists Skinny Puppy, whose *Evil Dead*–sampling *ViviSect* VI threatens to awaken any uninterred corpses within earshot. Operatic caterwauler Diamanda Galás—possibly the most terrifying woman alive—created a gnarly *Masque of the Red Death* album trilogy that turns the AIDS epidemic into an apocalyptic anthem for an undead empire. Her unmistakable polyphonic voice was sampled by Wes Craven to give his zombies perfect pitch in *Serpent and the Rainbow*.

Black Sabbath, Deep Purple, and AC/DC wedded horror to heavy metal, and by the '80s, no serious band could move T-shirts without a zombie mascot. Iron Maiden had Eddie, Megadeth got Vic Rattlehead, and Metallica has Lars Ulrich. Cannibal Corpse, Death, every third adult male in Scandinavia, and the Japanese cosplay critter act Zombie Ritual give a good/bad/ugly spectrum of the zombie death metal phenomenon.

Hip-hop has its own "horrorcore" school, such artists as Insane Clown Posse, D12, Eminem, Geto Boys the Gravediggaz sampling John Carpenter's "Halloween," but the reverence for zombies seems to be mostly a white, suburban affair.

Cheap, short, and nasty, zombie uprisings are the prefect subject for music videos. Genuinely repulsive Rick Baker zombies turn up in Michael Jackson's Grammy-winning 1984 *Thriller* video, but only to bust into a dance routine. Greg Kihn's "Jeopardy," Gorillaz's "Clint Eastwood," and Metallica's "All Nightmare Long" each feature zombies, while the Canadian indie-pop act Gob's "I Hear You Calling" pushes the envelope with zombies playing soccer.

COMICS

Next to movies, no medium has shaped and served the cause of the zombie more than the comic book. EC "suspenstories" anthologies *Tales from the Crypt*, *Vault of Horror*, and *Haunt of Fear* delivered righteous revenant zombies justice in four colors until crackpot psychiatrist Fredric Wertham's *Seduction of the Innocent* linked comics to juvenile delinquency and sexual deviance. Paranoid and overwrought, Wertham's attack was backed by EC's rivals DC, Archie Comics, and Timely (which would become Marvel), and the draconian Comics Code shut the Cryptkeeper down.

The dead could no longer walk, let alone spill blood, in comics. Juvenile delinquency persisted, and one wonders how much more shrill Wertham would have been, had he but know how many EC readers would go on to make horror movies.

Scads of second-tier companies such as Charlton and Gold Key cranked out tame code-compliant horror, but publisher Jim Warren reclaimed horror comics for the adult market with black and white magazines *Creepy*, *Eerie*, and *Vampirella*. Like EC, Warren artists such as Frank Frazetta, Reed Crandall, Richard Corben, and Bernie Wrightson gleefully depicted zombie slaughter, but they faded into mainstream shadows next to such underground fare as *Skull* and *Slow Death*, brought to you by Ron Turner's legendary Last Gasp Eco-Funnies. Corben, Jaxon, and Greg Irons's counterculture zombies here might have been on some serious acid—certainly, the artists themselves were tripping balls—but they're still in the karmic blowback mode of EC and Warren, just with full-blown fucking, intestines by the score, and a prophetically raised middle finger at the Establishment's doomsday shenanigans.

Underground and indie zombie comics persisted in various scattered titles like the short-lived but glorious *Twisted Tales*, *Taboo*, *Death Rattle*, *Gore Shriek*, *Bone Saw*, *Doomed*, and the like gave free rein to such highbrow trash artists as Charles Burns, Stephen R. Bissette, Ashley Wood, and J. O'Barr, creator of the ultimate badass revenant zombie comic, *The Crow*. Many hidden gems of this era survive in such trade paperback collections as *The Mammoth Book of Best Horror Comics* and *Zombie Factory*.

Marvel and DC leapt into horror with the relaxed Comics Code of the 1970s, but their tragic zombies are green and leafy—Man-Thing, Swamp Thing, and the Heap all owe a heavy debt to Theodore Sturgeon's "It." DC's *Weird War Tales* offered endless variations on zany Nazi Hail Mary victory schemes involving zombies, vampires, dragons, and the walking dead. Mostly, horror only serves to spice up the superhero model for these companies, but Marvel has struck unexpected gold with its *Marvel Zombies* series, which turns the heroes of the Marvel Universe . . . into zombies.

Hard-core, Romero-style survivalist zombie comics such as *Deadworld* serialized ordinary folks coping with a zombie apocalypse came and went through the '80s, and Romero himself took a hand in writing the miniseries *The Death of Death* in Toe Tags, a DC project, in 2004–05. Robert Kirkman's *The Walking Dead* has patiently sketched out an epic six-year sojourn in gut-muncher country, and done what few comics can boast. Not only does it command readers who dislike zombies, it has hundreds of thousands of folks reading who don't like comics.

The ongoing zombie renaissance has finally brought the undead into the spotlight, and the reanimated have finally moved from the cane fields to the killing fields. With his noir-inflected *Criminal Macabre* mutations of classic monsters, Steve Niles has given gore-hounds a Kolchak on crack with his occult gumshoe Cal McDonald, and kept reinventing zombies with Bernie Wrightson in *City of Others* and *Dead, She Said*. Loving spoofs such as Bob Fingerman's *Recess Pieces* and Eric Powell's gorgeous *The Goon* give zombies a painterly beauty and slapstick sensibility that by no means renders them harmless. Hellboy creator Mike Mignola has helped lift zombiekind to its highest pinnacle of achievement in Emperor Zombie, the urbane nemesis of steampunk secret agent the Amazing Screw-On Head. Unlike his vulgar flesh-gobbling forebears, Emperor Zombie (voiced by David Hyde Pierce in an animated version) sublimely smokes the brains of his victims.

You've come a long way, baby.

GAMES

The hardest-working targets in the video game business, zombies have shown the most bankable vitality, and the least diversity, in the video arena.

With almost no outstanding exceptions, the video games give us plague zombies, because they are the plot, and anything—a trip to the mall or across town—becomes a harrowing, gory adventure. Arcade shooters such as the crude *Chiller* (1986) and side-scrolling occult battlers such as *Ghosts & Goblins* (1985) threw shambling corpses and vomiting graves at the player, but true creeping fear only began to mount in the PC era. *Zombie* (1990), *Alone in the Dark* (1992-present), and *Doom* (1993-present) brought first-hand zombie carnage to desktops and devoured workplace productivity like so much raw meat.

Video games have changed zombies to suit their own ends, and diversified the zombie line, if only to give gamers new things to shoot. There are vanilla slow zombies, very fast zombies, fat zombies who spray shit on you, and big, badass mutant zombies who take all your quarters. But not much real evolution.

Next-gen arcade shooters such as House of the Dead and console franchises such as Resident Evil and Silent Hill honed zombie horror to its base ingredients: move and shoot, kill and survive. This skeletal subgenre, called "survival horror," in turn begat action-driven tie-in films and comics that, like Japanese anime, hewed to cherished stylistic rules—object-oriented plots, clichéd stock characters, level bosses—in defiance of story logic and plausibility.

Tie-in video games reward zombie fans' insatiable lust to relive their favorite flicks with endless seqeuls that run on when the movie revenues sputter out. Ash fans can wallow in *Evil Dead* games *Hail to the King*, *Fistful of Boomstick*, and *Regeneration*, whereas Romero sued the producers of *Dead Rising* and *Dead Rising 2* for cribbing their gory jaunts in zombie-infested shopping malls. The Romero-sanctioned *Land of the Dead: Road to Fiddler's Green* failed to touch the defendants' stellar sales' figures.

Tongue-in-cheek parodies such as Stubbs the Zombie in *Rebel without a Pulse* and such tweakings of the genre trappings as *Bioshock* and *Dead Space* may yet give the zombie genre some food for thought, but the bleeding edge of zombie games demands not more innovation, but only heightened tension and realism. The current champion, *Left 4 Dead*, ties players together to fend off blitzkrieg waves of highly motivated plague zombies (whose unnerving postverbal growls were voiced by Diamanda Galás's artistic heir Mike Patton of Mr. Bungle, Faith No More, and Fantomas). *Left 4 Dead* and its forthcoming sequel, along with the hugely hyped *Burn, Zombie Burn* and the MMORPG *Urban Dead* show no slack in the public appetite for shooting zombies, so long as the experience keeps getting more like real life . . .

And so, in conclusion:

The endless useful permutations of the walking dead continue to diversify and beguile because they *are* us.

And nobody really gets tired of looking in a mirror, or marveling at one's own shadow.

ACKNOWLEDGMENTS

Without a doubt, this book represents the most grueling production challenge of my publishing career. (If I told you how quickly this all went down, you would not believe me, cuz it's fucking insane.) So why was it also one of my life's most exhilarating experiences?

For starters, I want to thank Dinah Dunn, my fantastic editor at Black Dog and Leventhal, for coming to me first, and braving the entire bedazzling journey at my side; Lori Perkins, my excellent agent, for making the play; Chris Kampe, Anthony Gambole, Tori Goodfellow, and Cody G. for phenomenal research assistance; the good people of Shocklines, for pivotal suggestions; my beautiful family and friends, whom I love; and all the writers, estates, and representatives who granted me the right to share these astonishing stories.

I would also like to acknowledge all the great writers who, for one reason or another, I was *not* able to include: Brian Keene, Anne Abrams, Elizabeth Massie, Ed Bryant, Gary Braunbeck, John Langan, Tim Lebbon, *everybody* from my previous books, the Bizarros (my new favorite literary movement), the hordes from the all-zombie Permuted Press, all the hundreds of writers who have poured their hearts into forging fresh zombie nightmares over the years, and Craig Spector, who was there when this all began.

And finally, I dedicate this book to my beloved pooch,
Scooby Hamilton,
who would love to gnaw on all those bones.

STORY COPYRIGHTS